Philip Boast is the author of the panoramic epic, CITY, the story of Judas Iscariot's thirty pieces of silver. He has also written the Ben London trilogy, LONDON'S CHILD, LONDON'S MILLIONAIRE, LONDON'S DAUGHTER as well as GLORIA and most recently, THE FOUNDLING, all of which are set in London. He is also the author of WATERSMEET, a West Country saga, and PRIDE, an epic novel set in Australia and England. He lives in Devon with his wife Rosalind and three children, Harry, Zoe and Jamie.

RESURRECTION

Philip Boast

HEADLINE

First published in 1997
by HEADLINE BOOK PUBLISHING

First published in paperback in 1997
by HEADLINE BOOK PUBLISHING

10 9 8 7 6 5 4 3 2 1

ISBN 0 7472 5379 X

Typeset by Palimpsest Book Production Limited,
Polmont, Stirlingshire
Printed in England by
Clays Ltd, St Ives plc

HEADLINE BOOK PUBLISHING
A division of Hodder Headline PLC
338 Euston Road
London NW1 3BH

For my son
Jamie

Prologue

Aioula

London, Midsummer's Day 13,000 years BC

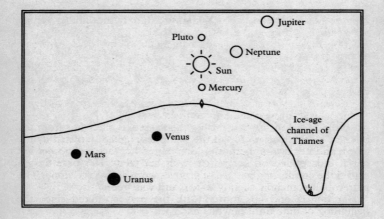

London, Midsummer's Day

Fifteen thousand years ago nothing moved, only the wind sweeping across the two hills, and the wind was hard.

Far below, by the river, a human figure appeared. A man was witless or lost to come out on such a night. Clad in flapping skins, the figure clambered upward from one rock to another, making the precarious journey from the darkness of the river-gorge to the darkness over the plain.

Pale with snow, the greater of the two hills rose in front of her.

She bowed to the wind, and climbed.

Aioula, a girl in the first flush of adolescence, sheltered from the blizzard by the rock on top of the hill. She laughed, terrified by the storm and her own impetuosity. She patted her face to find her left hand, then pulled off her mitten with her teeth. Her bare fingers traced the comforting pattern of grooves worn across the stone. The pattern felt somehow slightly warm, and was free of snow.

Her fingers and lips moved with the prayer offered since the beginning of time until now, its end.

Don't let him die.

The hills and the wind and the sky would live for ever, but love had only a day.

There was no sign of the hunters, or of the great rhinoceros, and the last night of the Moon had passed.

Aioula's right hand clutched her skins around her body, the fur worn inwards, the leather by now stiff with windblown ice. Her breasts and hips had filled out and her hair was night-black, tightly braided with finely ornamented bone pins. Her skin was as dark as her mother's had been and her mother's before her, as though made for the warmth beyond the Sunrise hills. But her eyes were shocking.

Aioula's eyes were pale blue.

She had been born on such a night as this and her great-father, Chlud's father, had named her for the call of the wind. But to the old women clucking over her mother she was Moon-Eyes, and they knew the own-child would have many children and much heartache.

Aioula blinked. By looking slightly away from the place she discerned the new day rising out of the earth, a faint line of grey ice flying on the wind.

No shapes moved against the wind, neither human nor animal.

3

Make Keear kill. Make him live.

Shivering, she kept her vigil at the stone. For her to return to the valley alone would be weakness, an admission that she could not make her prayer strong enough. They have made the kill, she told herself, and waited. Her stomach moved. She was very hungry.

If the hunters had not found shelter, behind or inside the body of the kill perhaps, they would die.

And if the men died, the women would die. Aioula would not bring forth own-children. No own-man would know her. At the thought of it she felt water slide down her cheeks. She touched its precious salty taste with her tongue, marvelling.

Today would be colder than water up here, she knew. The soft fresh snow ceased, but the wind from the midnight hills still blew out the hard ice picked up by its breath. The ice-wind sang to Aioula. Its voice rose and fell, sometimes whistling like the song in reed-pipes, now sounding as low as the solemn tusks of bone, now rumbling like the drumming in the earth.

Aioula's wide, full lips moved soundlessly as her fingers followed the rhythm of the grooves in the stone.

Make Keear succeed. Make his success bring him to me.

The pattern worn into the stone was too fine to take the fingers of men. The earthstone was the women's secret. Not a month passed without someone climbing up here in hope of comfort or succour, to beg, or to offer her life for her own-child, to place a curse or to lay one, or to see the shape of tomorrow, to rub their prayers into the stone.

Flesh and blood and prayer were harder than stone.

'Bring Keear to me,' Aioula prayed. 'Make Keear deserve me. No man is stronger than Keear.'

Worn almost as deep as her fingertips could reach, the grooves zigzagged across the stone. The meaning was obvious, infinitely reassuring. The twelve grooves were the years a woman could hope for of childbearing life. Each groove came to twelve peaks, the twelve moons of her fertility each year. The moons rose highest in the spring, the wisest time. Around the sides were scratched twelve rows of twenty-nine notches, one for each daylight in the month. Their raggedness, longer in summer, demonstrated even the length of daylight.

Summers lasted all year back then, and men and women were giants full of meat in the days when the message in the stone was begun. Now midwinter froze even through midsummer.

'Let Keear make me his first woman,' Aioula said fiercely. She pressed her forehead to the stone with the intensity of her left-handed prayer. 'Stone, give me sons to keep him. River, make me the only woman in his eye, first and foremost above any other. Wind, make him true to me, or destroy him.'

The stone drummed faintly against her forehead.

4

Her eyes flickered.

The wind said, 'What will you give me?'

Aioula snatched back her head. She had almost slept.

She stood. The wind was silent. In front of her the unconquered Sun was born, but though His heart blazed furiously above the distant slopes He threw little heat. She threw back her hood, shadowed her gaze with her hand, and carefully examined the landscape of home that daylight revealed around her.

Two-Hills was well named, standing at the centre of the huge marshy bowl of Aioula's world, the world of her mothers and great-mothers until the beginning of time. This hill was named Gog, which still meant shelter, though there was little enough shelter now. The lesser hill sent its shadow into the valley and across the frozen brook between the hills towards her but the shadow did not reach her. Together the two hills stood like milky white breasts, guardians of the river-gorge below.

On Aioula's right hand the gorge curved away in each direction, deep with shadow, connecting Sunset to Sunrise. Beneath the Sunrise the treeless promontory once called Wolfwood made the river-gorge curve around its cliffs on three sides before continuing its winding course. Over many lifetimes, like the fingers in the rock, the Great River had rubbed its way down, patiently wearing its channel through sand and clay and flints to the hard chalk far below.

In flood the river must have been immense, overflowing with sand and gravel and mud in its battle with the sea. Even within living memory the waterlogged marshland up here, held back from draining by the flood-sand and gravel banks, teemed with food.

But now the sea was returned to the earth and the river torrented far below on its journey. The almost impassable gorge cut Aioula's world in two. Confined, her people eked their existence from the soggy tundra, the network of boggy ponds and brambly islets between the gorge and the midnight hills. Other low gravel hills stuck out of the lumpy, intricate terrain here and there. It was easy to get lost on such difficult ground without a vantage-point. Aioula surveyed the heights for some sign of movement, but saw none. Beyond the midnight hills, cliffs of ice made the sky glow with a pale light, and nothing lived.

There was not enough for Chlud's people to eat. There was not nearly enough.

Each year the snow fell deeper, the ice froze harder.

And then, five daylights ago, M'a saw the great rhinoceros lumbering in the distance, shoving aside the slush with her shaggy snout, chomping the thin sharp grass and nettles below, lumbering forward. Shoving, chomping, lumbering.

The name M'a meant small, or lesser, and he was stunted like a dwarf, so at first no one believed what he said he had seen. M'a ran down from the rim and scampered among the women by the river, shoved at the ground with his little bowed forearms in imitation of the great beast, chomped his yellow mouth, lumbered with slow broad strides as best he could, and they laughed.

When they understood, they shrieked for their men.

The men came out yawning, then feverish exitement gripped the huddle of huts. Aioula fetched Keear's spear, pressed it into his hand, looked him in the eyes. A rhinoceros was hard bitter meat, but life itself, and would strengthen Chlud's people for the coming deep winter. Through the short hectic summer no part of the beast would be wasted, not even the grass in her guts. The women would labour to fashion her thick, stiff leather into pots. Her heavy bones would be splintered for a thousand uses, needles, hooks, barbed spear-tips for fishing. Her heart and womb would be offered to the Yenush for blessing, a fortune-totem to bring more luck, more kills. Everyone was intensely excited. The greatest prize, her horn, would go to Chlud, a fearsome knife to be retained by him or bestowed on the bravest hunter. All this that the men would achieve was eagerly discussed by the women as though it had already happened.

Keear and the others fetched their spears and hunting-skins as the shadows of night rose from the ground. The little hunting party of five men set off nevertheless, Keear the youngest running after them with Aioula's token, her lucky fish-tooth, rattling in his pouch. He turned and waved to her, running backwards, acknowledging her in front of everyone, and Aioula's face had flushed as red as the Sunset. The girls her own age jostled her sourly, small boys whistled and jeered. Their mothers grinned and exchanged nods, sent glances at Aioula, old women of twenty-five remembering the heat of their youth.

But the hunters did not come back.

The snow covered their tracks.

Each night the Moon shrank smaller and rose later, dying. To Aioula each increasing darkness lasted for ever. Still the hunters did not return. The sixth night was moonless, and the storm broke, and Aioula could bear to lie without sleep no longer.

Clad in flapping skins, she had clambered up the precarious path from the river-gorge to the plain, and she had prayed here at the stone on the hilltop, and she had felt the drumming in the earth, and she had listened to the wind until the Sun was reborn.

Chlud crouched in the narrow passage that would lead him to the womb. As always when he approached this wonderful, terrible place, he was afraid. But his demeanour betrayed no sign of his awe and excitement. It would be beneath his dignity.

'Boys, come.'

A man such as he did not let himself down in front of two small round-eyed boys dragging their feet in terror of their initiation ceremony.

Aioula's father was deep in middle age. Though he was still broad across the shoulder, Chlud's beard and barrel chest and wrinkled loins were grey. He believed this last fact was known only to his fourth woman, a girl no older than Aioula, but anything one of that sex knew all of them did.

He was growing old.

He crawled forward on his arthritic knees, deeper into the earth, an old man grunting with the effort, as naked as the night he was born. He had broken most of his teeth and even the choicest food was a trial to him. The muscles of his arms, once stronger than any man's, had lost their fat. But the strength of his personality was undiminished and formidable.

Still, among themselves the young hunters called him Greybeard behind his back. They belittled his moods as mere petulance, decried his past deeds as old wives' tales. He had seen the angry looks sulking in their eyes. Trouble was coming.

Greybeard had done his best for his people. He would not give up. He would not relinquish his place, even though he could not hunt the rhinoceros.

The hunters were gone and perhaps they would not all come back. It was his chance, perhaps his last chance, to assert his authority.

Greybeard stopped, puffed. He listened to the heartbeat from the womb. The drums thudded faster in excitement. His approach in the tunnel was sensed.

The two small boys crawled up behind him. One of them was the runt sired by M'a. M'aro and Qeet, son of Qeetlal the hunter, panted the same breaths. They were as close as brothers though so different in size. Their moccasins remained in the entrance, the ancient custom. One of them moaned. Barefoot, they knew what was demanded of them.

Good. They were more afraid than he. Greybeard grunted.

'Come.'

He lowered his head and reached into the dark, shivering with fear not of death but of the mystery of life that lay ahead of him. His heart trembled in fear of the unknown.

His probing fingers touched the tusk. 'Yaa!' he cried. The boys clutched one another.

Greybeard felt the jagged curve of skull, ancient and split, that guarded the way. He felt to the sides. The eyesockets were larger than his hands. The tusks were straight, and pointed at his heart.

Greybeard took hold of the elephant's skull and lifted it by the tusks. It took all his strength. He grunted his command. When the boys did not move he grunted again. The boys scurried beneath the skull, crying, scrambled towards the red glow of the womb beyond.

They were much too young. Their little penises jiggled beneath them like hairless twigs, sapless.

Greybeard's arms quivered with the weight of the skull. He turned unsteadily, his shoulders scraping chalkdust from the wall, then lowered his burden. Instead of facing outward in all its terror and awe, keeping out, the skull faced in.

None would leave this place without permission.

Greybeard took three steps, grabbed each boy's shoulder firmly until they were calm. He walked forward with them at a solemn pace. Together they entered the cavern.

The boys cried out at once. They lowered their heads in dread, peeped through their fingers. Sacred flames flickered on the left and the right.

Greybeard gazed around him. The walls of the cavern were alive with game. Reindeer. Bison. Horses. Elk. Bears. Other animals he did not recognise were caught in mid-leap, glistening with animal fat. The wealth was beyond counting. There was not room to contain all the spirits and their rich fat bodies overflowed the curves of the chalk boulders. A flint took on the shape of a living eye, a crack became a jagged spear.

Boys always tried to run, he knew. It was their instinct. Greybeard gripped them hard.

'Boys, stand.'

Colours like this were not to be had now. Browns, yellows, black, blood-red. Once wanderers, soothsayers, came from the highlands behind the Sunset and from the mountains behind the Sunrise, sometimes bringing pouches of fabulous powder to exchange for food. Old though he was, Greybeard could not remember it for himself, neither had his father nor his great-father.

But here, he knew, was the living proof of the fireside tales.

'I bring you boys!' he called out. 'Give me men.'

There was no response.

He stared at the wall. Hunters well knew that something which did not move could not be seen. Even though he knew the Yenush was present he could not see her, part animal, part forest, part earth. Between the line that was the snake and the chalk boulder of the Sun, part of the head of a deer turned. Greybeard saw her now. The boys shrilled in fear. The deer's hoof changed, became the knee of a woman.

It was a place of power indeed. No other woman was allowed to enter the shrine and leave alive.

The shaman – the shaman was always a woman – stepped forward. The contours of the wall and her immobility no longer concealed her. The Yenush was huge and ugly, mother of the womb, deformed by her fertility. A tongue of her prolapsed genitals hung through her braided pubic hair, as if she were endowed as a man as well as a woman. No one had given Chlud's people more children. Her belly swung as though still heavy with own-child, her breasts sagged with their weight, her thick flabby legs barely supported her swaying bulk.

The shaman straddled the place between life and death.

She summoned him in her high rasping voice. 'Great hunter.'

Greybeard bowed his head. 'Great Yenush.'

She held out her hands for the upturned skulls, brought forth from the dark by the spirits of horse and fox. The Yenush lacked the bright yellow ochre, almost infinitely precious. Instead she dipped her hand into the skull to her right, carefully daubed the right side of her body with yellow clay, the colour of the Sun, of life. Reaching to her left, she scooped crushed and soaked leaves of isatis from the deformed skull of poor Kalaa, sister of Teewit, and painted her left side with blue woad, the colour of death. With her fingertips the Yenush striped her cheeks in the same manner.

She held out her hands, yellow palm up, blue palm down, offering death and life.

'Great Yenush, great mother from whom we come and return, give me new life for old,' Greybeard requested formally. 'Make these boys men. They are no longer boys. Make these men hunters.'

Everyone knew their place in the ceremony. One of the scrawny old men in the shadows, Kirik the father of Teewit the father of Keear, gave a signal. He possessed authority and the drum fell silent. Two or three younger men, crippled in eye or arm or heart, carefully arranged the red pelt and bones of a deer around the chalk boulder, the rock of life and death. They lifted the skull of the deer on top of the boulder, adjusted its position with tiny movements until it was properly placed. The knee of one of them clicked and he made an expression of pain.

The Yenush gazed at Greybeard. She had taken sanctuary in the cavern since Sunset, as was her duty, and her eyes were watery with firesmoke. She wiped them without moving her gaze. 'Infants,' she grated contemptuously. 'Now you call infants boys, and boys men.'

Greybeard shrugged. He had no choice.

The charred skulls of great hunters who had gone before were brought out and propped around the walls in witness.

With delicate barefoot steps the boys hunted the deer made of skin and bones. No living deer had been seen all summer.

The Yenush murmured scornfully, 'You make them hunt dead flesh, Greybeard.'

The elders watched the mock hunt impassively, but Greybeard was ashamed.

'Something must be forced to happen,' he muttered.

The Yenush's chins quivered as she breathed. She stopped, alarmed. 'That is not wisdom.'

'Bring us the great herds,' Greybeard said simply. He knew she would oppose any change he proposed, and gave her a choice. He spoke through the corner of his mouth so that his words should not be read by the elders. 'Bring us back the great herds as you have promised to do, so many times.'

The Yenush sucked in a deep breath between her blubbery lips. What was Greybeard's purpose? She had known him all her life and his cunning was almost equal to her own.

'Such a great promise is not easy to bring forth,' she exhaled at last. 'Even for one so great as I am.'

Greybeard said, 'Great Mother, I cannot watch my people starve and die.'

'*My* people,' the Yenush said jealously. 'You are only the man of a day.'

'You do not live among them as closely as I do. I cannot wait and neither can they. We are thin. We feel the cold inside us.'

'You are soft. Have faith.'

'I am here. I have brought you new life here. Help me.'

The Yenush observed the ceremony. 'Doubt wriggles in your heart. You concern me.'

Greybeard said, 'I ask myself a question. Support me in this, great Yenush.'

The boys stepped back from the bones. Their dance was finished. They crouched nervously for approval, but the Yenush did not move.

'I have heard no question, Greybeard.'

Greybeard said, 'I ask myself what is best for us all. Not just for you. Not just for me. Everyone. What is best for us?'

The Yenush said, 'Believe in me.'

She braced herself on her stocky legs and held out her fists, a squat indomitable figure. She opened her palm towards the boys. Yellow.

Life.

The small boys grinned, exchanging glances, then saw the Yenush's cold, calculating eyes. M'aro and Qeet pushed their faces in the dust. They did not understand the disagreement between the two powerful adults but they understood it was serious. Greybeard was standing up to the Yenush.

'I do believe.' Greybeard bowed devoutly. No man was capable of disbelief in desperate times. But his back was tense.

Impatiently the Yenush clicked her tongue, the signal. The fire was kicked out, the ceremony moved forward. Greybeard grasped a brand of rushes rubbed with fat. The fat hissed in the flame, the melting oil flared. The boys lifted their dusty faces and peeped around them.

Greybeard raised the flames high above his head. He stood like the reborn Sun. The shadows around him swung as he waved his arm back and forth, the flames roared as they chased the burning brand. M'aro and Qeet stared around them in awe.

The shadows shifted and it seemed the cavern was alive with movement. The blank arch of the chalk roof, too high for men to reach, became the open plain racing beneath the sky. Around the walls deer and wolf began their intricate dance, old as time. The eyes of lion and bison gleamed, opening. Their limbs filled with blood. Nostrils flared, jaws stretched wide.

Greybeard stood still. Everything stopped. The boys stared. The childish stick-spears, flintless, quivered eagerly in their hands.

Greybeard turned to the Yenush. 'They are ready.'

'They are too young,' the Yenush said. But then she stood aside.

Greybeard pushed the small boys past the boulder to the far end of the cavern. What they had seen as one more shadow became a tunnel, narrower and lower than before. The larger boy, Qeet, hesitated. Suddenly M'aro went first. His shadow scuttled in front of him, jagged and distorted. Qeet followed him, then Greybeard, bent almost double, holding the flames above his head.

The tunnel ended and he stood up straight. 'A great hunter knows all secrets,' he said.

This chamber was smaller, its pale chalky walls dark with thousands of stick-figures, men with spears, crudely drawn with charcoal and fat.

'This is the place?' Qeet asked fearfully.

Greybeard said nothing.

'Is this the great secret?' M'aro demanded. 'Is this all?'

Greybeard said nothing. The Yenush stood up beside him, expressionless.

'It's all there is!' Qeet laughed, relieved. 'Men like us!'

Greybeard said, 'No. You have not reached the end. You are not men yet. There is a deeper place, the deepest. I have been there. You, too, will see and understand.'

He pointed with his head at a shadow. They discerned the tunnel at the far end, even lower than the entrance.

'Go forward into the dark,' Greybeard commanded. 'Hunt the great prize, prove your courage, and become men.'

The boys dropped to their knees. M'aro looked back, his face pale but determined, then wriggled out of sight. Qeet followed him, his movements faster, trying to catch up in the dark. The sound of their scuffling faded.

'They will fail,' the Yenush said inexorably. 'When you bring light they will run away without their spears and shame you.'

Greybeard knew it. In his heart he knew it.

He grunted with age as he got down on his knees and wriggled forward. The flames burnt his shoulders and the chalk bit at his elbows and knees.

Greybeard stood up, bringing light to the final chamber.

The boys crouched in the middle of the chamber, seeing nothing. Greybeard held up the flaming brand. He did not move, but the flames roared bright in a sudden gust of air.

Qeet screamed. He gibbered, and the hair stood up on the back of his neck. The tusks of a huge mammoth encircled them all.

The mammoth's mouth gaped red and black over the boys, taller than they.

Qeet dropped his spear and ran. He pushed past Greybeard. His kicking white soles disappeared in the tunnel. He would not stop until he was out. They never did.

Greybeard held out his hand to try to stop the smaller, more spirited boy, who might have been brave in a year. But M'aro writhed out of his grip and was gone.

Alone, Greybeard stared up at the great beast. One way or another, he knew he was here for the last time. He threw down the flames and they died.

Greybeard held his arms wide to the darkness, revealing his heart. Nothing happened. He stood alone in the deepest place in the earth. The mammoth did not speak to him, only gusted its slow breaths.

Greybeard understood. The tears ran down his rough cheeks into his grey hairs. He knew what he must do.

On the hilltop Aioula shielded her eyes against the Sun, feeling His glorious radiance like a fire on her bare face. Where His light touched the front of her body the frost became water dripping down her skins. She undid the bone toggles and slipped off the clumsy outer layer. Above her leather-strapped fur boots, the bare flesh of her knees and thighs warmed in the Sun. Her body was clothed in deer hide, black and soft with age, laced with leather thongs. It had been her mother's. Across her breasts she wore a bone necklace grooved like the pins that held her hair.

Aioula examined the bright silence of the morning. Nothing moved. The rhinoceros had hunted the hunters or the wind and the dark had taken them.

She would have no own-man, no own-place, no own-children. All she had dreamed of for her life would never happen.

This lacking was often among the women. There were always too many women. They made the best of it as second woman or third, and so the all-children were born. Chlud's people needed life greatly, for death had grown more powerful than life.

Keear was dead.

But Aioula had said, 'I love Keear.'

Keear had been young and playful, but already he had been the surest hunter. His muscles were strong and he had shown their hardness, and the other youths respected him. He had looked at Aioula and accepted her charm-tooth and run backwards for her. When he returned she would have taken him. One day, Aioula knew, Keear would have been acknowledged in her father's place, Chlud's people would have become Keear's people, and she, Chlud's daughter, would have borne Keear's children.

Of course the bloated Yenush, ever jealous of her influence that hung like a pall over the women's lives, would have opposed such a powerful union. To keep her grip she would have punished Keear somehow, and perhaps Aioula too.

But Aioula had dreamed, 'Love will find a way.'

Aioula had imagined her children bringing forth great-children, seen generations of her children stretching into the distance. She would never die.

But now Aioula stared at the Sun glaring above Two-Hills and Keear was dead and everything was impossible. She would grow old.

The lesser hill, M'agog, remained frosty with shadow on the side towards her. Dull thickets of dwarf birch pointed their branches where the wind had gone. Something moved among them. Even now, in the depth of her despair, Aioula's heart leapt.

But it was only a skinny hare. The cold had killed all the rabbits but hares survived, and she watched it bound downhill. In the valley between the two hills it stood on its haunches, whiskers twitching.

Then the hare did something remarkable. It jumped the frozen brook and scampered uphill towards Aioula. The snow clung to its paws, she saw herself in its eyes. She reached for a spear but had none, only traps of woven grass in her pouch. She snatched up a pebble.

In the thickets where the hare had first appeared, snow and frost showered as the branches were knocked aside, without sound at this distance. A line of shapeless figures appeared and trudged down the bare slope.

Aioula remembered the hare. Its footprints ran within a man's reach of her.

She shielded her eyes with both hands, staring, and the pebble she had forgotten dropped on her nose. All her attention was on the men.

Five men had gone to hunt the rhinoceros.

The men came into the Sunlight one by one, grew shadows. Three, four. The fifth man followed them, moving not like Keear but Keear's father. He was playing a joke that he had not seen Aioula. The men followed Qeetlal the leader, crunched carelessly across the stream, worked their way along the flank of the hill below her. They did not look around them, heads down, spears trailing. The breath puffed like fog over their faces but she recognised Keear clearly now. Aioula's excitement opened inside her like a flower and she could contain herself no longer.

She ran downhill screaming. She trailed her heavy furs from her left hand, she waved and called. The men glanced at her but did not respond.

'Keear!'

He would not stop his joke, would not pay attention to her. She danced lightly backwards in front of him, just as he once had to her, then threw her arms around his shoulders. Instead of picking her up

Keear staggered. He lost his footing and sprawled. Aioula laughed but he did not pull her on top of him to play at looking between her breasts. He turned his head aside, got to his feet without her. He said nothing. Aioula spoke. 'I thought you were dead.' She turned to the others but they trudged on. Keear stood looking down at his feet. His voice was low.

'There was no kill.' He would not meet her eye. He walked away from her. He did not ask why she was here.

After a moment Aioula caught them up. 'But you are alive.'

She smiled but they did not return her smile.

Keear stopped. He stared at her. 'Don't you understand?'

He looked so cold. She reached up to touch his cheek or his mouth with the warmth of her fingertips. He struck at her with the haft of his spear and stepped over her. She went after him and walked beside him. 'I will try to understand.'

Keear was silent. Then he muttered, 'You cannot.'

All that mattered was that they were alive, but Aioula saw how deeply the men were ashamed of their failure to bring food home, how deep their hurt and anger ran, how easily it might turn against anyone but themselves. She rubbed her side meekly, head down.

'The rhinoceros was not worth having.'

She glanced up at him. Keear muttered, 'It was braver than brave and stronger than strong and we were frightened.'

She hated him to admit that. She spoke firmly. 'You, afraid.'

But Keear's pride did not return. 'When it charged at us our spears could not pierce its flesh. Its horn was as long as a man, its body made the sky dark. The ground shook. We could not get away from its nostrils and its horn and we knew we would die.'

'But you are here.'

'Its eyes were small and when it turned away we followed it for a day. But we knew that if we caught it we would die.'

'There will be another rhinoceros.'

Keear shuddered. 'We saw nothing but ice and snow.'

She took his hand. 'You have come back tired. After you have slept—'

'This was four days ago. We slept last night on the other hill.'

Aioula let go his hand and stared at him. 'You slept!'

He shrugged. There was shelter.

Aioula struggled to understand. 'You slept. You were afraid to come back. I waited all night in the storm.'

Qeetlal stopped and the men halted, made impatient noises for Keear to catch up. The frozen river behind Aioula's hill was larger than the brook in front, and its deepening valley had worn into the rim of the gorge. Once it must have launched itself out as a waterfall but now only a stream of dirty water slid from under the ice. Red with windblown brickearth, the ice was filthy with grit and the shadows of boulders trapped in its cold heart.

Keear's mouth moved, and finally he spoke at Aioula. 'I was not afraid to come back. I am not afraid of anything.'

Where the waterfall had been a sloping jumble of boulders remained, the path into the gorge. Keaar joined the men handing themselves down the precarious descent. Yellow meltwater sucked and trickled beneath their feet, then they reached the steep dry path carved into the cliff-face. Aioula watched until they were only bobbing heads. Terns fluttered and shrieked around them, disturbed from their bespattered nests in the cliff.

Aioula followed the men quietly. Her feet and hands knew the way down. She felt numb with cold but she was not cold. The cliffs and the roar of the tumultuous white river below rose around her, the familiar chalky scent of its spray washed over her. Here was home. She turned downriver and the water raced and foamed past her footsteps on the shingle. The sky was winding like a bright blue stream above the dark cliffs, mimicking the river's course. The Sun's light had not yet touched the ground, but the cliffs curving behind her burst into fire, orange and blue.

She watched the men crouch among the white rocks, drink from the milky green pools. They glanced at her as they drank. The huts were a little further along the gorge, their knotted peaks barely distinguishable over the rocks. Any moment now the hunters' return would be sensed and the people would come swarming and there would be no more time for reflection. The hunters got to their feet, slapped at the midges attracted to the warmth of their faces and their rancid skins. Qeetlal jerked his head, spoke in a flat hard voice. 'Keear.'

Quickly Keear ran back to Aioula. She looked away. He threw down his spear, gripped her wrists. His voice hissed earnestly. 'Aioula, be careful. You have made Qeetlal very angry. You would have been more than afraid!'

'I would not have been ashamed of being afraid.' Aioula let Keear remember the storm. She let him think about her alone in the blizzard. 'I waited for you. It was for you.'

Keear pretended not to understand. He let go of her with one hand, bent and picked up his spear. Then he snatched her close in his elbow and smiled. 'You are warm, Aioula. You are beautiful. Even your strange eyes are beautiful when you look at me. And you are Chlud's daughter!'

The men grunted, then again watched her and Keear with their steady brown gaze. Keear let the hardness beneath his furs touch her, smiling. Qeetlal nodded his approval. The men were getting their spirit back with the heat in their loins.

Aioula called out at the top of her voice. 'See, the people come! The hunters are returned!'

The children heard her at once, of course, and ran over the rocks with eager whoops. As they jumped, the Sun limned their flying black

15

hair with gold. They gathered round the unresponsive hunters, the youngest arriving last; they tugged at the flapping pouches, the empty bags. They looked for a heavily laden pole-sledge. The eagerness left the children's faces, gave way to confusion. There was no meat. They stilled and fell quiet. Still the hunters said nothing, and the silence was very deep. The children's energy left them and they shrank in on themselves, thin and hungry, an accusing half-circle in front of the hunters. The hunters did not swing their sons on to their shoulders. No one spoke.

One little boy sat down and cried.

The adolescent girls came running gracefully along the beaten path, almost soundless in their moccasins, some of them still clutching whatever task they had been set. They stared over the heads of the children at the empty-handed hunters.

The little boy's cries could not be ignored. They went on and on until an older boy cuffed him, and one of the silent skinny girls, Ara who was normally the most garrulous, picked him up and cuddled him. But his cries would not stop.

Aioula took the infant, stroked his hair. She responded to Ara's whispered question. 'There is no cache of meat. There is no kill. They were afraid to return. They slept.'

The hunters pushed forward along the path. The children let them past, gathered behind them, followed them. Huts of arctic birchwood and hide, so familiar as hardly to be noticed, came into view. The settlement straggled along a mossy platform of chalk and gravel thrown up beyond the river's reach. The place was so old that the overhang of chalk cliff was dull and streaked with the soot of cooking-fires. The first finger of the Sun reached through the peatsmoke, threw a brilliant wedge of light along the gorge as though the air were solid.

The women of childbearing age came out of the huts and watched. Everyone stopped what they were doing. The women crossed their arms. There was nothing to cook.

Then Ara ran forward. She screamed, 'They slept!'

Suddenly everyone was shouting. The sound fed on itself, rose up like a flock of birds. The children cried with hunger and could not be heard. Their mothers put back their heads and tore their hair, opened their shifts to the freezing air and squeezed their dry breasts, showing no milk in the nipples. They jeered and spat white spittle because they had no milk.

The hunters pushed through, heads down, at first silent, then defensive, then violent. The spitting stopped. Someone threw a stone, and it clattered against the chalk cliff. There was a horrified silence.

'Enough.'

Chlud, leaning on his spear, stood in the entrance to the cliff. The entranceway, the height of a man from the ground and sloping upwards from a ramp of stones, was as tall as a man but barely wide enough to take his body. Its feminine form was unmistakable, to be entered only by men.

Chlud gazed down on his people in front of him. His hair, his beard, his chest, his loins were grey. The two small boys, Qeet and M'aro, wriggled out past him and scrambled down the ramp. They put their arms over their heads and ran to their mothers. The mothers slapped them then fought between themselves, pulling hair, each blaming the other for her son's failure.

Qeetlal stepped forward from the hunters. He called out to the figure in the cliff. 'Greybeard.'

Greybeard ignored him.

Qeetlal called out his challenge again, loudly and deliberately. '*Greybeard!*'

Standing in such a holy place, Greybeard would not respond to the insult, but his face flushed dark red. He stepped delicately down the stones on his scrawny legs. The joints of his fingers stood out like white knobs around the haft of his spear. The two women stopped fighting and fell back with the others as he approached.

Aioula saw her father's face and knew his anger pulled him forward. Qeetlal half raised his spear in threat. He too was angry, humiliated, dangerous, and he was in his prime. Aioula was afraid for her father. She was afraid for Keear, who had felt obliged to step forward beside his hunt leader. She pushed through the crowd but they held their places eagerly, jostling. Someone jerked her hair and she turned in a flash of pain, faced her father's third woman. The crone's cheeks were gnarled by bitterness, her twisted lips nagged her envious complaints. 'Where have you been, girl? Do you not think of others, Moon-Eyes? Do you think only of yourself? What of your work?'

Aioula pulled herself free. She dared shout out. 'Father!'

She stumbled into the clear space. She was too late. Greybeard no longer had his spear. There was a hiss in the air.

Qeetlal stared at the spear through his chest. Everyone knew the signs. His breastbone was shattered, he was unable to speak. He raised his eyes to the cliff where the Yenush stood in the entranceway, the Great Mother both sexed and sexless, extravagantly female in shape yet now sterile.

She turned her left side towards Qeetlal. Blue for death.

Qeetlal died. His body dropped forward. The women spirited it away for preparation according to the Yenush's orders. His own-woman was beaten away with stones. Keear and the other men laid their spears at Greybeard's feet, pointing away from him.

Greybeard's temper fled. He looked weary. He raised his voice and spoke to all the people with the stern dignity of which he was capable. 'Now listen to my words! In the womb I have seen the truth. Only when the Sun returns all year will the animals come

17

back and bellies be full and peace restored. We must move forward to another place.'

But he was interrupted by a furious shout.

'No!' The Yenush strode forward. She waddled powerfully on her massive legs, her breasts and belly swinging. The flesh jumped on her thighs and neck. She pointed her staff at the cliff, the entranceway, hinted at everything that lay beyond. 'This is our place. Without it we are nothing.'

Greybeard explained simply, 'It is your place, great Yenush. But these are my people. The power of the Yenush is great, but has not prevailed. My people hurt with hunger. We must live where the Sun lives. We will begin our journey tomorrow. It is the truth I have seen and I have spoken.'

The people murmured and did not disperse. They thought about this strange idea of leaving the place they knew. The young men and boys were excited but the older women shook their heads. Everyone looked at the churning emerald-green rapids and foaming spray and wondered how they would cross the river, and how they would climb the sheer cliffs on the other side with all they must carry.

The Yenush spoke. 'This is blasphemy. Without a place there is no people.'

'The people will make another place, Great Mother, and children will be born.'

'I will not permit this madness. Our journey will have no end and no peace. You are only a man, and old, and you will die and we shall be nowhere, rootless.'

Greybeard's spear was brought back to him. He took it with sadness. 'The Sun will prevail in me until my task is done.'

The Yenush observed his determination. Her eyes flicked cunningly in their rolls of fat. 'Then you know the price you must pay the Sun.'

Greybeard knew. He groaned. 'I have no son.'

The Yenush pushed her lips close to Greybeard's ear. 'But you have your daughter.'

Strong hands seized Aioula.

The Yenush took Greybeard by the shoulders. She spoke the Law. The people murmured the words as they were uttered.

'To obtain what is most desired, what is most loved must be offered in return. This is the purification and the Law.'

The people repeated, 'This is the Law.'

Greybeard spoke in a broken voice. 'It is the Law. She is my greatest prize and gift.'

Aioula struggled, kicked, shouted out to Keear.

Keear did not hear her. He looked away. He did not see her.

Ara smiled. Now she would have Keear.

Aioula was given over to the women. The women screamed and beat at her, tore her skins from her. They dragged her by her hair.

Keear stood aside. Aioula was pulled backwards along the ground, her face in the dust, her hands tearing at the moss. The women kicked her to make her let go, the fear and bitterness inside them given voice by their treatment of Aioula, Greybeard's loved daughter, his sacrifice for his people. They scratched her long legs, her fine breasts, they hated her. Her eyes were the colour of death. She killed her mother by her birth. She ate with her death hand.

They cried out, 'Moon-Eyes!'

Greybeard watched them. They had forgotten their fear of the journey.

They broke her nose. Aioula heard the bone crack. The children beat at her with sticks.

Aioula writhed forward on her elbows. Keear stepped back. She inched towards him. He turned on his heel and for a moment the Sun gleamed on his curly black hair, his shoulders. He shrank between the heads and shoulders around him until she could not see him.

Aioula closed her eyes.

Now the Yenush, her expression vengeful, stood behind Greybeard's left shoulder.

Greybeard raised his voice. 'At Sunset darkness will fall for Aioula my daughter and dawn will not come for her. For three nights and three days she shall lie in the darkness without the Sun, without water, without food, and her body shall be dead. Alone of women, she shall be placed in the ground of the sacred place with all honour, and her life shall come back to us in the shape of the herds of deer we shall hunt in the lands of eternal summer. This is my will, that my people may live.'

The Yenush bowed her head and intoned the blessing.

'*Aram menaht menou.*'

Aioula would be dressed as though for her wedding – but not to Keear. She stared around her in a daze, trapped.

She was lifted by her elbows and watched her bare feet walk, unresisting, to the pool in the Great River. Old women unafraid of touching her body scrubbed her with their wrinkled hands, swapped jokes and cackled about her as though she were not there, were already dead. They tried to scratch off a mole. They pushed their fingers between her legs to show their domination, broke her virginity. The cold water congealed the blood dripping from Aioula's nose and numbed her cuts and injuries. She could not respond. She hardly felt the icy splashes but her body shuddered in the brilliant cold Sun. Her teeth chattered. She could not stop them. She could neither pull forward nor draw back from what was happening to her.

What happened, happened.

The ritual was her fate and she could not turn aside.

The old women guided her inside the hut where Qeetlal's washed body lay, curled on his right hip, his knees drawn up to his chin. His flesh was daubed with yellow clay and he had been dressed again in his skins to keep him warm. His vacant eyes stared at Aioula.

The Yenush opened the flap and peered in. She grunted. Men came and took Qeetlal away. The drums began. Later the drums stopped.

The crones worked busily, combed Aioula's hair, braided it in a way she did not like, pinned it. Her hands moved uncertainly in complaint and were slapped away. They bustled out and left her alone. Aioula sat without moving, naked.

Greybeard ducked through the flap. He laid his right cheek against his daughter's right cheek, then his left cheek against her left cheek, and she saw the tears standing in his eyes as he observed her.

'Thus I saw you born, Aioula.'

He dressed her in a smock of tawny deerskins, laced them loosely down each side. The old women returned and tutted at his knots, retied them. The Yenush came inside. The shaman examined Greybeard's preparations with merciless glances, as though even now he might be bullied into giving up. Greybeard wept aloud. His tears dripped on Aioula's face.

He placed the skull of a doe on Aioula's head. The skin had been replaced as though it was alive, and the deer had shiny black river-stones for its eyes. A halter was placed around its neck.

Aioula no longer existed. She was the deer.

The Yenush led the procession outside. The halter tugged, and Aioula knew she must follow. Another halter was dropped over her head, leading back. She heard her father's solemn footsteps pacing behind her. The last Sunlight glowed on the rim of the gorge, everything below fell into shadow, the light failed. The flaming brands carried at the head of the procession seemed very bright. The people gathered, silent witnesses. She saw Keear at the back. The Yenush mounted the ramp of stones and abruptly the darkness of the entranceway hid her.

It was not too late. Aioula whirled. She shouted, 'Keear!'

Keear looked frightened. He shook his head. Someone – Ara – whispered to him. Keear cleared his throat and called out, 'It is for the good of the people.'

He did nothing. Aioula stared at him. The halter jerked her forward again, then again, and she stumbled into the darkness. Men's voices chanted, and the drum drummed in the earth.

'Fear nothing, daughter!' Greybeard said.

Aioula was not afraid. She was angry. She gazed blankly at the skull of an elephant, but it held no meaning for her, no fear. The passageway was ribbed like the inside of a body, dug by the hands of men with antler-horn. Soon the passageway opened into a cavern. Dust puffed over her feet, settled on her toenails. Old men came forward and spreadeagled her body on a rock, tied back her wrists and ankles with thongs. More thongs were tied across her breasts, pulled cruelly tight. The halter was passed between her breasts, dragged taut into her crotch and tied off beneath her, biting into her softest flesh. She lay unable to move, staring up at the colours that covered the walls and roof. Aioula understood that this was the place of life and death. Here she would die of hunger, but long before that she would die of thirst. Before that she would die of cold, or perhaps suffocation.

The fires were kicked out. Her father's voice spoke in the dark. His hands touched her for the last time. 'Farewell.'

Then there was nothing but the sound of footsteps retreating. Distantly came the sound of stones being piled in the entranceway. Then there was nothing at all.

Aioula closed her eyes, opened them, closed them. She was blind.

The stone was hard.

She screamed her fury. Her scream echoed.

She sobbed and the sound of her sobs came back to her.

She listened to herself breathing. She breathed in and held her breath. She breathed out.

She hated Keear with a hatred that made her skin burn hot. In the dark she saw him turn away from her a hundred times. She hated him. Then she pitied him. Then she hated him and pitied him again. Thinking of him made her angry. She would not think of him.

Was it daylight again outside, or had only a moment passed?

She had not suffocated yet. The air was clean and fresh.

The rock hurt her back. She tried to turn over but the thongs held her securely.

Something moved on her chest. It was the place her father had touched her. Aioula did not dare hope. She bent her head forward, felt with her chin. Instead of her own flesh she encountered smooth bone. The point of the bone pricked her and she felt a trickle of blood run down her neck.

Her spine cracked and she rested her head back on the rock. She panted, then craned forward again. This time her chin felt the broad handle, bound with plaited grass. The thin bone blade sliced at the skin of her neck.

Here was her death. Greybeard had paid the price, but he had denied the Yenush complete victory. All she had to do was jerk her head forward and she would die with no suffering.

Aioula lay without moving a muscle.

Her heart beat. The arteries pulsed in her neck. Her tongue moved and she felt her teeth against her tongue, and then she licked her lips. She breathed in through her nostrils, then out through her mouth. She saw Keear in the dark, turning on his heel away from her, the dying Sun gleaming on his curly black hair and fading on his shoulders as he shrank into the shadows.

The knife pricked her chin.

Aioula twisted her head to the left, arched her back. The knife did not move, then slid forward. Its point touched her right ear, but the handle was still caught between her breasts. She lifted her buttocks, legs quivering with the effort. The knife-handle rolled against her left breast, then slid over the smooth curve of her flesh but would not fall, held by her smock. The knife would not come free. She jerked, panted. She felt the perspiration slide up her spine. She jerked her whole body and the knife slid down the line of her jaw, clattered on to the rock beside her shoulder.

She held her breath, prayed the knife would not tumble further to the floor.

Let me live.

She felt the knife against her left shoulder. Her left hand could not reach it. Her fingers clawed, the thongs bit into her wrist as she pulled with all her strength, but they would not give way. Instead she rolled to the left, felt with her nose, and the tip of her nose touched the knife. Her right arm cramped, pulled her back. She straightened her arm, trembling, and prayed to the stone on the hill somewhere high above.

Let me struggle. Give me strength. Let me succeed.

Perhaps the Sun had risen, but she could imagine nothing but darkness now. She pushed patiently at the knife with her nose, guiding it towards where she believed her left hand was.

She felt smooth bone under her fingertip.

With her fingernail she scratched at the blade until it came forward into her grasp. She gripped the handle tight in her palm and rolled back, exhausted.

She woke. She twisted the handle so that the blade lay against the thong knotted around her wrist. She could feel the cold bone against her skin. The edge would cut her own flesh too.

She cut.

She slept with her head on her shoulder. The thong broke finally and her hand flopped down, waking her. She cut her other hand and her ankles, neck, breasts, crotch free with quick agonised slashes of the knife. She bent over like an old woman, took a few aching paces in the dark, fell.

She rubbed her joints until they loosened.

She was very thirsty. She licked the blood from the gashes in her arm. Its saltiness made her more thirsty.

She moved around the cavern, feeling her way by touch along the invisible walls. Here she touched air. It was the entrance passage. She imagined the heavy stones piled up outside and her breath jerked in and out of her nostrils as she fought the feeling of being trapped. Then she continued her journey around the wall.

Her breathing stopped. Her hands touched nothing again.

She felt the rock around the nothing. It was another tunnel.

She explored twice more around the perimeter of the cavern, until she was sure her sense of direction had not deceived her.

She sat down on the floor by the tunnel and crossed her legs. She felt for flints in the chalk, prised them free. She laid one in the palm of her hand and held one in her fingers, knapped them together with a particular flicking motion. When nothing had happened after a while she changed the one in her fingers for another.

A spark shot up, illuminated her hand for an instant, drew a Sunrise trail across her eye. She blinked again and again for the pleasure of seeing the vision repeated. Gradually it faded and she was alone again.

She gathered the pieces of wood from where the two fires had been. She made the flint spark. She chipped until her fingers were raw, then changed round, then changed back again. She fretted a piece of wood into tiny threads of tinder. Finally one spark did not die. It grew, caught. She blew on it softly, unable to bear the brightness of the insubstantial flame, and the wood began to burn.

Aioula raised the burning branch above her head and looked around her in awe. Now she understood. The cave was alive.

The Yenush spoke.

'The Sun is dying. The third day is at an end. Give up your madness, Greybeard.'

The Great Mother still believed that her twelve families would not set out on their journey, Greybeard realised. She did not see into the hearts of her children as deeply as she thought she did. Already the change had happened. Greybeard waited on the ramp and saw the huts lying dismembered, bare chalk between them, the skins piled on the long poles. Each family had bound their hut-poles together at the front to make a travois the men and boys could pull. Pots and ropes had been tied aboard, every possession that could find a place. They would carry their homes with them. Newborn children would be hefted on the mothers' backs, everyone else would walk. Greybeard knew the old ones would not survive. Already his eye saw that the arrangements were too heavy and clumsy for the rigours of the journey, but he knew his folk. It was best that the people learnt lessons for themselves, after they had set out. They would whine and complain, but by then it would be too late to turn back, and they would be obliged to discard everything that was not essential in order to keep up. From time to time they would rest—

The Yenush spoke.

Greybeard worried how they would cross the river. A young man carrying a spear could leap from rock to rock and make it across somehow, no doubt, and find a way up the cliff beyond. But the main party would have to walk towards the Sunrise until a crossing-place—

The Yenush struck his shoulder. She repeated the words she had spoken as though he was deaf.

'When the Sun accepts the spirit of Greybeard's daughter, then the omen is good.' Again that cunning light in her eye. 'I have promised the people that their journey to the plains of the Sun will be brief and joyful.'

Greybeard had heard her making trouble with these extravagant promises he must disappoint. He watched the gathering shadows calmly. Many would fail. Handsome Keear sat by the Great River doing no work, useless. Ara waited near the youth, talking with her body as well as her smiling lips. She was pretty. She would not be satisfied with that one for long. Greybeard sighed.

'Our people will journey for many years, Great Mother. They will freeze in the cold and burn in the heat. Many will die and many will be born.'

The shaman no longer bothered to hide her spite. 'You will not see the end of what you have started.'

'I will see.'

The Yenush stamped her ashwood staff in frustration. 'Madness!'

Aioula crawled in the tunnel that led further, deeper.

She knew she was dying of thirst. Her tongue had thickened until it filled her mouth, her swollen lips split but leaked no blood. She crawled after the tiny flickering straw-flame that her fingers held up in front of her. Its light scratched her dry eyes, but she would not stop. She followed the wind that blew the flame, keeping its breath on her face.

Aioula felt beyond fear. She marvelled at everything she saw.

The flame shrank to an glowing ember. She felt quickly in her smock for another twist of dried grass, blew it to life. She had only a handful left.

After a while she understood that the stick figures were hunters. Some held their spears like great men, others had been killed by their prey. The more she looked, the more she saw. This was not a story of one time but of a thousand generations of time. She was looking at the story of a family.

Smiling, she reached out to touch them.

The flame flickered and she lit another, crawled forward to the next tunnel.

Aioula was very tired now. She looked up dizzily. A bull mammoth must have been the last sight of many men, and somehow they had distilled their awe and terror and desire in here.

There was no way out.

She had reached the final place. She leant against the wall. Then she sat, rested her head against the line of the tusk, and her eyes closed.

She dreamed of Keear, saw him turning away, and her hatred burnt her.

The grass twist burnt her fingers. She woke, fumbled in her lap for her little store. Only one small twist remained. She lit it.

The mammoth breathed and the flame fluttered, almost died.

The mammoth breathed through its mouth.

Aioula crawled under the upraised trunk. It was not real, she saw, only the curve of a huge chalk boulder cunningly used. The mouth was hollow. She stood up inside the mouth of the beast. She climbed the sloping tunnel of its throat.

The Sun died. Greybeard ordered the stones rolled aside from his daughter's tomb. Old men lit tapers of twisted brushwood and formed a procession around the Yenush. The flames flickered briefly around the entranceway as they filed inside.

Greybeard stood in the night. He watched the stars winding above the canyon. Soon the stars would pull the new Moon up by the horns. The wind returned, blowing pale shreds of snowcloud, and he remembered the wonderful, terrible night of his daughter's birth, the call of the wind, her mother's dying screams, Aioula. Aioula.

The Yenush returned to the entrance. 'She is gone!'

Greybeard pulled himself back to the present. 'But she cannot be gone.'

The Yenush stood aside. Her face was white and her eyes stared. The old men scampered out past her. They hid their heads. Greybeard picked up a dropped taper and followed the fat woman into the cavern.

It was empty.

The Yenush cried out, 'I am afraid!'

Greybeard shook her, but she merely looked up at him. Her lips moved, terrified.

Greybeard took his courage in both hands. He bent double, peered into the tunnel at the far end, waved the flames in front of him, saw nothing. He shouted to frighten the spirits of the unborn and the dead. He went forward at a crouching run. The flames tried to blow in his face and he waved the taper from side to side. He smelt his hair.

There was no one alive in the next cavern, only the thousands of people on the walls. Greybeard's lips drew back. He was as terrified as the fat woman.

He crawled on his belly into the next tunnel. The breaths of the great beast blew past him and the flame guttered.

Greybeard came to the deepest chamber. He stood up, and the curling painted tusks of the great mammoth seemed to encircle him around the walls.

The mouth of the mammoth gusted its slow breaths.

Greybeard looked up at the eyes, the great uplifted trunk, then returned his attention to the mouth, red and black. He opened his own mouth and spoke one word. 'Aioula . . .'

Greybeard returned the way he had come. The fat woman waited outside on the ramp, shaking. The stones were already being piled up. Greybeard stepped over them and shook his head.

'Her body is nowhere to be found.'

'It is the worst possible omen—'

'We must leave now,' Greybeard said.

'She is seized by the gods below the earth. The people must go also, quickly, quickly—'

The fat woman's voice rose, but Greybeard spoke with dignity. 'At first light it shall be as you say.'

The beast was dead, its breath was cold.

Aioula lay in the belly of the mammoth. Many people filled the walls around her. They were not stick people. They had breasts and buttocks. She saw a woman wearing a mother's apron and pouch, her children around her. She saw no men, only women and children. Aioula smiled, touching the outlines of their hands daubed on the walls, drawn around with clay or charcoal. Children's hands, women's hands. Her own hands fitted into them.

She slept. The wind breathed on her head. Something woke her, distant voices echoed. Her eyes widened but she could not see, the flame was exhausted. She lay in the dark comforted by the invisible folk around her, the generations of women and children rising up and going forward, long dust.

Why had the men been so afraid of this place?

Or had they simply forgotten it?

Aioula smiled. Everything would be revealed in the moment of her death.

A glow suffused the cavern she had come from. A shape fluttered in the dark, glittered on her eyelash. She blinked and felt a bead of water melt on her cheek, but the glow remained. She heard shuffling movements echo in the tunnels and caverns, the marvels all around her that she would have discovered, had she lived.

A terrified whisper came to her, multiplied and echoing. 'Aioula . . .'

She held her breath.

The glow of firelight faded away. The crash of stones blocking the distant entranceway came to her after a while, then there was only silence and dark. She lay back and something fluttered on her forehead. A bead of cold water trickled into her eye.

Once Aioula had seen a butterfly. It was the most beautiful thing she had ever seen. Now she felt them fluttering, teeming invisibly around her, alighting on the backs of her hands, her raised face, her eyelids, soothing the aching bruise of her nose. She stuck out the tip of her tongue. A flake of soft crystal dissolved and her tongue sucked its moisture.

These were not butterflies. They were snowflakes.

Truly this was a place of marvels.

Aioula held up her open palms into the dark and the snowflakes fluttered against her skin, melting. She licked her hands, held them up for more. She found a place in the dark where the snowflakes flew down thickest, flying on the breaths of the mammoth, hovering around her everywhere she touched. She wiped her hands on the wet rocks and lapped them dry. She scooped a handful of slush and drank it greedily, grunting like an animal.

No longer thirsty, she was curious. She reached up into the snowflakes whirling down, touched nothing solid. So the chamber was taller than she. Feeling round her with her feet, she found that some rocks had fallen from the roof. She climbed them, teetered with outstretched fingers.

Her fingers slid along carved chalk, slipped upward, felt nothing again.

There was a cleft in the top of the roof. Dimly she sensed the grey dome of chalk and the snowflakes that whirled around her, dark crystals fluttering in a silvery mist somewhere high above, swirling down and down until the largest settled on her upturned face.

It was the first night of the new Moon. She saw moonglow filtering through clouds of snow.

The Moon had always been her friend. Aioula fetched more rocks, pulled herself up.

She began her climb towards the Moon.

The climb was much longer than she had thought. In places the cleft was wider than her reach, she must cling to one side or the other. Sometimes she climbed with her arms and legs braced tightly against each side, working herself up the middle. Once the walls closed so narrowly against her shoulders and hips she feared she was stuck. But the tube of pale jagged chalk soon gave way to clay, smoother and more crumbly, but footsteps had been cut and there were handholds. Once water poured into a slit by her hand as she reached up, and she had to climb through the splashes and spray pattering down from above where the holds had been washed away. She came to the place where the water poured out of a groove, pulled herself up between dry walls above. There she rested, soaked and shivering, rubbing her shoulders and legs to restore warmth. The snowflakes had stopped falling.

She was thirsty again, but she had only to reach down into the spurting water, cup her hands, and drink. She stared in amazement. She was holding a piece of the Moon in her palm. Looking up, she glimpsed a patch of stars and a glaring horn of the Moon surrounded by black. It was high above her, and disappeared abruptly when she moved her head by even an eye's width. But it was there.

Aioula climbed with all her strength. She had climbed so far that she must be high in the sky. The clay gave way to soil with roots and white tubers in it, nurtured by the warmth below the ground, growing towards the light.

Dawn had come to the upper world.

The shaft opened into a narrow cavern little longer than a hut. Its roof was stone. At one side of the stone the rich red brickearth had fallen away from the roof, making the hole through which she had seen her saviour the Moon, and now blinding Sunlight beamed.

The hole was not half the size of her head. When she tried to widen the aperture only pebbles and grass trickled down. She could not force even one shoulder into the gap. Her way was blocked.

Aioula lay looking at the little cleft of the sky. She was exhausted.

The Yenush, clad enormously in black furs, leaning white-faced on her staff, clambered up the slope. No one ever came up here, there was no point. The people called it Chlud's Hill in deference to his stature. The flood-terraces left by the Great River were too steep for her and she put out her hand imperiously. A boy helped her. A group of loyal old men nervously awaited her approach on top of the hill.

She recovered her breath. 'Well?'

Kirik pointed.

The Yenush kicked the snow from the stone. It was covered with strange grooves as wide and deep as fingers. Twelve by twelve by twenty-nine, and hundreds more going down into the ground, too many to recognise. But she understood at once.

She touched its surface longingly. She had known nothing of it, nothing. How could she have been so blind? She had never looked, never sought, never found. Her beliefs had been sufficient, and should have been sufficient for everyone. The Yenush clenched her fists, dropped her staff, and her voice gave vent to a great, formless scream.

She knew what the stone meant. The women, her own women, had betrayed her. The true religion had not been sufficient for them, they had chosen to believe there was more. She would make them rue their independence, their loss of faith, she swore it. She called them back.

But it was already too late. The path from the cliff was empty, and the last of the women toiled from sight around the side of the second hill, beneath the Sunrise.

The fat woman's lips twisted vindictively. 'This is the false god that has deceived us. Knock it down.'

She put out her hand and gripped the boy's shoulder with her fingers. She hobbled downhill after the people with all her strength. Behind her the old men shrugged. They kicked obediently at the stone until it fell over.

The stone in the roof fell over. Soil and pebbles rained down around Aioula. Complete darkness again surrounded her.

After a while she reached up, worked patiently with her fingers. More soil tumbled down. The stone's twisting fall had loosened the rocks around its base. She prised them away and the stone creaked, but it did not move again. Suddenly dirt showered around her, then she saw the sky.

She jumped up, clawed her hands on the side of the hole, pulled herself out on to the hilltop.

The great brown land stretched around her in all directions, vast, windy and deserted.

Aioula was entirely alone.

She screamed. She raised her fists and dug her fingernails into her hands until the blood ran down her arms. Her screams echoed between the two hills. She cursed those who had left her.

Make me live.

Clad only in a deerskin shroud, the figure of the girl dug in the floor of the womb. At first she shivered, then her work warmed her. A hand appeared in the earth. She took it in both her own hands, tugged, but it would not move. She recommenced her work, scooped away the chalk that had been stamped down. Again she gripped the hand and it moved. Suddenly the arm that was attached to it came up clad in fur, then the whole body came up showering chalkdust, its knees still bent to its chin.

Make me strong.

She unstrapped the thongs and toggles, pulled off Qeetal the hunter's cold furs, wrapped them around her own body. She tied them tight with jerks of her fist. Now her skin was warm.

But she was still cold inside.

She took a flint, sliced a strip from under the thigh, ate. The blood was good. She looked around her as she ate. This was a good place.

Her jaws stopped. She stared up by the flame of the burning taper. As the flame moved, so the animals moved. The herds began their migration, the multitude of them flowed like liquid between the hills and spread out across the plain, reindeer, roe deer, red deer, faster and faster. Wild horses neighing, the thunder of their hooves. A panther dropped from a tree onto the shape of a man.

She finished eating, then wiped her hands on her furs. The rocks that sealed the entranceway were too heavy for her muscles to shift. She made her way back through the caverns, then climbed the shaft to the top of Chlud's Hill. The Sun hung in the mid-afternoon, giving her time to get down to the gorge and back again. She descended the slope of the hill, took the precarious cliff path down to the settlement.

One look at the heavy boulders sealing the sacred entranceway convinced her that there was no hope of opening the cavern again. The settlement was gone as though it had never been. Apart from useless things left behind, a few broken poles, discarded flints, scraps of bone, the place of Chlud's people gave no sign it had ever been inhabited. It never would be again. Only a forgotten fire still guttered on the moss.

She kicked it out and climbed back to the top of the hill.

The Sun died, and the Moon was born.

Alone, Aioula clung to the cliffs, reached out for eggs without falling, sucked them where she found them. Once she caught a puffin in her bare hands.

Alone in the river's icy spray she crouched on a chalk boulder, and speared a salmon as it leapt. She found freshwater mussels in the pools and cracked their shells. She gnawed pine-nuts and hazel-nuts.

Two-Hills shimmered in the brief warmth of summer. Ice was only a finger's reach beneath the ground but midges, gnats, mosquitoes swarmed above the myriad shallow ponds in whining clouds. Pond-weed and sedges, campion and plume-thistle, tormentil, silverweed, patched her land with garish colour. Berries flourished in brilliant haste before winter's return. Buttercups nodded their yellow heads, and rue, sorrel and thrift grew from the moss over the ice.

The first snow fell, and stole summer overnight.

Nothing moved except the hare. Like the others of his breed who lived here, he had no tail. His whiskers twitched and he crouched on his haunches, sensing danger. But there was no danger, only the faint scent of his own kind. He scratched the snow with his forepaws, nibbled the revealed shoots beneath, bobbed forward.

A woven grass noose flicked over his head. He ran. It was too late.

The hunter was dressed in hareskins that hid everything but her pale blue eyes. She lifted the hare by his kicking back legs, chopped with the side of her hand to break his neck. Loosening the slip-knot as she walked back to the smooth snowy hilltop, she pulled up the square of thatch that hid the hole in the ground, dropped inside. The air coming up from below, which never changed temperature all year round, was warm enough to melt the snow on the stone. She unfolded the clay that hid the glowing embers of her fire and blew them to flame, skinned and cooked the hare, and ate.

But the hunger in her belly did not diminish. It was another kind of hunger. If she'd had no food, she would have dreamt of eating. Since she had no man, she dreamt of children.

In her dreams she saw them as vividly as the painted children in the cavern far below, and when the dreams were worst she went down and tenderly placed her hands over the outlines of their hands, as if by the intensity of her act of will she could bring them to life again inside her, bring them to birth again of her own body.

She awoke alone, hunted alone, ate alone. She would grow old alone, break her bones alone, die alone.

Lean and strong, she climbed out of the hole beneath the stone, replaced the thatch to keep her home tidy and safe. The wind made her furs flap as she leant on her spear, gazed towards the Sunrise as she always did. This morning was different.

She watched a man walk down the slope opposite her. She knew that walk. She said nothing. She watched him slither across the brook, by now frozen again. She let him search around the flank of the hill, then waited. Finally she permitted him to see her.

He toiled uphill. He halted and put back the hood from his handsome face, taking in the curves of her body, then smiled nervously. He cleared his throat.

'Aioula, don't look at me like that. It's me, Keear.'

Part One

Ellen

London, 22 December 456 AD

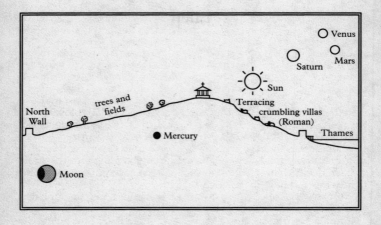

Midwinter's Day, AD 456

'London!' Ellen called. 'Mother, I can see London!'

The covered wagon jolted, blowing snow through the speak-hole over the driver's head, and Ellen dropped back on to her couch. She spluttered but Mother ignored her in the gloom. The child sulked, wiped the snowflakes from her cheeks and forehead, pulled herself on tiptoe and again squeezed her small determined face, ringed round with dark curls, into the speak-hole cut below the wagon's curving roof. From this bright vantage-point her pale blue eyes stared over the driver's frozen leather cap, the stench of his breath blowing past her nostrils in white puffing clouds, his thick hands wrapped with strips of frozen filthy leather lying in his lap, the frozen harness stretching from them to the snow-covered mules swaying wearily in front, faithfully following the line of carts ploughing into the snow.

Ellen decided that the heavily laden carts, covered with tarpaulins tightly roped down, looked like snails.

'Mother,' she called down, 'we're carrying our house on our backs, aren't we, just like snails do?'

Camilla sat unmoving in her priceless, threadbare blue gown. She would have brought her whole house with her if she could, brick by brick, and the rich black Fenland earth it stood on too. Her long white hand rested on her needlebox as though to restrain it from jumping away. Her household goods, thrown higgledy-piggledy around them, jangled and shook with the jarring of the unsprung wagon. She ignored everything bumping around her as calmly as though she sat in her bedroom. Her lips were white, her eyes dark brown holes, her wig piled up and carefully pinned. But she looked like a woman who has lost her life.

'How dare they?' she murmured. 'How dare they? Don't they know who we are?'

Ellen could not bear to listen. She pressed her face tight to the speak-hole.

The veils of snow shifted, and London changed into nothing more substantial than a line of trees.

The driver's head lolled. He was sleeping, exhausted.

Again came the crack of whips. The solid oak cartwheels – only one cart, immediately ahead of them, had spoked wheels with iron rims – rumbled like thunder on the broken snowy paving of Watling Street. Ellen heard the calls of the frightened drivers to one another, imagining attacks from the woods, or from culverts under the road, or from the bushes that had grown up like snowy mounds between the trees and the road. Sometimes there were bushes standing in the road, and the carts knocked them down. Far back a horse neighed, perhaps Father's, he was always where trouble was.

The shouts of running men drew closer behind them, catching up. The thin tinkle of swords sounded like breaking icicles. Someone screamed.

But still the driver snored. She reached through the speak-hole, nipped between her fingertips the hairs sprouting from his ear, and pulled.

'Faster, quick!'

The man woke with a yelp, cursed her, then saw who she was. Nevertheless he cursed her again in rough British. 'Do that again, you tiny bastard, and I'll kill you myself, that I will.'

Such insolence was startling, but still her mother did not respond, and Ellen knew they were in the hands of these ruffians. She was twelve years old and took refuge in her mother's Roman. 'Watch your tongue, you,' she commanded tartly, but he only laughed because she sounded so old-fashioned.

Ellen eyed the villain with uncertain glances, wishing she knew his name. She did not know any of the drivers' names, or from which hole on the estate Father had dredged such dregs. They were all dirty and smelly and all the same, all mortal property, slaves. 'What's your name?' she demanded.

'Hardalio, me.'

She threatened him imperiously, 'Attend to your task, Hardalio, or I shall tell my father, and Celatus Felix Caepio will have you flogged!'

Hardalio stuck out his tongue at the mention of her father's name, made the dreadful sign of the Evil Eye at her with his first and last fingers, and with his knuckles knocked the little hatch closed in her face.

Ellen gasped. She dropped down on the gilded horsehair couch set along the left side of the wagon. Her mother sat on the right-hand couch. Their knees touched as they were jolted from side to side by the motion of the vehicle, then their eyes met.

'Mother, will we die?'

'Of course not!' Camilla lifted her hand, her first helpless gesture. Her jewelbox chattered and spilt. Ellen collected handfuls of the stuff and Camilla draped herself with what she could, glittering necklaces of Empire workmanship, heavy gold bracelets, her rings, earrings. Ellen hugged her, wriggled into the warmth of her lap. Camilla looked down at her, and her expression softened.

'One day, my fierce daughter, everyone dies.'

'Not you, and not me,' Ellen said sleepily, and drew her black eyebrows together.

'Don't worry. Your father will see to us both before anything bad happens.'

Ellen imagined dying. She closed her eyes, and slept peacefully.

How little she knew of anything! Camilla stroked her daughter's curls and again her face became empty, drained of forcefulness. Her jewelled ears still heard the shrieks of her little maid Amanda Adelphia and the roars of Aeges's barbarians blundering through the fountains and trellises of her courtyard garden, heard their shouts of rage echoing in the deserted rooms and bare kitchens. She saw the flames rising through the thatch roof of the villa Celatus and the brightly painted walls blackened and burning, then the outhouses burning, the barns burning, everything burning. Her teeth chattered with anger and loss.

'The world is turned to fire,' she murmured. 'How dare they. How dare they!'

Aeges's raiders were the Wolves. Further south were the Stallions, the Horsemen, the Proud Tyrants and any number of other tribal gangs from the Continent, working alone or in alliance. Britain had few villages, and one by one the great landowners negotiated away their huge isolated properties field by field, or had them taken by force. Each year brought the continental invaders further inland, and by this time resistance was useless. Felix had ordered the carts, loaded by household slaves who by now were almost certainly dead or in chains wishing they were dead, to be hidden behind the slope of the vineyard. And it had been his idea – of course – to leave nothing for Aeges and his men to find in the house but an amphora of strong wine.

But it was the hardest time of the year for a journey. A hard time, and a long journey, and everything they could carry with them piled up in the line of wheeled vehicles bumping miserably into the rain and mud. Thirty-three carts of every sort had left the ruins of the villa Celatus, rattling on two wheels or four, solid or spoked, all of them old, a motley collection of heavy farm drays with sides and without them, wagons with roofs and wagons without, even an old chariot or two. Behind them Felix ordered the canal sluice gates broken down, drowning the orderly fields his family had cultivated for three hundred years or more. If he did not have them, no one would. Felix did not look back.

Fenland rain and fog hid the convoy, and the wine bought them a day clear of pursuit.

The coast was islands and floods. Refugees travelled across country towards the free British ports of the west.

But barbarians lived like animals anywhere in the undergrowth between the British towns. At Dunstable two nights ago the convoy found the Icknield Way, the old grand highway to the west, blocked by fire, looted wagons, Aeges's blond drunkards with bloody swords dripping in the rain, Aeges himself standing taller than his Wolves, and Camilla could not stop Ellen seeing the stripped mutilated bodies of people like themselves. After that Felix ordered the covered wagon containing his wife and daughter into the middle of the convoy, the place of least danger, and turned downhill into the sodden valleys of the south. 'It seems our pursuers got ahead of us,' he'd shrugged in that definite way he had, and his black cloak swirled. 'So we shall pick up the road to the west near London.' Nothing would defeat him. Camilla had loved him so much that she had wanted to enfold him in her love like his cloak.

But each milestone was further than the last. The endless rain turned to endless snow, and Aeges's attacks on the rearguard began again. That same afternoon the people of St Albans blocked their broken town gates with a rubbish of beams and smashed carts, their small ragged figures scampering along the ramparts, and a man claiming tribuniciate rank stood on the roof of an apartment block shouting at the travellers to go away. 'Have mercy, in God's name!' Felix roared, but they threw stones. The local *tyrannus*, Elafus, needing what little winter fodder he had, could offer little more than shelter in a decayed villa and a shrugging exchange of bad news.

Yes, the world is turned to fire and ice. Camilla felt Ellen's hand curl sleepily around her own in that way she'd always had, and she gripped as tightly as she was gripped, closing her eyes to the pain of her arthritis.

Ellen peeped from beneath her eyelashes. Mother slept, or perhaps she too was pretending, as she had last night. Had either of them slept at all, enduring the long slow climb towards the staging post at Brockley Hill, the drivers looking over their shoulders every step of the way, the whips cracking, the animals slipping and falling in the snow as darkness fell? Ellen had not.

Just before they had arrived, Father's black horse burst forward through a flurry of snow. He gripped one of the four saddle-horns and leant across, saw Ellen's little face pressed to the speak-hole, raised his sword and promised her exultantly, 'We shall see London and the road to the west in the morning!'

Ellen had watched him with a radiant expression. He'd struck the horse's bare flanks with the heels of his stiff leather boots, and the horse shot forward.

But the staging post was abandoned. They sheltered in the derelict stable and drank from the well. Nothing else remained of the place. Father prowled outside, guarding the guards so that they should not run away. He never slept.

At first light she'd peeped through the doorway and seen him standing alone on the empty road. Ellen was too much in awe of him to approach. During the night Father had exchanged his cloak for the heavy woollen overcoat, his hooded *byrrus britannicus*, its warm folds secured by a tasselled rope around his waist. Away from his land he was no longer a *tyrannus*, and his own clergy had run away before the final attack on the villa Celatus, but she thought he looked a little like a priest. She dared not move in case he heard her. Her muscles stiffened. She watched breathlessly as Father put back the bulky cowl on to his shoulders, which seemed enormously broad and strong against dawn's grey line. Bareheaded, he dropped to his knees and clasped his hands in prayer. He uttered the Christian mantra, 'Rotas. Opera. Tenet. Arepo. Sator.' But Father was not facing west like most Christians. Ellen decided he had probably forgotten which direction that was.

Then the sun rose in front of Father, flashing rays for a brief moment beneath the snowclouds, and his silhouette lifted its arms. He bowed his head three times. 'Soli Invicto!'

The sun climbed into the clouds and winked out. The snow began again. Father got to his feet, beat his sword on a shield to rouse the groaning drivers, and the moment of calm and peace was gone as though it had never happened. Eighteen carts, double-loaded, remained of those which had left the villa Celatus. As the column breasted the hilltop Ellen had kept her face pressed at the speak-hole, excited to see London, the hub of all roads, in the distance as Father had promised her.

London, she'd called. *Mother, I can see London!*

But London had changed to nothing more than the line of trees falling away towards the snowplain below, and Hardalio the driver had been asleep.

Now Hardalio rubbed his ear, still cursing her for waking him.

The four-wheeled wagon creaked and banged, and the cacophony of iron pots and pans inside made a din like a sutler's cart. Ellen had wrapped them in a whole wardrobe of Mother's bright tunics and gowns, anything she could find to muffle the noise, but nothing worked. On the top shelf, protected by a fillet of wood and tied tightly with twine, Mother's ornamental Nene Valley unguent pots – possibly from the hands of Vediacus himself – that once contained valuable perfumes, spices, oils, medicines, jingled like tiny musical instruments. The set of copper colanders and strainers that Mother claimed was a hundred years old swung clinking from the hooks beneath the shelf, silver cutlery clattered in a box, and a helmet – they'd thought it was lost – gonged hollowly as it rolled on the floor. Ellen put out her foot and stopped it. The spindle and bone weaving combs for cloth were crammed in one corner, the embroidery frame wedged on top of them. She had been told that the furniture and rugs, the heavy farm implements, everything else they would need to start their new home across the sea in Brittany, had been flung into the other carts. No one talked about her toys or her nurserymaid, Monica Numidea.

There was a loud thud on the side of the wagon. The driver lashed the whip and the motion redoubled, then they heard cries rising all around them as though the trees had come to life. Hardalio shouted at the mules, 'Yi, yi, yah!' The wagon jerked, bounced, threw mother and daughter painfully against one another, threw them apart. With frightened faces they hung on to the shelves. Ellen caught the little sieve that jumped off its hook, then had to grab with both hands against the vibration of the wheels, and the sieve was flattened by something else falling.

'Oh, I hate this!' her mother exclaimed. 'I wish it was over!' She screamed as her pots crashed down and shattered, tried to gather up the sharp pieces between her forearms, shouted as everything else fell down around her.

The wagon veered from the highway, following a steep local diverticulus of the sort lately called a lane. The sounds of skirmish and pursuit faded behind them. Ellen jumped up to the speak-hole. 'Hardalio, stop!'

The wagon careered through a tumbledown hamlet of the window-less thatch huts favoured by Saxon farmers, scattered chickens and children, and came into the trees again where there was little snow. Ahead, the carts pulled into a loose circle near a stony mere and the wagon joined them, then the last carts drew up behind.

The noise stopped. Everyone touched their ears as though they had fallen deaf. A bird clattered in the reeds, breaking the intense quiet.

'By all the angels of Hell,' Hardalio swore in a shaky voice, 'the pagan piss-drinking bastards nearly had us! What's got into them? Why us? Why don't the bastards pick on someone else?' The other drivers murmured, shook their heads, looked fearfully up the lane. 'Where's the guard? Jesus' blood, don't our three-named master pay them enough?'

'Where is my father?' Ellen called out in a high voice. 'Where are we?'

Hardalio recovered his composure. He scratched his ginger whiskers. 'As for the first, why should I care? As for the second, Caesar's Pond.' He wound the reins around the whip-holder, jumped down. He nodded at the filthy scratching urchins who stared curiously from the trees, barked a few words and received a reply, threw a stone to scatter them. 'Stone Mere, to these blond bastards. Mere's their name for a pond, see.'

Camilla opened the rear door. Her hair had escaped from under her wig. One chestnut curl stranded with silver hung over her eye. 'Stanmore? You mean you speak the Saxon tongue?'

Hardalio shrugged. 'English, which is mostly what we get in the Fens, but it's much the same.'

'Then I'm amazed my husband has trusted you!'

Hardalio grinned. He broke a reed and stuck it in his mouth. 'Well, he can't be choosy about his help now, can he?' He jerked the reed with his teeth in salutation, stuck his thumbs through his string belt, and wandered off among the men peeing against the beech trunks. Camilla bit her tongue, ignored them. If they were anything like the brute Hardalio – and she could see they were – they would not bother to obey orders from her. Here she was merely the wife of Celatus Felix Caepio, his shadow. These days, she knew, even slaves thought they were as good as their masters. Some had changed sides and become masters, and many masters were slaves. Everything that had once been an advantage, manners, accent, breeding, was now a disadvantage. The world was upside down.

She thought, where is Felix?

Suppose Felix is dead?

Ellen watched her mother's lips soundlessly moving. She listened to the men's nervous laughter about their escape, their jokes. Everyone had a story to tell. Someone was trying to hammer a crooked wheel straight. It was the cart with spoked wheels.

She asked, 'Can I get out?'

'If you must.'

Mother stayed at the wagon, but Ellen knelt by the pool. 'Mother? Aren't you thirsty?'

Suppose Felix is dead? Camilla felt sick. She noticed the spear stuck in the side-beam of the wagon. Her legs began to shiver, then her whole body gave a shudder, and now she had started she could not stop herself. A hand's-breadth above or below . . . she imagined the point thudding through the thin planks into the back of Ellen's neck, or between her shoulderblades. She pulled her cloak over her head to hide her feelings.

Ellen called from the pool, 'Have we escaped?'

'Escape?' Mother threw her a haunted look from beneath the cloak. That look said they would not escape until they were safe in Brittany. The free ports of the west were at least a hundred miles away and Camilla doubted the roads. She doubted ships and the wind even more. She hated the sea.

She said firmly, 'As long as your father is alive we are safe.'

Ellen wiped drops of water from her lips. 'Why won't the Saxons leave us alone? Why won't they stop? All this fighting for a set of silver spoons and some ploughs.'

Camilla was vague. 'There are always rumours . . . Lies.'

'Can't we just give them to him?'

Camilla said simply, 'How dare you believe your father would submit to anyone.'

'Aeges must be mad.' Ellen noticed her mother's wrists trickling with blood, ran to her. 'You've cut yourself! Haven't you seen your arms?'

Camilla realised it for the first time. She stopped trying to tie the cloak and it dropped down. The mass of jewellery draped over her azure gown made her look privileged, ungrateful, pathetic. Old. The lines intensified on her naked face, bereft of makeup or youth, as she remembered scraping up her broken pots. 'I shouldn't have tried to . . . but you can't get them any more. It's only scratches. Oh, Ellen, I should never have left my home!'

'Our home,' Ellen said.

Camilla steadied herself. 'That's what I meant, of course.' But suppose Felix was dead? What would they do? The circle of thought went round and round.

The drivers waited by the lake scratching themselves and yawning. Mostly they were dressed in sacks, torn bits of leather and fur. A few took pitchforks and spades for weapons and stood peering back up the lane, increasingly anxious. Ellen wrung out a rag at the pool and calmly wiped the splinters from her mother's cuts. A mule whinnied softly to its friend by another cart. Half a dozen men tried to lift the cart with the crooked wheel then called for a hand. Hardalio obliged, braced himself. He muttered at the unexpected strain. 'What's in these things? Stones?'

'Hup, easy, easy,' someone grunted, then cursed his back. 'Bit more – bit more. There.' The spoked wheel came off, thudded on the ground. The men lowered the cart carefully and it canted over. 'Don't ask,' the man advised Hardalio, favoured his aching back, then knelt to help the men working on the wheel. Hardalio twitched the reed between his teeth, his eyes moving between the men busy at their work and the heavily laden cart. One of the knots holding down the cover had come loose. He thought about ploughs and silver spoons.

The men by the lane discussed sending up a scout. They couldn't decide who should go. There was no one to give them orders.

Ellen said, 'Mother, are you frightened?'

Camilla answered in a high, quick voice, 'You must never be frightened.'

'I am.'

'Of course you are, but you must never admit it. You must conceal everything important. I have brought you up as a lady, Ellen, and we are surrounded by enemies.'

It was not ladylike for a girl or a woman to wear gloves, only workmen did. Ellen pulled her long sleeves over her hands, hiding them to keep them warm.

'Good manners. That's better.' Camilla tried desperately not to keep looking at the lane. She controlled her shivering by an effort of will and pointed her head at the debris littering the inside of the wagon. 'We'll have to clear up it up ourselves, I suppose.' Neither of them mentioned Amanda Adelphia or graceful black Monica Numidea, the household slaves and all the others on the estate who'd had to be left behind. Then Camilla spoke out. 'There just wasn't room. The barbarians are too greedy and lazy to damage skilled farmworkers, valuable property.' Both females were silent, remembering Amanda's shrieks. The Wolves had come faster than expected, Mother had tripped and fallen, and Father had ordered little Amanda Adelphia back to the house for something he had forgotten. Monica Numidea had insisted on going with her friend.

Their shrieks lasted for an hour, buying time.

Mother looks ill, Ellen decided. It was more than just her swollen ankle. Camilla was about fifty years old. Without her busy household and its complicated daily routines, worries and concerns, she had nothing to do. Her life was out of her control and she was a different woman. Her mouth had wrinkled, sour with loss and the bruising indignities of the journey. Her eyes kept flicking towards the empty lane and Ellen really thought her mother might go mad. 'I'll clear the mess up,' she offered. Mother glanced at her impatiently, then returned her gaze to the lane. Ellen busied herself setting things to rights in the wagon, though she knew as soon as they set off it would all fall down again. She found every last one of the little pots broken but she didn't have the heart to throw the pieces away, knowing such fine work would never be seen again.

She heard a commotion outside and jumped down, ran to her mother. Shapes moved in the woods. The men fell back fearfully, but suddenly Camilla rushed forward, pushed them aside.

'Felix!'

Father walked backwards from the shadows beneath the trees. His sword was broken; only the leather-wrapped handle hung forgotten from his hand. His horse was gone, his dagger-scabbard empty. He carried a dripping bundle across his shoulders, wrapped in his cloak. He did not look at his wife.

Camilla hung on to him. She could not let him go. Her hands clung to his arms, she touched his face appealingly. The silver crossbow brooch that clasped his *byrrus* at his throat looked unsettlingly like the shape of a crucified man. He knew what his wife was feeling. He rebuked her gently, 'Camilla.'

She broke down. 'Felix, I thought you were dead. I thought you were dead.' She dropped to her knees on the dead leaves and snow. He turned away to deal with more important matters. She raised her voice when he could not pay her enough attention.

Father called to Ellen in a low voice, 'Look after your mother. Hush.' He was concerned that her hysteria would infect the men.

Ellen put her arms round her mother's back, patted her as though comforting a child. Camilla sobbed. 'Hush, Mother. Hush . . .'

'I'm sorry,' Camilla whispered. 'I'm so ashamed of myself.'

Father swung the burden from his back. His brown eyes, almost black, had taken in the situation in the clearing at once. In the British tongue he rapped out orders to the drivers. 'You lucky men with pitchforks, stand between the track and the carts. The rest of you fall back. Water the mules from pails, don't unhitch them. Jump to it!' They jumped.

He glanced at Ellen. Suddenly he smiled, and Ellen smiled back at him, basking in his attention. Camilla looked from each of their faces and back to the other, hushed by their silence. Her fingertips touched her lips, excluded.

The moment broke. In Roman, still the language of military men, Father bellowed for his German mercenaries in the trees. 'Leubasnus, Dannicus, to me!'

Nothing moved. A blackbird foraged in the dry leaves.

Leubasnus's voice called out, 'Dannicus is captured. How is Maduhus?'

Father knelt beside Camilla. He moved her hands aside tenderly and examined the bundle he had laid down. With an expression of compassion he closed the folds of his cloak over the staring mutilated face.

'Maduhus is dead.'

He stood. Tiredness did not touch him. Everyone in the clearing watched him, everyone depended on him. Father was no taller than other men, but he made them seem shorter than he. He was broader and heavier than they. His eyes were restless with vitality, dark brown, almost black. Strikingly for a man of his age, he had all his teeth, and his hair was black to the roots.

He ordered, 'Leubasnus, deploy your men in the trees on each side of the track!'

'Men? What men?' Leubasnus was almost hidden by trees and shadows, but they recognised his battered glinting helmet. He still clung to the title of *foederatus*, and he looked like the ghost of a Roman centurion, but his tattered greasy *sagum* cape was stolen and his boots were a dead man's. Other mercenary *foederati* shifted in the trees behind him. Their eyes found the bundle that contained Maduhus. 'You've killed my best men,' Leubasnus called sadly. 'All my double-pay *duplicarius* troopers are dead. We have fulfilled our duty to your gold and your name, and to our pride.' He listened as a forsaken cry echoed between the bare trees. 'Dannicus!'

Father offered, 'Share Maduhus's clothes among you. All the wine you can drink when we reach the sea. More money.'

Leubasnus spat. 'What good are wine and clothes to dead men? You have destroyed us.' He raised his arm in farewell, and his men melted away after him.

Camilla said, 'But they can't leave us.'

Ellen understood how her father's mind worked. 'They won't,' she said. 'They'll change sides.'

Father nodded. 'I would.'

Camilla could not understand treachery. She said, 'But we trusted them.'

He shrugged. 'It will take them a while to convince their new masters of their sincerity. By the time they do, we shall not be here.' He watched the men repairing the wheel, raised his voice. 'Hurry!'

Ellen brought him a skin of water from the pool. Father leant alone against the wagon and she watched him drink. For the first time he looked tired. She washed out the rag and bound the cut on his left hand which he had not noticed. He grinned at her, then ouched as she pulled the knot tight.

'Hush,' she said without thinking, but he was not offended. He laughed, tousled her curls.

'Camilla . . . your mother wanted a boy. But I think you're stronger than a boy, aren't you, Ellen?' She smiled, excited to see her reflection in his dark eyes. They were widely spaced and sensitive, all his concentration upon her. 'How old are you now? About eleven?'

'I'm twelve, Father.'

'Have I missed you already?' His gaze flickered. He sounded sad. 'You know what may happen to us.'

She tugged the spear and said fiercely, 'I'm not frightened of anything if I'm with you.'

He looked at her appraisingly, then his eyes narrowed. He stared over her head at the broken cart. The men had lifted its side, the spoked wheel was knocked back on the axle. Now the driver complained about his back and a second man knelt, hammering the wooden peg that locked the wheel in place. A third man whistled softly to himself, his fingers busy at the back of the cart.

Ellen followed her father's gaze. She said cheerfully, 'That's Hardalio.'

Father didn't hear her. He had put down the water-skin and prowled forward without a sound, like a hunting animal, across the leaves and stones. Hardalio hummed to himself, his fingers busy at the knot. The knot came free, the canvas flapped down.

The cargo shone.

Hardalio stared. He swore. He reached out his grasping hands. He did not look behind him.

Father knocked him down. He flapped the cover into place and jerked the knot tight. He picked up Hardalio by his ear or his hair, Ellen couldn't tell which. Hardalio struggled. Father put his face close. He whispered.

Hardalio howled, shockingly loud. 'See nothing, I didn't! I didn't!'

Father moved. Hardalio squealed like a pig. Father's knee stuck in the small of Hardalio's back. He twisted Hardalio's arm, and Hardalio screamed until he had no breath.

Father said, 'Now.'

Hardalio gasped. He whooped for air, squealed, 'Gold. Gold!'

Father whispered, 'That's all you saw?'

'Yes, yes!' Hardalio screamed again. 'Gold, that's all! A few lumps of brown leather! Skin! Nothing!'

Father reached for his sword but his sword was broken. He felt for his dagger but his dagger was lost. He took the tasselled rope at his waist, dropped a loop over Hardalio's head, pulled the golden tassels tight. Hardalio clawed the rope. Father stood on Hardalio's feet to stop him kicking. Hardalio's struggles weakened. He hung limp.

Father did not let the body go. He stared from left to right at the men gathered around him. Father made a low growling in his throat and chest. Ellen thought he sounded like a wild beast. The men looked uneasily at the woods, the lake. Christianity was the surface of their religion, but the older spirits of trees and pools, stones and sky and sun, were still gods. The word *pagan* meant countryman. Like most of the great landowners, beneath his house-chapel and quarters for Christian clergy Father had preserved a Deep Room for pagan rites, its walls decorated with swastika and leaf patterns, Jupiter in the guise of a bull, other beasts, and much more.

Father growled. Ellen ran to him carrying the spear. Father dropped the body and took the spear. The silver cross flashed at his throat. He growled, 'Now get back to your carts.' He turned his back on the men.

No one looked at Hardalio. Then one driver stepped over the body and returned to his cart. He swung himself aboard, clicked his teeth and lashed the whip, and the cart jerked forward to the head of the column. One by one the other drivers followed.

Father hefted the spear. He watched Ellen with that same appraising look in his eye. Then he said, 'Well done.'

He hugged her, lifting her feet off the ground, and Ellen thrilled. But she went on in her practical way, her voice muffled by his *byrrus*, 'Who will drive our wagon now?'

Father laughed. 'Ask me no more questions,' he said.

One of the men with pitchforks came out of the trees. A bald, fat man, he dragged something behind him that struggled and bit. 'Look-a-here what I got me, Magister, ears flapping trying to overhear us! A Saxon brat. Knaves, they call themselves.' He cuffed the filthy blond boy until the knave hung quiet, snivelling.

Father knelt and said kindly, in English, 'What's your name?'

The knave spat and was cuffed. Father asked him again.

'Wixan, us,' the boy said proudly.

'That's his tribe.' Father shook his head. 'Your own name, knave. I won't hurt you.'

'Wemba, me, myself!'

'Spirited lad.' Father pointed to the body of Maduhus. 'Ellen, bring me his boots.'

The feet were cold and stiff and the boots did not come off easily, but Ellen did as she was told. She did not have to touch Maduhus's skin. Father took the boots.

'These are worth much' – he searched for a word – 'much barter. They are yours if you help me.'

The knave grabbed at the boots but Father held them back.

'Uphill there are men who want to kill me. I do not want to go that way. Is there another way I can go?'

46

The boy did not take his eyes off the boots. He pointed at the far end of the clearing.

'These people live in villages,' Father told Ellen and the driver in a low voice. 'They avoid towns and main roads. They forge their own primitive pathways through the forest.' He asked, 'Is the' – again he searched for the word – 'is the *lane* wide enough for carts or only for feet?'

The knave shrugged. He said a word. Father asked, 'Hunig? Does that mean honey? Hunigpotte?'

'Honeypot Lane, he calls it,' the driver spat. 'Means it's deep mud, Magister. These pagans mean what they say. Sticky as honey, see.'

Father thought about it. 'But today the mud will be frozen hard.' He tossed the boots to the knave. 'Yours.'

The driver called cheerfully, 'Want me to do him in, Magister?'

'No, let him go. He's a brave lad, and I hate a useless death.' Father muttered to Ellen, 'Aeges and Leubasnus will be after us soon enough. But they still have no horses or mules, so we'll stay ahead of them.'

He swung himself on to the driver's bench of the wagon. 'Ellen, inside, and look after your mother.'

'But Father, I could help you—' Ellen saw his look and bowed her head.

Father said gently, 'Nothing is more important than obedience. It is your absolute duty to your family, Ellen. The daughter becomes the mother. One day, you will be her. Do you understand?'

'Yes, Father.' Ellen stood watching the heavily laden carts pulling forward, rocking along the narrow lane. She wondered what they contained that was more important than all their lives. She wondered what Aeges and Leubasnus knew that she did not.

'Ellen!' Mother clicked her fingers frantically from the rear door as the wagon jolted from the clearing. Ellen ran forward and jumped aboard. Mother wrapped her arms around her. The wagon swayed gently, sleepily, across the forest floor of leaves and pine needles.

Ellen murmured, 'Mother, what did Hardalio see?'

Mother said, 'Nothing.' She closed her eyes and stroked her daughter's curls. 'Nothing.'

The wagon gave a terrific lurch across a tree root and everything that had been put up fell down at once. Ellen scrambled on the couch, pressed her face to the speak-hole. Honeypot Lane led from the forest into lighter woodlands, probably Roman fields left untended for generations and grown over, only older trees and lines of mossy stones showing where their boundaries had been. The road was frozen hard as Father had promised. Occasionally the convoy passed desultory groups, farmers working with an axe or two. Fields deserted less long had reverted to impenetrable brushwood and bramble, only a narrow path hacked between them for the lane.

Father noticed her little face peeping from the speak-hole. He nodded to the left. 'Saxon lanes wander like drunken men, but we're keeping roughly alongside Watling Street.' Ellen glimpsed the straight line of the military road flickering through the trees and snow.

'Is Aeges over there?'

He nodded. 'Somewhere. And my old friend Leubasnus, the traitor.' He took mercy on her. 'Open the hatch if you like, get a better view.'

Ellen popped open the roof hatch and stuck her head and shoulders outside. She rested her elbows on the roof. Now that she could no longer depend on Mother – rather, it seemed, Mother depended on her – she felt like an adult. She leaned closer to Father. The snow blew thinly in her eyes. She blinked, thinking she saw something move on Watling Street. She said, 'Do you think Aeges has given up?'

Father shook his head.

From time to time they passed paths leading towards the Roman road, most with a hovel or two thrown up nearby, a few pigs, chickens, children roaming about. The half-dozen fields looked like tiny miserable holes hacked out of the woodland, incorrigible sticky clay showing through where the wind blew away the snow.

Father hauled on the reins. The nine carts in front had stopped and the lead driver pointed at the marshland ahead. He spoke to someone yellow-haired and sullen, shrugged. 'These folk call it the Brent river. He says there's no way across.'

'Watling Street.' Father nodded up the path to their left, lined with bare oaks. He held the wagon back, then followed last behind the carts. He pushed the spear into the whip-holder and lashed the whip.

The path skirted oak pools and marshes. Everything was ice, or they would not have got through. The carts pulled uphill towards the Roman road. The whips cracked like snapping fingers in the grey air.

The lead cart turned right. Watling Street stretched like a ghostly white spear through the gloom. The culverts were blocked and the carts splashed through the River Brent washing across the roadway. Here there were no people, no dwellings, only the empty road. Far behind them Ellen glimpsed the glow of fire, and the veils of snow burned orange from the ground to the underside of the clouds.

Father had seen. 'They've burnt the staging post at Brockley Hill.'

Mother overheard him. She called, 'Everything is turned to fire. I said so.'

Father said grimly, 'Fire and blood, the torrents of Satan. And the fiery flames shall eat up the foundations of the earth, and the rocks shall burn like rivers of pitch.'

Mother's voice called up, 'It is the end of the world. It is as it was foreseen in the Prayer of Thanksgiving.'

Father shrugged. 'It's always the end of the world.'

The carts came to the River Kilburn and splashed to the other side. Father looked back. 'Here they come.' The tiny forms of men swarmed across the Brent, silent at this distance. Yesterday he had cut the throat of every mule that fell so it should not be put to use by their enemies. Aeges and his Wolves still waged their ragged pursuit on foot. Such feats were a test of manhood and comradeship to them, and their stamina was formidable. Felix could see their breath and the heat of their bodies hanging like mist above their heads.

He cursed them.

The carts were strung out now. The wheels rattled on the broken stones.

'Not far to the road to the west,' Father said. Then he stood up on the seat, roaring. The lead cart had reached a large geometrical stone and instead of turning right at the crossroads, turned left. The seventeen carts following hesitated, then turned after him.

Father dragged on the reins. He halted the wagon on the elbow of the junction. He stared. He said, 'My God.'

The road to the west was blocked with people, hundreds of people, thousands. The broad mass of them moved slowly, flowed wearily from the trees on one side into the trees on the other. Weapons had been thrown away anywhere. The wail of children filled the air, and the groans of wounded men and the women who helped them rose up like the lowing of cattle.

Felix knew he was seeing more than a defeated army. He was seeing a migration, a whole defeated nation on the move.

There was no way through. People fell into the ditches and lay dying. Someone called out in a British accent, 'Plague!'

Father covered his mouth. Ellen watched him. She did the same.

Together father and daughter looked from the mass of people on their right, to the Wolves approaching behind them down Watling Street, then to the empty road to the left and the town about two miles away.

Father cracked the whip. 'London. We'll take ship from there!'

The pale walls of London shimmered between the bare black treetops. The grey-green Thames curved out of sight behind the town, reappeared in the distance. Beyond the hilltops of the horizon a great column of black smoke hung motionless, wider at the top than at the bottom, looking solid enough to overbalance on to the white forests below.

The wagon slowed a little, plunged down through the River Tyburn, then the mules pulled for all they were worth. The Wolves behind did not slow for the water. They ran so close now that Ellen could hear them grunting. An arrow whickered, glanced off the wagon roof, a long splinter stuck up. Ellen ducked inside, grabbed an iron saucepan to throw. It bounced off the roadway and the leading man jumped it, lost his rhythm, fell back. The others ran past him with their elbows tucked in to their sides. Aeges sprinted in front of them. She recognised him because of his height. His long straw-coloured hair flew behind him.

Ellen ducked down. 'Mother! Quick!'

Mother passed up whatever came to hand, bigger saucepans then smaller ones, and Ellen threw them. They rang like gongs. The gridiron, a copper *caccabus* cookpot, grandmother's *thermospodium* food-warmer, embroidered cushions, rugs, finally the precious set of sieves and colanders. Aeges dodged them or knocked them aside with his sword. His eyes stared with his effort, straining. His lips opened to show his honey-blackened teeth. He had stained his face with red powder to make himself look terrifying. He beat at the back of the wagon with his sword. He reached out, his fingers snatched at the rear door. It swung open.

Mother screamed.

Aeges lunged forward, clung to the step.

Ellen flung the cutlery box. It caught Aeges in the chest. The silver spoons exploded round him like spray. He let go, fell away, rolled over and over in the road like a snowy white sausage.

Mother slammed the door closed.

A roan horse stood patiently by a dead body. The horse shied as the carts rolled past and a man wearing a helmet caught its reins.

Ellen clung to the roof. The two hills of London rose above them, then the town's massive ragstone walls, and the carts bounded downhill almost out of control into the valley of the River Fleet. All around them was a huge graveyard, headstones and grave markers humped everywhere beneath the snow, bits of broken statuary sticking up, a woman's stone hand, a stone sword, stone heads with haughty stone eyes. The carts' brake-poles dragged in the groove cut down the centre of the road, the sparks flew up like brief lives. Below, a wooden bridge leapt the Fleet. A party of workmen sent from the town hacked at the supports with axes. They saw the carts coming down and tried to wave them away, then abandoned their work and retreated towards the gate opened for them, built later than the others, and even after all these years still called the New Gate. They gathered in the shadows and shouted threats.

The carts thundered over the bridge. The timbers rocked alarmingly. One railing collapsed. The roadway slanted, showering snow from its sides, but held up.

'Father!' Ellen shouted. A man on a roan horse rode up behind them. Ellen recognised the glinting brass helmet. 'It's Leubasnus.'

Father lashed the whip. But the carts lost speed, labouring uphill. The heads of the exhausted beasts tossed from side to side. Lather trickled from their nostrils and streaked their flanks.

The workmen ran behind the walls of London and turned back, pushed at the gates to close them.

Father stood on the seat. He roared, 'Open them in God's name or

50

I'll kill you all. I'll kill your wives. I'll make slaves of your children.' He gripped the cross at his throat. 'I swear!'

A man appeared on the bastion high above. He wore a gown of white wool.

Leubasnus rode up alongside the wagon. He swung his sword. The metal flashed.

The man in white watched the scene below him, then raised his right hand. The men opened the gate. The first carts rumbled, echoing, into the tunnel cut through the thick wall.

Again Leubasnus swung his sword at Father. 'For Maduhus!' he cried. 'For Dannicus!' Ellen reached down for something to throw but found nothing. 'Traitor!' she screamed.

Father took the spear from the whip-holder and thrust it through Leubasnus's face. The horse stopped, then turned and galloped away carrying its grisly cargo.

The wagon thundered into the tunnel. The gates slammed closed behind them. Father pulled on the reins. He looked around him. He sighed a deep lungful of air and hugged Ellen tight.

Then a voice called from above, 'My dear Felix, my brother in Christ, I see you are alive. Welcome to London!'

The sky above the battlements gleamed with the setting sun. Ellen shielded her eyes and watched the man in white bless them from the parapet. He held a shepherd's crook in one hand. The sun limned the strands of his silver hair. He held out his arms to take in all of them, even the drivers, as he called down, 'I am Mansuetus, Archbishop of London, Metropolitan Bishop of Maxima Caesarensis. Welcome, welcome, all of you, to the City of St Peter and St Paul. Alleluia!'

His image nodded to itself, as though acknowledging his shadow cast over them, then he turned and squinted at the sun, shielding his eyes just as Ellen did. He stepped from the battlements to the bastion on his right, and they saw his shadow moving across the gatehouse windows as he started down the stairwell inside.

'You lucky lads,' Father called to the drivers, though he looked surprised that the archbishop had bothered to notice their sort. 'A blessing from Archbishop Mansuetus. Worth an extra year on your miserable lives, I'd say.'

'That's nothing,' the lead driver bragged. 'Me, I was baptised by the hands of Bishop Germanicus of Auxerre, at St Albans, where he routed those heretic Pelagist bastards by the power of his voice alone. You didn't get any better than St Germanicus on this earth, I'll tell you. Immortality, his touch was.'

Father chuckled, then wound the reins around the whip-holder. 'Yes, but you still have to die first.'

'I'm a good Christian, sir, the best that was ever born. My old master never had to beat *me* to get me to a Christian service . . .'

The man's bragging bored Ellen. She jumped on to the dirty

roadway, gazed around her excitedly. London, City of St Peter and St Paul, was all she had imagined. 'Father, I'm glad we didn't go to the west!' she exclaimed.

He looked interested. 'Are you?' he said.

The City was huge. The perimeter cradled a whole different world safe inside its huge walls and forts and staked ditches, quite different from the wasteland of moor and forest beyond the fortifications. Ellen saw painted houses with tiled roofs, distant palaces, terraced fields, rows of trees, a grid of roadways running in orderly lines in every direction. She had never seen anything so wonderful.

She clapped her hands and brown London ravens flew up, circled with heavy claps of their wings against the white sky.

Then she noticed that the ground and roadways nearby were covered with litter that no one bothered to clear up. Ditches blocked with rubbish overflowed where the sun touched. A low raggle-taggle of thatch huts and stalls had grown out of the mud near the New Gate to take advantage of the trade it provided, but when she looked more closely she realised the thatch was black with rot. One hut had collapsed. A cockeyed mossy sign above a deserted booth proclaimed, 'Senacus Makes the Best Shoes. Soles Drawn and Fitted.' A dog watched them without barking.

Mother ran to Father and embraced him in public. She wept openly, though whether from relief that they were saved or from the loss of her silver spoons, Ellen could not tell. Typically, Mother turned on her. 'Get out of the mud! Look at your shoes!'

Ellen sulked. She muttered that she'd get another pair from Senacus. She jumped on to the verge of broken paving-stones, piled up for some roadworks or other that had not occurred. Most of the workmen had drifted away, but a few slipped out and through the giant gate she saw them working again with their axes to destroy the bridge. They did not seem accustomed to the labour and she wondered if they had the skill to rebuild it once it was gone. Without the bridge the road would be useless. She did not understand how the people would get across.

She looked around her. 'Father! Where are the people?'

He shrugged.

They heard rubbish kicked aside in the stairwell and Mansuetus emerged. The archbishop was still a considerable, muscular figure of a man, but less imposing close to than from afar. Ellen was disappointed to find him only human, about fifty years old but looking older. First among whatever bishops of southern and western Britain were left alive, the pontifex had long silver hair that crawled with fleas like any man's. His white Roman gown was ancient, faded to the colour of oatmeal, blotched and spattered, the elbows and collar clumsily patched. The rough wool was shiny with dirt where his neck and wrists protruded. She thought the yellow stains down the front looked like egg. His sacred *pallium* cape, its once pure white

52

supposedly received from the hands of the Pope himself, was yellow with damp. The hem of his scarlet cloak dragged in the mud. In truth the Church was so poor that no British bishop had travelled abroad on his own purse for longer than anyone could remember.

The archbishop drew himself up with tattered grandiosity. 'Celatus Felix. You may approach us.' Father went to embrace him but Mansuetus held out the back of his hand. Father kissed his ring. 'Felix, you old heretic,' Mansuetus said with genuine fondness, now that Father had shown respect.

'Heretic? The way I recall it, I was not alone in heresy,' Father growled.

'That Pelagist business. You aristocrats. I never supported it.'

'Of course not. You always support the winning side.'

'One does not become archbishop otherwise.' The pontifex tapped Father's chest. 'I should be merely like you, a collector in a time without values, a rich man in an age without money.'

'A landowner with no land.'

'I'm sorry to hear that, Felix. Truly. Friends in childhood remain friends for ever, wherever their footsteps take them. God has brought you and your soldiers back here in our hour of need—'

'Soldiers?' Father said. 'My soldiers are dead, Pontifex. My own centurion tried to assassinate me. These men? Slaves. Some are *coloni*, tenants who have lost their farmsteads.'

'And you have brought with you carts full of weapons, swords, spears, arrows. Felix, you are resourceful as ever! We hope to repair a ballista—'

'Ploughs,' Father said. 'Farm implements. Household goods.'

Mansuetus laughed. Then his expression fell uncertainly. He looked stunned. 'Felix, surely you are not serious?'

Father said, 'Don't you know me after all these years?'

'We shall make a new life!' Camilla burst out.

Father grunted. 'My wife you know, of course.'

Unlike her husband, Camilla covered her head and knelt devoutly before kissing the archbishop's ring. She wept. 'I can't help it. Felix, stop me. It's been such a long journey. I can't stop.' But she pressed her knuckles to her mouth and she did stop. Her eyes moved as though seeing some terrible vision inside her head.

'I remember you as you were, Julia Camilla,' Mansuetus said gently. 'A night's sleep will bring you back again. And my prayers. Your own efforts will not be sufficient. The sacraments of the Church—'

'Yes, Pontifex, pray for me,' Camilla whispered. 'I'm weak. I need your help.'

'Just as we need men of Felix's energy and experience to help *us*.'

'Only with worldly matters, it seems,' Father said.

'All matters, worldly or not, are the province of Mother Church. The world *is* the Church.'

Father said firmly, 'And this, Pontifex, is my daughter.'

'I'm Ellen,' Ellen said. She kissed Manuetus's heavy ruby ring, tasted her mother's tears on the stone.

Mansuetus stroked her hair, called her child. Then he looked at her more closely, with sudden interest. 'Ellen. Of course. I remember—'

'She doesn't know,' Father said. 'She was only about three years old. She has no memory of that time.'

Mansuetus acquiesced. 'If you insist. The hospitality of my palace is yours, of course, for as long as you stay. And you will stay, I know.'

Father grunted, 'We leave tomorrow. As soon as my wife is rested.'

Mansuetus said smoothly, 'As you wish.'

Ellen noticed that the archbishop's solid gold shepherd's crook, the crozier that was the symbol of his authority over his flock, had peeled like flaking skin to reveal the glued wood beneath. The wood was aspen, like the Cross, but the shine had been nothing more than gold leaf. Mansuetus followed her eyes. He rested his hand lightly on her shoulder. 'Walk with me, child.'

Ellen asked, 'Father?'

Father shrugged his permission. He jumped back on the wagon and the drivers cracked the whips, setting off uphill after him. Once he had come to London regularly on business, and he knew the way.

Alone with Ellen, Mansuetus looked back at the gate. It was being closed. He called the foreman to him. The man ambled over, waved a salute.

Mansuetus said impatiently, 'Well, Coroticus? Is it finished?'

'Aye, Pontifex, it's done.' Coroticus pointed to the massive gate and gatehouses about three hundred yards to the south, lying between them and the Thames. 'And I've got Lud's bridge down too.'

'Then the roads to the west are cut off.'

'That they are, Pontifex.'

'Proceed with your other work, loyal Coroticus.'

Mansuetus grinned at Ellen, thinking that she had not heard, or that she didn't matter. He pressed down on her shoulder, turned awkwardly on her axis. 'I have rheumatism in my legs. All this infernal mud and damp.' He shifted his weight between her shoulder and the shepherd's crook. They walked slowly after the carts. 'Look at them all, in this day and age! Eighteen . . . nineteen vehicles including the wagon,' he marvelled. 'It is such a relief to meet cultured people again.'

Ellen didn't understand. 'Yes, Pontifex.'

'Your wonderful parents.' Ellen had supposed all parents were the same, huge booming figures rarely seen. She had been much closer to Monica Numidea. 'Tragic to see them running for their lives like this, brought low. Still, obviously they've saved everything they can, and I bet that's a fair bit.' She wondered at the envy in his voice. Mansuetus staggered. 'Steady, youngster, not too fast.'

Ellen walked slowly. 'There wasn't room for Monica,' she said. 'Or for Amanda.'

Mansuetus said, 'Who were they?'

'Ours.'

'Oh, slaves.'

'They both had little girls my age and I played with them sometimes. They were my friends.' A hill stood in the sunlight in front of them. They climbed out of the shadow of the gatehouse into the orange rays of sunset. Ellen glimpsed the muddy Thames shining on her right, beyond the river wall.

'It is our misfortune to be born in times of such confusion,' Mansuetus said. He tried to touch the girl's sadness at the loss of her friends. 'The papacy is the ghost of the deceased Roman Empire, sitting crowned on the grave thereof. But Rome will rise again, child, and smite the barbarians.'

The girl's sadness did not change, but she was respectful. 'Yes, Pontifex.'

They crossed a canal on a fallen treetrunk and Ellen wondered where the houses were.

The archbishop followed a path that cut short across the sharp corner where two Roman roads joined. He knocked aside dead brambles with his crook, then pointed at a tumbledown wooden structure erected in the corner of the field. 'A refugee church. The remoteness of country folk makes them more devout than the people of London, no doubt, but more likely to be led astray by strange beliefs. I have received them here in their distress and corrected their ways.'

'Yes, Pontifex.' Ellen wondered why the archbishop spoke as though he had no subordinates, as though he did everything himself.

Mansuetus mistook her curiosity. 'For example, many wrongly believed – as St Paul the Sword, first missionary of Christ, found among the people of Ephesus and Corinth – that John the Baptist, not Jesus, was the Messiah. They worshipped the Baptism of John not the Baptism of Christ!' He shook his head. 'Other refugees believed that James, the legitimate brother of Jesus, was the Way. Some believed in the Virgin Birth but not the Crucifixion, or that our Lord Jesus married Mary Magdalene like an ordinary man. The Arian sect completely denied the divinity of Christ. The Pelagian heresy, most subtle and dangerous of all, gained a fearfully strong grip in all the twenty-seven dioceses of Britain.'

'Yes, Pontifex.' The archbishop had called Father a Pelagist – and Father had called the archbishop one.

'But St Paul teaches us the truth, child. Jesus proved He was the

Christ by the manner of His death. He did not die in defeat. Death was His victory.' The old man's fingers trembled on Ellen's shoulder. '*Jesus Christ is alive.*'

To Ellen the archbishop's hand felt very heavy. To her, events four hundred years in the past were a very long time ago. She was hungry.

They came near the top of the hill. Everything below was drowning in shadow. The hill was stepped down to the river wall in a series of level terraces, natural features long ago made precise by Roman engineers. Each flat terrace was held back by a wall about ten feet high. A street with shops, houses and gardens ran along each one, neatly separated, with connecting roads at intervals. The canal descended between the terraces in a series of low waterfalls, providing water for houses, public fountains, a large green-and-blue public baths near the river wall. Down there Ellen saw a gatehouse had collapsed into the Thames, revealing lines of wooden quays staggered along the mud beyond the walls. The wharfs were abandoned, warehouses roofless and derelict. Tiny figures swarmed around the baths. Men and women worked without barrows or carts, carrying armfuls of rubble to the breach in the fortifications. They piled their tiny stones in the gap and returned for more. The curved roof of the baths fell in.

The pillar of smoke still stood in the distance to the east, blocking the first stars. Ellen remembered Father's words. *London. We'll take ship from there!* Watching the frantic activity, it took her a moment to realise what she did not see. She asked, 'Where are the ships?'

Mansuetus looked exhausted. 'Did you not hear me, child? Jesus Christ is alive.' He pointed beyond the western wall to the ruins of an octagonal temple, already looted of its stone, a small wooden church built inside it. 'Even beyond the walls of London. Do you not see the holy church of St Bridget? Londoners call it St Bride's. Built over the pagan temple of Brigantia, whose name – and place – we have appropriated to our own . . .'

Ellen said, 'But where are the ships?'

Mansuetus said in a low voice, 'What is your father really carrying in those carts?'

She looked uphill. The carts, followed by the wagon, passed through the gate into the courtyard of the archbishop's palace. Her father jumped down.

Ellen looked from her father to Mansuetus and said firmly, 'Ploughs.'

Mansuetus said, 'Ploughs.' He resumed his slow progress. 'Not one ship has come upriver all year. Not one. And now—' He hesitated. 'It is God's will, our punishment.' He smiled at her and kissed her forehead. 'I remember when we had olives.'

He walked uphill. Ellen wondered what olives were.

The archbishop's palace was not as impressive as his manner

suggested, a single storey of dirty white stucco walls beneath a shallow terracotta roof, a low portico entrance with incongruous white Purbeck marble columns, once painted ecclesiastical scarlet but now peeling. The double doors were decorated with brass studs. Windows to each side had curved tops of red London brick. There was no glass in them. Low winged corridors had been added to each side, state rooms here, a stable there. The carts were drawn up in front of the building, around the icy green pool connecting two dry fountains, alpha and omega, the beginning and the end. With much shouting and pushing the mules and donkeys were unhitched and hobbled in the goats' field. The archbishop's ostler scratched his ears, yawning, and found what fodder he could in the corners of his empty stable. The drivers wandered downhill to find women and beer.

It was almost dark, but now the courtyard was quiet Ellen still heard the tiny shouts of the figures working below, and the clink of their pathetic armloads of stones into the wall.

She found her mother in a bare room lit by a single candle. The underfloor heating did not work. Damp streaked one wall and there was a bird's nest on the window sill. Since it had a mosaic floor and no furniture, the room echoed. The archbishop's slave, a blunt-browed boy with a drippy nose, listened to Camilla's complaints. A blanket must be hung over the draughty window.

'What?' he said.

Camilla pulled the only stool to the middle of the floor and sat on it. 'Ellen.' She snapped her fingers. 'You will attend me. Archbishop Mansuetus keeps Roman hours.' She meant he would eat soon, at the ninth hour, the fourth after noon. 'It is already late. This blue gown will have to do.' She wore it with her linen shift showing beneath the hem in the manner of respectable women from time immemorial. Ellen salvaged a pair of red anklestrap shoes from the wagon and for the first time her mother smiled. She had taken off the mass of jewellery that she had worn to keep safe, but then couldn't resist the matching wheel-and-crescent necklaces for good luck. Her mood mellowed, but they found no saffron for her eyes. 'Do you remember, I had a whole bed of saffron in my garden back home?' Ellen had watched Amanda work many times and knew it was not necessary for her to speak. 'I wish I'd saved some seeds,' Mother said wistfully. 'I don't know where I'd obtain more now.' As always, thinking about small things cheered her up. They had no black *stibium* for her eyebrows and no sheep's wool for the *oesyspum* face cream either, and Ellen did not think the goats wandering in the corridors would do. Mother's wig was lost, probably she had thrown it at the barbarians in her panic which she was so determined to forget.

But her hair was terribly white. Ellen hid her shock, combed soothingly. Mother settled back and closed her eyes while her white locks were pinned. The brass mirror was bent and Ellen went to search for whatever she could find, but she made certain she did not find a mirror that would reveal the truth to her mother. The palace had no lamps – they had not been made for hundreds of years – but Ellen took the tallow candle and dripped a little fat from it, mixed it with soot from the flame, and anointed Mother's eyelashes and eyebrows in superior black arches. They had no rouge so Mother squeezed her lips to redden them.

'How do I look?'

Father came in. Ellen knew that he saw at once how white Mother's hair was, how deep her lines, but his smiling expression did not change. 'You look much better, dear. Do you feel better?'

'Of course. Don't make a fuss.' She hung on his arm. 'Please, Felix. Don't embarrass me. My weakness was momentary, I assure you.'

'All right. But you will say if you feel too tired.'

The archbishop's steward poked his head through the doorway. 'He's holding the service in the house-church tonight.'

Father was surprised. 'Not at his cathedral, St Paul's? But surely the crowds—'

'There's only you three. The old boy's past it, he can't fight any more. Last week he sent his archdeacon, Riocatus, to prepare his palace at Fulla's Ham upriver. King Fulla he calls himself, a baptised Christian though he don't speak a word of British. *I* wouldn't trust him.' The steward picked his teeth, looked over his shoulder as though he had more important business elsewhere. Chicken feathers stuck to his clothes and hairy forearms. 'Country bumpkins like you don't see it at all, do you. You never do. Until it's too late. London is a corpse. We're dead.'

'My wife requires a bed-couch,' Father said quietly.

'Good luck to her, that's all I can say!'

Father grabbed the man by the neck of his tunic, pushed him back against the carved door. The wood splintered, rotten.

'Leave him alone, dear,' Camilla said. 'It's quite all right.'

The steward straightened his clothes and grinned. 'Tell you something. You know what the English call us? Welsh. It's the same as their word for slave. You think about that.' His gaze lingered appreciatively on Ellen. 'Christian they're not.'

'Get out,' Father said.

Camilla whispered, 'We're safe in London. We're safe here.'

Ellen looked through the window frame. It was dark outside but a line of fire shimmered along the distant hills beyond the river, and above them the stars had gone out.

She hurried after her parents. They found Archbishop Mansuetus in a small room set aside as a church. The archbishop prayed in the usual Christian *orans* position, arms outstretched and hands upraised. Ellen followed her mother, covered her head in imitation. A wooden crucifix of the shape that had lately become popular stood on the table. At first it seemed that worshippers earlier in the day had left offerings in the little shrines to the saints along the walls, pieces of bread and bowls of wine, but as she bowed to each saint Ellen realised that the bread was hard as stone, and the wine had dried to sticky resin.

Father murmured, 'Cult of the dead.' Camilla threw him a furious look. She knelt devoutly behind the archbishop, hands raised in submission.

Mansuetus prayed in the Roman language. 'Sovereign Lawgiver, let us in Your earthly City see sin not as wilful rebellion but as the inevitable result of Adam's Fall, and let the sacraments of Mother Church redeem us. Let us not argue among ourselves. Give me strength, Lord, for it is impossible to eradicate all errors from obstinate minds at one stroke. It was in this way, step by step, that You revealed Yourself to the Israelite people in Egypt, permitting the sacrifices formerly offered to the Devil to be offered thenceforth to Yourself.'

'Amen,' Camilla said, then looked round.

'Amen,' Father said.

They followed Mansuetus into the dining room. There were no couches. Several tables had been pushed together to make a long eating-place. The light flickered from candles stuck in wooden bowls. The painting on the ceiling was almost black beneath decades or perhaps centuries of tallow-smoke, impressive by virtue of its obscurity. The lunettes of religious paintings along the wall, mostly in red and yellow ochre, were simple garish cartoons by comparison, but the plaster flaked to reveal older, darker scenes beneath.

Mansuetus seated his guests around him at the head of the table. He kept his scarlet cloak over his shoulders for warmth. The steward and the boy with a cold brought in roast chickens and black bread, wooden grail-platters of oatmeal porridge and grail-mugs of goats' milk, then turned their backs and sat among the household servants and slaves gathering at the foot of the table. The servants took knives from their clothes and talked loudly as they ate, running their greasy fingers through their hair.

Mansuetus blessed his meal. 'Chicken. Rather a treat. There is no law and order in London. I have a boy doing nothing but guard the hen-coops. The cockerels wake me before dawn every morning.' He apologised because there was no salt. Ellen gnawed hungrily at the tough scrawny meat. The men brought pitchers of beer for themselves, and their laughter became uproarious. There was no more milk. Father ordered the steward to bring him a pitcher of beer. The man pushed a slopping pitcher up the table with his elbow, offended by the interruption. Father glanced at Ellen and she stood obediently, filled the archbishop's grail-mug, then her parents'. Camilla made a face, unused to the taste. It was raw beer, cumin or honey being unavailable, so strong that it was almost undrinkable.

Father ate his porridge hungrily. He'd always had a good appetite.

Mansuetus watched him eat, then drained his beer, threw the dregs on the floor in a sudden lapse of good manners. He looked round for more drink, but Ellen was already refilling his grail.

'You don't miss anything, do you, child?'

'No, Pontifex.' Ellen lowered her eyes obediently. By God's command the archbishop's word was law. Even a question from him was a statement of truth. Only he or his bishops could perform baptisms, and a man empowered to lead people to God was incapable of lying, and never wrong about anything. 'Please sir,' Ellen said, 'I am not a child, I am a girl.'

Father burst out laughing. 'That's true!' he said. 'She's twelve. Old enough to marry.'

The archbishop banged his grail on the table. The noise was loud and the group at the bottom end looked round, then got on with their own talk.

Mansuetus said, 'I will not be contradicted, not even by my oldest friend, who thinks he knows me better than he does.' His voice was thin and as harsh as an accusation at Father. 'Have you really changed your beliefs? I doubt it. You remind me of another man with the strength of an athlete, and the same fondness for oatmeal porridge.'

It was an insult. He leaned back and Ellen wiped up his spilt beer.

Father said, 'Obviously you mean Pelagius.'

'Yes, your friend Morgan, the Welsh monk, who among his rich friends styled himself by the learned name Pelagius!'

Father said mildly, 'A liking for oatmeal porridge does not condemn me. Surely this is in the past, my friend. Morgan the heretic monk has been dead for more than thirty years, and you and I were both very young men.'

'You even wrote passionately in his defence, under the name Caelestius – not very difficult to see through to your real name, Celatus Felix.'

Father said, unafraid, 'I wrote in support of Morgan's *Commentaries on the Thirteen Epistles of St Paul*, as I recall.'

Mansuetus snapped his fingers for Ellen to refill his grail. The wind blew through the empty windows of his palace, and now he had started he would not stop. 'You and your showily dressed clique, you always had too much money, and too much influence, and too many gods. You were clever and frivolous and insincere. The preaching of St Germanicus, true soldier of God, the one God, one Way, put you in your place.'

Father growled, 'Insincere? My showily dressed clique, as you put it, welcomed you among us when you thought we had the winning side of the argument. You now deny what you then believed, but I do not understand your bitterness. Morgan was declared heretical by both Pope and Emperor. The views of St Augustine, so vigorously argued at St Alban's shrine by St Germanicus, have won the day.' He spread his hands. 'I accept that they are the true belief.'

'No.' Mansuetus shook his head angrily. 'They are the Truth. Do you still not understand the difference between mere belief and the Truth, the Way, the Light of Mother Church?'

Camilla bowed her head. 'Of course we do.' She looked up helplessly. 'I do not quite understand – what is it exactly between the truth of St Augustine and the heresy of Morgan the monk—'

Father spoke forcefully. 'Morgan believed that people can improve themselves by their own efforts. We ought to do good of our own will, without the need for the intervention of divine grace. And if we *ought*, then we *can*.'

The archbishop shook his head. 'St Augustine understood that Man is born sinful, of woman. The Garden of Eden is the true account of Man's fall into sin. Man's violent and depraved nature cannot be redeemed except through the sacraments of Mother Church.'

'The Garden of Eden,' Father said firmly, 'is a parable of human freedom.'

There was a fight at the bottom of the table. The men pushed one another rowdily, then laughter broke out and they settled again.

'My brother bishops of the Empire believe nothing good can come out of Britain,' Mansuetus sighed, 'and I think the wickedness of your beliefs, your mere *beliefs*, Felix, proves their point.'

Camilla said bravely, 'My husband is the most religious man I have ever known, Pontifex. To question is not to doubt, is it? To acknowledge the marvellous complexity of God is not heresy, surely?' She looked to Felix for guidance. 'Is it?'

Mansuetus snatched Ellen's hand. 'And what do you think, child? Do you question everything and see the truth of nothing, as your father persists in doing?'

Ellen looked him in the eye.

'There is one question I would like to ask you, Pontifex.'

Mansuetus laughed indulgently. 'Ask away!'

'Where are the ships?'

Mansuetus stood abruptly. He muttered the *benedictus*. The meal was over.

Father said, 'Ships?'

Mansuetus said, 'Surely you know.'

'There aren't any ships,' Ellen said.

Camilla cried out, 'But there must be!'

Father turned to the men at the other end of the table. 'Is this true?' They shrugged. Father pulled one man to his feet, looked into his eyes, pushed him down.

'There haven't been any all year,' Ellen said. '*He* told me.'

Father turned towards the archbishop.

'It's true.' Mansuetus looked smooth. 'Felix, I assumed you knew. You must have seen the refugees.'

'I'm used to the sight of refugees,' Father growled. He strode to the head of the table.

Mansuetus sat quickly. 'Touch me and lightning will strike you dead, I swear before God.'

Father gazed from the window. The line of fire along the distant hilltops had separated, approaching, dropping sparks into the forested slopes of Valle Dei below. The sparks flickered like eyes in the black night, then gleamed into new life. 'The fishing village at Greenwich is burning.' A gush of sparks rose up silently. 'They're burning the wharves, the landing stages.' Burning boats drifted in their reflections on the river. 'The people must be trying to swim across the old ford to the Isle of Dogs. It's too far to see.' Father turned abruptly. There were tears on his cheeks. He did not brush them away.

Mansuetus spread his hands unctuously. 'You mean you really didn't know? There has been a great battle at Crayford, the staging post only fifteen miles away. Kent is overrun, the east is cut off. The Christian forces are defeated, nothing now stands between the Stallion's pagans and London. An attack is inevitable. At Aylesford we were defeated last year, we are cut off to the south. The British fell back on the City or ran away through the woods, naked, with only their swords. This is worse.'

Father said, 'The men went to fight at King Arthur's side in the west.'

'If you believe he exists.'

Father said, 'I do.'

'The City must be defended at all costs.' Mansuetus cocked his hand to his ear and they listened to the shouts of the working party at the breach in the wall. 'Their families are probably dead, or caught up somewhere in the raggle-taggle army of refugees you saw. None of them will ever meet up again, you know. They might search for their children, their wives, but they will never find them, not in this world.'

'But they'll try,' Father said. 'Not even your command will keep them within the City walls when they think of their loved ones, Archbishop.'

Ellen said, 'Father—'

Mansuetus raised his voice. 'My good Christian Londoners have nothing to worry about. I have taken every precaution for the defence of our City. We have God on our side.'

'Why are you not rallying every able-bodied man to the walls? You need a man every four feet to defend the battlements—' Father stopped, seeing Mansuetus's smile. 'No. This is not my battle.'

'Father!' Ellen tugged his sleeve. 'I tried to tell you. He's had the roads to the west cut off. I heard a man called Coroticus tell him so. All the bridges are knocked down.'

Mansuetus said, 'To keep the barbarians out.'

But Father understood. 'No, to keep the people in. That's your plan, isn't it, Mansuetus? We're trapped. We have no choice, we have to fight for our lives.' He bit his lip, then turned furiously. 'What are these men doing lounging about here? Why aren't they working their balls off? Where are their weapons?'

'We bless you, Felix,' murmured Mansuetus, speaking in the archepiscopal plural. 'As soon as we saw you, we knew we had won. Alleluia!'

'Felix,' Mother whispered. 'What are we to do?'

Ellen had wrapped herself in a blanket on the floor. She pretended to be asleep, listening to her parents' whispers in the corner of the bedroom.

Father murmured, 'What else can I do? We've nowhere to go. Almost half a ton in each cart, the axles bent or worn, men and animals exhausted. He's a sly one—'

Mother hissed, 'You must not say that word of Archbishop Mansuetus!'

'I had the advantage, or disadvantage, of knowing him before he was an archbishop,' Father said dryly, 'when he was just a man.'

'But now he is a man of God.'

'He's still sly.'

'Ssh, you'll wake her.'

Both adults were silent.

'I don't trust him,' Father said. 'We're completely in his hands, though. I stand and fight.' He sat up, the blanket falling from his shoulders. He had found a sword. The metal gleamed in the moonlight. He tested the edge with his thumb.

'Won't you at least try to sleep?'

'There's too much to do.' Father stood and went to the broken door. It squeaked on its hinges.

'I love you.' Mother's voice trembled. She sounded so vulnerable that Father hesitated. She said, 'You won't let them down, you know. You're a greater man than your ancestors.' She said again, 'You won't let them down.'

'I won't.' He nodded and went out, and the door squeaked closed.

An owl hooted, and Ellen slept, and a cockerel crowed. Mother snored.

It was still dark. Ellen turned over and tried to sleep again, then sat up wide awake. The window was grey and she put her hand where the glass had been. The carts were grey lumps round the ornamental pool. Father sat on the basin of the dry fountain to the left, keeping watch with the sword in his hand. The morning was cold and clear.

His dark figure moved and she heard him yawn. The sword clinked as he laid it on the stone, ducked his head in the icy water of the pool. He swept back his hair, took up the sword again and crossed the courtyard. He opened the gate and stood looking out, then slipped through.

Ellen went to the door but it squeaked when she touched it. Mother muttered uneasily in her sleep. Ellen tiptoed to the window, swung the frame open, and let herself down on to the paving. Without warning the bird's nest fell on her hair and she sneezed. One of the lads left guarding the carts opened one eye, turned over, went back to sleep.

Ellen crossed by the pool, her footsteps soundless on yesterday's snow. The dog sleeping by the portico ignored her. The gate was ajar and she slipped through on to the road. She pushed back a goat that tried to follow her.

There was no one outside. Even the works downhill by the old baths were silent and still. Beyond the Thames and a brief jumble of decayed wharves and buildings, fires sparked far away across the grey marshes, but the ring of southern hills showed no sign of life. The barbarians are closer than last night, she thought. The fishing village trailed thin threads of smoke, no new fires. London Bridge spanned the river like an ungainly wooden centipede standing in a mirror of itself. The drawbridge was raised.

Ellen was wiser now. The drawbridge was raised not only to keep the barbarians out, but to keep the Christians in.

She fitted her feet in her father's footsteps, and followed them uphill with very long strides. Almost at once the wall of the archbishop's palace angled away from her, and she saw St Paul's Cathedral on the summit of the hill.

It was larger than a barn, but not much. Heavy and squat in the Roman style, the walls were of patterned brick in chevrons and diamond shapes, and the roof was tiled. The curved western end faced her, doorless.

But Father paid no attention to the cathedral. The houses below interested him more, the sudden leap of a cat on to a broken wall took all his concentration. He stopped as though listening, then strode past the cathedral's far end and the corner hid him.

Ellen followed his footsteps alongside the building. She was at the top of a snowy field, so stony that perhaps it had once been paved – probably it had been used for preaching to unbaptised crowds between the cathedral and the street of ruined houses. Some of the houses were very old, roofless, the walls falling in. She looked at the black-and-white cat. It jumped down into the rubble and disappeared.

Ellen paused. She glimpsed cellars dropping down beneath the houses, the outline of shadowy rooms behind dark windows. Bare fruit trees rustled, the remains of orchards. Ellen was suddenly sure, perfectly sure, that there had been herb gardens here once. She could almost smell the dense mingling fumes of aniseed-scented elecampane, minty hyssop, fragrant pellitory, the penetrating gingery odour of silphium. She saw them growing in her mind's eye, their vivid tangled colours multiplying, spores drifting lazily in the breeze, the drone of bees.

It was summer.

Ellen blinked.

She was back in the snow.

She shivered and pushed her chin deep into the throat of her gown. She did not look at the houses again. The first rays of the sun touched the orange roof of the cathedral, sparkled from the broken glass in the clerestory windows. She followed her father's long strides to the corner and peeped round.

The broad paved area facing the eastern end of the cathedral was smooth, unmarked, white with snow. Her father's footsteps crossed the snow to a raised plinth of tiles in the centre. As was the case outside almost all churches, this was the baptistry. On the stepped platform of flint blocks, which only priests, catechumens – converts about to be baptised – and baptised Christians were allowed to ascend, stood a lead font as long as a man. The font was inscribed with the holy alpha on the left, omega on the right. *I am the Beginning and the End*. In the middle was blazoned the chi-rho monogram, the symbol of Christ. Beneath it was carved *Vivas in Deo*. May you live in God.

Below, on the stone block that supported the font, eight Roman letters had been deeply chiselled. *RESURGAM*.

Father's bulk obscured the legend as he climbed on the plinth. He deliberately faced east, away from the Cathedral. His wet hair sent dark trickles down his *byrrus britannicus*. He held out his arms.

'Rotas. Opera. Tenet. Arepo. Sator.'

Ellen stared past him. As her eyes adjusted to the light her father became only a shadow beneath the brilliant dawn sky. The hillside fell away in front of him, its slope speckled with old houses and apartment blocks. Ragged thatch farmsteads scattered here and there among the fields were connected by enormous roads, far more than necessary. Streams ran from the culverted north wall of the City into the bottom of the valley, joined, flowed between the two hills to the Thames. The far side of the valley rose up covered with houses, shops, the private churches called *parochiae*, arcades of tile roofs leading to the huge square forum on the summit.

Sunlight glinted behind the ruined colonnades. Ellen drew a deep breath. She knew what was coming.

The sun flashed above the broken roof of the forum, bathed the two hills in yellow light.

Father called out, 'Soli Invicto, Soli Invicto, Soli Invicto!' He bowed his head three times to the Unconquered Sun.

Ellen understood. Midwinter was past, a new year was born. She called out eagerly, 'Is it Christmas?'

Father whirled, sword in hand. His eyes were wild. 'Emilia?'

They heard the dog barking in the archbishop's courtyard.

'It's me, Father. Ellen. It's me.'

The mad look left her father's eyes. 'Oh. I thought – for a moment—'

'I'm sorry I startled you.'

'It was long ago.' The energy left him. He looked drained.

Ellen went over to her father. She asked, unafraid, 'Why do you pray to the sun?'

He sheathed his sword, regained his gaiety. He picked her up as though she were a child. 'Because God has many faces, that's why! And all of them are wonderful and dreadful, Ellen, just as we are.'

'The archbishop said Jesus Christ is alive, although he was crucified four hundred and twenty-five years ago.'

'He is.'

'The archbishop really meant it.'

'So do I. Jesus ceased to be a man about a century ago, when he was officially decreed Jesus Christ Son of God by the Emperor Constantine at Nicea. Constantine was later baptised into the Christian Church.'

'But Jesus proved he was the son of God right from the start, when he rose from the dead and people saw him.'

'Ellen, all our churches, pagan or not, offer their people salvation in the afterlife in return for belief in the church and obedience to its teachings. Mithras, Serapis, Isis, Atis, Cybele, Bacchus, Serapis, Sol Invictus. Usually the divinity himself, or herself, conquers death and thus promises followers the hope of doing the same.'

'But that's only belief,' Ellen said. 'What about the truth?'

'Truth? All his life Constantine prayed to Sol Invictus, the Unconquered Sun, but he was still a good Christian. In battle the Cross appeared to him in a vision, and he won a great victory.' He touched the clasp at his throat, its silver worked into the anguished shape of a crucified man. 'That is why nowadays the Cross is so important to us. You saw the archbishop pray to one last night.'

Ellen was happy. 'You know everything.'

'Does it seem so?' He sounded sad. 'That's because I'm older than you. But one day you will be as old as me.' Then he chuckled and she cuddled him close, having him all to herself, basking in his attention. The sun warmed them. Behind them the cathedral dripped where the sun's rays bathed its eastern face, probed fingers of light between the pillars to illuminate the brick arch of the doorway.

Ellen murmured to his chin, 'Father?'

'Yes.'

'Why does it sometimes feel as though we've been here before?'

'Everybody feels that sometimes. It doesn't mean anything.'

'The archbishop said truth was different from other things. Truth is just one thing, and if it isn't perfect, it isn't the truth.'

'I heard him.'

'He said that truth was what *really* is. He said it's so obvious that hearing it and seeing it and believing in it isn't enough, it simply is, you can't help knowing it. It's all around us, everywhere.'

Father gave her a respectful look. 'Perhaps that's what he said. He didn't say it as well as you.'

'I'm more than your daughter, I'm your only child. I'm your son as well, because there's only me. I'm all you have.'

He sat on the step, settled her in his lap. He sighed. 'Mother could not have more children.'

'Did you want more?'

'We had wanted a child so very badly.'

Ellen put her arm around his shoulder. 'When I'm grown up you'll tell me everything that you've never told anyone else, won't you? I mean,' she added, 'except Mother.'

He murmured, 'Perhaps I have a secret from your mother.'

'What?'

'Nothing.' He put his head on one side, listening to the dog barking.

Ellen said precisely, 'What is it in our carts that is so wonderful?'

He sighed. 'I don't know that it's wonderful, Ellen.'

She gave him her impatient look. 'What did Hardalio see?'

'I don't know. Us. I mean all of us. It's been in my family for so many generations, it's part of us.'

She bounced excitedly. 'It's money, isn't it! How much?'

'He might have seen money.'

'Enough to be worth dying for?'

'I suppose that what he *thought* he saw . . . yes, it was worth risking dying for. That was the choice he made.'

'What did he see exactly?'

'I think he saw exactly what he hoped to see, Ellen.'

She grinned. 'In his wildest dreams?'

'Yes. In his wildest dreams.'

'I'm not sorry he's dead,' she said unsentimentally. 'He called me a bastard.'

She looked round with a shock, hearing footsteps. She wriggled out of her father's lap.

'Felix, it's you.' Archbishop Mansuetus leant on his crook. 'And the dear child. I thought I heard someone talking.' Father stood to go, but the archbishop gripped his sleeve. 'Well, my dear *magister militum*, can you save my people from the barbarians?'

'Yes. If anyone can. If they will fight.' Father sniffed the air impatiently. 'What's that smoke?' He pointed beyond the curve of the Corn Hill where a black column rose against the dawn.

'The barbarians have burnt our signal station at Shad's Well, as you can see. We no longer have any information on anything that is happening outside the City.'

Father raised his sword in salute. 'I leave my daughter in your care, old friend.' Mansuetus held up his hand and Father kissed the ring. Then he did something extraordinary. He bent down to Ellen, hugged her and kissed her face.

The archbishop drew his cloak around his shoulders, watchful as ever. 'Trust in me, Felix.'

They watched Father run between the ruined houses towards the men working on the riverwall. He reappeared in the distance and his shouted orders carried faintly through the still, bright air. Hefting stones, he hurled them into the breach to set an example. Busy bustling figures obscured him as the work was rekindled by his enthusiasm, the mules and donkeys rigged with wicker panniers and led down from the goats' paddock. Even the archbishop's goats were pressed into service. But Mansuetus did not take his eyes from Ellen's face.

'If anyone can hold the barbarians at bay from the City of St Peter and St Paul, it is your father.' The shadow of the Corn Hill dropped down the slope in front of them as the sun slanted higher. Mansuetus glanced at her again, pointed. 'Do you see my church of St Peter, Ellen?' He bent down to her level and she followed his gnarled finger. 'Raised with stones from the forum.'

Ellen turned on him. 'It's all ruins, isn't it,' she said bleakly. 'The whole City looks real, but it isn't. It's an illusion.'

'We shall fight to the last man, the last woman, the last child.' The archbishop's finger followed the shadow of Corn Hill to the left, where the amphitheatre was just coming into the sun. Its tiered walls glowed as smoothly as though newly built at this distance. Beyond loomed the huge square citadel that dominated the City. The parade grounds were plain untrodden snow. No cooking-fires smoked outside the mossy barrack blocks.

Ellen said, 'Is there anyone there?'

Mansuetus gripped her shoulder, turned her towards his cathedral. 'Look. What do you see? This glory is no illusion, it is as real as the Kingdom of God. St Paul's. St Paul of the Sword, the instrument which beheaded our martyr.' He patted the squat redbrick pillars. 'These will stand for ever.'

'Yes, Pontifex.'

'Come.' He tugged her impatiently and Ellen followed him into the shadows. 'This is my narthex, my threshold. My church is a basilica, like the one in Rome.' He lifted the beam and one side of the double door, little higher than a man, swung open. Mansuetus leaned his weight on her shoulder. When she hesitated he grunted for her to go inside.

Ellen looked around her in the musty gloom. The nave was as long as a stable or *palaestra*, an exercise hall, but chilly. The only light came from the clerestory windows gaping above the pillars that separated the side aisles. Mouldy faded frescos along the outer walls showed richly clad men and women with their arms outstretched in prayer. Part of the ceiling had fallen in, revealing the underside of the rooftiles. Ceiling-plaster and broken glass lay heaped on the flagstones.

She turned to go out, but Mansuetus gestured at his raised throne in the chancel. He sat in it, higher than her even sitting, and he looked so lonely that she was sorry for him.

'All my life I worked for this.'

The archbishop's throne was made more impressive by the curve of the apse rising above it. On the curve was painted the head of Jesus Christ, tightly braided hair, dark brown eyes, long nose and small mouth, clean-shaven, with a cleft chin. Ellen stared.

Mansuetus stepped down beside her. He murmured, 'Powerful, is it not?'

She nodded, finding it difficult to look away.

He took her elbow. 'This has always been a place of religion. Can you not feel it? Even pagan religion, my dear. This building was dedicated to the god Mithras before the statues were smashed and it was purified, and re-consecrated to God. A temple to the goddess Diana once stood on this holy ground, long ago. Some people still call this the *Domum qui fuit Diane*. The church built on the temple to Diana. It seems the temple was burnt.'

'How do you know?' Ellen wanted to pull her arm from his clutching fingers, but she was afraid he would take offence.

'White Purbeck marble columns survive from the ambulatory – the best examples are used in my palace – but additional fragments, exploded by heat, sharp as knives, kept turning up when the catacomb was dug.'

'Catacomb?'

'Since the Romans were expelled fifty years ago, there has been no prohibition on Christian burial within the City. For those who can afford it. I myself shall sleep down there one day.'

'Sleep?'

'Death is sleep.'

He crossed between the pillars into the side aisle on the right, beckoned. Going to the far end, he opened the door to the sanctum. A curtain kept the room private from prying eyes when the door was open and he swept it aside. Ellen looked past his shoulder. The sanctum was bare except for old rubbish.

Mansuetus bent, then complained. Her back was younger than his. He handed her his shepherd's crook, pointed at the floor. 'There.'

Ellen inserted the ferrule of the stick into a groove between two flagstones. Nothing happened. She didn't know whether to push or pull.

'Pull.' He put his hand over hers.

Ellen pulled with all her strength. The flagstone grated, then rose smoothly, counterbalanced. Steps led down into the dark.

Mansuetus lit a candle, took back his crook, and went ahead of her.

It was not dark in the catacomb. The floor was shiny, a brightly coloured carpet of hard, shimmering mosaic pieces that reflected the candlelight with bright gleams. The catacomb was narrow, much longer than it was wide. The polished floor-mosaic tailed off before reaching the far end, replaced by dull lumps stripped from old houses, baths, pavements. Stretching away from the steps, the two long walls were at first luminous with patterns of religious scenes from the Old Testament, Moses in azure and gold carrying the Ten Commandments, Elijah rising to heaven on a fiery golden chariot. 'Paintings in stone,' Mansuetus murmured. The walls changed to dull yellow and brown further towards the end. The artist had run out of colours. The plain end wall had been rendered with smooth yellow mortar, blackened and stained as a tooth.

Mansuetus tugged Ellen after him. Niches were dug along the side walls. Heavy lead coffins were placed in them, heads to the west in the Christian custom. 'My predecessor Bishop Restitutus,' Mansuetus said with satisfaction. The stone base was deeply carved with the word RESURGAM. 'Here is Bishop Exsuperius.' The wooden coffins near the western end were much poorer in style, more recent inhumations. Ellen tripped over broken mosaic. The last coffins were elm planks roughly nailed. Shoved several to each niche, they were cramped and crowded and jumbled together, but even the last carried the same inscription as the first.

'Fortunately the air is strangely dry down here,' Mansuetus said. '*Resurgam*. It means resurrection. I shall rise again.' He gestured at the empty end wall. 'I shall have my niche cut here, pride of place. Here I shall sleep at the head of my congregation, and in this position I shall be awakened on the glorious and terrible Day of Judgment. There shall be no doubt of my status.'

He wiped the mortar with his knuckles in a peculiarly delicate gesture, as though already seeing himself lying in the blank wall, bony hands clasped across the hoop of his ribs, his fingernails fallen through on to his spine, his sacred *pallium* neatly folded beneath his skull, waiting for eternity.

He watched Ellen.

'You are beautiful, bright as a flower.' Mansuetus touched her chin with his fingertip, lifted her face. 'It is your morning in the sun. I too was young once.' His lips cracked in a smile. 'Lie down.'

Ellen looked at him steadily.

He laughed to reassure her. 'You must do as you are told. You are so full of life, you have so much to learn. Lie down!' He pressed his hand on her shoulder. 'Lie down as though you were dead.'

Ellen took a step backwards. His grip tugged him after her.

'Mother will be wondering where I am,' Ellen said. 'She'll be worried.' She twisted from his grasp, ran to the steps.

'How dare you!' Mansuetus shouted. He hobbled after her. 'Who do you think you are?'

Ellen stopped with her foot on the third step.

'No one!' Mansuetus shouted. 'Don't you know the truth? You're no one!'

Ellen ran.

Ellen ran through the open gate into the courtyard. The carts were still drawn up around the archbishop's foul green pool. Mother saw her through the window. 'Ellen!' Clothes flapping, she hurried down the steps of the palace. 'Where have you been? I've been looking for you everywhere.' She enveloped Ellen in her embrace and her body heaved with hidden emotion. 'You mustn't leave me. It's been awful, awful. That awful dog woke me.'

'Father will be back soon.'

'Yes. Yes, of course.' Camilla steadied herself. 'Archbishop Mansuetus was very kindly doing up one of the knots that came undone on that old dray, and the dog was barking at him and wouldn't stop. How's my little girl? You look so pale.'

The yard was silent and still except for their voices. Ellen looked round, wondering what had changed. She said, 'Where are the guards, Mother? Where is everybody?'

'Yes,' Camilla said eagerly. 'That's another thing. The men are gone. I noticed at once. That horrible drunk steward, everyone. Even the poor boy with a sniff. There's no hot water. I called and called but no one came—'

Ellen picked up a spear. 'But who will look after the carts?'

Camilla stared around her. 'Your father will know what to do.'

Ellen looked through the gates. She saw no one. She called over her shoulder, 'Where are Father's slaves? Where are the drivers?'

'You know what they're like,' Mother said. 'Curse that silly girl Amanda Adelphia for running back and getting herself killed.'

Ellen said harshly, 'And curse Monica Numidea for running back to save her, is that what you mean? And their children for getting killed too—' She gave up struggling with the beam. It was too heavy for her to lift across the gates.

'I'm sorry,' Mother said. 'I forgot you saw all that.' She cleared her throat. 'But the fact remains, someone has got to get me my hot water.'

But Ellen gripped the spear tight. She was white-lipped with determination. She sat on the rim of the fountain where her father had sat, watching the gate.

'You know me,' Mother said. 'If I cannot wash, I simply die.'

Ellen said nothing, then jerked the spear-tip at the pool. 'Father washed his head in there.'

Mother made a sharp noise. Ellen did not budge. No smoke rose from the chimney at the back of the palace. Ellen said, 'You'll have to find a pot or a saucepan to boil the water in, and you'll have to light the fire first.'

'But I don't know how to light a fire.' Camilla shuffled up the steps. 'We'll have to find someone to give orders to,' she said.

Ellen sat in the deserted yard. She held the spear first on one side then the other, trying to feel masculine and responsible. She was probably holding the spear the wrong way and wouldn't scare anyone. Suppose she had to fight? She wrapped a blanket round her shoulders to make herself look more formidable.

The gate creaked and her heart leapt into her mouth. But it was only the boy with the drippy nose. He was carrying a hare, swinging it by the back legs. 'Oh!' he said, dropping it at the sight of her. He backed against the wall, eyes wide, fixed on the point of the spear.

Ellen advanced on him fiercely. She demanded, 'Where have you been?'

He prodded the hare with his clog. 'Dinner.' He yelped. 'Dinner! Don't hurt me!'

'Where is everyone?' She jabbed him, then asked again.

He said sulkily, 'Ran away.'

'Why?'

He eyed the spear, held up his hands in submission. He slid his shoulders along the wall as far as the gate, pointed through. Ellen stood in the road. Below her the broad suburban terraces dropped away down the side of Lud's Hill as neatly and regularly as steps. Now that she knew what to look for she saw that the rows of houses were dilapidated, disused, with tiles missing from the roofs here and there, the windows long ago broken by looters, storms or children. Melting snow gathered in pools around the blocked drains, made miserable streams through doorways and gardens. Some dwellings, those enclosed by defensive walls, had been converted into apartments, domestic enclaves with proper doors and glass in the windows, and stood out neatly from the decay around them. She thought one inn by the canal looked particularly smart, smoke in the central-heating chimney as well as the kitchen, and old men on the gate.

'You're not looking right,' the boy sniffed. The gap in the river wall was now plugged by rubble from the Baths, the last raft-load of headstones and statuary being poled down the River Fleet from Newgate cemetery to finish the work. She saw no sign of Father, but in the distance her eye detected men moving busily on London Bridge, throwing up a palisade to supplement the drawbridge. 'My father's there,' she said.

The boy sounded awed. 'You must have eyes like a hawk.'

'No. It's where I would be if I were a man.'

He sniffed. 'Anyway, you're holding that wrong. Thumb and forefinger like that. That's it.'

She ignored him. The River Thames must have a tide of sorts, because the water level had dropped. The river was very broad and so many islands, mudbanks, sandbanks were showing that it was difficult to tell where the south bank began. The quays at the south end of London Bridge were built out from the tip of the largest island, which had inns and decrepit shopping arcades peeping among the willow trees and brambles. Enormous causeways, the work of giants, strode away across the marshes, gigantic roads joining the chain of islands like a string of beads.

The boy watched her. 'Them roads don't go nowheres now.' She narrowed her eyes, catching glints of movement in the marshland between the roads. 'See them? That's them.' The boy gave a satisfied sniff, pleased to show off his knowledge. 'They're coming.' She stared. He pinched his nose, snorted on the road. 'Nothing'll stop them now. London's had it.'

She whispered, 'How long?'

'By now, tomorrow' – he pointed at the sun – 'they'll be at the walls.'

'My father will defend the London Bridge to the death. He'll burn it down if he has to. The Thames will protect the City.'

The boy shook his head. 'See, at low tide, like now, they'll use the old ford at Greenwich. No deeper than your neck, it isn't.'

She pointed at the City's east wall looping in the distance. 'But there's forts and bastions all along that side.'

'Or they'll cross upstream, the gravel bank at Thorney Island. Don't even get their knees wet. Come round behind us . . .'

'You've given up already,' she said.

'I know when I'm beat. I'm off to join King Arthur's cavalry.' The British had stolen the enemy's word for cavalry, not the Roman *equites* but the English *cniht*. 'One of King Arthur's knights, I'll be.'

She said contemptuously, 'Not if you know when you're beaten.'

She stared at the marshes. The British were once renowned horsemen but the English, Saxon and Jutish clans advanced on foot, weaving dark spidery lines across the patchwork of snow and islands, reaching forward towards London like a spreading net. They made their own lanes twisting and turning between the foreign Roman roads, which they did not use at all, preferring to get their own feet wet in their own way.

'They got webbed feet,' the boy commented. 'Born in water they are. The sea's over their islands, that's why they're here. Our hills and valleys and woods is strange magic to them.' His brow furrowed. 'Why aren't you crying? You should be! Don't you know what they do to Christians?' She made no reply. He offered, 'Look, I'll let you come along with me.'

'*You* would let *me*—'

He said cockily, 'Ay, I would.' She jabbed the spear. He lost

73

his cocky grin and stepped back nervously. 'Ay, careful with that, you'll cut.'

She said, 'What's your name?'

'Patrick, I am.'

'Just stop talking and run away, Patrick!'

His face contorted into an enormous angry sulk. 'What's your name then?' he demanded. 'Who do you think you are? We're all the same now.' He went to the gate. 'I'll just take a little something to help me on my way—'

Ellen got in front of him. He stepped to one side but she kept ahead.

'I've had enough of this,' he said, and pushed her.

She jabbed with the spear. She felt nothing through her hands, only the faintest quiver. He shouted and scrambled back. She saw the blood on his arm. I really did it! she thought. The breath panted in her mouth.

She told him, 'Touch those carts, I'll kill you.'

He grabbed his arm. He bit his lower lip between his teeth and doubled over. She held the spear in both hands, ready for a trick. He put up his good arm to ward her off and backed away from her. He was crying. His sobs were genuine and she softened, then hardened her heart.

'I mean it!' she said.

'Daddy's girl.' He stumbled away, then shouted from the street corner, 'Bitch!'

She jerked her spear and he ran away.

Ellen stood in the courtyard. A dog stole the hare and she heard the snarls of the mongrels tearing the carcase. She leant back against the gates and closed her eyes.

When she opened them smoke was rising from the chimney. Mother had discovered how to light the fire. Ellen found some steps where she could look over the street wall. Nothing moved in the City. The sun hung over the river, beginning to slant down the sky now, so it was past midday. She shivered and wrapped the blanket around her shoulders, grateful for its warmth as afternoon shadows filled the courtyard. The drains stopped trickling and ice formed on the pool. She took a turn round the yard to ease her muscles, returned to her place on the wall. She imagined Father returning and his pride in her when she told him she had been looking after everything. Was there anything more she should do, something she had forgotten? She checked the knots on the carts but all were tight and secure. Again she returned to the wall. The smoke had gone from the palace chimney. Mother had let the fire go out. Perhaps she had baked bread. Ellen's mouth watered at the thought of the hot soft bread but she was determined not to abandon her post.

Mother did not come out.

Ellen was thirsty but she didn't like the look of the pool water. She tightened her grip on the spear. A few people came into sight on her left, weary men pushing handcarts uphill from the Walbrook stream between the two hills. The broad road towards Lud's Gate passed near the archbishop's palace. Women and children walked beside the men, some herding geese, helping push the barrows when the slope was too steep. One white-haired fleshy man caught her eye, obviously he had done well, perhaps a shopkeeper or apartment speculator by his hard manner. All at once he slipped and his barrow ran backwards, caught his hip, overturned and broke the wheel. Everything rolled off, his family's whole life made suddenly visible to Ellen, bundles of clothes rolling, a broken picture, a stool. His wife cried out like an angry bird. No one stopped to help them, and Ellen crouched behind the parapet, watching, helpless. The family moved within the growing stream of refugees salvaging what they could, knocked open an empty yellow house, stored whatever they could not carry to come back for later, closed the door neatly and Ellen saw them make a note of the place. She watched them shoulder their heavy burdens and trudge forward. Almost at once they stopped, exhausted. The mother picked out whatever more she must sacrifice and her boys ran back and hid it in the yellow house. The fleshy man limped forward with his remnants and did not look back.

The crowd reached Lud's Gate but the gates were shut. Ellen made out Coroticus and his men standing in the shadows, hands on swords. The people gathered on the military road that ran behind the walls, growing in number, piling up, pushing forward. Archbishop Mansuetus came on to the battlements above them, harangued them in a reedy voice. She knew he was begging them not to leave. The crowd swelled, frantic newcomers jostling the earlier arrivals, there was a fire on Corn Hill. Men ran forward and tugged at the gates. Mansuetus waved his arms, offering his congregation eternal life in the Kingdom of Heaven if they would stay. He would stay. He would fight to the last breath. He roused their spirits with the Church's battle-cry. 'Alleluia!'

But the crowd surged towards the gate, sullen, sluggish, irresistible. Coroticus and his cronies were swept aside. A scream rose. The swords flashed, hacking into the crowd, and all at once a roar went up, and the crowd became a mob. The mob poured forward by sheer weight of numbers, geese flew into the air, the gate was dragged open somehow. Coroticus struggled free, hid in the gatehouse. Archbishop Mansuetus cried, 'Alleluia.' Once on the slope the mob could not hold back. Handcarts bounded out of control, crashed into the headstones, broke. Men, women and children fell forward, slipped, slithered towards the broken bridge over the River Fleet. More tumbled after them. They scrambled among the timbers trying to find a way across, fought for coracles, rafts, anything they could drag on to the mud and ice. A wharf gave way, plunged a hundred people into the icy river. Their heads bobbed, hands thrashed, their struggles weakened. Their faces went wearily into the water, and gradually everything fell still.

Ellen put her fingers in her ears. She squeezed her eyes shut, but she could not make herself blind to the dreadful sight that she still saw, or deaf to the cries that she still heard.

She looked up with a gasp. It was evening, the tide was full, and Father was coming up Lud's Hill from the Walbrook. He walked alone, with long confident strides, and again she thought how like a monk he looked in his *byrrus*, its tasselled cord swinging, the hood flapping on his shoulders. Only the sword gave him away.

He saw her and waved, and she realised he was exhausted. His hands were grey with pulverised ragstone, red brickdust streaked his hair, and he had lost one of his sandals. His bare foot slipped on the ice. She ran down and pulled the gate open for him. He came inside, took in the situation in the yard with one glance, nodded. He realised what she had been through. With one arm he lifted the heavy beam that had defeated her and dropped it in place across the gates.

Ellen said, 'Now we're safe!'

He went to the pool, leaned over the balustrade, dunked his head through the green scum. The muscles of his neck worked as he drank thirstily. Ellen watched him. She knelt beside him and drank too. The water tasted cold.

She realised he was watching her.

He shook the water-drops from his head. 'Nowhere is safe, Ellen.' He put back his hair with the palms of his hands, then wiped his fingers from his eyes to his chin, looked at her steadily. 'This is the second time you've done well,' he said. 'You looked after the place.' Then he murmured, 'My little girl.' He tousled her hair, grinned. 'Whoever would have believed it? Camilla was right about you after all.'

Ellen bowed her head, made more pleased than words could say by Father's praise, and when she hugged him she felt so close to him that her arms might sink into him.

He laughed, put his hand behind her head and pressed her to his side.

'My Ellen,' he said. 'My Ellen.'

She found him another sandal, too small, and they walked to the wall. He swung himself up on the step. 'This is where you kept watch?'

'Yes, all day!' Ellen told him about finding the men gone, her fight with the boy, the terrible sights and sounds of the people drowning by Lud's Gate. Father stared, following her words. The river had taken its dead but survivors still moved in the swamp, searching for a way across, or loved ones, or something lost. A hollow booming sound echoed through the failing light. Coroticus had closed the gates.

Ellen whispered, 'Father, why is there so much I don't know?'

He took a deep breath, then merely said, 'Because you are only a child.'

Ellen shivered. The air was grey and suddenly she was very afraid. 'Will I die and never know?'

'How is Mother?'

Ellen said obediently, 'Worried about you.'

'This is very hard for her.' He grunted, stared to the west. The sky was black night. 'Do you hear it?'

She strained. 'It sounds like a huge flock of birds.' She wondered. 'Or a pack of dogs?'

The sound that came to them rose and fell with the evening breeze.

'It's people.' Father pointed. On Corn Hill a house sprang into view, burning. They watched the flames spread along a row of houses. The street burnt like a finger of fire but the flames could not jump the broad gardens, faded away. Bonfires grew up like bright stars trailing sparks, outlining the shape of the hill.

'Why are they doing it, Father?'

'They don't know what they're doing,' he murmured.

'Mother says it's the end of the world.'

He shrugged. 'When people lose faith, they destroy what they most love.' He roused himself. 'Come on. They won't burn St Paul's, they're too afraid of God's lightning. We'll hide the carts in the cathedral.' He glanced at her, his eyes moving in the firelight. 'I told you, Ellen.' He sounded dreadfully weary. 'Nowhere really is safe. And you can depend on no one but yourself.'

She squeezed his fingers tight, understanding.

Working in the dark, they found the gate to the goats' paddock open, and they could only find two pairs of mules in the paddock. Father hitched them to the first two carts. Mother came to the top of the steps, leant on the pillar. 'Felix! Thank God! I've had a dreadful day.'

He went to her. Camilla was wearing her blue gown and she had again draped herself in masses of jewellery to keep it safe. She hugged him and he kissed her, sniffed her breath. 'Don't look at me like that,' she said. 'It was the only thing there. You know how I hate beer. It was awful.' He picked her up and swung her on to the driver's seat. She held the reins genially.

'Just sit there,' he said, and paid her no more attention.

He bundled a straw torch, bound it, lit it and opened the gates. The two carts bumped into the road. He walked ahead of them, and by the flames of the torch guided them across the top of the hill to St Paul's. The carts fitted through the double doors with a hand's-breadth to spare. 'Back them into the side aisles.' Father unhitched the mules. Their hooves banged loudly on the flagstones. He called to Camilla, 'My dear, you will stay here.'

'But suppose someone comes?'

'Scream.'

She showed a flash of her old fire. 'But my place is at your side!' Then she closed her eyes. 'All right. This once.'

Ellen followed her father back to the palace. They hitched up the mules and repeated their journey, then seven times more. By now it was long after midnight and only the wagon remained in the courtyard, its roof too high to fit through the cathedral doors. Father wedged the doors closed from the inside and carried Mother out by the side door. She woke and insisted on walking. They wheeled the wagon across the palace courtyard and left it by the stable wall, working in the dark. The torch had gone out, but by now Ellen sensed her way. The City slept as quiet as if exhausted. She heard the mules snorting softly in the dark, followed their sound, unharnessed them and let them lead her to the goats' field. She rattled the gate to check it was shut then looped a length of hairy rope round it to make sure. She hung the harness in the stable, felt for an armful of dusty straw in the last manger, dropped it over the fence.

In the courtyard Mother and Father talked in low voices. Mother was ashamed over the matter of the beer and leaving Ellen alone to guard the courtyard. Father murmured something. Camilla hissed, 'But it does matter. It matters to *me*. I let you down.'

Ellen said, 'I've put the mules—'

Father looked up sharply. 'Sssh.'

Firelight flickered beyond the walls. They heard footsteps and Father drew his sword. The gate creaked open.

Archbishop Mansuetus came into the courtyard. He saw them and stopped. Two young acolytes from parochial churches supported him. He held up a torch of blazing straw and the red flames illuminated him from above without mercy. He looked like a man made of blood. His face flickered with shadows, doubt, uncertainty, the face of a religious man who has seen into the pit of Hell.

'Did you see?' He raised his voice. 'Did you see?'

Ellen said, 'I saw. You could not stop them.'

'They wouldn't listen. It wasn't my fault.' Mansuetus staggered, looked around him dully. 'Where are the carts?'

Father said, 'I have removed them to the cathedral for safekeeping.'

The archbishop nodded. He called for his servants but was not surprised when none came. His lips moved, complaining that his cardinals and canons had all fled. He ordered his acolytes, 'Help me to my room.'

Father called, 'The barbarians will reach London Bridge tomorrow. You and I shall face them there, the holy cross in your hand, a sword in mine.'

Mansuetus halted on the top step. He spoke without looking

round. 'They crucify Christians upside down in mockery of our God.'

'Alleluia.'

Mansuetus bowed his head. 'We are all human, Felix. Merely human.'

He went inside. The glow faded. They did not see him again that night.

Father shouted. Ellen tried to wake. Her eyes were gummed together by sleep. She struggled, throwing the blanket and the pile of Mother's old gowns aside. She sat up blinking on the hard, cold mosaic. The weather had changed, the sky was grey. Snow had fallen in the night, speckled the pattern of the floor, made a pale half-moon beneath the bare window. The window sill was fat and white.

Ellen shivered and drew the blanket around her again. Mother sat up in the opposite corner, wearing the same expression as her own.

'What?' Mother said.

'I thought I heard a shout.'

'It must have been a nightmare,' Mother said. She looked at the rumpled clothes beside her, and her face changed. 'Where's your father?'

Ellen hobbled to the window, her muscles stiff with sleep and cold. Three sets of footsteps crossed the courtyard and the gate was open. She rubbed her legs and ran to the door, looked down the corridor. A goat was eating the plaster. Father ran into the far end of the corridor. He called, 'Is he with you?'

'Who?'

'Mansuetus, that's who. My God!' Father swore. The goat dodged away in front of him as he came down the corridor. 'He's not in his room. I've checked the dining room and the house-church—'

Ellen said, 'There's footprints in the yard.'

Father stormed past her, stared from the window.

'But he can't leave us.' Camilla trembled. 'What will we do without him?'

Father slammed his fist on the window sill, sending snow flying. 'My God, that's not what I'm worried about.' He was too large to get through the window. He stormed between them out of the room. Camilla and Ellen looked at one another. They listened to his footsteps running in the corridor, the smaller sandal making a slapping sound.

Camilla said, 'I still cannot believe that an archbishop—'

Ellen ran to the window. She slammed the frame open and jumped down into the yard. Father bounded from the portico, followed the footprints to the gate. They turned uphill to the cathedral. He glanced at Ellen. 'Look after your mother.' He ran uphill with long strides.

Ellen hesitated, then raced after him. Snowflakes clung to her eyelashes. The ruined houses fell away on her right. Father followed the footprints to the side door of the cathedral. Ellen ran up to him. He did not seem at all surprised to see her.

No footprints led away from the door.

She panted, 'They're still inside.'

Father pulled the handle but the door did not move. He ran round to the front of the cathedral. 'No. We're too late.'

The double doors hung open. Hoofprints and the tracks of two wheels crossed the smooth fresh snow of the baptistry. Father called, 'He can't be too far ahead of us.' He ran inside, checked the cathedral's side aisles, counting. 'Sixteen . . . seventeen. One gone.' He clenched his fists. 'But which one?'

He pulled Ellen with him into the snow, slammed the double doors. The wheel tracks followed the white road downhill, swooping towards the dark line of the Walbrook flowing along the valley. Father ran between the wheel tracks and Ellen ran after him. The rooftops that had seemed so small rose around them. This had once been a busy area but now the silence was intense, the only sound that of their running feet. The main road bridged the Walbrook and climbed Corn Hill, but the wheel tracks turned to the right. A smaller road followed the brook's course downstream towards the Thames. They ran between once grand houses, broken fountains built to take advantage of the fresh water, roofless public latrines, gaping public baths. Ellen slipped and Father lifted her, ran with his hand on her elbow.

She said fiercely, 'I won't fall over again!'

'I might,' he said mildly. 'You could hold me up.'

They ran past an old temple of Mithras, an outline of snow in the grounds of a Christian parochial church. A massive stone gateway guarded the entrance to the governor's palace. The buildings stopped as the river wall towered over them. The culverts were blocked and the Walbrook had flooded, spreading a long marsh behind the wall. The ground level had risen and the brook leaked across the road, overflowed through the watergate where the wheel tracks led.

They splashed through the tunnels beneath the wall, ran on to the quays beyond. They skidded to a stop on the edge of the creaking timbers, stared.

The broad Thames lapped in front of them. The empty dray stood abandoned beside a landing stage. The mule flapped its ears, already asleep.

A rowing boat, deeply laden in the water, pulled between the mudbanks towards the main channel. Its form grew faint between the veils of snow crossing the grey waste of the river, but Ellen made out two young men in priestly garb tugging awkwardly at the oars.

Father roared at the top of his voice, '*Maaan-suuu-ay-tuus!*'

The figure in the stern of the boat twisted, clung to its shepherd's crook. He said something and the acolytes redoubled their efforts at the oars. The boat angled upstream, the tide gathered behind it to help it on its way.

'*MAAAN-SUUU-AY-TUUS!*'

Mansuetus waved. He settled himself comfortably and did not look back again.

'He took my gold!' Father shouted. 'He took my gold!'

Snow hid the boat, and when it lifted the craft was no larger than a water-spider in the distance.

The snow came down again. 'He's gone,' Ellen said.

Father stood on the timbers projecting from the edge of the quay, and for an incredible moment Ellen thought he really would jump into the water and go leaping across the islands until he had retrieved what was his. No, not what was *his*, Ellen corrected herself. What was in Father's care. She remembered Mother saying, *You won't let them down, you know. You're a greater man than your ancestors.*

Perhaps by allowing what had been in his care to be stolen, he had let his ancestors down. Perhaps Father felt he had let down his own father.

Ellen gripped his hand but he didn't feel her. His face was a furious bruise of anger. She stood beside him as motionless as he, until she could not help shivering.

He said gently, 'Are you cold?'

She shook her head. Her teeth chattered. She said, 'Are you angry with me?'

'No. I am pleased with you. I am angry with the archbishop, and I am angry with myself.'

'Why?'

'Because I trusted him.'

She thought about it. 'But he admitted he was only human. I feel sorry for him.'

Father said, 'No man who claims to stand between me and God can admit he's only human. I should have known he had lost faith in himself.'

'I should have known too,' Ellen confessed. 'Yesterday morning the dog barked. Mother said that one of the knots had come undone on the dray.'

He looked at her admiringly. 'Clever girl, though.'

Ellen shone.

'He'll be past Thorney Island in an hour, with Riocatus at Fulla's Ham before dark,' Father said philosophically. He seemed calmer now, as though he had decided it could have been worse. 'Rub your hands like this, keep warm.' He crossed the uneven timbers, flapped the limp cover and unknotted ropes off the dray, dropped them in the water. He found a silver coin caught in the bare boards, all that remained of the heavy load.

'Father, what did you mean in the cathedral when you said, *Which one?*'

He flicked her the coin. She caught it, stinging her numbed hands, examined it eagerly.

'I wasn't sure which cart he'd taken, you see, Ellen.'

Ellen saw the coin was engraved with the figure of a woman kneeling before a Roman war galley with many oars.

'Who is she?'

'She is London, Ellen.'

'I didn't know London was a girl.'

'Always.' He grinned and unhitched the mule, slapped its rump. The mule looked at him reproachfully, used to people, then ambled away in search of grass beneath the snow.

'But why is she kneeling to Rome?'

'The British always hated Rome. Roman soldiers. All the Roman bureaucrats and rules and regulations. Roman laws and Roman customs. We even preferred our own homegrown version of Roman Christianity.'

Ellen understood. 'Pelagius.'

He nodded. 'Morgan, as we call him. Just like today, in those days ordinary people hated speaking Latin, wouldn't live in Roman houses if they could build British thatch cottages, hated doing everything the Roman way. So, a hundred and fifty years ago we put up our own Emperor. The Roman army were lucky with the weather, landed near the Isle of Wight to put down the rebellion. The British and French troops were routed and slaughtered beneath the walls of London, like a public show for the citizens. Naturally, Londoners decided they had been on the winning side, and struck this coin to compliment the victor.'

Ellen smiled, touched the figure of the girl with her fingertip. '*Redditor Lucis Aeternae.*'

'Restorer of the Eternal Light.' He dropped the mule's harness in the river, held out his hand for the coin. 'Shall I throw it away?'

Ellen clenched it tight. 'How valuable is it?'

He laughed. 'Only as much as it is worth to somebody, of course.'

'Worth Hardalio's life?'

He said flatly, 'Ask Hardalio.'

He put his shoulder to the wheel. The dray rolled to the edge then caught on the low bulwark, its shafts pointing over the water. 'Push!'

She hesitated. 'What was it carrying?'

'Nothing very valuable.'

'You said gold.'

'Yes, some gold and silver ingots. A chest of money.' He grunted, shoved with all his strength. 'A not very good figure of Apollo in onyx with gold trimmings. Now *help*.'

They both pushed. The dray rocked forward over the edge, tumbled outwards, splashed. Ellen watched the bubbles.

'I see,' she said, disappointed.

Father grinned. 'Most people would call it a fabulous fortune.' He dusted his hands. 'Archbishop Mansuetus could not resist what he saw. What he could reach out and touch. Does that answer your question?'

She said, 'A fabulous fortune? Is that really the truth?'

He put his hand on her shoulder. 'Oh, Ellen, the truth.' He shook his head. 'Come, my no-longer-a-child. Let's get away from here.' Together they splashed under the watergate, went to the steps up the wall. She climbed after him. The steps were worn into scoops by use and there was no rail. Now that she was close she saw that the whole massive wall, ten feet thick and more than twenty feet high, was cobbled together from ragstone lumps, rubble, headstones, old pieces of statuary smoothed and made faceless by time and weather. A fingerless stone hand stuck out of the rough mortar. Here was part of a wreathed head.

She followed the wet prints of her father's sandals, one small, one large, along the walkway.

He leaned on the parapet looking out, spoke to the roofless warehouses below them, and the River Thames.

'I owe you the truth, Ellen.' He turned to her. His mouth moved but she saw he could not go on. 'You are not ours in the way you think you are.'

She bowed her head. The toes of his left foot stuck forward into the snow, black with cold. She unstrapped the sandal and took his foot in her lap, warming it. He gave no sign of pain.

'You are my daughter, Ellen. But you are not Mother's daughter. Do you understand?'

'You feel like ice.'

He tried to wriggle his toes. 'They're numb. Did you understand me, Ellen?'

'Yes.'

'Yes! Is that all you feel?'

'You said you had a secret from Mother. What can I feel? She doesn't know, does she. You haven't told her.'

'That I am truly your father.' He shook his head. 'Father . . . Mother, we have used them as terms of convenience. Because we wished, how we wished, it was true. But Camilla could not conceive.' He hissed as pain flowed back into his foot. 'You're hurting me.'

Bastard. 'Did the slaves know? Did they?' *I am his bastard*.

'Slaves always talk among themselves.'

She said bitterly, 'If you knew she was barren you could have divorced her.'

'I loved her.'

'Even now?' She stepped back without looking at him.

'Even now, because Camilla needs me more than ever now. I have never let her down, Ellen. Not that she knows of. Ellen, look at me!'

83

She looked at the river, the sky, the hills.

'You must never tell her.' He took Ellen's head in his hands, very gently, irresistibly, and made her look at him. 'Never tell her.'

Ellen's eyes filled with tears. She said fiercely, 'Why not, if it's true, why not!'

'Because it would not be fair on her.'

'Because it wouldn't be fair! What about fairness to me?' Ellen struggled to understand. 'What about *me*?'

'Camilla believes you are nobody's child. A child of the gods. No one could have been a better or more loving mother to you than she has been. She found you, we adopted you for our own, her love and kindness sustained you, a homeless waif. To tell her that I . . . I had betrayed her with another woman three years earlier, a younger woman, a beautiful woman . . . that you by a terrible, wonderful chance were my own bastard child, lost and found in the ruins of the house where your real mother and I loved . . . that would be very unkind, an unkindness Camilla does not deserve. Everything she believed in overturned, not what it appeared to be, even her own husband, her own family? I am not nearly so cruel as to tell her the truth.' He touched her tears. 'You even cry like me.'

She brushed away his hand. 'Did you love my real mother too?'

'Yes, I did.'

'Did?'

'She has been dead for nine years at least. I am resigned to her death. I searched for her when you were found. No one remembered her.'

'Who was she?'

'Nobody. A no one.'

Ellen said, 'Her name was Emilia. You said her name.'

He swallowed. 'Emilia. Yes.' He touched her hair. 'You have her hair, her eyes. You are her image. Her smile. The moment I saw you, I knew.'

'Was she in London?'

He pointed at Lud's Hill, the squat cathedral, the streets of decaying houses around the hilltop. 'There.'

Ellen trembled. 'Were you staying at the archbishop's palace?'

'Yes.'

'Did you see her when Mother was with you in London?' Ellen could not hide her outrage, her despair. 'Did you sneak from Mother's bed to your lover's bed? Did you lie with her while Mother slept?'

Father tied his sandal calmly. 'No. I travelled alone. In those days there was still trade, wool business to transact with the *hyparchos* and *kommerkiarios*, exchanging our Fenland bales for manufactured work from Byzantium.'

Ellen's voice shook. 'Do you know for sure that I am yours?'

'You are your mother.' He looked at her blue eyes and smiled as though seeing the past in the present. 'She lives in you.'

Ellen touched her face. She thought, I have my mother's eyes, I have my mother's skin, perhaps I think like her. Emilia cried and laughed as I do. I stand in her reflection as clearly as London Bridge stands in itself in the River Thames. But I don't know her and I never will.

Father stroked her hair. 'Her hair was as black as yours. But she wore hers to her waist.'

Ellen stared at the pale slope of Lud's Hill. She cried. I remember, she thought. Somewhere inside me I remember.

Father returned to St Paul's, but he sent Ellen back to the arch-bishop's palace. Deep inside he still felt guilty. He didn't want Camilla left alone.

The kitchen was a dreadful mess. Ellen did her best to set it to rights, finding embers in the hearth and blowing them to life, adding fresh logs to the fire. The pots and saucepans had been looted by the servants, but she found a good iron pan rolled under the massive stone table. She laid her finds along the wooden worktop, an old linen table cloth, second-rate cutlery, wood bowls and water-pails. The barrel of mouldy brown flour was half full. Perhaps my real mother worked here, Ellen thought as she worked. Perhaps she performed these exact tasks I'm doing now, measuring out the flour, adding water using this ladle, kneading dough. Perhaps with me swinging in her belly as she grunted at her menial tasks.

Perhaps with me watching her, a toddler two or three years old, learning this.

She spat on the hearth and her spit sizzled, bubbled quickly over the stone without friction. Hot enough. She pulled the dough into lumps to make rolls, flattened them into discs to cook more quickly, pushed them into the oven with the long-handled peel.

Camilla lifted the curtain hung over the kitchen doorway, watched her. 'You're terrifically good with your hands,' she said. 'I couldn't get the fire to stay in.'

She sat on the three-legged stool by the table, watching. Ellen milked the goat in the corridor to get away from her adopted mother's eyes. In the storeroom she found an overlooked tub of salt, a precious commodity. The chickens had been stolen from the coop but a basket of eggs remained. There was a well in the back yard and she filled the pail, tested the eggs in the water. They sank, fresh. She put them to boil in the iron pan. 'What's the matter?' Camilla asked. 'You can tell me.'

'Nothing. I'm tired.'

'I can't believe we'll be stuck here for long, can you? Something's bound to turn up. We'll be on the road to the west in a week.'

'Yes.' Ellen faced up to the word. 'Yes, Mother.'

The door-curtain flapped in the wind from outside and Father came in. Camilla ran to him. 'I've been so worried about you!'

'Barbarians are crossing the islands within half a mile of London Bridge.' He sat wearily on the three-legged stool. In private he showed his tiredness, putting his elbows on his knees, resting his forehead sleepily on his knuckles. He swayed.

'Stay with us,' Camilla said simply. 'You mustn't go out.'

Ellen spooned eggs from the pan. Father turned to the table, reached into the tub for a twist of salt between his fingers, ate the eggs like a starving man. Ellen withdrew the crusty rolls from the oven. The pewter spoons had pointed handles and Father pierced his empty shells superstitiously, the habit of a lifetime, and she knew his mind was busy with a hundred plans.

'You don't have to go,' Camilla said. 'It isn't your battle.'

He ate a piping hot roll between mouthfuls of the goat's milk.

Camilla begged him. 'Felix, if you are killed, I shall die too.'

Father helped himself to another roll. There was nothing he could say to help her in her anguish. The outer door banged and he stopped chewing. Footsteps sounded in the corridor and Coroticus came in. He looked around him wildly.

'Coroticus, you have blood on your sword.' Father spoke in British, coldly. 'Are the Saxons within the walls?'

Coroticus shouted, 'Where is he?'

Camilla cried out hysterically. 'The archbishop's gone!'

Coroticus roared. He slashed with his sword and the milk-pitcher clattered from the table. Ellen picked it up. Coroticus brandished his sword. 'British blood, this is,' he panted. 'I followed orders. I didn't do nothing wrong. I'm blessed, I am.'

Father said calmly, 'The enemy is not us.'

'The bastard's stabbed me in the back. I know that now. All his talk, it was just talk.' Coroticus waved his sword aimlessly. 'He's betrayed us. The forum's full of people and they're screaming.' He turned earnestly to Father. 'Me and the lads, we don't know what to do.' He dropped on one knee and waited for orders.

'We have our swords,' Father said decisively. 'We'll rally them at the forum and fight on London Bridge. Find a holy cross.'

Coroticus saluted and ran off to search the rooms.

Father said nothing, looked at his childless wife and his daughter.

'You can't leave us,' Camilla said.

'I'm not leaving you,' he said. 'I have to go.' His eyes followed Ellen to the storeroom. 'Ellen understands.'

She came out holding a leather bag, opened it. 'I found you some proper shoes.'

Father pulled them on, grinning. 'Fit as good as if drawn for me.'

'Senacus the shoemaker drew them, I expect.'

He laughed. 'You don't miss much.'

'You'll be back,' she said.

He hesitated. 'Look after Mother.'

'I promise.'

'And the carts.' He embraced them both. 'You are of more value to me than anything, my real treasure. My family.'

He was gone and the curtain flapped down behind him.

Camilla spoke in a ghastly voice. 'He won't come back.' She did not cry. Her skin squeezed into lines, suddenly she was an old woman. She opened her mouth and blinked, dry-eyed, but the lines did not disappear. Loss and emptiness drained the life from her features. Ellen helped her to the stool.

'Did you hear him, Ellen? He won't come back.'

Ellen busied herself with whatever work she could find for her hands, stoked the fire. She boiled more eggs, put as many heavy bread rolls on the platters as she thought they could eat, put the rest in a bag with the salt for later. She filled the bag with whatever odds and ends came to hand, searched out smoked cheeses and enough smoked meat to fill another bag. She tied the bags off with rope and came back to the kitchen. The eggs were ready and she made Camilla eat. 'Salt?' Camilla ate listlessly with the pewter spoon. 'Pierce the ends for good luck,' Ellen said sharply.

'It won't make any difference,' Camilla said, but she did as she was told. Her teeth could not handle the crusty bread so Ellen spooned the fluffy inside for her.

Camilla swallowed her last mouthful. She looked a little stronger now. 'What are we going to do?'

'Wash,' Ellen said, pouring the water that had boiled the eggs into a bowl. They washed and dried their faces and felt better.

'What now?' Camilla said.

'I must feed the mules.'

Ellen crossed the yard. The snow had stopped and patches of sunlight circled the distant ring of hills, flowed like brilliant ripples across the churned grey marshland. She stopped. Spears and battleaxes glinted, shimmered between the snakes of black water, gathered together and took on the shapes of the islands. Ellen went on with her search for straw but she kept glancing up. She wondered how many men stood beneath that shimmer, first bright, now dark, then bright again as the sunlight swept across them.

More than a thousand, she thought. More than ten thousand. Perhaps much more.

They reached the south bank of the Thames and she made out individual figures jumping from island to island, tussock to tussock, wading across streams not feeling the cold, breaking down Roman quays and revetments to make huge communal bonfires. The bonfires spread along the south bank as far as the great lake opposite Thorney Island, which from this height could just be seen as a dark stain of bare oak, elm and alder around the curve of the river, with the long island of Eia lying beyond. The Saxons, Jutes and English swarmed across Thorney ford, so many of them that the trees seemed to move. The first bonfires sprang up on the north bank.

Ellen stared. She shook. She made herself turn back to her work.

There was no hay or straw to be found for the mules, none. No rope held the gate closed now. She let the gate swing wide, freeing them. She watched the mules canter downhill. Her eyes narrowed.

Men were coming uphill. She could see the spittle clinging to their beards.

They were British. Ellen hid behind the courtyard wall. She thought she recognised one of the drivers. Some of the men broke away to chase a mule. The others pushed forward, pointed at the roof of the archbishop's palace. Ellen looked up.

They had seen the smoke drifting from the chimney.

She ran back to the kitchen. Camilla said in a frightened voice, 'What's wrong?'

Ellen grabbed the bags of food, swung them from her shoulder by the ropes. 'Men.' She picked up the pitcher of water and what was left of the pitcher of milk, pushed them into Camilla's arms. 'Men are coming!'

'They can help,' Camilla said, misunderstanding.

Ellen shook her head vigorously. The spear was propped in the corner and she gripped it in her left hand.

Camilla said something else but Ellen interrupted her. 'No. We're going to do what Father told us to do.'

'The carts,' Camilla said instantly, realising. 'You're right. Nothing else matters.'

Ellen kissed her. 'And you, Mother.'

Camilla stiffened. 'Don't you worry about me. I know my duty.'

Ellen ran into the yard. She could hear the shouts of the men coming round the back. She beckoned Camilla, who plodded after her, not fast enough. Ellen slipped to the gate, peeped through. The road was clear. She took Camilla's elbow and left the gate hanging wide.

Camilla looked back. 'We'd better close it.'

'They'll break it down. Once they start breaking things, they won't stop.' Ellen peered round the corner of the wall. Beyond the ruined houses the cathedral straddled the hilltop. She saw no one, tugged Camilla forward. They hurried across the open space to the cathedral's side door.

Camilla regained her dignity. 'We should enter the Church of God in the proper manner, through the front door, not creep in like thieves—' Ellen pulled her inside. She wedged the door closed. Camilla covered her head piously.

Their footsteps echoed in the deserted nave. The carts made dark mounds along the side aisles. Afternoon light slanted pale fingers from the clerestory windows, glowed round them in the dusty air, made the shadows darker. Ellen took blankets from beneath the drivers' seats of the carts, arranged them in a corner near the main doors. She checked the hard oak wedges that Father had again hammered in place this morning. The doors too were massive beams of oak. She threw her shoulder against them but they yielded not a fraction of an inch. Camilla sat on the blankets and arranged them around her.

'One just has to make the best of it,' she said.

The sunlight fingered the archbishop's *cathedra*, his throne of scarlet and gold that shone on its podium raised in the apse. Ellen ran to it. Her face contorted and she pushed at the throne with all her strength. Camilla shouted, horrified. Ellen's feet skidded. The throne toppled slowly forward, fell upside down. One of the arms broke off and rattled on the flagstones.

'How could you?' Camilla said, but she did not stand up. 'What are you doing? That's sacrilege. Blasphemy.'

'It's not blasphemy,' Ellen panted. 'I love God, but I hated *him*.'

'You're upset.'

'So are you.' Ellen knelt beside the older woman, put her arms around her. 'But I'm not like you, I can't help showing what I feel.'

Camilla patted her, then Ellen slowly realised the older woman was crying.

'I've lost my husband, Ellen.' Camilla held open her arms, showed her naked breasts. Her opened mouth gave vent to the formless groan of her grief. 'I've lost my husband and he won't come back.'

She rolled on to her side, drew up her knees. Ellen touched her but the old lady shook her head. She pulled the blankets over her, wanted to be alone. Ellen listened to her sobs mingling with the distant shouts, jeers, the sounds of household goods being thrown about in the archbishop's palace.

She noticed a small entrance in the wall near the cathedral's double doors. A narrow stairway led up inside the wall. Like all Roman steps, they were cut very steep. She glanced back. Camilla had cried herself to sleep.

Ellen climbed up to a shallow room running the width of the portico. The roof angled down into the floor at each end, but the middle was high enough for her to stand upright. The circular stone window set in the pediment showed the eastern part of the City, Corn Hill sloping down to London Bridge, the warlike barbarian bands congregated along the south bank. She stayed, watching. The drawbridge in midstream went down, a white dot crossed over London Bridge. After a while the drawbridge was again raised.

Ellen leant her elbows on the stone coping. She stared.

The white dot moved easily across the islands, came into clearer view. Ellen realised she saw a knight on horseback. His Roman armour, perfectly preserved, flashed like the sun. The knight lowered his long cavalry spear, or lance, set the white horse galloping forward among the gangs. A wave of swords rose up, fell back in front of him. Arrows curved in the air but could not hit the knight on the white horse. The spent arrows dropped in the crowd, no more were loosed. A wide space opened up and the horseman galloped back and forth. No one dared bring him to battle. He dropped the white lance, drew his sword, pranced his horse in circles, but still no one offered combat. The knight turned his horse on the south end of the bridge, dared them to cross past him as the drawbridge was lowered. No one came forward. The knight turned his back in final mockery, the drawbridge came down, and he trotted his horse to sanctuary across London Bridge.

The drawbridge was raised behind him. Nothing more happened.

Ellen's attention was drawn to the east, more barbarians coming up from the Isle of Dogs. They reached the red cliff that bordered the north bank of the Thames and came forward, foraged around the gutted signal station and farmsteads, now deserted, that had tilled the fertile alluvium near the river. Following the paths between the roads radiating out from the City, they reached the walls and flowed peaceably around the long northern curve.

Ellen stretched her stiff muscles, bumped into a door behind her. Startled, she opened it and looked down into the nave. Camilla slept thirty feet below. A rickety timber walkway served the clerestory windows on each side of the main roof. The boards creaked when she stepped on to them. More plaster fell from the ceiling, littered the debris already fouling the walkways. She held on to the rafters and inched forward, knelt at a draughty north-facing window.

Far more men and women, their dogs and children scampering with them, moved outside the walls of London than inside. A thin stream of Londoners ran along the top of the wall shrieking and throwing whatever came to hand, but the barbarians kept out of range and ignored them except for abuse, gestures, laughter. To Ellen they did not look like warriors. Without their war leaders, the kings and earls and aldermen, they seemed as peaceful and amiable as cattle, farmers with swords. Their dirty women waddled beside them with swinging breasts and hearty rumps, their sandy-haired children screeched insults in English. From time to time a family stopped and made camp, another struck camp and moved on. It was poor ground, boggy moorland over solid clay, sure to break backs and ploughs. Sometimes a gang of louts pushed through shouting orders, whacking people aside with shields and long flat knives, making way for a warrior of importance, perhaps a knight or the landless nobles called *gesithcund* men, their cloaks secured by large showy brooches.

Ellen heard crashing noises close by. She crossed to the south side of the clerestory, looked over the ruined houses to the archbishop's palace. The shadows of men moved past the windows and doorways. For some reason, or perhaps no reason, they had pulled one of the gates off the hinges and set it alight. She watched a man climb the roof, straddle the apex and throw down roof-tiles. The men in the yard threw things back at him. He slid off and wandered about, kicked bits off the wooden drinking-troughs and mangers, then found a length of timber to use as a club, continued his work with a passion. By this time the wagon had been hauled away. The remaining men loaded the pannier-baskets of a mule with whatever they came across and left. The passionate man lay down in the yard and went to sleep. The western sky filled with colour.

It was dark. Ellen heard a woman screaming, running footsteps. They came close by the cathedral, faded away. More footsteps came running, a group of them, then continued on their errand without stopping. From another direction came a burst of laughter. Ellen strained to make sense of what was happening.

It was much later. She tensed. Shadows moved stealthily across the baptistry paving. She heard the furtive clinking of hammers and chisels. She went down. Camilla was terrified, the whites of her eyes showed in the dark. She had woken from her dreams and thought Ellen had left her. She clung to Ellen as she once had to Father.

Someone scratched on the double doors.

A loud banging filled the cathedral with echoes. The doors held but dust showered down, hissing. Abruptly silence returned. 'Sssh,' Ellen whispered. They listened to footsteps moving around the walls. The handle of the side door rattled all at once, but the door held firm. Silence again, and they thought they had been left alone. Then they heard a stone strike near the apex of the roof and skip down the outside before falling to the earth.

Someone shouted irritably. The man who had thrown the stone was called to give a hand. A grating, dragging sound crossed the baptistry. Ellen whispered, 'They're stealing the font.'

Camilla's whisper was incredulous. 'But why?'

'It's made of lead. Lead is useful. No one can make it any more. What we've got is all we've got for ever.'

'A holy baptismal font.' Camilla shuddered. 'At least they didn't break into the cathedral.'

Ellen remembered what Father had said. 'They're afraid of God's lightning.'

The whites of Camilla's eyes blinked. 'Then thank God they're Christians.'

'As long as they stay Christian,' Ellen whispered.

They counted out the blankets, shared them equally, wrapped themselves like equals. Both lay awake trying to sleep. Camilla kept sitting up. An owl hooted. The new moon rose, illuminated the clerestory windows. A dove, the cathedral bird, fluttered between the arches of light thinking dawn had come, then fell quiet.

Ellen returned to the clerestory. She found a comfortable place among the roof-supports and leaned back. She kept watch. The

City lay soaked in blue moonlight below her. She heard a woman's terrible screams, children crying, shouted curses then a rising babble of rage, shrieks, howls, like a city of devils.

Silence returned.

Ellen stiffened, sat up. A shadow of something not human, with four legs, standing upright with two heads, crossed the baptistry. She gazed with round eyes as it staggered, separated into two halves. With relief she realised it was only two men, one helping the other. They disappeared below the roofline. She ran down as a knock came on the side door. It was repeated. One, then three. Trinity, the Christian signal. She kicked out the wedges, the door opened, and her father stumbled into her arms.

'Father!' She took his weight, looked round for her adopted mother.

He had more important matters on his mind. 'Coroticus, stay with me.'

The other man backed away. 'Sir, I won't. I've never seen anything like what I saw today. That's the bravest thing I ever saw.' He sounded dazed, uncomprehending. 'But a man's got to look after himself.'

His shadow turned and ran.

Father called out, 'Coroticus!' But Coroticus just ran faster. Snow kicked from his heels, the ruins hid him.

'You're hurt,' Ellen said.

'No, I'm tired.' Father leaned back against the door, closing it. 'It's just my leg. An arrow. A scratch.'

His *byrrus* fell open. Beneath it Father wore silver armour, the finest work Ellen had ever seen. The rough wool slipped over its polish as though fine as silk.

Ellen busied herself, tore a strip of linen from her shift. 'You're lucky it's only a cut, it didn't go through.'

He grunted.

She spoke without looking up from her work. 'You were the knight on the white horse.'

He shrugged.

She murmured, 'I know it was you.' Her voice rose. 'Why did you do it?'

The echoes woke Camilla. She threw off the blankets and ran towards them, gown flapping, a ghostly figure running in the moonlight. She stopped.

'It's me,' Father said.

Camilla took his face between her hands almost reverently. She gazed up at him. 'You came back.'

Ellen looked at them both. She thought, Father looks as weary as she does. She fetched the pitcher of goat's milk. Despite the cold it was already rancid, but he drank thirstily. Camilla went for a blanket.

Ellen whispered, 'Why? Why did you do it for these worthless people?'

He bent his head close. Just the two of them, the family, her adopted mother excluded. He whispered, 'To show it can be done, Ellen. All around us in chaos, disorder, despair, but—'

Camilla put the blanket round his shoulders. 'There. Keep warm.'

He squeezed her hand. 'Bring me some cheese, if you have any, or sausage.'

'We found some smoked meat,' Camilla said eagerly.

'Yes. Please.'

They watched her search for the right bag, pick at the knot.

He whispered, 'How is she?'

'She is surviving.'

He sighed. 'You realise there is no hope of our leaving the City alive.'

'If we left the carts . . .' Ellen said.

He shook his head. He would not discuss it.

'We could hide them,' she said.

Again he shook his head. 'Even the cathedral's not safe.'

'I know a place.' She led him to the sanctum, opened the door, swept the door-curtain aside. She pointed at the floor. 'There.'

'The floor?'

'That's what I mean. No one would know there's anything there.' Ellen pulled down the rod that held the curtain, inserted it in the paving.

She pulled. The counterbalanced flagstone rose up smoothly.

Camilla came in holding a piece of smoked meat between two fingers. She looked at the steps leading down. 'What's that?'

Father grinned at Ellen. He laughed. 'The very place,' he said. He took the meat, and ate.

'You're my daughter all right!' Father walked along the row of carts, flapping the covers off them. 'Yes, you're my daughter all right.'

Ellen gasped. Down one side of the nave gold shone darkly in the moonlight, silver shimmered, cart after cart after cart was revealed loaded with shining things, more than she knew how to see or what their names were. Her lips moved wonderingly. Gold chalices. Silver grails intricately worked. Cups big and small. A *lanx* platter. Gorgeous coloured glass of every hue. Bowls embossed with silver and gold. Coins, medallions. A box fell open, spilling jewels. Ellen filled her hands with them, staring, unaware of her father watching her.

'It's all true, Ellen. It's all real. It's all exactly what it appears to be.'

Her lips moved but she could not speak, could not look up from the gems in her hands.

'It's the treasure of Toulouse, Ellen. It was stolen by my ancestors many hundreds of years ago, the fabulous looted wealth of Greek temples, oracles, pagan shrines. Golden calves, gods wrought in the shape of every jewel and every precious metal worshipped by men and women.' Ellen realised he was standing beside her. The rope-tassels of his *byrrus* swung gently from side to side with his breaths. He had taken off his armour. It lay in the corner like a discarded silver skin.

Camilla had found a cupboard of votive candles in the sanctum and carried them below. Candlelight flickered up the steps as she moved about down there.

'A fabulous treasure indeed. Too much to use, too much to show off. Much was lost, or paid for the protection of the rest. Much found its way to Galatia, the Celtic tribes there which our name Celatus remembers, our Roman and Celtic blood combined. Much went to France, later to Spain, thence by sea to the Wash of Britain, finishing its journey by Fenland canal.'

'You worship your ancestors.'

'I know where I come from so I know who I am.'

Father crossed to the other side aisle and jerked the ropes free from each cart over there, flapped the covers off the cargoes. His face gleamed as he worked, now illuminated by reflections from below as well as moonlight above.

'Marvellous, is it not?'

Then he stopped by the spoked wheels of the last cart. He unknotted the rope with difficulty, carefully lifted the cover aside.

'But this is what Hardalio died for.' He beckoned. 'Ellen.'

Ellen crossed the nave. She rested her hands on the side of the cart, stood on tiptoe. She looked inside.

Two heavy banks of gold ingots glimmered at her dully, making up the weight.

The rest was nothing but a cargo of brown leather.

'This, Ellen,' Father said quietly. 'This is what you protect with your life.'

Ellen staggered under her burden. Sneezing, she helped her father pile the old goatskins and cylinder-shaped pottery jars out of the way at the far end of the catacomb. Around them, on top of them, almost hiding them, grew a breathtaking hoard of valuables. Ellen struggled down the steps with a gold candlestick almost as tall as herself. Camilla stopped her and stuck a candle in it.

'Might as well make it useful,' she said.

'Yes,' Ellen said. 'Yes, Mother.'

'You've changed,' Camilla said.

'She's grown up.' Father descended the steps crabwise, pulled something heavy after him.

'Is that all?' Camilla said. 'I know that.'

He tugged and an enormous chest embossed with gold and jewels appeared, bumped down after him. It thudded, breaking a piece off the mosaic floor, and it took all three of them to carry the chest to the far end of the catacomb.

Ellen returned upstairs for more. Already her legs and back were aching, but she thought, if I *ought*, I *can*.

She picked up a large silver censer, but Father laid his hand on hers. His gaze was level. He made sure he was alone with her and spoke seriously.

'When I die—'

'You won't die!' Ellen's voice trembled and she realised how exhausted she was.

'One day all this is yours, Ellen.'

'But Camilla—'

'No, Ellen. It's not Camilla's. It's your responsibility. You are my blood, my own flesh and blood. There is no connection between your adopted mother and me but earthly love. But *you*, you are my family.'

'But—'

'You, Ellen. Remember.'

'Yes, Father.'

Ellen worked. Her eyes were half closed. She yawned, stumbling. Each time she passed her father on the steps he said something to make her smile, lift her spirits, but she grew very weary. She dropped down and he let her sleep for a quarter of an hour, then shook her awake.

'What?'

'I must go now,' he repeated. Thin grey light showed in the clerestory windows. 'It's dawn soon.'

'Will the Saxons attack at dawn?'

'If they don't, I will. If I find some men to stand with me.'

She said sleepily, 'I'll stand with you.'

'You're too busy.'

Ellen groaned. Her task seemed endless, she hardly noticed him go. Gold ingots, though small, were worst because they were so heavy. She piled them beneath the niche of Bishop Restitutus. She stopped, realising something had changed, but she was so tired it took her several moments to work out what it was.

Before he left, on the smooth wall of yellow mortar at the far end of the catacomb, Father had scratched five words of equal length.

ROTAS
OPERA
TENET
AREPO
SATOR

Ellen asked her adopted mother, 'What does it mean?'

Camilla said, 'Your father will tell you when he gets back.'

Ellen noticed that underneath, close to the floor, Father had scratched three more words, though equally meaningless. Then she recognised the symbols for alpha and omega above and below, the beginning and the end.

$$\alpha$$
aram menaht menou
$$\psi$$

'Your father will tell you everything when he gets back,' Camilla repeated without opening her eyes.

'He will come back,' Camilla said. 'He said so. He promised us and he kept his word last time. He'll be back. Is it dark up there?'

Ellen came down the steps from the sanctum of the cathedral. 'Yes, it's dark.'

'You've been up there all afternoon, you know.' Camilla had tried joining Ellen in the clerestory, but she had no head for heights and quickly fled below. She felt safe in the quietness of the catacomb.

'I've been keeping watch.'

'Did you see anything?' Camilla busied herself moving things about.

'The Saxons are all around the City. The peaceful ones have camped along the strand to the west, round the curve of the river as far as Thorney Island. The warlike ones are still gathered round the south end of London Bridge. They're not Saxons, they're Jutish or English, I'm not sure.'

Camilla nodded, humming. 'Have you seen any fighting?'

'No. But British raiding parties are moving about the City, looting mostly. They fight when they meet.'

'I think this here, don't you?' Camilla moved the candlestick to the other side. 'Or there?'

Ellen was too tired to care. It was much warmer in the catacomb than in the nave or the draughty clerestory, and she felt her eyes closing. She rummaged in a bag and ate some cheese. She held out a wedge but Camilla shook her head. 'You'd better eat,' Ellen said, 'you're getting thin.'

Camilla looked pleased. 'Yes, I want to look my best for when your father comes back.' She touched her silver hair. 'I might pin it up. I mean, since I've got it, I might as well draw attention to it.'

Ellen drank a little water, offered the rest to Camilla.

'Or does it make me look too old?' Camilla made a face at what was left in the pitcher. 'I could wear my chestnut wig. It's human hair.'

'I'll pin your hair up tomorrow, if you like.'

'Yes,' Camilla decided. 'There's nothing like having one's hair done to make one feel better.'

Ellen finished the water. She lay down on the blanket and closed her eyes.

Camilla said, 'Pinned at the front or the sides, which do you think he'd prefer?'

'Oh, Mother, leave it alone!' Ellen said.

Camilla looked as though she had been struck. 'You're quite right, of course.' She pinched the candle and darkness fell.

Ellen woke.

'Is he back?' whispered Camilla's voice. 'It must be the middle of the night. I thought I heard his footsteps.'

'I didn't hear anything.' Ellen turned over.

'Suppose he was knocking on the door and we didn't hear him down here?'

Ellen said patiently, 'That's why I've left the slab open at the top of the steps. We'll hear him, don't worry.'

Don't worry, she said, but she was very worried.

'He'll be back soon,' Camilla said. 'I have faith.'

At first light Ellen climbed to the clerestory. She half expected to see Father kneeling on the steps of the baptistry to greet the new sun. No one was there. It was a raw cold morning, promising snow. Grey campsmoke rose from the marshlands and drifted over the City. The Saxons on the strand were upping sticks and following the smoke northwards. Ellen returned downstairs. Camilla had found her ornamental hairpins, her brushes. She smiled at Ellen's face.

'Cheer up, don't worry! I know your father better than you do.'

Ellen thought, do you?

Camilla settled herself comfortably on a very precious gilded couch with tasselled bolsters of imperial purple. She patted her hair for Ellen to start. 'I know your father and believe me, my girl, he teaches cats to land on their feet.'

Ellen brushed her adopted mother's hair. 'Yes, Mother.'

'It won't bother me at all if he doesn't come back today. What is important is that we are ready for him when he *does* come. Coil it before you pin it, dear.'

'I don't think the Saxons are going much further west,' Ellen said as she worked. 'I think they've turned north.'

'They're totally unpredictable.'

'Perhaps they heard about the plague.'

Camilla laughed. 'Really, Ellen, you're such a little misery this morning.'

'We saw plague among the retreating British.'

Camilla said firmly, 'Cowards running away will make any excuse.'

'Yes, Mother.' Ellen looked for more pins. She pointed again at the words her father had scratched on the wall. 'Won't you tell me?'

'They're nothing important.'

'The last words Father wrote before he left, not important? Rotas, Opera—'

'A Christian mantra, my dear. Arepo the potter tends the wheels carefully. No man is more religious than your father, but he has always been led astray by that sort of clever nonsense. It's a palindrome.'

'Palindrome?' Ellen returned with the pins.

'The words have no end. Their beginning is the middle and their end is the beginning.'

She doesn't know what they really mean, Ellen realised. My father spoke them to the rising sun, and she doesn't know that either. Did my real mother, Emilia, teach them to him? Was that something else she did, besides conceive me?

Yes, Ellen realised. Because Emilia loved my father as deeply as he loved her. Through these words he was remembering their love. Ellen's hand trembled.

Camilla hissed warningly as the pin scratched. 'It's a code. What your father calls a pesher, a secret meaning concealed within an obvious meaning. I made PATERNOSTER out of it, Our Father. One sees what one wishes, I suppose.'

'And the others?'

'What others?'

Ellen pointed. 'The final three words, of course.'

Camilla noticed them for the first time. 'Aram menaht menou? More clever nonsense, no doubt. Your father understands Peshito, one of the ancient languages in which the Old Testament of the Bible was written. The alpha and omega are Christian, the beginning and the end.' Camilla made a vague gesture. 'I don't pretend to understand that sort of thing. Your father does.' She repeated, 'Ask him when he returns.'

Ellen finished and stepped back.

Camilla admired herself in a jewelled mirror. 'There. I told you I'd feel better.'

'I've got to get some water.'

Camilla hummed cheerfully.

Ellen took the pitcher and went up the steps into the nave. Snow whirled down from the south-facing clerestory windows, settled on the flagstones, outlined the empty carts in white. She climbed into the clerestory, saw only the snowflakes swirling around the hilltop, everything else white and still. She went down and let herself out, pulled a fold of her gown over her head against the falling snow, and hurried across to the archbishop's palace.

It was deserted. She passed the black skeleton of the gate, still smouldering, and crossed the yard on muffled footsteps. The snow lay even deeper round the back, by the well. She let the pail down on its rope but there was no splash, only a soft thud. She jiggled the rope. The pail would not fill.

She wound the handle. The pail came up empty.

Ellen leant over the edge.

For one dreadful moment she thought the body was her father. The man she had seen drop down asleep in the yard, the day before yesterday, stared up at her from the water with his arms outstretched. His face was black and his neck was swollen as thick as his head.

Ellen covered her mouth. She backed away from the well.

'Plague.'

She was shaking. She took her hands from her mouth. They had brickdust on them from the lining of the well. She rubbed them in the snow until her fingers were numb. She tasted the brickdust on her mouth, rubbed her lips until they bled.

She told herself, I didn't touch him.

She went to the ornamental pool and ran with the filled pitcher back to the cathedral.

'I thought you were him!' Camilla said. 'I just had one of those feelings, you know how one does? I can't explain it.'

Ellen leant back against the door. 'We can't go out again. There's plague in the City.'

Next morning the snow had stopped, but there were footprints all round the cathedral.

Ellen stood in the shadows behind the clerestory window. Nothing moved in the white world outside, but she was afraid of being seen. She crouched forward, reached out quickly, scraped snow from the rooftiles into the pitcher. When she had collected all she could reach she crept along to the next window. The rafters creaked. Slowly the pitcher filled with snow.

Camilla called up from the nave, 'Can you see him?'

'Sshh.' Ellen put her finger to her lips.

'Just check if he's coming up the hill, would you?' Camilla said.

Ellen looked out of the window obediently. She shook her head.

'He's busy.' Camilla returned to the catacomb.

Ellen went down. The two women sat with the pitcher between them. Slowly the snow softened, melted.

'I don't think he's alive,' Ellen whispered. 'I think he would have come back by now. I don't think he's going to come back.'

'Have faith,' Camilla said simply.

Ellen returned to her lookout in the clerestory. Beyond the city walls the north was unblemished white, only a few smoky camps here and there. Along the south bank of the Thames old women moved like ungainly crows, sent foraging by the warriors at the bridge. There was no sign of any fighting there. Cattle and sheep from Kent, the spoils of war, were herded across the marshes in preparation for a feast, and then lines of women slaves roped together, and the fires grew brighter.

That night the two women heard British men in the Walbrook

valley yelling and hooting as if in imitation of the revelry across the river. The sounds came closer, footsteps all round the walls. Ellen stood in the nave. Above her the clerestory windows glowed orange with the blaze of torches outside. 'I think there's hundreds of them,' she whispered, and Camilla nodded. The shuffling footsteps gave way to loud calls, people showing they weren't afraid, then came the mocking hoots they had heard earlier from the Walbrook valley. Some brave soul kicked on the cathedral doors. Laughter.

Stones were thrown at the roof. A roof-tile broke, slid down, crashed on to the ground. A hail of stones followed. More tiles gave way, showered through the fiery light into the nave, shattered.

'They're drunk,' Camilla said. The terrible banging noise began on the doors, and she clapped her hands over her ears. This time the mob had carried heavy stone hammers with them. This was not the first church they had broken tonight. Dust jumped from the door-beams.

Ellen pulled her adopted mother into the sanctum. She slammed the door and they looked at each other with staring eyes.

'Your father would know what to do,' Camilla said.

'I know what to do.' Ellen pulled her adopted mother down the steps into the catacomb.

'But we'll suffocate,' Camilla said.

Ellen crouched on the bottom step. 'That's better than what they'll do to us.' She pushed upward with the rod.

The flagstone rotated, slammed into place over their heads.

The candle flickered, then the flame held steady.

Camilla slumped on to the couch. 'Our own people. I'm ashamed. What are we going to do now?'

Ellen took the blankets and the pitcher of water, and carried the two bags of food to the couch.

'Have faith,' she said, and Camilla smiled to hear her own words come back to her.

'Now we both have faith.'

Ellen walked to the votive candle burning in the candlestick as tall as herself, halfway along the catacomb. 'We wait. I don't know how long. We'd better make the most of the air.'

She blew out the candleflame.

It was dark.

'How long has it been?' came Camilla's voice again.

'Don't keep asking.'

After a while Camilla's voice again came out of the dark, as though no time had passed. 'You're stronger than me, you know. You sounded just like your father.' Suddenly, without warning, her hand gripped Ellen's. 'Suppose he comes back while that dreadful mob are in the cathedral?'

Ellen opened her eyes and closed them. It made no difference to the blackness of the dark. 'He'll know how to deal with them.'

They sat in the dark, breathing steadily. The silence was intense. Camilla sighed loudly. 'Do you think they're gone?'

'No, they're not gone.'

'I can't hear them.'

They listened to the silence.

Ellen murmured, 'We're ten feet below the ground.'

'Do you think they're desecrating the cathedral?'

'Yes. They're determined.'

'It's a good thing we saved everything. Do you think God's lightning will destroy them?'

'I hope it will. I've been praying for it.'

'I shall never understand evil,' Camilla said. 'I just thank God there's a God and everything comes right in the end.'

Ellen lay down on the blanket. 'Better get some sleep.'

Camilla settled her head on the bolster, drew her legs up on the couch. 'I'm so cold. Come up here and cuddle me like you used to—'

'When I was a baby?' Ellen said without thinking.

Camilla said nothing and Ellen hoped she had not heard. She scrambled on the couch and Camilla made space for her, flapped her blanket over them both.

After a while Camilla said, 'No, I couldn't cuddle you when you were a baby because I didn't know you when you were a baby.'

Her voice was strong. She had decided.

Ellen thought, what am I to say to her? She doesn't know the whole truth, she only thinks she does.

'It's very simple,' Camilla said. She moved beneath the blanket, hugged Ellen tight. 'We are your adopted parents but we love you as much as if you were our own. We love you as much as Jesus does. Your father and I – I mean Felix and I – we could not have children.' She wept.

Ellen lay staring into the dark. She didn't know what to say. *Father could.*

Camilla made herself calm. 'I wasn't always like this. I'm sorry. It's been difficult . . . difficult. Everything changes so quickly nowadays.'

Ellen stroked her. 'If I was not born . . . where exactly did you find me?'

Camilla sighed. 'Imagine me as I was, Ellen. In the prime of my life—'

'As you still are.'

'No. I was in the prime of my life, forceful and proud in reflection of a forceful, proud, respected husband. Accustomed to having my every order obeyed, to having everything I demanded. Except a child of my own. Some women are contented with their lot. But my lack spread like an infection within me, poisoned my every happiness, made my good life worthless. I even argued with Felix, blamed him for my emptiness, I was so bitter, unhappy. I mocked him. I thought only of myself, not the misery I was causing around me. In fact that was a kind of pleasure, for it made my own misery more bearable.

'As a matter of course, on those rare occasions when I accompanied Felix on his visits to London, we accepted the archbishop's hospitality. In those days, nine years ago, it was still safe for a woman to travel about the City in a sedan chair carried by slaves. Even then London was only a shadow of its former glory, perhaps only a shadow of a shadow, but it's all relative, isn't it? Naturally, one was carried by sedan chair to worship at the cathedral, and made one's prayers, and received one's blessing, and was carried away also by sedan chair. Of course there were distressing sights and armed guards were required. There was a place . . . I forget why we went that way.'

Ellen cleared her throat. 'Nearby?'

'You may have noticed those dilapidated houses. It was summer, wonderful herb gardens run riot, the scent of wild flowers, beehives abandoned long ago except by the bees. Pathetic little gardens still lovingly hoed and tended by itinerants, the most disgusting dirty people you ever saw. Made themselves scarce when they heard the tread of armed men, I'll tell you. Then we passed a place where there was nobody. Crooked walls, timbers fallen everywhere, no sound but bees droning. And a baby child, about three years old, playing in a cellar open to the sky. You looked straight into my eyes.'

Ellen said, 'Where was my mother?'

'You had no mother. You had no one. You looked up at me with those blue-moon eyes of yours and you reached out to be picked up. And I reached out through the curtain of the sedan chair, and I picked you up. And you would not let go of my hand. You curled yourself in my lap as though it was the most natural place in the world and went to sleep, but still you would not let go.' She sighed. 'It was your will that made Felix and me a family, Ellen. The child not the parents. You kept us together.'

Ellen listened for sounds from above but there was nothing. 'Did you try to find my real mother?'

'I am your mother now,' Camilla said. 'Whoever she was, she couldn't look after you.'

Ellen thought, *Emilia*.

The two women, adopted daughter and foster-mother, clung together and tears streamed down their faces in the dark.

Ellen tried to remember the mother she had never known. *Emilia*.

Ellen and Camilla did not know how much time passed. They lit the biggest candle from time to time. Next time they drank a sip of water, took a mouthful of goat's cheese, put the candle out. Sometimes they ate a strip of smoked meat, also goat, and wetted their mouths with water. 'We've been here for ever,' Camilla said. 'It must be day.'

Ellen said, 'Which day? Tomorrow or the next day?'

'The candle's almost done.'

Ellen blew it out.

At last they tried to eat the bread. The rolls were so stale that Ellen pounded them to breadcrumbs with the base of the candlestick. They ate but there was not enough moisture left in the pitcher to wet their lips. The candle guttered, flared up, went out.

Camilla said in the dark, 'He'll be there.'

Ellen crawled across the floor. She found the rod by touch. She stood on the bottom step and reached up with the rod into the dark.

She found the place, pulled the rod.

Nothing happened. She tugged with all her strength.

'It won't—' she grunted. 'There's something—'

She threw back her weight. The flagstone grated, shifted, gave way. In its place light poured down, tumbling bricks, a cloud of glaring white dust. Ellen climbed, blinking, into the light of day.

Camilla called up, 'Can you see him?'

Ellen turned slowly, looked round her. She stood in blinding sunlight striking across piles of rubble.

The cathedral was gone.

'It's gone,' she called down. 'It's gone.'

'It can't be.'

Ellen said, 'There's only us.'

There was no roof, no walls. The pillars of the narthex and the nave pointed at the sky. Bits of brickwork stood up like jagged teeth where the building had been strongest. The carts had been dragged away or burnt. Only the floor remained, strewn with bricks, tiles, all that had fallen down or been thrown down.

Camilla climbed into the open air.

'It's impossible,' she said.

Ellen turned. To the west a remaining fragment of brickwork rose above her like half a cracked and broken dome, fragile and improbable as an eggshell, part of the apse. The painted head of Jesus Christ now looked out across this scene of desolation, the bare snowy hilltop where St Paul's Cathedral once stood. His brown eyes were pocked by stones chucked by the mob. His mouth and nose were missing. Damp segments of Christian plasterwork had peeled, dropped away to reveal the ancient dark head deliberately obscured beneath the later work.

The handsome features of Mithras the God of Heavenly Light, Saviour from Death, once more stared along the ruined nave.

Ellen waited for hours, watching for movement. Fresh snow had fallen but there were no footprints. Nothing moved anywhere on the slopes of Lud's Hill. No one moved in the Walbrook valley. No one moved on Corn Hill. A single thread of smoke faded away, and then nothing moved at all.

Half a mile to her left, the walls of the amphitheatre had also been ransacked. One massive set of tiers remained, ranks of stone seating clinging to it right to the top. Beyond the amphitheatre the gates of the citadel hung open. The day turned grey and sullen. Everything was frozen, motionless.

She thought, it's impossible to imagine anything in London moving again, except falling down.

Camilla shuffled up the steps, wrapped her in blankets.

'We survived,' Camilla murmured. 'He will. He'll be back. You are watching for him, aren't you, dear?'

She returned down the steps to the catacomb, cleaning up.

Ellen moved suddenly. She took the water pitcher, filled it with snow from the baptistry, left it on the steps for Camilla to find.

She shrugged off her blankets and slipped away between the ruined houses.

A man's foot stuck out of a doorway, heel up. Ellen stopped, covered her mouth, then hurried past. She followed the battered back wall of the archbishop's palace, heard low calls ahead of her. She crouched, then crept forward to the corner. The road to Lud's Gate passed in front of her and she saw the cart with spoked wheels at the door of the yellow house. A family worked to load the cart. She recognised the hard-faced shopkeeper limping out, a carpet rolled over his shoulder. He dropped it in the cart, returned for more. His sons hurried back and forth, their mother snapped out orders. When the cart was full the sons pulled between the shafts and the cart inched ahead, then slowly rumbled forward. One wheel squeaked. The shopkeeper closed the door of the yellow house, then shrugged and kicked it open, walked after the cart. Ellen shrank back, heard the cart as it squeaked past, then watched it lurch downhill. Lud's Gate was open. The bridge was still down but a pontoon of treetrunks had been thrown across the Fleet. The family unloaded the cart, carried the stuff piecemeal across the wobbling trunks, manhandled the cart across, loaded it again. The shopkeeper and his family turned their backs on London. Through the open gate Ellen watched the cart bump from sight along the deserted strand.

She pushed at the gate. It swung slowly at first, then with increasing speed, closed with a hollow booming noise. Snow showered from the roof of the gatehouse and brown London ravens clapped into the air, surveyed her beadily from the peaks of the bastion towers.

Ellen climbed on to the wall and followed the high walkway to the Thames. She thought, the mudbanks and islets look like the backs of huge animals grazing underwater. The barbarians no longer scavenged along the south bank, which was deserted, though she saw warriors gathered by London Bridge. Ellen turned along the river wall, crossed the makeshift repairs overseen by her father.

A cormorant splashed for eels. She found the Walbrook watergate hanging open, although she and her father had left it closed.

She closed it again, and walked on. She closed each watergate that she came to. The Kentish and English warriors were spreading along the south bank. She wondered if they had seen her. They beat their long knives on their shields. The rhythmic throb pulsed across the river.

Ellen came to London Bridge.

Here, if anywhere, she would find her father.

The drawbridge was raised, the Bridge Gate was closed and barricaded in the river wall. But no one manned the barricades. Massive oak piers and elm piles supported the snowy roadway of the bridge, which reached out across the river empty except for spent arrows, carts overturned by the defence, a few crumpled ragged bodies. The defenders were gone from the palisade. Even the elm towers that protected the drawbridge were abandoned.

The King of the Barbarians walked on to London Bridge.

He came to the gap and the river swirled beneath him. He stopped, and the rowdy noise of his warriors beating their shields stopped with him. He looked up at the walls of London without the slightest sign of admiration, fear, or defeat.

'We are at peace with walls.' He kicked aside the snow, spat on the gravelled roadway, turned his back on the City. His men opened in front of him, fell in behind him. '*We are at peace with walls!*' Within a few minutes they had spread out from the islands, shrinking, dwindling.

Ellen watched until they were all gone.

She heard the harsh croak of a cormorant. A fish splashed in the sullen grey surface of the river. Swans paddled by a mudbank. A snowflake blew into her eye and she blinked.

She walked to where the wall turned sharply north. Here was the most heavily defended side of London, with forts every few yards, but all were empty, all useless. She picked her way between the rubbish thrown down the stairwells, closing the great gates as she went. Below her she saw the roof of the Christian community called All Hallows and she heard a few dogs barking, but there was no other sign of life. Ellen walked to the Colchester Gate, closed it. The forts stopped, the swamp beyond the northern wall long considered a sufficient defence. There was no sign of human life as far as her eye could see, only snowfields and oakwoods. She closed the citadel gates one after the other. She put her shoulder to the New Gate, and it boomed closed.

Ellen had come full circle around the city.

She walked back to the hilltop of St Paul's. She sat on the steps and put her chin in her hands, watched her adopted mother work.

'I know what you're going to say,' Camilla muttered without looking round.

'I don't think there's anyone left alive in the whole of London.'

Camilla swept busily with a besom. 'I know what *I* believe. He'll be back, you'll see. He'll be back.'

It was summer. Bees droned in the ruins. Ellen walked the narrow overgrown lanes calling up at the houses. She called out the same name over and over. Sometimes a strange mood settled on her, and today was one of those days. Her throat was sore.

'Emilia . . .'

Her calls echoed off the mouldy plaster of roofless rooms, set mice scuttling on the mossy timbers, but there was no reply. 'Emilia. Mother.' In her heart of hearts Ellen knew there never would be a reply. Everything was up to her now.

But her real mother was here in spirit. She felt it in the familiarity of these places where she hunted for her mother, the twisting overgrown passages, broken courtyards. She knew her way between them as if by instinct. The scent of herbs blowing on the warm breeze made her swallow with longing, remembering. Sometimes Ellen could almost reach out and touch her happy childhood. It was still here, as though she might come round a corner and find herself playing in the ruins. Look up at herself with her blue eyes. Hold up her left hand trustingly to be picked up, squeezed tight, taken away. Become her adult self.

I'm back home, Ellen thought, and realised it was true. Part of her had always been here. She had always carried the place she had been born inside her.

Ellen leapt deftly on a wall, crouched, then let her long legs carefully down the other side. She had grown her black hair to her waist, and it flowed smoothly as she moved. A warm dead hare swung by its neck from the girdle of her tunic. She crossed a grassy lane to the grassy houses growing out of the other side, where creepers hung like heavy smoke from the chimneys, and an elm tree grew gracefully from a bath room. On these excursions she always tried to come back with something useful, a samian pot or a copper pin or a pair of tweezers, once a whole box of dentist's tools. She stopped, seeing a red pottery handle sticking out of the moss.

She bent forward and examined it eagerly, showing the backs of her thighs to the warm evening sun, then knelt. Her fingers scooped delicately at the soil, she dug as expertly as a hare. She clapped her wrists excitedly, held her lower lip lightly between her teeth as she worked to free the buried amphora. She exposed the neck, grinned.

The seal was good.

Sealed amphorae were the most exciting. They could be any size from a cistern down to a small pot. It was impossible to tell what they contained. If the wax or pitch seal around the stopper had held good – if not, the contents were liable to smell worse than the body she had roped out of the drinking-well – if the seal was good, there was a chance that what was inside, though often mysterious, would also be good.

She took a knife from her girdle, peeled the pitch away from the stopper, then inserted the point into the rim and prised the stopper off. She caught it neatly, sniffed it and laid the stopper on the grass. Not too bad, but definitely not olive oil. She slipped her knife back in her belt.

She put her nose to the opening and inhaled. Not fish paste. She sniffed closer. Something strong and bitter, almost pungent. She reached inside, felt something wet, about the size of a grape. She looked at it in her fingertips, then tested it between her front teeth. Soft, hard in the middle. She spat out the stone, and chewed. She made a face, then her mouth filled with the salty flavour.

She thrust her arm inside, pulled out a handful, pushed them into her mouth. She ate luxuriously, spitting out the stones, then reached for more.

Something was behind her. She turned quickly.

Nothing moved. The sun stuck out of the roof of the archbishop's palace like a bloody breast, its lower half jabbing gleaming spikes of red light through the missing tiles. Everything pointing towards her was deep with shadow.

She put back her hair, tried to lift the amphora. A City of grass, and broken bricks clinging together, and stonework held by crumbling mortar, and trees working their way gently and implacably through deserted rooms towards the light, and branches creaking, and leaves rustling, was full of sounds both natural and half natural. Doors banged in a wind of a certain strength from a certain direction, no other. Other doors banged when the wind changed, or gusted. After a hot day like today the buildings moaned and settled themselves into the cool of evening as though they were alive.

She looked round slowly. The last light of the sun flashed on a window. The window tapped, then rattled in the breeze. That was all.

She replaced the stopper and swung the amphora over her shoulder, made her way to the place where the back wall of the palace had collapsed. She stepped through. Camilla was drawing water from the well. Ellen swung the pointed end of the amphora into the soft soil, propped it against the parapet. 'I'll do that.'

'What?' Camilla squinted. 'Oh, it's you. I don't know what's the matter with things these days.'

'Water's getting heavier, that's all.' Ellen pulled easily on the rope, stood the pail of good fresh water on the rim.

'Is it? I can do that,' Camilla said fussily. 'What have you found?'

Ellen showed her the amphora. Camilla sniffed. 'You know I can't smell.'

Ellen reached inside, pulled out a black handful.

107

Camilla said, 'Olives!'

She sucked one between her gums, spat out the stone. 'Olives! Perfect olives! Quick, plant it, we'll have an olive garden.' She helped herself to more. 'I can't eat just one, can you?'

Ellen chewed one carefully, savouring the taste. 'So these are what olives are.'

Camilla reached inside, pulled out her arm black with liquor to the elbow. 'Thousands of them!' she cackled, and skipped. 'Roman food again. You don't need teeth for Roman food,' she added accusingly when Ellen replaced the stopper. Ellen grinned, swung the amphora over her shoulder and carried the slopping pail in her free hand, and Camilla followed her back to the palace, complaining.

Long ago they had decided to live in the kitchen. The men who first looted the place, and the mob who followed them later, had naturally concentrated on the best rooms. Whatever had not been carried bodily from the reception area, dining room and house-church had been smashed. Rain poured through the broken tiles when it was wet. Many of the painted frescos had fallen in one piece face-down from the damp walls on to the hard mosaic floors, where they stayed, forgotten. Chickens roosted where once the archbishop had prayed, and a covering of dark earth grew up, made of manure, decayed straw bedding and mud, so that already the doorways seemed unnaturally low. Damp had got to the rafters and the roof groaned on windy nights, bending, bowing. It had not fallen in yet.

The kitchen, built on the back of the palace to reduce the fire risk, was different. It had its own roof and its walls were stout, rendered with mortar. No one important ever came in a kitchen, it had never contained any precious objects, so the looters had neglected it. But a kitchen was full of useful things, everything two women needed to live comfortably. And the log-fed hearth kept it warm through the coldest winter.

There was even glass in the window, admittedly greenish and ripply, but adding immeasurably to the feeling of closeness and companionship between the two women.

They argued all the time, of course.

Ellen propped the amphora in the corner and slopped water into a pot to heat. Camilla watched her beadily. London hares had no tails, unlike the superior Fenland variety. 'Miserable little thing,' Camilla scoffed. Ellen slit the belly of the hare and gutted it into a smaller pot. She took out the gall-bladder, squeezed the contents from the gut, added the heart, liver and kidneys and the head for stock, added nettles for tenderness, then covered them with water and put the pot to boil. Camilla needed her food soft and strong.

'That the best you could do?' she demanded. 'Hardly more than a leveret, that is.'

Ellen skinned the hare, jointed it and added it to the vegetables which she cut for the larger pot, leeks, onions, hazelnuts, finally lovage and chives, all found growing along the streets of the City.

A shape moved in the window. Ellen jumped. 'Did you see?'

Something in Camilla broke. 'It's him!' she shouted. She clenched her gown in her fists. 'It is him, your stepfather, quick, quick—'

'It was just my shadow,' Ellen decided, but she allowed herself to be pushed to the door. She peered out into the night. 'There's nothing.'

Camilla called, 'Felix, is that you?' She pushed Ellen out. 'Quick! You have young eyes.'

Ellen stood in the dark. The window cast a glow. In the soft soil beneath it was a bare footprint.

Ellen looked around her, saw nothing but the dark. A brick clattered in the distance.

She put her own foot in the footprint, then rubbed it out with a quick, almost savage gesture. She went back inside. She shrugged. 'You imagined it.'

They ate their supper in silence.

Camilla put down her spoon. 'But there was. There was somebody outside.'

Ellen shrugged again. 'You're always saying that. I wish you'd eat. You're thin as a stick.'

Camilla sucked another mouthful, then rested her spoon. 'I'm so worried about the' – she wouldn't say the word – 'g-o-l-d,' she confessed.

Ellen laughed, shook her head. 'It's safest left where it is. Best to forget it.'

'How can I forget it? When you're out I worry about it all day,' Camilla said. 'It's our responsibility. I lie awake all night and worry about it.'

Still Ellen shook her head. 'Gold is no use to anyone.'

'Neither is a newborn child, but they grow up.'

'No one would steal a baby.'

'I stole you,' Camilla said quietly. A single tear trickled down her scrawny nose, dripped from the tip. She stirred her soup. 'Now I'm afraid, Ellen. I'm old. And so afraid. You wait till you're my age, you'll know what it's like.'

Ellen lost her appetite.

Father said, *This is what you protect with your life*.

'I'll go up there in the morning,' she said.

Camilla squeezed her hand gratefully.

Ellen was up before dawn. She lifted her shoes in her fingers and stole from the kitchen before Camilla woke. The grass was wet with dew beneath her bare feet. She sat on the step and pulled on her shoes, slipped away through the mist.

She turned uphill and climbed out of the mist almost at once. The grassy green curve of Lud's Hill stood against the blue sky. Below her the mist stretched from left to right, a snaking white cloud following the course of the invisible Thames below it. Around the great bowl of London, distant hilltops speckled the mist like a ring of islands.

She reached the top of Lud's Hill, found a stick and pushed her way through the brambles and saplings. The sun rose above Corn Hill, struck level rays through the cloudtops swirling around her. The Walbrook valley beneath her, bruised with misty shadows, decaying buildings, filled with light.

Ellen stopped. Stones grew up through the brambles. She thought she was somewhere on what had once been the baptistry. She glimpsed a shape in front of her and climbed on the plinth that had supported the font. Here she had seen her father praying to the Unconquered Sun. There was so much he could have told her. Ellen realised that despite all she had learnt about living from day to day, and keeping food in her mouth, and keeping warm at night, she knew almost nothing important.

She bowed to the sun as her father had.

She turned round. The rubble of St Paul's was nothing but mounds of grass. What remained of the apse had blown down in last winter's storms and already the stones were a bed for stinging nettles. Weeds and brambles filled the nave, each evenly spaced pillar stood like a ivy-clad green trunk, neither stone nor tree. One corner of the sanctum wall was thicker than the others and rose to a jagged peak twice the height of Ellen's head. Years ago she had found the stone cross that once surmounted the cathedral, crawled up there and wedged the base of the cross into a cavity between the bricks, leaving it standing crooked but defiant. Now creepers flourished all around it, but the cross still stood.

It's still, she told herself, glancing up, the highest point of the cathedral.

The rod was concealed in the wall beneath the cross. Taking it, she swept aside the clematis and honeysuckle, found the flagstone beneath, brushed away the mud. She inserted the rod. The stone creaked, rotated, opened.

She went down.

The air was not musty. Ellen had brought a piece of glowing charcoal in a small iron keep-fire. She lit a candle and walked down the catacomb. Bishop Restitutus. Bishop Exsuperius. She nodded to them like old friends, not for the first time wondering why the catacomb was so obviously overcrowded at the far end, the side walls crammed with niches, recesses, alcoves, instead of being dug forward beyond the end wall. But here was the gold.

It had not been touched, of course, nor would it be. No one would ever know of this place. This enormous, useless fortune would stay here for ever, slowly sinking deeper beneath the earth. Until the day she died it would stay in her care. She had given her word.

Only with death would her responsibility be relinquished. No woman could live for ever.

The gold, silver, jewels, gleamed and shimmered and sparkled all round her by the light of the candleflame. But she was drawn to the one place that was dull.

This, Ellen, Father said. *This is what you protect with your life.*

Not the gold. Not the silver. Not the jewels. This.

Ellen leant forward. She reached out towards the mound of brown leather placed out of the way at the farthest end of the catacomb. Brown skins. The strangely shaped cylindrical jars with three quadrangles stamped on them, that looked as though they might be useful for storing something in the kitchen. She stretched out her fingertips, touched a piece of soft skin frayed by age. Wind gusted on her face, and the candle blew out.

She drew back.

She laughed, startled by the sudden draught. The keep-fire had gone cool and the candle would not catch. No matter. There was enough illumination coming down the steps for her to make her way back to the entrance. She climbed into the green lushness of the cathedral ruin, pushed the rod, and the stone rose into place.

She returned the rod to its hiding place in the wall.

Now, as she crossed the nave and jumped on to the grass from a mouldering foundation of the cathedral, the draught that had blown out the candle was explained. A wind gusted past her, pulling the mist into streamers. The muddy Thames appeared below her, grey-green, sparkling in the breeze, and the green streets of the City waved their treetops and roared in the wind, elm and oak and beech sounding like huge green fountains, rowan and holly bright with red berries as bushes of flame.

Camilla hobbled into sight by the wall of the archbishop's palace. She was wearing her ragged red gown and her jewellery hung from her emaciated figure. She saw Ellen and waved, then leant on her stick, face quivering, waiting for Ellen to reach her. Ellen hurried.

'Whatever's the matter?'

Camilla licked her lips. 'So it wasn't you. I thought it wasn't.'

'What are you talking about?'

Camilla tugged her sleeve and Ellen followed her past the wall. 'And the pail's in a different place, too,' Camilla grumbled. She stopped at a wary distance from the kitchen door, pointed her stick.

On the kitchen step a large pike, mouth gaping, teeth shining like pins, lay on a carefully arranged bed of freshly cut parsley and rue. The staring eyes were clear and moist. Ellen touched the scales with her knuckles. 'Still wet.'

Camilla looked around her. 'If not you,' she said, 'then who?'

They put the fish on the table and looked at it.

'You did see something last night,' Camilla said accusingly.

'It is not him!'

'It is,' Camilla said plainly. 'It's a gift from Felix.'

'It might as well be from my real mother,' Ellen said angrily, then sighed. The two women, young and old, sat looking at the fish, united by hope.

'It's magnificent,' Camilla said. 'You've never caught one as good as that, you're not strong enough. Thirty pounds at least.' She added cunningly, 'We could stuff it with olives. Olives aren't fattening, neither is fish.'

'Someone is watching us,' Ellen said.

'Yes, dear, He is watching over us, and when we die we shall go to His Heaven.'

'That's not what I meant.' Ellen went into the storeroom, fetched a copper *sartago* long enough to poach the fish. 'Somebody was watching me yesterday evening,' she admitted.

'English farmers sometimes come into London for bits of iron.'

'Somebody was outside the window last night. I didn't want to alarm you.' She told Camilla about the footprint. 'Not much larger than mine.'

'That's not Felix.' Camilla drew her gown anxiously around her. 'He has big feet.'

'I can't think of any reason for anyone to hang around our window, or give us a fish.'

Camilla fetched a blanket and hung it over the window, cutting out the daylight. They sat in the gloom watching the fish poach.

'Felix's gold!' Camilla exclaimed. 'You weren't seen?'

Ellen shook her head. 'No. It's safe.'

Camilla said tremulously, 'I think we ought to move back in there. It's cool in there. No flies, no mosquitoes. Peace and quiet.' She sighed longingly, and closed her eyes. 'I'm too worn out to eat.' She doesn't do anything all day, Ellen thought, she's worn out with waiting. Ellen watched her, flaked mouthfuls of cooked fish from the bony pike, nibbled them herself, but Camilla would not eat. The fish grew cold.

It was dark. Ellen went to the door, closed it, returned to her stool at the table. Camilla had not moved.

Ellen said gently, 'I'm never going to see my real mother. I know that now. I accept it.'

Camilla sighed.

Ellen said, 'Now you must accept the same truth about my father – my stepfather. He is dead and you have to accept it.'

'He's not dead.'

Ellen said firmly, 'If he was alive he would have come back by now.'

Camilla's eyes became enormous in her thin face. 'But you have found your mother. Look at you, Ellen.' She hobbled to the window,

112

pulled down the blanket that covered it. Ellen's reflection stood in the glass. 'Look at you! Are you me?'

Ellen looked at herself, her wide blue eyes, high cheekbones, her hair curling like a glossy black wave from her high forehead into the small of her back.

'Your breasts. Your hips. The shape of your hands, Ellen. Look at the way you smile. You're not me. Do you see her?'

Ellen breathed, 'Yes.'

Camilla gripped Ellen's hands. 'You *have* found her. She is alive.' She rested her scrawny head on Ellen's shoulder. 'Now, permit me, in return, my one small piece of mercy.'

Ellen stroked the old lady's flimsy hair, just as she had seen her father do. *You even cry like him, Ellen.*

She looked at her own reflection in the glass.

'He is alive.'

Next morning Ellen opened the kitchen door and looked out. Her foot knocked against a basket on the step.

Ellen dropped the basket of red apples on the table. The two women looked at them. Ellen picked one apple out. 'Still with the dew on it.' She ate it.

Camilla said fretfully, 'What does he mean? What does he want of us?'

'He probably wants to get you to eat!' Ellen said. 'One day a gust of wind will blow you away.'

'Take them outside,' Camilla said dully. 'I can't bear to look at them.' She fumbled for her stool and sat on it.

Ellen came back later in the day but Camilla had not moved from her stool. In the afternoon she pretended to eat a little fish soup, and she really did eat an olive or two, chewing nostalgically, her youth more real to her than her old age. Then she made up her bed near the hearth and lay down as if she was cold, and closed her eyes before darkness fell.

Ellen watched her in despair. She cuddled the old lady, but Camilla lay like rags.

She can't tell me what it was really like to be her when she was young, Ellen realised. It's still there inside her but it can't get out. When Camilla dies, all her memory, all her emotion, all she was, is gone in an instant. She is erased.

Unless what Christians believe really is true, that she'll wake on the Day of Judgment remembering all that happened before, and be cast down to Hell for her sins, and lifted up to Heaven for her love.

Was my father really a Christian? Could a man really be a Christian and of every other religion as well?

What did my father truly believe?

Ellen thought her thoughts and watched for a shadow outside the window.

She kept to her normal evening routine, washed herself at the well, returned inside. She slept through the hours of darkness and woke at the first hint of light. Instead of using the kitchen door she went out front, paused behind a pillar of the portico.

She crossed the courtyard and slid quietly behind the wall.

Almost at once she heard footsteps toiling uphill, and the sound of sloshing water. Someone was humming. There was an extra loud splash and a curse, then the nasal humming resumed. Ellen waited until the sound drew level with her.

She drew her knife and held it point upwards in her fist, teeth bared.

She jumped out.

'Hoi!' shouted the young man, dropped the leather bucket he was carrying, sent foam and writhing shapes washing across the roadway. He scampered instinctively on to the kerb to keep his bare feet dry, then flushed, looked angry to regain his composure, and eyed her with bravado.

'Still don't know your name!' he said.

He'd practised saying that, obviously. She put her hands on her hips. 'Who do you think you are, scaring us?' she said contemptuously.

He deflated. 'You don't remember me? You stole my hare. I thought you'd remember me.'

She recognised his eyes. His nasal voice was familiar. But he was a lot taller, thinner, and his hair touched his shoulders.

'Yes, and I stuck my spear in your arm!'

'Patrick, remember? I've still got the mark.'

'What are you doing here?'

'Thought you'd say that. Unfriendly, you are.'

'You'd better pick up your eels and be gone,' she said, and flashed the knife threateningly.

'They aren't my eels. They're yours. Don't be like that, bringing them to you, I was. Nice surprise, bit of fun.' He watched her face. 'Friends, aren't we? The fish, apples, that was me. You got them, didn't you?' He remembered the eels and chased after the wriggling shapes in the gutter, snatched them up by the heads, stood with half a dozen tails jerking from each hand.

'Fun,' Ellen sneered. 'You were spying on us.' She picked up the bucket and filled it from the pool in the yard. He followed her with his eyes, watching her legs, her sway. She held up the bucket and he remembered her face, grinned at her cockily.

'Only spying on the pretty one!' he said.

She scowled. 'Why exactly did you come back?'

'Oh, I don't know. Thought I'd give it a go, you know? This and that.' He dropped the eels in the bucket, slapped his hands. 'Oh, and I might see you.' He glanced in her eyes for a moment and she knew that was the truth.

But he baffled her. 'You came back just to see me?'

'Bet I did.'

She spread her hands uncomprehendingly. 'Why?'

'You're going to invite me in, aren't you?'

'No,' Ellen said. 'Go away. Go away, we don't need you.'

Camilla appeared in the doorway. She bent over her stick, peered front of her. 'Ellen?'

'Ha!' cried the young man victoriously. 'Ellen, is it?' He ignored her frown, called over her head to Camilla, 'Pleasure to meet you, my lady.'

Ellen said over her shoulder, 'It's the boy with the drippy nose.'

'Come on, Ellen, your old mother wants to meet me. Patrick, I am, my lady. A Christian, me.' He hitched his thumb in his belt. 'Look what I got for you. Both of you ladies. Eels.' He held up the bucket and bowed.

Ellen and Camilla looked at one another with an expression of perfect understanding.

'You can't come in,' Camilla said. 'Go away. We don't want you here.'

Patrick returned his attention to Ellen, winked chummily. 'Up in the middle of the night to catch the tide, I was, trapped these eels for you special, knew you'd be grateful—'

'Trying to worm his way in with us,' Camilla said.

'Where are you living?' Ellen asked.

He made a vague gesture. 'Down by the river.'

'Get back there,' Camilla said. 'Off he goes!'

'But—'

'Wait,' Ellen said.

He turned back at once, eager as a puppy dog. 'I can be useful about the place. Look at that roof, drips when it's wet, I bet it does. You know, clear up, look at this mess—' He picked up a piece of timber easily and they saw how vigorous he was.

Ellen said, 'You'll have to do as you're told. When you aren't working, you stay down by the river, and you don't bother us. Agreed?'

'Whatever you say.'

The two women sat with their heads together, watching him.

Patrick worked mornings and afternoons at first, but only mornings now the mess in the yard was cleared. He patched the worst holes in the roof with tiles stripped from the stable. He'd made a good strong ladder from trees and rope and climbed it carrying the tiles on a hod. He saw their faces at the window and waved. Ellen looked down, blushing.

'Look how strong he is,' she said. She watched him climb on to the roof, his muscles working in the sun. He took off his top and threw it down.

'He knows you're watching,' Camilla said.

'I'm not watching. What is there to watch?'

'He's a man,' Camilla said. 'He's an outsider. What about us?'

'I know.'

'You're not sounding like you, Ellen. I thought you were so tough-minded and nothing fooled you.'

'He doesn't fool me.'

'The roof still leaks,' Camilla pointed out. 'I got wet when it was wet.'

'He's interesting, that's all.'

'He's got less sense than you! He's fey and feckless.'

'Well, he likes me. Why don't you like him? He's always got a kind word.'

Camilla sighed. 'He just wants to talk his way between your legs.'

'He hasn't.'

'Ellen, don't you understand? He's a man. He's a *man*.'

She said, 'He's useful.'

Camilla snorted. 'Already he isn't working as hard as he was.'

'He eats everything I put in front of him, which is more than you do. And he talks to me.' Ellen's voice rose, heated. 'He doesn't complain all the time!'

Camilla sat perfectly still. Then she reached out and touched Ellen's shoulder.

'I am not angry.' Ellen's flushed cheeks made her eyes look very blue. 'I'm not angry and I'm not stupid. I would never let you down.'

Camilla touched her fingers to the back of Ellen's hands. Her fingertips quivered, wrinkled, dry. One hand slipped and Ellen realised the old lady was nearly blind. She was pretending to see.

Camilla whispered, 'I'm not old. I'm trapped. Inside me I'm still young, and I know things you should know.'

Ellen moved impatiently.

'I know what you feel,' Camilla murmured. 'I wish I could make it easier for you. Their minds are not like ours, Ellen. Sometimes Felix took me as though I was only a sack of flesh, yet he loved me. Other times he was the sweetest, tenderest, lovingest man I ever dreamt, and I went to bed alone. I love him. But a man is not a woman, Ellen. He is as different from us as a dog is from a cat.'

'Don't worry! I know what Patrick's up to. He'll have to work harder than that.'

The young man waved from the roof. Ellen ignored him. He grinned, dashed the sweat from his forehead. 'He's an idiot,' she said. 'I know what he wants.'

Camilla said implacably, 'Make sure he doesn't get it.'

This, Ellen. This is what you protect with your life.

Ellen burst out, 'It's not fair! I won't take a vow of celibacy, wear a veil like a nun, just because you—'

Camilla wrapped her cold bony fingers round Ellen's warm hands. 'Don't let him into your heart. He'll eat you up until you're gone, and your life won't be your own. Drudgery. He'll take everything you have.'

She said, 'Perhaps I want to give it to him.'

'*Do not fail in your trust.*' Camilla dug her nails into the backs of Ellen's hands. 'Are you strong, woman? Are you strong enough?'

'Now you do sound old,' Ellen said spitefully. Pain glistened in the corners of her eyes but she wouldn't cry out.

Camilla released her. 'Old,' she said, 'and wise.'

'And sad,' Ellen whispered, and wouldn't talk any more.

'Dying,' Camilla said aloud. She closed her eyes wearily. 'I wish I could save you from all you must suffer.'

Ellen sat up in the night. She was alone. She felt her aloneness like a coldness in the air, though the kitchen was warm. The hearth glimmered, casting gleams where Camilla slept. The dark shape of rumpled blankets was different, silent, still.

'Are you awake?'

There was no reply. The underblanket was cold. Camilla often went to the latrine in the night, her bladder and bowels were weak. Ellen bound her hair through a silver ring, slipped her gown round her, made her way into the corridor as she pinned it. She came to the door-curtain of the latrine.

'Are you all right?'

She looked in the latrine, three seats along each wall, but it was black dark. She felt in each place to make sure. Empty.

She let the door-curtain drop and went to the dining room. She had been afraid one night she would find Camilla collapsed on the floor, and she swept ahead of her with her feet in the dark. Obviously Camilla was very ill, her face was skeletal, everything was painful for her. Sitting down, standing up. Breathing in, breathing out. Sometimes she wandered in her agony thinking she would meet Felix, or she wanted to ask Archbishop Mansuetus when he was holding the next service, or in her cracked voice she summoned Amanda Adelphia and Monica Numidea to do her hair, as if their raped and savaged bodies had not lain unburied in the ruins of the Villa Celatus these seven years.

Sometimes Camilla went into the bedroom they had first occupied, and lay as though wrapped in Felix's arms.

But she was not here.

Ellen went quickly into the back yard. The night held itself perfectly still and quiet under the stars. Far away across the marshes a male bittern boomed its call, unnaturally loud.

Above her, candlelight moved across the top of Lud's Hill.

117

Ellen ran. She jumped the rubble of the collapsed wall that Patrick had not yet repaired, among all the other things Patrick had not yet found time for. She ran uphill.

The candleflame hovered between the houses, then flicked between the trunks of young trees. Because of the trees' shade on sunny days, their leafy tops almost touching, the undergrowth no longer grew so wild and tangled beneath them. A bramble looped over a black tree branch towards the starlight, and Ellen hissed as its thorns snagged her hair.

Now the candle moved among the broken pillars that lined the nave, some fallen one on the other like dominoes, others held up by the grip of the creepers encasing them. The leaves shone round the candleflame like green eyes, illuminating Camilla's hobbling figure, her spine humped between her shoulderblades, a blanket draped over her head.

Ellen followed her, thinking, should I wake her? Is she sleep-walking?

Camilla stopped, listening. Then she mumbled to herself and trudged forward.

Her fixation on moving back into the catacomb had become an obsession. It was the last place she had seen her husband alive, and Ellen thought the old lady could not now help returning here, as if this demonstration of her faithfulness could bring about his own return. Several times Ellen had come upon her in daylight and guided her away from the place.

'We mustn't let that young man see our secret, must we?'

Each time the old lady agreed.

But each time she came back. She could not stop.

Camilla looked round sharply, grown cunning. Ellen dropped behind a mound, closed her eyes so that they would not reflect the candlelight.

When she opened them the rod stuck out of the ground and Camilla hobbled down the steps into the catacomb.

Ellen trod quietly across the grass. Candlelight glowed up the steps.

Ellen went halfway down, crouched so that she could see beneath the roof.

Holding the candle above her head, Camilla walked the length of the glittering catacomb. Her small figure bowed to various gold and silver crosses. She talked to herself, surrounding herself with murmuring echoes.

Ellen descended another step.

At the end of the tunnel Camilla halted. She pursed her lips, shaking her head to and fro as she argued with herself. Ellen thought, she thinks she's arguing with my father. She stepped silently on to the floor of the catacomb.

Camilla stopped arguing. Then she leant over the one place

that did not shine, and touched the candleflame to the mound of skins.

'No!' Ellen shouted.

Pale fire guttered around the frayed papery edges of the leather, caught, burst into soft transparent flames.

Ellen ran down. 'No.' She pushed Camilla aside and the old lady fell like a bag of bones. Ellen grabbed the blanket from her shoulders. She beat at the flames. Fire licked the fine hairs on her arms, the heat tightened her face. For a moment, leaning forward to reach out, she thought she would fall forward on to the skins, into the flames, and be engulfed. Her shoes skidded, she pushed at the mound with her left hand. It rocked back, and by the light of the fire that was burning them she glimpsed what lay between the skins.

They were more than skins. They were pages, scriptures.

Each scripture was black with words.

The stack slid aside, knocked one of the cylindrically shaped pots piled behind. The pot teetered. Ellen heard her hair crackle, smelt it burn. She threw the blanket forward over the fire, fell back. The pot tumbled past her outstretched fingertips, broke on the hard mosaic floor, and something black rolled out of the middle. She watched it bump from sight among the treasures and smoke.

The flames died beneath the blanket. It was almost dark again.

Smoke rose through the glowing candleflame, thinned, clung to the roof of the catacomb, slowly cleared.

Ellen coughed. Her face and her left arm itched where the flames had touched her, and her frizzed hair stank. She pulled the stinking blanket off the scriptures, then sank to her knees beside the old lady.

Camilla said, 'It's time you knew the truth.'

'The truth, stepmother?' Ellen coughed. 'Now you sound like my father.'

She went rigid, realising what she had said.

'Your father?' Camilla closed her eyes. Her eyelids fluttered. '*Your father?*'

'I wish I could bite off my tongue.'

Camilla lay with her eyes opened, staring up. 'No. It's best to know. Felix is your real father? The Lord moves in mysterious ways.' With tiny jerks she turned her head towards the pile of skins. 'Did you save them?'

'They're safe.'

'Then you have made your choice, Ellen.'

'You deliberately tried to burn them!' Ellen demanded angrily, 'What were you doing?'

'I did it for you, Ellen.'

Ellen stood. She felt too shaken to talk, but Camilla gripped her arm.

'Help me.' She struggled to her feet beside Ellen, tottered to the couch with purple bolsters and gold tassels on which she had once spent so much time. She half fell across it, without strength. Then she eased herself back against the bolster, made no further attempt to move. 'I'm done.'

'You can't stay here,' Ellen said, alarmed.

'I shall stay here for ever.' Camilla groped for her stick. Ellen saw it lying on the floor and fetched it. Camilla gripped the familiar comforting shape of the wood. She sighed with relief. 'Time for me to die, time for you to live. I'm not sorry. I'm worn out. Nothing works. You'll know what I mean when you're my age. My life's a trial, every day.' She chuckled. 'You look like you've been struck by lightning, Ellen! Your hair's standing up. You burnt your arm, your face. It must hurt.'

'No, it feels—' Ellen shrugged. 'I'm numb.'

'It'll hurt tonight. You'll have to mix the herbs yourself.'

Ellen said, 'You'll help me.'

Camilla smiled. 'Tonight I am at peace, asleep in the arms of the Lord.'

She exhaled with open eyes, and Ellen thought she was dead.

'Bury me here. Bury me in gypsum plaster to keep me whole, so that when the great and glorious day of the resurrection comes I shall rise not as bones, but in the flesh.' Camilla blinked herself back to the present. 'Yes, bury me here where Felix will find me. Your father is close, Ellen. He's very close.'

Ellen took her cold hands. 'You're cold.'

'I thought you said you were numb, Ellen . . .' Her gaze changed. 'My God, Ellen. Look.'

Ellen looked across the shining heaps of silver and gold to where the skins lay, the mound she had knocked over showing its pale interior, page after page inscribed in neat columns.

'No!' Camilla said. 'Look at *you*.'

She touched the front of Ellen's gown, which fell open where the pins were loose, revealing the line of angry pink skin where the flames had touched. Ellen gasped. The pinkness was turning red, darkening. Blisters rose on her injured flesh. The gown hung open from her neck to her crotch. The line stretched unbroken even beneath her girdle.

She gasped, 'I'm frightened!'

'Look at your hands. Look at your arms.' Camilla stared, the candlelight reflecting in her cataract-whitened eyes. 'The flames went up your sleeves—'

Ellen stared at herself. The blisters ascended the inside of her arms to her breasts, joined together over her heart. She held out her arms, shaking.

'It's a cross.'

'It's the Cross.' Camilla shivered as her fingertips touched the blisters. 'Oh, Ellen. Who are you? What have I done?' She traced the line with her palm. 'It's a stigma. I've heard of such a thing, all Christians have. I've never seen one.'

'It doesn't hurt.' Ellen wrapped herself in her gown, clasped her arms tight around her. 'It doesn't hurt!'

Camilla said with longing, 'Let me see it. Please. Please.'

'No!'

'It's a miracle.'

'It's not a miracle.' Ellen stepped back as though stepping out of her skin. She shuddered. 'I don't want it. It doesn't mean to be that shape, it doesn't mean anything.' She looked again, examined her hands. Her voice changed. 'It's gone.'

Camilla reached forward, felt Ellen's smooth white skin from belly to breasts. 'It was there. I touched it. It was real.'

Ellen pinned the gown tight.

'Your father will understand.' Camilla slumped back on the bolster. She looked exhausted, transparent. 'He understands it all.'

Ellen glanced at the scriptures. Some were wrapped in linen coverings, three quadrangles carefully woven into them in blue linen thread.

'Even those?'

Camilla muttered, 'They are scriptures from the Dead Sea. They are the scrolls taken from the scriptorium at Qumran by the sons of Celatus, your father's ancestor, four and a quarter centuries ago.'

Ellen reached out. The skin was light and flexible, pale yellow away from the edges, which were darker. She shivered as though a cool breeze blew on her. Suddenly the piece of scripture fluttered, and she put it down. 'Four and a quarter centuries ago? How do you know so exactly?'

'Because that is the date of the crucifixion of Christ.'

Ellen stared at her. Camilla lay against the bolster with her eyes closed, ancient, inscrutable.

'Your father knows which are goatskin, which are gazelle skin. He knows that the quadrangles are the ground plan for the Temple of God to be built at the End of Days. He told me more than I could understand. He knows what the writing means.'

Ellen peered. 'It's strange letters.'

'Hebrew. Jesus spoke Aramaic, which uses the Hebrew alphabet. The writings are in various languages, some formal, others colloquial.'

'Colloquial?'

'Informal. As spoken. There's even a Latin Vulgate Bible, though that must have been added later. A very early Septuagint Bible, Greek. Another in Peshito. Two hundred psalms of King David. The Lost Gospels. The Celatus family are always collectors. Magpies. Insatiable. That's Celtic blood for you.' Her eyelids flickered as she struggled to control her wandering mind.

Ellen thought, do I believe a single word she says?

Camilla breathed through her mouth.

Ellen opened a folded skin, pointed to a word that occurred several times. The four letters were angled, not squarish like the others. 'Why is this one so different?'

'Your father will tell you it is the tetragrammaton, the sacred name of God, that may never be uttered aloud.'

'But I thought His name was God.'

'Not to the Jews.' Camilla grinned vacantly. 'There is always more, more than we can imagine.' Her stick dropped to the floor and Ellen picked it up.

'You said *the sons of Celatus. Celatus?*'

'Celatus the Galatian. Red-headed like all Galatians.'

Ellen remembered, my father mentioned Galatia. *I know where I come from so I know who I am. Our Roman and Celtic blood combined.* 'What more do you know?'

'Only what your father told me.'

'Speak with my father's words.'

Camilla's voice strengthened. 'The Black Book—'

'Please. Start at the beginning.'

'Galatia is a mountainous country far to the north of the Holy Land. The pilgrimage of Beloved Celatus from the Galatian town of Ancyra to Qumran is a long and dangerous journey for a Gentile, a non-Jew. Celatus rests at Jerusalem, then on the appointed day departs the Holy City, rides his mule down past the hovels of lepers and the blind, the cesspits and the leather tanneries, and takes the road to the east.

'This road leads across the wilderness of Sodom to the great white monastery at Qumran, the remote nationalist outpost of the Essenes, where Beloved Celatus the Gentile is to be baptised by Jesus.'

'Baptised by Jesus himself!'

'Yes, at the hands of Jesus the Saviour, *Christos*, the Christ. None of the other prophets, not even John the Baptist, would baptise a Gentile. But Jesus baptises them. Saves them. Because without Gentile money and political influence, the coming Jewish rebellion against Rome is bound to fail, along with its Messiah. Pilgrims like Celatus bring great gifts of money that benefit the monastery and pay for the work of the scriptorium. All donations, all earnings from the perfume gardens and farmland and tithes from peasants, go to the coffers of nationalists and zealots. Within the walls there are no sexual desires, no women, and everyone wears white. Through the pilgrims and their money, for hundreds of years a community in which no one is born has found a way to live for ever. The early Christian Church was founded on the wealth of Qumran.'

'Is this in the Gospels?'

'Christianity sprang from Judaism and its founders were Jewish, Ellen. Yet they murdered our Christ. Don't forget that.'

'But the Gospels—'

'The first Gospels in our Latin Bible were written down forty, fifty years after the events they describe. They are copies, copies of copies. Good copies, no doubt, just as I am a good Christian. All my life, Ellen, I have known that what I was reading was more than belief, more than fact, it is simply the truth. I accept it and I am bound for Heaven. But your father is always . . . different. Restless. Doubting. Unsatisfied. Infallibly curious.' She tried to excuse him. 'It is his nature, given to him by God. The deadly sin of curiosity.' Her voice was a papery sigh. 'It worries me. What I will tell you is written . . . all written somewhere among those papers. Everything is there, Ellen. I warn you. Precious knowledge. Knowledge that fascinated your father. He understood its power. Knowledge that perhaps a true Christian should burn.'

Something crunched beneath Ellen's foot. She remembered the pot that had broken, and crouched, swept up the pieces with her hands. She said, 'But it's in another language, no one can read it, so it's no harm to anyone.' She prompted, 'So, red-headed Celatus takes the road to Qumran . . .'

'The road winds between sun-baked hills and groves of Jerusalem Apple. Usually the pilgrims travel in bands for protection. Perhaps Beloved Celatus gets over-confident so near the point of his journey. Perhaps his mule goes lame. Perhaps he's old and grows careless. He's ambushed by bandits. Killed. His money stolen.'

'Such a long journey, and he never reached Qumran after all.'

'Pilgrims from Pontus found his mortal body on the second day, buried him beneath a heap of stones in the large cemetery at Qumran, and later returned home bearing the sad news. Next year Celatus's twin sons, Justius and Terentius, undertook pilgrimage in the springtime to pay their respects at their father's tomb and be baptised in their turn.

'But they find Jerusalem packed solid with Jews arriving for the Passover. It's the second Friday in April and there's not a room to be had anywhere within the walls. Anyway Justius and Terentius hate the rituals of the Jerusalem Temple, rejected by Essene teaching and scorned by Jesus. They're strong young men, red-haired and determined like their father, no doubt, and probably as hot-tempered and impulsive as he in his youth, so they decide to set off for Qumran immediately. The road's busy with Jews coming the other way to celebrate the holy feast. Then a white-faced runner catches up from behind, from Jerusalem.

'Jesus is crucified. He's dead.

'Justius and Terentius are shattered by the news. They can't go on or turn back, there's nothing for them in Jerusalem and now nothing at Qumran. They take room at the inn at Bethany while they discuss what they must do. In any event they cannot travel the next day, the Sabbath, so it is Sunday morning before they decide they must continue to Qumran, and set out on the road.

'And they see Jesus walking on the road with them. There is no doubt it is Him. Many see Him. Jesus Christ is alive, He is risen from the dead. His forehead is scratched, His hands and feet and side are mutilated. He is dressed in white. His hair is braided for the tomb. The dust clings to His sandals and flies cling to the sweat and blood on His face.

'The brothers kneel before Him and say, "Lord."

'He says, "I am with you always, to the close of the age."

'He walks forward, but when they follow Him across the top of the hill the road is empty as far as they see. The other travellers returning home fall back to the right and the left to their villages, fearful, whispering of what they have seen. The word spreads. No one comes from the houses to greet the strangers, everyone is afraid. Even dogs do not bark at the two brothers. In the heat of the day they stumble into an orchard, and sleep drops upon them.

'At evening they wake, thirsty, and drink at a stream. The full moon climbs in Libra in front of them, the stars guide them through the night, and at dawn they climb to the sterile plateau where the Qumran monastery stands, its walls as white as salt, high above the fertile green shores of the Dead Sea. To the east, overlooking the sea, is the field by the potter's kiln, the camp of Gentile pilgrims, who are considered unclean by the Essenes. But the brothers find the camp deserted, and only a forest of bare tent-posts remains. The fields on the slope are together called the Field of Blood because blood from monastery sacrifices is permitted to fertilise them. But the kiln is cold, no Qumran pottery or manuscript jars will be fired today. The potter is fled. No farmers hoe the fields, and the wind blows dust over the cemetery beneath the cliffs.

'The brothers call out, but Qumran is deserted. Not a single person remains. And then they hear the creak of a rope.

'From one of the tall tent-posts hangs the body of a man by his neck. His belly is burst open from his crotch to his heart, his guts are dropped on the ground. The stink of him is death itself as he blackens in the sun. This is Judas, arch-celibate leader of the scribes in the scriptorium for which Qumran is famous. The brothers turn away, they cannot bear to witness the terrifying look on his face. Judas Iscariot, betrayer of Jesus of Nazareth to the wicked High Priest, is dead.

'Justius and Terentius knock at the monastery gate and enter, but still there is no one. It is as though a whirlwind has blown through the place. The wind draws the brothers forward, up the steps. The money tables in the lower third of the courtyard, where peasants should queue to pay their tithes, lie scattered in the dust. There has been an earthquake and the Jewish baptismal pools, not normally seen by Gentiles who are baptised in the Dead Sea, are cracked and empty. The brothers are drawn forward between the white buildings, the wind breathes on the backs of their necks. Gentiles are forbidden here, but no one turns them them back. There is no one in the vestry. For a Gentile to enter the Holy of Holies is death. But they find no one inside here, only the wind.

'The brothers climb a circle of stone steps to the second floor. They are in the scriptorium. Is this the very room where Jesus, risen from the dead, confronted His betrayer? The wind whirls fragments of parchment round the lecterns where the scribes worked, scatters their pens, sends their fine knives for the trimming and ruling of skins tumbling into the black ink spilt across the floor. Along the walls are shelves containing hundreds of scrolls, some rolled up tightly into cylinders and inserted into pottery jars, some loose, fluttering, unravelling, and one flies up in the wind flapping like a wing around the brothers, thirty feet long or more. They look at one another, understanding, for it has long been known that nothing of the Word of God falls to the ground. They seize the biblical scripture and roll it carefully. Justius looks at his brother as one sentence, written perhaps a hundred years earlier, catches his eye. "And he shall be called a Nazarene . . ." The brothers realise that here is the treasure of Qumran. Not its wealth in silver. Not its way of life. It is these priceless scrolls, their priceless gift of knowledge. Knowledge . . .'

Camilla's mouth opened. Her breath rattled.

'Knowledge. The Gospels of the Eleven Apostles. Eyewitness accounts of the true history of Jesus's ministry.'

She was dying. Ellen knelt beside her. 'And the brothers made their way back to Galatia? And so, through marriage, the scrolls were passed down?'

Camilla exhaled. 'Aaaah . . .' Her breath faded away.

Ellen shook her. The old lady's body felt no heavier than paper. 'Why did my father and his father's father and their ancestors never share them? Why did the family keep their knowledge of the scrolls to themselves?'

Camilla gasped. Her eyes opened wide.

'Among them are works of blasphemy. Terrible blasphemy to believers. The War of the Sons of Light against the Sons of Darkness, together with the secret peshers for all its meanings. The Manual of Discipline. The Book of Hagu. The Apocrypha. Scriptures from outside the Christian canon written as though they are the words of God. Ideas. Knowledge. Facts. Reason, not what we know to be the real truth. Diaries. The Lost Gospel of Judas . . . the Black Book . . . the Black Book . . . Do you hear the wind?'

Ellen listened. 'I don't hear anything.'

Camilla stared beyond Ellen's shoulder. She smiled. 'Look. He's standing behind you. There he is. It's your father.'

Ellen looked round. The steps were empty.

Camilla smiled peacefully. Her face shone. 'I told you he'd be back.' She dropped her stick, reached out her hand.

Ellen held her stepmother in her arms. Camilla's life was gone.

Ellen sat with the body of the old lady in her lap. It weighed nothing, skin and bone, a few tattered bits of jewellery clinging to its ears and neck and wrists. She closed the eyes. For nine years, from when Ellen was three until the age of twelve, the old lady had played the part of Ellen's mother to the best of her ability. She had not been perfect, but she had done her best. Even in the shadow of death, right or wrong, for better or worse, Camilla had done her best. Ellen laid her on the couch as though she were asleep.

'I loved you,' she said, and looked round her.

Now she was alone.

Bury me here, Camilla had said. Bury me here where Felix will find me. Tonight I am at peace, asleep in the arms of the Lord.

A faint grey light glowed down the steps. Soon the night would be over, and Patrick might come up from the river. He might stumble across the entrance to the catacomb. The thought filled Ellen with horror. She saw him forcing his way inside, ransacking the fragile treasure, taking whatever he wanted, scattering the rest, burning the scrolls for firewood.

She pushed the mechanism. The flagstone dropped down, hiding the place from the light of day.

Down here it was still night.

Camilla's dying words laid a heavy burden on her.

The end wall, rendered smooth with mortar, was the obvious place to dig the recess for the body, and again Ellen wondered why the place had not been dug out by the workmen who first constructed the catacomb. She looked for something to dig with and her foot knocked against pieces of the broken pot. She remembered the cylinder of rolled skin that had fallen out. She knelt, her face close to the floor looking beneath the various glittering objects, and spied the dull scroll resting where it had bumped into a golden cross. She could just reach it, rolled it towards her with her fingertips. The gazelle skin was black outside but when she peeled the corner back a few inches, without untying the ribbon, she saw that the inside was still white as ivory, the ink black. But the Hebrew scripture meant nothing to her.

This, Ellen. This is what you protect with your life.

She nodded. Her father had understood these complicated signs and meanings, and they had been precious to him, so they were precious to her. These were his sacred trust in her, left in her care until he returned, and she would never let him down. She closed the scroll reverently, bowed her head, crossed herself. Obviously the skin could not be replaced in its broken pot, but she spotted a tall gold reliquary, shaped like a house or temple, richly ornate in the eastern style of Byzantium, heavily studded with rubies, that made a fitting place. She placed the scroll inside and closed it with a gold rod that made a second hinge, locking it. Her knees cracked as she stood up, made stiff by the cold mosaic, and she remembered Camilla.

She dusted herself down and looked for something to dig with, found a square bronze platter to use as a spade. She decided to dig the burial niche below the *Paternoster* her father had scratched on the end wall. Aram . . .

She whacked the wall, and the heavy platter clanged, rebounded. The wall was hard. She found a dreadful-looking silver spike from some pagan ritual, chipped its point into the blackened mortar. It crumbled away, revealing something hard beneath. By bad luck she'd started where there was a stone. She chose another place and chipped. Hard stone again, but this time a long tooth of mortar broke free. She dug her fingers into the cracks, pulled the mortar away.

The end wall was a single boulder. That was why the workmen had stopped.

There were grooves in the stone, probably roughly cut by the workmen as a key to hold their mortar. On impulse she pushed her fingers inside. Uncannily, the wavy lines fitted as snugly as though made for her, the interior of the channels rubbed smooth as if deliberately polished.

Ellen grunted, worked hard with the spike, levering, prising the mortar. The *Paternoster* broke into pieces, fell around her, though it left its scratches on the stone. She shook the mortar-dust from her hair. More grooves and lines appeared as she worked. She laid bare a slab of stone taller than herself, part of the foundations for the cathedral perhaps, she thought, holding up the weight of a building that no longer existed.

Twelve by twelve by twenty-nine. She crouched, noticing how the grooves went into the floor. There was plainly more of the boulder to be found under the clay and chipped mosaic.

Ellen settled back on her haunches. She shook her head. This stone was massive. She could not bury Camilla here.

Then she noticed how the edge angled away at the bottom left. Perhaps she had found a corner. She jabbed the spike and the point sank into soft clay.

Ellen leant forward excitedly. She stabbed the spike in front of her, working round the side of the boulder. At first there were fragments of white marble. The archbishop had said there was once a temple here. As she worked further the fragments stopped. The wall pushed her shoulder on one side, the boulder on the other. She worked at arms' length, then wriggled forward, widened the niche she was making. Dry powdery clay fell on her head, the dust blew past her.

The spike sank into the clay as deep as her fist. She blinked as cool air wafted in her eyes.

She stabbed the spike forward, and again it went in easily. She opened a hole about the size of her face.

Ellen put her face to the hole.

Nothing. Solid black.

She wriggled backwards, snatched the candle out of the candlestick. She returned to the niche and crawled forward holding the candle in front of her. Tallow dripped on her hand. The candleflame brightened, fluttered as she pushed it through the hole. Ellen squeezed her face forward beside her arm.

She saw walls.

She drew back, withdrew her arm and the flickering candle. The air was fresh. She panted with excitement. But she was afraid. Then she told herself, if I *ought*, I *can*. She twisted awkwardly, kicked with her feet to open the hole. Then she squeezed her shoulders past the stone, and pulled herself through.

Ellen stood up in a room with walls of rough-hewn earth. She held up the light of the candle. The floor was white and crumbly, dug somewhat deeper than the catacomb, but not nearly as long. The catacomb was like a tunnel but this was a pit. The stone crossed part of the roof at an angle, covered with thousands of markings that she did not recognise, and they had been cut, not worn nearly as deeply as the grooves on the other side. She decided that the floor had once been much deeper, or else the room was dug by people much shorter than herself.

She grubbed her toe into the white crumbly floor. She was standing on bones, hundreds of bones, so old that they were turning to stone. She bent, picked up part of a skull, a horn, a flat tooth. Ox skulls.

But these petrified remains were much larger than anything she had seen before. A Christian God had never made animals like these.

A whole gigantic skull was placed in each corner, horns curved forward, eye sockets staring.

Nobody had been here for a long time, it seemed. Ellen picked up a bone necklace made of sharp teeth she did not recognise. The dried grass stringing them fell to powder at her touch. She rubbed her fingertips thoughtfully, then something glinted, catching her eye.

She picked up a cheap bronze brooch, corroded, but the sort of ornament ordinary servant girls like Monica Numidea had worn, and precious to them. Probably it was not much more than ten or twenty years old. It had been carefully placed over rough, untutored letters scrawled into the stone. Ellen stared. *Aram menaht menou*. The same words, the very same words her father had written much later, in the catacomb.

Ellen turned the brooch over and over in her fingers, then clenched it tight in her fist. *Aram menaht menou*, the connection between her parents.

'No,' Ellen whispered. 'It's me. *I* am the connection.'

Her mother, Emilia, had known of this place. It must have been she, untutored though she was, who had taught the words to Father. But she had kept this place hidden even from him, the man she loved.

The brooch was her mother's. Ellen was sure of it. She opened her hand, pressed the rough metal to her lips.

'Mother.'

She laughed in wonder, looking around her. Here Camilla would rest in peace. Here was the perfect hiding place for the gold and everything else, and no digging for her to do.

With a grinding sound the flagstone rotated, closing the darkness in the ground behind Ellen.

It was a brilliantly sunny day. She moved between the grassy mounds that covered the top of Lud's Hill. Oak and elm trees waved their shade over her. She stopped, resting one hand on the bark, her eyes narrowed against the silver curve of the Thames below her. With her other hand she shielded her eyes from the sun. The shadow of the river wall looked very black, underlining the glare of the river. There was only one gap, through the opened West Watergate, where the canal flowed out on to the mudflats. Broken landing stages stood like black spiders in the bright water. The shadow of a man sat out there, swinging his legs in the glare, fishing.

His head moved. Patrick was always thinking of her. Looking for her.

She stepped from the trees, crossing the slope. He saw her and waved. She did not respond. He decided she had not seen him, checked the nets he'd strung between the pilings, swaggered through the gate. He'd expect to come across her near the archbishop's palace, quite by chance. Just happening by. Eyeing her appreciatively. Must be something I can do for you.

He sometimes used a room at the back of the yellow house. He did not know she knew. From there he watched her coming and going, he saw her every time she used the well. He thought he knew everything about her.

Ellen walked between the ruins behind the back wall of the palace, found a path through the brambles that had conquered the road, came to the yellow house in a glade of elms. She could hear Patrick swearing as he climbed. With him everything was eff this and eff that, the English words he'd picked up outside the walls bartering fish for corn from the farmer on the strand. She stood in the back room of the yellow house and watched him through the window. Patrick's curly head bobbed into view, pushing his way through the bushes that had grown over the terraces, and she admired his strength. He grunted as he heaved himself up the fallen stones. Each time the canal flooded, which by now was each time it rained, the neat terraces softened and crumbled, sloped downhill a little more. The indistinguishable mass of houses and inns, shops and places that had probably been shrines, were gradually sliding downhill as they decayed, becoming part of the mud that inched towards the Thames, piling up in the swamp behind the river wall.

Ellen moved from the window. He could not see her. There was a couch in the corner, padded with straw. She sniffed a pot filled with cold porridge, made a face. She sat out on the shadowed doorstep. Yes, from here she could see the mossy palace, the kitchen window, the well.

She waited.

Patrick walked straight past her, his mind busy with his own thoughts, his muscular legs in blue breeches carrying him to the road. Then he sensed her sitting quietly behind him, and turned with a shout.

'Effing Jesus—' he cried. 'It's you! Quiet as a cat, you are. You might cough or something.'

She watched him without emotion in her wide blue eyes. Then she gave him a very small smile. 'You live here sometimes, don't you, Patrick.'

He demanded, 'What of it?' He licked his lips.

She did not change her smile, at her ease, showing perfect indifference to him.

He said, 'Convenient for me if there's any work to do for you girls, it is. How did you know?'

'It's dirty. It smells.'

'Thought you didn't know about it.' He tried to read her eyes. 'Haven't seen you for a week, thought you were ill. Hurt, maybe. Worried, I was. Didn't you hear me calling?'

He wanted to sit beside her on the step. She made him wait. Then she moved a little, so that the space was still too small. His hip touched her as he sat.

Most of the time Ellen had been down in the silence of the catacomb. She had come out only at night, so that Patrick should not see her and become curious about the hilltop.

'My adopted mother has died.'

'The old lady's dead?' He tried to absorb this information, but all he could think of was Ellen, her warm hip against his. 'I could have done the shovel work – that's what I got these for!' He braced his broad shoulders, grinned, then saw her expression. 'Well, very sorry about her, I am.'

She glanced at his face. There was no harm in him.

He thought she would weep. He moved awkwardly, then put his arm round her.

'So,' he said impulsively, 'just us then.'

He kissed her. After a moment she looked down. 'It's too soon. I don't know what to do—'

'That old woman isn't around any more to say I can't have you!'

She said, 'Patrick!'

'Marry you.' He kissed her hair, inhaled her woman's smell. 'I'll look after you. I'll do anything for you.'

'I don't know.'

He rushed, 'I love you and I always have!'

She looked him straight in his desperate brown eyes. 'Love me?'

'Love.' He reddened. 'I'm not afraid to say it. Love. God, let me touch you now, I've got to have you, Ellen, don't, I can't wait—' He rolled on to his knees in front of her like a dog that she had taught to beg, his eyes yearning and moist with desire, staring at her tunic as though already gauging the weight of her breasts.

She said, 'Love?'

'You've always known it.' But he looked questioningly into her eyes for confirmation. 'I've always been good to you, haven't I? Fish, plums, oysters—' He wrapped her in his arms and they rolled back against the doorpost. She laughed. 'Don't,' he said fiercely. He fumbled his mouth on her lips, his hands searched her breasts, moved greedily to her legs. His lips slid from hers and he mouthed her nipples like a hurtful baby, pushed his blunt hands up her tunic, kissed her thighs while he held her sitting against the doorpost, frightened his moment would pass before anything happened.

Ellen watched him kiss her. She observed the frantic pleasure he took in something as ordinary as her legs. If I'm careful, she thought, I can make him do whatever I want.

He jerked the rope round his waist to free his breeches. She squeezed him lightly down there and his face contorted anxiously. He swore, grunted rhythmically like an animal, then cursed himself. He turned his head away in embarrassment. She stroked his hair.

'Now, Patrick.'

'Something's happened,' he blurted, bright red. 'I can't. You were so beautiful. Just let me hold you close.'

If I'm careful, I can make him do whatever I want.

'Yes,' she purred, 'I am beautiful.'

She held him. Her heart was not here in the bright sunlight. The stain of cold semen darkening Patrick's blue breeches neither dismayed nor disgusted her. Legs apart, she gazed uphill at the ruined cathedral, the cross wedged crookedly into the last mossy corner of standing wall. Her heart was in the glittering dark.

'Emilia?'

It was the coldest winter for years.

The woman's voice called again, 'Emilia . . .'

The child played Emperors, scrambling up one snowy mound after the other, surveying the walled City as though it was her own. The bitter wind flapped her rags. Good clothes were getting very hard to come by, and even the best finds dug up in boxes were rotted if damp, and if dry had the moth in them. In winter the ground was either frozen or mud, and there were no finds at all.

'Emilia!'

'Yes, Mother.' Emilia wished Theo, son of the Englishman who farmed the strand, who was her age and sometimes came sneaking within the walls, was here to play with her.

Ellen's voice shouted, '*Emilia!*'

'I'm here!' Emilia waved cheerfully. 'I'm playing!'

Even the short climb up Lud's Hill had left her mother desperately weary. The wind dragged out Ellen's hair like a white flag. She stumbled, then leant back against an elm.

'Come down here, *at once*,' she ordered gruffly.

Emilia sulked. Mother was cruelly short-tempered since Father died, almost two years ago, which was for ever to a child. Being the only child, and worse, a daughter, meant all the work and all the blame if Mother's commands weren't finished *exactly* to order fell squarely on Emilia's shoulders. Sometimes she hated her mother.

Theo, who lived in a warm timber cottage with a sunken floor to keep the wind out, thought they were both mad to live in a draughty stone room tacked on the back of a palace built for giants, not men, in a City that was the work of giants. He was too shy to say so, because Emilia stuck up for her mother fiercely. The huge raven-haunted walls of the City, enclosing nothing but silent mossy ruins and forest, frightened him with their strangeness, and he would have stayed outside them except for Emilia.

Emilia, too, was afraid. But she was afraid she would never succeed in living up to her mother's standards. Winter was always the worst time, when the cold hurt Mother's bones and made her more irritable than ever. Theo's mother never made him wash, though his parents worked him to the bone during harvesting and ploughing. He often ran away when his mother called.

Emilia turned from thinking of him. She stared into the icy wind from the east. The massive forum and St Peter's basilica still gave shape to the forest on Corn Hill – her mother had patiently taught her all the names – and the Walbrook winding below was dark with meltwater, not as cold as the white slopes of Lud's Hill. Marsh and forest had hidden the strange straight lines of Roman roads – Romans, she knew, were the race of people Theo called giants.

Always know more than others think you do, Ellen had whispered. And always keep it to yourself.

Lately some farmers had moved in and built huts near the amphitheatre, whose tiered walls could again be seen since the farmers had felled trees to make fields. Their footpaths went winding around the curve of the walls and foundations, and they had cleared the central area, using it as a night stockade for sheep and cattle. Pigs rooted for acorns in the forest between the amphitheatre and the citadel. Sometimes in the summer tribes from distant places, coming together along scattered paths, camped within the citadel to trade, negotiate marriage, and impress, departing when the leaves fell.

Emilia saw the look in her mother's cold blue eye and jumped down. Ellen held out her arm. 'Help me.'

Emilia took her mother's arm and they followed the path meandering between the elms and the mounds of snow. Ellen's knees were inflamed and her weight pressed hard. 'How soon it goes,' she muttered. 'Everything that once seemed so solid. Even a life. Gone in a flash.' She looked around them, marking the place, and Emilia wondered if the path were quite so aimless as it appeared. 'Do you know where we are?'

'No, Mother.'

'St Paul's. This is St Paul's.' Ellen's hair was long, silver-white. She saw Emilia looking at it, and the old woman's lined face smiled. 'Once my hair was black, like yours.' She touched the little girl, stroked her hair fondly. 'Do you love me, Emilia?'

Emilia hugged her.

'Tell me the truth, Emilia.'

Emilia gave her mother a frightened look, realising she was being treated like an adult. 'Yes, but not when you're nasty to me!'

Ellen chuckled. 'I know I'm like that sometimes, but it's for your own good. I know sometimes I tell you too much and it's too difficult and I shout at you. Children always irritate their parents. But I always love you, do you understand? You are my daughter, you are my life. Everything I do, I do for you.'

Emilia was terrified. 'Are you going to die?'

'Not until I have told you something first. It's a secret, Emilia.'

The child's face was radiant. She clapped her hands excitedly. Like all children, she loved secrets.

Ellen looked at her sadly, remembering herself.

She left the path, tugging Emilia after her across tree roots, bending under branches heavy with snow and ice. Ivy stems trailed in front of their faces and Ellen pushed her way through.

'No one's been along here for years!' Emilia said excitedly.

'No one has been here for longer than you have been alive, daughter.' Ellen stopped, frowning as though she had lost her way, then pushed aside a last screen of ivy. A piece of wall was revealed, topped with a cross. Emilia looked at it without comprehension.

Ellen pulled a rod from the wall, pushed it into a place in the snow, pulled it. The ground opened like a grave. Snow and soil showered on to the steps that led down into the dark.

'When I die, Emilia, this secret lives in you.'

She reached inside, pulled out a stump of candle. It was made of animal fat and the wick was a twist of braided grass. She took something from her clothes, held it in her palm. 'Do you know what this is, daughter?' Emilia shook her head. 'It is a keep-fire.' Ellen lit the candle, took a firm grip on Emilia's wrist, and led her down into the empty catacomb.

'This is your sacred trust, daughter.'

Emilia looked around her, revolted. 'But it's dead people.'

Ellen walked to the far end. She touched the stone.

Then she knelt and dug in the corner, made a hole. She pushed her arm inside and Emilia realised there was nothing there. Ellen pulled out handfuls of clay, then lay down and crawled through the gap.

The candle flickered in the wind from the hole. Emilia shielded it, alone, more afraid than she had ever been in her life. Then she crawled into the dark after her mother.

Ellen sat on the petrified floor of the room beyond, treasure piled around her to the roof. Her face turned towards Emilia, the candleflame lit its reflection in her eyes.

Emilia whispered, 'It's all the treasure in the world, isn't it?'

Ellen spoke.

'I buried my adopted mother here. Perhaps my real mother lies here, too.' She raised her finger, pointed to the stone slanting above their heads. 'I carved this word.' The letters cut across the odd faint collection of suns and moons and stars made by earlier hands. Emilia's tongue moved as she read the word.

RESURGAM.

'It is a Latin word, Emilia. It means I shall rise again.'

The child shivered in awe of all she saw around her, and of all she felt as its secrets were revealed to her.

Ellen drew a deep breath. 'Have you heard of Jesus Christ?'

'No, Mother.'

'Not many people have. Listen to me, for this is the truth.'

She sat on crossed legs, and light flooded into her face, or perhaps it was only the gold and silver.

'Once upon a time there was a man called Jesus, and he died but now He is alive.'

Emilia stared over her mother's head at the letters cut in the stone. She wondered how long it had taken her mother to cut them so deep. She touched them with her fingers.

Ellen gripped her hand fiercely, turned her towards the one place in the room that did not shine.

'But this, Emilia. *This* is what you protect with your life.'

Part Two

Alia

London, Easter 604 AD

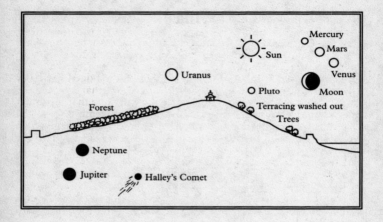

Easter, AD 604

The girl ran through the forest.

She did not know how old she was, for she could not count. Her name had no shape to her, because she could not read, but the sound of it was *Alia*, like the cry of a bird. No one knew the forests of London as well as Alia.

Alia ran as fast as the wild deer. Her slim body dodged flawlessly between the huge trunks of oak and lime and elm that rose around her. She skipped the gnarled roots knowing each one that lay in her path. Though she was not very tall, she jumped nimbly on to the alder that had pulled down a tangle of young green foliage when it fell days ago. She paused on her knees, perfectly balanced on the slanted trunk.

Alia listened.

Motionless as an owl, her outspread left hand rested lightly among the leaves and tender buds. Alia became the forest, receding into her surroundings like any other woodland creature. Only her eyes moved, questing, and her nostrils flared almost imperceptibly with each breath, searching the air.

Over the high part of the day the sun had glowed hot and hazy, but now the wind was cold, brushing the gooseprickles on her skin with its invisible touch. The whites below her eyes showed as she looked upward. Muddy clouds roiled above the treetops. She read the patterns in the shreds and whorls of pale vapour, the glowering thunderbellies pregnant with rain.

Alia smelt lightning.

Tree trunks flickered in the glare, black bars standing between her and the edge of the clearing. She blinked as grey daylight returned. The scent of apple blossom blew past her and she snatched at the wind, sniffed the tiny white stars of blossom blown from the orchard. Thunder rolled across the two hills of London and the great armies of the gods fought in the sky. Swords as long as the world clashed, sending lightning sheeting through the clouds.

Coming closer.

Alia jumped down, covered her ears against the coming crash of thunder, ran forward. Shadows leapt around her as new lightning flashed across the clouds and the clearing.

On the edge of the woods stood, for an instant, the shadow of a man among the tree trunks. On his wrist a bird fluttered nervously,

137

a jay, loyal to him against every instinct of its nature. The man was clad in tattered scraps of bullhide held together by thongs, broad-shouldered, legs braced apart as if to receive the storm. His greasy black braids hung to his waist, swinging as he walked forward into the clearing. He called her name in a lost voice. 'Alia.'

Thunder rolled, but still his lips moved.

She ran after him down the slope, tugged his elbow, but Rowan did not feel her. He walked steadily on to the hoed field, trailing deep footprints across the strip of green shoots from seeds so painstakingly gathered and saved, nearly half last year's crop returned hopefully to the unforgiving earth. He plodded forward with grim determination.

Here, away from the shelter of the trees, hard rain fell. As she struggled after him Alia's shoulders were soaked in an instant, icy trickles worked down her back, and she knew the rough oily wool would not dry tonight. The rain worked cold fingers into her hair, cut off short at her neck by Rowan's razor-edged *seax*, the long knife that swung at his belt.

Clay and brickearth stuck to his studded bullhide boots. He swung each leg heavily forward and she realised he had decided to search for her among the apple trees. Alia skipped in front of him, waved her arms. She skidded on the slippery clay and almost fell backwards. He would have walked over her.

'Alia!' uttered the jay harshly, then uttered her name twice more, like its natural call.

Rowan stopped. Apple blossom stuck to his wet face and he blinked the raindrops from his gentle eyes, as blue as his sister's. Lightning flashed. A thin scar started in his hair, deepened, puckered the corner of his left eye, scored a lived cleft down his cheek, and his lips had split open and peeled back, exposing the rows of his top and bottom teeth. His teeth were white, not one of them broken.

He put back his head. 'Storm's coming!' he said.

Alia covered her hair with her hands. 'It's here. The storm's here. Come home.'

Rowan grinned. Rain trickled down his teeth, the gleaming drops hanging motionless in the flickers of lightning. 'There's a battle coming, Alia. Battle!' Thunder crashed and they both flinched.

'Come home.' Alia took his hand but he stood like a rock.

'You're always running, Alia. Alia the deer. Why is Alia always running?' The jay hopped warily on his thumb, bobbed its head, raised and lowered its crest. Rowan looked at it, and suddenly the bird took all his attention. He talked with clicks and soft calls, his head on one side, the rain dripping from his ears.

'Rowan,' Alia said gently, 'Mother's waiting.' He allowed her to take hold of his sash-belt. Alia led him forward and he plodded obediently after her. At the edge of the field she stopped him and wiped the mud off his boots. The worst of the storm had passed and he looked longingly after the lightning flickering across Lud's Hill. Corn Hill was lost in cloud and the day was dying.

'Battle!' Rowan called. He promised her seriously, 'I will protect you, Alia.'

'I know.' She touched his ruined face sadly. 'I know you will.'

Alia took him by his belt-clasp and he stumbled uphill in her footprints. The cottage lay half hidden in the trees at the top of the field. Nearby a mulberry tree was burning, struck by lightning. Its fruit had sustained the silkworms and now they were all burnt. The branches upraised in the flames looked odd and disconcerting.

'Look!' Rowan pointed. 'The tree is a burning man, Alia.'

She turned him towards the cottage. Steamy white smoke was beaten down the steep thatch roof by the rain, blew around them, and they coughed as they came to the ancient bronze-studded door that Rowan had found somewhere in the forest and laid lengthways across the entrance. It was a good cottage, not one of those shelters of boughs lashed together and any old grass chucked on top. Edna's man, Alia's father, had built his home with proper iron tools, and the beams and corner-posts were properly shaped and pegged. The yellow riverside thatch was weathered black but the low eaves still curved up over the doorway, making enough headroom to duck through without crawling. Originally her father had made a door, too, of sticks and thatch, as his father had before him, going back into the mists of time.

Alia could not remember her father. In Middlesex, the kingdom of the Middle Saxons that lay beyond the City walls, her English father had been of the *cotar* class, a cottager. He had moved his dairy herd from the Strand into the neutral ground of the City, safer for an Englishman, during Middlesex's war with Essex, and Edna took him for her man. First among the kings of Essex was King Sabert. Sabert built a summer *sele* or hall of reclaimed timber in the old citadel to impress his sub-kings, thegns, *gesithcund* men and the great families of the area, Gill's people at Ealing, Gumen's at Harrow, the Mimms further north and all the others. But Sabert's war went badly for him. He grudgingly vowed allegiance to King Athelbert Oiscing, the old king of Kent, as his *Bretwalda* or over-king, in return for the old man's religious warrior fanatics who ate the flesh and drank the blood of their god, fought like demons and did not fear death. In victory Sabert calculated the interfering old man, who now styled himself King of the English, would soon die and relieve him of his obligation, but Athelbert's conversion to the new religion had greatly prolonged his life, and now it was said he would live for ever. Meanwhile Sabert tightened his grip on his new territory, and when Alia's father displeased one of the king's sons, in a business transaction, he simply disappeared. No one knew what happened. Bodies were often dropped from the city wall into London Fen, the marsh around the mouth of the Fleet river, or perhaps Alia's father was sold as a slave to the Frisian traders from the king's wharf at London Bridge, a man with no name and no past, and by now had no more memory of his previous life or of Alia than she had of him. She knew she would never know.

'Ha!' Edna, her mother, sat on a stone in the middle of the sunken floor. She stirred the fire glumly with a stick, sitting with her legs apart to make the most of the heat. She peered up at them as they squeezed past the door. 'So you found the worthless lump,' she croaked harshly, slapping Rowan's leg with the stick. 'Where was the idiot? No, don't bother to tell me, I don't want to know.' She pulled her scratchy woollen shawl closer to her neck, returned her attention to the fire. Part of one wall had fallen in and the wind blew through, making the flames flutter. The daubed clay had cracked from the wall, showing the burning tree like a glowing mesh outlined between the wattles.

'I found him in the orchard,' Alia said quietly. The housecow stood in the corner, chewing quietly, brought in early lest she be stolen. Rowan leant against her for her warmth, his big body shivering with cold and wet. He was not allowed at the fire without his mother's permission. He coughed at the smoke swirling into the roof, the rain dripping through. Chickens roosted on the rafter-poles, confused by the early darkness of the storm. The housecow lowed at Rowan softly, recognising him. Alia said, 'Rowan was looking for me, Ma. He was worried.'

'I sent *you* to look for *him*,' Edna snarled. 'I'm up to here with both of you.' She pulled angrily at the greasy woollen scarf that muffled the lower part of her face, jerking a wider gap to speak through. They saw her toothless mouth moving in the hole. 'Where's my food?'

Rowan nodded eagerly. 'Rowan caught a hare.'

'The idiot knows I can't eat hare,' Edna snapped. 'Too stringy!'

'Yes, he knows.' Alia circled the fire warily, sat lightly on her stone on the far side. 'He knows a lot.'

'Listen to my arse speak,' Edna snorted. 'It speaks better sense than you and smells worse. I'll trust my arse any day.'

Alia said, 'Just listen to what he has to say, Ma.'

'I never listened to your father. Why should I listen to my son, the idiot?'

'Rowan took the hare to the Westwatergate,' Rowan beamed. He was lost in the world of his story and saliva trickled down the bone of his chin. 'There was a skin boat pulled up on the beach and there was a fisherman and he said, all right, my boy, you give me one of them, and I'll give you one of these!' He reached into his pouch and proudly pulled out the trout he had bartered.

Edna got up and slapped him. 'One single trout.' She slapped his face from side to side with her hands and Rowan tried to protect the bird on his wrist, cupping its fluttering, frantic form under his pouch.

Edna sat down and looked helplessly for her stick. Tears stood out in her eyes. 'I hate you. I hate you because you're stupid.'

'I'm sorry, Ma.' Rowan's teeth opened. He was crying. 'Rowan's sorry,' he moaned.

'Shut your noise.'

Alia said, 'He can't.'

Edna said irritably, 'Tell him to hold his breath or I'll turn the pig to bacon.'

Alia reached behind her, picked out a piglet from the mess of straw. The piglet squealed, its tiny black trotters kicking, and the sow grunted. Alia brushed the piglet's ears with her lips and it fell quiet. She glanced at Rowan and drew a deep breath. Rowan understood. He took a breath, held his finger to his lips. He stroked the bird, smiling, lost in admiration of the jay's pinkish-brown plumage.

Alia looked at Edna more closely. 'Cut your mouth, you have.'

'No I haven't,' Edna said defensively. 'It doesn't hurt.'

'Cut it with your fingernail just now,' Alia said, 'when you pulled your scarf, remember?'

'Don't feel a thing,' Edna grunted. 'Fry my fish, you lazy whore.'

Alia glared. 'I am not a whore.'

'Wish you were! Get something back from you, you useless mouth. I'll use you or sell you, one or the other, whatever's best. Fry my fish!'

Alia glanced at Rowan. 'Breathe.' She found the dripping, still angry. 'Ma, I'm a virgin.'

'That's what I mean, got to make the best of yourself.' Edna was pleased. 'Still got value, good for another cow if we play you with a bit of sense. You trust your old ma.'

Rowan said numbly, 'Ma, don't.'

Edna enjoyed herself. 'Thinks she's better than me just because she's young and running about. Well, young Alia, you need a good big cock up you to teach you you're no better than the rest of us and keep you in one place. I'd do it myself if I was a man.'

Rowan begged, 'Ma, stop it.'

Edna chuckled. She threw the fishguts to the dog. They listened to the fish fry. The dripping hissed in the raindrops from the roof.

Alia warned, 'You shouldn't talk like that in front of him.'

Edna belched and they smelt beer. 'I don't mind making an idiot angry. Shame to me, he is.' She raised her voice. 'Shame to his mother, you are, idiot. A whole hare for a piddling trout. Gives me a bad name. Idiot.'

'He isn't an idiot,' Alia said.

'He's soft, he is. Soft in the head and soft between the legs. He hasn't had a woman since he got a sword in his face.' She turned and called out loudly, 'Have you, idiot?'

Rowan smiled uncertainly.

Edna found a wooden platter. She wiped it smooth with her elbow, put it on her knee and gnawed the fish. Alia took the head and ate it, moving her tongue in the fine succulent cavities and hollows. Edna finished and belched. She turned to the breeze blowing round the door and cursed it. Rowan crunched the bones. Edna did not move. Her gaze past the door had become perfectly fixed. Suddenly she gripped her stick tight.

'Family together,' she said. 'Gather round. Strangers coming! Rowan, your sword, get it now.' He hated the sword and complained but she shoved him fiercely. He pulled down the rusty blade from the rafters. Edna stood, peered through the gaps around the door. 'It is, it's strangers. It's a man on horseback.' Only the greatest warriors and thegns rode horseback. 'Two squires walking behind.'

Alia struggled to see. 'It must be a great man.'

'They're the greatest thieves.' Edna shuddered fearfully, but then her peeping eyes recovered their eager light. A great man was a danger, but also an opportunity. A man of importance gave gifts of land and livestock. He might take Alia for his concubine. The loss of a daughter was often the mother's profit. Edna squeezed past the door into the rain, bowing and fawning to stop the horse.

The great man on horseback wore a scarlet woollen robe whose weight, heavy with rain, bowed his shoulders. He was small and dark, a foreigner from the hot lands. A large jewelled ring adorned his hand on the reins. His feet hung limply and his free hand clasped his belly. Edna noticed how pale he was beneath his complexion. He was runny in the guts.

'Sire,' she called, 'shelter here a while—'

The great man ignored her, lost in contemplation of the burning tree. Alia noticed he wore no sword, unheard of. Something was very strange about him. She tugged her mother but Edna snatched her arm away, stumbled forward into the mud and rain. 'Sire, I shall warm wine from my own vineyard, send out my most beautiful maiden daughter here' – she jerked Alia forward – 'and with delicate skill her virgin fingers shall pick you meadowsweet and rue, and I shall grind a preparation of white powder, my mother's own recipe, to set you right in a trice—'

The great man without-a-sword looked at her wearily. He held out his hand with the ring on it and Edna, baffled, curtseyed until her bottom went into the mud.

The man sneered, '*Paganus.*'

It was a foreign language but his contempt was clear. *Pagan*. The two boys standing behind him, wearing bleached white robes foul with mud and travel, looked at one another. Alia decided they were not quite like squires, there was something different about their eyes, humility and arrogance mixed. The red-haired one on the right, with only one hand, stepped forward. He spoke to Edna in a broad Kentish dialect, not local, but recognisable English that she could understand.

'The rain was sudden and we are lost. Abbot Mellitus, ordained by God through His servant Pope Gregory, and further through his servant in the English nation Archbishop Augustine of Canterbury, to be consecrated Bishop of London, humbly commands you to show us the road to the *sele* of King Sabert.'

Edna was confused. 'Road? Abbot? Bishop?' All these words were foreign.

Alia pointed. 'It's that way.'

Edna hissed at her, trying to hold the travellers back. 'Alia, my daughter, sires, will show you the lane when you have rested.'

Mellitus spoke heavily accented English. 'Is this tree yours, woman?'

'Held by me and mine by right of the king, sire,' Edna said anxiously. 'And the vineyard. It's the only one, though they say there's another on Corn Hill, but I wouldn't know that.'

Mellitus said, 'This tree is a sign from God.' He turned to his acolytes. 'The world is full of signs of God's will, if only our eyes can see.'

The acolytes bowed their heads, dripping in the rain. 'Yes, your grace.' Although the flames were dying down the tree seemed to grow brighter as darkness fell.

Mellitus said, 'The girl shall guide us.' Again he offered his hand.

The acolyte who had spoken before said quietly, 'You may kiss the bishop's ring.'

Edna shrugged and kissed the jewel, impressed by its size. The bishop made a vague sign and kicked his horse forward. Alia ran ahead. They entered the trees at once and he called, 'Are you sure this is a path?'

She bobbed, smiling, with a flash of her eyes and teeth. 'I come this way every day, your grace.'

'Your grace.' He laughed, acknowledging his title, and said something in the foreign language. He added in English, 'You learn quickly, for a girl. Tell me the name of this place.'

Alia was confused, thinking everyone knew. 'Lud's Hill, your grace. Some call it St Paul's.'

He was surprised. 'St Paul's? Why?'

'I don't know, your grace.'

Mellitus twisted in the saddle. 'Amazing,' he said to the acolytes in the foreign language, but the word was similar. Alia skipped across the tops of shiny white stone that stuck out of the forest floor like stepping stones. Mellitus paused, pondering, then called to her, 'Do you realise these are marble, my child?'

'Your child?' Alia stopped, balanced alertly on the last column. 'I'm not your child, your grace.'

Mellitus beamed paternally. 'In the eyes of God you are. I have no wife, no children of my own. All children are children of my flock. I am here as God's servant doing God's work on earth. You are my child and it is my Christian duty to bring you to God your Father.'

Alia did not comprehend a word of sense.

'I don't know what marble is, your grace,' she said. She led the way forward through the trees across the hilltop.

Mellitus fell back. He groaned and clutched his plump belly. After a moment, with a furious gesture to his acolytes to stop, he scrambled off his horse, waddled into the trees where they could not see him, and they heard him relieving his bowels. The acolytes pulled hoods over their heads against the rain. Silence fell and the sound of water dripping through the trees was very loud. The horse snorted, then they heard Mellitus cry out. 'Child!'

Alia ran to him past the tree. The bishop crouched with the wings of his scarlet cloak folded over his knees to free himself behind. His mouth was open and he stared. 'Child?'

In front of him, rising little higher than his head, a corner of crumbling, weather-softened brick stood out of the forest floor. It was topped with a stone cross.

'This is a holy place,' Alia said. She wondered what he had seen that was so important. 'People know of it.'

Mellitus stared, amazed. One of the acolytes picked leaves and wiped the bishop's backside, held his cloak respectfully off the ground as Mellitus walked forward. 'His Holiness the Pope is infallibly right, of course, but truly this *is* the City of St Paul. It is a miracle that has brought me to this exact place.' He glanced at Alia, marvelling. 'A miracle, child!'

'Yes, your grace.' Alia wondered what a miracle was.

'Beautiful!' Mellitus snapped his fingers for joy, turned in a circle on the forested hilltop. 'It is the perfect place!'

His acolytes scampered behind him, and Alia watched as though they were mad.

'Here,' Mellitus said. 'Here I shall build my church.'

He fell on his knees in prayer.

When he finished he held out his arms and the acolytes lifted him back on the saddle, a flap of leather laid across the back of his horse with a heavy burden of saddlebags.

The rain had stopped but the trees were still dripping as they came out of the forest. Alia led the bishop's party forward and downhill among the patchwork of tiny strip-fields that lay between the villages of London. Labourers of various classes, all of them intensely aware of their order and rank – the lowest families born to slavery because descended from Roman slaves, above them the men, women and children reduced to slavery as prizes of war, then peasant serfs with some rights, then villeins and cottagers and free men with more rights and some obligations, though not as many as their lord – tramped wearily back to their hovels as darkness fell. They would sit, drink, eat, fornicate briefly and sleep like the dead in the dark, and get up with the sun. The villages lay around them black in the night, grown up away from the lanes and paths for protection. Alia led the bishop's party carefully, finding a dry lane through the marsh. 'They say there is a road built by giants beneath here,' she said over her shoulder. 'That's why the path is dry.'

'God has made us a dry path to lead us to King Sabert that His Will be done,' the bishop said firmly. 'Our most excellent son, the glorious Christian King Athelbert of the English, will pay for my great cathedral where his nephew King Sabert will be baptised into submission to the mighty Lord and God Jesus Christ.'

'Well, the path is dry,' said Alia. She heard the ring of swords from the ivy-clad amphitheatre, warriors testing their mettle by the glare of braziers before the camaraderie of an evening's beer, rich red meat, whoring and bragging about whoring. Alia hurried. Mellitus grunted as his horse trotted to keep up with her lithe, shadowy figure. Ahead of them rose the citadel.

Mellitus covered his nose. He could have found the place, even in the dark, by the stench through the enormous gateway. A king must hurry constantly across his kingdom to keep ahead of dirt, disease and rebellion, bullying tribute from his sub-kings in the form of hostages, food, drink, shelter, women and other entertainments for the court and his hangers-on. But a Christian king would be guaranteed the support of the Church.

Alia covered her nose. 'If the king is not here, he soon will be.'

Mellitus looked round sourly. The gates, if there ever had been any, were long gone. Bonfires burned in the lane wandering beyond, their dim glow illuminating the banners of the great families above various mossy timber halls scattered higgledy-piggledy here and there, dwarfed by the massive ancient ramparts.

Alia said, 'They come here to trade.'

'A church is the proper place for trade,' Mellitus said.

He rode forward. Alia followed reluctantly. Roars sounded and the street smelt of beer and vomit. The shapes of people shoved past her in the dark. A group of men tried something with a girl and she screamed with laughter. Mellitus turned to Alia. 'You have been a good and faithful guide and I shall pray for your soul.' He opened the pouch at his belt and threw her something which she caught. Alia turned the object over curiously but she could not eat it. It was worthless. Mother would be angry.

The people were jostled apart and a great man preceded by guards with blazing tapers rode by. Mellitus, though affecting humility, called out with the firmness of a man of equal or greater rank. The man with guards became deferential at the mention of King Athelbert's name. Mellitus held up a cross like the one in the forest, but very much smaller, and in his other hand he held up an idol of a man in painted wood. A crowd had gathered and Mellitus raised his voice above their gathered heads.

'This is our great King and Lord Jesus Christ. We pray Thee, O Lord, in all Thy mercy, that Thy wrath and anger be turned away from this City and from Thy holy house which I will build, for we are sinners. Alleluia.'

Alia slipped back into the shadows and stole quietly away.

Rowan sat on guard outside the cottage, his forehead pressed against the pommel of his sword. The moonlight had swallowed the stars and covered the clouds and treetops with silver, but barely revealed the rusty blade of the sword. Once no man had been stronger with such a heavy weapon, and few men quicker. Rowan had been proud of his skill in single combat. But in battle that did not matter, only butchery and chance.

Alia stood among the trees and listened to him weep. Rowan, in his present helplessness, was haunted by the dead he had killed. Rowan's sword had cut apart husbands from wives, fathers from sons. He had killed women and boys and daughters. He had raped girls and killed children.

He remembered them.

'Alia?' He dropped the sword and clung to her. But the sword would not drop. It stuck in the wet earth, swaying between them.

'I'm back now, Rowan.' All she could see of him in the dark were his moonlit eyes, the weak tears trickling on his cheeks. He lifted her easily off the ground, clasped her gently to him. His love was full and uncritical and as innocent as a child's, she knew. 'The men have gone, Rowan.'

He put her down. His teeth gleamed his smile. 'Alia is clever.'

That was an astonishing thought. No other man but Rowan could have thought that thought.

'Rowan is clever too,' she said.

'But Alia led them away from here.' He jumped as Edna growled from the cottage. It was time they went inside. Their mother, they knew, would not tolerate being unaccompanied, fearing her children were plotting against her.

Edna watched them come in. She was lonely and she grumbled to herself because they had not been looking after her. She huddled herself closer to the fire to keep them away from the warmth. Both her children were idiots. Alia, the younger, conceived when Edna was already feeling like an old woman, had been born an idiot. Without her mother, that girl was nothing. Alia was fey, a dreamer, and the work that was demanded of her turned her to skin and bone. She would starve herself rather than submit to her mother's will, and she had not found a man. Edna watched the girl circle the fire as warily as always, then perch herself primly on that little rock. Edna spat at her for her defiance.

'What did he give you?'

Alia looked rebelliously into the fire.

'Not even a kiss?' Edna snatched with her fingers but Alia jerked back quick as a bird, so that Edna's hand caught the corner of her mouth. Alia hated having her hair pulled, which was why Edna did it. The two women glared at one another with hostile looks. Edna changed her attack.

'I'll sell you if you don't start pulling your weight.'

She grinned, and Alia knew she would do it.

'He wasn't that sort of man!' Alia said hotly.

'Men are all that sort of man. What did he give you?'

Alia shouted, 'Why do you always think so badly of me?'

Edna grinned her grin wider, as though her accusation was vindicated.

'It's nothing—' Alia ducked her hands over her hair as Edna snatched, but instead Edna caught her by her clothes, dragged her forward over the fire, and something shinier than bronze fell out on the floor. Edna pushed Alia back, satisfied. She rummaged in the matted straw and muck.

Alia straightened her smock. Her mouth had swollen where Edna struck her. A strip of skin hung from Edna's knuckle, pink against the dirt. Edna ignored it, her tongue moving between her lips as she studied the find between her fingertips.

Alerted by her mother's attention, Alia asked, 'What is it?'

They all peered through the firelight and smoke.

'It's shiny like the sun!' Rowan gasped. Edna shoved him back.

'It's not a piece of the sun. I know what it is. It's called gold.'

Alia shook her head. 'I never saw anything like it before.'

Edna said, 'I've seen it. That's gold all right.'

She turned it over, then back again, and they tried to understand the patterns stamped on each side.

'There's a man's head,' Rowan exclaimed.

'It's King Athelbert's head.' Edna bit the flap of skin off her hand without thinking about it. 'It's Christian money.'

Alia said, 'Money?'

They gazed at the coin.

'You bargain with it instead of bartering,' Edna said. 'It buys things.'

'It can't be worth anything, it's so small,' Alia scoffed. 'It doesn't weigh as much as an egg.'

'This, my girl, is worth whatever someone will give you for it.' Edna snapped her fingers closed over the coin. 'And the man without-a-sword gave it to you. What did you do?'

'Nothing!'

Edna scoffed, 'Nothing.'

'I showed him the way, that's all.'

'That's all?'

'He called himself a Christian and he called me his child—'

'The cheek of him!' Edna examined the coin privately in her hand, holding it so they could not see. She closed her fingers possessively, deciding. 'He must really be a Christian, like King Athelbert. That's the way they speak. Abbot and bishop and grace might be Christian words.'

'He said King Sabert must submit to Jesus Christ,' Alia said.

Edna grunted. 'To King Athelbert, more like.'

'What is a Christian?' Alia asked.

'Christians don't believe in this world, they believe in the next. They don't believe in our trees and ponds and clouds like everyone else, they've got one God you can't see who made everything.'

'Bishop Mellitus said God was angry with us because we were sinners and might destroy the City.'

'I'm no sinner!' Edna said fiercely.

'I know, Ma, but he said he was going to build a holy house here.'

'Christians call that a church.'

'Yes!' Then Alia remembered another word. 'He said King Athelbert would pay for his great cathedral. That must be what he was carrying the coins for.'

'Cathedral?'

Alia said, 'And I showed him where.'

Edna said softly, 'Where?'

'It's the holy place on top of the hill. Bishop Mellitus called it a miracle.'

Edna stared at her.

Edna was afraid.

She lay awake in the night thinking about Alia and what she had done. The fire had died down. Edna rolled over, poked the embers with her stick. Is she like me? Edna wondered. How much of a woman is my daughter?

Then she thought, gold has come back to London.

There is gold money, so soon there will be more gold money. Money breeds.

The stick slipped and Edna's hand went into the fire. She held it in front of her face and stared at it curiously, then rubbed the glowing embers off her fingers. Her flesh seemed burnt but there was no pain, none at all. Her fingernail looked loose. She felt her forefinger with her tongue and the nail twitched temptingly. Now she had started she couldn't leave it alone. She caught the quick between her gums, pulled. The nail peeled off on her tongue. Edna prodded the fire to make a flame and examined her bare finger. Then she wrapped each of her hands in strips of cloth to hide them.

She lay back and waited for dawn with her eyes open.

The cockerel crowed, then came the familiar patter of chickenshit as the hens woke. They fluttered down from the rafters, stirring dust and straw. Rowan yawned, stretched like a baby, rolled over and went back to sleep. Edna kicked him, 'Get up!' without getting up herself. Rowan sat up scratching straw from his hair, stood up as big as a giant. The dog peed on the doorpost then sat yawning like a man. Rowan scratched the dog and smiled as it jerked its hind leg in time. He let out the housecow and hobbled her to graze.

Edna watched all this.

Alia woke silently, rose without a sound. Edna watched her lift the hatch that covered the sousterrain. Alia knelt, scooped out grain from the hole with the brickearth-clay pot fired by the potter on the Strand. Oswald the potter lived near the old dairy farms, the old *wyches* known as Aldwych. He added dung to darken the finish and show off the white mica specks. Oswald gave his pots in exchange for fresh eggs and sweet red apples, and wanted to give Alia to his son Osric, but Edna would not allow her to be given outside the walls of the City. Still, flaunting her had gained Edna a collection of pots.

Alia poured the grain across the ragstone quern, pressed the stone down, rotated it with all her strength to make rough brown flour. If only she was as strong as me, Edna thought. I birthed my babies without a cry. Edna hated the thought of her child being a weakling. 'Can't you do better than that?' she snarled.

'You were pretending to be asleep,' Alia said. She worked no harder. Perhaps she could not. The sinews stood out on her thin white arms. Edna remembered when her own arms had been white and slim like that. She could not bear the grating, rumbling sound of the quern and Alia's gasping breaths.

Edna shuffled outside. A mass of greasy rags, deeply hooded like many women to hide the signs of her age, even her face and hands covered, she stood in the spring sunshine looking into the forest over the hilltop. Her husband had cut this assart-field into the trees. Edna remembered when it was nothing more than a glade, and she had lived here with her mother in a turf hut. Now birds stole grain from the field and nested, thieving fragments of straw and twig from the roof of the cottage her husband had built. Edna cawed like a crow and they flew away.

In the distance a boat lowered its mast and slid beneath the tree trunks of London Bridge, newly repaired. London Bridge was always falling down, always repaired. The boat emerged from beneath, made of wood not skin, foreign, almost square in shape, bluff-bowed, flat-bottomed. Frisians, then. The sail, red with pitch to stop it rotting, rose again at once, good seamen. Coracles paddled alongside the vessel in hope of first trade. The Frisians beached their craft on the yellow Strand, trading cod and bits and pieces for slaves and wool. Occasionally, nowadays, there were two or three boats on the sand and the beach resembled a marketplace, an emporium.

Children and women ran down, the traders tossing out bits and pieces to draw a crowd quickly. Some of the jostling women were London wives, no doubt, and their children spoke German as easily as English, and dreamed of sailing away to sea with their fathers.

She watched Rowan return to the cottage. Lent his strength the quern began to speed up, rattling and banging, and Edna heard her children laughing. Her frown grew deeper at their irresponsibility, risking the precious quern she had dug out of the forest. Edna had seen a new quern of lava rock, sold by Rhinelanders sailing from the edge of the world, fetch the best part of a smoked pig on the beach at the London Emporium. She shook her head, muttering her anger.

Alia constantly defied her. That thin little thing. Edna's rage goaded her like a hot blade.

Not only rage. Envy.

She strode towards the cottage, but before she could interfere Edna heard the clop of a horse. She stopped. The man without-a-sword was riding among the trees. She watched, only her eyes moving as he rode back and forth across the top of the hill, sometimes in plain view gazing round him, sometimes hidden. She heard his horse even when she did not see him. He reappeared among the tree trunks, reined in at the top of her field. He crossed his arms and surveyed the forest as though he owned it, a plump Italian nobleman with short legs, a foreigner. Edna had heard from Edwen, a sempstress, that King Sabert had sworn an oath on the solemn *cavea* of the amphitheatre to convert to Christianity.

The Italian bishop of the Universal Church dragged on the rein, kicked the horse into a trot down the field, trailing deep brown hoofprints among the green shoots. He did not notice Edna watching him, a woman of no importance. His acolytes walked after him, heads bowed, following without a word.

Edna's head turned slowly, watching them out of sight. Then she went into the cottage and swore at Rowan and kicked him and pulled Alia's hair because they were idiots, one born and one made.

But she kept looking over her shoulder.

The next day, Edna was woken by the sound of axes. She hobbled outside. Gangs of slaves chopped the trees. She sat on a stump and watched them. Later the men stripped off and their shoulders reddened in the sun striking into the cleared ground behind them, flashed from their axes in front of them. They drank massively at midday and through the heat of the afternoon, their shaved heads pouring with sweat, muscles pumping. They were slaves taken by King Sabert in the Middlesex war, not yet redeemed, and many were striped by whipmarks across their blistered shoulders and thighs. Some renegades dragged heavy lumps of wood behind them to stop them running.

Each day they returned and each day the elm trees creaked and fell, the greater knocking down the smaller, and each day Edna sat on her mossy stump near the top of the field and watched their work without a word.

Alia and Rowan watched her from the cottage doorway. Their lives revolved around her.

'She loves the trees,' Rowan said.

'She doesn't love anything,' said Alia. He shrugged. No one did. Then the jay fluttered on to his wrist and he smiled.

'Rowan does!' he said.

Silent and unmoving, Edna watched the trees fall. She watched them stripped of green foliage into huge bonfires, the leaves burning to fertile ash. Bushes and roots and dead twigs blazed. A fog of white smoke grew up, hung over the hilltop. When the wind turned the smoke drifted around her in choking clouds. When it blew to the north it revealed the summit of the hill now bare on top and ringed with trees like a monk's tonsure shaved clean of all but the ring of hair. Mellitus too wore the devout tonsure. Morning and evening he arrived and stood bareheaded, the shaved circle of his skull sunfreckled and browning, hands clasped in front of him, watching his labour progress. The bald hill would be visible for miles around.

'It is more than a church,' Mellitus said. 'My cathedral is a symbol of God's will on earth.'

The bark was peeled off the fallen trees. The trunks were roughly sliced and shaped by men with adzes, stacked to season in the sun. On days when the smoke cleared the air was heady with the scent of fresh golden timber. Rain fell and the stumps were dragged from the ground by mules and the lowest slaves, dull-eyed limp men and children who struggled interminably with the wet roots and mud. The mud and ash slid downhill with the rain.

Edna sat watching, a dark figure muffled in rags. The green crop tended by her children grew up around her.

New men arrived, with spades. They levelled a flat rectangle of ground in the curving hilltop. Edna sat up, the sweet stink puffing out of her clothes whenever she moved. She watched alertly as a line of holes was chopped from right to left along the levelled ground. She stood up, watching them closely, but the men stopped. They began another line of holes to match the first and she observed them with narrowed eyes.

'They're digging the foundations of the cathedral,' she grunted to herself. 'Cathedrals have foundations. They'll carry the weight of the walls.'

Her explanation satisfied her.

Next day the men dug through a layer of brick and plaster in the soil, the paint still clinging to it. They pulled the first of the stone statues from the ground, a woman of pure white marble, her arms posed as though flexing a bow and arrow. Edna dozed, bored. Throughout the afternoon the workmen dug up other statues blackened by fire, mostly with the arms and legs broken off. Lying among this ancient marble the workmen turned up human bones, green and mouldy and soft as the soil, tens, perhaps hundreds of them, as though a congregation of worshippers had been slaughtered here before human memory began. Mellitus arrived on his horse. He looked shaken. He ordered the statues smashed and the bones thrown away.

Edna sat holding a leg-bone in her lap.

'You can dig there all you like,' she muttered. '*I* don't mind.'

She watched Alia coming up the field. Even tired as she was, the girl moved with a lithe ease that Edna watched with bitterness. The bile rose in her throat.

'Alia!'

Alia hardly heard her. She was weary after a day pulling weeds and the strangling bolters from the crop, and the flowers whose pretty petals would poison the whole harvest, and chasing the scavenging magpies away. She saw her mother and ignored her. But when she turned to go into the cottage Edna came up behind her and gripped her wrist jealously.

'You'll sit with me. It's time we talked.'

Alia gasped at her mother's smell. It was the smell of rotting pork.

Alia did as she was told. Obeying Edna's orders was her life. She sat beside her mother on the tree-stump, a hand's-breadth of air separating them, while the long summer evening turned very slowly to dark.

The men stopped work when it was dark.

'You've guessed,' Edna said.

The two women got up. They went inside and ate crusts and a broth of pork bones as they always did. Rowan fell asleep.

Alia could not sleep. She lay on the floor without turning over. The night was solid with heat, too hot for a fire to kill the insects. Even the hens could not sleep, shuffling on the rafters, and the cockerel kept crowing for dawn.

Alia held her wrist where her mother had touched her.

'You must have guessed,' came Edna's voice.

'It's not true.' Alia moved her head slightly. She waited until the grey light of dawn leaked through the walls. Now that dawn was really coming the cockerel slept, silent.

'You mustn't tell the idiot,' Edna said at last.

'Then it is true.'

'He'll tell anyone. But I can trust you, can't I, Alia? My own daughter. My own sex. Yes, I can trust you to keep a secret.'

There was a smacking sound. She was licking her lips.

Alia shuddered. 'You touched me. You knew, and you touched me.'

'Don't worry about me.' Edna grinned. 'I'll get better. I'm getting better already. Always been strong as an ox, me.'

Alia's face contorted with revulsion. She rubbed her wrist in the straw.

'No one gets better from leprosy. You touched me. I'm dying. You've killed me.'

'Everyone's dying.'

'It's leprosy! Not of leprosy.'

Edna didn't reply.

'You'll be surprised, Alia, when you've got it, it isn't as bad as it sounds.' Edna's voice filled with envy. 'Don't make such a fuss. You're so sorry for yourself.' She sat up, and her jealousy ran away with her tongue. 'You had youth, everything. You won't use the thing between your legs but it's all we've got, it's *all we've got.*'

Alia said, 'There must be more than—'

'There's nothing. You won't let Osric bed you. You could even have had the bishop, *he* was taken with you—'

Alia shouted, 'And you would!'

'Yes I would! I would!'

They shouted at one another, and Rowan groaned in his sleep.

Alia hissed, 'And Osric too, you would. I've seen the way you look at him—'

'No. He's too young.' Edna remembered. 'But I've had his father.'

Alia stared. She shook her head. 'You're disgusting.'

Her mother spoke furiously. 'I've survived! I've kept us together! When *he* came back from the war an idiot' – she jerked her elbow at Rowan – 'who looked after him? Me! I wiped his arse!' She struck her chest with her bandaged hand. 'Our family! *That's me!*'

Alia groaned.

'You had your chance,' Edna said calmly. 'Why shouldn't you know what it's like, getting old, what I'm going through?'

'Why can't you love me? What did I do?'

Edna said savagely, 'It's what you don't do. You aren't as strong as me. You're weak, Alia. You're soft. You don't deserve all I've done for you. All you ever did is let me down. Grow up, child.' She crawled painfully to her feet. 'Besides,' she threw over her shoulder, 'I only touched your sleeve. Your precious virgin body is safe from me.'

She went outside.

Alia uttered an exclamation of disgust. She tore off her clothes and stood naked, shivering despite the humid animal warmth of the hovel. Rowan snored. She found a pair of his black leather breeches, a tunic of black hide, broad-shouldered, tattered, but she tucked the strips tight at her waist. She was gasping as though she had run a race.

Edna walked slowly towards her tree stump. Alia ran after her, barefooted in the dew.

Edna wiped a dry place on the stump and sat. She pointed uphill.

'They'll start work soon.'

Alia sat on the grass away from her, so that she could not be touched. She was thirsty but she could have licked the dew. She was hungry but she could have returned to the terrible hovel for food. She did not know what to do, except follow her mother.

She said, 'Leper. You know you'll be stoned out of the City.'

They watched the men arrive. The work began.

Edna said, 'No. I won't. Not if you don't tell them.'

Trunks of elm with the bark still on them were stood in pits to make the corners of the building. The carpenters staggered in the mud that covered the hilltop. Teams worked to form joists, split planks. Other men made pegs or bored holes laboriously.

Edna unwrapped her hands. Her scarred fingers, covered with suppurating burns, worked to unpeel the muffler from her face.

She turned to Alia. 'You won't tell them, will you, Alia?'

Pieces of flesh hung from the muffler. Edna's face was eerie, as white as snow. Her hair was gone. She had cut her left cheek without realising it and her skin had rotted like the injuries on her hands.

'I'm so sorry!' Alia said. She reached out to put her arms around her mother, then drew back, terrified. 'Oh, Ma. I'm so sorry.'

'Keep your pity for yourself,' Edna said. 'Death. This is all it is. It's happening to me while I'm alive, that's all. Rotting and decay. There's nothing more, nothing on the other side. I'm seeing all there is. There's nothing.'

The sun rose but was extinguished almost instantly, and the rain began.

It was a wet month and there was mould in the crop. Bishop Mellitus had a vision that the bad weather was because the workmen were not working hard enough and God was showing His anger. Edna watched the planks pegged hastily together, the walls rise. Several times the planks sprang loose or slipped down because no one had done such large work before, and there was much scratching of heads. The men working on the roof cursed the rain and wind and the men on the ground cursed the mud. Nevertheless, the shape of the cathedral began to emerge from the earth that supported it and the trees that formed it. A doorway was cut in the western end, wide in hope of admitting many people, and Edna frowned. This would be a church for worshippers, then, as well as priests. Slaves arrived hefting stooks of thatch on their shoulders, reeds cut from the river. After the harvest men arrived to try their hands at thatching. They had thatched nothing larger than their own cottages before, but they climbed the precarious ladders and began their clumsy labours.

Only a king could arrange all this effort, Edna thought. King Sabert must be a great king.

It seemed everyone was agreed on that.

But Mellitus arrived and spoke to the acolytes. 'God's cathedral is far greater in size than the *sele* of King Sabert, for it is God's work being done here. When the baptistry is built, King Sabert will submit to be cleansed and baptised a Christian on the Day of Dedication of St Paul's Cathedral, and receive the white Bread of Life.'

The roof was covered and the earth floor of the cathedral dried, was stamped flat. Edna watched and listened as a column of laden donkeys toiled up the hill, flanked by Benedictine monks dressed in black, and many servants and attendants, slaves. Mellitus greeted the great man who rode at their head, embraced him. 'Liudhard, my brother in Christ!' It seemed Liudhard, a Frenchman, was King Athelbert's personal bishop. Edna eavesdropped.

Liudhard, long-nosed, with his hair braided and pinned, brought sad news. 'The Lord Augustine, Archbishop of Canterbury, died on the twenty-sixth day of May. He is now called the first archbishop of Canterbury. There will be no archbishop of London, only a bishop.'

But Mellitus hardly heard him, stood with his eyes fixed on his cathedral whose half-thatched tower rose between the trees.

Mellitus murmured, 'But London is a greater city than Canterbury.'

'But Canterbury, my dear Mellitus, is the capital of King Athelbert. Augustine consecrated Laurence as his successor in his own life-time.'

'Laurence!' Mellitus said, dismayed. 'He performs no miracles.'

Liudhard was a supporter of Laurence. 'He is blessed with humil-ity, not the sin of pride, the weakness of the Lord Augustine. Powers to perform miracles are entrusted by God solely for the salvation of Christians, which do not forget Pope Gregory warned him . . .'

Mellitus, warned in his turn against pride by the powerful bishop's allusion, dropped to his knees in prayer, his figure shrunken in the shadow of the cathedral he had built.

They're just like us, Edna thought. She spat, watching them. They fight to keep their heads above water, and scramble on each other's shoulders, and push one another down as best they can to their own advantage, just as we do.

The two men went into the cathedral. The doors had not been made yet. After a while the donkeys were unloaded and she watched with more interest, hearing what the pieces were named by the monks. Everything was necessary for the worship and service of the Church. Altar coverings. The altar itself, made in several parts cunningly slotted together. Sacred vessels and ornaments, vestments for priests and clergy, relics of the Holy Apostles, all were carried reverently inside before darkness fell. Two carts arrived carrying stone landed by ship from France, a heavy font and a massive stand to support it, work far beyond the ability of an English stonemason, even if one could have been found. These two pieces alone were left outside the cathedral.

The two bishops came out, spoke a while, gave orders, and rode off to the citadel. Mellitus had consecrated an outhouse attached to

King Sabert's *sele* as St Alban's Church, where the two men had been granted quarters, and rows of tents erected for their servants. The monks followed them, praying, and shadows filled the clearing, now deserted of life.

Edna crept forward. She was afraid, because it was said the Christian God protected His buildings with angels and lightning, and it was well known that the Bread of Life conferred superhuman strength on Christians.

Edna peered through the doorway. The place was dark inside, with only slits cut for windows, without glass of course, letting in more wind than light. The treasures had been placed in the gloom at the eastern end of the cathedral, where the two acolytes slumbered on guard.

Edna was confused. It was said that Britons in their mountainous wastelands built their churches with the chancel, the holiest place containing the altar, at the western end. These British bishops had not accepted peace with their fellow Christians over such matters as this and the date of Easter, and more than a thousand British monks and bishops had been massacred accordingly while praying, since praying was fighting without bearing arms. St Paul's had been built firmly in the new Roman Catholic style with its doorway to the west, and the altar would be placed at the east end, towards the rising sun.

Edna worried. Something was wrong.

Rowan, of course, put his finger on it first.

'She's as if she's sitting on an ants' nest!' he said, worrying about his mother. Anyone could see that Edna was obsessed by the building of the cathedral, and the more she worried, the more her children worried about her. Slaves thatched the low square tower near the eastern end. Others knocked together doors out of boughs and planks, trying to make them fit the entrance, but no one had any experience of work on such a scale, a church built for ordinary people.

The strange building looked almost finished, but Edna did not move from her tree stump. She watched the work intently, and Alia and Rowan, in her thrall, watched her.

'She can't feel anything,' Alia said. 'She can't feel pain. Not even discomfort.' She glanced at Rowan but said nothing more. Mother had entrusted the secret of her terrible illness to Alia alone, her own sex. Alia could not share it even with her brother.

'You keep looking at your hands,' Rowan said. The jay balanced fastidiously on his arm. 'Your wrists.'

The first sign of leprosy was a patch of white skin.

Alia looked into her brother's split, battle-scarred face. How much did he know? The jay pecked a piece of grain from between his lips and he smiled sunnily.

'It's hard to catch,' he said. 'It takes a miracle.'

Alia said loyally, 'What are you talking about!'

'Leprosy.' He held his finger to his lips with the childish excitement of sharing a secret. 'Sssh . . .'

Alia gave a sigh of relief. She had not realised how heavy a burden her silence had grown for her. 'How long have you known?'

He let the bird flutter away and pored over his hands, his wrists. 'You worry like this.' He looked miserable.

'I don't have it,' she said.

'I know. It takes a miracle.'

'You don't know about miracles.'

He touched his face. 'One of King Athelbert's Englishmen did this to me. So he was a Christian. Only Christians do miracles.'

Alia laughed.

'Every day that I am alive,' Rowan said, 'is a miracle.' He held out his hand, and the bird returned to him. He grinned, then put back his head to the clouds. 'It's going to rain.'

Alia stared at her brother, closest to him but wondering now at how little she really knew him. When Rowan was carried home almost dead, a piece of his brain had shown open to the sky. The place had been stitched over with skin by Edna's mother with bone needles, catgut and ancient skill, and he had survived, though only half the man he was. But Alia realised how much more clearly she saw him now his natural kindness and gentleness were revealed than when he had been whole, invulnerably shielded by manhood, aggression and strength. And he saw into her more clearly than men ever could, yet he was a man.

She looked at him closely, then kissed his cheek on the scar.

'Who must you take?' he asked bluntly.

'Ma says Osric, if I can make him come to me.' Rowan did not remember him, so she added, 'The potter's son.' She waited awkwardly. 'I would value your opinion.' When Rowan stared blankly she said, 'What do you think?'

'He is no worse than any other.'

Rain began to fall and the slaves thatching the tower gave up their work, sheltered waiting for the rain to stop. Mellitus arrived and they looked busy. Edna ignored the rain. A team of workmen trudged through the downpour carrying shovels and pointed digging-axes over their shoulders. They looked round for orders. Mellitus trotted his horse through the puddles by the west front, gauged the distance to the doors and the size of the font.

'Here,' he said, pointing at a place in the mud. 'Build your foundation well, for baptism is the foundation of our Church.'

Edna stood. Alia and Rowan, sheltering in the cottage doorway, chuckled at her obvious agitation. 'It's the ants again,' Rowan said.

They heard the foreman complaining. 'Bit late in the day for heavy work, it is, sire.' But Mellitus rode away.

'Your king is baptised here the day after tomorrow,' he called over his shoulder. 'Make your excuses to him.'

The foreman waited until the bishop was out of sight between the trees, made a rude gesture, then yelled at his men, and they dug. Their shovels threw out mud and soil, then roots, and reached the gravel.

Edna stood in the rain sheeting down. She walked forward to the labourers.

'What's she doing?' Alia whispered.

Edna said something to the foreman. He shook the rain out of his hair, shrugged without looking at her, kept on with his work.

Edna pulled his shoulder. He paid her a moment's attention, knocked her down, and went back to his digging shaking his head, and his men laughed. The raindrops bounced on their backs. They dug in the ground to their knees now, tossing out shovelfuls of gravel and clay. Edna lay where she had fallen, then crawled forward again. Rowan went to her, placated the foreman and lifted his mother effortlessly to carry her to the cottage, but she beat at him. He put her down and walked back to the cottage alone.

Edna sat in the mud with her arms clenched over her head, watching the work.

The men struck stone and groaned. They tried to work round it then waited for orders and stood shrugging, trying to cover their heads against the rain. The thatchers had already gone home.

'All right, we'll do the bastard tomorrow,' the foreman swore. 'Get off, you lucky bastards.' The men dropped their tools and were gone. The foreman touched his amulet superstitiously at Edna, then skirted round her and followed them away, a lonely figure dwindling into the shadows cursing his bad luck.

Darkness fell and Edna did not come back.

Alia searched. She found Edna sitting where she had been left, a darker shadow in the dark and rain and mud. 'Ma, come home.'

Edna looked up through the greasy droplets trickling from her hood. The gleam of her eyes became cunning. 'It's you. Is the idiot with you?'

Alia was too tired to argue about *idiot*. 'Rowan's in the cottage, Ma.'

'Will you let Osric take you for his woman?'

Alia said, 'I don't know that he wants me.'

'Wants you! Right to the bottom of his balls he wants you. Haven't you seen his eyes? You haven't seen how he follows you with his eyes? You can do what you want with him.'

'He doesn't love me.'

'Love you! He loves you and you'll love him, soon as you feel how hot he wants you.'

'I hate talking like this. Oh, Ma, it isn't the same for me as it was for you. We're different people.'

Edna said clearly, 'You must have children. You want children, don't you?'

'Everyone wants children.'

Edna pulled aside her hood, revealing her ravaged complexion to the rain and the moonlight above the clouds. 'Did I want you? Don't give me any more of your clever, cold answers.'

Alia eyes filled with tears. 'Yes. I do want children. Why?'

'That's all that matters,' Edna said.

She pressed on her knees and got to her feet, sloshed forward through the mud and puddles. 'Fetch me a bowl of fat and a stalk of straw and the flint from the cottage. *Do as you're told!*'

'But Rowan—'

Edna interrupted her. 'It's dark and the idiot sleeps in the dark. Tell him nothing.'

'But why?'

Edna snarled, 'Because he's a man.'

Alia did as she was told. She returned holding the bowl of fat and dry straws under her cape. Edna waited for her at the edge of the trees, well clear of the pit the men had started. The wind was driving the rain across the clearing, rattling on the cathedral walls. Edna called so that Alia could find her. She sheltered from the rain by the ancient, tilted corner of brick wall. The mossy stone cross had been removed and placed on the tower of the new cathedral, the height of six men above the ground. Alia stumbled in the dark, almost touched Edna before she realised she was there, drew back with a cry.

Edna paid her no mind. 'Fetch me one of those spades.' Alia splashed loyally through the rain to the digging, came back with a broad-bladed iron shovel. Edna prodded the grass. 'Dig there.' Edna fumbled in the wall as though expecting to find something concealed between the bricks. 'Work harder.' She felt for a branch of the size she had in mind. Alia struck stone, stepped back helplessly. 'There's stone everywhere here,' Edna said. 'This place is a mess of stones. Come here, cut this wood for me. Trim it to the thickness of two fingers. No, better make it three of yours.' She seized the prepared stick. 'That'll do.' She pushed the stick deep into the ground, pulled at it clumsily with her bandaged hands. 'Pull!'

Alia pulled. She stepped back. 'I'll fetch Rowan—'

'*No!*' Edna seized the stick, dragged it back. Her bones clicked with the effort.

Both women pulled with all their strength, and the ground opened. Steps led down.

Alia murmured, 'I've walked here a thousand times, and I never—'

'Mother to daughter,' whispered Edna. 'Daughter to mother to daughter. This is what we pass forward.'

Alia stared into the darkness beneath them.

Edna put her foot on the top step. She mouthed incantations similar to those she used on the crops and in the orchard. 'Out, *thyrs*. Out, *Grendle*. Out, *Drake*. Smile on us, *Erce, Erce, Erce*, mother of the earth—' She moved down the steps and disappeared.

Alia looked round her at the rain and trees, terrified to be left alone, terrified to follow her mother into the ground.

Tinder sparked down there, then the straw wick pushed into the bowl made a small yellow flame, illuminating Edna's rheumy eyes. 'Come on down,' she beckoned. 'Nothing to be afraid of down here.'

Alia knelt. A *thyrs* was a goblin that lived in a hill. The fearsome Grendle was the most famous, and the story of its battle with Beowulf the warrior was still chanted by storytellers round bonfires while wakeful children listened, wide-eyed, from the shadows beyond the flames.

Alia called, 'What's a *Drake*?'

'A dragon. Beowulf fights the fire-breathing dragon—'

'But that's just a story—'

'Everything old is true, Alia. The dragon destroys the countryside after its *noth* of treasure is plundered from the mound where it lived' – Edna uttered the chant – '"ancient, proud in its treasures".'

Alia said, 'I'm afraid.' But she went down.

She was disappointed immediately. Her mother's flame lit part of a tunnel. The floor was covered with dirt, soil, stones that had fallen from the vaulted roof. It was a place, not a dragon's lair, only a place that had obviously been dug out by hands, and she drew a deep breath of relief.

Edna said, 'My own mother said this work was dug by giants. She believed that until her dying day. But me, I don't know. She was just an old girl jealous of whatever she had left, worn out by care. Liked to play the treasure up a bit I expect, for my benefit. I was younger then, believed everything I was told.' She turned to Alia and spoke so directly that for once Alia did not doubt her honesty. 'Best to believe in nothing, Alia. Then you don't get fooled.'

She operated the lever and the steps rose, showered wet soil, last year's leaves and mould. It closed and the sound of the rain and the wind in the trees was suddenly absent. A few drops of water dripped down in the silence, stopped.

'Yes,' Edna said loudly, then lowered her voice. 'Best to believe in nothing. Didn't do these folk no good.'

Alia called, 'Folk? What is this place?'

'It's a grave, that's all.' Edna walked down the tunnel, the straw-light flickering in front of her. Alcoves along the walls held mounds of dust, meaningless. Then Alia gasped as her mother's dragging foot revealed shiny lights beneath the dirt.

'Is this the treasure?'

'No. It's just the floor. There's a foreign word for it, I forget.' Edna shrugged. '*Mosaix*.'

Alia touched the floor. She swept her hands out, revealed part of a brown eye made of tiny squares of shiny stone, then an eyebrow, then braided brown hair, all in coloured stones.

'It's lovely,' she whispered.

'Come on!' Edna hissed. 'I haven't got time.' She stopped at the end wall, coated in crumbling mortar as soft as cake, revealing the solid stone beyond. Alia held up the bowl but Edna hissed for more light down here. She crouched in the corner and scrambled forward, disappeared round the side of the rock.

Alia crawled after her mother's feet. The draught blew dust that Edna had disturbed into her face and she coughed. When she opened her eyes she was in a pit of bones and gold.

Edna watched her, bright-eyed in the reflections piled around them. 'Bit dusty,' Edna said. She toyed with the private parts of a silver statue, rubbed a golden grail on her sleeve. The cup gleamed, encrusted with jewels. 'It's real, Alia. It's as real as you and me. Gold. Rubies.' She held out the cup but Alia shrank back. Edna laughed at her daughter's awe and fear. 'I felt like you, first time.'

Alia whispered, 'How often have you come down here?'

'Hardly never. No need. Wasn't worth anything, see. Until now.'

Alia sat on the floor of crushed bone. In the four corners were placed four huge skulls with curving horns, their empty eye sockets set to observe every point of the room, so that Alia thought of them at once as guardians. The stone that slanted across the roof was marked with grooves, patterns, all sorts of shapes without meaning. Wonderingly her forefinger traced out an *R*, its sense long forgotten.

'But why would someone bother to do this?'

'Who knows? Don't mean anything,' Edna said. The heat of the flame had melted the fat and she poured the oil into the golden grail. The burning straw bobbed, flared up. The rubies gleamed like spattered blood.

'It meant something to your mother,' Alia said.

Edna shook her head. 'It was just dirty old dusty metal to her, all this. But it was in her trust, see. She'd sworn to protect it with her life.'

'Even though it was worthless?'

Edna chuckled. 'Why should I care why she did what she did? I got more sense. This stuff isn't worthless now, that's the point. Not now there's King Athelbert's gold coins in the City.'

'But you could make many gold coins out of this . . .' Alia voice faltered. 'Everything.'

Edna's muffler moved. She was grinning.

'That's right. I'm rich. I can sell this stuff to a merchant.' She took a roll of skin and lit it. The skin burned with a papery transparent flame, filling the room with light.

Alia whispered, 'Mother, don't you see how beautiful these things are?' Alia struggled to explain her feelings, failed. 'Special.'

'You sound just like my ma. Don't be so humble. She was an idiot, too, and so was grandma, and now what? I've got idiots for children. I'm the only one with sense round here.' Edna patted the stone roof. 'Now listen. Them men were digging just on the other side of that. Tomorrow they dig through, and what do they find?'

Alia shrugged. 'The gold.'

'*My* gold,' Edna said. 'But they won't. They'll find an empty old bone-pit, because we're going to move all this into the tunnel, and seal up the passage past the stone, and they'll never know' – she threw down the burning skin as the flames reached her hand – 'what they missed.'

Alia looked round her. She had never dreamed of such lovely things. 'You're going to need Rowan's help.'

'No.'

'But—'

'I'll tell you one thing I've learnt that's always true, Alia. A woman can never trust a man. The only person you can trust is yourself.'

'Then the only person you're left with is you.'

Edna said rapidly, 'I need your help tonight.' She held out the grail. 'I'll give you this if you'll help me.'

Alia said simply, 'What would I do with it?'

'Sell it to one of the bishops or the king, you idiot!' Edna was enraged by Alia's stupidity. 'One day this will all be yours, don't you understand? Everything I haven't sold, yours!'

'But I haven't done anything for it,' Alia said.

'You're a fool.'

Alia turned the grail curiously in her hands.

'I'm going to be made a Christian,' Edna said. 'The bishop will do it. A Christian lives for ever, and I'll throw off this little illness, and I'll be rich.'

Alia said, 'Did you swear the oath? The oath you said your mother swore to the gold?'

Edna shrugged. Then she said, 'Yes. She made me swear that oath.'

'To protect it with your life.'

Edna said very quietly, menacing, 'Yes. I swore.'

Alia said, 'Selling it isn't protecting it.'

Edna pulled the bandages from her hand. The strips peeled off one by one, blackened where the flame had caught them. 'All I have to do is touch you.'

Alia shuddered. She said, 'I don't think you know what you're doing.'

'I know exactly what I'm doing.' Edna pulled Alia by her cape, dragged her across the floor. 'Tomorrow they'll dig into here! They'll find it if you don't help me! *Help me!*'

Alia tried to tug out of her grasp but Edna snatched a handful of her hair, pushed her forward. Golden pots fell with her on to the pile of skins. Edna held her down.

'Swear it.'

Alia struggled away from her mother's hand, the smell of smoke clinging to the shiny flesh.

'Swear it!'

Alia screamed, 'I swear!'

Edna twisted her hair. 'With your life. Swear it.'

'I swear it! With my life I swear it!' Alia screamed, then sobbed.

Edna pushed her away. Alia stumbled into the corner.

'Now you have to help me, girl. You swore.'

'*You* didn't keep the oath,' Alia sobbed. She slid down the wall on to the bones. She rubbed the pieces of charred skin Edna had burnt, felt them turn to soot between her fingertips. She closed her eyes, frightened and lonely. The skull moved slightly beneath her. Alia's eyes opened wide. The tip of the horn came down gently on to her shoulder. She stared at it.

'I'm no fool,' Edna grunted. 'You don't catch me exchanging a hare for a trout. Work to do.'

Beneath Alia the petrified jaws of the skull opened slightly, the flat teeth trickled dust.

Alia said, 'Ma.'

More teeth appeared in the opening mouth, and the dust blew outwards.

Edna picked up a gold thing on a golden chain, swung it experimentally, wondering what it was.

The horn moved across Alia's shoulder to the side of her neck, pulled her close. Air puffed from the eye sockets into her eyes. Wind from the mouth blew dust on her hands as she tried to push away. But the skull was heavy.

Alia shouted. She jerked her head away, scrambled backwards.

Edna remarked jocularly, 'What's the matter? Your face is white as mine.' She picked up the skull by the horns. 'Don't worry. It's nothing.'

Wind gusted into the chamber. The corner collapsed as though there was nothing beneath it. Edna shrieked as she sank into the floor. The skull flew up from her arms and fell on top of her, tumbled away past her into the darkness below her kicking feet. She clung to the sides of the hole with her elbows, screamed herself breathless. Then her mouth gulped open. She held out her bone-white leprous hand to Alia, her eyes both domineering and appealing. 'Alia.'

Alia crawled obediently towards her. A bone slipped beneath her hand, its pale shadow fell over and over into the darkness beneath them.

'Alia, save me. I'm so frightened to die.'

Her mother's hand reached out. One of Edna's fingers was gone.

Alia gave a cry.

Then she gripped her mother's hand tight.

The soft cold flesh slid through her fingers. Edna went down shrieking. Her bone-white face stared upward, dwindling, disappearing far below. Alia saw nothing. The shrieks faded into the dark. Stopped.

Rowan was dreaming.

He was often not sure when he dreamt and when he was awake. For him there was little difference. The creatures of the night hid in the walls during the day, and the men and women of the world of day slept with the sun at night. Day and night were equally strange. For him, real life was often as surprising as a dream, and he never knew what was going to happen next. He was dreaming now – or perhaps that meant he was awake. He must be awake, because he was fighting, lifting his rusty sword with all his strength, and goblins and elves and sprites invaded every nook and cranny of the cottage, their fierce eyes blinked in every shadow, coming forward, filthy beards, shaggy ears, dribbling lips, raucous voices babbling, claws grasping towards him, shaking him, and he heard himself snoring.

Rowan woke.

The goblins' voices screamed at him. He shouted back.

'Wake up!' Alia shouted.

He groaned.

'Wake up, Rowan. It's all right.'

'Am I awake?' he asked fearfully. His leg was pinched, hard. 'Ow.' He rubbed the place, blinked his eyes open. 'When is it? Is it dawn?'

Alia held a golden grail encrusted with jewels, and a flame rose from it. He smiled and she smiled back. Her reply came in a form he could understand. 'It's like dawn because it's time to get up, Rowan, but it's late at night.'

He peered round him, looking for Edna's sleeping form by the fire. 'Where's Ma?'

'She's hurt and we've got to find her. I need your help.'

Rowan stood decisively. 'Here's help!'

She brushed straw tenderly from his hair, then held up something that flashed. 'Do you know what this is?'

Rowan grinned, knowing the answer. 'King Athelbert's coin, that is.'

'You're right. Take it.'

He took the coin, turned it over wonderingly, because he had not been allowed to hold it before. He looked at Alia clearly. 'What's wrong?'

'This is what you must do for me. Run down to your friend the fisherman and when he gives you his longest rope, give him that coin. Then bring the rope to me by the cathedral. Run all the way.'

Rowan took his orders as sternly as a warrior. Then he asked with childlike simplicity, 'May I take my sword? There are elves and goblins in the dark . . .'

Alia suddenly realised how brave he still was. 'Yes. Of course.'

Rowan swung his rusty old sword from the rafters and drew his *seax* too. She heard his footsteps running downhill, the dog scampering after him barking with excitement.

She put her hands over her ears, hearing her mother's screams going down into the dark as sharply as though they were still going down.

She prepared several pots of fat to use as lamps, lit one, then blew out the flame that burned in the grail. She poured out the hot oil, wrapped the cup in cloth and hid it beneath the grain in the sousterrain. If anything, now, the rain outside was heavier. She hurried to the shelter of the trees and waited there. Rowan's panting breaths sounded almost immediately and she gave a low whistle so that he found her. 'You were quick.'

'I ran all the way,' he puffed, a wild-eyed figure with a blade in each hand, dripping rainwater, and a ship's cable slung over his shoulder. Its coils looped almost to the ground. 'It's the longest he had,' Rowan panted. 'He wouldn't accept the money. He asked me to just take the rope and go.'

Alia stared at him, then her nervousness bubbled up inside her and she did what half an hour ago she had thought she never would again. Alia laughed. The tension released inside her until she didn't know whether she laughed or cried.

'That's better,' Rowan said, and tossed her coin back to Alia. 'Now, where is she? Is she badly hurt?'

Alia wondered how he would best understand what she had to say. 'Rowan. Listen to me.'

He settled at once, told her seriously, 'Rowan listens.'

'What I am about to show you is my secret and you must never, *never* tell anyone.'

He breathed, 'You mean it's family?'

Alia sighed with relief. 'That's it exactly, Rowan. It's family.'

She pulled the lever. The steps opened, leading into the ground. To her surprise, Rowan accepted the remarkable sight at once. 'Down there?'

'Did you know this was here?' she asked softly.

He gave her a strange look. 'Such places are all around us, everywhere, Alia.' He shook the water from his hair and went down first.

Alia stood behind him in the tunnel. She had been prepared for Rowan to be very frightened, but he stood looking calmly at the shining place on the floor her hands had earlier swept clean.

In his turn, just as she had, he caressed the bright coloured stones. 'They're lovely, Alia.'

She crawled ahead of him round the rock, showing him the way into the pit. Rowan looked about him with innocent wonder, then picked up a bone in one hand, a gold platter in the other.

'You know what this is, Alia?'

'Yes, it's gold.'

'No. It's a miracle.' Rowan looked everywhere, marvelling. 'This place is a miracle. It's beautiful.' He touched the shapes cut in the stone and a smile spread across his face.

Alia said guiltily, 'Something very bad has happened. It was my fault.'

Rowan pulled her gently. She realised that he did not think what had happened to Edna was important. She stared at him uncomprehendingly. Rowan took her hand.

'Don't,' she said, 'I—'

He pressed Alia's fingertip to his face. She felt his scar and he flinched, every touch hurt him. He said quietly, 'The width of a fingernail this way, Rowan loses his eye. The other way and my nose is gone. A breath deeper, and my skull is shattered.' He opened the leather covering his chest. The scar curled down past his nipple, puckered like a kiss over each broken, mended rib.

Alia understood what Rowan was showing her, the incredible chance that had left him alive. She asked, 'What happened to the man who did this to you?'

'My sword-point ripped him open as I fell. There is no difference between good and bad, Alia. My miracle was his death.' He let her go.

Alia said impulsively, 'Rowan, are you a Christian?'

He crawled the the edge of the hole. 'Do you think it goes down far?'

Alia crouched beside him.

He said, 'Rowan tries to forgive every wrong done to him. Yes, Rowan is saved. Rowan knows there is a God and the world shows signs of His purpose.'

'You never told us.'

'I was never baptised. Would Ma have understood?'

They stared into the dark.

Alia murmured, 'I tried to hold her but her hand slipped through mine.'

'You touched her?'

Alia nodded. 'Do you think I – the white patches—'

He hugged her deliberately. 'Alia is a girl but she is braver than any man I know. And that is all I know.' Rowan leant over the edge. He spat but they heard nothing. He called down.

No echo returned to them.

He took a bone, dropped it into the dark. They listened.

Alia took the dish and poured flaming oil from the lip. The streaks of flame seemed to go down for ever, bottomless.

Alia said, 'Suppose she's alive? Lying on a ledge somewhere, hurt perhaps, suffering, unable to call out.'

He sat on his heels, watched her steadily with his gentle blue eyes. 'Do you really want her back?'

'I love her. I hate her sometimes. But I can't imagine being alive without her.'

'You are too used to being hurt, Alia. She was not a perfect woman.' He sighed, heaved the rope off his shoulder. 'Rowan will climb down.'

He shook his head, then grinned, seeing that Alia had already tied one end of the rope round herself.

She wouldn't let him argue. 'You're stronger,' she said, 'but I'm lighter.'

Any other man would have been humiliated and refused, but Rowan saw her common sense. He pulled the knot so hard she grunted, then lifted her over the edge.

She kissed his hand. 'Hold tight.'

He gave her the lamp, then handed her down into the dark.

The flame flickered in the draught from below and Alia cupped it in her hand. Her other hand clung tight to the comfort of the rope. The blue-grey clay walls of the cleft closed around her, silent and heavy. A sloping ledge rose towards her and she pushed off from it with her feet in a shower of red brickearth, looked up. Rowan's arms moved rhythmically, lowering her. The ledge cut across his face glowing in the dark above her and suddenly she saw nothing but blackness up there.

The flame she held took all her attention, very bright and precious. 'Rowan?' she called.

The rope stopped.

'All right,' she called.

The rope dropped her down again. Pebbles and flint and fragments of mica glittered in bands in the clay, as if deliberately laid down that way for a purpose, separated by bands of mud. She could not imagine why.

It was a long way down.

'I can see the marks of the tools that dug it,' she called, but he did not reply. The ribbed walls of the shaft rose steadily round her, showing the pecks and grooves where it had been dug out or widened.

'Men did this, Rowan. Perhaps the same men who dug the tunnel.' Alia tried not to think of Edna's horrid goblins and dragons. She knew of many shaft-graves in the City where people still threw down pots, carved stones, incense-burners, altars to this and that religion, and coins, and babies, and the decapitated heads of loved ones, just as they had in the old days. But such places were normally dug – and not dug as deep as this – from a holy glade, its entrance-hole surrounded by bowers of interleaved branches where the mourners grieved and cast down their offerings.

A chert boulder appeared, seeming to rise up as she dropped, and Alia pushed off it with her feet, swinging in the dark. The boulder disappeared above her. The flame swung back and forth in the air with her movement. She nerved herself to call down.

'Ma?'

Alia thought she heard a reply, then realised it was only the chuckle of running water. The walls gleamed, wet, and trickles dripped down. She held the flame beneath her cape as a stream spouted from the wall, fell past her into a channel it had worn in the other side. Alia pushed away from the slanted wall, walking backwards, then hung again by the rope.

A glow appeared beneath her.

'Rowan?' Alia called up but heard nothing, only the sound of water becoming faint above her, and still the rope jerked rhythmically, lowering her down. 'Rowan!'

The glow from beneath grew brighter and rose around her, redoubling the power of the flame.

Alia reached out, licked her fingers. Chalk.

The walls were now pure white chalk such as boats brought from Kent, the same white chalk that was rafted down the River Colne. Alia touched the pale boulders as she dropped past them, marvelling. How had the people who dug this known what they would find, how had they known they would find chalk? The chalk boulders showed the jagged marks of digging underneath their sides, not on top, as though they had been dug out from below not above. That was impossible.

Alia stared between her feet as the darkness beneath her gave way to shadowy grey outlines. The shapes grew brighter and clearer, difficult to recognise from above, then she realised she was looking straight down on a pile of rocks. Before she was quite ready her feet touched the top and she stood up. The rope looped as her weight came off it, then stopped as Rowan realised she had reached the bottom.

Alia untied herself. She looked around her.

She stood on the rocks that had fallen from the chalk dome. The dome curved down on each side of her. It was the roof.

She scrambled down the rocks to the floor.

Edna stared up, her face screaming. She lay on her back with her arms beneath her, her body transfixed by a horn of the skull on which she awkwardly lay. She was dead.

Alia bowed her head. She stepped past the body, held up the flame.

A woman watched her.

Alia sensed her shape out of the corner of her eye, and turned slowly.

She was a young girl outlined in black. Next to her stood a taller girl with breasts, slim hips, buttocks. Beside this girl, no taller than her, stood a plumper figure wearing a bulging smock or apron. Alia's gaze travelled along the wall. The next girl stood at the centre of smaller versions of herself, her hand pointing towards the head of the tallest child, perhaps the eldest, perhaps actually resting her hand on the child's head with maternal pride. Watching them stood an old woman, her hair and eyes bare white chalk.

Alia's hand shook helplessly. The flame quivered as the oil spilled. She thought, someone is here before me. Perhaps they are still here.

She called out, 'Who's there!'

Echoes burst forward around her, as though many girls cried out with her voice. Alia turned round and round, the candleflame stretched out to one side. She glimpsed shapes sweeping giddily past her, women and children and strange unnatural patterns without sense.

Alia fell to her knees. Her head span.

Something touched her. It was the end of the rope looping and twisting like a snake across the floor.

Rowan's tattered boots stuck down from the roof. His legs appeared, his knees pressed tight on the rope, then his body. His head peered down, the *seax* clenched between his teeth. He had tied his rusty sword by a thong to his wrist.

He grunted, seeing her. He let go of the rope, jumped down the pile of rocks, leapt nimbly from the last, and crouched with his sword in one hand and *seax* in the other.

He glanced briefly at Edna. 'She's dead.'

'Our mother is dead!' Alia said. She threw her arms around him.

He squeezed her with one arm, looking calmly over the top of her head, then sheathed his sword. 'This place means us no harm.'

'It is a terrible place!'

'Look at this.' He pointed, and Alia saw there were many more people than she had noticed. They filled every nook and cranny of the wall, their figures large and small, close and distant, young and old.

'No men,' Rowan said. 'Only women, only children. Where are we?'

Alia shook her head. She tugged his elbow, led him to the place she had first seen, the family of girls standing watchfully on the curve of the wall. 'I don't—'

But Rowan understood at once. 'It's not many, Alia. It's one. One life, one girl.' He knelt, touched a circle Alia had not noticed. 'This is her. She's a baby.'

Alia stared. 'Yes. I see her now.'

'Here the baby becomes a child. Grows into a young woman.' He moved along the figures. 'Here she has her own babies. Her

169

family growing round her. Her children have children. She grows old and goes into the ground and her family lives on, going forward as she did.'

Alia stared, entranced. 'Who is she?'

'Rowan thinks she's all of them.' He walked round the curved edge of the chamber beneath the dome, staring up. 'Thousands of them.' He sniffed the patterns of charcoal, brown clay, ochre. 'Long ago.'

His voice faded as he went behind the pile of rocks. Alia called out, 'But who are they?'

Rowan came back to her. 'They're you. They lead to you. In you they are still alive.'

He reached his hand out, covered one of the odd-looking patterns she had noticed earlier, and suddenly she realised the shape was a hand traced round with charcoal. He murmured, 'It's not Rowan.' He took Alia's hand and fitted it perfectly inside the outline on the wall. 'They *are* you, Alia. They are your life. They are why you are here.'

Alia laughed. The soft echoes of their murmuring voices ceased and the walls trilled with her silvery laughter. Rowan grinned. He looked around him with an expression of the most wonderful, simple humility.

'This is your place, Alia. You are part of this. You always have been. Here you stop running.'

'This is where we hide the gold,' Alia said, and closed her eyes. She sat on a rock and yawned. It must be very late at night, but it was always night down here. She listened to Rowan's footsteps exploring behind the stones. The flame of the lamp he held moved with him, swinging shadows across the walls. Her eyes flickered tiredly. 'We'll lower it on the rope,' she called.

'There isn't much room in here.'

Now that she was resting Alia's body weakened. Her legs shook. The smell of her mother's body rose up strong and sickly around her, like honey left too long in the pot. She called, 'How could she believe in nothing?'

His voice came back. 'Rowan says, don't think about her any more.' She heard his boots scuff as he knelt down. He was silent. The flame dimmed.

'What is it, Rowan?'

He did not reply. Alia pushed on her knees and stood. She felt better keeping busy. She found Rowan crouched in the angle between floor and wall, his hand out as though feeling something invisible. He held the lamp in the place and the flame guttered, sparked.

'Don't let it go out!' she cried.

'Rowan followed the wind,' he smiled. 'It led me here.'

She sniffed the clean air. 'There's a passage.'

'Rowan knows there has to be, or the wind does not blow.' He pulled aside lumps of chalk and the rest fell forward, rattling from sight down a slope. He coughed, waved his hand in the chalkdust blowing in the draught.

She said, 'I'll go.'

'Rowan's sister does not take Rowan's place in danger.' Rowan took his lamp in one hand, his sword in the other. He pushed his shoulders into the passage and slid down the slope.

Alia stared after him. The flame reappeared almost immediately at an angle below her. She saw Rowan's boots and realised he was standing in a lower chamber. She called, 'What—'

Rowan gave a shout of fear. The lamp went out.

Alia called. She heard Rowan crying. She fetched her lamp and came back, held it in the sloping tunnel. Its walls too were ribbed, dug by men.

'Stay there,' she called. 'Don't be afraid.'

Alia wriggled inside the chute, then slid down.

She stood up in a second chamber. Rowan sat, knees drawn to his chin, rocking against the far wall. His lamp lay broken where he had dropped it, the oil staining the dusty floor. He had wrapped his arms round his knees and buried his head between them. His sobs echoed between the dark walls of the chamber.

She cradled him in her arms. 'It's all right, Rowan. Sssh.' She stroked his hair and glanced at the fierce animal on the wall. 'It's nothing. You're not frightened, are you?'

'No!'

'I'm not frightened,' she said. She lit the remaining oil in his lamp from her own. 'We're going to go back now.'

Rowan shuddered. He peeped with one eye, then crawled across the floor. He wouldn't look up at the tunnel, painted like an opened mouth. She guided his shoulders inside and he stood up, wriggled up the slope, whimpering. His feet kicked, and Alia was alone.

She looked behind her. 'There's room in here,' she said. Her words sounded so ordinary that she fell silent. By the single flickering flame the silence and darkness of the cavern became immense, overwhelming. Another tunnel led out on the far side, and she imagined tunnels and chambers going on and on down into the earth, each one darker and further than the last.

Her curiosity became intense, and she smiled. If only—

'Alia!' cried Rowan's voice, panicking.

Alia turned away, and crawled back to her brother.

He would not look at her at first, sitting with his hands over his eyes on the pile of stones, then he whispered, 'Did you see it?'

'What?'

'The elephant.' He tried to explain. 'There's an elephant carved on the wall of the old amphitheatre.' He pointed. 'Down there was an elephant.'

She laughed.

'We're in the elephant's mouth, or its belly,' he said. 'It's eaten us.'

He had come so far, almost as far as she. But she realised Rowan felt little of what she sensed here, that she felt beating in her body and bones and blood.

'It wasn't frightening, Rowan. I thought the elephant was beautiful.'

'Beautiful!' he cried. Shuddering, he threw his arms round her, clasped her to him.

She remembered Edna hissing, *A woman can never trust a man, Alia. The only person you can trust is yourself.*

'I trust you with my life,' Alia said. She closed her eyes and hugged him tight.

Rowan tried to understand. 'Mother said there was nothing more. Nothing on the other side. She saw all there was and there was nothing.' He shook his head. 'But there's this.' He looked around him in bewilderment. 'She was wrong.'

Alia realised, I shall never be as completely close to another man, ever, as I am to Rowan now. He needs me for everything, needs me as completely as a child does. He will never let me down. He will never lie to me, and he'll never lose his temper with me or argue with me, and he will never do anything to hurt me. For him, it's enough that I'm me. That's all I have to be. True to myself.

She patted him gently. 'You have work to do.'

'We'll never get everything down here tonight.'

'Perhaps we'll have another miracle.'

Rowan took hold of the rope. He glanced back at her as he hauled himself up. She did not really believe in miracles.

But he did.

The work was the hardest they had ever done, harder than the awkward ox-plough, harder than the back-breaking labour of hoeing, harvesting, threshing. And there was no time.

Alia was afraid from the start that she would fail, or that Rowan's strength would fail him, or that the rope would break, or that the workmen would suddenly dig through the roof of the pit. She imagined them flinging Rowan down the shaft, looting the treasure for themselves. She waited in the cavern, staring up into the dark shaft, and knew this was happening high above her. She imagined them sealing the shaft. But then she heard the rope coming down with more glittering stuff tied to it, she pulled the knot free, jerked the rope twice, stacked the stuff round the pile of stones while she waited for Rowan to lower the next load down. Again her doubts assailed her, but again the next load of baubles and trinkets arrived safely.

To go up, she knew, widen the crooked passage into the catacomb and carry or drag the treasure in there, would take longer than this. The next load swung down, a golden house, and she grabbed it. Besides, she knew, the shallow catacomb might well be found, but

172

the cavern was safe. She sat wearily, and realised she had slept for a few moments.

Rowan came down. His hands were wrapped in sheepskin to stop rope burns, now shiny across the palms with wear. His hair dripped and his shoulders were dark with wet. He pointed up. 'It's dawn and it's still raining.' He had been outside, fetched a shovel from the pit. From a bag he handed Alia a pot of milk still warm from the housecow, a couple of eggs, a mouldy crust of bread. Alia ate ravenously.

'The men won't work while it rains, will they?'

'No, not as long as it keeps raining.' Rowan used the shovel to scoop a shallow grave in the chalk. They piled stones over Edna's body. Alia wondered what she should say about her mother. Graveside eulogies often went on for days.

Rowan leant on the shovel. 'Rowan says, she tried her best, but she would have been a better mother if she'd been a Christian.' He picked up the last, largest stone and laid it on Edna's face, then smacked the chalkdust from his hands. 'Rowan says, back to work.' He swung himself up on the rope, then climbed the shaft using handholds and footholds that had been cut in the walls and boulders, chipping them out where necessary because they were too small for him, as though cut for the hands and feet of women.

Alia groaned, and worked.

Once a tall silver pitcher broke free, fell rattling and banging from the top of the shaft to the bottom. She picked it up and stood with the dented shape hanging from her hand. She was dazed by exhaustion and supposed Rowan was the same. Nothing more came down for a while and she dozed beside the piles of gold. It was neither warm nor cold in the cavern, and the air was dry.

Alia woke. The rope hung from the shaft, swinging slowly. A bale of skins was suspended from the knot. The rope creaked.

She called up, 'Rowan?'

'It's all right!' he called cheerfully. He slid down the rope, jumped from the skins on to the pile of stones. 'This is the last. It's night again. The men won't work now.'

Alia touched them. 'This is what she made me swear on.'

'Skins?'

'To protect them with my life.' Alia thought. 'It was these. Not the gold.'

Rowan grinned and peeled one of the wads open. 'They can't have meant anything to her.' He looked at the marks, scratched his elbow absent-mindedly. 'This is writing.'

In the whole nation of the English, the number of men sufficiently learned to write and to read what was written could be counted on the fingers of two hands. Alia and Rowan stared at the skins. Gold was cheap, if there was enough of it, and after their labour neither of them wanted to see anything made of gold ever again. But Alia reached out and touched the scuffed, scrawled leather. She could not understand the marks, but she understood their importance. 'Writing!' she whispered. Such rarity was valuable beyond price.

She thought, they're old. Everything old is true.

'Ma burnt one and she died,' she said, nodding. 'That's why she fell and died.'

Rowan stepped back from the skins with a respectful look. He turned to her for guidance.

'I'll put them below the elephant's mouth,' she decided. 'That's the safest place.' Rowan shook his head. She realised he would not go down there again even if she ordered him to. 'You go back up,' she ordered. 'I'll do it and meet you up at the top.'

Rowan waited anxiously for Alia to climb back up the shaft. At last he saw her face below him, her pale hands moving for holds in the clay walls. 'Hurry!' he whispered urgently. She gripped the rope tight and he pulled her up as easily as a fish on a line, clasped her round her waist, swung her on to the bone floor of the pit. 'Sssh.' He tied off the rope around the blade of his sword, then wedged the sword across the mouth of the shaft.

'Hurry, Alia. They're here.'

Alia looked up. Faintly, on the other side of the stone slanting above her, she heard the clink of digging-axes.

The floor of the pit was now bare, a mass of bones. Rowan threw them across the top of the shaft, skulls, leg-bones, horn, anything that came to hand, then smaller pieces, fragments of shell and spine. They coughed in the bone-dust, covered their mouths. More dust showered from the roof, then the point of a digging-axe pierced through. They heard a man grunting. The point was withdrawn, and a blinding wedge of sunlight slanted down from the hole.

Rowan pushed Alia back round the stone, followed her, remembered the lamp and went back for it, grabbed it, scrambled after her. They heard many axes ringing on the roof of the pit, and white dust swirled in the bars of sunlight. Rowan turned and scrabbled and shoved with his hands, filling in the short passage after him.

He backed into the catacomb, stood doubled over, his hands on his knees, gasping. His hair and eyebrows were white with dust.

'See? It rained all yesterday,' he croaked.

'So? Rain?'

'Rowan calls that a miracle.'

He took her elbow. They let down the steps of the catacomb carefully and crawled up among the trees. Rowan pulled the lever closed then threw it away, and they kicked soil and moss over the place. They started dusting themselves down, then Alia fell still. They watched quietly as Bishop Mellitus rode past the cathedral. He reined in near the workmen and the foreman begged his pardon.

Mellitus dismounted. He stood on the edge of the pit of bones.

'Ox heads, my lord,' the foreman said. 'Bearing the marks of sacrifice, I'd say.'

Mellitus turned from the font to the cathedral, then back again.

'Cover them up,' he said quietly, 'cover them up. My church is built on a profanity.'

Alia and Rowan heard the men groan at the extra work. They watched as the pit was filled in and covered with the heavy French stone slabs of the west-facing baptistry.

The lowest slaves climbed earliest to the hilltop, shuffling from the riverside mists long before dawn on the Day of Dedication of King Athelbert's second cathedral and the baptism of King Sabert. All ranks of slave were released from their forenoon labours by his decree. 'That the king can utter such a command and be obeyed demonstrates his power and importance,' Alia said, impressed.

'It tests the loyalty of his thanes, who will lose half a day's work,' Rowan said practically, understanding such matters. With ferocious looks, hand on his *seax*, he guarded their cottage and precious orchard from the low classes filing uphill. He had hidden the cow and the pig in the deepest brambly undergrowth by the Walbrook, and the dog snapped and growled by his ankle.

Alia hid a smile. Rowan was very protective of her.

'Perhaps you would like to hide me by the Walbrook too,' she said.

'Rowan knows his duty.'

The sun's light struck along the tree-clad slopes of Lud's Hill. Alia watched the people milling up the path. After the highest ranks of slave came churls, slaves who had won their freedom, and then a few shabby British monks and travellers, dignified and polite in their manners, careful not to provoke hostility so far from home. Then came the freemen, low *geburs* and cottagers and superior *geneats*, farmers who owned land and rights, and the thanes who were wealthy men, several of them making the journey from estates beyond the City walls. Alia saw a merchant from the Strand, wearing a dyed wool cloak but with a face like a thief, touting for business with a bag of English shillings.

She whispered to Rowan, who nodded reluctantly. She slipped through the bushes and ran between the trees to the top of the hill, where the elmwood cathedral stood in its clearing. The yellow walls and yellow thatch looked almost white in the sun among the tall green elms. On top of the thatched tower stood the stone cross that Alia herself had shown Bishop Mellitus.

Families of ordinary people camped under branches propped together among the trees, worshipping their gods as they always had, interested to see the new ceremony. Smoke and the smell of roasting meat rose from their fires like a sacrifice. Children ran about or watched seriously. All round the cathedral the mud was covered by the huts and tents of the servants and monks attending the Bishop of Rochester and the Archbishop of Canterbury, who had arrived yesterday after a long journey.

The people stirred, staring towards the busy gateway of the citadel.

Young warriors, the *geogoths*, came first along the trail from the citadel, knocking people aside to make way. Away from the king's hall they were permitted to carry their swords and knives and limewood shields. Alia swung herself into a tree and from the bough, silent as a bird, watched them swagger with their weapons below her.

Now the elder warriors who had proved their valour in great wars trooped from the citadel, and the crowd fell back. The aldermen followed, looking at the strange new cathedral or not, as it pleased them. Behind them, slipping on the muddy track, came the king's trumpeter and drummer, then singers to praise his deeds, followed by the king's standard-bearers carrying his gold standards, painted banners, and the ceremonial spear known as the *tuf*, symbol of old King Athelbert's favour.

King Sabert's bodyguard marched from the trees. The king rode on horseback, a large man in a large wooden saddle. His woollen cloak was long and pure dark blue, a rare and difficult dye, showing his greatness. Over his face he wore a tall bronze helmet. Golden boars decorated the cheek-pieces and another stood on the crest, gold tusks shining.

After the king came the bishops, last and greatest because closest to God, walking on foot with ostentatious humility.

Alia noticed Ricula, Sabert's mother, standing near the cathedral. She was too old to walk but her face was still hawkish and powerful, King Athelbert's sister, English and obviously Christian, for she had not allowed her son to marry her after her husband's death as was customary and polite. But where was King Sabert's young pagan wife?

For the first time Alia realised that there was more going on than she saw. A king, for all his power and glory, was buffeted by factions on every side, and must leap from compromise to compromise to keep his throne. No wonder such men longed for the simplicities of war.

Alia wondered, where is Sabert's young queen? Where are Sabert's sons? If a king died peacefully one of his sons was often elected to the kingship. At length she noticed the queen waiting near the baptistry. But the queen was surrounded by her women, and her three sons were nowhere to be seen.

The king dismounted and the queen bent her knee, handed him a cup to drink. She went to the bishops and offered drink to them also, but they refused, unsure of the custom. The women knelt before them, insulted, but the bishops thought they were offering homage to God and blessed them.

The bishops of the Church of the English filed into the cathedral to pray. The king gestured the women out of the way, took off his helmet and stood with his arms folded. The sun grew very hot and some people held their clothes over their heads for shade. Others lay down to sleep. Flies buzzed and smoke rose from the cooking-fires.

The convocation of bishops, led by a cathedral virger carrying a rod, came outside. The company of devils that inhabited empty structures had been driven out. The cathedral was consecrated and Mellitus wore the *pallium*, a circular white lambswool cape embroidered with four crosses woven by the virgins of St Agnes in Rome, formally consecrated by his synod as the cathedral's first bishop.

Acolytes came forward. Without laying hands on the king, speaking tactfully through the reluctant queen, they arranged that he was divested of his sword, helmet and cloak, and led him into the cathedral. Sabert looked for his followers. Spittle clung to his beard as he spat. His bodyguard and aldermen hurried after him.

Mellitus called out in a loud, robust, accented voice – English was his fourth language – 'I dedicate this great church, this sign of God's Will, in which I pray He will vouchsafe His Truth to us by means of a miracle' – a ripple of excitement ran through the crowd – 'I therefore dedicate this cathedral in the name of St Paul of the Sword, and I name this the City of St Paul, for the enemies of a Christian king are the enemies of God, and should they dare to enter these walls His sword will strike them down.'

Alia listened enthralled. Mellitus had claimed the whole City as the cathedral precinct of St Paul's. He promised a City of God where a devout Christian king was guaranteed the support of the church authorities. King Sabert had given away the City, but got what he wanted in return.

The king was led outside wearing a simple linen smock, showing his white neck and skinny legs. Mellitus ascended the steps of the baptistry before the barefoot king. Under Christian precedence even a bishop, below his archbishop, exceeded a king in rank. The king stormed up the steps and climbed into the font like a man getting into a bath. Mellitus, being of a monastic order, immersed him completely in symbolic death, burial, and resurrection.

Mellitus cried out, 'Do you believe with all your heart that Jesus Christ is the Son of God?'

The king spluttered. He hated water like a cat. 'Yes.'

'You say, I believe—'

'Yes, I believe with all my heart that Jesus Christ is the Son of God.' King Sabert climbed out and shook his feet dry. 'I pray for long life for my lord King Athelbert,' he growled. 'Now give me the bread.'

A humble wooden platter was brought forward. Sabert drank the Blood of Life and reached hungrily for Christ's flesh, the Bread of Life. A precious fragment was placed on his tongue.

He raised his arms and his men roared. Sabert's closest followers, who wore his ring on their swords, came forward to be baptised and eat the strength of the holy bread like their leader. Bishop Liudhard, King Athelbert's personal chaplain, looked sour. He mistrusted mass conversions.

But Mellitus spoke enthusiastically. 'Though fewer than a thousand people live in our City—' No one understood *thousand*, so he began again. He praised Sabert as a Christian king, a man of family, a giver of rings, a distributor of treasure. Sabert understood, and grunted for his baptismal gifts to the Church to be brought forward, rings, silver plates, rich vestments, a gold collar for Mellitus.

'I accept these gifts for the poor of Christ.' Mellitus blessed a ragged man who had been baptised, then ordered a silver plate to be broken up and distributed among any Christian poor.

Sabert gave a signal. Slaves, more gifts, were herded across the mud by Frisian traders. Mellitus examined them eagerly, aware of their importance. Taken after a skirmish, these slaves, like many others, would be shipped to Europe and trained as English-speaking Christian missionaries before being returned.

'The borders of the Diocese of London are the borders of my kingdom,' Sabert proclaimed. 'To St Paul's I give my manor of Tillingham in Essex. To the bishop I give Stepney and the districts of Middlesex to the north and west of the City Wall. I permit the canons of St Paul's to accept and hold property independently of the bishop and grant them the forests called Willesden and Harlesden, exempt from Forest Law and royal hunting privileges.' Alia gasped at Sabert's generosity. Stepney alone was a huge area of woodland supporting several villages. Harlesden was fine pigwood, Willesden even better. At one stroke the cathedral was wealthy, its importance declared.

Bishop Liudhard rose to his feet. 'In addition our most glorious suzerain, King Athelbert of the English, grants to the cathedral of St Paul's the district of Southwark and lands and manors south of the river.' Alia thought she saw a look of cunning cross King Sabert's face. Perhaps he still calculated the old king would die, and the kingdom of Essex would grow at the expense of Kent.

Sabert said, 'Bishop Mellitus, you are given permission, as you have asked, to take over the temple on the Strand and consecrate it as St Martin-in-the-Fields, and to make a church of the travellers' shrine at Thorney Island.'

Mellitus made his response. 'Thus King Sabert, great giver of gifts, receives the greatest gift.' The bishop took a silver cross and strung it on Sabert's helmet. 'It is the gift of eternal life. Because God chose you as king, it behoves you to teach your people to follow Christ, which is the gift of Christianity.'

A finger-bone of St Paul was lifted from a reliquary and Sabert kissed it. 'I swear it by St Paul.'

Mellitus intoned, 'A king is Christ's deputy. You will zealously avenge offences against Christ. In return a king cannot be expelled from office, for you rule by the help of God and the favour of the divine grace.'

A man heckled from the crowd, 'How do we know all this about God is true?'

His face was warty and people drew back from him. Sabert drew his sword, glowering, but Mellitus said humbly, 'Come forward, *paganus*.'

Alia looked down from her tree branch. The man who had been called walked below her and another man took his place. She watched him rub dung over his face and squint anxiously at the bright sun.

Mellitus spoke again to the pagan. 'Our Lord says, Take My yoke upon you and learn of Me, for I am meek and lowly in heart.'

'What's it worth?' The man stuck his thumbs through his belt. 'If you're so meek, why should we listen to you?'

Mellitus said calmly, 'I am a mere man, I know. Whatever powers I have received from God are entrusted to me solely for the salvation of my people.'

'What powers? What people?'

'Christians.'

'I was born with these horrors!' The man showed his warts to the crowd. 'Go on. Do your magic for me, if you're so close to God. Get rid of them.'

Mellitus was undisturbed. 'I cannot save you, for you have not been brought to salvation with the Sacrament of Baptism.'

A voice cried out below Alia, '*I* have been saved! I am a Christian! But I have a demon within me—' The English voice rose to a scream, and people nearby scrambled back to get away from him, and even Alia drew up her legs. 'The demon took my sight!'

'Come forward, my brother in Christ.' Mellitus nodded and an acolyte guided the blind man into the clearing. Flies buzzed on his filthy face and his eyes were turned up, white. The acolyte drew back in revulsion from his breath.

Mellitus dropped to his knees in front of the man. He bowed his head. He clasped his hands in prayer. The crowd fell silent.

'O Lord,' cried Mellitus, 'O Lord, on this Day of Dedication, grant me a miracle to silence the unbelievers. O Lord, let me bring them to Your grace. O Lord, let the beliefs and humility of those who can heal this poor blind soul be accepted as pleasing to God, and therefore to be followed by all.'

Mellitus reached forward and gripped the man. The blind man screamed as the demon came out of him. A woman in the crowd shrieked and fainted, seeing the creature. Everyone saw something. The eyes of the blind man blinked, filled with colour.

He looked from Bishop Mellitus to St Paul's Cathedral.

'I can see,' he said. 'I can see.' He rubbed his eyes and tears of joy streamed down his cheeks. People looked at one another and moved curiously from their bowers towards the baptistry.

'Alleluia!' cried Mellitus.

Alia looked for the warty man but he was gone. When she looked back she could not see the man who had been blind. Both had disappeared as though they had never been. She swung down from the tree branch and approached the baptistry among the others. One man with a ginger beard called out, 'Yes, but what about a sacrifice?'

'Jesus Christ sacrificed his life for you—' Mellitus turned as there was a swirl in the crowd. The three sons of King Sabert pushed angrily through. They had been hunting and one, Sexred the eldest, still carried the hawk on his wrist, its jesses trailing.

'Saba!' The boys went to their father, calling him by his personal name. 'Saba, why did you do this without telling us? Why would you not permit our mother to tell us? It was a trick, Saba, don't you see? The man was English—'

Mellitus said, 'It is you who are blind, children. You are as blind as was the blind man before God drove out the demon.'

Saeward, the youngest son, shouted, 'We have our own gods—'

Mellitus said firmly, 'You are forbidden to worship idols even if you are not Christian.' He turned briskly to King Sabert.

Sabert looked from the bishop to his sons. All their names began with S, showing his family pride. 'Sexred, Sebba, Saewa, my sons whom I love. Listen to him. In matters of faith the bishop speaks with my words. In matters of the sword you listen to me.'

'Amen,' Mellitus murmured.

The boys stormed away furiously and gathered round the queen as though protecting her.

Like many others, Alia remained quietly near the font watching the ceremonies. The monks, celibate priests in sacred orders and the married clergy below them in rank, gathered in front of the cathedral and sang psalms, preached, and said mass. Converts were taken inside to make their offerings at the altar. The merchant in the dyed cloak was welcomed for the people his trade would bring to the cathedral. The merchant saw the advantages at once. The trade attached to a king's court was constantly on the move, but a church stayed in one place. Soon stalls and markets would grow up around the walls, and the clergy would witness transactions and seal documents, drawing people into the Faith. Alia blinked. The sun felt like a hot hand pressing down on her head, and the bright business of the day and the splashing people and the chanting priests receded into the distance.

Alia was intensely aware of birds calling in the trees, the deep green of the forest, the smell of the soil beneath the grass where she was standing. Beetles and tiny ants toiled between the blades of grass. A slow-worm slithered over the toe of her deerskin shoe and for a moment Alia saw everything that was real. There was no sound, only a man frozen with his drenched head in the font, his legs caught in mid-kick, the priest's face withdrawn and immobile as his nostrils flared, suppressing a yawn. She blinked and they were gone, life had flashed forward, transparent, fleeting. She blinked, reached out, but they were already somewhere else. Drops of holy water showered from a man's head and his wife embraced him.

Beneath them Alia saw the pit of ox-skulls and the shaft going down into the solid earth, permanent, massive, silent, real.

Voices babbled and the day shone brilliantly. People were drifting away. Noon had come and they must go. The imperfectly seasoned walls of the cathedral creaked in the heat of the sun. The priest yawned.

A hand touched Alia's shoulder. 'I remember you, my child.' She turned to see Bishop Mellitus. He smiled. 'You are the girl of the burning tree. You led me through the forest to the cross.' He nodded at the cathedral. 'This is your place, for without you it would not be here.'

Alia threw herself on her knees.

Mellitus said wonderingly, 'You have come to Christ. You are of the Faith.'

She shook her head. He took her by the hand and led her up the steps to the font.

'Do you believe with all your heart that Jesus Christ is the Son of God?'

Rowan had grinned when he heard the news.

She'd said, 'Will you be baptised too?'

Rowan had shaken his head. 'Both of us know what the real miracle was, and it wasn't the blind Englishman.'

'I know.'

'Rowan and Alia know the real miracle was the day of rain that happened before. Just a day of rain. Nothing more.'

Alia nodded. 'Even as Bishop Mellitus baptised me, I still felt that God is far more wonderful than even the bishop knows. I felt it strongly.'

Rowan's eyebrows had drawn together in his most intent, most childlike expression.

'Then Rowan too will allow himself to be baptised.'

But they were busy winnowing the crop for the next few days, and when Alia and Rowan walked to the hilltop all the tents were gone from around the cathedral. The consecration feast which had lasted three days was over. The visiting bishops, their slaves and attendants and the Benedictine monks were all gone. The mud had dried to summer dust but no one had filled in the cesspits. Alia and Rowan picked their way carefully between the dumps to the cathedral door. Rowan carried a squealing piglet to offer at the altar. A merchant waiting outside bid him two hands of first-lay hens for the pig, knowing he'd get a better deal out here than afterwards, from the Church on whom his livelihood depended. Rowan shook his head and the man offered three more fingers, then spat as the girl led her idiot brother into the cathedral. The merchant knew the cathedral kitchener, working in a turf hut set apart from the cathedral because of the fire risk, had no use for an unfattened piglet and would demand a clutch of eggs as well as the thirteen hens. The merchant weighed the pros and cons. On the one hand, his brother worked a patch of pigwood by the Walbrook for his lord, and an extra piglet might be fattened on the sly. On the other hand, it was risky. The merchant ran after the two parishioners and added one more finger-hen to his count.

But a virger saw, and chased him out of the cathedral.

Looking around them, Alia and Rowan advanced slowly across the floor of beaten earth. Being inside a building so huge – huge enough to take all the people living in the City in worship – filled them with awe. Most houses were also barns, but this House of God was larger than any barn. All the produce of London could have fitted in here – they saw a man offering a woven basket of green apples at the altar, and the priest tried to keep the basket too. The man, who had already exchanged a handful of apples for an egg with the merchant, hurried outside with the basket over his head. They heard the merchant offering him something for the basket; worshippers often needed a container to make their offerings look more special, and the apple-farmer sounded interested. His wife wove osier baskets skilfully, he said, and could easily make more than she needed. Their voices faded in the sunlight outside, negotiating a deal.

Alia and Rowan trod forward among the animal bones and apple cores left by worshippers. The walls of the cathedral were starred by sunlight peeking through cracks and knotholes. There were no seats and the priest helped himself to an apple, as Alia supposed he was legally entitled to do – offerings to the Church were divided four ways, between the bishop and his household, the buildings, the poor and the clergy. The priests of St Paul's lived like monks, though not bound to a rule. Alia watched the priest lean against the wall eating the apple with obvious enjoyment. He sensed her attention and raised one shoulder to finish the fruit secretly, as though guilty of a serious crime. When the flesh began to take pleasure, then sin was born.

Bishop Mellitus stood at the altar, his white *pallium* and formal cassock streaked by the grimy pawing fingers of pious folk. He looked weary but recognised Alia immediately. Rowan made an offering of the squealing piglet, the priest made the sign of the cross, and a boy was sent running outside to exchange the noisy animal with the merchant for something quieter. Alia spoke. At her urging the bishop agreed to baptise Rowan, and thus erase the atrocities of his warrior life that had tormented him. 'My brother is simple, your grace, yet wise.'

'Through simplicity we achieve wisdom.' Mellitus led Rowan to the font, immersed him. The bubbles cleared from Rowan's face, revealing him plainly looking up through the holy water. Mellitus lifted him. 'The Church may not punish him, or even appear to punish him, for sins committed unknowingly before the purification of baptism. For Adam and Eve taught us, in the Garden of Eden, that knowledge is the essence of sin.' He scratched himself uncomfortably at some irritation behind, suddenly frail and human.

Alia said, 'You have no one, no wife, no children, to wash your dirty robes? Even sailors sleeping on the shore have women who wash their salt-stained clothes.'

Mellitus looked startled. 'But you are not a low slave or a washer-woman.'

'Nevertheless.'

'Then this offer is a gift of love to Mother Church?' He nodded. 'I gladly accept!'

Over the next few weeks Alia saw clearly that the bishop, surrounded by staff, priests, virgers, canons, converts, each busy day full of care, was lonely.

Each week before the Sabbath, Alia walked up to the hilltop to wash the bishop's clothes. She watched Mellitus changed by the difficulty of his labours, losing his plumpness, and in the first year his face aged into the folds of a hard lifetime. His wooden house, erected in a fortified private compound or *bur* just to the south of the cathedral, was called a palace to assert his rank and importance, and so show off the contrast with his personal humility to best effect. Alia washed his cassock and rubbed the wool with a hot stone to take out the wrinkles. She was so quiet and attentive, after the barracking of his noisy serving women echoing from the back room, that during the evenings the bishop asked Alia to bring his food to table when he dined alone, and talked to her as though he talked to himself. She did not understand much of what he said. She was important, she knew, only because she listened. A wooden church was being built around the pagan sanctuary on the Strand, and the bishop would consecrate it to St Martin. 'I shan't live long enough to see St Peter's consecrated on Thorney Island, I fear.' He suffered great pain from gout, and Alia picked autumn crocus in the woods for a balm to relieve the worst of his attacks. One of the joints in the bishop's left foot swelled and she propped his foot on a stool, bandaged the foot tightly with strips of linen. Mellitus watched her fingers work, the firelight flickering in his eyes.

'Alia.'

He said nothing more, so she asked, 'Yes, your grace?'

'Why are you not married, Alia?' He laughed at her confusion. 'You should be!'

She concentrated on her work. 'Why does your grace not have a wife?'

'Because I am married to Mother Church and my flock is my family. But you are a young girl. If you do not have children, my child, you will lose your chance. You will be like me.'

It was late. The bishop reached out longingly to touch her black glossy hair, which Alia now grew to her shoulders. She felt the brush of his fingertips, then he snatched his hand back, crossed awkwardly from the eating-table to his bed. He sat with a groan, nodded his dismissal. When she hesitated, seeing his illness, he waved her away, shouted in a high voice.

'Go! Go, Alia, quickly!'

The next day Alia washed his clothes as usual, and saw the stain of a dried emission encrusting part of the bishop's undershirt. She stared, incredulous and disgusted, her mind in a tumult. Even a bishop, she realised, raised so far above other men and even above the king, could not withstand his bodily appetites. He would be unclean until sunset today, although the Church would still permit him to administer the sacrament. A bishop was married to the Church, yet his bodily fluids had overflowed as surely as though he had lain with a whore. The force of the body was irresistible in men.

She prodded the stain briskly into the pail of washing-water with her stick. I am not a man, she told herself. A woman was permitted to receive the mystery of Communion even when unclean with her monthly courses, though it was not encouraged. Alia remembered the bishop reaching for her hair, how abruptly he had then drawn back. She gave a provocative little smile as she worked, amused.

Her breasts felt hot, and she imagined the bishop kissing her nipples.

Alia shocked herself. She clapped her hands to her cheeks, covered her bosom with her elbows. He was thirty years older than she.

If you do not have children, my child, you will lose your chance. You will be like me.

Alia thought about children. She thought about herself growing old, gnarling and bending inward on herself like her mother, her life withering inside her, thinking only of herself. Alia would die childless.

She thought about the gold. The gold did not matter. She thought about the writing, but she could not read. But children. Suddenly Alia saw herself as Rowan had seen her, a child growing into a young woman, her family growing round her, her children's children growing, her family living on when her own life passed away. She remembered Rowan fitting her hand inside the hand painted on the wall.

Alia tried to imagine life without children.

Rowan met her outside to walk her home in the dark. She could have run the distance to the cottage in a long breath, but her brother was her closest kin, responsible in law for her safety. For the same reason that it attracted trade, a church attracted thieves, harlots and scum, and a wooden stockade behind a thorn hedge was being built round the cathedral grounds to keep order. Bolts were fitted to the doors and a whipping-post set up for the correction of offenders, the merciful beatings charitably administered to save the wicked from hell-fire.

They walked in companionable silence, then Alia said decisively, 'Rowan, what happens to us when we die?'

Rowan knew the answer to that. 'We are reborn on the Day of Judgment.'

'I mean to our earthly bodies.'

'We are the earth, Alia.' The dog ran out of the cottage and licked his hand, tail wagging. 'We go on and on.'

'Then who should I marry?'

Rowan chuckled. 'Oswald the potter has always liked you, as you know. His son Osric will do whatever his father tells him.'

'Osric is strong,' Alia said. 'His teeth are good.'

Rowan agreed. 'And his sisters have all birthed strong children.'

Alia decided. 'You are my brother. You will have to do the talking for me.'

Rowan was alarmed by her impetuosity. 'But what about love?' he said.

Next morning Alia dressed in her cape that reached almost to the ground, though they could feel in the mist that it would be a hot day. She probed the grain stored in the sousterrain and pulled out a package wrapped in sacking. She put it under her cloak. Rowan walked with her.

They followed the crooked path downhill to Ludgate and came from the trees as the mist pulled back. The river wall bulked against the sky, its long length stained black at intervals from the smoke of villages that had grown up in its shelter. The culverts were unblocked and the drained marshes made fine market gardens. Cottagers tended beans, peas and lentils, and a few apple and pear trees grew in the cottage garths to shade the thatch dwellings. The City was not so much a town as a sprawling farm enclosed by the gigantic circuit of defensive wall. But no enemy had sailed up the Thames within English memory, Alia knew, and probably never would. Holes were battered through the river wall wherever it suited the fishermen to come through. The cathedral had built its own landing stage, St Paul's wharf, for the use of the growing number of clergy coming and going to Rochester, Canterbury, the great bishoprics in France, even as far as the greatest in Rome. A boat landed oysters for the bishop's table – Mellitus was no meatless British bishop, he ate in the Roman style, and anyway he did not regard oysters as meat – while the captain haggled with the bishop's proctor over the cargo of malt barley and rye he would receive in return.

Alia and Rowan came to the shanties by Ludgate. One of the tunnels beneath the gatehouse was blocked by rubbish but the other was wide enough to drive a cart through. The roof got lower as the road rose, thick with dirt, and Rowan complained as he bumped his head. King Sabert's laws decreed that Roman roads be kept clear of houses and trees, but now the City fell technically under ecclesiastical jurisdiction the legal position was uncertain. Since St Paul's was built and the Church took the City under its wing, and owned most of the surrounding lands, London had ceased to be like any other town of the English nation.

Alia and Rowan walked under the walls, then took the slippery pathway down to the River Fleet. A causeway had been thrown across London Fen, then a steep bridge of tree trunks for boats to pass under even at high tide. It was new, paid for by merchants beginning to trade with the City and the cathedral. Alia looked back. From the Fleet Bridge St Paul's looked like a thatched, ungainly beacon on its bald-topped hill.

Out here, along the Strand, was the real centre of London. The Strand was still famous for its dairy farms, but to English ears the Saxon words for dairy farm and port sounded the same. The farms still clustered along the crest of the fields, but London's port, in the Emporium, was where everyone gathered. It was the height of summer and boats were drawn up higgledy-piggledy on the sand, some of them smaller than a man, others with a crew and a hut on the back. The noise and smell of the shore, fish and mud and hot bodies, washed over Alia like a tide. Herds of animals lowed, barked, squealed or whinnied according to the nature God gave them. Sweating slaves pushed past Alia loading slaughtered carcasses packed in salt, straw for smoked bacon, then scampered the other way rolling barrels of oysters and the salted cod the Frisians called *bacalhau*. Come winter or a storm, all this activity would cease, frail and brief as the life of a gnat. But the weather had been fine and leather tanners worked in a mist of smoke and stench and bubbling cauldrons, scraping skins busily and hanging them out like clothes, shouting cheerful greetings to everyone whether they knew them or not. Alia thought she would be sick with the smell.

Tanneries had been thrown up on each side of Oswald's hut. Once this had been a prime piece of ground, a low well-drained gravel knuckle close to the river, yet sheltered by the higher land behind. Now the cauldrons blew their stink across his land whatever the wind, and he had no recourse in law. The tanners had cut down the trees to feed their fires, and the path was almost a street. Oswald worked outside to attract passing trade. He was a tall bald man, with black eyebrows, and they were drawn together. He looked sad.

'Good day, Oswald,' Rowan began.

'Fine weather,' Oswald said. He turned his pots on a turntable with expert flicks of his fingers, working the wet clay. 'Sorry to hear about your mother. Fine woman, she was.'

'Yes,' Rowan said. Alia had put about the story that Edna had drowned.

Oswald got breezily down to business. 'Well? What can I do you for?' The English liked this sort of conniving jocularity but Rowan did not know how to handle it.

'I'm giving away my sister,' he said awkwardly.

Oswald looked at Alia as if for the first time. 'And I thought you just wanted to haggle for a pot,' he bantered. He stilled, studied her alertly. 'You've grown up, you have. Wouldn't mind marrying you myself, I wouldn't.' He grunted, unsettled by her calm manner. 'So, young Osric, and Edna's girl. Well, I don't know. Are you a good girl? Good enough for my Osric? Is she intact?'

'I am a virgin,' Alia said.

'Good. Don't want my boy reaping where another man's sowed.' Oswald came to the point. 'What dowry did your ma leave you?'

Alia unwrapped the grail from the sacking. She placed the gold cup carefully on the turntable. It span in the sunlight, flashing. Oswald's eyes widened. He swore an oath to Thunor and snatched it out of sight before it was seen.

'By Thunor,' he repeated shakily, then scratched it with his fingernail, soft yellow metal, even softer and heavier than lead. Real gold.

'It's mine,' Alia said.

'Where'd you steal it?'

Rowan leant across the table. 'It's hers.'

'There's one condition,' Alia said. 'It will be a Christian marriage, properly recorded on tallies in the cathedral. My husband will live in the City. Rowan holds my mother's cottage, my husband will build a new cottage where I choose.'

The potter cleared his throat. She had named two or three conditions saying they were one, just like a woman. His eyes blinked yellow in reflection of the gold, then he shrugged. 'All right. I wouldn't wish this stinking place on anybody.' He bellowed over his shoulder, 'Osric!'

The youth who pushed the curtain aside was so handsome that Alia stirred. He was tall, with blond hair and his father's black eyebrows. So he'll lose his hair like his father, Alia thought.

'I remember your mother,' Osric said. He looked at Alia appreciatively. 'You're prettier than her.' Alia could see he was attracted to her, and that made him all the more attractive. She moved slightly and his eyes followed her.

'Don't be impolite, Osric,' his father said, and cuffed him with the back of his hand. Oswald tapped the grail, cleared his throat again. Osric's eyes widened and he reached out, but his father gripped the cup tightly to his belly. He spoke to Alia. 'You do know what this is worth?'

'No,' Rowan said.

Alia said, 'It's worth a husband.'

Oswald glanced at his handsome son. 'It's more than he's worth,' he muttered.

Mellitus had seen this a hundred times before. The English were an uncouth race, and he baptised Osric without delay. 'If I wait to offer him the mystery of redemption,' the bishop confided to Alia as his friend, 'it may be too late for him to be redeemed.' He sighed, because she was obviously incapable of seeing that Osric would cause her trouble and heartache. 'If they cannot contain, let them marry.' A priest was present, so it was proper for Mellitus to hold Alia's hand, and he did so, with a kindly light in his eyes. 'Why does a woman marry the man she does?'

'I want children,' Alia said.

Mellitus was touched by her simplicity. 'Then, if you are not moved by lust or a desire for pleasure, the union will be made in heaven.'

Rowan blurted, 'But she does not love him.'

'After I am married, I will love him through my children,' Alia said fiercely.

'She is too good for him!' Rowan exclaimed, but both men knew better than to try to change a woman's mind. Alia knew exactly why she was doing everything she did, but they did not. To them she was mysterious.

She pointed out the precise place she wanted her marriage cottage built, in a small elm glade near the bishop's ramshackle wooden palace – though a small stone hall, made of stonework plundered from old ruins, had recently been added – and since she was plainly determined, Osric shrugged his assent to whatever she wanted. He was too lazy to bother arguing with her, and anyway he'd already learnt if she didn't get what she wanted one way she got it another. 'She got me, didn't she?' he laughed, throwing back his long, fine blond hair. It was impossible for her to dislike a man who was so happy in himself, who liked himself so much.

Rowan helped Osric collect timber and thatch, interlacing branches to make neat walls, seeing something he needed in the shape of each tree. In fact Rowan ended up doing most of the work as Alia had known he would. The cottage had a traditional sunken floor, and when Osric was called away to his father's on business, which meant drinking with his friends or boating for fish on the river, Rowan dug the sousterrain in the usual place by the back wall. Alia inspected his work. 'Deeper,' she said.

Rowan looked at her sadly. The fishing trips of Osric and his friends were often accompanied by a girl or two. Osric thought Rowan was a fool and not a whole man, and so never asked for his company, but he often bragged of his exploits to make Rowan admire him.

Rowan said, 'Alia—'

'Deeper,' Alia said. She would not let him talk. Osric, a normal hot-blooded man, even in his absence was like a wall that had come between them.

'Rowan loves you!' Rowan said. 'Rowan cares for you. Rowan would die for you.' He gave her a suffering look. 'Not Osric!'

Alia ran to him, hugged him. 'Sshh,' she whispered. 'Dig deeper. Quick, before he returns.'

'They're never dug this deep,' Rowan grumbled. 'It makes too much work getting the last of the grain out every year—' He saw the look in her eyes and did as he was told. 'You won't see him again today,' he muttered, 'and tomorrow he'll be late because of his headache.'

Alia just smiled that small, secret, birdlike smile of hers.

She came back later. Rowan stood up to his head in the hole and she went down the makeshift ladder. Without a word she took his spade and stuck the iron shoe into the side of the sousterrain, worked her way slowly forward.

Rowan scratched his head. 'Why are you going so slowly?'

Alia looked furious, then laughed. 'Because I'm not as strong as you,' she puffed. 'Make sure he isn't coming.'

'Nobody digs them like this,' Rowan said when he came back. 'What are you going off to one side for? Nobody'll ever see it, I'm going to line it with boards like everyone does, to keep the mice and mould out.'

Alia stabbed with the spade, pushed through the wall of the sousterrain into the catacomb. She crawled through and pointed up at the heavy stone slab directly beneath the wall of the cottage, that formed the roof of the catacomb and the underside of the steps. 'Oh!' he said. 'Rowan wondered why you chose this place.'

'Exactly.' She jammed the mechanism with stones. It would never move again.

'Now Osric will never know,' she said intensely. 'Hide it with stones and earth. Stack boards in front of the place and fill it with grain.'

Alia sat in her doorway inhaling the smell of fresh wood. 'This is my house,' she said.

From where she sat she could see the cathedral through the trees. In a year its elm walls had weathered to dark gold, and the thatch was green with moss, black with damp. Already it looked ancient and permanent, as though it had stood here for ever. She grinned, seeing that the urchins who hung about the place, already called cathedral sparrows, had cheekily picked the bark from the massive tree trunks that supported each corner and the tower. Above the height a child could reach, the smooth peeled wood turned again to rough bark.

They would find some way of going higher, she knew, swaying from one another's shoulders or clinging to a pole, scattering with excited cries when a virger chased them.

For her wedding day Alia wove a garland of flowers for her head. The Church tolerated such pagan customs, weaving them into its own beliefs to let the minds of the English grow accustomed slowly to change. But Mellitus was not standing at the altar.

'Where's the bishop?' Rowan demanded.

The priest, Cuthbert, frowned at the interruption to his Latin. He was a gaunt, devout man who did not care for the English language in a holy place.

'Did you not know?' Cuthbert murmured, dominating them with his humility and yet his knowledge of far-off places. 'Mellitus has been called by God to impose on the British and Irish bishops the customs of the Universal Church. In Rome he will acquaint the Pope and the council of bishops of Italy with the affairs of the Church of the English.'

'Don't matter!' Osric called, then walked to Alia's side with great dignity. Not for the first time Alia realised he was most dignified when most drunk. Their hands were placed together, and they swore that they were not related by grandfather or great-grandfather, and they were married, and were one flesh in the sight of God.

Osric and his new wife walked back to their cottage with his friends and feasted and drank until everyone fell down, and then Osric closed the door of the bridal bower firmly in Rowan's face.

Rowan stepped over the snoring men and women and went back to his own cottage, where he milked the housecow and ewes, collected the hens' eggs, and lay quietly down to sleep alone among the animals.

'But she does not love him,' he whispered.

It was soon obvious that Osric, in the memorable phrase of the English, was all cock and crow. He was proud of his virility, and he shouted it out. Big happy Osric, outgoing, backslapping and surrounded by friends, was the one who came first to everyone's eye. His quiet wife in the background was ignored, a dutiful presence. Her long black hair, beautiful eyes and reserved manner made her a target for his cronies, but she was always faithful to Osric. When Osric dropped down drunk she turned his head so he did not choke. She listened loyally to Osric's bragging. When Osric's father died she consoled him. When Osric tore himself on the plough she bound his arm in the blood, and prayed for him, and the demons did not corrupt his flesh.

Rowan watched them while he worked in the field, and he could see Osric's cottage from his own. He visited his sister when Osric was fishing and they talked.

She came to the point. 'Why do you never come and talk to me when Osric is here?'

Rowan was embarrassed. 'Osric is so marvellous. Quick. Full of life. I can't keep up with him.' Rowan lied awkwardly. The truth was that Osric had told him to keep off.

Alia said decisively, 'I want to see you often.'

'But Osric—'

'I am with child,' she whispered, then smiled.

Rowan and a crone from the village by Westwatergate attended Alia's lying-in. The child was a boy, almost bald, but with fine blond strands. Rowan and Alia glanced at one another and both thought the same thing together, and both laughed together. 'Don't, it hurts,' Alia giggled, then they both looked at the baby again and broke out laughing. 'Looks just like his father!'

Osric came in. He pushed angrily past Rowan. 'What are you doing here? I won't have another man looking at my wife. It's disgusting!' When Rowan didn't understand, Osric's shouts took on a hard edge. 'Get out!'

'Osric, it's all right,' Alia murmured. 'He meant no harm.'

Osric snatched up his son and kicked the door closed behind Rowan.

Osric named his son Oscoifi, and his second son Osred. Rowan watched the boys play, but they were frightened of him because of what their father said. Osric doted on his sons, teaching them all he knew, often taking them fishing in his tiny coracle on the Sabbath, sometimes drifting on the tide's flow as far as Thorney Island and the tiny church in the trees there – not consecrated by Mellitus, as he had foreseen, but by one of his priests, Peter – and then the coracle would return gently on the ebb to Westwatergate or St Paul's wharf, the young boys curled asleep in their father's lap.

'You see, his sons are everything to him,' Alia murmured. 'He is a good father.'

Rowan turned her face towards him, her flesh purple with Osric's beatings. 'Yes. Rowan has seen him with them. Osric is a good father. But their mother—'

She smiled. 'I am with my third child.'

But this time the baby was a daughter. Osric sulked. A girl was a useless mouth, and would cling to her mother, and would have to be found a dowry. Alia named her girl Elwynne. 'Now you will have to work harder,' she told Osric.

He smacked her but this time Alia did not cover her face. She fell back with her children. 'Let them see,' she said.

'Quiet your noise,' he threatened, 'or I'll wipe your nose with this.' He showed his fist.

It was evening and the last of the sunlight barbed the cottage walls.

'Stop it,' Alia said. 'Get back to work. Weeds in the crop. Burrs in the hay.' Her cheek had swollen as though she held a mouthful of porridge. He gave her a smack on the other side to even her up.

'You go on and on and you never give me a chance!' he shouted. He raised his hands over his head to hit her again. The lines of hard living and anger made his face old. His baldness had started like a tonsure, and now his hair hung down in filmy veils over his ears and from the nape of his neck to his shoulders. Alia threw a pot at him. It broke. His sons shouted at him. Alia threw handfuls of straw, chaff, choking dust.

Osric stumbled outside roaring with anger. A shadow rose up in front of him.

Osric screamed in fear. He felt himself seized by the throat, lifted, pushed backwards against the wall of the cottage. He stared at the point of a *seax*, razor-sharp, that came towards his eyes. He was so terrified that he could not cry louder than a girlish whisper.

Rowan rested the tip of the *seax* between Osric's eyes. Osric wept. He begged. The point pricked the skin and a thread of blood crept down the ridge of his nose. The most frightening thing was that Rowan said nothing, nothing at all. It was getting dark. Then Rowan spoke.

'Rowan says, be a good husband.'

Osric dropped to the ground. He curled up.

Rowan slipped his *seax* cheerfully through his belt and offered Osric his hand, pulled him to his feet. 'Rowan will help you pull the weeds.' He clapped his hand to Osric's back, and the two men walked downhill. 'We can get the top end of the field done before night . . .'

Alia watched them. The two boys ran after their father, instinctively understanding him, and she knew they had forgiven him already. They would grow up like him. Alia held little Elwynne in her arms, and the girl's eyes followed their movements through the twilight. She too was watching.

'I have you,' Alia whispered. 'I have my daughter.'

When she was old enough to walk, the growing child often accompanied Alia to the bishop's palace. Bishop Mellitus had long ago returned from Rome, where at the Pope's command he headed the council drawing up regulations for monastic life and discipline, and he was spoken of as the next Archbishop of Canterbury. But his clothes still needed washing. When he had time Mellitus liked to talk to Alia at his fireside. 'Alia?' She jerked, staring at the fire. 'Sometimes I wonder, Alia, what you are thinking.'

It was a cold afternoon, the last day of February. 'I'm sure I was not thinking about much at all, your grace.'

'Your face does not tell me. You women are masters of disguise, you know.'

'I'm sure we don't mean it, your grace.'

'Tell me the truth, now,' the bishop scolded her with a smile, and his eyes twinkled beneath his white hair. 'What were you really thinking?'

Elwynne played behind his chair, not understanding a word.

'The truth?' Alia drew a breath. The bishop's window had glass in it, curvy and ripply to be sure, but she could just make out the snowy shape of the cathedral. 'The truth is, I was thinking that I still feel that God is far more wonderful than you know.' She added, 'With respect, your grace.'

But Mellitus hardly heard her. He had seen something moving in the glass. It was the shape of a running man. 'What's this?'

Father Peter burst into the room. Snow speckled his shoulders and pink head.

'King Sabert is dead!'

Mellitus looked wary and thoughtful. Then he relaxed. 'It makes no difference. We knew this moment must come. We remain under King Athelbert's protection.'

'You mean they did not tell you?' Peter wrung his hands. 'One of the cathedral sparrows found me in prayer at Thorney Island! I have run all the way. The word came from Kent. King Athelbert has been dead a week and is in the ground.'

The bishop limped to the window. His gout was troubling him, but he remained calm. 'All is not lost. The succession—'

Peter said flatly, 'Athelbert's son has already declared himself king and married his mother according to pagan rites.'

'This cannot be true.' Mellitus groped for his chair. He came to a decision. 'Call my servant. Bring me my shoes.'

The priest cried, 'Don't you understand? Your servants have fled. Everyone is gone. They're running for their lives, and urchins and thieves are ransacking the kitchen and stealing everything they can pick up or tear down—'

'Calm yourself,' Mellitus said. 'Alia, kindly bring my robes. I shall go to the *bur* of King Sabert and pray for his soul.'

Peter shouted, 'It's not King Sabert now, it's King Sexred, and he's already married his mother the queen and she never was a Christian, she's behind this, and if Sexred doesn't cut your throat his brothers will – they say you bewitched the king with magical spells—'

Mellitus said, 'Then I shall go to the cathedral and offer solemn mass there. They won't dare make trouble in God's house. You will accompany me.'

The priest backed to the door, eyes staring, then turned and ran. 'Peter!'

There was no reply. He would not stop running until he got to London Bridge.

Bishop Mellitus reached out to Alia. His hand shook. He was pale as death, but his voice was firm.

'Alia, will you help me?'

Alia fetched his cassock and *pallium*. She brought his stout shoes, knowing the snow was deep, and helped Mellitus dress himself in the substantial pomp of Rome that the British found so offensive. 'I will not give one inch,' Mellitus said. 'God is with me.' But still, Alia saw, his hand shook. She lifted Elwynne on to her hip and accompanied the bishop through the snow to the cathedral. As they went between the cathedral doors she looked down the pale slope of Lud's Hill to the black river below, bare of boats.

At first she thought the cathedral was empty. Then she saw a priest with one hand guarding the altar. This man was the red-headed acolyte she remembered from the day of Mellitus's arrival. He grinned, and she knew he recognised her. 'The alpha and the omega,' he bowed to her. 'You are fated to be here at the beginning and the end, it appears.'

'Our congregation seem to have deserted us,' Mellitus said. 'Is your faith strong, brother?'

'Prayer is my sword.' The priest held up the stump of his wrist.

Bishop Mellitus coughed. His coughs echoed. 'Let us celebrate mass, and our congregation will come.'

But the congregation did not come. Instead a low murmur grew beyond the cathedral walls, then shouts, and the flames of blazing torches. 'It seems the news from Kent has reached the City of St Paul.' Mellitus continued to speak, but his voice was drowned. A crowd shoved through the doorway, poured along the nave, men with firelight glittering on their swords. Elwynne began to cry. Alia stepped back to the rear wall of the cathedral, quieting her, felt the wood hard against her shoulderblades.

King Sexred pushed through the throng. He shouted at Mellitus. 'Give us the bread!'

The bishop continued to speak mass quietly.

'It made our father Saba strong!' Saeward shouted, standing in front of his brother to shield him from the bishop's magic. 'Give it to us!'

Mellitus looked up. 'If you will be baptised—'

'We won't!' the youngest brother shouted.

King Sexred shouted, 'Give me the white bread!'

Mellitus stood firm. 'If you reject the Water of Life, you cannot accept the Bread of Life.'

The three brothers shoved forward. They drew their swords in the cathedral and there was a clanging all round the walls as their followers did the same.

'Take care,' Mellitus warned, 'lest God strike you down and in His wrath He shall strike down your halls and He shall rot your flesh in His damnation eternal, and He shall condemn your wives and your children to cursing your names and wailing and suffering and their souls burning in the fiery furnace of Hell for ever.'

The men threw their torches against the walls, and smoke poured up.

'Stop!' Mellitus cried.

King Sexred and his brothers seized the altar. 'What is not given us, we take.' They grabbed the silver grail-platter and pushed the dry bread into their open mouths, and men running after them did the same, and the altar went over with a crash. Everyone started fighting for the bread across the dirt floor.

Alia felt a door behind her. She ran outside. The air swirled with smoke. The priest and Mellitus, his *pallium* flapping over his head, lifted their skirts and ran out past her. Alia picked up the *pallium* but they were gone.

The cathedral was burning in the snow. The timbers creaked, then the heavy stone cross plummeted through the roof in a roar of sparks.

'Alia. Alia.' Rowan found her sitting by a tree. The flames rose almost as high as the trees. He took Elwynne gently in his arms, and found she was asleep.

Many years passed, enough to last a lifetime.

'One day,' Alia had said as she walked among the smouldering, blackened timbers that first morning, 'one day they will come back, and the cathedral will rise again.'

She closed the gate in the hedge, and thorns grew over the gate.

She waited for Bishop Mellitus to return to the City. Sometimes she heard that he was alive. There was little trade even on the Strand nowadays, but a Frisian trader had heard of him in France. The pagan King of Kent was said to have repented and been baptised, but the people of London, guided by the priests of the gods of this world, refused to allow Mellitus to return. A travelling priest told Alia that the old man, so crippled with gout that he could no longer walk, had been consecrated Archbishop of Canterbury, and years later, when Elwynne was a young woman choosing her husband, Alia heard that he had died.

Elwynne, too, gave birth to two sons and a daughter, and Osric died, and Rowan married a buxom big-hearted West Saxon woman who'd had her own children and loved him with hugs.

Each Christmas Day Alia walked to the top of the hill. The Bishop of Winchester, expelled from that city, had purchased the bishopric of London but done nothing. Each year Alia came to the impenetrable tangle of thorns. Without the cathedral's trade, the London Emporium and St Martin-in-the-fields flourished. Each Christmas Day she returned carrying the same package on her arms, and waited from dawn until sunset.

Slowly, together with Christianity, wealth began to flow back into the City. Each year she heard workmen's hammers in the frosty air, knocking at the old forum on Corn Hill for stones for one or two new buildings, the grandest of them standing with two storeys and roofs of wooden shingles among the thatch cottages. And gradually the ragged rows of cottages straggling along old Roman roads became streets running from nowhere to nowhere, and the pathways winding through the woods became lanes without beginning or end.

Alia saw her grandchildren born, and she saw the plague come to London. The plague was a time of miracles, and monk-kings, and nuns returned to the ancient Christian monastery by the City wall at Barking. Alia saw their smoke rising beyond the curve of Corn Hill. But that was not what she was looking for.

Still she watched, and waited.

Each Christmas Day she rubbed at the white patches on her hands, but it was only the cold.

I'm old, she realised, but I feel the same as when I was young.

Alia walked to the hilltop with Ebba, her great-granddaughter. The girl was so young and vibrant that she moved almost too fast to see, a flash of rosy cheeks and bright blue eyes. Alia pursed her lips and nodded, remembering.

'Now?' Ebba laughed, and Alia realised that time had passed while she stood witless in the doorway of her grandson's house. 'Now,' Alia said, and the young thing whizzed around her laughing and chirping, and Alia gave up the package wrapped in a faded piece of silk that she held in her left hand. 'Careful. I remember . . .' And she did remember buying that piece of silk from a trader in the Emporium, when she was young. She remembered everything as clearly in her mind as though she were still there, and felt how hot the sun had been in those days. 'I do remember.'

Ebba took the package in her left hand, and her right arm supported her grandmother. The walk to the snowy hilltop, that once Alia had run in a few breaths, was now very hard, very long, very cold.

'One day,' she quavered, 'one day they will come back, and the cathedral will rise again.'

'One day?' Ebba laughed, and pointed. 'They're back already!'

Monks filed on to the hilltop, tonsured heads bowed, and gathered in prayer at the thorn hedge. Two monks led a horse uphill, and two monks followed behind. In the bumping litter dragged by the horse lay a man.

The monks stopped the horse by the hedge, and helped the man who lay in the litter to his feet. He was tall, and very sick, but his eyes blazed with strength. He saw Alia at once. 'Who are you?'

'I am Alia.'

He stepped towards her, supported by monks. 'I am Erconwald, a prince of Kent. By the grace of God, by Archbishop Theodore, I am consecrated Bishop of London to raise a cathedral of stone near this place.'

'This is your place,' Alia said. 'This is St Paul's.'

'No, my cathedral will be dedicated to the Apostle to the Gentiles.'

Alia smiled. 'He is St Paul. Your cathedral is St Paul's.'

Erconwald studied her. 'You are a Christian.'

'For seventy years.' Alia turned to Ebba. 'Child.'

Ebba held out the package.

Alia took it on her arms. She tried to curtsey, then presented it to Erconwald. He examined the wrapping, not understanding. 'This is silk?'

'Look inside.'

The monks shouted. One of them had stumbled against the hedge, and a gate creaked open behind it, then fell from its broken hinges. The monks pulled at the hedge, revealing undergrowth beyond like a secret garden, a few weathered stumps of burnt timber, a stone cross.

Erconwald looked back to the package in his hands. He unwrapped it and held up a white lambswool cape marked with four crosses, one shoulder still streaked with soot.

'That is the *pallium* of the first Bishop of London,' Alia said. 'You are the second.'

Erconwald looked from her to the *pallium*.

'I shall wear it with pride.'

He looked round as workmen toiled up the hill, stonemasons, carpenters, adzemen and sawmen, chisellers and shapers, gougers and drillers, a smith and a kilnmaster.

'Here,' Erconwald called them. 'Here is the place.'

Alia let Ebba lead her home. No one was there, taking advantage of the few hours of winter daylight to work in the fields. Alia settled herself by Elwynne's hearth. Her bones felt very old. With an effort she flapped aside the mat that covered the boards of the sousterrain. Last year had been a poor harvest, and it was more than half empty.

Ebba was worried. 'What is it? Are you ill?'

Alia reached forward, touched the child's supple skin. Ebba's cheeks were flushed, her young body quivered with life. She moved like lightning, bringing a stool for Alia to sit on, a bowl of broth to warm her.

Alia caught her to make her still, stroked the blonde hair out of the child's blue eyes. She pointed at the sousterrain.

'The boards on the right, child, nearly underneath the wall. Lift them out carefully, carefully.'

'But—'

'Do as I say.'

Ebba laughed, not understanding, and Alia was sad. These were the last carefree moments of the child's life.

'There is something I will tell you, child. There is more than you know.'

Part Three

Edith

London, St Valentine's Day 888 AD

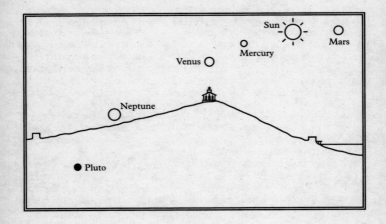

St Valentine's Day, AD 888

Wolf saw her first.

He was sixteen years old, and he saw her long before she saw him. He knew her name long before she knew his, knew her tragic story from years ago, when they were children. Wolf had loved her all his life. The sight of her always struck him dumb like an intoxication, empty inside, dull as a cracked bell without her. His stepfather, who used him as an apprentice, had already arranged a good marriage and the dowry would pay for the new tools. Because he could never have the girl he loved, Wolf pretended not to notice her. Whenever she was near he let his friends talk while he was silent, and she hardly seemed to notice him, and he pretended he didn't care about her. He forced his eyes not to see her.

But she was all he saw.

Hiding behind the baker's house in the still, snowy morning, he watched her walk from her uncle's house to the cathedral. Then from the cathedral she turned downhill towards Carter Lane, coming closer.

He ran away on silent footsteps. He would be busy when she saw him.

The night was endless. Edith woke for the hundredth time. She touched the heat of her left breast as gently and earnestly as if she touched her own heart, felt the painful outline scrawled on her flesh.

Her straw mat rustled loudly as she sat up. She listened, motionless, the back of her hand rising to her mouth, hardly daring to breathe. On the other side of the wattle half-wall that divided the cottage and gave her a measure of privacy, her uncle's snores stopped.

He grunted as he turned over, then his snores began again.

Shivering, Edith lifted aside the thin blanket that covered her. Holding her breath, she rolled on to her knees on the dirt floor. Beyond the window, barred to keep out thieves – this had once been her mother's house – the poorly fitting night-shutters revealed the first line of dawn, so faint that the mist of her breath obscured it in the bitter cold. Nearly dawn. Nearly time.

Edith felt in the dark, put her hand flawlessly on the clay lamp she had placed so carefully last night. Before she stood, she took a moment for prayer.

Dear God, giver of all good things, do not let my uncle, dear kind man though he is, and full of peace, be the first man I see today. Make him sleep this morning! Though I love him almost like a father, this is the most important day of my life.

In return she promised God a King Alfred penny for the offertory after the creed, and she thought of promising Him anything He demanded of her in a sign – a dozen *Aves* for seeing a flock of a dozen birds, for example. Then she drew back with typical caution, wary of promising too much. Londoners' most hectic and extravagant prayers, their pleas and promises against fire and sword, had not stopped the Vikings. Even Bishop Swithwulf's shouted excommunications were meaningless to the raiders. Edith's father was spreadeagled on Paul's Cross, his breastbone split with a blow of the axe, his living ribs pulled open to make the Blood Eagle, a warning to others not to hide their money from the invaders. Edith's two brothers were killed with axes, her elder sisters and her younger sisters who ran screaming in the street were raped and put either to the blade or under the hammer, sold as slaves. Edith had never seen them again and would not recognise them if she did.

Edith and her mother had hidden, and Mother had not died that day.

In those days, God had almost broken the English despite their prayers.

Edith covered her eyes so she would not glimpse her uncle by mistake. She reached around the half-wall, touched the mouth of the lamp to the embers of the fire. One of the dogs whined, licked her hand affectionately, gave her its paw to hold.

'Down, Tawny. Down, boy,' she whispered. She averted her eyes even from the male dog.

Hiding the yellow flame behind her hand, Edith withdrew behind the screen. A girl would be wisest and warmest to wear sheepskin boots and greasy woollen knee-length tunic and leggings on such a day, but then she would not be treated like a lady. Edith pulled off her smock, touched the pale curve of her bare left breast over her heart.

She had written his name there. The sharpened quill had scored her flesh.

Wolf.

Edith pulled on Aunt Winifrid's linen shift over her head, then the dyed light blue gown, once the bishop's property no doubt, that reached almost to the ground. The clothes worn by men and women were almost identical. The patches were of slightly different shades but that would not show under the cape. She stroked her cheeks to make them bloom, spat to clean her mouth. She took the tiny bronze mirror in her left hand, held it in the lamplight. What would a man see when he looked at her? Her eyes set wide apart, deep blue with the pupils inclined towards the inner corners, adding to the catlike intensity of her gaze. She brightened her fierce concentration with a smile, took the horn comb and swept back her hair, which was even longer than a man's. Her mother's hair had been almost pure blonde, but long black strands grew in Edith's, more each year.

A man must be made of stone not to notice her now.

For the first time in her life, Edith put on the headband and veil her mother wore the day she was wed. A veil was the sign of a great lady or a nun, the symbol of chastity. For a common orphan girl of no rank to claim the veil on any but her wedding day was an outrageous presumption. Great humility was expected of women, and under Wessex law even King Alfred's own wife could not call herself his queen.

But today was different. Today was St Valentine's Day.

The first man Edith saw today would be her Valentine, and if it was God's will their names would be drawn together in the lottery, and they would be bound in companionship for as long as the festivities lasted. It was the only way a girl with no dowry except a hovel might catch a respectable husband, their union blessed by God's dice.

Everyone knew that even the birds in the air found their mates on St Valentine's Day, and many witnesses attested to that fact.

Edith blew out the lamp and moved silently to the door. The walls were thin but the door was heavy to stop criminals breaking in. When the hinges creaked Uncle Benedict's snores stopped.

Aunt Winifrid, Mother's younger sister with no child of her own, stirred on her mat by the fire. She sat up and whispered, 'Good fortune be with you, dear Edith!'

Uncle Benedict woke beside her. 'Wha'? Cock-crow already, it's not?'

'She's gone, sweet husband,' Winifrid murmured, rolling into him, and her hand behind her back gestured to Edith, go!

Edith closed her eyes tight. She slipped outside quickly, and closed the door behind her with a gasp of relief.

The street was empty. The mud was frozen, the wheel-ruts more than a foot deep, hard as grey iron. Edith walked head down lest she see anyone, her shoes crunching on the frost. A cart, stuck to the wheel-hubs, stood abandoned where it froze. The snowy cottages and conventual buildings, both public and private, and the infirmary with its single tiny window, looked like loaves of white bread. Over the pointed stakes of the stockade rose the snow-heavy roof of Bishop Heastan's wooden palace and the outhouses and guesthouses that sloped against it for support, and the longhouses around it.

Above the bishop's roof loomed St Paul's Cathedral, pale as a ghost in the dawn. Edith supposed it had always stood here just as it was, but for a moment its walls of stone and brick, the rows of thin round-headed windows and massive, blunt-headed thatched tower, the weathered stone cross above the narthex at the western end, seemed to quiver as though insubstantial as a dream.

She realised she was looking through the heat rising from the baker's furnace. As she walked past the side chapels he called out a good morning. She called back cheerfully but blinkered her eye so that she did not see him. 'You're my Valentine, you know!' the fat baker called out in his rollicking, jolly voice.

'You and your seven children,' Edith called. The first fans of sunlight illuminated the sky above the cathedral. It was the hour of Prime and a flock of rooks spilled from the tower, circled higher to catch the sunlight. Seven rooks. What sign could that be? That she could expect seven children?

The baker's merry laugh followed her down the street. 'Oh, *my* wife wouldn't mind a rest from me. Three babes in the last three years. I'm not married today, how about that? It'll be me who draws your name from the box, I'll be young again and slim as I was, don't you worry . . .'

Edith passed out of earshot and he watched her from sight, then tended his oven. Festivals were busy days, and people drawn to the cathedral from all over the City for the lottery would pay money for bread, not barter like the locals. And his wife expecting their eighth child, babes following times of prosperity as surely as day followed night . . .

Edith glanced up as the eastern end of the cathedral, the rounded apse, was touched by sunlight. Crossing the hedges and ditches that bounded the lands held by various lords, she turned downhill to Carter Lane. In the three years since the Vikings were thrown out of London by King Alfred, the Christian God was praised again and it was safe to walk even between the villages. With law and order came trade, started off by the public *burhworks* of the king and the City's aldermen. With the Strand settlements and the marketplaces of the London Emporium devastated, their people slaughtered, trade was moved within the City walls. Teams of men owing *burhwork* to the king walked from Harrow, Stanmore, Edgware, from the great lookout mound dominating the Thames at Tothill, the islands of Fulham and Eia and Thorney and from many hides and villages further afield, and needed housing while they worked at rebuilding the defences of the City. Blacksmiths arrived to forge iron spadeshoes, hammerheads, adzes and axeheads. Butchers, bakers and fish-sellers set up stalls near the camps. The ditches being dug or cleaned out in front of the City walls required carts to move the soil, so in Carter Lane heavy cartwheels were hammered together from slabs of oak, carpenters turned hubs and axles, sawmen cut planks and men with drawknives smoothed them. Oxen were needed to pull the carts, so for the first time an ox cost more than three slaves.

But today was St Valentine's Day, and Carter Lane was silent and still. Only a single line of footprints in the snow, widely spaced as though made by a running man, crossed in front of Edith. She saw no one. The footprints ran ahead of her as though leading her forward, zigzagging between the half-finished carts and baulks of cart-timber along the street.

She turned the corner into Paul's Wharf Lane. The footprints skidded and there was the outline of a hand in the snow where the runner had slipped, recovered. Paul's Wharf Lane dropped down Lud's Hill towards the river. The slope was steep and perhaps once, by unimaginable labour, was bordered by level terraces, now blunted by time, but still cottages clung to the lines of flatter ground. All but the last few stands of trees had been cut down for firewood or blacksmiths' forges, and by the charcoal-burners whose smouldering turf mounds blew smoke and steam across the snow.

The footprints ran in front of her, skidded again, then disappeared between two cottages.

Edith walked slowly, heard the busy snicker of a blade starting on wood. She came towards the corner of the cottage, hesitated, then took a long step forward past the wall.

She saw him.

Wolf was almost fully grown, a little over five feet tall, so he would be taller than she when he stood. He sat in the yard behind the low wattle fence, pulling the drawknife carefully along a plank of wood, working on the frame of a wagon. Edith knew everything about him, just as she knew everything about his work – St Peter's Minster on Thorney Island was permitted seventy wagonloads of firewood each twelvemonth from the parish of St Mary of the Holy Innocents on the Strand, and the priests required a new wagon. Wolf's stepfather Hewald was one of the few carpenters skilled and conscientious enough to attempt the heavy four-wheeled wagons with all the difficulties of suspending, pivoting and steering the front wheels. Hewald was a cold, withdrawn, resourceful man who lived for his work, all his love going into the wood. Wood came to life in his hands. But Edith hated him because he made Wolf unhappy. She could see, by Wolf's meticulous pulling of the drawknife, by the way he would not look at her, pretending to concentrate on his work, how unhappy he was, and her heart went out to him.

Edith spoke bravely.

'You are the first boy I have seen today.'

Wolf stopped the drawknife. He swallowed. His face was pale with cold except that his cheeks bloomed from his exertions. His eyes were blue, deep and sensitive, gorgeous.

He would not look at her, but took her in with small glances from the corners of his eyes.

She put back her veil, revealing her face, her frank gaze. He said nothing.

'Are you shy?' she blurted, intensely disappointed by his timidity.

He coloured, returned her direct look. 'You are the first girl I saw today, Edith.'

'On St Valentine's Day.'

Now that he had started the words tumbled out of him. 'I looked for you!' he confessed. She smiled, her spirits lifting as he went on. He knew who she was, she was not alone. 'Edith, daughter of Wyn and his wife Hild—'

She said, 'Wolf, son of—' Edith stopped, appalled by her blunder. The man who would have been Wolf's father had been drowned by the Vikings and it was possible Wolf was a rape-child, though his mother had always denied her shame. But she was dead now.

The occupation had lasted more than ten years, and everyone had something to hide.

Edith said gently, 'Wolf, child of God's mercy.'

His sad expression changed. His eyes gleamed, he filled himself with the look of her in the first rays of the sun. He leant towards her over the fence.

A door creaked behind the cottage.

'I shall be with you!' he whispered urgently. 'I shall pray for the chance—'

'I shall pray that you are the one—'

'Yes, as shall I!'

'Wolf shall be the only man I see.'

Edith heard footsteps coming round the side of the cottage. Her fingertips brushed Wolf's face, and he was hot as a fire.

He whispered, 'We are the same. You and I.'

'I shall see you there!' she whispered, and fled.

She ran downhill, blind. He loves me, she thought. She pressed her fingertips that had touched him to her lips. Everything in the world is good!

A workman shovelling stones by the river wall eyed her and shouted something crude. She didn't care. Now the marshland built up behind the river wall was thoroughly drained, the old Roman military road had reappeared, called Thames Street. Down here a lady's veil and clothes attracted attention and catcalls. She made signs and crossed between the piles of slag behind the smithies' roaring furnaces, climbed the steps to the wall. She imagined Wolf following her, he could not take his eyes off her, he pushed between the workmen hardly seeing them, only her.

On top of the wall the sun rose in Edith's face. The river was a blinding sheen and in the distance the palisades of London Bridge, newly repaired and fortified, hung like a skeleton between the river and the sky.

She turned, but did not see him.

His stepfather, she realised, had deliberately made him stay back to work. He worked Wolf too hard.

Edith walked. The king had introduced time, with candles a man's foot in length made to burn an inch every hour, so that the wages of craftsmen could be regulated by hours of equal length, and so that monks knew the hour of their prayers and would not displease God

206

by lateness. But the monks insisted that God must be worshipped according to a calendar of hours of length varying between summer and winter. Everyone counted the hours in a different way. Edith must meet the girls like herself on London Bridge not more than an hour after dawn, but dawn was timed from St Paul's, closer to God, not from down here by the river where the sun rose later. Edith was afraid she would be late. She hurried.

Wolf would be waiting at St Paul's. His would be the only face she saw, she knew. She had promised.

She stumbled where the road along the top of the wall sagged. Extra courses of stone had been laid, and in places the battlements were made of timber until stone could be found. Elsewhere the gaps were plugged with rubble and grey mortar. Edith bent to rub her ankle and for a moment she was a young child here, holding earnestly to the keep-rope tied to her mother's knee, the day the Viking longships came.

The ships, hundreds of them, rowed slowly on the tide past the river walls of London, no bridge to stop them, and she had thought how beautiful they were with their dragons' heads and ranks of shields, and not understood the terror she saw all round her. The Vikings beached their 'dragons' on the Strand and plundered and burnt the old port as they had before, but this time they could not take hostages because of the panic, and they cut down every man, every woman, every child running towards the walls of the City. At first it seemed the prayers of the Londoners and Bishop Swithwulf were blessed and that the Sword of St Paul and the Angels of God would smite the invaders. On a bier adorned with lemons and roses, as though He had just died, priests carried the waxen effigy of the dead Christ from St Paul's through the streets, where the crowd thronged forward and covered it with kisses. The Vikings fell back from Ludgate and Newgate, were thrown down the slope, drowned in the Fleet by the weight of their battleaxes that they would die rather than relinquish, and the water floated with a brown scum of blood.

Edith looked across the Thames and the islands, smelling the wet tide and mud and gravel, remembering.

The dragons drifted downstream in defeat, then the drums roared and the oars plunged into the water, pulling for shore. The high prows of the dragons nosed towards every weakness in the wall, rode up over the beaches and burning wharfs, and in the smoke came the warriors. The smoke blew over the City, and silence did not fall all day, or all night, or all the next day, while Edith hid with her mother in the dark.

Mother had whispered, 'It was like this in your grandmother's day, the first time the Vikings burnt London. Nothing changes.'

Edith shielded her eyes from the sun. The other girls, skipping and jumping on the bridge, clapped their hands excitedly and shouted

207

for her to hurry. She ran across the timbers and the wagoner flicked his whip impatiently. Behind the wattle stock-fence the five girls greeted her, laughing for joy to be chosen on St Valentine's Day, poor orphans like herself picked for their virtue, girls of each shape and size draped in every sort of clothing and one in rags, one girl with straw still clinging to her hair, a lumpy girl with saucy eyes, a thin downcast girl lost in some private misery, a girl with sheepskin boots kicking snow in her excitement, and Edith in her robe.

A man wearing a dyed cloak kept an eye on them, penned where they were like animals, knocking back young men who grabbed squeezes or stole kisses. 'Enough of that!' he said. A priest knelt in front of the oxen praying. Over the side of the bridge hung the cage where a woman guilty of murder drowned as the tide rose. By the rope knotted to the railing a group of hearty witnesses and an official gathered and watched the girls, grinning and choosing their favourites, shaking their heads at the others' choices. A red-faced toothless man pointed at Edith. 'Wearing the veil to hide her face!' She must be ugly and they condemned her unanimously. 'So ugly you'd kiss the wrong end by mistake!' they decided. An old woman passing scolded their fat bellies and dull wits. The priest said, 'Amen.'

The sun rose above the spars that operated the drawbridge, and the girls were shepherded into the wagon. It set off, rattling between the fish-sellers and pigmen of Belinos's Gate, past the king's Custom House and the royal wharf, where sweating men unloaded barrels of wine and boxes of saintly relics, past the hall where the moneyers worked. This was the richest and most populous quarter of the City and the girls clung to the bars, looking out for husbands, showing off and catching if they could the snowdrops, 'Mary's Tapers', that elder women threw as reminders of purity. One young girl wove a garland in her hair, unconcerned by the jolting of the vehicle, then glanced at Edith and smiled. Guards jogged alongside, knocking with sticks at the crowd of youths and boys and yapping dogs who ran after them. In old times the St Valentine's procession took in every church in the City, and now the Vikings were gone the Church was determined to re-establish its grip. From All Hallows in Barking to St Ethelburga's at Bishopsgate the priest hung on beside the driver, trying to add dignity to the gaiety. The wagon bumped along the intervals of street that accompanied each clump of houses and the market stalls round the churches, toiled up Corn Hill, made a circuit of the gigantic headless pillars of the forum and St Peter Cornhill, bumped down the other side with the priest clinging to his seat. The driver missed some of the many tiny private timber churches and was called back angrily, then the cart bumped up from the Walbrook valley on the strip of Roman road, turned between the trees along Wood Street and lurched on the track round the tiny ancient church of St Alban where, by legend, a king's palace once stood.

King Alfred's new wooden palace, of course, was built on the hill beside St Paul's Cathedral, making visible the king's closeness to God. The cart rattled among the people milling on the cow pasture, the Folkmoot where the people of London gathered for civic meetings. By the north wall of the cathedral the Vikings had pulled down the stone cross from the roof and planted it in the soil. Here they crucified their victims, or shot arrows into them, or split them in Blood Eagles, each way of death more savage than the last. Edith closed her eyes. Here her father died, and she heard his screams still, drifting down through the earth to her hiding place.

The Vikings, believing in the family of their own gods, killed the priests but did not burn the cathedral, which they decorated with herbs and charms to Woden, and fierce idols of their great father. Any cathedral or church was a *terribilis locus*, a place to strike awe, a replica of heaven. But monasteries, monks and priests were put to fire and sword.

When the Vikings were gone the stone cross was re-blessed by the new bishop and, once more ineffable and divine, was hoisted back on the cathedral roof. But the circle of bloody earth was still called Paul's Cross.

The wagon lurched round the western front of the cathedral and halted at the foot of the porch. By popular tradition common people called this ground the baptistry, and it was paved with gold long buried beneath the deep mud trodden across it by devout feet. Nowadays, except on White Sunday, baptisms were performed within the cathedral, so the priests called this open square the atrium.

The atrium was thick with people, so many people that a fog rose above them in the cold air. The common people shoved forward between the cottages, clergy houses and stalls on three sides of the square, flowed round the bishop's palace behind its high palisade south of the cathedral and the king's palace to the north. Edith looked for Wolf but all she saw were eyes looking at her body, gauging the size of her breasts and her warmth of heart. Sellers hawked beer, hot chestnuts and chops, dogs snarled over the bones. Children played catch-he on the cathedral steps and a canon lashed out smartly with his wand, putting a stop to the silliness.

In the chaos and brutality of the preceding years the festival had turned into a kind of foxhunt after the chosen girls. Now a grim-faced priest who could write vernacular, his fingers inky and his lips red with cold, took down the names of hopeful lads on slips of torn paper. Wolf was not among them. Perhaps he had arrived earlier, but still she did not see him in the crowd. Then Edith noticed that this year most young hopefuls were being turned away by the priest, and angry mutterings started because of the cathedral authorities' new rule of seriousness and virtue. No one who had missed a service of Sabbath worship since the last St Valentine's Day was allowed through. Several gangs of youths pushed through the crowd then stormed off shouting it was no fun. She noticed Father Daniel watching quietly and he acknowledged her with a small nod. During the slaughter of priests Mother had taken him into her cottage until he could escape to Winchester. A quiet, bookish, celibate man made remote by his calling, he could never be kin. Yet she thought of him as kith, like a very distant well-intentioned uncle, and she suspected it was by Father Daniel's recommendation her name was in St Valentine's box as a girl of godliness and virtue.

Father Daniel bowed his head in prayer, and sank back into the shadows.

Bishop Heastan strode on to the cathedral porch. He stood on the top step, a stocky man with the high aquiline beak of all King Alfred's kin, glorious in costly purple, sublime with shining silver and gold, metals precious because closest to God. His use of them and his power over the sacred ceremonies of the Church elevated him above other men. A bishop was no longer a man for he had endured the sacrifice of consecration, the symbolic death that transformed him visibly into God's earl. No undyed goats' wool habits such as the British monks wore for the Bishop of London, no wooden plates or cheap copper candle-holders for St Paul's. Like nearly all bishops Heastan was a nobleman born to power, and his diocese controlled immense and growing estates north of the river, though as a matter of practical politics the south bank was now ceded to the Bishop of Winchester and Lambeth was snapped up by the Archbishop of Canterbury. 'Get on with it,' Edith overheard the bishop grumble at his archdeacon. 'I'm cold.'

The girls were tugged out of the wagon and pushed along the step below him. Heastan preached to the crowd while the porch-candle in its huge gold candlestick burned down by an inch. In the atrium the hard frost melted under the weight and warmth of all the people. A woman fainted, a pregnant girl was harried away, unclean because close to childbirth. Male babies older than thirty-three days, and girl babies older than sixty-six days, were permitted into the vicinity of the cathedral. Many families brought a nursemaid with them, an infant guzzling on her breast, since few men suffered the Church's edict and slept apart from their fathers' wives until the child was weaned. Toddlers were lifted on their fathers' shoulders, put down again when they grew too heavy. Junior clergy round the edges made sure no one slept, others at the front held the crowd back from the steps with cracks of the rod. Edith searched the crush of faces anxiously for Wolf, his particular expression that she could have picked out from a thousand faces, his fine pale cold complexion and rosy cheeks, his lovely eyes, the quiet tenseness of his look resting on her.

Nothing. Edith felt sick. She realised, he is not here.

Panic filled her but it was too late to run. She stepped back, bumped into the bishop.

Heastan noticed her for the first time.

She trembled. 'Forgive me, lord.'

He forgot her at once, a common girl dressed above herself. He turned to his archdeacon and Edith heard him mutter, 'Are the boxes ready? Add the names of the young men who are chosen, and bring the boxes to me.'

The archdeacon beckoned. The red-lipped priest put down his quill with finality and latecomers were turned away groaning with disappointment.

Wolf had lost his chance.

The red-lipped priest carried over the two caskets, one with male names inside and the other female. He displayed them, open, to the bishop. The crowd roared with excitement as the bishop blessed the slips of paper. 'I beseech Thee, Lord, that Thou wouldst bless this Thy creature of paper. I bless thee, O thou paper creature, in the name of our Lord . . .'

From now on, everyone knew, whatever happened was not chance but a sign of God's will.

'Close the boxes! Shake them well!' the bishop commanded loudly. Then Edith heard him mutter to the archdeacon, 'So, what was done before to the honour of demons, I now do to the honour of the Virgin. Still, it's a disgusting pagan ceremony, the Lupercal, whatever we call it. Not one of these poor girls will retain her virtue tonight, mark my words.'

Edith wondered what the Lupercal was. It sounded Roman. Perhaps the festival had not always been dedicated to St Valentine.

The archdeacon murmured, 'The potential for wickedness is denounced in all your pulpits, your grace, as per your instructions.'

'Bad customs must be altered slowly,' muttered the bishop. 'Gradually adapted and made harmless. It seems they cannot be abolished *per se* by edict.'

'The people have taken marvellously to your patronage of St Valentine,' murmured the archdeacon flatteringly. He spat something distasteful from his mouth. 'And, after all, the Church is no longer giving tacit approval to a mating of courtesans to brutes. Only good Christians are chosen, and this must have an improving, civilising effect to the benefit of the Church.'

'Next year I won't use living girls,' the bishop grunted. 'I'll have saints' names put in the box. People can draw a saint's name at random and offer prayers to him or her, and be satisfied with that.' He grunted again, and drained a gold cup of mead to moisten his throat.

The girl with saucy eyes winked at Edith. 'Don't sound like much fun,' she whispered. '*I* wouldn't be satisfied holding a cold dead saint, I'll tell you.'

Edith supposed such disdain for the hallowed saints whose shrines and relics, the miraculous stone sarcophagus of King Sebba and the healing horse-litter of St Erconwald which decorated the side chapels of the cathedral, was close to blasphemy. But she was too frantic with anxiety even to be horrified, imagining herself snatched into the pawing embrace of some whiskery brute, losing Wolf for ever just when she had risked everything to get him.

She hardly heard, overcome with misery, as the first name was plucked from the box and called. It was not Wolf's. A muscular lad wearing a leather apron, probably a smith, swaggered on to the steps. A cheer went up. The box of girls' names was shaken and he plunged his hand in, pulled out a slip of paper. He stared at it dumbly, wondering what writing was. The priest took it and called a name. The saucy-eyed girl embraced Edith and rushed to her new companion, who took her arm with a hearty grin, seized her behind and bussed her lips with ragged yellow teeth for the crowd. A virger pushed them on their knees to pray.

The priest dug into the box, the long sleeves of his cassock flapping, pulled out the second name. This man was older, well dressed and with no need of a dowry, his wife probably killed by Vikings or plague. His eyes were mean and darting. He kept looking at Edith, trying to pierce her veil with his gaze. But when the girl's name was called, it was not hers, and the thin girl was pushed forward. She dropped on to her knees in prayer.

The third man was pocked by some childhood disease, but he had a kind smile and the girl who had woven a garland for her hair curtseyed very prettily to him, and he looked amazed to be so lucky. She laughed, taking his hand first, and the crowd roared their approval of the match. The fourth man struck his fists in the air to proclaim his victory and the awkward girl bumped into him, chosen. Everyone looked from the vivacious girl in sheepskin boots, Leoffla, towards Edith silent and mysterious in her veil. The fifth man was called.

He was nobody, a glazier from out of town, and the Londoners booed but Leoffla hung on to him tight, standing on his feet to hold him down. A glazier was a rare and skilled craftsman, and when times were good for such men they were very good. Edith swayed, watching their happiness. The sixth man's name was called and it was Wolf's name.

He ran shyly up to her, gazed at Edith with quiet firmness. Then he took her hand and with his other hand removed her veil. 'Didn't you see me?' he whispered. 'Why didn't you look at me?' Then the shouts of the crowd drowned his voice and she watched him laughing.

Edith drew him tight to her and kissed him on the lips. 'I love you.'

He put his lips close to her ear. 'You're just like me,' he whispered.

'Am I,' she said, offended.

He whispered earnestly, 'I love you. We're the same because love makes us the same.'

He was right, she realised. She did know it. She felt what he said as well as heard his words. She touched his shoulder. 'You're all right,' she said.

He said, 'You're perfect.'

A virger led them up the steps to pray. They entered the cathedral as reverentially as souls entering heaven. All round them were marvels. The floor was red, the roof painted blue as the sky, the walls were plastered and painted. There was coloured glass in the tall thin windows so the sunlight they threw down was wondrous and mysterious as a palace of rainbows, filling the cathedral with miracles. On each side were the tombs of great kings and saints, and the altar glittered with a glory of gold.

I do love him, Edith thought, and she gripped Wolf's hand so tight that her fingers cracked. He ducked his head in prayer, but she saw he was breathing as quickly as she. A relic of St Valentine was brought forward and they kissed the saint's bone with their lips. Wolf watched her. She thought, he's thinking the same as me!

'How did you do it?' she whispered.

'Do what?'

'You know what, your name chosen!'

Wolf said seriously, 'I prayed.'

Yes, that was some of what she loved about him, his seriousness. She winked playfully, but he did not.

The bishop addressed them. 'There is a word in the holy language which you will hold in your minds. That word is *decorum*. Decorum is what is proper, suitable, and seemly. It is what the Church demands. You are sinners, but do not sin. Be pure in heart even though temptation is all around you today.'

Edith squeezed her eyes shut in the intensity of her prayer. I am pure in heart, because nothing can be purer than love.

The bishop dismissed them and they were led outside. People ran forward and the roar and heat of the crowd rose round them, they were pushed and pulled into the warm rushing embrace of the festivities, jostled from side to side by well-wishers, and a hissing hard-eyed woman touched the hem of Edith's cape to steal some of the magic of St Valentine. Priests formed a cordon round the wagon, trying to regain their influence, pushed Edith and Wolf holding tight to one another into the wagon on top of the others. They clung to the bars gazing at one another as the wagon banged and thumped round the churches back to London Bridge, but everything outside passed in a blur for Edith. For a moment her attention was snatched by a juggler tossing three knives and three balls. Next she heard the man with mean eyes demanding the thin girl stop crying, but she cried louder. Someone handed in a jug of mead and the garlanded girl plumped her man's hand firmly up her thigh, and the wagon bumped them from side to side, and singers and storytellers pushed so tight round the vehicle that Edith could not tell where in the City they were, and the people ran with them in a solid mass, blowing horns and drunk and happy and free for a moment of troubles and fear. A mêlée of muddy boys chased a leather head in one of the muddy play-fields near London Bridge, and suddenly the wagon drove inside a hall, knocking away part of the doorway, but no one cared. Everyone staggered to the table and ate meat. A slim youth was allowed to draw his sword without a fine and sword-danced on the table until he fell off and everyone laughed because he burnt his arse on the fire. The chosen of St Valentine were escorted to the lord whose table it was and he greeted them with dignity, so drunk he could hardly move. Wolf did not drink. He did not let Edith away from his side.

When dark showed through the broken door people snored on their elbows, slumped forward until their heads bumped the table, dropped from the bench and curled comfortably among the bones and mugs and matted straw covering the earth floor, snored louder. The crackling fire died down, slumbered quietly while Edith and Wolf talked. The garlanded girl elbowed the man lying beside her. 'Now you'll have to marry me,' she prattled brightly.

Wolf went outside and Edith stood beside him looking up at the stars. He put his arm round her. 'You broke your word,' he joked. Even Wolf's jokes were serious. 'You said you'd see me, and you didn't. You said I'd be the only man you saw, but instead you saw every man but me.'

She said, 'You hid.'

'From you?' He shook his head. 'Never.' He held her hand. 'Never.'

'You're lovely,' she said. 'Don't make promises. You don't know me.'

But still he didn't kiss her. 'I know you.'

'I don't want you to have to promise things.'

He played on the bishop's words. 'I'm pure in heart even though temptation is all around me tonight. The angels—'

'I'm only human.'

They walked beyond the houses, following the lane home by starlight.

'Not to me,' he said.

'Just skin and bone,' she said, rubbing her shoulder against his, but he twisted and instead of pushing him away she turned into him.

'You're as perfect as the stars in the sky,' he said. He kissed her. They both stepped back. He held both her hands.

'We can't go home,' she said. 'It's St Valentine's night, it's different from every other night. Let's walk all night.'

'Marry me.'

She laughed, turned in a circle.

He turned with her. 'Marry me. Don't say I don't know you. That's why I want to marry you. I know you, I'll *be* you.' He stopped her, spoke to her face. 'Do you want to be alone? You *are* lonely, aren't you, Edith?'

'But my uncle – and your stepfather—'

He interrupted, 'You didn't see me, you didn't see me at the cathedral because I was standing too close to you.'

'How close?'

He touched her with the whole length of his body.

She whispered, 'How did you get your name in the box, really?'

He kissed her for the second time, less clumsily. 'I told you. I prayed. I prayed for you.' He kissed her chin, her ears, more cleverly. 'Do you believe how much I love you?'

Edith struggled to separate herself from her feelings but she could not. She felt herself rushing forward, she hung on to him. 'Yes. I do.'

They had crossed the Walbrook. The lane led uphill between cottages and trees and bushes, dim outlines in the starlight, the Thames winding below them like a ribbon of stars. Wolf was so confident. Edith gave herself up to his arms, felt the weight of her hair slipping down her shoulders as he kissed her jaw, her neck, growing skilful now, subtle and delicate, thinking only of her. There was nothing casual about his need, he touched her. She put back her head, gasped as a spark flared in the sky, trailed coloured fire like the light she had seen stream through the cathedral windows.

He saw. 'You know what that is? It's a soul rushing to heaven.'

Wolf enfolded his hands in her hair, kissed her throat. His freezing hand touched her breast. She felt tree bark and brambles behind her, thorns and frozen twigs, sniffed the smell of urine here where people had relieved themselves earlier.

Edith said, 'Stop.'

He stopped.

'It's wrong,' she said. She hugged him. 'We love each other. We're worth more than this. I don't know how many people have been here. I'm special, Wolf.'

He said, 'I've lost you.'

She stroked his hair and adored him. She whispered, 'I'm special because I have you. I have so much to give you.'

But he didn't understand. 'You don't care about me.' He didn't move a muscle, didn't feel the tenderness of her caresses. 'I got up in the dark, I froze just to see you leave your uncle's house this morning. You walked in the shadows by the cathedral, hardly looked at it like you were part of it, and you didn't see me watching you, and you talked to the baker and you didn't hear me.'

'Wolf, child of God's mercy,' she whispered. She slipped her hand in his as if it were he who decided to walk uphill, walked with him as if it were he who led her. No lamplight showed between the shutters of her Uncle Benedict's house. Wolf held back miserably when she turned by the door as if to go in. Before he could speak she covered his lips with her hand. 'Sshh. He's a light sleeper. Do you love me true and for ever?'

He sounded shaken by her intensity. 'Yes, truly and for as long as I live.'

Over them on the hilltop the cathedral was a dark hole punched among the stars, the one single candle burning inside barely illuminating the windows, and she thought it looked like a huge ship that had come to ground on the hill, like some mighty Noah's Ark.

'No!' She shook her head. 'Only until death, that's marriage. I said love. Love is for ever.'

'I wish there was a moon, so I could see you properly. You sound so lovely.' His eyes and smile gleamed in the starlight, she felt his warm breath on her ear. 'I love you truly and for ever.'

She knelt by the wall and reached down, pulled open a hatch almost under the wall. 'The cottage has been built and re-built many times. My father used this as a grain store, but Uncle Benedict sells the portion his lord does not take to the baker, who pays with bread.' She pulled her gown to the knee, backed swiftly down the steps tugging him after her, she would not let him go. 'Most people are turning these places into cesspits, there are too many people fouling the woods, but this one's too close to the house.' She added, 'Thank God.'

Wolf overcame his fear of close spaces and looked around him. The place brushed his shoulders and smelt musty. Cobwebby plank walls were revealed as she sparked a flint, caught the flame in the mouth of a dirty copper lamp. He closed the hatch and turned to embrace her, but she was not there.

A few dry-rotted planks lay on the floor where she had pulled them from the side, and he glimpsed her hair as she ducked through the gap. Wolf shrugged, swung his leg through and ducked after her. A clean draught blew in his face, warmer than the snow. Her obvious excitement excited him and as he went after her his erection was so hard it hurt him. He rapped the tip of his bulging breeches with his finger-knuckles to make it go down, but his blood was up. He knew what was going to happen.

Edith turned, sweeping the flame round her in the dark, and its hot light fluttered in her eyes.

'Look around you—'

'I'm only looking at you,' he said. He dimly sensed the place was very large, the flame did not illuminate the walls behind him and in front of him, only darkness, solitude, and she was very beautiful.

'My love,' he said. 'My love.'

'I will,' she said. 'I will marry you.' Edith kissed her fingertip, pressed it to his lips. 'Look where I wrote your name.'

He took her in his arms, kissing her breast, and the flame went out.

Somewhere above them a priest, his sandals smoothly kicking the hem of his cassock, crossed the red gypsum floor of the cathedral and examined the night-candle. It had burned down to the hour of Nocturn. He lit a fresh candle and went to summon his brothers sleeping in the *claustrum*, the clergy house, to prayer.

His tiny figure came dimly from the cathedral side door and closed it carefully behind him, keeping out demons. No larger than an insect, he shrank smaller across the pale snow of the atrium. The yellow glow of his candle was extinguished by the vast icy radiance of the stars, and his shadow winked silently from sight.

There was no wind. The stars did not flicker.

The root of an elm tree hung down through the roof of the catacomb. It grew slowly, not seeming to move. Soon, in a matter of years, it would reach the floor, and crack through the mosaic to the soft nutritious earth below.

I am pure in heart, because nothing can be purer than love.

Love was not what she had expected. Edith had watched animals mate but people were not animals, because animals could never go to heaven and people might, if they were baptised, virtuous, shriven. The pain was atrocious, burning and ripping at the same time. Surely there was no sin in it, for she felt no pleasure. She held the holy word in her mind, *decorum*, and for Wolf's sake she made no sound, clung to him tight to move with him, trying to ease the anguish the thrusts of his love caused her. She felt guilty because she wanted to show how much she loved him. She bit her lips and the tears slid from her eyes in the dark, where he could not see how she suffered beneath him. When she groaned with her tearing pain he heard groans of pleasure that added fuel to his desire, and he rode her harder. She cried out and he grunted with delight, forcing himself forward in his moment of ecstasy, and spurted his sauce into her like a bull.

And she loved him.

He lay with his face against her ear, almost asleep, then rolled off her. Edith pulled her gown, covering her knees. The draught made her breasts cold where he had licked them and she put them back inside.

His voice came. 'Edith. My Edith.'

'Yes. I am your Edith. I'm yours.'

'You're lovely.' He struck the flint and lit the lamp, propped himself on one elbow by its flame, studied her. He licked the tears from her cheek.

'It's supposed to hurt,' he said tenderly. 'Do you believe now how much I love you?'

'Yes.'

'I am you, aren't I. And you're me.'

She wondered how he didn't know what she felt. 'I am,' she said.

'I love you, Edith.'

How many times had they said that word *love* tonight? She cuddled him close, showing how much she loved him, feeling her blood and his semen trickle cold on her legs.

His head moved. He was looking over her shoulder. 'Well, where's this?'

She murmured, 'My secret place. No one knows it. Only you, now.' She hugged him earnestly, making him look at her, showing how much she trusted him.

'That sticky hairy thing between your legs is your secret place,' he said. He added, 'Was.'

'Don't speak like that.' His words hurt but she wanted to understand what he meant. 'You liked me enough just now.'

'That's true,' he grinned. 'I'd like it again, too.' Just when she thought she understood him, he slipped out of her grasp. Edith wanted to talk to him about getting married. There were more than seventy wooden buildings in the cathedral's *haga*, the hedged precinct, and Uncle Benedict, God willing, could take over a hearth in the longhouse serving the bishop's palace, a step up in class and much more convenient for his workshop than the cottage. Aunt Winifrid would be pleased to get away from the cottage, the roof was so low that horses of great men sometimes helped themselves to mouthfuls of thatch. Much repair and a skilful carpenter was needed . . . Edith smiled at her husband-to-be, the skilful carpenter. Wolf would work at his stepfather's during the day, and improve the cottage on long summer evenings. There would be children, and chickens, and dogs . . .

Wolf kissed her lips and stood up. He pulled up his breeches, then reached to touch the roof as though reassuring himself of its solidity. 'So, it really does exist,' he murmured. He took a few paces along the catacomb, stopped, turned back to the light. 'This is why the Vikings tortured your father. They believed the old stories.'

'No!' Edith was shocked. 'He didn't know of this place. Only Mother did.'

'They thought he knew.'

'No. They—'

'That's why they killed him, Edith. Everyone knows that. Because he wouldn't talk.'

She repeated what, as a child, her mother had told her. 'My father was the bravest man who ever lived.'

Wolf and Edith thought about her father spreadeagled on Paul's Cross, his insides hanging between his legs, his exposed heart beating frantically between his lungs, and she remembered his screams echoing from above.

'He couldn't tell them because he didn't know,' Wolf said gently. He picked up the lamp and walked with it down the catacomb. A few paces further along the floor was a mass of stone and plaster where a tree root had pushed through the vaulted roof. He stooped reluctantly, feeling the darkness pressing down on him, then picked his way carefully forward. He stood straight with a relieved sigh and she watched him examine one of the niches in the wall.

'Bones,' he called. 'It's only a cemetery. Where's the treasure?'

Edith sat up. 'What treasure? I'm the only treasure down here.' She held out her arms. 'Come back to me.'

He looked ahead into the darkness, then brushed past the tree root and returned to her. 'There's supposed to be treasure. The atrium's somewhere above here, isn't it? Stones made of gold.'

She nuzzled him. 'Aren't I treasure enough for you?'

He chuckled with pleasure. 'Yes. You are.' He touched her legs, looked horrified. 'Blood. Have I hurt you too much?'

She kissed him. 'No.' She wondered if he fully appreciated the magnitude of her gift.

'You'd better wipe it off,' he said, then returned to his original subject like a dog to its bone. 'How do you think a rumour like that started?'

'I don't know.'

'No smoke without fire.'

'I don't know any rumour.'

He nodded, then smiled. 'Anyway, you're right. You are my treasure. My wife.' He touched her left breast, the raised weal of his name written there. 'So that's what my name looks like. I have a wife who can read and write. You're far above me, I'm a lucky man. There's a lot I've got to find out about you, isn't there?'

She provoked him. 'I thought you knew everything.'

'Yes, but everything about a woman is a surprise.' He lifted the lamp and she knew he was going to talk about treasure again.

She said quickly, 'Wolf, how did you get your name in the box?'

'I told you, I prayed. The power of prayer.' He looked into her steady gaze. 'What's the matter?'

'Nothing,' she said saucily. 'No smoke without fire.'

'Do you really want to know?'

She was eager. 'I want to know everything about you.'

He said bitterly, 'You're saying you're allowed to have secrets, but I'm not.'

'Yes,' she laughed. 'I'm not a man.'

'I bribed the priest to write my name and hold it in his sleeve.'

'But that's impossible. A priest—' Edith shook her head. 'How much did it cost? An offering to the cathedral?'

'A kiss.'

She laughed again, then stared at him silently, remembering the red-lipped priest.

'I did it for you,' Wolf said. 'It's disgusting. The whole business was as disgusting as going with a whore.'

Suddenly Edith understood him. She was sure he had never been with a whore, he was too shy. He gave her that gentle, blinking look from the corners of his deep blue eyes. She took him in her arms. 'Oh, my poor husband. Our prayers would have been sufficient. You didn't believe in yourself. But God hears, God listened to my prayers. Our names would have been chosen anyway.'

Wolf stood. 'It must be very late.'

'It's very early,' she whispered. 'We're at the start of our life together.' With her fingertips she stroked the sensitive, gorgeous angles of his face, kissed the little upward twist in the corner of his mouth, she couldn't bear not to touch him. 'I believe in you. I believe in you enough for both of us.'

Finally she let him go. Wolf watched her hunch down into the short tunnel that led to the cellar. He licked his finger, rubbed the dirty lamp, stared at his reflection in the golden gleam. Edith called to him.

'Coming,' he said.

He covered the gleam with dirt and crawled after her. He smiled and kissed her. It was nearly dawn.

Edith was wed in her headband and veil. The marriage was witnessed by a priest, and Aunt Winifrid as her closest kin, and Uncle Benedict as her formal male guardian. A copy of the marriage agreement between Wolf and herself was deposited in the cathedral. Edith paid her King Alfred penny into the offertory, just as she had promised that St Valentine's Day, and like most young women she was pregnant when she took her wedding vow. A wife could not be divorced for sterility, for the gift of life was God's. Without children, a man had no one to take over his business or feed him in his old age. It was best to be sure from the start that God Himself blessed the union.

'I caught you the very first time,' Wolf whispered proudly. The divine spark of the husband's semen contained the child, a tiny perfect replica of himself inside it like a seed of grain, and the wife's body was merely the ploughed field, the human soil which nurtured her husband's homunculus for nine months. Her earthly flesh no more created the child than wood creates flame, and the baby would be born from her body between piss and manure, tainted and unclean, merely human.

Edith never felt healthier than when she was pregnant. Everything worked perfectly and she was radiant. All the bad things that could have happened, all the obstacles that could have been thrown in their way, had not. For instance Uncle Benedict, now that he had given up her interests, might have been difficult to remove from the cottage, though it was Edith's holding through her mother. Such difficulties often did happen. But by good fortune Benedict was offered the room he coveted in the longhouse and firewood in winter – no small concession, as the bishop levied a shilling on every cart of firewood that passed through Bishopsgate – and Winifrid purchased a better position in the bishop's household, so they jumped at the chance. Edith agreed to make over her mother's cottage to Wolf for his lifetime, just as Mother had to Father when she married, and Wolf would make no payment provided he rebuilt it in good house style, with gables, a perfect arrangement for a penniless carpenter. Several other houses had been put up in the street, one of them with two storeys.

Her greatest piece of good fortune was that Wolf's stepfather, Hewald, made no attempt to forbid the match. He'd had his eye on a girl, Frea, who brought with her a dowry of two mancuses of gold, or so he said. It was Wolf's main worry, Edith knew, that he would be forced into a marriage for the sake of the business. But he spoke with Hewald the carpenter earnestly, several times, and finally Edith watched the two of them sitting over a table with their heads together, Hewald still angry at first, Wolf persistent. The older man listened quietly, drinking his beer, then acknowledged Edith and spat on his hands. 'The poorest business deal I ever made in my life,' he said, then his big face grinned.

'The best,' Wolf said. He took Edith's hand but continued his male banter. 'She loves me. She needs me.'

Edith played her part, elbowed his ribs, pouted, and Hewald laughed and watched her calculatingly. 'You'll do,' he said, then embraced them both. 'I'll make him work, mind . . .'

She asked Wolf afterwards, 'What did you offer him?'

He looked blank. 'It was obvious that I love you, that's all.'

Wolf complained that marriage was the most exhausting time of his life, but he was a hard worker. All day labouring in his stepfather's service, then the long summer evenings working on their house, left him little time for love. Edith was ashamed that his lovemaking caused her such pain – it was no easier for her than the first time – and often when Wolf slept she stole from his side and washed herself quietly, rubbed raw, bleeding. His pleasure was her pain, and she felt too guilty to tell him. She asked the priest what she had done wrong. He gave her various penances to perform, and she did feel a little better.

By seven months the straw mat on the floor felt very hard under her back. Her belly already felt so heavy she could not get comfortable whatever position she lay in. 'I'll make you a bed,' Wolf promised.

'My house first,' she said.

He kissed her. 'Ours.'

'Our child's.'

He kissed her again, more passionately, running the palm of his hand gently over the swell of her belly. He was a fine husband, and mounted her, and Edith gritted her teeth. 'Is something wrong?' he asked.

'Oh, I do love you!' she cried.

Even the weather was perfect that summer, with plenty of sun for the vines, apples, pears and cherries, yet enough rain fell at night to feed the field crops. The street turned to white dust and Wolf coughed as he worked on the new house. Edith had worried about living in the cottage while the work went on but Wolf simply started the new house around the cottage. Workmen who owed him favours dug holes for the posts, or he paid them with pieces of joinery, wooden latches, hinges. Wisely Wolf covered the cellar with stout timbers lest someone fall down and pursue him in the Folkmoot for their injury.

'Besides,' he whispered, stroking the black-stranded blond hair over Edith's ear, 'that's our place, the palace of our love.'

She loved it when he spoke so romantically, it sent a thrill up her spine, and he knew it. If ever they argued, he knew how to get round her.

Being entirely of wood, the structure of the new house rose with amazing speed. It stood like a skeleton around the cottage, and Edith grew used to stepping over baulks of seasoned timber, trestles and yellow chips of wood, and the smell of sawdust which made her sneeze, and the smiles of strange cheerful men she did not know, who knuckled their foreheads respectfully as she passed and obviously, from their grins, told quite a lot about her by the size of her belly.

Edith pushed her hands into the small of her back and straightened with a groan. Work on the new house had paused and the men were all out at the harvest, where she would have been but for her swollen, plodding condition, all but the lightest work now beyond her. She weeded the herb bed of her back garden or garth, which stretched nearly two hundred feet downhill, though little wider than the house. On each side of the central path grew the onions and leeks she had planted, garlic, and cabbages. Edith sniffed the herbs whose scent clung to her hands, sage, rosemary, marjoram, thyme. Downhill stood the mulberry tree, obviously once riven almost in two by lightning but now covered with fruit, where a nightingale sang. At the end of the garden was the cesspit, rubbish dump, compost heap, nothing wasted. The hedge that bordered the holding was a profusion of elder-berries, hazelnuts, sloes, strong weeds like fennel and borage to mask the taste of high meat, and the damp back wall of the cottage was heavy with pellitory. Every spare scrap of ground was covered with London rocket and thick tangles of wild flowers, stinging nettles and dandelion for wine and soup. Bees droned around the fig and apple trees that appeared and flourished without being planted, like ancient memories rising from the soil. The scent of herbs grew stronger, became overpowering, suffocating. Edith put the back of her hand to her head. There was a bump and she realised she had fallen. She called out.

Edith realised she was in the cottage, faces around her, and she blinked sleepily. 'How did I get inside?' she asked.

'I carried you,' Wolf said. He looked afraid. 'You frightened me.'

'I heard you groaning,' a woman's voice said proudly. She lived at the next cottage but one, her jolly face as red and round as an apple. Her name was Leoba and she was crippled in the legs. 'She don't sound right, I told myself, and I shouted, and in the end everyone came running. Didn't they run! I'm a good shouter.'

Edith gripped her hand in thanks, then looked down. 'What happened?' she asked Wolf, alarmed. 'Our baby—'

'Babe's fine,' Leoba said. 'Kicking earlier, felt it.'

'You fell asleep, wife, that's all,' Wolf said. 'You must have fallen and bumped your head. Don't do it again!' he pleaded.

'I feel better now,' Edith told him. 'I do.'

'Are you sure?'

She squeezed his hand gratefully, drifting, dozing.

Leoba stroked Edith's tummy reverently, feeling for kicks, but the baby was asleep like its mother. 'Had seven little ones myself before something went wrong,' she told Wolf, then thumped her useless legs. 'I'm a practical sort, birth calves and ewes as well as my own and others', I know most things about it. Don't let it happen without me here, master.'

'I won't,' Wolf said. Leoba's son helped her outside and Wolf closed the door, relieved to be alone. Edith was talking in her sleep, fretting, worrying.

'Wolf?'

'My love?' He crouched beside her. A faint raised line had appeared down her forehead, making her frown deeper.

Edith murmured, 'How will we pay for our house?'

Did she think money grew on apple trees and apprentice wages? 'Don't worry,' he murmured. 'My stepfather Hewald is helping.'

She drifted into a deeper sleep and he wondered if she had heard him.

But in the morning she awoke normally, her frown was gone and she said, 'I'm so glad Hewald is helping. He's a good man.'

Wolf promised her, 'The outside of our house will be finished by the time our baby is born.'

Edith had recovered her sense of humour. 'You'd better hurry up!' she said.

The harvest ended and Wolf went back to his carpentry at Hewald's. The season cooled and Edith planted root vegetables until Leoba saw her and told her off at the top of her voice. Edith retreated inside. Wolf would have to plant the vegetables and do her work as well as his own, but no one could have been a kinder or more thoughtful husband, and he never complained. Edith loved him so much that she actually cried from happiness and her own inadequacy, because the baby took all her strength. Even poor Wolf's lovemaking stopped, not because of her

223

pain or the awkwardness but because she was afraid of hurting the baby.

She strung her clay loom-weights to weave wool as best she could, but even light work exhausted her. The house walls enclosed the cottage, making it very gloomy inside. Edith had nothing to do but sit and worry. It poured with rain outside, though the rain made little sound, falling not on the cottage but on the thatch roof of Wolf's house above. Edith stood in the gap between the cottage and the house. The timbers that stopped people falling into the cellar had been removed, and only the flimsy hatch remained.

No one was about. Grunting, she lifted the hatch and went down.

Almost at once she came out, telling herself off because the lamp was not where she thought she left it. She fetched a tallow candle and went back down, closed the hatch after her, and lifted the planks from the side. She recovered her breath then went through to the catacomb.

Nothing had changed, it was as it was nine months ago. She touched the hard shiny floor, the place they had lain together, conceiving together, rubbed clean of dust by their passionate bodies.

Our place. She remembered Wolf's words fondly. *The palace of our love.*

His footprints tracked across the dust, scuffed where he had bent beneath the tree root, as clear as though he were still here. His footprints stopped where he had examined the niche.

Bones. It's only a cemetery. Where's the treasure?

Edith held up the candle and waddled to the end of the catacomb. On the end wall was carved Menaht, Menou, and other words she could not make out, perhaps a nonsense rhyme to lull children to sleep, as her mother had lulled her. On the left, partly obscuring the words, was a pile of earth solid and compacted with age, a spade left standing in the top. Its iron shoe was perfectly preserved by the dry air. The handle was short, too short for a man to use comfortably unless he was the size of a woman, and the shoe was small, as though forged for a woman's strength.

The earth had been dug out to make a tunnel beside the stone.

Edith turned away. Nothing had been touched here for years.

Still, there was no harm in taking another look.

She knelt awkwardly. All at once she felt something grip her insides. A band tightened across her tummy and her bowels cramped. 'Not here,' she groaned, but she really thought she couldn't wait. Then the band loosened and the need passed. She put her hand under her tummy and her eyes widened.

'O Lord, not now.'

She held up the candle with one hand, the other supporting her tummy, and waddled back along the catacomb as rapidly as she could. What a fool she was to come down here! The second cramp struck as she crouched under the tree root. She shuffled forward, groaning, trying to keep her knees together. The third cramp came more quickly still, in the cellar. She forced herself to wait, sweating despite the cold, breathing through her nose, trying to hold back. She should have time to get up the steps, get the hatch closed behind her before the fourth cramp struck. She felt a little better, quickly dropped the planks in place, lumbered up the steps. She heard the hatch bang closed and staggered forward.

She collapsed in the vacant doorway of the house as her waters broke. She shouted Leoba's name, then her agony began.

Voices came to her.

Wolf was holding her hand. 'Can she hear me?'

Yes, I can hear you.

Leoba the cripple shrugged. 'She's exhausted, this one.'

Edith's eyelids flickered, stilled. Her body stiffened in the last contraction, her muscles quivering weakly as they tightened. But this time her back did not arch from the mat. She was giving all her strength, but one of her legs flopped slackly.

'A night and a day and half the night,' Leoba said. She held up the ringed candle. 'The darkest hour of the night.'

'Light more candles.'

'Master, this is the time for them to die, mostly.'

'She'll live,' Wolf said. 'She's determined and she's pig-headed and she knows what she wants and she won't die.' His voice rose, blurring, he was shouting. 'I've never changed her mind on anything and she wants to live. She'll live.'

Edith tried to speak. Someone put a cloth soaked in wine vinegar into her mouth, trying to slake her thirst. Edith felt herself begin to swallow the cloth, then her tongue slipped back in her throat. Fortunately Wolf noticed and plucked the cloth out and she heard him cursing someone she could not see, then she felt his lips against her ear. He was saying my love, my love. She tried to smile for him but vinegar trickled from her lips.

Wolf spoke across her to Leoba. 'Can't you do anything?'

Get it out, get it out.

Leoba said, 'I can save the mother or the babe.'

'Save her,' Wolf said.

'The babe's head is stuck. If I cut the mother I'll kill her. If I pull the babe's head I'll crush its skull.'

'Save her,' Wolf shouted.

Edith opened her mouth. 'No, save my baby.'

Leoba held up the wooden forceps from the byre.

Wolf leaned across Edith so she could not see what was happening.

'Do as I said,' he instructed Leoba quietly, and Edith screamed.

Leoba worked the blunt forceps round the baby's head. She was not strong enough. One of her sons helped. Someone put more logs on the fire and sparks rushed up, casting a ruddy glow. 'Holy Mother, holy Lord,' Leoba recoiled. 'Look at this! O Lord our God forgive us.'

Edith's naked body was transfigured. A raised red stripe ran from her forehead to her torn vagina, as though she had been whipped. Another, with drops of blood squeezing through its flesh, was ripped from wrist to wrist up the inside of her arms, across her breasts and her heart.

One of Leoba's boys shouted, 'It's the Holy Cross! It's the Sign!'

Leoba grabbed him with her muscular right arm. 'Get the priest. Run to the cathedral and get the priest. Any priest. Run!'

Wolf held tight to his wife. 'What is it? What's happening?'

Leoba lowered her head, got back to her work.

The priest came running, his prandial porridge still clinging to his chin. 'My poor Edith,' Father Daniel said compassionately. She was the clever girl whose mother had taught her to write vernacular, and he had taught the child Latin while he was in hiding. Edith was a phenomenon, a woman able to read and write in a kingdom where only a dozen or two dozen men were blessed with such ability.

She touched his wrist in a grip as fluttery as a bird's wing. 'Father Daniel?'

She was dying. He made the sign of the cross and gave her extreme unction. 'Look at her, Father,' Leoba grunted. '*Look* at her.'

Father Daniel stared. He touched the girl's body wonderingly. A woman in childbirth, every function exposed, was strangely sexless, her body as innocent and instinctive as a child's. He touched her skin reverently and felt no guilt.

'It's the stigma,' he marvelled. 'I've heard of stigmata. There are priests who drip blood from Christ's wound in their side or the nail holes driven through His hands, or bleed about the head from the Crown of Thorns. I've never seen it.'

Leoba said, 'It's fading.'

'I can't see anything,' Wolf said. 'What is it?'

'It's nothing,' Father Daniel said decisively. He turned to Leoba. 'It's a temptation, a vanity. Say nothing of it, woman.'

Leoba shook her head. 'All right by me,' she grunted. 'Enough miracles and shrines at every crossroads already, if you ask me.'

'But I did see what I saw,' Father Daniel whispered. 'I do believe. God is real and He is the truth. God be praised.'

'The babe's head's coming—' Leoba gasped, showered with blood as the dead baby slid forward into her arms. She dropped it with the forceps on the floor, tugged gently at the cord that led into the mother's body. 'If the afterbirth sticks she'll die too.'

Father Daniel prayed on his knees, then jerked back. Edith's eyes stared into his own.

'Baptise my baby,' Edith said.

The soul of an unbaptised baby was blind and did not know which way to turn towards the Light, and was taken down to suffer the torments of Hell for ever.

Father Daniel whispered, 'Edith, your baby is dead.'

Edith summoned her strength. '*Baptise my baby!*' she screamed.

Father Daniel nodded soothingly. He picked up the child, staining his cold hands with blood and slime. It was a girl.

The baby hicked.

The baby cried.

Father Daniel trembled. 'It's alive.'

'*She's* alive,' Edith whispered.

The priest cradled the huddled body to his cassock, unstoppered the vial of holy water, sprinkled the wrinkled forehead before life departed. The child weighed almost nothing. 'I baptise you – what name, what name?'

'Aine,' whispered Edith.

Wolf gripped her hand, understanding. 'Aine, queen of the fairies.'

Father Daniel intoned, 'I baptise you Aine, in the name of the Father, the Son, and the Holy Ghost. Amen.' He could see the poor thing was terribly hurt, her head dented and distorted by the forceps, and her blue eyes were started open as if in anguish.

'Wrap it something warm, you idiot!' Leoba shouted. The cord moved in her hands and the afterbirth slithered out like a liver.

Edith moved weakly, reached for her baby. Father Daniel handed the child down gently. Edith kissed the top of Aine's head and closed her eyes. Daylight showed in the doorway.

Leoba held the afterbirth between her arms, panting. 'I lied,' she confessed. 'I only did animals before.'

'She's the prettiest little thing that was ever born,' Edith murmured. 'Aine. My Aine.'

'And mine,' Wolf said. He watched unsentimentally as his infant daughter sucked her mother's breast. Edith's breast was still heavy, her nipple engorged, brown. Aine grinned at him and burped milk. Wolf touched the breast, enfolded its tip between his fingers, squeezed lightly. Drops of milk trickled into his palm.

Edith nuzzled him. 'Yes, and your Aine too.'

'Ours,' Wolf said.

'Yes, husband.' Edith shifted uncomfortably from his hand. Wolf licked his palm.

Edith forgot him and studied her baby lovingly, feeling even closer to her because of all they had been through together. Aine's enormous baby-blue eyes had not faded with the months, she looked exquisitely vulnerable with her snub nose, button mouth, tiny dimpled chin. The forceps had scarred and dented her head, distorted her skull where she was dragged from Edith's womb, but that too made them closer, joined them in a special way. Aine's hair had grown long, black and blonde like her mother's but with more black, the shade Leoba called night and day. The voluminous fine hair was gradually hiding her injuries.

Wolf said, 'We share everything, don't we?'

Edith smiled, rubbed noses. 'You are my husband. Without you I'm nothing.'

He rubbed her breast longingly, and did not smile when she drew away. He rolled aside from her on the mat, prodded the fire with a stick. The house was not as warm as the cottage had been, and now that leaf-falling was well set in and the season had changed to winter back in the middle of September, according to the Church's regulations, the nights were sharply colder.

Edith spoke, embarrassed. 'She's made it sore. I'm sorry.'

It meant more than that to him. 'Don't you love me, Edith?'

Aine was almost asleep. She was a light sleeper.

'Of course I love you!' Edith whispered.

He turned. 'But you won't—'

'Sshh, you'll wake her,' Edith hissed urgently. She was tired and Aine had been fretful all day, feverish.

He said firmly, 'But we don't sleep together as man and wife.'

She pointed out sensibly, 'We can't, until Aine is weaned, it's against Church law.'

'I'm dying for you. Yesterday I heard of a woman, a carter's wife whose baby died, she has milk, she could—'

'No,' Edith said fiercely. Aine cried. Edith jogged her. 'Now look what you've done.' She saw the anger and hurt on Wolf's face and tried to explain to him in a way he would see. 'I do love you, but we can't risk having another baby.'

Incredibly, he blustered. 'That's the first I've heard of it.'

'Leoba said.'

'What about a son? One day the business will be mine, and then my son's.'

Edith lifted her tunic, revealed herself to him. 'Look at me!' she cried.

He glanced, looked away, prodded the fire.

She said, 'I'm so sorry.' Wolf would have no son. She thought, of all men he will understand. But she was afraid of losing him.

Wolf went to the door and looked out at the night, then came back again, speaking bitterly. 'I don't know what I believe, Edith. All the time it's your child, not your husband.'

Edith laid her baby to sleep. She put her arms round Wolf. 'Our greatest love must be for God who made our world, and made us, and gave us our daughter.'

'I gave you our daughter. If only I had given you a son!'

Edith said gently, 'I love you, but I cannot in the way we did. You don't need to have my body to love me.'

He looked at her steadily, silently. 'Touch me,' he said.

She hugged him. 'I'm touching you, I love you.' But he pulled at his breeches and hung out of them, pressed her hand against him.

'Kneel, open your mouth,' he said eagerly.

She tried to explain. 'But I love you.'

He said in a rising voice, 'This *is* love—'

They both looked round as Aine whimpered. The child's eyes stared open, blue, sightless, then rolled up in her head. Her little limbs whipped from side to side. Edith burst into tears and threw herself beside the tiny struggling figure, grasped her, tried to shield her head from banging the floor. Aine grunted like an animal, chuckled, laughed. She moaned like a tormented adult, the most frightening sound of all.

'Baby, baby,' Edith murmured. Wolf stood by the door as white as a ghost. 'We've sinned!' Edith shouted at him.

'We haven't done anything wrong,' he said.

The child's struggles faded, she fell silent. She seemed to drop into a deep sleep.

'A demon's got into her,' Wolf said. 'It's her.'

Edith was terrified that he could even think it. 'No. She's not possessed. The same thing happened to me, once, remember?'

'You only fell asleep in the garden, it was the heat.'

'Leoba heard me groaning like that. I had cuts on my hands from brambles.'

He looked at her doubtfully. 'You didn't remember anything.'

Edith stroked the hair from Aine's forehead, kissed the sunken marks. 'She's sleeping peacefully. Perhaps she won't remember anything either.'

Aine woke normally in the morning and suckled cheerfully, a normal child none the worse for her experience. Wolf hesitated, though it was dawn and he should be on his way to Hewald's workshop.

'Edith, my love, don't grow too close to her, in case she dies.' He sighed. 'Perhaps we won't have any more children. I couldn't bear to hurt you. Forgive me for last night, I couldn't help myself.' He fumbled for words. 'It's because I love you, I need you so much.'

She reached up and put her hand behind his head, kissed his lips. 'You're a wonderful husband.'

He shrugged. 'I'm a man.' She waved to him as he set off between the houses along the snowy street. Edith watched him out of sight, then saw smoke drifting from Leoba's roof, wrapped Aine well against the cold and carried her across. She confessed to the crippled woman the dreadful thing that had happened.

'It is a demon,' Leoba confirmed. She shivered a blanket round her shoulders, sitting where her son had put her by the fire, her face blackened by smoke. 'Children get fevers and the demon gets in them.'

'It isn't a demon,' Edith said.

229

'But you yourself—'

'Not in my baby,' Edith said firmly.

Leoba coughed. 'Have it your own way. But even women hand down bits of themselves to their children. My son don't look one sniff like his father. Looks like me! Anyone can see that. My nose, even got my bad temper. Part of me's alive in my son, that's what I think.'

Edith said despairingly, 'Then whatever is wrong with Aine is my fault.'

Leoba picked her nose. 'Or your husband's fault.'

'No, it's not Wolf.'

Leoba sucked her finger. 'Fools about them, we are.'

'They're stronger than us, and that makes them closer to God.' Edith lowered her head submissively. 'Our king is a man. So is our bishop. Priests are men, men are the shape of God. Jesus Christ looked like a man.'

Leoba put her hands on her hips and laughed, her legs dangling uselessly beneath her from the stool. 'All I can tell you is this. My husband, God rest his soul, did what he was told every day of his married life, and a happy man he lived and died.' Her laughter turned to racking coughs. She waved Edith away.

'You're ill.' Edith was concerned.

'I'm going to God,' Leoba said clearly. 'Talk to Father Daniel. You can trust that one. He likes you. He didn't run around shouting and make his reputation when he saw those marks on you, whatever they were. He loves you in his way, near as a man of God can.' She gestured to be shown the baby, smiled at Aine's sleeping face.

Edith brought the dying woman a broth of beefbones most days of the winter. She decided not to speak to Father Daniel because Aine's possession had not happened again before the Sabbath, then it was raining when she next saw the priest, and then all month passed and Aine's attempts at crawling turned to tottering steps, her exclamations became words, and Edith forgot she had ever been ill.

Leoba died on the fourth Sunday in Lent, a beautiful spring day. She was buried in St Paul's cemetery, and Edith and Aine stood hand in hand by the little wooden cross. Edith had wound a necklace of daisies and dandelions for the child to hang over the crosspiece. 'Do it now?' Aine said.

'I'm praying for her soul,' Edith whispered.

Aine clasped her hands and closed her eyes, the sun hot on their faces. A mass ended in the cathedral and a priest ran out and played a pipe from the elm pulpit on Paul's Cross, so that people coming out wandered over to listen, and instead found themselves listening to his sermon. 'Smell flowers,' Aine said, and Edith looked at her sharply. Aine fell among the wild flowers and weeds as though she was dead. She writhed as the demons came into her. Spittle foamed from the child's mouth. Edith was terrified. She picked Aine up, clasped her struggling body tight so that no one would notice, or they would think she was playing, and ran in despair back to her house.

Edith knelt, praying, and watched Aine fall into a deep sleep.

Later the little girl woke and ate a few spoonfuls of soup, drank a few mouthfuls of beer. Edith said anxiously, 'Don't do that again.'

Aine said, 'Do what, Mummy?'

Edith would stare at her, watching her sleep. She was afraid to let Aine out alone. Suppose Aine was possessed whilst playing outside and other children saw? The word would spread like summer fire, no mother in her right mind would let her child near a possessed girl. Shouts and stones would begin from the older children, mothers snatch their youngsters inside, doors and shutters slam. Edith herself would become suspect. What secret sin had she committed, so that God obviously punished her through her daughter?

Edith whispered, 'I have done nothing wrong.'

Father Daniel had been called to Canterbury, and there was no one else she dared talk to.

Wolf had finished the heavy work on the house, but completing the inside had taken much longer than he hoped. With the return of prosperity to the City and the cathedral the markets swarmed, but a stallholder who was clever at catching or selling fish, and the smiths and bakers who laboured all hours at forge and oven, did not often have the time or skill to construct quarters for themselves, their family and trade. One house often attracted another beside it, and two houses sometimes started a row of dwellings. The street grew, and a good carpenter was in demand. Hewald charged for new services and raised his prices one way or another. Most trees in the City had been chopped down for building or firewood and now timber must be fetched from outside the walls by cart, so woodcutters and labourers, carters and tolls must be paid. The treeless moorland to the north of the City was grazed by sheep, the forests and pigwoods further out were protected by laws. Londoners had long ago been granted hunting rights over a vast area, without which the City would have starved, but every right to chop wood must be paid for. It was too much time and trouble for most people to do everything for themselves. Hewald purchased cutting rights to a wood on the island of Eia, too marshy even for pigs, and shipped the cut timber from the minster's wharf on Thorney Island to St Paul's wharf, to the profit of both St Peter's Minster and St Paul's, and bought himself a new leather jerkin on his profit. Wolf worked hard for his stepfather, often not home until after dark even in summer, and up before dawn. In a year or so he, too, bought himself a calfskin jerkin.

Edith watched Aine. She hated to leave her daughter alone even for a minute. Both of them were alert to the slightest sign of possession, the smell of flowers, sometimes the appearance of flashing lights like water sparkling in the sun. At once Aine and Edith would run home, shut the door, bolt it, and wait fearfully for the possession to begin.

Aine was six years old, and each time the attacks were stronger, and left her weaker.

Edith and Aine got up together, were never apart during the day, slept together. There was never a moment when Edith was not watching for telltale signs. Mint was sometimes sprinkled in the cathedral before mass to freshen the air, and Aine smelt it and Edith, panicking, rushed her outside. Nothing happened. Wolf was so calm about Edith's fright that she wanted to scream. She brushed Aine's hair anxiously from her eyes, cleaned her face.

'Mummy, don't . . .' Aine said.

'You fuss over her too much,' Wolf said. 'It's embarrassing. You embarrass me in front of my friends. They think I'm married to a madwoman, the way you go on. It makes me look stupid.'

The more Edith cared about Aine, the more he was distant and genial. 'You're all right, aren't you, Aine?' He tousled her hair.

'Don't do that!' Edith said.

He shrugged. 'By the way, that old grain cellar, we don't want it any more, do we?' The hatch was under the floor behind the hearth in the house, where the wall of the old cottage had run. 'I'll fill it in, part of it must be under the woodshed, we don't want any accidents.'

Edith tried to think of something other than Aine. 'But it's where we first loved,' she said dully. 'Our love is down there.'

'All right,' Wolf agreed. 'I'll leave it then.'

Edith watched him set off to work, trying to see the shy youth she had married, trying to remember herself when she was young. Aine looked up, smiled brightly, and slipped her hand into her mother's.

As soon as his wife started that little word *But*, Wolf knew she was lying.

But it's where we first loved. Our love is down there.

He turned back when he was out of sight.

The moment she'd said it he knew there was something more down there. She was keeping something from him. *Our love*, she said. Love? The bitch had no idea what love was, all she thought of was herself not him, the useless mouth not him, she had no idea how hard his life was, and he slept with himself all night. Wolf had learnt that the truth was this. Life was divided into three classes of people. Those who fought, those who prayed, and those who worked.

He worked. God, how he worked. But a great warrior could rise to be a thane or an earl. A priest could rise to be a bishop. A poor man could rise to be a rich man.

It rarely happened, because life was unfair. Men fell much more often than they rose. But Hewald was no longer as poor as he had been. In fact, compared to his penniless condition of seven or eight years ago, Hewald was well off, with two carts, a boat, a field leased to him by the cathedral as a timber-yard. He had enough to want more.

I started him off, Wolf thought jealously, remembering the lamp.

With Edith's kisses still warm on his lips all those years ago, before they were even married, he had run the copper lamp to a man by London Bridge. Not copper. Gold. That was how Wolf had married the girl he loved. Enough gold to buy Hewald's permission to marry, enough gold to start Hewald's carpentry shop, and enough gold left over to buy timber for Edith's house. Edith had believed Wolf's cock-and-bull story about his stepfather helping them from the goodness of his heart because she believed people were good at heart, she was too romantic to know what they were really like, she believed Wolf's story because she believed in *him*. She hadn't seen through it even though he didn't make a word of sense. She was a fool, deserved to be lied to. Had she *really* wondered where he got the money to buy all that valuable timber, felling rights purchased, trees chopped, trimmed, dragged, loaded, boated, unloaded, carted laboriously to the top of the hill for her house? Had she given it a moment's thought? No, she trusted him.

'That's right,' Hewald had reassured him ponderously, in their cups. 'They think wood grows on trees.' It was the funniest joke Wolf had ever heard. He laughed so hard he choked on his beer. Hewald wrapped his work-scarred hands around his mug, watching the young man with sharp businesslike glints of his eyes. 'By the by, where *did* you say you got it?'

Wolf was instantly sober. 'What's that?'

Hewald covered Wolf's hand with his own. 'One thing I'll tell you, my handsome boy. Wood grows on trees but gold lamps don't.'

'I told you, I found it,' Wolf said in a high voice. With men he was a bad liar. He paid for another pitcher of beer with his last coin. Hewald shrugged agreeably and allowed himself to be drunk into his evening stupor, and Wolf felt the money well spent. But he had to use all his strength to tug himself free of his snoring stepfather's grip.

Wolf hid behind the cathedral. In a few minutes, he knew, Edith would take his daughter to mass and prayers, followed by the service of All Saints today. They crossed the atrium and he watched the two of them go into the cathedral. He went home the long way round the building lest they saw him through the doorway, then he cut across the cathedral priests' precinct called the Pater Noster with their *claustrum* on the north side, hurried along the street to his own house. The bakehouse door was open and the baker waved to him. Bakers were always nosy. Wolf pretended he was going back for something forgotten at home. As soon as he was out of the baker's sight he left the street, climbed the wooden fence behind his house.

The dog stopped barking, licked his hand quietly.

Wolf went into the open-fronted woodshed, scrambled over lengths of tree branch waiting to be sawn for winter, pulled them away. He tugged at an old plank of wood and it slid aside. He looked round to make sure he was unobserved.

He dropped into the hole.

Darkness closed in on him at once. He hated the dark, the deep sharp stench of the soil, kept his eyes focused on the bright square of daylight above him. His heart hammered as he pushed his hands into the darkness, fumbling for the candle and flint he knew was there.

The yellow, smoky flame rose. He sighed, kissed his finger and brushed it through the flame in thanks, then dismantled the plank wall.

In the catacomb he stood upright. The candle threw a glowing sphere of illumination around him. The floor was shiny where he stood, and his footsteps from the night he had first loved his wife led beneath the tree root. With the passing years it had grown down almost to touch the floor.

Wolf drew a deep breath and realised how silent it was down here without the sounds of life above, birdsong, wives gossiping, children playing. He heard a cart rumble overhead and smiled as the comforting sound made the darkness seem less dense. He pushed past the root and followed his footprints to the niche.

There were four sets of prints. His own left and right feet going, then coming back.

And another set of prints, smaller than his own.

Edith's.

Wolf was outraged. Edith had come sneaking down here without telling him, her husband. Her footprints snaked into the dark and he followed them, treading in them as well as he could, past rows of niches and dry bones. There was a wall and a mound of earth. Here, her prints turned back.

Something darker caught Wolf's eye. The mound had been dug from somewhere. There was a low tunnel beside the rock.

He looked round anxiously. How long had prayers taken, how long would the benediction to All Saints last? Not much longer, surely.

He crouched reluctantly then crawled inside the tunnel, holding the candle in front of him. He hated this. The roof was stone covered with writing that he could not read, the words scraped his shoulders. Past the stone the roof changed to clay and gravel. Bits of pottery stuck out of it, faded redbrick and lumps of painted plaster, even an old broken shoe, infill that had been chucked down long ago. The floor looked like crushed bone.

The tunnel ended abruptly in a deeper darkness. An ancient sword, pure rust, was wedged across the darkness. A cobwebbed rope was tied round the knobbly black sword-blade, hanging from it into the dark.

Wolf reached down. There was nothing.

He peered down, saw nothing.

He dropped a stone down, heard nothing.

He touched the rope. It was heavy. He lifted it and it felt dry as dust. His elbow touched the sword and the blade snapped, showering rust, and the two halves tumbled into the dark.

Wolf sat with his legs over the edge, holding the rope. He pulled it up hand over hand, sneezing at the dust that puffed out of it, his hands reddened by the hairy strands. Gradually the rope grew lighter, relieved of its own weight.

There was nothing on the end, only a chalky whiteness.

Wolf stared down. He knew he had found the entrance to the underworld, perhaps an entrance to Hell itself. It might go down and down to the end of the world.

He stopped swinging his legs and pulled himself back from the edge, taking his weight on his hands. He cursed as something cut his palm.

He licked his palm, cursing, then stopped. Among the shards of bone and marble glinted the object that cut him.

It was a jewel, red as a bead of blood.

He examined the ruby between his fingertips. It was small, broken from a setting perhaps, but undeniably a ruby.

A ruby such as kings and bishops and magnates wore. Rubies made a glory of the cathedral's altar crucifix and church plate without end. Rubies were Christ's blood. Wherever rubies were found gold and silver and crystal were nearby, the precious elements of which God built Heaven.

The rain poured down. It had rained for days, and even inside the house with its thick thatch roof and sturdy walls everything felt wet, even the floor was soft with damp beneath the mats. Aine lay deeply asleep on her mother's canvas mattress under a mound of blankets, her face pale and peaceful. Edith knelt beside her. She was praying. She was at the end of her tether.

'What if you die?' she whispered. She touched Aine's forehead, put her fingers in her daughter's hair, felt the dented bones. This time the demons had been most cruel, flinging Aine from side, arching her back until it seemed her spine must crack, Edith had hardly held her down. The child's demented strength was simply terrifying, and Edith was too frightened to cope with it alone any more. 'What if you die next time?'

Edith came to her hardest decision. She must share her secret.

She picked up Aine. The child hung sleepily on to her neck. Edith swung her cloak over her shoulders, then lifted it over their heads as the rain was so heavy, drumming over them as she hurried along the muddy street to the clergy house. Aine hung awkwardly, heavier than she looked. Edith clasped her tight but one of her feet trailed in the puddles. The cloak slipped and rain trickled down the child's sleeping face.

From the firelit clergy house, the Camera Diane, a boy's sweet unbroken voice chanted psalms. Through the slatted shutters she saw Father Daniel, his cheeks and chin dark with growth so close to his fortnightly shave, eating at the top table in the refectory. The priests and canons of St Paul's lived by the *Institutio Canonicorum* and the Rule of St Paul's which regulated every detail of their lives, from the time and duration for the emptying of bowels to the washing of hands to make them pure again in Heaven's sight.

It was a wine day and Father Daniel lifted his cup with both hands to show his humility as he drank. The bishop in his palace ate fresh salmon and pigeon, no doubt, but below Father Daniel the rows of novices and petty priests at the long mess-tables made do with communal messes of herring as usual, dividing each mess into four equal portions to go with their quarts of beer. It was April and the servant brought Father Daniel a whole young plaice, its tail hanging off one side of the plate, the first of the season. He took one of the filthy knives supplied and cut the white flesh expertly, ate indifferently, so as not to show gluttony. He saw Edith watching him. Poor people gathered at the door nearby scrounging for leftovers. What the hungry priests left was shared among other guests, then the servants removed the messes, gobbling broken meat and fragments of fine conventual loaf into their mouths as they passed behind the priests. The leftovers were shared among the grooms and after them the valets, then the lowest staff and their working wives and their urchins the cathedral sparrows, before the remains were slopped into five-gallon *ollas*, buckets for the paupers. Father Daniel spooned a few mouthfuls of pottage, oatmeal spiced with salt, pepper and saffron from Africa, then drank a pint of beer for his thirst and speared a pork fritter on the point of his knife as an afterthought. Still swallowing, he came into the shelter of the doorway and reached out into the rain, placed his hand on Edith's head.

'What can I do for you, my child?'

'It's Aine!' Edith said. Everything she had held back welled inside her, the tears and raindrops streamed down her face. 'It's Aine and she's sick and she's going to die.'

Father Daniel touched Aine's lolling head. 'She's only asleep.'

Edith trembled with the child's weight, could feel her slipping down. 'It's worse every time. *They* come to her.'

'They?'

Edith whispered so that no one but the priest would hear. 'Demons.'

She got a grip and hefted Aine up with all her strength. The child's head rested sleepily on Edith's shoulder.

Father Daniel was moved to sympathy. 'I know you are a good girl, Edith. I shall pray for her soul.'

'No!' Edith cried. 'Pray for her to live. Let me take her to the cathedral *medicus*. Give me permission.'

Father Daniel drew her into the shelter. Any priest was permitted to cut and burn, but a disease never had a natural cause. Illness was always a sign of God's purpose. He was reluctant to call the *medicus* because to treat illness was to defy God's will. He would be guilty of hubris, the sin of pride.

Father Daniel watched her sadly. A mother was always desperate for her sick child. How many times had he stood here and listened to a mother plead for her child's life, beg for a priest's privileged prayers? Through a priest's prayer many such women could be persuaded to accept their grief and loss, be made quiescent by promises of the child's coming happiness in Heaven, and in the end acquiesce peacefully in the child's death. Sometimes he could even bring them through acquiescence to affirmation, a kind of positive cathartic joy in God's plan, and he wondered how best to bring Edith forward.

He looked into her eyes. 'My child, I—' He stopped as though she had slapped him. What he saw in Edith's eyes was not pleading or submission or supplication. Edith was angry. She might explode with anger.

'It's not right,' she said. He tried to explain, but Edith would not let him speak. 'She suffered. She fought. She nearly died when she was born. She nearly died after. You all said she'd die, *you* did. She didn't. Don't let her die now.' Her loud tone, the rage rising in her words, was attracting attention. People were looking round. Father Daniel realised that whether she knew it or not Edith, the quick, clever, quiet girl he remembered, had grown into a dangerous woman. She shouted at him, 'Do something!'

'My dear Edith—' Father Daniel stopped. He thought of the ulcerated shin-bone of his left leg that had made his life at Canterbury a torment. Finally his agonising varicose ulcers – a condition which afflicted priests and monks more than common people – were treated with white wine and a secret recipe of spices, herbs and powders prescribed by the archbishop's *medicus* and mixed, at appalling expense, by his apothecary. The leg was better now. But he remembered his pain. It was impossible not to feel for Edith's pain now. 'Yes,' Father Daniel agreed. 'I will do what I can. We have a shin-bone of St Paul in the cathedral, and that may help.'

'Tell me what I must do,' Edith said earnestly. 'What prayers, penitences. I'll make whatever gifts I can. Only let my daughter live.'

'Those things will be the most important,' Father Daniel agreed, 'but we shall consult the *medicus* as well, on my authority. He has treated the king for nervous disease.'

'Successfully?'

Father Daniel looked surprised. 'Yes. King Alfred has made gifts of land to the cathedral.'

Edith drew a deep breath. 'Thank you, Father.'

He shrugged his hood over his head and led her through the

puddles towards the infirmary. The child kept slipping down and several times Father Daniel paused in the teeming rain while Edith struggled to lift her. Finally he sheltered in the infirmary porch, then went inside as she came up the steps, and she followed him.

Father Daniel waved his hand through the smoke. Some priests and important visitors kept their chambers here, more comfortably than in the clergy house. A young priest lay dying on straw, the lobes of his ears turned out, the harbinger of death, and a novice kneeling beside him prayed for his soul. Two old men sat by the fire, watching the newcomers jealously, then moved to protect their beds. The infirmary butler came forward, but bowed and returned into the smoke as Father Daniel called for the *medicus*.

'I am Father Adlard.' The priest stepped from the hut erected in the corner of the building. He spoke to Father Daniel in an appraising, authoritative manner. 'I prefer to be called the infirmarer. A *medicus* is a cross between a saint and an enchanter, but I am a physician trained in Rome, at the school of Galen. I am also the cathedral's librarian. One day we shall have a library like the libraries in Rome.' A priest who held one office was fit for another. Rank and seniority mattered, not skill, as the actual duties were performed by subordinates.

'My apologies, physician. I have been away.' Father Daniel bowed respectfully, but Edith said, 'Galen?'

Father Adlard noticed her. 'Who is this?'

'It is a woman,' Father Daniel murmured, and expertly navigated the web of favours and influence by which everything important was achieved. 'It was I who brought those books from Canterbury.'

'Ah!'

'This poor girl is Edith, a carpenter's wife. Her mother, who is with God, preserved my life at the risk of her own. I would return what I owe her memory through the blessing of your skill on the child of her daughter.'

Priests talked in a way that seemed deliberately difficult to understand, but Edith saw the infirmarer was complimented, for he preened visibly. Aine's weight overwhelmed her and she fell to her knees. The infirmarer called his butler, pointed at the child's head to show where he wished to examine. The butler held the hair aside.

'My master Galen was the prince of physicians,' Father Adlard said, pointing for another place to be shown. 'He taught us that every part of the body is perfectly adapted to the body's needs and therefore is an expression of God's will, part of His preordained plan. Veins and arteries contain blood from the liver and lungs. Animal spirit is formed in the brain and distributed by the nerves, which are hollow. It is the brain and nerves we are concerned with here. My dear brother—'

'Please address your remarks to the woman,' Father Daniel said.

Father Adlard glanced at Edith. 'Your daughter—'

'Aine.'

He stopped, irritated by her interruption, then obliged her. 'Aine has the Sacred Disease. She is merely asleep and she will wake. That is my diagnosis and my prognosis.'

'Waking does not heal her,' Edith dared say. 'Soon everyone will know, don't you understand? They will know her to be possessed by demons. Father Adlard—' She clasped her hands in prayer. 'Drive them out. Make her clean.'

'There are certain substances that will purge demons,' Father Adlard said. He clicked his fingers. 'I will instruct the apothecary to prepare aloes, rhubarb and terpeth so that she vomits out the demon filth that has collected inside her, and a lotion of lead acetate to cool her brain. A surgeon will perform a seyney on the girl.'

'Seyney?'

'A bloodletting.'

'Will it heal her?'

Father Adlard looked offended.

Father Daniel gently took Edith's shoulder. 'All healing is through God. You must be obedient.'

'Then give me prayers and penitences, and I shall make gifts—'

'I think, woman,' Father Adlard said over his shoulder, 'that your sort will find the apothecary quite expensive enough.'

Aine's eyelids fluttered as she woke. 'Mummy?'

The surgeon was a butcher, a man not shy of working with flesh. He flashed knives of every sort in his apron. Aine screamed. 'It's for your own good,' Edith said, but she could not watch the cut. Aine screamed again. The blood dripped noisily into a bowl. 'It will make you better,' Edith whispered. The child looked at her tearfully.

'Dark blood, see,' the butcher grunted. 'No vitality. Best got out.' He slipped his knife back in his apron, held out his hand for money, and promised to come back and stop the bleeding that evening.

'Before my husband gets home,' Edith said.

The butcher shrugged, interested. 'Don't know about it, eh?'

'He doesn't know about the expense,' Edith said.

He spat. A woman who lied to her husband about one thing would probably end up lying about everything.

Soon a cathedral sparrow, a breathless dirty-faced boy of about six, arrived with a sauce of strong-smelling herbs and purgatives from the apothecary. He accepted a mouthful of black knyten loaf washed down with beer as a tip, and a kiss from Edith on top of his head because he was young, then scampered cheerfully on his next errand. Meanwhile the apothecary waited outside, holding his hand through the doorway for his payment in silver pennies.

The expense was huge.

There were few ways for a frugal wife to be more frugal. Wolf often ate at the workshop where he worked so hard, and breakfasted there

239

too, rising with the first birdsong. Sometimes it seemed he was hardly home. Edith almost stopped eating, or slipped what she had to Aine. Edith's face became gaunt, her teeth loose. In the summer she grew vegetables in her garth for sale or barter, and whatever was left over or too rotten to find takers she ate. Strangely, her teeth firmed in her gums and she felt well, but she remained painfully thin.

'Skin and bone, you are,' Wolf said when he noticed. There had been a time when he noticed everything about Edith, how she walked, how she smiled, everything. She looked at him wearily.

'You look fine,' she said.

'I don't spend all my time on my knees.' He glanced at the cathedral and she realised how her prayers, Aine beside her, had excluded him. 'See any less of you, Edith, you might as well be a nun.' He did not ask about Aine's health, hurried out. He had no time for them. Nowadays Wolf was always hurrying. Sometimes the man he had become seemed nothing like the man Edith married, and a world apart from the boy she had dreamed of marrying. We have grown up, she realised sadly. Edith wished with all her heart she had wise Leoba to talk to. Wolf was twenty-five, middle-aged, the first flecks of coarse grey over his ears, and he did not look like a carpenter. This morning to go down the street he wore a new blue woollen cloak of the short cut that English merchants had made famous, and Edith had not seen him wear such fine quality before. Money jingled in his silk purse, business was going well. Householders waved to him. From St Paul's chapter he had leased a house shaded by an elm tree across the street, then sub-leased it for an income. Edith realised that he had hardly looked at herself or Aine. As she grew careworn he was even more handsome, reaching towards the prime of his years. Life was good to a man.

Edith looked in her bronze mirror. In her youth a girl had all the advantages, but to a middle-aged woman came all the disadvantages, the loan of her youthful beauty was called in, her muscles lost their grace, her body its life. Yet a man had vitality enough to sire children at twice, three times her age.

Edith gazed at herself starkly in the mirror. Something moved in her reflection. She looked down at Aine and smiled fondly.

But Aine was old enough to look very, very frightened. 'Mummy, I smell flowers.'

The child's head snapped back and she dropped like a stone. She bit her tongue and pink bloody froth dripped from her lips. Her head slammed from side to side and Edith lay on her to ease her struggles, wrapped her in her arms. 'Oh baby,' she cried. 'Baby.'

Aine slept. It was a terribly deep sleep. She looked exhausted.

Edith called out of her doorway, sent one of the cathedral sparrows for the physician. She had always paid him promptly, and Father Adlard came at once, his young assistant scurrying in front of him.

Father Adlard pointed with his staff and the assistant opened Aine's mouth, examined her head.

'It was much worse,' Edith said numbly. 'I've never seen it so bad.'

Father Adlard looked at her consideringly. People were not of the same value. The word of a nobleman was worth more than the word of an ordinary man. A greater man would be fined more for a crime than a lesser man. A man was worth more than a woman. This desperate woman kneeling in front of him could not be helped. He gestured with his staff and his assistant stepped back at once.

'This case is hopeless,' Father Adlard said. 'She will die.'

'Can you do nothing to help her?'

The physician shrugged, put his hands together in prayer, and turned to go.

Edith snatched his sleeve. 'You helped the king with gold pills.'

'The value of a king's body is measured in thousands of shillings.'

Edith said, 'She's worth more than that to me.'

The physician tugged impatiently. His sleeve pulled free of her grasping fingers.

Edith called after him, 'Suppose she were a princess?'

He flung over his shoulder, 'In that case it would be proper of me to recommend quicksilver.'

The assistant closed the door behind him. The sound of their footsteps faded.

'Quicksilver,' Edith said. The liquid metal was as fabulous and expensive as gold.

She knelt in the shadows behind the closed shutters of her house. She touched Aine's forehead. The heat had left her. After a little while Aine's eyelids fluttered and she woke. She yawned, smiled. 'I was dreaming,' she said.

Edith said haggardly, 'Are you better?'

Aine was silent for a while. She sat up, put her arms round her knees, and wept. 'I didn't know it happened, Mummy. I couldn't help it.'

Edith cuddled her. 'I know. I don't blame you.'

Aine blinked away her childish tears. Her blue eyes looked enormous in her elfin face, the tears clung in gleaming drops to her eyelashes. She clung to her mother for reassurance. 'It will be all right, won't it, Mummy?'

Edith said, 'Yes.'

'Are you sorry for me? You won't leave me, will you?'

Edith squeezed her tight. 'I'm not sorry. I'm angry.' I *am* angry, she realised. I'm losing everything that matters to me. My beauty, my husband, my daughter.

Her lips and teeth hurt, pressed hard together. Her hands tightened into fists. She was not very strong, and they trembled. Something her mother had said to her long ago, down there in the dark, came back to her.

If I can, I ought.

'I won't leave you,' Edith repeated. 'I'll buy all the quicksilver you need, and make you well.'

She shuffled forward on her knees as though still praying, but pulled Aine after her. Together, Aine following her mother's example, they lifted the mat behind the hearth. The earth beneath had been stamped flat over the years and peeled in hard flakes between their fingers. Edith felt for the iron ring of the hatch, prised it up. She dragged with all her strength. Aine watched then copied her, helping. The matted soil clung to the hatch as it rose, then slid round their feet. Relieved of its weight, the hatch swung up easily.

They looked down into the old cellar.

'I'm sorry, Aine,' Edith said sadly. She stroked the child's flushed, excited cheeks. 'I was a little older than you, almost of a certain age, when my mother showed me this place. It's our secret.'

'I like secrets!'

'This is the secret you protect with your life, Aine. You must never talk of what you see.'

Aine said practically, 'Why not?'

'Because one day it's yours.'

'I have the Sacred Disease,' Aine whispered, trying to understand secrets. 'That's our secret too, isn't it? Even Daddy doesn't know about that.'

Edith thought about it. 'He does know. But he doesn't really believe it. He thinks it's just the woman's weakness I had. Once I fell, cut myself on brambles. That's all he believes.'

She lowered herself into the ground, held up her arms for Aine, and for a moment their heads touched.

'I have dreams, Mummy.'

'So do I. But your father doesn't,' Edith said. She realised how bitter she sounded. 'Not since he was young.'

'I'm dreaming now,' Aine whispered. She held up the candle as Edith pulled the planks from the wall, lifted her through the gap. Then Edith stopped dead, staring past her.

'What's happened?' Edith cried, confused. Her determination fled, her confident expression was replaced by uncertainty and fear.

Where the elm root hung from the roof of the catacomb, a wooden ladder now stood. Aine watched her mother walk past the shiny patch on the floor, touch the ladder as though she could not believe her eyes. Footprints trailed from the lowest rung of the ladder into the dark. Aine began to cry, upset that her mother was upset. Edith climbed the ladder, pressed her hands against the wooden hatch set across the stone vault at the top. The stout beams of the hatch stood firm, bolted closed, or with a heavy weight placed above.

'It's all right. It's all right.' Edith came down, hugged her daughter. 'Don't worry,' she said, and Aine knew she was very worried. Edith took the candle, and they both stared at the footprints leading away.

Aine whispered, 'Whose are those?'

'Someone who has found their way down here.' Edith gripped Aine's hand tight, led her along the catacomb. Their feet fitted easily in the footprints. Edith saw that the spade was gone from the mound of earth and new earth had been scattered about. The tunnel beside the stone had been much enlarged, shored up with beams. Timbers had been laid crossways along the floor.

She went through.

Aine slipped after her, then gazed in awe at the grooves and signs scrawled over the roof. She fitted her finger into the curves of a letter carved deeply into the stone. Her tongue moved between her lips as she read the rest of the word. It made no sense to her.

RESURGAM.

Edith stopped. The darkness at the end of the tunnel was now covered by a sturdy oak hatch, as if to ensure that no one should fall. She glanced back absently. 'It's Latin. *Resurgam*, I shall rise again.'

Again she looked at the hatch and wondered what to do. 'You'll have to stay here,' she told Aine. 'I'll go down alone.'

Aine said, 'But you said you wouldn't leave me.'

The thought of helping a ten-year-old child down hundreds of feet of rope chilled Edith. She was afraid neither of them was strong enough, and she imagined Aine falling. She imagined them at the bottom without the strength to climb back up.

She murmured, 'You see, I need you at the top because I need you to pull something up on the rope—'

'Pull what up?'

'Something that will make you better, Aine.'

Aine shivered. 'You're doing this for me.' She looked up at her mother, her eyes luminous with candlelight.

'Yes,' Edith said simply. 'I'd do anything for you.'

Before Edith could move Aine bent down and lifted the hatch, pulling, then as it came up she pushed it back, and it thudded on its hinges against the wall. For the first time Edith realised Aine's thin body was becoming lithe, grace flowing into her slim muscles.

She was old enough.

Aine put back her hair from her eyes as she looked down. 'There's no rope,' she said. She braced her legs across the hole and jumped down lightly from sight.

Edith screamed.

Aine stuck her head out of the hole. 'Don't worry,' she said sunnily. 'There's ladders.'

A lamp had been left at the top of the shaft. They lit it from the candle and Aine went quickly down the ladder on to the platform of planks below. It creaked, taking her weight. She dripped burning oil from the lamp over the edge and glimpsed ladders crisscrossed below her, shrinking smaller, fading, going down into the dark.

Edith climbed carefully down beside Aine. 'Someone's been busy.' Together they peered over the railing. 'I'll go first,' Edith said.

But Aine went first, dropping down the ladder easily to the next platform below them, then the one below that. Only the golden circle of her hair showed, and the long fluttering flame of the lamp. Edith touched one of the oak support posts that had been driven sideways into the clay wall. It was well placed and firmly anchored, and the boards had been meticulously pegged to it, good solid workmanship. Edith covered her mouth with her hand, trembling.

Aine called up.

'Coming,' Edith said.

She climbed down the ladders, their angles cleverly using the walls of the shaft to good effect. Sometimes, where it was convenient, steps had simply been cut down the wall, then the ladders began again. Edith heard the sound of running water. Aine waited for her on a platform, hardly more than a ledge, wedged across the top of a greenstone boulder.

Aine stood quietly. A sapling had been tied between the supports, making a railing. 'Who did this?'

Edith replied, 'Someone who knew what they were doing.'

'How much further? Will we get wet?'

'So many questions.' Edith closed her eyes, but when she opened them Aine was already far below her again. The falling water glinted in the lamplight as it sprayed down beneath the ladders. Edith climbed after her wearily. Suddenly the water slid into a channel it had smoothed in the wall, disappearing as abruptly as it had appeared. Its rushing sound faded above her as she descended. Edith looked down. A radiance grew everywhere beneath her, the lamp's flame illuminating white walls of chalk.

Aine had stopped. She called up, 'What is it?'

'It's nothing,' Edith called. 'There's nothing down here to worry about.'

She came down to the last ladder. It stood on a pile of boulders beneath a dome of chalk. She crouched, trying to ease her quivering calf-muscles, watching Aine hold up the flame, the girl's shadow moving one by one along the figures that stood in the wall.

Aine reached forward with her left hand. She placed her palm and fingers carefully into the outline of a painted hand. Then she turned away, the precious moment was gone, and for the first time she seemed to notice the glittering piles of gold thrown down everywhere around the boulders.

But not as much as much as there had been, Edith saw. Dark holes showed where stuff had been taken away, knocked over, looted.

She gave a cry. 'He's taken some. It's gone!'

'There's enough for anyone,' Aine said quietly.

But Edith sounded horrorstruck. 'Don't you understand? It's my sacred trust. These don't belong to *me*, they're not *my* possessions. They're not mine!' She stared round her. 'He's been here! There was a silver statue where you're standing—' Edith dropped the candle, put her hands in her hair. 'Looted. Gone. Spent it on himself. I wondered how your father got that cloak. Lord, how can I have been so blind about him?'

Aine looked round her calmly, then relit the candle from her lamp.

Edith said, 'He deceived me.'

Aine said, 'I can smell flowers.'

Edith stared at her, numb. 'You can't. There's no flowers here.'

Aine inhaled calmly. 'I can smell the scent of the flowers, can't you?'

Edith held her tight. She tried to make Aine lie down so that she would not hurt herself when she fell.

'It's all right,' Aine smiled. 'I'm fine. Everything's all right. Can't you scent all—' She frowned, trying to see them. 'Buttercups. Purple plume thistle. Sorrel and rue.' Hundreds of plants and flowers and herbs, many more than she had names for. 'Pine needles—'

'Stop it!' Edith said. 'It's mad, talking like this. Look where we are.' She threw herself on her knees, praying. Aine looked over her mother's head at the gold. She walked slowly round the cavern.

'The gold isn't it,' Aine said.

Edith repeated, 'One small thing, that's all I have to sell to make you better.'

'But the gold isn't what's wonderful,' Aine said. 'There's more. There's—'

Edith grabbed a gold grail, clasped it to her chest. 'This will save your life, Aine. I'd do anything to save you.'

Aine knelt by the wall. A sloping tunnel led to another chamber. She slid down, stood. She held up the lamp and smiled. A fabulous beast, like the ones Arabian merchants described in their stories of far lands, and monks painted in the borders of their books, encircled her with its tusks. Its tiny red eyes squinted down on her but she felt no fear.

A pile of dirty skins had been thrown down in the centre of the chamber.

Aine walked round them, round and round, the flame flickering above her head.

Above ground the day was sunny and windy, swans circling on the rising tide between the islands, and Edith walked to London Bridge. She had wrapped the grail-platter in a sack like any old junk, but she hurried with it clasped tight to her breasts. Aine walked beside her, a dagger pushed through her girdle, her slim

245

hand resting ready on the handle. The fresh breeze from the east that had brought the ships upriver blew in their faces, fluttered their cloaks behind them. Edith looked at Aine's hair flying, the blue determined glow in the girl's eyes, and realised Aine would use the weapon without hesitation if anyone accosted them. But everyone stepped out of their way, mother and daughter hurrying along the wharves, weaving between the men unloading the ships. A smelly tub unpacked barrels of herring at Belinos's Gate. By a heavily built Norse boat beached on the mud men haggled over the price of walrus tusks, antlers, seal-oil. Saffron, spices and precious rare goods from North Africa and Arabian Spain were declared and taxed on the deck of the strange-looking gilded caravel lying at the king's Custom wharf.

The two women came to a house with two storeys, climbed the unfamiliar stairs up the outside, stood uneasily on the first floor. The roof was tile not thatch, and echoed. People pushed past them, a dog growled. The merchant wore a cloak trimmed with fur. He noticed the two women then ignored them.

The Danish wars had made the traders coming and going past Edith and Aine into rich men, though the pirates that infested the Thames, and the storms that stirred the shallow waters of the estuary into wild fury, might make even a burgess poor again at a moment's notice. Sometimes a few City families banded together to share the risk of a voyage, their mutual distrust allayed by their common heritage, but mostly a man's fortune and his life hung on the fate of his own single vessel.

Edith pushed forward among them. 'Good day.'

The merchant eyed her. 'A day is not good until it is ended.'

Edith slipped the gold platter from the sack. The merchant yawned, hefted it, tested it with his thumbnail, examined the top and bottom with sharp glances, yawned again and pushed it back. 'I have seen many of these Christian holy grails.'

'You hardly examined it!' Edith said. 'It's not stolen.'

'My name is Lothere and my word is good.' The heathen smiled at Aine, and she tightened her hand on her knife.

Lothere picked a fishbone from his mouth, belched, then said, 'Shillings.' He flapped the fingers of his hand a few times, making his offer so that it should not be overheard by the others.

Edith said uncertainly, 'Is that fair?'

Lothere shrugged. 'I don't handle these any more, there's a glut on the market. I'm doing this as a favour to you at this price.' He smiled, picked his slimy brown teeth with the fishbone.

Edith said, 'Those others, were they sold by a man in a blue cloak?'

The merchant yawned again. 'I buy from whoever sells, I sell to whoever buys. I don't judge a man by the colour of his cloak.' He closed his mouth with a snap, shaken by the anger in Edith's eyes.

'Yes, a man in a blue cloak. Sometimes another man, scarred hands. I don't know his name.'

Edith said, 'I accept your offer.'

Outside, her face was frantic. 'It was him. He's been selling it here. And Hewald too. Scarred hands! They're both in on it. How could they do this to me?' She wailed, 'I'm a fool.'

'What will you do?'

'I love him,' Edith said quietly. 'Even after all he's done to me I still love him.'

People were starting to notice them. Aine held her mother's hand and Edith looked at the purse of Lothere's shillings as though seeing them for the first time. She gripped Aine tight and they hurried to the moneychangers at the church by the bridge, changed the shillings into English dinars, then spoke to people on the wharf. A black-bearded man with a flowing robe, and yellow-stained lips and fingers, was pointed out to them. In this tiny swarming village by London Bridge Edith was sure everyone knew everyone else. Bales of wool were loaded on to the Arab boat, now afloat on the tide. The Arab sat in a hut on the stern listening to what Edith had to say. A boy placed a bowl of bright yellow eggs in front of him. He selected one and peeled the shell, flicked the pieces to the seagulls. Even the white of the egg was bright yellow, Aine saw. He offered it to her with a smile, uneasy at doing business with a woman but doting on the child.

'Quicksilver?' he asked Edith at last, casually. 'Then, she must be most precious to you.'

'I'll pay whatever price you ask,' Edith said, putting the bag of dinars on the table.

The Arab covered the bag with his yellow fingers. 'By coincidence that is exactly the price I had in mind.' He sent the boy to fetch a crystal vial of heavy silver liquid. 'Precious metals bring enlightenment to the soul. A little of what overheats the body does it good. The mercurial anima is the power, essence, nature and quality of all living things. Mix the quicksilver with powdered chalk. It will make a grey elixir that this poor afflicted girl will take as pills, one a day or before an attack.'

But I smelt the flowers in the cavern beneath the dome, Aine remembered. And I was not afflicted.

She followed her mother home. Edith crushed the quicksilver with chalk, gave Aine a little on the point of a knife. Aine made a face. 'It tastes horrid.'

'That means it's doing you good,' Edith said. Her face looked drawn and weary. She was thinking about Wolf coming home and what she would say.

Aine lay down quietly and closed her eyes.

'*But I did*,' she whispered to herself. '*I did smell the flowers.*'

She rolled on her side, slipped the pellet from the corner of her mouth into her palm, and pressed it into the soil of the floor.

She woke. It was night and her father was laughing insincerely. Aine recognised his tone at once. 'Edith, Edith,' came his voice reproachfully. 'Don't you trust me?'

Aine peeped beneath the curtain. The fur trimming his expensive blue cloak gleamed in the firelight.

'I trust you and I love you with all my heart,' Edith said. 'You are my husband. But—'

'Then there is no more to be said.'

He sat on the stool, and she pulled off his boots obediently.

Then she spoke with her head down. 'But you stole from me.'

Aine listened.

Her father's voice came angrily. 'How dare you speak to me like this? You are my wife. You *are* me, my flesh. Everything of yours is mine.'

Aine watched his eyes. His eyes were anxious, calculating. He was not angry, she knew, he was blustering. He was frightened. Perhaps he was frightened of Hewald. Or simply of himself, the position his greed had got him.

Edith whispered, 'The gold is not mine. When I sold the grail today I was stealing, yes, as you have been stealing. But you have stolen more.'

Aine shifted on her knees behind the curtain, watching intently.

Her father drank a cup, handed it to Edith for more, wiped his lips. He exhaled noisily. 'I did it for our child, Edith, don't you understand?' He didn't mention Hewald. 'All these years you knew of the treasure and you did nothing with it. Why? Because your mother said so! Nothing for Aine. Until your guilty conscience, watching her suffering, drove you to it.'

'That's unfair—'

'Unfair! Have I married into a family of Furies? Your mother listened to your father's screams while he was tortured to death and did nothing!'

'She didn't know—'

'Don't tell me how holy you are, you're as bad as me.' He held her earnestly, ignoring the cup. Then he smiled, spoke easily. 'We took the gold together, you and I. At separate times, that's all. We do everything together. I love you, Edith.'

Aine watched him kiss her mouth with his eyes open.

Edith softened. She closed her eyes, even stroked his hair. He stepped back and she refilled the cup. Then a remnant of her anger flickered, unsoothed, and she became insistent. 'But you mustn't go down there any more.'

'Agreed,' Wolf said cheerfully. He returned to his stool, slapped his knees. 'Agreed!' He held out his arms for her to come to him.

'Not even once,' Edith said.

He frowned at her presumption in again telling him what to do, then made the sign of the cross in front of his chest. 'Cross my heart and hope to die.'

'And Hewald. He must swear too.'

'He doesn't know where I got it. He helped me handle the stuff, knew where to get the best prices, that's all.'

She looked relieved, sat on his knee like a child, cuddled him. 'Husband, I'm so glad you've explained everything. Can you not claim some of it back? Explain that it was not yours to sell?'

He looked incredulous, then said flatly, 'You are an ignorant woman. You don't know how hard life is. I built this house, I sheltered you from everything. We won't speak of this any more.'

'Promise me you'll try.'

'Why do women always try to bind us with promises?' Aine heard how angry he sounded again, and he blustered, 'You deceived me, Edith.'

'I deceived you!'

'You kept the gold secret from me. I found it for myself. I thought we didn't have secrets, Edith. I thought our hearts were open to one another.'

Edith looked miserable. Aine wondered why did she did not see how he manipulated her. Mother was still a woman in love.

Wolf said angrily, 'How do you think we have lived so well? Listen to me, Edith. Think of all it can buy. A few more trinkets, that's all I ask. A man who owns five hides of land is assessed as a thane, and sits at the king's table as a man of consequence. I have three hides of land, I own the living of three families. When I own five hides men will pay their respects to me. My word will be worth something. I will be a man of value. And you, Edith, my wife, will glow in my reflection and wear a lady's gown as a right, not as a cheat.'

Shaken, Edith remembered the gown she had dared to wear on St Valentine's Day so long ago. It still rankled him. She wished she had never given herself airs. She said, 'You won't go down there again. Not for one penny. Promise me.'

But he pushed her away furiously. 'I already promised!'

'Promise me again if you love me.'

He said nothing. She waited. He shouted, 'I promise it.'

Edith came to the curtain. She would check Aine was asleep, but as she reached out for the curtain she glanced back.

'I do love you, husband. That's true and that's all that matters.'

She pulled back the curtain and looked down. Aine lay peace-fully asleep.

Aine lay awake. Why did Mother believe everything Father promised her? Aine had seen the look in his eyes. Did he really love her as he swore he did? Aine felt as though the ground had dropped away beneath her and everything she had known was changed. *Almost of a certain age*, her mother had said. Aine struggled to understand.

Truth was hard. She knew that from the long sermons at the cathedral. She knew it from learning about God. How could her father be telling Edith the truth when his loving words came so easily to him, with a smile and a kiss? Why did Edith refuse to see her husband was lying to her, cheating her?

Aine lay in the dark with a protective, jealous light in her eyes for her mother.

Father was a man, and she tried to see him not as her father but like any other man. He had laid his hands on a fortune in gold, *their* gold, gold that men coveted above all other things, even women, for gold bought women. He probably thought of nothing else, probably dreamt of nothing but gold, saw nothing but gold. Not his family. Not his wife. He had plundered and sold enough to feed his hunger, he had almost the whole hoard in his grasp after all his labour and preparation and deceit – and now he so easily stopped, and promised no?

She thought, only Mother stands in his way.

Mother believes everything he promises her because she has to. She's afraid not to. Once she sees him as he really is all she's gone through for him, everything she's done for him, even the love she feels for him, is a mistake.

She feels *she* is the guilty one.

Aine heard someone stirring, peeped beneath the curtain. Her father sat up scratching his hair. He slid from under the wool blanket carefully, not to wake his sleeping wife, and stood in his underclothes. He scratched his armpits, yawning, looking down at Edith. Nothing could be more innocent than the sight of him dressing in the early morning, moving round quietly not realising he was observed.

Aine peeped at his calm, handsome, masculine face. She wondered what he really felt in his heart, what he was really thinking behind his wide, honest eyes. He looked confident and prosperous, he moved with certainty, hefted the heavy handle of his dagger and pushed it into the matching silver-chased scabbard at his waist. His cloak swirled as he turned, sending pieces of straw chasing across the floor.

He looked like a man of birth, not a carpenter.

His grey shadow walked along the street in the fog of dawn, and she slipped after him behind the grey dwellings. He stopped at a house and drank a jug of beer, ate a plate of bread and sprats. He looked round, but Aine hid. His footsteps went past the wall and she heard him turn the corner into Paul's Wharf Lane, crept after him. The sun glowed across the mist rising from the river and Hewald, coming up on horseback, called him. Aine watched behind a stook of hay. Hewald dismounted and clapped Wolf across the shoulders, smiling. Wolf shook his head. Hewald's face drew inwards, growing in power. His smile turned into a grimace filled with lines. He pulled Wolf's shoulder back with his hand, talking rapidly, and Wolf could not shrug him off. The horse cropped the verge, filling its mouth with buttercups while the two men argued. Wolf shook his head for the second time.

Hewald let go the rein, staring at Wolf, then drew the nail of his thumb across his throat.

Wolf looked down. Hewald laughed abruptly and tugged the horse after him towards the longhouse, which had been divided into workshops. After a few moments Wolf, too, followed.

Aine wondered what she had seen. She was afraid.

She ducked back along a ditch, bent double, then walked home. Before she could speak Mother told her off for playing outside, treating her like a child, then kissed her and fetched the grey powder. The bitter metallic taste filled Aine's mouth. When she was not watched she spat it out in the herb-beds of the garth, but the taste stayed with her all day.

Hewald drawing his thumb across his throat.

When her father came home, Aine watched him. He tousled her hair. He ate his supper by the candle, meat for the second time today. He saw her looking at him and winked at her. Aine was sent to sleep. Through the curtain she heard him talking to Edith about various desultory matters. He sat by the fire for a while then went to bed. The straw beneath his palliasse was new and he complained of its sharpness, sneezed. Edith's voice soothed him. Later their snores came.

Aine lay awake, then slept late. She woke with the bitter taste still in her mouth, sick with it, and Edith gave her more of the precious grey powder. Aine spat it out running into Paul's Wharf Lane. There were places a child could innocently go, hide, play, that an adult never could. She played in the ditch among the wild flowers, glancing up from time to time. Around Hewald's workshops straggled the miserable huts with sunken floors where the slaves and their families lived like animals. Down on the river a boat arrived laden to the gunwales with timber from Thorney. Ox carts with slatted sides heaved the wood uphill where the trunks and boughs were sawn and shaped in the yard, but that was all. The workshop was not as busy as she had imagined. Several times her father or Hewald came out and shouted orders. A surly labourer was whipped but the oxen were carefully fed and watered. Several times men came on business and Hewald and Wolf fawned on them. The sun went down. Aine returned home and Edith pulled her ears and shouted at her for not telling her where she was going. 'What do you think you were doing?'

Aine shrugged.

'Playing! I was worried to death about you,' Edith said, relenting. 'You're overheated.' She stroked Aine's forehead tenderly, then stared at the pale strands clinging to her fingers.

'What's the matter?'

'It's nothing, dear. Just a few loose hairs.'

Next morning Aine spat out her medicine and was violently sick. She played in the ditch hidden behind the boundary mound, weaving flower-chains which she hung round her neck, watching the longhouse. Her head ached and though she put the flower petals to her nose she could not smell them, only taste the bitter quicksilver. All day she was too sick to eat, and she followed her father home feeling thin and weak. He stopped at the house by the elm tree, went inside to check on his sub-tenants.

Aine waited nearby with her head between her knees, wishing he would come out.

She sat up. Darkness had fallen and she could hardly see the house. She was sure the door had not moved. She crept forward and pushed it with her hands but it was fixed, made of oak, bolted or barred on the inside. She heard footsteps and shrank behind a wall. The bolts banged and Wolf came out, looked round him, locked the door with a smith's iron key.

Aine ran. She was home before him. She watched him steadily all evening, shivering, eyes blue and steady and enormous in her distorted head. Wolf would not meet her eyes. He grew irritable with Edith and Aine was sent to bed.

'Stop it,' Edith said in the morning. 'What is it, Aine, some sort of game you're playing? You're annoying your father.' She took the vial which she had hung round her neck on a leather thong, made up the grey powder and held it out on a spoon. This time Aine pinched it between her fingers and put them in her mouth. 'It tastes horrid!' she exclaimed, which was what Edith expected. But Aine kept her fingers pinched tight, and later she washed the powder off her fingertips in the water barrel. She gazed at her reflection. Her forehead showed the odd silvery sheen that the Arab had assured Mother would be the sign of the divine quicksilver doing her good. Aine rubbed it with her hands but her hands shook, and the sheen remained.

'I'm turning to silver,' she whispered.

That evening she saw her father return not to his own home but again to the house by the elm tree. Again he bolted the door as soon as he was inside. Darkness fell and the moon rose above the villages of Corn Hill. A single light gleamed in the tollhouse by London Bridge, then at each City gate, and at each tower along the wall to show the watch was kept. The gates were closed but the lights on the towers remained, glittering like a ring of eyes protecting London. Wolf stayed inside the house for about an hour. When he came out he looked round him carefully and locked the door with the iron key.

Aine waited behind the elm tree. His footsteps faded.

She climbed along a branch to the shuttered window, prised the slats open with a stick. Bars of moonlight illuminated the interior. The house was a shell, nothing inside but bare earth floors awaiting occupation. She peered, just able to see a piece of wood clumsily covered with soil close to the wall beneath her.

She was sure it was the top of the hatch whose underside she had seen set into the roof of the catacomb.

Aine breathed quick breaths. She pushed the shutter closed. She ran home.

In the morning, alone with her mother, she asked, 'Do you remember the tree root?'

Edith, mixing the grey powder, gave her daughter a brisk no-nonsense look. 'I don't know what's got into you these past few days.' But Aine could see she did remember the tree root.

Aine said fiercely, 'Why won't you see how badly he treats you!'

'Life looks so simple at your age. One day you'll understand.'

Aine stamped her foot. 'I *won't* understand. I won't try.'

Edith held out the spoon of medicine, trying to overcome her young daughter's tantrum with a loving smile.

'I wish you were angry again,' Aine said. 'I won't let anyone treat me the way he treats you. I'm never going to get married.'

Edith looked impatient at Aine's wilfulness. She pushed the spoon forward.

Aine said tearfully, 'He's lying, Mother. He's lying.' She knocked the spoon from her mother's hand.

Edith stared at the precious powder scattered on the floor. 'Look what you did,' she said. She cried, trying to scoop it up in her palms, crying as though her heart was broken.

'I'm sorry, I'm sorry!' Aine ran out, appalled.

She sat cross-legged by the ditch, watching the activity in the longhouse with steady eyes. The sun grew hot and she wove a garland for her head, twining the stems of buttercup and celandine, hedge-mustard, ox-eye daisy, dog-roses and cat's-ears, bittersweet, speedwell, self-heal and black horehound, until the petals and leaves shaded her eyes. Down by the river a lord's reeve inspected a fisherman's eel catch and claimed the lord's share. A larger vessel rowed downstream, the mast put up beyond London Bridge, then was made to moor at the king's Custom wharf, its cargo valued and taxed before departure. Clouds came up and the wind rose, ruffling the river's perfect reflection of the sky, and everything turned to grey waves of wind and rain. But the air was warm and Aine sheltered behind a boundary oak. The leaves did not begin to drip around her until the light was failing. Her father came from the longhouse, looked up at the sky with his cloak flapping. He talked to someone Aine could not see. He shook his head, then ran his hands through his wet hair, nodded. He hurried away uphill.

Aine took a step to follow him, then shrank back as Hewald came out of the doorway. He wore a long hooded travelling cloak fastened about his neck with a gold torc. He sheltered beneath the eaves and put back the hood, shouted for slaves. Ragged men dashed forward into the downpour and splashed about, pulling oxen from the paddock, harnessing two pairs of the strong, slow beasts. Hewald cursed their efforts impatiently. The slaves teamed the oxen to the heavy four-wheel wagon, then one of them crouched and made a stirrup of his hands for his master's boot. Hewald climbed aboard the wagon, cursed them again and sent them scampering away.

Alone, he pulled his hood well forward against the rain and lashed the whip, sending spray from the backs of the oxen. The animals jerked against the harness, grunted, and the wagon lumbered slowly on to the street. As it turned uphill past the boundary oak Aine circled the broad trunk, keeping the opposite side from Hewald the carpenter as the wagon creaked past.

The rain soaked her instantly as she ran after the lumbering shape towards Carter Lane. She lost sight of the wagon in the jumble of buildings around the bishop's palace and the cathedral. The markets had all packed up hours ago but left their mud and refuse behind. A black broad-shouldered pig grunted and trotted hungrily after Aine, then stopped to bite something more interesting in the mud. The wagon's ruts filled with rain and she followed them close by the streaming walls of the cathedral. The water pouring from the thatch gleamed like a veil in the last of the light. The wheel-ruts found the street, bumped between huts and hovels towards the houses.

The dark outline of the wagon stood beneath the shelter of the elm tree at the empty house. Hewald moved between the open door of the house and the wagon, loading blankets aboard. They looked very heavy, and the pouring rain made them heavier. Hewald grunted, slipping.

A corner of the blanket he was carrying flapped down and something gleamed gold inside. He flapped the corner quickly back in place, slid it on the back of the wagon and looked round him carefully. His cloak opened and Aine saw a long sword at his waist. Raindrops trickled down her nose, dripped from her chin. Hewald rested his hand on his sword-pommel, then shoved the cargo forward on the wagon and went back in the house.

Before he reappeared Aine slipped across the street. She was afraid she would find her mother still crying, or furiously angry, but instead Edith ran forward instantly and hugged Aine's wet frail body against her own warmth, pulled her to the fire. 'You're soaking. You're shivering. It's raining. Have you been trying to punish me? Your hair's black with wet. I've been so worried—'

'They're stealing everything,' Aine said. 'Don't you see?' But Edith had closed the door. Aine said miserably, 'He promises you he won't go down there any more but he doesn't mean it, he's down there every day. He says he loves you but he doesn't know what it means. He's stealing everything of ours!'

But Edith wrapped her in a blanket. 'You're my little girl,' she murmured. 'I've been so worried. I hate you doing this, Aine. Forgive me. I just want what's best for you.'

Aine pointed through the window slats. 'Look.'

Edith stared at the fire. 'You've got to stop this, Aine.' She gripped tight, but Aine snatched her hand away. She backed past the fire, then dropped to her knees and swept her hands through the straw, found the ring, pulled it.

'Don't!' Edith said.

Aine snatched a piece of burning branch from the fire, dropped down. From the cellar she looked up at her mother's face, then ran into the dark.

'Don't! Stop!' Edith's cries followed her, fading.

Aine held up the flaming branch. The catacomb was empty. She heard no sound but the crackling of the flames. She pushed past the elm root to the ladder, discarded sacks lying round its foot. Ropes led up it to a pulley hanging from the open hatch. At the top of the ladder was the empty house.

Aine put her foot on the bottom rung. She climbed up a step, then another. She could see the roof of the house above her. She put her foot on the third step. It creaked.

There came the sound of rain and Hewald's voice grunted, 'Wolf? Last load!'

Edith came into the catacomb carrying a lamp, ducked past the root. 'Aine! What are you doing?'

Aine swung all her weight on the ring that secured the lid of the hatch. The pulley came loose, fell past her on the ladder with a noisy clatter, trailed a mess of uncoiling ropes. 'Wolf?' Hewald's voice hissed from above. 'What you at, old cock? Leave the rest, my man on the gate comes off at midnight—'

The lid swung down, cutting him off. Aine snapped the hook over the ring, securing it. She stepped down beside her mother.

Edith quietly picked up the pulley. She understood clearly that such things were used for hoisting heavy loads. She had seen builders use pulleys to swing the stone cross back up to the roof of St Paul's. Now she examined the cleverly worked mechanism as if to find an excuse for it. She put it down slowly.

'I love him,' she said. 'Wolf loves me. He loved me here. There's so much you don't know. You're so young.'

'Every evening he brings up stuff from below, all he can carry,' Aine said. 'He made a store of it here, loaded it into sacks. Tonight Hewald brought the wagon.'

'But Wolf—'

'They're going, don't you see? They're leaving us!' Aine looked round her. Her eyes widened, realising. *'Where is he?'*

A glow of light appeared at the far end of the catacomb.

Leave the rest, my man on the gate comes off at midnight—

Hewald stepped back from the lid, stepping back faster and faster until his broad shoulders banged into the wall of the house. It cracked, cheaply built. He stared at the lid and wondered what had gone wrong. Then a cunning look came into his eyes.

One way or another he would have got rid of Wolf anyway. Cut his throat or broken his head, that man was too pretty to last, and he had a conscience. No room for that with the load they were carrying.

'Suits me, old cock,' Hewald whispered. He saluted the lid mockingly, pulled the hood over his head and splashed outside into the rain. Time to spare before midnight.

Lightning flashed and something gleamed gold on the back of the wagon. He tossed a sack over it, swung himself on to the seat, lashed the whip, and the heavy vehicle rumbled downhill.

Aine ran down the catacomb towards the glow. She crouched, pushed forward round the rock, held up the burning branch in front of her as she crawled. The flames singed her arm.

The hatch at the end was open and light flickered up from below, growing.

She stared down the shaft. Her father stared up.

Neither moved. He stuck his candle on the rail of the platform beside him. The ladders slanted into the gloom beneath him. The candleflame and the burning branch fluttered in the draught from below. In his arms he held a tall reliquary of gold and rubies, the most precious object Aine had ever seen.

He smiled.

He kissed the gold reliquary and put it down between his feet, slowly.

He reached forward and gripped the ladder with his hands, put one foot on the bottom rung, staring up at her, smiling, but she saw into his eyes.

He took the first step up.

Aine shouted. She tried to slam the hatch but it would not move. Edith held it tight, open. Her knuckles stood out white from her hand.

'I love you, Wolf,' she called down in a lost voice. 'I'll never love anyone but you.'

He smiled with all his teeth, making soothing noises, climbing up the ladder towards the two women easily, step by step, not alarming them. The silver-chased handle of his dagger glinted in his belt, and his hand touched it as he climbed.

'Edith, Edith,' he said. 'This is the palace of our love. Do you remember?' He reached up, pulled himself up another step.

'I remember everything,' Edith said.

Again his hand touched the handle of his dagger. Aine knew what was happening. His muscles tensed, she screamed at him, he rushed up the ladder with all his strength and speed. She threw the burning branch. He warded it off with his forearm, shouted as the falling branch knocked the candle into the dark. They heard the branch rattling down the ladders crisscrossed beneath him, throwing off sparks, then it fell free, its flame pulled out behind it like a comet's tail. Aine snatched the crystal vial of quicksilver from her mother's neck, flung it down and it struck his face, whirled into the dark. Now the only light came from Edith's lamp, illuminating his cut face and his clawed hands and his dagger as he lunged towards her throat.

Edith slammed the hatch.

She fell across the hatchway to hold it down with her weight but it lifted an inch. Wolf's fingertips groped through the gap. Both women screamed.

Aine dropped across her mother, shot the bolt, and they piled earth across the top of the hatchway until they could see nothing but earth, and the hatch did not move again.

Aine sat up. The two women embraced each other so tight they almost hurt one another, both determined, and both with a kind of cold anger growing inside them to retrieve what had been stolen from them.

'Hewald,' they said.

Hewald was only just in time. 'You're lucky my replacement's late,' grumbled his man on Lud's Gate. Hewald tossed him a gold coin.

'Yes, I am lucky,' he said. He looked back. Something was wrong.

It had stopped raining and the moon shone between moon-coloured clouds. The fat tollman bit the coin suspiciously, weighed it in his palm. Hewald flicked the whip impatiently, but the gate remained closed.

'His legs again I expect,' the tollman remarked. 'Always having trouble with his legs.' He took an age shoving past the wagon. 'What's the hurry, then?'

'Just open the gate.' Hewald threw him a handful of pennies. 'Here, for the other lads.'

Infuriatingly, the tollman bent down to pick them up. 'I'll make sure they get them,' he said. 'Don't you worry.'

Hewald glanced behind him. 'Open the gate!'

'Very expensive, this job is,' said the tollman agreeably, 'but always a pleasure.' He opened one side of the gate barely enough to let the wagon through, stood yawning. He watched the wagon bump down the steep hill to the Fleet river, the oxen digging their legs into the mud between the piles of rubbish, holding back the vehicle from running over them. Carrying a weight all right. He heard the whip lashing and the rumble of the wagon crossing the bridge of tree trunks, and the beasts grunting as they pulled uphill along the Strand towards the old wych.

Then he heard footsteps running and shouts from the other lads.

A girl jumped the toll, dashed through the gate, knocked into him. His big belly sent her sprawling. But she was up in a flash. She ran downhill with the moonlight showing her pale legs.

'Hoi!' he shouted. 'Stop! Thief!' The lads were already running after her, a chase with legs like that at the end was always good sport. He wished he was thirty years younger, then tightened his belt, threw down his cap, and thumped after them.

Hewald lashed the oxen until their backs were black with blood under the moonlight, but they walked no faster. Soon he'd afford horses. He looked back, saw torches burning in Lud's Gate. They started off, came streaming downhill to the Fleet. He lashed the oxen and they plodded forward. He should have paid for horses. The ruins of Old Wych rose around him, spears of charred timber, broken frames. By his left hand the moon gleamed like silver on the Thames. Round the curve of the river he glimpsed a yellow light or two, the West Minster on Thorney Island. Once he came down off the spine of the Strand he would find nothing but marshes on each side, the islands of Eia and Chelsea, Putney and Battersea. He would not be able to turn away.

He twisted round. Lights crossing the Fleet, more coming through Lud's Gate. A hue and cry.

Hewald dragged on the right hand rein, turned north through the ruins. This was dangerous ground. There were abandoned wells for the oxen to fall into, old post-holes to break their legs. Away from the road a man was supposed to shout or blow a horn to show his presence, or be taken for a thief. Hewald grunted with dark amusement. He'd stolen a greater fortune than most men had the guts to dream of, and now his greatest risk was falling in with thieves.

Or simply getting lost on this winding path.

The oxen tugged wearily uphill. The ruins fell behind him. In the fields a church with a square tower painted by the moon's glow stood alone, and he glimpsed the Oxford lane beyond it. Hewald cursed, hearing distant shouts. Everywhere round him now were old boundary mounds, easy to jump across and escape on foot but impossible for the wagon. He thought he saw shadows running in the fields, men or deer. He threw back his hood, wiped his hand across his eyes, but could not be sure.

Torches flickered behind him in the ruins of Old Wych.

He turned towards the church and lashed the whip. Even the meanest church had a hedge round it to keep out market stalls, or traders touting wares on the convenient tombs and gravestones. It would be a good hiding place while the chase went past.

Hewald pushed through the gate and the oxen plodded into the churchyard.

The shouts were closer now. He thought he saw some men run by the church, wondered if he had disturbed graverobbers.

Then nothing moved in the churchyard of St Martin's-in-the-fields.

Hewald jumped down from the wagon into a mound of soft soil, recoiled at the smell. Then he stepped back with an exclamation, for he had almost jumped into an open grave. The moonlight revealed the body of a man or woman crumpled in the earth, it was impossible to tell which.

Someone shouted, 'There she is! Catch her!' Hewald heard cries, but it was only the sound of the chase baying after one of their own.

They would come back.

He dragged the blankets and sacks and gold and silver off the wagon, dropped them into the grave until the body was completely covered by the golden weight and the grave glittered with jewels, precious metals and packing straw. With his feet he kicked soil over the top, then found a spade and finished his labour. He smoothed it carefully so that the mound would look as neat as any other.

A sapling grew nearby. He pulled it out and planted it where he had dug, so that he would know his work.

He opened the gate and slapped the oxen to send them on their way. He would spend the night at the West Minster almonry, or under a tree if he had to, and return one dark quiet night at his leisure.

He walked a few paces from St Martin's then shrank back against the hedge, seeing a girl's pale legs. It was Wolf's brat, the sick daughter who would never be good for anything. He grasped the pommel of his longsword, lifted it the first six inches in case she saw him.

But the girl saw the empty wagon bumping in the field and ran after it. Another woman followed her more slowly, Edith, the bitch whose marriage had started the whole thing off. Hewald let them get on with it. He turned away, followed the hedge round the corner to the road, and walked a few paces.

'Oooh, that's a nice piece of work,' said a low voice.

Two men came from the shadows by the road, daggers drawn.

Hewald turned. A third man stood behind him.

'Gold, that is,' the first man murmured. He reached out and fingered the torc at Hewald's neck.

The torc was of no account, a plated gift from his wife, he had forgotten it. 'Gold?' he said. 'But this is *nothing*—'

Fingers snatched the torc from his neck. Hewald tried to draw his sword but the blade would not come out quickly enough. A dagger slid softly under his ribs, the wind bubbled from his lungs.

Hewald lay on the road, his life draining away. His sword was gone. He felt his body being stripped of everything of value, cloak, leather scabbard, leather belt, smock. His body jerked and he supposed they were pulling off his calfskin boots, and when that was done they would throw him in the ditch, and the badgers would come, but by then he would be dead. In his last moment he sensed something more. He tried to see it.

Darkness.

The darkness pressed in on Wolf like an intolerable weight.

He screamed Edith's name. She did not come.

He sobbed for his daughter.

He begged for their forgiveness. He begged for their love. He begged for them to let him out.

He was afraid of the dark.

He bent his head under the hatch and heaved with his shoulders, his hands braced on his knees. The hatch would not move. Sweat and tears dripped from his face. A tendon tore in his leg and the ladder broke, dumped him down on the platform below.

He lay weeping in the dark.

Far below him glittered a spark of light. It was the branch Aine had thrown down. His eyes narrowed. Perhaps there was another way out.

Yes, perhaps there was another way out.

It was a long way down in the dark.

Wolf climbed down. Sometimes his leg hurt. Sometimes he imagined shapes in the dark, but the spark of light drew him down. He heard the chuckle of water, and when the darkness was silent again he found his lips were dry, and realised he had forgotten to drink. He was very thirsty, but he was afraid to climb up again.

He could hear his breathing now, echoing, and suddenly there were rocks under his feet. The branch glimmered dully to one side. It burnt his hands when he lifted it but he would not let the sweet light go. He blew on the embers, laughing when the first yellow flame appeared.

It went out.

He stared in the dark. He fixed all his concentration on the one remaining spark. He blew gently. The yellow flame curled dully over the charred wood, rose.

He found the candle, but the fall had shattered it to pieces.

Wolf straightened slowly. He looked round him. He realised he had never really looked round before, never seen all of this. His eyes had been filled with the gold. The gold was almost gone now, making more space, and he saw the shapes along the walls. He wondered what they were.

'The more you look the more you see,' he whispered.

He moved forward then sensed someone standing behind him, and the hairs rose on the back of his neck. He turned, but it was only his shadow.

The flame fluttered in front of him. Here was the way out. He knelt in front of the tunnel sloping down, leading deeper.

The wind breathed in his face like a deep sigh.

Deeper . . .

He whispered, 'The more you seek the more you find.'

The flame flickered and he blew it anxiously, then slid down farther and farther.

It felt as if many days and nights passed, but it was always night down here.

'It must be nearly dawn,' Edith said. She sat by the hatch and picked a burr off her ankle. Her feet were soaked with dew. 'He's been down there nearly all night.'

They glanced at one another with frightened looks, then cleared the earth from the hatchway. Weariness and all they had lost had sapped the anger and determination that had kept them going. Aine squeezed her mother's hand. She voiced what both of them were thinking.

'What if he's angry with us?'

'I don't know.' Edith shrugged. 'I suppose he'd be right. It meant so much to him. I'll always feel as though I let him down.'

'What will he do to us?'

'I don't know. I suppose that's up to him. He can do whatever he wants. He's the head of the family.'

They sat in silence for a while, afraid to open the hatch.

Aine murmured, 'Do you think we'll ever get it back?'

'The gold?' Edith shook her head. 'Hewald must have had another accomplice, a second wagon. No, Aine. It's gone. I lost it. I've betrayed my mother's sacred trust, and I've nothing to hand down to you.'

'I wonder,' Aine said, and it was she who reached forward and opened the hatch.

No one was there.

She called down. No one answered.

She went nimbly down the ladder, missing the broken rungs, and called up from the platform. 'He must have gone right down.'

'Wait for me,' Edith said.

Aine picked up the gold reliquary and shook it gently. Something soft bumped inside but she couldn't open it. She rested it in the crook of her elbow, holding the top against her hand with the lamp, and started down. On the way she drank thirstily from the stream, then looked round her in the cavern beneath the dome.

'He's not here.'

'Wait,' Edith called down.

Aine skipped down the pile of rocks. She walked round the walls, smiling, inhaling the scent of lilies, campion, tormentil and rue. 'Can you smell them?'

'What?' Edith said. She came off the ladder and backed nervously down the rocks.

'Flowers!' Aine called gaily. She knelt by the entrance to the sloping tunnel, the flame gleaming in her eyes, then slid down.

'Wait!' Edith called, then crawled after her.

In the cavern with the big animal, Aine's lamplight already bobbed on the other side. It went almost dark and Edith held up her own lamp, following. There was another way out. Edith ducked down grumbling about her knees, came into another cavern, but Aine was already gone. The walls were covered with stick-figures such as children draw. Edith did not want to look at them. For the first time she shouted, really shouted at the top of her voice. 'Wait!' She groaned when there was no response, then crawled forward after her daughter into the next tunnel.

Aine stood up in a high cavern. She looked round her in wonder, then turned back to her mother. 'It's marvellous,' she whispered. 'Look!'

But all Edith saw was the figure of her husband, his arms around his knees, sitting quietly on the rock slab at the centre of the cavern. She approached him but he did not move. His eyes were huge and black, the pupils expanded for total darkness, filling the iris so there was no room for colour. Beside him rested the charred remains of the branch that had brought him this far.

She touched his motionless face. 'Wolf,' she said.

'Father,' Aine said, putting down the reliquary on the slab.

'Husband.' Edith took him in her arms and he rocked like a baby. The lamplight shone steadily in each eye. Edith took his hand, then recoiled. It was terribly burnt. She said gently, 'We're taking you home.'

They lifted him. He shuffled to his feet, gave Edith his hand. He smiled trustingly.

Aine said, 'He needs you for everything.'

They walked towards the tunnel a step at a time, and as they helped him climb slowly towards the daylight the feeling grew on Edith that she held the hand, not of her husband, but of the son he had always wanted.

Even when she was very old – and people who survived their birth and childhood often lived to be very old, as had her father – Aine's hair remained as black as it had gone that night, from the quicksilver perhaps, or perhaps some more ancient memory in her blood. The gold that her father had plundered and lost was never found, and to the end of his life Edith loved him and washed and wiped and dressed him, innocent as a baby as he was, and as helpless.

It was a golden age. For sixty years London was prosperous and at peace.

Aine kept her word and like most women of her class she never married, though she made her decision from choice. With her strange beauty she did not lack for suitors, but she was determined to live her own life herself, and turned down all offers of favour. She cared nothing for the men who loved her, all her love went into her children. She brought her family up very poor, almost destitute, but she never sold the reliquary that could have fed and clothed her daughters, neither did her eldest daughter, nor her grand-daughter, black-haired as herself and blue-eyed, Ethel.

Now it was Ethel's turn to shriek and swear her way through childbirth, and Aine sat on the bench in the garth, the scent of flowers and herbs wafting round her old bones on the warm easterly wind of a summer's evening.

She smiled as Ethel emitted an enormous shriek. Normally there would have been laughter and complaints about the girl's noise from men playing peg-and-hoop or drinking beer in the busy rutted street, but it was a time of plague and the street was empty. Even the women stayed indoors, remembering their own time, but they did not allow themselves to become too fond of children.

Lately the Walbrook valley had been built over with houses spreading down the two hills of London, joining those spreading back from the waterfront. Even her old eyes could see that despite the many gardens and fields the larger streets were solidly lined with thatched dwellings, their roofs glowing in the setting sun behind Aine, the Walbrook valley filling with shadow. The smoke of many cooking-fires rose out of the shadows, then flames licked up.

'Fire,' Aine said. 'Fire!'

Along the Walbrook, the flames jumped from roof to roof as darkness fell. She wept for the poor people in the confusion as street after street turned to fire, fanned by the wind, the flames racing along the streets leading uphill towards St Paul's Cathedral. Her daughter came out and hugged her.

'She's a girl. Ethel's had a baby girl and named her Paula, after the saint.'

'Get her and her baby out of the house!' Aine said. 'Get them into the garden. Make shelter, bring pails of water! Call out the men to save the cathedral.'

'God won't let the fire reach the cathedral, Mother.'

Aine glanced at her and said an extraordinary thing. 'I don't know God.'

The cathedral began to burn very late in the night. Teams of men toiled with buckets and hooks on long poles, tearing down the burning thatch, but soon the heat was too intense. Bishop Dunstan stared with his arms crossed, a tiny dark shadow in the glare of the conflagration, watching the walls slump outwards like weary beasts as the mortar crumbled in the heat, and the cross fall burning from the roof to shatter on the steps.

By morning it was all over, and only smoke remained.

Dunstan turned silently to the canons, the petty canons, and the priests of St Paul's. The clergy house, his palace, all the hovels and huts and houses and outhouses that had clustered around the cathedral, were gone. An owl hooted, mistaking dawn for sunset after the brilliance of the night.

Dunstan said, 'I shall build the cathedral better.'

A priest called, 'Better?'

'Closer to God,' Dunstan said. 'Taller. Greater. And without a roof of thatch.'

A baby cried. 'That is a sign!' Dunstan said, and life began to return to the stricken faces of the clergy. He called for holy water. 'A new baby, a new cathedral. Bring the child to me.' He smiled into the blue eyes of the strong young woman who was presented to him. 'What is your name?'

'I am Ethel.'

'And what is the name your baby will take to God?'

Ethel whispered.

Dunstan nodded. 'I baptise this child Paula in the name of the Father, the Son and the Holy Ghost. Amen.'

The priests gathered round wonderingly, looking at the new baby.

Next year Dunstan, the founding father of Westminster Abbey, was consecrated Archbishop of Canterbury, but he kept his post as Bishop of London, and the new cathedral proceeded to his design. Bishop Mellitus's cathedral had been built in a month, its successor in a year or two, but Dunstan's was planned on a grander scale to the glory of God. The ground was levelled over with dark charred earth and burnt stone. It took almost a a decade for the new building to rise in place of the old cathedral, palace and houses, covering where they stood with wide flagstone floors, walls of smooth Kent stone and rows of tiny windows beneath a tile roof.

Meek Paula devoutly swept floors in the service of the cathedral all her life, and never had children.

But her robust sister Agatha, born thirteen years later and her mother's favourite, birthed five sons and finally, at the age of thirty-five, a daughter. The daughter drank as hard as her mother, ran away with a pagan Dane called Konal for love, and after his death returned in disgrace but unrepentant, carrying his child who was baptised Astrid.

Astrid's fourth daughter was named Elfrida. Her elder sisters all died before she was five, and her two brothers were killed by Norman horsemen. Elfrida grew up like an only child, grew up so close to her mother that people said you couldn't slip a piece of paper between them. They were like twins in everything but age, and Elfrida was at least as strongminded as her mother. Everyone agreed on that too.

In the year 1087 Astrid and Elfrida, hand in hand, watched St Paul's Cathedral burn to the ground for the third time.

Part Four

Eleanor

London, Candlemas Day 1142 AD

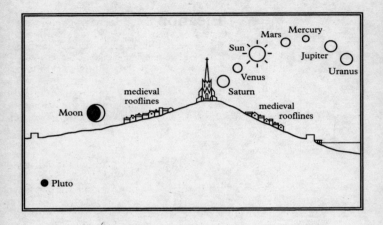

Candlemas, 1142

Brother William of Westminster Abbey, a thin fine-looking man with a large head shaven round his crown, his skinny body hidden beneath his bulky monk's clothing for the sake of his modesty so that he was entirely concealed from his chin to his sandals – except for his inky hands clasped devoutly in front of him, and the pouch of writing tools hanging from his white wrist – hurried from the library in the Bishop of Winchester's house at Southwark, hurried along the arcade wondering at the amusement he caused among the bishop's servants, for his long garments and hurrying walk made him look as though he ran on wheels not feet.

Brother William was late again.

It was the fault of the books.

He begged God's forgiveness for that unworthy thought. God saw every man's thoughts as clearly as words written in a book, knew the innermost secrets of every heart. Every man, every woman, every child was an open book to God.

People were God's books.

Last year there had been a terrible fire at Winchester and the cathedral was much damaged. Its precious store of books, manuscripts and illuminations had been brought here to Southwark for safekeeping. Winchester was under siege in the civil war that divided the ruling classes of the country, and the books had not been recalled. Such an opportunity might never occur again, and every day since the summer Brother William had been permitted to examine them and employ the humble skills God gave him on the restoration of marked or sooted works.

He skidded down the steps into the snow, but God held him up, and crossed the great courtyard past the women's prison. The cold was bitter and he resisted the temptation to blow on his hands, hurried smoothly forward – the dragging hem of his garments erased his footsteps from the snow – into the bishop's park. The bishop was the king's brother and this seventy valuable acres along the south bank of the Thames once grew food and herbs for Bishop Henry's table, grazed beef and pork among rows of chicken coops, even had a rabbit mound, but now it was a more profitable mess of tumbledown shacks, including the bishop's twenty-two brothels, and numerous taverns both attracted by the bishop's wealth and contributing to it. Brother William hurried past the unconsecrated cemetery where the bishop's whores were put to rest when their work was done, open-legged and unloved in death as in life. A woman scurried past pulling a boy on a string, his eyes sewn shut, and a man threw a pot after her.

These lost souls needed God so much it terrified Brother William. No wonder He had turned His back on them. They damned themselves with every mortal breath they took, and would suffer the fires of Hell for eternity, ripped by hooks and flayed by demons.

He hurried past the Clink prison. For three hundred years erring priests, monks and friars had been imprisoned here, scourged with rods until their penance was complete. Today a monk sat with his legs in stocks, the heavy iron collar called a ferramente – his work as Papal Legate had introduced the bishop to the Italian language – fastened round his neck. The jailer charged threepence for its fixing and threepence for removal. Brother William was not a rich man – his earthly father was a Ludgate baker – but neither was he entirely without means, and unusually he was paid a small wage by the abbey for his skills. He enquired of the brother's sin, was shocked, yet found a farthing to press into the man's hand towards his redemption.

'Bless you, brother,' the monk whispered, then both men started as a bell clanged. Bells ruled every day of a monk's life on earth, handbells of dorter, frater, chapter and church, the great tolling bells of the tower. Bells at midnight for the first and longest service of the day, then after Matins came the bell for Lauds, bells calling the faithful to Prime, then bells for public and private masses, the bells for Tierce, Nones, Vespers, Compline.

The bell in St Mary Overie's blunt Norman tower clanged eleven times. But was that candle time, or the eleventh hour of the day? Brother William had been so engrossed in intellectual work, starting before daylight, peering at texts with his large blue eyes strained and watering, that he had lost all idea whether it was morning or afternoon. Bells all over Southwark took up the refrain at ragged intervals, further confusing him as he hurried forward. Churches often used candle time, whereas the sacred life of the abbey was regulated by hours of varying length, depending on the judgment of the subsacrist who rang the bells. Winter hours were short and started at dawn, and he had no idea whether it was eleven o'candle in the morning or the eleventh hour, only an hour from sunset. Frosty clouds obscured the position of the sun. 'Is it morning or afternoon?' he cried out to a man shovelling snow.

Priests knew everything. The man rolled his eyes, wondering what answer was required to this test. 'Forenoon?' he said cautiously.

'Thank God!' Brother William would not now be whipped by the abbot for lateness, but he hurried anyway from force of habit, and came to the Thames by Great Pike Ponds. The pools, kept free of ice by urchins with poles, swirled with the fins of fierce pike destined for the bishop's table. Lesser fish, carp, trout, for lesser people, were accommodated in smaller pools.

Brother William stopped, and stared across the river in awe. The Thames was ice.

He had been born into a time of miracles. Within living memory, only three years after St Paul's was burnt, London Bridge was swept away in floods, and its shabby timbers on his right still looked cobbled together from old bits and pieces and every species of rot. In 1114, the same year the Thames first froze, the tide fell so low that people strolled across the riverbed downstream of the bridge. Now the Thames was frozen again. William gazed at the people walking on the ice, an idea coming into his mind as he watched a gang of lads skate past on sharpened beefbones. They slid their sticks after a bundle of rags, turned like a flock of birds and skimmed towards the vessels frozen at Queenhithe on the north bank, once called King Athelredshithe. English names were gradually being replaced with their civilised French equivalents either deliberately or by tax collectors and clerics unable to comprehend English accents.

Above the cranes, pulleys and masts rose St Paul's, the greatest project of this age or any other since the beginning of the world. Already its huge white bulk of French stone on the hilltop dominated London's skyline of a hundred church towers, though only the cathedral's eastern end was roofed and the massive white lantern tower was incomplete. One day – and Brother William prayed he would live to see that glorious day – the huge tower would be topped by that marvellous innovation, a spire, though incomparably taller than any other spire, and made taller still by the hill on which it stood.

The spire of St Paul's would prick the face of God.

Brother William's idea would save him the bridge toll. He would walk across the ice. A few hungry ferrymen, their boats frozen solid, demanded payment for helping people on to the ice but the nearby wooden stairs were unattended.

Brother William crossed himself and walked on the ice.

The freedom and strangeness of the broad expanse was wonderful. His sandals slipped slightly and he could not help enjoying himself. Skaters swooped round him on the clear ice of the middle, children threw snowballs near the banks. He slipped and fell on his hands, thanked God for making him humble as he scrambled to his feet. His feet went off in opposite directions and he sat down. Someone in a striped cloak skated flawlessly past him in a tightening circle, helped him up, skated away without stopping.

'Bless you,' Brother William called, red-faced. The fellow in the striped cloak waved casually without looking round.

Brother William walked steadily and ahead of him the curve of the river opened up, a few dark buildings dotted along the snowy slopes of the Strand leading his eye to the island of Westminster and the abbey that was his earthly life. The proud and wilful people crowded within the City's black ancient walls on his right worshipped commerce as easily as God, but Westminster was pure, God and King united in glory. Westminster Abbey rose above the double wooden roofs of the Palace of Westminster.

Brother William heard a loud crackling, felt heat on his face. A huge bonfire had been built on the ice and vulgar people clustered round its warmth practising the inevitable pursuits of Londoners, buying and selling, watching a bear-bait, drinking bitter four-day-old beer, eating hot nuts and flirting. Brother William paused, marvelling how God did not allow the ice beneath the fire to melt. For a moment he wondered why it did not, then chastised himself for sinfully demanding reason from God. His sin was serious because the powers of human reason were feeble and easily deceived, but true faith could never be deceived. In effect his thoughts had doubted God, however unintentionally, and by inviting deception he had invited the devil into his heart. He must confess the crime and probably he would be whipped for it. He slithered on his way.

A man looked away from the bear-bait and called out cheerfully, 'I wouldn't cross that patch if I were you.'

Brother William paused, not liking the man's familiar tone, then walked away. No one would harm a monk, he was protected from injury by his monastic garb and the crucifix at his neck. He heard laughter behind him and turned to reprove the people at the bonfire. The ice crackled.

The ice broke. Brother William tried to step back. He skidded forward towards the brown foam, turned and clung to the jagged ice rising behind him. The ice slid deep into the water like a knife, the water flooded like a numb weight round his legs, rose above his waist, his chest. His teeth chattered. He tried to shout for help but the ice rotated, came down on top of him, shoved him down.

The ice settled smoothly in place, Brother William underneath.

'Fourpence he don't come up,' the cheerful man said.

'A cup of chestnuts if he do,' cried the chestnut-seller.

A girl with a sooty face put her arms round the cheerful man. 'He won't come up. There he is.' The monk's face slid under their feet, carried downstream by the tide beneath the ice. 'Holding his breath,' the cheerful man said. 'Come on, fourpence. Tuppence then.'

'God looks after them,' the chestnut-seller said. 'God helps them.'

Brother William heard their voices mumbling through the ice. Water rushed in his ears. He beat the ice with his fists but made no sound.

'He's a dead 'un,' the girl said. The air rushed from the monk's lungs, making an opaque silvery bubble that obscured everything but his nose and his fingertips sliding silently along the underside of the ice. The people drifted back to the warmth of the fire.

Brother William felt the darkness beneath him become more real than the smeary daylight receding above him. His arms floated out limply. He felt himself going down into the dark and he could not help himself. Everything was peaceful, and a light grew, and the light was God. Brother William smiled, for God was exactly as he had imagined Him, with long white hair and a robe of stars.

The ice rang. The water chimed with heavy blows, two, then three. A hand reached down through the hole chopped in the ice, grabbed his hood, plucked him whooping into the air and grey freezing daylight.

William lay shuddering on the ice like a landed fish. He gasped, choked disgusting river water. A striped cloak swam into view. A nasal, foreign-sounding voice said clearly, 'You owe me a new sword.'

William stared up into the face of a Jew.

A Jew was unmistakable. Jewish nose, black Jewish eyebrows, black Jewish hair curled in oily locks, glinting brown Jewish eyes. William recoiled.

His life had been saved by a Jew.

William was twenty-three years old. The Jew was no older. His lips curled in a calculating Jewish smile.

No, it was just an ordinary human smile. 'I'm Joshua, son of Master Abraham.' He offered his hand, pulled William to his feet.

William said, 'William.' His wet clothes hung on him like iron. They weighed a ton.

Joshua grinned. 'Walk, William, don't freeze.' He put his hand under William's elbow. 'That's it. One foot. Now the other. I was joking about the sword, it is well made. The hilt of a sword is not meant to be used as a hammer, that's all.'

'You saved my life,' William said.

Joshua shrugged. 'Undoubtedly.'

'You're a Jew.'

Joshua laughed. 'Undoubtedly!'

William meant, a Jew does not do something for nothing. He struggled to understand. 'I have no money.'

'Neither do I. My father has all the money. He is a money-lender.'

'You're proud of it?'

A wary edge touched Joshua's smile. 'And you are a monk, I see. You should not believe everything you hear about us.'

'But the Jews—' William struggled to put everything he knew about the Jews in order.

Joshua said, 'Christ was a Jew, you know. Not a Christian. My name, Joshua, means Jesus.'

William, shuddering with cold, gaped at him. No wonder such men were considered dangerous. A Jew, any Jew, had committed the sin of unbelief, but kings and magnates gave them rights because they borrowed money from Jews. By law Jews could not be killed for being

Jewish, could not be forcibly converted to Christianity, their children could not even be taken from them and baptised to save their souls. They could practise their religion but must not attempt to spread it. Jews were subject to perpetual servitude and their possessions were at the king's disposal, except he must not take so much that they were deprived of the means of life.

William pulled his arm away from the Jew. A monk knew nothing in life happened by accident. Everything was ordered, everything had a meaning. Every breath he took from the moment of his birth to the moment of his death was planned, part of the cosmic order of preordained events. At his baptism his godparents had made promises on his behalf, oaths that bound him legally for life. Baptism could never be renounced, it was for ever. The Church was everything, birth and life and death and the promise of life after death.

But there were the Jews, the licensed enemies of God.

Joshua said, 'I suggest you warm yourself at the fire.'

'What?' William said.

'You're shivering.' When the monk did not move Joshua bowed, swept his hat so low it touched the ice, and skated smoothly away.

William called after him, 'Thank you.'

Joshua lifted his arm in acknowledgment, then the skaters swirling on the ice hid his showy striped cloak and William could not see him.

William had thanked a Jew for saving his life.

He plodded along the ice towards Westminster. A monk was bathed four times a year, at Christmas, Easter, high summer and the end of September, and his linen underclothes were not yet greasy enough to be waterproof. His outer habit steamed visibly, and he felt cold enough to die.

He had said *thank you* to a Jew, one of the murderers of Jesus. He would rather have drowned.

He scrambled up a landing stage into Thieving Lane, which curved behind the riverside palace to the abbey. Many of the cottages belonged to the abbey's hereditary reeves and servants – some monks followed in each other's footsteps, too, father and son, though celibacy was the Rule, and rather than put away their wives or concubines priests who lived in sin paid a fine to the king on the thirtieth of each November, for his connivance. Other cottages belonged to the abbot's men-at-arms, or to pensioners. The abbey's brothel, the Maidenhead, was quiet at this time of day. William crossed by the fishponds, hurried past the vineyard. Carts crunched through the snow from Convent Garden and the more distant manors along Watling Street belonging to the abbey, and winter vegetables and bavins of firewood were thrown down outside the kitchen. The cellarer marked the old wooden fee-tallies, then pulled out a purse of money as well. Nowadays the abbey must often pay money for what it used. Boys and women, familiars, swung chickens through the kitchen doorway for slaughtering, for the *Regularis Concordia* allowed monks to eat only two-legged animals. William had missed dinner and they were preparing supper. Abbey sparrows ran past him laughing, boys who were part of the chaotic army of unskilled labour required by any great building or organisation, paid in food and sent on the most menial tasks, probably now to clean the night latrine whose frequent blockages embarrassed the monks. Barrels of beer were rolled from the brewery, churns from the buttery. The churning women cursed the cold weather because it set the butter hard.

William realised he was horribly late, and ran as best he could between the massive stone buildings. He could not possibly present himself before the abbot wet and shivering, and he ran upstairs to change at least his outer habit. The Rule allowed a monk into the dormitory during the day but he must not linger. The dormitory was a vast room divided by blue muslin curtains hung from poles. He came to his own cubicle and closed the curtain to preserve his modesty, undressed quickly, feeling intensely nervous without his underclothes. He stood naked, rubbed his body dry with a blanket, hopping busily from one foot to the other to keep the Rule against lingering. Fortunately he had another outer habit, sent away to the chamberlain's department to be repaired, returned yesterday. But he had no dry undergarments.

Bells tolled the fifth hour of the day.

No time. William wrapped his outer habit thickly around him, tied it tight, and ran like the wind to the day stairs. Brother Thomas was coming up and William walked past him slowly and decorously, then sprinted past the refectory. He forced himself to walk calmly by the cloister. Nearby a monk knelt stripped to the waist, his flogging watched by a circle of monks, whipped by his accuser.

William rounded the corner and ran, paused to recover his breath, then walked slowly to the door of the abbot's lodgings and entered quietly. The prior pushed through the waiting squires and beckoned him upstairs alone, to a large room where the abbot welcomed him in heavily accented English. An abbot was allowed to speak in a voice of normal loudness, which sounded intimidatingly loud.

'Brother William. Stand by the window that we might see you.'

William shuffled forward. He was acutely aware of his nudity beneath the scratchy outer habit. A draught blew against his legs. Though shivering, he began to sweat in fear.

Abbot Gervase de Blois was plump, and Prior Osbert de Clare was thin. The prior saw to the everyday running of the abbey, the abbot dealt with larger matters. Abbot Gervase waddled past the table with the expansive manner of a man who has just eaten a pound of finest conger eel fried in butter, and wore a robe of three furs trimmed with snow-white budge, the softest underbelly of lambskin. Prior Osbert was almost hidden behind him, a nervous, obsessed and frustrated man, his face lined by the Vatican sun. The prior had recently returned from his latest fanatical mission to Rome, cultivating cardinals and papal clerks in his efforts to have Westminster Abbey's founder, Edward the Confessor, canonised as a saint to the glory of his abbey.

In French Abbot Gervase grunted at the prior, 'This is our man?'

'The one,' murmured the prior. 'William of Ludgate. My finest one.'

'One of your wiry breed rather than mine, I suspect, my dear *prieur*.'

The prior bowed, drawing the barb from the provocation by taking it as a compliment. 'Obedient and thorough indeed, *mon abbé*.'

William followed the foreign conversation raggedly. Many men could not understand the language of their masters at all, and few Frenchmen bothered to learn the vulgar tongue, English.

At last de Clare murmured in English, 'Brother William is to be complimented on his silence and patience.'

Abbot Gervase came close to the window, eyed William. 'Are you ill? You're shaking. Are you afraid of me?'

William shivered. 'I'm not ill, Father.'

De Clare murmured smoothly, 'Brother William is more at home with books than people.'

Gervase snorted. 'Do you know how old you are?'

William bowed his head. 'I am in my twenty-fourth year.'

'Then you will be professed as a priest next year, if you are worthy.' The abbot spoke to de Clare without turning round. '*Is* he worthy?'

William whispered, 'I am not—'

De Clare interrupted. 'He will be, if he continues his excellent work.'

William was confused. To him the organisation, transcription and elaboration of books and documents in the abbey's extensive scriptorium was a labour of love to the glory of God. But de Clare looked sly, and the abbot's smile was conniving.

'I'm sure he will live up to our expectations,' Abbot Gervase agreed, sounding pleased. 'Trustworthy, of course?'

'Trustworthy, obedient, discreet.'

'Then God has sent us the perfect man. Our decision is blessed.'

William wondered what was expected of him. He was prepared for any test. He would have held his hand in the candleflame had he been instructed. The abbot was father of the abbey's family, his interlocutor to God.

Abbot Gervase spoke authoritatively. 'Brother William of Ludgate, we are lending the skill God has given you to the Dean of St Paul's and the service of his new library. The old library as you know was destroyed in the unfortunate small conflagration of eight years ago, when the smith's house caught fire. Though most of the books and charters were saved, thanks be to God, they have remained in a sad state of disorganisation.'

The cathedral's store of richly illuminated bibles and religious works was second to none, and William did not know whether to be delighted at his opportunity or sad. 'But my work at the Bishop of Winchester's palace—'

'Is finished. This is more important.'

'Is essential,' de Clare said.

William had no choice but to obey, in heart as well as mind. No man's skill was his own. His whole life was one of service, he was a mere conduit for the talents given to him by God, not the owner of them.

William said, 'Yes, without question, *mon seigneur l'abbé.*'

The abbot looked at him sharply, wondering how much French the monk understood, but William bowed his head in humility and obedience to his superiors. The chantry bell rang beyond the window and his lips moved, singing the repetitive chant of the Benedictine Order that had been his life since he entered the abbey's tiny almonry school aged fifteen, lucky, gifted, intelligent, starving for knowledge. An empty vessel waiting to be filled. Seven years, two of them at Theobald's University at Oxford, had passed before he felt he had learnt enough to even begin to understand the meaning concealed in the simple chanted litany he heard now, and every day of his life.

'Does he understand us?' the abbot demanded sharply of the prior, in French.

'No. He worked on the forgery of the two French Great Charters. He has listened to us converse and picked up a few common words, that is all.'

'Then our Ludgate monk is a formidably quick learner.'

'That is what will make him so useful among the dean's papers. Let him once examine a charter or a history thoroughly, later it is his skill to copy it flawlessly from memory. I have seen it. He worked on the Mangoda charter that confirmed Hampstead belonged to our abbey. He did our work on the Great Charter of Edgar, the grant of Hendon to us by Dunstan, and Edward the Confessor's First Charter.' The prior switched to English. 'Brother William, you are loaned simply as a gesture of goodwill from our blessed abbey to the cathedral. That is all.'

William bowed to take his leave, but the prior called him back, spoke in an even lower voice.

'However, whilst you are there you will make it your business, without bothering anyone by letting them observe your interest, to examine certain notable documents most thoroughly. Especially those ancient Great Charters which substantiate St Paul's possession of their numerous estates around London, do I make myself clear? Examine their title to the lands claimed by the bishop, the canons, the cathedral itself, everything. Carefully note the form of words and the design of the seals of validity. During your research you will pay special attention to the canons of St Paul's supposedly ancient claim to Willesden, Harlesden, St Pancras, and the many estates in Middlesex which they hold to the detriment of our abbey.'

William asked, 'Is there some doubt as to the validity of these documents, *mon seigneur le prieur*?'

De Clare said smoothly, 'There may in the future be some doubt as to their validity.' He whispered, 'They may even have forged a Papal Bull to authenticate their claims. Even forged the signature of His Holiness himself!'

William looked shocked.

'It was the intention of our great founder, the Confessor, that his royal abbey should counterbalance the power of the cathedral that bestrides the City.' De Clare's thin lips twisted that the new cathedral would stand taller and greater than the huge buildings of his beloved abbey. 'However, lies have flourished and the truth must be established. Claims have been made on lands which we believe were granted to us by our founder.'

William nodded. In the past endowments of lands were granted by word of mouth. Later the verbal traditions were recorded on expensive parchment which rotted in damp and burnt in fire, got lost or stolen, or was eaten by mice and beetles. Lately good paper started arriving from abroad and a veritable copying industry had sprung up in the monasteries. A good scribe was as valuable as gold. Under the prior's direction, for the sake of clarity William had himself written many documents in the name of the Confessor and other people granting lands to the abbey.

Abbot Gervase said, 'You will begin your work at once.'

William thought of his bare legs. 'At once, *Abbé*? But today is Candlemas.' He faltered. The abbot's word was law. He backed to the door then burst out, 'But I have sinned! When shall I confess?'

The abbot glanced at the prior. 'The St Paul's matter is more important than a penance or a whipping. This cannot be serious enough to cause a delay—'

'I doubted God.'

The abbot beckoned impatiently. 'How?'

'There was a bonfire on the ice and the ice did not melt beneath it, and by wondering at the reason for this I doubted God and invited the devil into my heart.'

'Heat is vitality, and vitality is called to God. Therefore heat rises, Brother William. Therefore it did not melt the ice beneath it. Therefore you have not sinned. Go at once!'

William stuttered. His real sin today was almost incalculable, but he did not know how to express himself. Today he had allowed his life to be saved by a Jew.

Go at once! William bowed and ran. Brother Richard was coming upstairs and William's outer habit parted, showing his flashing legs as he ran down. Brother Richard stared after him, frowning. The *Regularis Concordia* specifically forbade monks from running or gadding about. 'Brother William—' he murmured reprovingly.

William ran faster. The snow flying from his sandals blew under his habit and clung freezing to his bare skin. He saw the stairs to the dormitory, then a line of monks filed round the corner, heads bowed, fingers touching the tips of their noses, which were blue with cold. The white breath rose above their heads like haloes as they stood about near the chamberlain's office, William's only hope of dry underclothes.

Today my life was saved by a Jew.

William sighed and turned away. Obviously it was the divine will that he must walk to St Paul's as he was. Therefore the mortification of the cold and the suffering and embarrassment and fear of discovery his naked body caused him beneath the draughty shell of his habit would be good for him, and therefore his journey would bring him closer to God.

All this land now belonged to Westminster Abbey by one means or another, but once everything in sight had belonged to St Paul's.

Shivering, William crossed the frozen River Tyburn on foot and walked up Charing to where the roads crossed. He turned along Akeman Street. Beyond the Stone Cross on the Strandway was the Church of the Holy Innocents, St Mary le Strand, and on his left he saw St Martin-in-the-Fields and the frozen orchards and vegetable patches of Convent Garden. The festive bonfires burning along the Thames ice blazed brighter as daylight faded. William's feet were numb, and he distracted himself by counting the churches connecting Westminster to the City. Between the churches one or two fine houses grew up like flowers among the hovels, mostly inns for bishops, cardinals and magnates visiting London, enjoying the clear country air between commerce and power.

William could smell the City from here. He dropped down into the foul rubbishy valley of the Fleet. The City's black walls and ragged skeletons hanging from the Holborn gallows rose above him, and beyond them St Bartholomew's Priory stood like mist amid pure snowy fields where the heretics were burnt. He plodded up the slope and came into the City through Ludgate, where he took his name. The two castles built here by Frenchmen, Montfichet with its tall round tower and Baynard's with the square barbican, added their threat to the White Tower of London in the east to remind unwilling Londoners who their masters were. Both castles were already decayed and the moats had been granted to the Bishop of

London. Workmen were busy dragging out stones for the rebuilding of St Paul's.

William raised his head. He looked up Ludgate Hill. With darkness falling behind it the Norman cathedral stood like a great white skeleton rising out of the hilltop, the western end which faced him less complete than the east, roofed only with wood and bare of pinnacles, its tiers of windows blank of glass and dark to the sunset behind him.

He clasped his hands and murmured quietly despite the people rushing past him, '*Domine labia mea aperies et os meum annuntiabit laudem tuam.*'

William struggled through the crowds to the side of the road. Christmas lasted longer each year. For devout Christians the festival ended with the Twelve Days, but for the generality of vulgar citizens Christmas lasted until today, Candlemas, when the candles were lit. William muttered, 'As Tertullian says in *Of Idolatry*, let those who have no light in themselves, light candles!' London was a city of snow and fire as darkness fell along the narrow streets, Carter Street so thick with crowds that people must walk on each other's shoulders or stay wedged where they were with heat and breath rising all round them, stuck like currants in the warm pudding of humanity.

William felt a hedge behind him and slipped beneath it into the deanery garden, which also was full of people. At once rough hands grabbed him and he was pulled forward by men-at-arms. The Rule forbade William to shout even when his life was in danger and he endured his treatment in silence, pulled this way and that like an assassin. The dean, dressed in furs, came out of the old thatched building and stood watching the scene below him, one valet pulling on his black gloves, another the glittering rings over the gloves, another adjusting the dean's hat. 'Who is that man?'

William was let go. He picked himself up from the snow and murmured, 'I am Brother William.'

'It's a monk!' one of the men-at-arms said. 'I never touched him.'

'A brave monk, it seems.' Dean Ralph de Langdon strode down the steps, looked appraisingly into William's face by the light of the flaming torches surrounding them, then put out his arms to be lifted on to horseback.

William murmured, 'I bring greetings from the Abbot of Westminster—'

'I've no time for that now,' de Langdon said. 'I know who you are. Hold to my stirrup, walk beside me.' He kicked the horse and the men-at-arms cleared a path ahead of them. 'I am building my new deanery here.' De Langdon waved his gloved, jewelled hand at a grand half-completed edifice. 'Magnificence pleases God, monk, whatever you say, for He is magnificent.' The men-at-arms shoved a clear path along the street and William clung to the stirrup to keep up. Torches and processions revealed the pattern of every City thoroughfare sparkling between the unlit mass of St Paul's and the distant Tower. More torchlit processions shimmered on London Bridge, and the sound of blasting trumpets carried even over the roar of the crowd. 'In honour of the Virgin, isn't it?' the dean grunted, staring over the heads of the people beneath him. 'Not many virgins here tonight. Give me St Valentine's and a dull box of saints' names. This disorder is altogether too popular.'

William murmured, 'Our Feast of Lights is also in honour of Simeon, who proclaimed "a light to lighten the Gentiles".'

'Don't lecture me, monk. Why is your face so sour? Don't you approve of torches?'

Torches were pagan, showering oily flame and stinking sparks around them, but candles were Christian. A pure white wax candle was a rare sight outside a church, and William watched the expression of wonder in the eyes of the children as the processions gathered in Candlewick Street, and the candles of Candlemas came together in a shimmering stream. The procession started towards St Paul's behind the Bishop of London, Robert de Segillo, and behind him came the dean and canons of St Paul's pushing forward, and then the justiciar of London and the vicecomes and the sheriff and all the jostling dignitaries, and then the merchant classes strutting as fierce and proud as those of high birth. A child put its hand in William's, walking with him, and William looked round wondering where its mother was. 'If only I had a candle I'd be happy for ever,' the child said, and William handed down his own. The child ran away joyfully shielding its prize from the wind, and William felt the warmth of his hand where he had been touched.

The procession toiled uphill from the Walbrook. The dark mass of the cathedral covered the starry sky and the dean dropped his hand on William's shoulder, guiding him. The south side of the cathedral precinct was a high stone wall. The fat grunting men leading the procession, and Giovanni da Crema the arch-celibate and woman-hater in his cardinal's purple hat, dismounted in the broad atrium, and the noisy crowd pushed after them up the steps into the cathedral.

The shouts were silenced, the candles were put out. The sound of footsteps was muffled.

William looked up, and fell in love.

Not a light burnt in St Paul's Cathedral. The interior seemed even larger than the exterior and was the shape of the Holy Cross, and everything inside was shadows, dark, incomplete, columns supporting no weight, dimly seen vaults curving upward into nothing. The giant windows revealed themselves by starlight, distorted, half finished, the walls jagged and full of gaps, pieces missing. The barrows and spades and hods thrown down in the side chapels might at any moment jump to life again and recommence their activity.

William gazed around him. He understood. The cathedral was caught for a moment in time, like a living creature holding its breath in the act of being born.

The devout footsteps shuffled forward. Nobody coughed. William reached the crossing at the centre of the cathedral. The partly completed tower, unroofed, open to the sky, was full of stars. He stared, marvelling, as one star detached itself from the sky and drifted down, grew brighter. Even the dignitaries stared up like children, sure it was the Star of Bethlehem. The silver lantern came to earth shining with crystal light like a star, and from the square fourteen-pound candle flaming inside it other candles were lit, and from them the flame was spread to others and carried round the cathedral by angelic novices and cathedral sparrows and smooth-faced petty clerics, until the whole cathedral blazed like a lantern with candlelight from two hundred and twenty candles and sixteen torches, and a further sixty candles were carried up the steps of the pulpitum to illuminate the completed sanctuary, the choir and the altar at the eastern end of the cathedral, the curve of the apse already painted a gorgeous rose pink like a dawning light.

As the crowd thinned William glimpsed the clever mechanism of pulleys and ropes that had lowered the silver lantern. It had not been magic after all.

Dean de Langdon crooked his finger, beckoning. 'You will make your lodging in a carrel by the chapter house as arranged. But first, monk, you shall marvel at the glory of our library.' All libraries of course shut at sunset, when the light failed. This would be a special visit. William, hands clasped in obedience inside his broad sleeves, hiding his eagerness, hurried after the dean up the broad steps of the pulpitum into the choir, past half-finished choir stalls, inhaling the smell of fresh-sawn wood that impregnated the dull chilly air. The sheer scale and ornament of the cathedral was a wonder to him, this eastern end almost complete to his untrained eye, the roof rising above tier on tier of pillars and windows and vaults seeming hundreds of feet high in the gloom. The whole edifice moaned and echoed as the thirty vicars choral, priests who deputised for absentee prebendaries, mingled their calls with the chantry priests chanting masses for the souls of the dead at many colourful chantry altars.

Near the bishop's throne the dean turned left behind the choir stalls to a door set behind the tomb of King Sebba, opened it, took a candle and climbed narrow steps set in the thickness of the wall. Through the tiny slit windows the choir and sanctuary already seemed a very long way down. William felt as though they were climbing as high as Heaven, and only when the dean grunted with amusement did he realise he had spoken his awe aloud. He glimpsed the tomb of St Mellitus and the gilded, jewelled pinnacles of St Erconwald's shrine far below, the saint's horse-litter whose touch healed the sick kept behind iron bars for security but opened for a fee.

The stairs led to a long stone gallery running below the clerestory windows. De Langdon turned away from the airy space on his right, unlocked and opened a second door, ushered William inside.

The library was a very long room but low on its outer side, set in the roof-space over the side chapels. Its sloping roof – the dean knocked it with his knuckles, 'lead, not thatch, no danger of fire!' – was heavily buttressed with stone arches, dividing the room into compartments filled with books. Desks set back to back and lecterns for copying were placed along the external wall where headroom was lowest, and books and rolls of papers were stacked along the high inner wall in profusion. Shelves of books. Aumbries with beautifully ornamented doors for the storage of books. Book cupboards with arched tops like windows, that spilled a flood of books and dust as soon as the hatch was opened.

'Heaven indeed,' the dean commented dryly, with a glance at William, 'if books are Heaven.'

'They are to me.' William realised that the position of cathedral librarian was of course held by a petty canon as a sinecure, an office obtained by birth not expertise, and that such men often held more profitable benefices in the City – the residentiary canons of the chapter doubtless kept the best cathedral livings for its own members – and the real work was probably done by assistants and inferiors. But for now the place was empty and the fireplace, the first he had seen, was dark and cold. The only light came from the dean's candle, though in daylight he guessed illumination would stream from the circular windows set between the desks in the outer wall.

'Our librarian is Balchus,' the dean said. 'I have spoken of you to him, of course – he is one of the wardens of London Bridge, and is busy with many other emoluments. His father is a mercer of note—'

William ducked beneath a buttress, stood up on the far side staring at a stone shelf on which rolls of parchment, papers, charters, and books beneath them resting on more papers, were tossed in confusion.

'I see why you need my help,' William said. He lifted various fragments, some of them scorched by fire, others nibbled by mice. 'This will take years. How—' He looked beneath, picked out a brilliantly illuminated volume among sheaves of water-blotched worthless stuff. 'How do you even know the works you possess?'

'We don't,' the dean shrugged. 'We need your organised mind to place things in order and hierarchy, Brother William, to prepare a written catalogue and sift the wheat from the chaff. In the confusion of the dreadful fire—'

'It would take a lifetime!' William said, appalled. Yet he was uplifted, almost intoxicated, for he opened a book at random and saw it was the *Breves Causae* of Eusebius, compiled in the fourth century and probably copied half a dozen times since, and if this was here perhaps Eusebius's *Concordances* were also somewhere nearby, though he did not see them. Instead he found a psalter and noted with incredulity the diminuendo of the opening letters, each smaller than its predecessor. 'I do believe this work is from the stylus of St Colum Cille himself!'

'Its value is what we need you to tell us,' the dean said, then smiled reverently, as though he loved books for themselves. 'You will commence at sunrise tomorrow?'

William bowed obediently.

The dean carried the candle to the door. William followed, then paused, clearly hearing a footstep tread behind him. The floor creaked. He turned slowly. No one was there. He smiled. It was impossible to imagine such a new building being haunted. He was tired.

A piece of parchment, dislodged from a desk by a draught perhaps, wafted from side to side to the floor like a falling leaf.

William picked the parchment up and replaced it on the desk. He went out and the dean closed the door and locked it with a loud click, then handed William the key.

The two women stood in the shadows at the end of the gallery. They heard the lock click and watched the two men enter the staircase, watched the glow of candlelight drop from sight. They leaned over the balustrade as the light appeared below, in the choir, and watched the dean and the other man walk through the pulpitum in the direction of the chapter house.

'Just a monk.' The older woman, Elfrida, turned to the younger. 'He's no one.'

The girl said nothing.

She had seen the way the monk looked at the books.

William was up long before dawn. He had woken at midnight for Matins as usual, but when the bell did not come slept again almost at once. Now his refreshed body fizzed with energy and pleasurable anticipation of the day, excited by the novelty of his surroundings. He threw off his night-blanket, shivered and wished he had his underclothes. He could not send for them – could not bear the humiliation of such an intimate confidence to a sniggering messenger – and he could not afford new ones. He had slept in his habit to save his eyes any inadvertent glimpse of his private parts, his *pudendum*, but the rough wool of the outer garment irritated his skin like a hair shirt. The itching would be good for his soul and he welcomed it. The carrel where he had slept was as small and bare as a monk's cell, but the bunk was made of wood not stone and the tiny window had glass in it, dimly revealing the dawn. He tightened the rope that secured his habit, made sure it would not flap open to reveal his bare legs, and stepped outside.

The old thatched chapter house nestled in the angle between the cathedral's south transept and its massive nave like a louse in an armpit. Builders' calls rang out around William, stones and loads of mortar were swinging on ropes like black dots against the flanks of the cathedral, tiny men sauntered among the pinnacles. A great shout went up and all work stopped almost as soon as it had started. Apparently the guild of masons had contracted as long for their breakfast as a man took to walk a mile. The masons sat round their huts gnawing hungrily at black meyne bread, making vulgar jokes. William, as part of the contract the abbot of Westminster Abbey had made with the dean for his services, claimed a white canonical loaf from the kitchener and two pints of best barley malt beer from the brewer. One of the kitchen sluts called him back and cut him a thick slab of red roast beef, but the Rule did not allow him to eat it, and when he explained she gave a kindly smile and pressed a hard-boiled egg into his hand instead.

William had hardly spoken to women and he didn't know how to deal with her kindness. 'Thank you, thank you.'

'It's only an egg!' she cackled. 'Don't mean we're getting married nor nothing.' William flushed red to the tips of his ears.

He found a place to eat. Thatch rooftops heavy with snow and smoke fell away beneath him to the Thames. Eel-catchers chopped lanes of clear black water in the ice to string their nets. Fishermen left their boats floating in the salty water downstream and pushed their baskets of fish under London Bridge on foot, cleverly avoiding the halfpenny a vessel must pay at the king's Custom House. William brushed the eggshell and crumbs from his hands and relieved himself privately in the latrine, knowing the day would be long.

The inside of the cathedral boomed with the cries of builders and tradesmen and lawyers pushing past him or touting for business. Hungry men hung about near the tombs that had been installed, begging for food. Old women or girls with babies waited at the chantries for alms. William surprised a man and a woman behind the choir stalls and they looked flustered, then devout. William took the heavy iron key from his sleeve but the door behind the tomb of King Sebba was unlocked.

The wall was thick and he left the hubbub below him as he climbed into the silence of the gallery and entered the library. The round windows, being north-facing, did not cast as much daylight as he would have wished, but it was clear and grey. The best places near the fireplace had already been taken by the regular rubricators – men working on chapter headings, titles, saints' names and important words in red ink – their copyists working beneath them, dough-faced, round-shouldered, their fingers swollen and deformed by the monks' curse, arthritis, old men by the age of forty and blind at fifty. Meekly

William absorbed their jealous looks. He knew he was looking at himself in twenty years' time. Reading and writing were a young man's skill.

The librarian, Balchus, stood at the lectern nearest the fire. William approached him and waited to be recognised. The librarian, a sharp-faced man with swollen apple-coloured cheeks and a bitter twist to his lips, examined minutiae in the chained catalogue in front of him. From time to time he leafed a page, and William was ignored. William wondered what happened to the smoke from the fire, since the air in the room was clean. He bent slightly, trying to see what was behind the grille that prevented sparks from flying into the room, and his interest became fascination. Thus ignored in his turn, the librarian turned irritably. He spoke as though he held a piece of sour fruit in his mouth.

'You are Brother William the monk, no doubt.'

William bowed. He murmured, 'And you are Balchus.'

'I have been expecting you. You are late.'

'My apologies, librarian.'

'Really I do not know what you are doing here at all.'

William said nothing, for Prior de Clare had instructed him to examine certain documents without letting anyone observe his interest, and he was bound utterly by the Rule to obey. Balchus continued grumpily, 'Anyway, you will take care not to disturb our important work. You will touch nothing, interfere with nothing. I won't have any gadding about. Any work you particularly request will be brought to you at your desk by one of my inferiors.'

'Thank you, librarian.'

'Do I make myself clear? No browsing!'

'Yes, librarian.'

Balchus, pleased that his authority had been established so thoroughly and accepted so meekly by the quiet monk, returned his attention to the messy catalogue in front of him.

William supposed that Balchus's difficult manner, if not born in him by God, was a result of the disappointments of politics. Perhaps bitterness towards Abbot Gervase of Westminster Abbey, a relative and strong supporter of the elected King Stephen of Blois, if Balchus was a supporter of the usurper Empress Maud. Her faction all but crowned her in London last summer, but the vulgar mob rioted and forced her to run for her life. Women had been kidnapped in the cathedral close and held to ransom by this faction or that. Men of importance ditched their friends with bewildering speed to stay on the winning side, but everyone hated a mob of common people asserting their opinions.

William kept his eyes down. 'Dean de Langdon promised me every assistance, Petty Canon Balchus.'

Balchus frowned at the mention of the dean. 'The only use of deans is to ask canons to dinner, and the only use of canons is to accept the invitation. I have promised you every assistance. That is all.' He beckoned one of the cowled inferiors carrying books. 'Show Brother William to the desk I have reserved for him.' Balchus smiled. His swollen mouth was jagged inside, brown rotting teeth without hope of remedy. He was in agony. William prayed for him.

The desk, of course, was the most unpopular, situated at the end of the library furthest from the fire, and was illuminated by a round window on its left. William thanked the inferior who showed him to his place but did not sit down. He asked, 'What do you think I have done to so offend Petty Canon Balchus?'

The figure mumbled. It was not here to think, only to obey.

Then William glimpsed a flash of eyes from the shadow beneath the cowl, and a voice spoke. 'Why should you have done anything, monk? Is life fair?'

The cowl turned away, but William stared. He had heard the voice not of a man, but of a woman. He whispered, 'Who are you?'

'I am your inferior. What book do you require?'

He whispered, 'I require your name.'

A library was a good place for whispers. It was expected.

She whispered, 'What book?'

'Your name before a book.'

She shrugged. 'I am Eleanor.'

Again he glimpsed her eyes, blue as his own, though she was much shorter, her head hardly to his shoulder. Her cowl was somewhat ragged above her eyes where the stitching had given way, perhaps just this morning, for her nondescript garment was so much patched elsewhere, and with such care, that it was almost all patches, but perfect. Her feet were bare, scabbed by splinters from the floor, but her ankles were slim and strangely white. William glanced at his own sandalled feet, scoured clean by the snow. She must live in the warren of tiny snowy streets that clustered beyond the cathedral precinct.

He whispered, 'But your voice is . . . *young*.'

She spoke from the shadow beneath the cowl. 'No, monk, I am old. Withered. Wrinkled.'

'You do not sound old.'

'You do not sound wise.'

'What does a young girl know of books?'

'What does a monk know of them?'

'If you are insolent again I shall report you and have you whipped.' William stopped. He realised that the inferior was laughing at him but making no noise. She covered her mouth with her fingers but he saw only the rags clinging to her arm beneath her sleeve. He whispered, 'Tell me how long you have worked in the library.'

'All my life.'

'No, tell me truly.'

She whispered earnestly, 'All my life, and my grandmother worked here – I mean in the bishop's palace, where the library was stored

287

in those days – until her eyes hardened against too much reading.'

'And your mother too, I suppose?' Most duties were hereditary.

'My mother is dead.'

'I see. I shall require rare and difficult works.'

'I know the place of every volume.'

That was a remarkable assertion. He whispered, 'But surely even the librarian cannot—'

She was contemptuous. 'The librarian knows almost nothing.'

'This library contains four thousand volumes, and uncounted numbers of documents, charters—'

'I know them all.'

William sat. He ignored her. 'You have committed the sin of pride. I shall pray for you.'

In front of him on the desk he found the communal inkhorn and stylus, but he laid them aside, preferring to use his own. He took his writing pouch from his sleeve and laid out his materials neatly. He let his inkhorn remain stoppered – the ink was his own concoction of charcoal, gum and spices known only to himself – and placed carefully beside it his own stylus and sharpening knife. He took out his lava stone for smoothing vellum, then his ruler and ruling knife, its tiny blade as sharp as a barber's razor.

He realised the girl was still watching him. She was waiting. She repeated patiently, 'What book do you require?'

He said impulsively, 'St Jerome's Vulgate Bible.' It was probably the most valuable book the cathedral possessed. She walked to the far end of the room and he followed her with his eyes between the stacks of books. Balchus was gone, but she asked permission of the collator in his place, bowed, and returned from among the shelves carrying a heavy, ornate book with a cured leather cover worked with miracles.

She put it down in front of the monk. 'Knowledge is not pride, Brother William, it is simply fact. Fact is fact. It is itself.'

William glanced up at her, but she could see all his attention was on the book. He had long fingers, cleaned so that he did not dirty the papers he held, and his nails were trimmed short for the same reason. The forefinger and thumb of his left hand were twisted together like man and wife, from so many years of holding the stylus no doubt. He touched the Bible tenderly – not reverently, yet. His joy was in the book itself, in the words and learning hidden inside it. The excitement of the book, the mystery. Once Eleanor had a little brother, Thomas, and she remembered his face shining with wonder, opening a piece of bread to find the currant hidden inside. A child's innocence and wonder gleamed in Brother William's face as he opened the book.

The child was long dead but the memory was still painful, and Eleanor said more harshly than she intended, 'Is that all?'

William gazed at the beautiful manuscript. His lips moved as he read.

Each day the monk returned to the library at dawn, immediately after the service of Prime. His bare white ankles flashed beneath his habit as he ran upstairs, always hurrying. It made her smile just looking at him. His breath usually smelt of kippers when he arrived so he had obviously made a friend in the kitchen, and Eleanor wondered who she was.

As always he settled in his place without looking at her, head down, busy at once.

Eleanor made sure that she, not one of the other inferiors, was the one his eye caught when he looked up to request a new work. She made sure he got the books he wanted. She made his life easier with small acts of kindness, arriving before him, making sure his stylus was sharpened in the way he liked it – remembering to cut in the opposite direction from usual, he being left-handed – and finding a cushion for his hard bench. He did not thank her, he obviously thought nothing of himself. Hurrying and busy, that's all he was. Every hour of every day organised and in its place. He bent forward over the pages, eyes peering much too close to his work, tracing his finger along the line, lips muttering. Then a slight jerk of his body back to the start of the next line.

Hour after hour he worked.

He ignored her.

Eleanor stood beside him, waiting to be noticed, then cleared her throat so she did not startle him. The monk blinked his large watery eyes, returning slowly from the world of books. She whispered, 'You are left-handed. The light comes from the window on your left, therefore your hand shadows your work. You're ruining your eyes.' She turned him to the desk behind him, so that the light came from his right. 'Now you are illuminating your work not your hand.'

He said, 'Thank you.' But he did not move his place. Her kindness had affronted him somehow and he settled obstinately back to his work as before. He was a stubborn one! Clever and stupid, as the cleverest ones often were. She watched him writing doggedly in the shadow of his hand and turned away, covering her mouth in amusement and sadness. He was a man who had no friends. He thought he had everything he needed.

William tried not to notice her. The inferior had a way of being quiet that was noisy, of being absent that made him watch for her return. He had to admit the cushion was comfortable. A monk was not supposed to be comfortable. And she had laid her hands on him without his permission, physically taken hold of his shoulders at the expense of his dignity, to make him sit facing the other way. The Rule forbade him to allow such intrusions into his privacy.

But she was right. His hand *did* shadow his work. William had never realised it before but now he saw nothing else. The shadow of his moving hand irritated him constantly. He wondered if he could turn to the other desk without her noticing. He would have to find some way of turning round without losing face, but each time he was about to drop his stylus she seemed to be watching him particularly. Silent. Attentive. Intrusive.

William often tried to catch the eye of one of the other inferiors to fetch a book, but somehow the girl – now he remembered her name, Eleanor – was always beside him first, head bowed and hands clasped obediently. Yet she so plainly disliked him, causing him all this distraction, interfering.

It was wrong, a woman intruding so much into a man's world, a library. Wars always brought women forward in place of men. He could not settle to his work, she was always in the corner of his eye.

It was on the tip of his tongue to demand that the collator have her removed. He would do it tomorrow.

His window dimmed and the rooftops spread out beneath him dropped into shadow. It was evening. Someone stretched, leaving. William hurried, he had much yet to finish. He realised the other desks were bare and the library was silent. A copyist's day, according to cathedral time, was only seven hours long in winter. He looked gratefully at the glowing light as a hand set a lantern in front of him.

Eleanor said, 'You must know my hand by now.' William never looked at her face, just the books her hands put in front of him.

He wrote busily. 'I know you by your voice.'

'I thought the lantern would help you.'

He grunted to thank her for her kind thought.

She whispered, 'Why do you never look at me?'

Talk was idle and idleness was the devil's work. When she repeated her question William covered it busily. 'Now, you have in your catalogue, I believe, some charters of lands with descriptions of their borders?'

She said cautiously, 'We have many charters.'

'You claimed you know the position of everything.'

'I do.'

'Better than the librarian.'

'Yes.'

'I require the Charter of King Ethelred to Westminster Abbey in the year 986 concerning the grant to St Paul's Cathedral of lands in Paddington and Hendon.'

Eleanor hesitated. Her cowl turned slightly towards the collator yawning at his lectern, half asleep.

She murmured, 'Why do you wish to see that?'

'Merely to make a fair copy.'

'It is forbidden for you to see such documents.'

'Why?'

Her eyes stared at him from the shadow of her cowl. 'You're absurd.' She shook her head. 'Are you genuine? I don't know whether to believe you or not!' But Eleanor remembered him with the St Jerome Bible. 'Books are everything to you, aren't they?'

She decided about him.

William watched her whisper to the collator, Syrus, already late to the chapter house for his dinner. He sleepily nodded permission and entered a line in his list of works requested. Eleanor returned to William and with a casual air slid a roll of documents in front of him.

But suddenly William was perfectly certain these were not the papers for which she had asked permission.

The collator walked down and she happened to drop another document over these others, concealing them. She murmured, 'Don't tell him.'

William whispered, 'What?'

'Don't worry,' she whispered, 'Syrus is lazy.' William had never lied or concealed anything in his whole life. Syrus advanced with big, slow steps. He asked William how much longer he expected to work. William apologised for his lateness, but confessed his work was very long. Syrus dithered. William added that the dean had given him his own key, if more important matters called Syrus, and he would lock up carefully when he had finished.

'If the dean says so . . .' Syrus said, and hurried away gratefully to his food.

William sat motionless. He was breathing heavily. Eleanor pushed the door closed with her foot. She broke the silence.

'See?' she said cheerfully. 'That didn't hurt. Natural liar, you are.'

William lifted the document she had dropped over the Ethelred charters. 'Why did you do that?'

'Isn't it obvious?'

'Not to me.'

'If he saw I'd given you the Ethelred Telligraph I'd be kicked out on my arse. I'd starve, so would my grandmother. We don't have an abbey to feed us and clothe us, Brother William, shelter us and wipe our bottoms every day, as you do.'

Her crudeness shocked him. William realised she was angry with him but he did not know why. She was not like a man. He squinted at the lanternlight, not looking at her directly. He asked logically, 'Then why did you risk bringing it to me?'

'For you.' When he said nothing she uttered an exclamation, then rushed on, 'Why did you ask for it?'

'Because it is my business discreetly to examine notable documents.'

'Why don't you ever look at me? Are you afraid of me?'

She knelt at the fire, threw back her cowl. She was as he had imagined her, young. Her hair was black, hacked short. He noticed nothing else about her. She looked like any ordinary slut and sometimes she spoke like one.

She said, 'Do I annoy you?'

He told her the truth. 'I hardly think about you at all.'

'That's not the truth,' she said. She mimicked his whisper. '*It is my business discreetly to examine notable documents.*' She spoke in a loud, normal voice that made him flinch. 'You aren't perfect, monk. You're just a thief.'

'May God forgive you. No man is perfect, but I am not a thief.'

'You are a monk of Westminster Abbey, a professional thief. Westminster Abbey is a forgery factory, it is well known!' She shouted and he clapped his hands over his ears. 'You forge documents and seals for yourselves and other abbeys or whoever can pay. You substantiate your claims to ancient estates with forgeries and lies. You even fabricate true history and twist it to your own advantage.'

William was stunned. 'That's untrue. Some matters are omitted from the originals and require addition or alteration. They have to be brought up to date—'

'You don't know what the truth is.' She looked into the flames. 'You don't think for yourself, you do what you're told. You obey. You know what's going on but you won't admit it, even to yourself. If only you'd open your eyes, look around you.'

She shook her head over his denials, not listening.

He whispered, 'Eleanor, who told you these dreadful things?'

She laughed. 'What do you think all these others do in here all day? They're busy forging documents on behalf of St Paul's!'

William could not believe her. 'You are a cynic.' He wavered. 'Anyway, it's not a crime.'

She grinned, surprising him. 'Yes, crime is an entirely respectable activity, if everybody does it. And everybody does.' Her grin widened. 'We've even got your Mangoda charter here, Brother William. It's perfect work. It's fooled everybody. You cheated a word here, changed a name there, added a nought to a number or took it away. It was your duty. You were just following orders, you believed everything you were told. Easier than thinking for yourself.'

He tried to see himself as she saw him. He said sadly, 'How do you sound so wise?'

She swept out her arm from the books in the library to the filthy rooftops littered below. 'Here's my education.'

'I don't do what I do for me, Eleanor. I do it for the glory of God and for Westminster Abbey.'

She stood and went to the door, then stopped by him impulsively. 'I wish you didn't love books.'

'I love God.'

'No, I think you just love books, Brother William. I think books are all you know.'

He sat alone by the lantern, working, and locked the door after him when he left.

Eleanor, cowled, silent, mysterious, on gliding footsteps, crossed the dark trampled snow of the atrium. She took a few steps along Bower Row, called by newcomers Ludgate Street, then slipped to the left, a few paces downhill into the narrow gap of Sporyer's Lane. This was the area behind the deanery called the Creed, the tangle of old clergy cottages built over and built up and falling down, leading to Carter Lane. The thatch roofs met over her head, then the cries of children, the clatter of metalworkers' hammers, and barking dogs, and the stench of urine and manure, the world outside the cathedral, closed foully round her like human soup. A hand reached out of the dark, gripped her wrist. A woman's voice spoke.

'Late, you, where you been?'

Eleanor tugged for possession of her wrist but Elfrida would not let go, dragged her forward into the firelight from an open door. A baby cried. Eleanor tussled, wrenched free. 'Leave me alone!'

'Good thing I waited,' Elfrida snorted. She breathed through her nose to keep the cold air from her tooth-stumps. 'Upset, you are.'

The door was slammed, shaking the thin wall. Eleanor walked between the tumbledown houses, acknowledged with sharp nods and glances people she knew. Elfrida caught her up, spoke with puffing breaths to walk so fast.

'You haven't. Not a monk. A *monk*! He must be rich.'

Eleanor turned furiously. 'He's poor as a parish mouse! He stayed late! He works! That's all he is and all he does!' She came to the doorway of her grandmother's house and ducked through.

Elfrida came inside. 'He's not for you. Them, they don't have balls. They're shrivelled off. They do it to the novices with string knotted tight. He doesn't need you, doesn't understand you, doesn't care.'

Eleanor found a slab of bread and ate. 'Grandmother. Stop it.'

Elfrida nibbled alertly. 'It's not love again.'

Many local folk found Elfrida, with her provocative Saxon name like a throwback to another age, strongwilled and threatening. Eleanor did not, and it never occurred to her this was because she was as strongwilled and determined as Elfrida herself. There was more than a little of Elfrida in her. The old woman once desired daughters with all her heart, but gave birth only to a son. Her son took a wife before he died, and Eleanor was his daughter. Eleanor's mother, after endless arguments about property and storms of tears, had lived in submission and terror under the thumb of her indomitable mother-in-law.

Eleanor's mother had never known the secret. She had never taken the oath. She had died as she had lived, an outsider caught between grandmother and granddaughter.

Elfrida thought about her Eleanor. She knew better than to attempt to terrorise the young girl, but all the same she knew something had come between them. Something, anything, was trouble. Always.

'I was close with my mother,' Elfrida murmured soothingly. 'Close as this, we were.' She pinched her thumb and forefinger inseparably. 'Astrid, her name was. Mind of her own. Your sort, you'd have liked her. She always got what she wanted.'

'Do you know how often you tell me this story?'

Elfrida had forgotten. 'My grandma's eldest brother – she had five – was Deorman. Rich, he got. Rich side of the family, lands everywhere. His son was Algar. Deorman made enormous gifts of land to the cathedral, and Algar was elected prebendary canon tout de suite. The year before the old cathedral burnt, that was. It was Algar what did so much getting the new cathedral started, that's why they're putting up the statue to him, and why his worthless grandson is a prebendary now, who won't give me the time of day.'

'I'm going to sleep,' Eleanor said. She drank her ale, pissed in the jug and poured it out of the window hole. She lay down. There came the sound of a brawl outside, then silence.

'I'm not good with women,' Elfrida said. 'Women are difficult. But men, I understand. I've been watching you watch that one. He's dangerous.'

Eleanor scoffed. 'Brother William, dangerous!'

'Dangerous to us. Dangerous if you let him be. If you love him.'

Eleanor turned over. She snored. Any obstacle her grandmother put in her path made her more determined than ever to get her way.

'I know you're not asleep,' Elfrida said. She was in her eightieth year and her every bone hurt as though it turned to stone. 'Once I was you, in heat just like you are now, I can smell you. I can see it in the way you're breathing, how your eyes move. You're tightening your lips. You're thinking about him all the time. You're trying not to listen to me, aren't you?'

Eleanor sat up. She hugged the scratchy buckram blanket round her rags. Her eyes grew large in her elfin face. '*You* really felt like this about Grandfather?'

'Wasn't I young once? No no, God save us, like you I was, plump with youth and flesh. It was another man.'

'Did you confess?'

'Like the king he was, like a rising sun. He was . . . he was everything to me.' Elfrida's expression soured. She shrugged. 'For a month or two.'

'It's not like that,' Eleanor whispered. 'It's nothing like that.'

'Talking to Henry of Billingsgate, I've been. His boy Peter of

Cheap has been eyeing you. Soft in the head as an egg, that boy, but good stock. He'll inherit a good fish stall in the Cheap, and his father's licence.'

'I don't want him. He's dull. He smells of fish.'

'Think of the future.'

'Future?'

'Children.'

Eleanor rolled back in the straw, pulled her blanket over her head.

'Let your monk go,' Elfrida whispered. 'He's not for you.'

William thought about what the library inferior had told him. It was morning and he pushed between the barrows weaving through the cathedral, blocks of stone swinging on pulleys high over his head, stepped round the piles of sand and carpenters' benches and ladders littering the whole enormous enterprise. It was magnificent to see simple faith in the Truth, the Way and the Light translated by the labour of mortal men into such a massive symbol of worship and eternal God. He walked seeing on every side of him the cathedral, not as it was, but as the St Paul's it would become, a vast white cross standing for ever on the summit of London. Here the new octagonal chapter house would rise, he was almost blinded by its brilliant stonework, and perceived the holy cloister surrounding it where the canons of St Paul's would stroll deep in prayer and theological discussion. Instead of the winter sky he saw the spire five hundred feet high in the clouds, pointing the way to Heaven. He imagined the spire and roofs clothed in an immense fortune of gleaming lead, and glittering golden shrines filling the sanctuary and choir, and the ornate tombs and effigies and brasses of great men yet to be born filled his mind's eye. Ordinary people would subscribe to chantry guilds for prayers to be sung for their souls until the Day of Judgment. He imagined the lady chapel extending the eastern end of the cathedral – there was already talk of a huge rose window – and the church of St Faith's demolished and re-consecrated in the crypt beneath St Paul's. And as St Paul's led Londoners to God he foresaw all the money and gold they would bring to God's glory, the fragrance of righteousness rising with the prayers of the wealthy and devout, the splendour that would be devoted to Christ within these walls, the pomp of the churches and palaces gathered round this house of God adding to the glory of the cathedral, until the cathedral was the City.

Lost in these thoughts he ran upstairs with the air cold on his ankles. The inferior was standing in the stone gallery, waiting for him.

'You don't believe a word I told you,' she interrupted his thoughts. 'You're lost in your own little world.'

'I will not be disturbed by you.' He stepped round her.

'And you've been eating fish again,' she said. 'Kippers.'

That stopped him. 'I never know what you're going to say. You're deliberately unpredictable.'

'Which girl gives you the extra food?'

He had never noticed her. 'I don't know. A slut. A kindly woman. She calls me Sweet William, like the flower. It's her joke, I suppose.'

'That's Mary,' Eleanor said with satisfaction. 'That's all right.'

'Why?'

'She's ugly.'

'My dear woman, I—'

'You never say my name. You don't notice much, do you.'

'Look around you. We inhabit God's house—'

'You don't notice me. You don't notice poor Mary.' She stared at him, then her teeth flashed. She was smiling. 'Why do you keep scratching? Your clothes itch, don't they?'

William forced his hands to be still. Her whole attitude was an unforgivable intrusion into his privacy, but still she regarded him with cheerfulness, with almost a proprietorial air.

He said angrily, 'They do not itch.' He frowned to intimidate her. 'Do you not know that you are God's temple and that God's spirit dwells in you? God's temple is holy, and that temple you are.'

'St Paul's letter to the Corinthians,' she said effortlessly, and accompanied him to the library door without being asked. 'We are living stones to be built into a spiritual house.' She added, 'I shall be that tried wall, that precious cornerstone, whose foundations shall neither rock nor sway in their place.'

He lost patience with her, pushed past her into the library. A woman had no right to quote scripture at him. 'I shall insist the collator have you removed.' But he did not.

Later Eleanor came to his desk. William continued working, ignored her. Her slim white hands appeared, slipped a small sheaf of papers in front of him.

'I'm sorry I offended you,' she whispered.

He worked.

He looked up only when she was gone, then worked again.

At the end of the day he remembered the sheaf she had left. It was a Saxon charter granting Fanton Hall to Westminster Abbey, written in Latin, supposedly original. It was probably sixty or seventy years old, the work of a monk like himself. He examined it closely, fascinated. Such documents were always important.

A voice whispered at his elbow, 'True or false?'

William jerked, startled. He had not heard her come to him.

'It's false,' he muttered.

'Your eyes are watering. You work too close to the page. False?'

He frowned at her interference, then explained. 'It dates from the time of Abbot Edwin, the last Saxon abbot of Westminster Abbey.' She settled on her knees beside the desk, as naturally as a pupil with her master. William glanced round the library, which was empty and dark with shadows. He was flattered by her pious respect and forgave her intemperate, intrusive manner of this morning.

'The Saxons wrote briefly, often in English. This is Latin, wordy Latin, made long to impress Edwin's new Norman masters by its weight with its veracity.' William hated admitting that to her, because he now recognised the practice as deceit, though made from the best intentions.

'So it is a fake,' she said bluntly. 'Your sort of fake.'

No one ever talked to him like this, but William talked only to men and perhaps her gender differed in mind as well as in body from his own. 'No, everything is not a lie, Eleanor. It's fake only because it purports to be a ninth-century original and is not. It's beautiful work, but yes, in that sense it's a *falsum breve*, a forgery.'

She breathed, 'How do you know?'

He tried not to think of her. 'As I said, Eleanor, the Latin is suspicious. The grammar is too good . . .'

'I see,' she whispered appreciatively. 'You're so clever,' she complimented him. Twice he had said her name.

He wondered how she had changed so completely from their earlier conversations. A smile flickered on his thin lips, and with her encouragement his animation grew. 'The shape of the letters is wrong, you see. We do much better work now—'

'Yes, I'm sure you do.'

'The actual grant of land may be true or not, because it would be based on a mouth agreement and written down much later anyway. It's impossible to know.'

William realised that he looked forward to this time of day when everyone had gone, and fell silent. Alone except for the inferior, Eleanor, who did not count, kneeling beside him. She admired his intellect with submissive glances. He supposed he must seem very superior to someone of her God-given inferior gender and status. Yet her presence filled the library.

She seemed sad at his silence. He supposed he had been interesting. He wished he could think of something more to say.

She whispered, 'But the Gospels were also passed down from mouth to ear for a long time, weren't they?' She paused respectfully. 'I mean St Luke didn't actually sit down every evening and write the Gospel of St Luke. When he was an old man he told people what had happened and the story got passed down among believers and written down years later.'

'St Paul's Letters were written first, about twenty years after the Crucifixion, in times of confusion. He is the first Christian. However, a Gospel is incapable of untruth. Each Gospel is in the Bible and every word of the Bible is true.'

'But the Gospels are not the same, are they? The stories disagree.'

'No, no. You see, Eleanor, everything is there to be interpreted. Neither prophecy nor the Saviour himself declared the divine mysteries in a simple manner to be easily comprehended by ordinary people, rather He spoke in parables. It is we who are imperfect because we cannot always see the truth.'

'Forgive me. I wished to understand.'

'You are only a woman.'

'Yes.' She touched the sheaf of papers and his eyes followed her hand. 'There is another item underneath which you may not have noticed, Brother William.'

She got up and went to the fire, warming herself.

William lifted aside Edwin's vellum charter. His expression became fixed. Then he peered close, his long thin nose almost touching the little jewelled book. Eleanor smiled to see his finger tracing the lines, his lips muttering the words, the jerk of his body to the next line. Lost in the book. The room grew dark and she brought the lantern to him. 'Mind your eyes.'

He blinked. 'What?'

'I brought you light to see.'

He turned the book to the light and read aloud, '"The torrents of Satan"—' He crossed himself at the mention of the Father of Lies, the Evil One. 'This book is called the Prayer of Thanksgiving, but—'

'Yes, I know.'

He read, '"And the torrents of Satan shall pour to all corners of the world. And the fiery flames shall eat up the foundations of the earth, and the rocks shall burn like rivers of pitch. They shall devour as deep as the great Abyss and vomit as high as the Sky . . ."'

William swallowed, touched the tiny book with his fingertip. 'It's describing the end of the world.'

Yet the book looked small enough to be carried in a lady's jewellery box, and perhaps had been made for that purpose. 'This is very old,' he whispered. 'The form of letters is archaic, in the same style as St Jerome's Vulgate, and the syntax is similar – translated from an original into Latin at almost the same time, perhaps.' He swallowed. 'That would place it in the fifth century, Eleanor. Perhaps the fourth.'

She didn't take her eyes from his face illuminated by the lantern. He remained silent. She said, 'It doesn't look that old.'

In fact, thought William, this book looks as though it was made yesterday. The leather is uncracked, the leaves supple, the delicate colours are fresh. I cannot believe this is a forgery.

Yet he could think of no other explanation. 'Eleanor, where did you get this?'

She smiled at his enthusiasm, and even more at his repeated use of her name. 'Are you really interested?'

'Interested!'

'Oh, it must have been lying around on one of the shelves somewhere. It's amazing what a library collects over the years.'

'I've never seen *anything* like this.' He shook his head in wonder. 'It cannot be wrong to read it. Adding to the truth cannot be damaging to true religion.' He gazed round the shelves and aumbries as though to see more wonders revealed to him by the library of St Paul's. 'There's more.'

'Is there?'

'This morning when we spoke of St Paul you quoted a precious cornerstone, a wall whose foundations neither rock nor sway.'

She turned away, treating him to his own indifference, warmed herself at the fire-guard. 'Did I?'

'That wasn't St Paul.'

'Wasn't it?'

He left the desk and hobbled to her, stiffened and bent at first by his day of unremitting labour. 'Eleanor, you will pay attention to me.' When she did not William actually laid hands on her, pulled her shoulder. 'Look at me! St Peter spoke of the living stone, rejected by men but chosen and precious in God's sight, in almost the same way. But you weren't quoting St Peter.'

'Perhaps I said what St Peter actually said, not the version that was written down later.'

He whispered, 'Beware of blasphemy, woman.'

'It can't be blasphemy if it's true.'

'*How do you know it is true?*'

She let his hands turn her. She smiled. 'I must have read it in a book somewhere.'

He stared helplessly at the confusion on the shelves. He knelt beside her. 'Eleanor. Please.'

She said tempestuously, 'You said you'd demand the collator have me removed! You don't care if I starve.'

He said, 'I do. I do care.'

'You need me. Who would bring you any further precious works the library may contain? Will you find them for yourself?'

'Surely you're joking.'

'You threatened me. And you threatened to have me whipped. You don't look at me, you ignore me.'

William was chastened. He placated her. 'I'm sorry,' he said. 'I was wrong, Eleanor.'

Next day William arrived early as usual, running up the steps to the library with his ankles flashing. He looked round eagerly.

Eleanor was not there.

He looked for the little book. It was gone.

William sat in the empty library. He wondered what had happened to her. Had his secret thoughts wishing her gone been granted by God, had she indeed been removed? *Nothing in life happens by accident, everything has a meaning*. He could not shake away the feeling he was watched – a feeling that was rightly and devoutly with him all his life in the Order, but now seemed especially intense.

The other copyists filed in picking bits of breakfast out of their teeth, grumbling about the food, their elbows and foreheads dusty from prayer, and settled to their work.

William too settled to his work, and gradually his own thoughts left him as he became absorbed, and he lost his identity to the books he studied. He looked round him stiffly, suddenly aware he'd been working for hours. He rubbed his aching eyes. Syrus the collator stood dozing at his lectern. William watched the rows of copyists hunched like him over their desks, elbows moving, fingers tracing, busy with their forgeries and deceits. He remembered telling Eleanor, *Everything is not a lie*. But now, looking at them so busily at work, he wondered if everything was.

William called an inferior to serve him but a boy's face peeped beneath the cowl, not Eleanor's. He asked where the girl was. 'A girl, lord?' William sent him away.

He worked into the evening and fetched the lantern himself. The fire had died to glowing embers. William looked round him to make sure he was not observed, then knelt curiously, peering upward to try to see what happened to the smoke. He remembered kneeling here beside Eleanor. A draught blew past him and he jumped to his feet. 'Who's there?' The library was silent and still. The door remained closed.

William returned to his desk but he could not concentrate. The silence was oppressive. He extinguished the lantern and went out, locked the door behind him. He had passed a sterile and unsatisfactory day and though he had laboured hard he had achieved nothing.

Tomorrow was the Sabbath.

After mass William hurried down the steps. The Bishop of London's prison occupied the cathedral tower on his left, and in the yard behind him shrouded bodies were unloaded into the charnel house for holy storage. He hurried past the cathedral brewery and the Camera Dianae, the canons' residence, and walked down Bower Row to his elder sister's house in Cecil's Lane. On weekdays the place was called the Ready and a market filled it to the house gables, but today it was quiet. Ramshackle taverns overhung the street to serve the usual trade. Agnes had married a taverner at Le Four Nuns. Her husband kept out of William's way but a torrent of children flooded downstairs then pressed themselves shyly round the walls, regarding the visiting monk in silent awe. Agnes wrapped her arms round him. 'Come as often as you like if you bring this sort of peace and quiet with you!' She was a large buxom hearty woman, with blue eyes in a bouncing red face, long black hair swinging in greasy plaits. 'Thin as a rake, you are! Feed you up.' She pointed proudly at the children and shouted their names, cuffed the ones that hung back. 'Come on, he won't bite you or bless you. He's still human, my little brother is. Still drinks beer.'

'He doesn't look like you,' the eldest girl said, dark-haired and serious. 'He's skinny.'

'He's got brains instead of these.' Agnes hefted her milky breasts and immediately there was a cry. 'Look out, now the babe's seen them.' She hurried out to the scullery in the yard and the baby was thrust into William's arms to hold. The serious girl showed him how to hold it properly. 'I want to be a nun,' she confided. The baby played with William's stubbled face and the children gathered round, crowding closer as their trust grew, until by the time Agnes fetched the roasted chickens indoors they were crawling over him laughing and shouting, and all that could be seen of William were his sandalled feet, and all that could be heard of him was his laughter.

They ate, and William looked round him at his happy sister's family, his own for a day. He saw the life he had given up for the love of God. The wife and warmth and children he would never have.

Agnes cried when he left.

It was already dark and snowing heavily. Time had passed so quickly. William walked into the empty cathedral and prayed.

At dawn he left his cold carrel and plodded through the snow, knelt for Prime, and climbed to his desk among the forgers working in the library. He forced himself to concentrate on his labours. The cowled figure of an inferior pushed past him.

He grabbed its elbow. 'Eleanor!'

It was she. Head bowed, she awaited his instructions.

'Where have you been?' he hissed. 'I looked for you!'

'You *really* looked for me?'

'I feared you had been dismissed. I feared—' The truth was that William had feared more than he could put into words.

She said, 'I had a cold.'

A cold! 'That's all? But why did you not send word?'

'It was only a cold. I did not think you would notice.' But she sounded pleased.

'Are you recovered?'

She glanced at the collator, whispered, 'If you have no instructions for me . . .'

William shook his head miserably.

She patted his hand, and he knew he would see her later.

All morning he watched the tiny figures of cathedral sparrows swarm across the precinct sixty feet below his window, legs of beef and carcasses of mutton running apparently by themselves from the butchery. Greasy cooking-smoke poured from windows around the top of the kitchener's tall building. It was a memorial Day of Dedication, not of the modern St Paul's which was not yet formally dedicated, but of an earlier cathedral on this site. A bell rang at noon, the sixth hour, and the benches scraped noisily as they were pushed back. The library was abruptly deserted for the special services of remembrance and the feast. Bellies would be stuffed with red meat and half a gallon of beer and no one would work this afternoon. William worked alone. Eleanor moved round replacing books in shelves and cupboards according to her own mysterious custom and without disturbance.

At last she stopped by him. 'Are you not attending the feast?'

He whispered, 'I am of Westminster Abbey not St Paul's.'

'Are you not well? You sound feverish.'

'I do not know if I am well or not.'

'You have done little work. You stare from the window like a blind man.'

He whispered, 'If you had that book, I'd look at it again.'

'The Prayer of Thanksgiving? I have returned it to its place. Surely there are more interesting things to look at,' she said insistently. She put back her cowl. Distantly they heard chanted responses rising from the choir. She closed the door, muffling every sound but the scuff of her footsteps.

'Books are my life,' William said.

She waited but he remained in his lonely misery. She bent down beside him, her mouth close to his ear, her breath tickled him. She was always either too close or too far away, perhaps deliberately she had no sense of his dignity. 'It is rumoured the dean secretly charged you to organise a verbatim and truthful catalogue of the library's treasures.' She slipped a small book bound in red leather and gold from her sleeve, placed it on the desk. When he reached for it she covered the slim volume with her hand until he looked from it to her eyes. 'Make sure you do not put this in your catalogue.' She withdrew her hand and left him to the book.

After a few minutes' study William came to her by the fireplace. He held the book flat on his hands as though it was almost infinitely precious to him.

'What are you doing to me, Eleanor?'

'Is it wrong?'

'No! It's right. It's marvellously right. Eleanor, this is a book of psalms.' He tried to make her understand.

'Like the Book of Psalms in the Bible?'

'These are all written by King David of Jerusalem. Personally, I think, it's not just his name added to give veracity to someone else's work. They're individual. There must be almost two hundred of them. I've never heard of any of them.' He showed her the book. 'Look, Eleanor. Translated into Latin. Forgotten.'

'I see,' she said. She smiled to see his pleasure.

'Look at the workmanship! Fourth century or earlier. This book was made for someone very rich – perhaps the same person as the Prayer of Thanksgiving, beauty and labour and care like this never came cheap. See all this gold leaf? That means the words are very valuable.' He spoke in a hushed voice. 'I'm holding the lost psalms of King David in my hands.'

They sat in silence for a while. She moved closer to him.

William murmured, 'This fire is a marvel. I mean, that it does not fill the room with smoke.'

'Have you not heard of a *cheminée*?' She pointed above the fireplace. 'There's a hole in the wall which goes up to the hole in the roof. One of the pinnacles, actually. A cylinder of air up which the smoke rises.'

He patted the wall. 'But it's solid.'

'The cathedral would be too heavy ever to stand if the walls and columns were really solid, William.' It was the first time she had said his name aloud, but he did not notice. 'William.'

'Yes?'

'A cathedral is a maze. At least as complex as a person.'

'People are made by God.'

'Like living stones be yourselves built into a spiritual house . . .'

'St Peter.' He finished the quotation. 'The stone which the builders rejected has become the cornerstone. A stone that will make men stumble, a rock that will make them fall.' He looked at her excitedly. 'What you said last week – almost the same words – the precious cornerstone whose foundations shall neither rock nor sway in their place—'

She nodded. 'Peter's Book.'

He cried out, 'Then there is more!'

'There's always more.'

He said anxiously, 'You're not lying to me?'

'No, William.' But she had been, at the start. She had used William's interest in the books to make him interested in her. But now she felt so close to him that his excitement infected her, became part of her own excitement.

He hugged the little book of the two hundred psalms of King David to his chest. 'You've actually seen it?' He begged her, 'You're leading me forward with little scraps of the truth—'

She whispered, 'The truth is that I have fallen in love with you.'

He laughed. 'Tell me the truth.'

'I will not live without you.'

But he kissed the book. He had eyes only for the book. He looked at her and saw the book.

'Would you believe the truth?' she said sadly. 'You don't hear. You don't see—'

He jumped up and went feverishly along the shelves. 'Are there more books? Show me everything!' He looked round.

She was gone.

Next morning William arrived in the library using his fingernail to dislodge a fishbone caught between his teeth. He stopped, staring. On his desk lay a single roll of dark skin.

The scroll was about a foot in length, a cylinder of skin rolled to the thickness of his upper arm. It was dark brown and the edges, which had once been sharply cut with a knife and ruler, were frayed and stiffened by age.

It was very old. At first William thought it was human skin, so smooth and fine was it to his touch. Long ago it had been carefully cured and scraped. William recognised the skill and care.

He thought, this is the work of experts. This skin was very valuable to them. Therefore the words it contains will be very valuable.

He worked his finger under the flap, peeling the end apart from the curve of the scroll beneath it.

The skin that had been closed to the air was ivory white. It was as white as his own soft, cold fingers.

He unrolled it carefully. In two places the scroll had been cut and extra lengths of skin sewn on with tiny stitches. He took the unravelled length and placed his inkhorn on the end to stop it rolling up again.

The scroll was about six feet long.

Its length was divided into columns, each about as broad as the page of a book. The lines of each column had been ruled by a knife with exquisite skill, marking the skin sufficiently but not penetrating it. The ink looked very black on the ivory white.

The text was meaningless. William did not understand a word of it. Not one single letter.

Except that at the top left, before the start of the script, in a different ink and hand, the word *Hagu* had been added in Roman letters.

Hagu.

He rolled it up carefully. He hardly worked all day for looking for Eleanor. She was not there.

Darkness fell.

William stood in the empty library. He had locked the door, locking himself in. He looked from the window over the rooftops of London below him. A gang of roughs ran along one street, knocking people over. A man carrying a long fiery flambeau led a group of pilgrims from Ludgate, toiling uphill towards the cathedral. A woman committed filthy acts in a doorway, shouting at her children when the door opened. William couldn't hear what she said from up here. His lantern went out. The fire had gone out hours ago. He stood in the dark.

From somewhere down the library, a door creaked. He heard soft footsteps. They paused, and he knew he had been seen.

'Eleanor.'

'You're shivering,' she said. She held up a lantern, illuminating him.

Yes, he realised he was shivering. 'Where have you been? Where do you come from?'

She shrugged. 'My grandmother has my cold. I had to look after her, she's nearly eighty years old. You see, once my family was rich but now we are poor. Our side of it, anyway. Her grandmother's brother was the father of Deorman—'

'I've heard of Deorman.'

'Yes, you must have forged his signature many times, on false grants of land to Westminster Abbey. Don't deny it. In a way I admire you for it. Your fanaticism. Deorman's son was Algar, a famous prebendary of St Paul's.'

'Yes.'

'So Algar is not my ancestor, not directly, but we are related. Sufficiently closely that, for example, the Church would not have permitted my grandmother, Elfrida, to marry him. My grandmother remembers Algar well, knew him very well, do you understand?'

'Understand what?'

'She loved him, William. Twenty years younger than he and never his wife, but she loved him. Algar the Prebendary, the founding Canon of the new St Paul's. Bishop Maurice the Norman and Algar the Saxon, they were the two who pushed the work forward, made this real.' She patted the wall. 'Without Algar's vision this would not be here.'

Religious phenomena, evidence of God, fascinated William. 'A vision was revealed to him?'

She looked wary. 'Determination. He was a very determined man. Obsessed.'

'A glorious obsession.' William looked round him, touched the cathedral's living stones. 'A vision from God.'

She said, 'No. A vision from my grandmother.'

William frowned reprovingly. 'Must I remind you that this is a holy place, not a place for jokes or laughter? It has been proved that Jesus Christ never laughed.'

She whispered, 'Would you recognise the truth if you saw it?'

He said, 'I'm sure—'

She shouted at him. 'You're blind and deaf and dumb! You have no feeling!' She fell silent. William stared at her as though she had struck him across the face. She whispered, 'Can a man only recognise the truth he believes he is looking for?'

He whispered, 'I am a man. What is *Hagu*?'

Eleanor took his hand. 'You must promise never to reveal what I will show you.'

'I am a monk. It shall be *sacerdos in aeternum*.'

'Swear it.'

'I have already sworn it.'

'Swear it!'

He smiled at her persistence. 'I swear.'

She led him by his hand to the fireplace. William bent his head beneath the angled buttress to its left, complaining as she tugged him forward. She opened the aumbry filling the niche behind the fireplace and its *cheminée*. The tall gilded doors swung wide, revealing the aumbry stacked with books. She knelt, not letting go of his hand or looking away from his eyes, and operated something William could not see.

There was a click and the lower shelves of the aumbry swivelled outwards.

Behind them was nothing.

She ducked inside, tugged him after her.

'We're going inside the *cheminée*?' he said.

'It is a pillar.' She reached back and pulled the door closed behind them. The lantern flickered in the draught rising past them to feed the chimney above them. William looked down. Steps spiralled downwards, round and round the inside of the pillar, sooty at first then clean, the stone grating under the wooden soles of his sandals as he hurried down after her, round and round, his feet almost touching her head. William grew dizzy. He heard fragments of singing, chanting voices in the choir. Someone close by muttered his allotted psalm, then the voices faded above them.

Now they heard muffled calls touting for business, lawyers offering torts and writs, the banging seal ring of a notary witnessing business. A voice grunted, 'Pretty girl like you.'

Eleanor whispered, 'We're in the crypt.'

The pillar was floored by a massive arrangement of stone slabs and struts. She pulled on a loop of rope and lifted a hatch, revealed a wooden ladder.

William followed her down the rungs. The air hung thick with cobwebs. 'Where are we going?'

'It's a catacomb.'

He said, 'What's that smell?'

'What does it smell like?'

'Unmentionable.'

'That's exactly what it is.' She pointed the other way. 'Shit. Sorry. The priests' latrine. Did you never wonder what happened to it, William?' He didn't answer. 'Oh, of course,' she said, 'monks don't do it.'

He coughed, then followed her lantern light brushing through the pale veils that hovered round them like angel wings in the draught.

Eleanor crawled beneath an angled stone, came to another hatch, this time of wood. Beneath it wooden ladders led down, crisscrossing into the dark.

Very dusty, very old. They creaked loudly.

William looked round him. He whispered, 'Is this *Hagu*?'

She glanced up, the lantern light flickering under her chin and nose and eyes, an elf's face. Then she crossed the platform to another set of steps, swung herself out, and continued down.

William followed the light into the darkness.

The wood beneath him turned abruptly to stone. He stood on a pile of chalk boulders, then scrambled down, looked around him.

'Why did Algar build his cellar so deep?'

Eleanor smiled. She crossed to a way out he had not noticed, ducked through. William followed her down a sloping tunnel. Another dark cellar lay beyond. She held up her lantern.

In the centre of the room a dark pile of leather was illuminated. For a moment William thought it was leather armour, then he fell on his knees with a gasp, recognising what he saw.

'Books,' Eleanor said. 'Scrolls. Knowledge.'

She watched his face. William's eyes were very blue in the lantern light and she saw the reflections of the books in them. A cobweb had stuck to the stubble on his jaw and she brushed it away. He did not flinch. She turned his face towards her but his eyes stared at the books.

'My God,' he said. 'My Lord. My dear sweet Lord.'

She fell on her knees with him beside the books. She did not look at them, only at William's eyes.

'What are these?' he whispered. 'Are they Apocrypha? Is the Hagu a lost book of the Apocrypha?'

'The Book of Hagu is the Book of Meditations on the Divine Law, written by Jews.'

He murmured, 'Jews!'

'You have not forgotten the Bible was written by Jews.'

'But our Bible has been purified by translation into our own Latin.' He reached out with trembling fingers, touched a fragment. 'This is the Jewish language. Hebrew.'

'Do you understand Hebrew?'

'No one understands Hebrew. One or two scholars in Oxford, perhaps, or Paris.' He murmured again, 'What are these?'

She repeated what her grandmother had told her. 'Perhaps knowledge a Christian should burn.'

'No, no.' He muttered feverishly, 'They're in a foreign language, they're no harm to anyone. Is the Book of Peter here?'

She whispered, 'I believe everything is here, William.'

He begged, 'Tell me!'

'No one knows anything. Only what happens is true.' She moved between him and what he was looking at. 'Look at me, William.'

He looked at her.

She said, 'They're mine. They're in my possession, not yours. Not yours, not the cathedral's. The Book of Mannasseh, the First Esdras, the Second Esdras that predicts the rejection of the Jews by the Church. The Prayer of Thanksgiving. The Wisdom of Solomon, the story of Susanna and Bel and the Dragon. The Manual of Discipline. The Wisdom of Jesus ben-Sira. The Song of the Three Holy Children. Bibles. I don't know what else. Some in Latin, some in language and writing beyond imagining.' She kissed his mouth, that was all. 'Not yours, William.'

William seized her with all his strength. The blood pulsed in their veins but he did not know what to do. The floor was hard. She lay back across the books, kissing him with her lips, her thighs rising beneath his garb, warmly caressing his bare body.

William fell.

'Marry me,' she whispered. 'Give it all up, be yourself, marry me.'

He did not hear her.

'Don't be a monk,' she murmured. 'Give it all up for love. Love me.'

Even as they made love, William's eyes had watched the books. Even as his body pulsed in his moment of passion it was not she he saw. He was overwhelmed.

William glanced at her while she talked. He pulled down another scroll, tried to read what was written on the outside. He pulled down another, then another. Some were wrapped in linen. 'What do these blue rectangles mean?'

She shrugged. 'They are statements of truth.'

'It's gibberish.' He put his hands to his head. 'Not one word makes sense.' He knelt. 'Look at this work, Eleanor. Look at all this! All the trouble they took. It must have meant everything to them, and I don't even know what it is.'

He carried on, finding a scroll of silver, then one of pure gold, on which only the purest truth could be written, but she hardly listened to him. 'You made love to me, William,' she murmured. 'We're joined. You can't make it not happen.' She caressed him but he did not feel her. He was so naked under his garb, deliciously male, stark yet vulnerable. Untouched until she touched him. She could change him. Yet his will and determination were equal to her own, perhaps greater.

Perhaps he was stronger than she.

Eleanor waited patiently. She did not believe so. He was the first man she had loved, the first man who had not used her for his moment's pleasure and forgotten her. Her thoughts became tinged with sadness.

I used you, she thought. I love you and I'll do anything to keep you.

She sat up. He glanced at her again, his attention caught because she was naked. She let him look at her. Probably he had never seen a woman revealed before. Now he had started, he would soon want to see her again. What he saw he would want to touch. Through her body he would learn to love her completely.

'I know what you're trying to do,' he said. He put down the golden scroll. 'I'm ashamed of myself. God forgive us. I must do penances until next Christmas.' So he still thought he could forget her.

'Christmas,' she murmured. She wrapped her clothes loosely round her. '*Dies Natalis Invicti Solis*, the birthday of the Unconquered Sun.'

He frowned. 'No, Eleanor. The day Jesus Christ was born and laid in the manger in Bethlehem.'

'And the day the god Saturn was born. And the god Attis, killed and resurrected in the spring. And the god Mithras. And what about Yule, the sacrificial tree on which men were hung?'

He said, 'Is this knowledge here?'

'It's all here. Everybody knows these things, though the Church denies them.'

'Because they are not true.'

'Decide for yourself what is the truth and what is a lie.'

'Mother Church teaches us—'

She sat beside him. 'Down here we are equal. Down here you are not my superior, William, you're part of me, I'm part of you.' She revealed herself matter of factly, his semen dripping from her. 'Don't talk to me of your penances. We both know you don't do them, you pay a pauper priest to fast on bread and salt in your place until your sin is wiped clean.'

'One man's penance is as good as another's.'

'No,' she said, standing. 'No, William, it isn't. What you do is up to you.' She wrapped her gown round her, knotted the rope at her waist.

He rubbed his face wearily. 'I don't understand you, Eleanor. This is the greatest treasure in the world, and yet—' He shook his head. 'You. Only a woman.'

'You swore an oath to me, William. *Sacerdos in aeternum*.'

'This must be kept safe in the library. Examined by scholars. Revealed to the world.'

'I showed this to you because I love you, William.'

'But—'

'I am yours but this is not.'

He bowed his head. 'But the truth is here, isn't it?' he said. 'The book that Peter actually wrote is here. The truth.'

'The fact.'

He murmured in an awed voice, 'Written standing next to God.'

'Written perhaps in the same room as Jesus Christ, yes. Peter's was the only one translated into Latin.'

'There are others?'

'Ten others. Eleven altogether. The books of the eleven true apostles. You recognise them by the linen wrapping sewn with blue rectangles. A dove signifies the Holy Spirit. Each apostle has his own emblem: Matthew a man, Mark a lion, Luke an ox, John an eagle. Christ was a man in his birth, a calf in his death, a lion in his resurrection, an eagle when He ascended to Heaven. Obviously the original collector understood Hebrew.' She kissed his cheek. 'You've been down here longer than you think, William. It must be almost dawn.'

He watched her find her clogs. He longed to stay here but knew he could not. Eleanor hopped from one foot to the other, putting her clogs on. Her every action marked her as merely human, nothing greater. William knelt beside the mysteries, praying, his lips moving and his eyes closed to slits, watching her. She turned her back on him and his pale hand snatched out, tore off a piece of scroll, slipped it into his sleeve.

He breathed heavily through his nostrils, praying.

The truth is here. God cannot have meant to place a woman as its guardian.

Everything I do, I do for You, O Lord.

Eleanor went to the tunnel that led upward. She held out her hand for him to help her up. William whispered, 'I do love you, Eleanor. I want to come down here with you again.'

She laughed excitedly.

Still no Eleanor.

Elfrida, bent and bowed with age, staggered from her straw pallet. She'd hardly slept a wink and she felt deathly. She waited shivering by the cathedral's west gate. Her eyes and nose streamed with her cold, she sneezed noisily, hawked on to the snow. Dawn rose behind the cathedral like God and the masons swarmed black against the light, busy as always, the sound of their hammers and chisels and shouts a constant refrain all her adult life.

Her granddaughter came down the steps of the cathedral two at a time. The bell clanged for Prime, but Eleanor did not look stiff with cold like someone coming from prayer. She walked fast, kicking the snow in front of her, her face flushed and eyes sparkling. Elfrida sneezed into her sleeve, not giving her presence away, and awaited her moment.

Eleanor came cheerfully through the gate. The old woman stepped in front of her. 'What have you done?'

Eleanor burst out, 'Everything you told me was a lie! He was marvellous. You're horrid.' Tears filled her eyes. 'I'd trust him with my life.'

Elfrida said implacably, 'You're giving everything away, you're a bitch in heat.'

'What about you and Algar?'

Elfrida groaned. 'That was different and long ago.'

'A married man, old enough to be your father!'

'You're letting your womb rule your heart and your heart rule your head.'

Eleanor's voice rose. 'I'd rather be as I am than dry, and withered, like—' They were having a blazing row in public.

Elfrida hissed, 'I've made a proposal to young Peter of Cheap—'

Eleanor pushed disrespectfully past her grandmother. She stormed down Bower Row, went from sight. Elfrida stared after her as long as she could, wiping her rheumy eyes.

She groaned again, praying. Thank you, Lord, for letting me grow old beyond the pain of earthly pleasures and desires, even though You grant me no peace, no forgetfulness. She sighed. 'Grand-daughter, granddaughter, you're just like me.'

William clutched the piece of skin inside his left sleeve. His guilt at his theft felt hot enough to burn him. Then he remembered last night and what Eleanor had done to him. He would burn anyway.

After Prime he rose from his knees and ignored the door leading to the library. Instead he hurried out past Paul's Cross, through the cathedral cemetery, took the north-east Little Gate into Westcheap. The market made a jostling mass of heads and shoulders streaming along the broad thoroughfare, the trampled snow brown with blood and offal, dogs running between people's legs, and a woman gave him an apple for his holiness. Terrified of being robbed, William caught the fruit with his right hand, clutched his left arm against his body, and blessed her.

He realised he was starving and surreptitiously crunched the apple as he walked.

Like most people, William of Ludgate had very little idea of London outside his own small piece. The first two people he asked in the tumult of sidestreets and market stalls had never heard of the district called Jewry, the third and fourth misdirected him to the Jews' Cemetery, and the fifth demanded to know what business an honest monk had with thieving Jews and usurers. One of the tanners working to the elbows in his stinking task at the Cow Face bellowed Jewry was only a few rods down the street, on his straw foot. William could hardly understand the man's accent, which was of Walbrook, and had no idea whether common folk meant by straw foot right or left. Stallholders changed their cries to French for a man passing on horseback, a man-at-arms beside him, and offered trays of warm gloves, mulled wine, spiced meat. A boy followed the horse with a spade. A pig sat in a butcher's cart with a red blanket thrown over it, looking as noble as an archbishop. The horse lifted its tail and the boy, his patience rewarded, caught the steaming *brancard* flawlessly on his spade, dodged away nimbly through the crowd with his prize.

The ironmongers pointed William to a narrow street on the left. William finished his apple and tossed the core to a beggar. He walked into the *vicus Judeorum* past St Olave's Church. There was still talk of making Jews, all property of the Crown, wear yellow badges and of enclosing their ghetto within high walls and gates. But even without battlements and guards, William felt he was entering a foreign country.

Even the air smelt different. Butchers worked with copper knives, spoke unintelligibly. Their strangeness and ritual manner were threatening – it was a matter of proven fact that a crime by one Jew was a crime by all – and William was acutely conscious of his crucifix and monk's habit. But no one molested him. In fact the strange-looking men avoided him, the chattering women fell silent and passed him with faces averted. Eventually William stopped a Jew with long black sidelocks, selling pieces of toasted rusk from a tray.

'I'm looking for the Jew Joshua. Do you know of such a man?'

The rusk-seller nodded patiently. 'Hundreds of Joshuas I know.' He tried to walk by politely.

'A young man, dark, intelligent.'

'Yes, ten or twenty of them – all good boys.'

William realised how close these people were. 'I mean no harm. He isn't in trouble.' He wondered what Eleanor, who knew the ways of the world, would have done. He paid for a piece of rusk. 'Wears a striped cloak? The son of Master Abraham, the moneylender.'

'Master Abraham! Now you say.' The man pointed cheerfully. 'Beyond the *scolae*, the synagogue, you find the messuage of Master Abraham.'

To William the Latin slang for a synagogue was a brothel, and the word for its congregation was harlots.

'Enjoy your food!' the rusk-seller called after him amiably, then broke into another language for his next sale. William was sure they were talking about him.

He threw the rusk away. It was common knowledge that the Jews stole the Host of consecrated bread – literally the body of Christ – from Christian churches. In secret ceremonies they stabbed it until it ran with blood, revenging themselves for the sufferings their crime of deicide had brought upon them.

William almost lost his nerve. He whispered, 'I must have been mad to come here.'

Master Abraham's messuage was a large jumbled building cobbled out of many dwellings. Its stained walls and tiny windows peeped in every direction. William went through the gateway into the yard. Stairways clung to every crooked wall. Children played in the yard and as they saw him their happy cries gradually ceased. They watched him, then shrank from sight.

A hand gripped William's shoulder. 'What are you doing here?'

It was he, the same curled locks, bright brown eyes. William cried out, 'Joshua. It is I. Do not grip so hard.'

'Quick, before my father sees you.' The young Jew pulled William through a doorway. They stood together in a low, small room. It was dusty, lined with boxes and wooden chests. William supposed them full of mortgages and bills of indebtedness. These were the first things to be burnt in times of trouble, so doubtless the Jews kept copies of them in safe places like this, among others.

Joshua released him. He sat on a creaky stool, made a foreign-seeming gesture of his hand for William to do the same. He wore a small cap on the back of his head. Everything about him, his striped cloak, his unfashionable clothes, his casual florid mannerisms, seemed deliberately designed to make him look more outlandish, more of an outsider from the country in which he lived. Even the way he rested his hands on his knees, palms open as if in friendship, was odd and different. Almost aggressive in its difference.

William sat.

Joshua said, 'So that is what a monk wears beneath his habit. Complete with foreskin—'

Bright with embarrassment, William flapped his garb over his knees. He said, 'You dare to mock—'

But Joshua interrupted, 'I do not mock. What more can I do for you, Brother William?'

William took a deep breath. 'You are plainly intelligent, and I know that I can trust you.'

Joshua said, 'How?'

'You saved my life. You wouldn't waste that.'

'Somehow I didn't think it was gratitude that brought you here. You aren't going to accuse me of poisoning wells, are you?' William knew that bad water, like bad weather, was always blamed on the Jews.

'You're the first of your race and religion I've ever spoken to,' he confessed. 'It's not as I thought. Why do I feel instinctively that you and I could be friends, and why do you make it so difficult?'

Joshua put his finger to his lips and opened the door a fraction. He checked through the gap, returned. 'You're not like a monk, Brother William.'

'And you are not like a Jew.'

Joshua said furiously, 'I am Jew, Jew, Jew. I am what I am. My father's cousin, Uncle Moses, was knocked unconscious, and when he awoke he had been baptised.'

William said gently, 'God be praised, he is saved.'

'He tried to drown himself but he was pulled from the water. When he renounced Christianity and his baptism he was burnt on a pole for heresy. Can I forget?'

William put his hands together. 'I will not forget that you have saved my life. Do you speak Hebrew?'

'Of course.' Joshua looked surprised. 'It is my first language, not English. And I speak French, because most of our loans are to important people.'

'At tuppence per pound per week.'

Joshua showed his teeth. 'A little less to Westminster Abbey, old friend. Is money what you need?'

'No. No one else in London speaks Hebrew.'

'Because London is your home. Not ours.'

William thought London was the centre of the world. 'Where is your home?'

'We have never left Israel. Our numbers there are small. But they represent the whole, and are entitled to be supported by the whole.'

William murmured, 'What does your father think of your ideas?'

Joshua said honestly, 'He thinks I am outspoken. I believe in the Jewish land, nation, religion, race. I am a nationalist in a foreign nation. But I am young. So whatever you want, say it before my father returns.'

'He would be angry if he saw me with you?'

'He would be angry with me. I am always in trouble, Brother William. I cannot afford more. I will grow into a man of many words and few actions, no doubt, and lose my idealism like my father. Hurry!'

William decided. He took the piece of skin from his sleeve. He bent forward carefully.

'It's dirty, but dirt doesn't take away all the holiness from words. It's not ornamented or coloured or illustrated. But that doesn't mean it has no value at all. Do you recognise this writing?'

Joshua took it. He laid the fragment on his knee and examined it closely, then asked William's permission and carried it to the window. He wiped the grimy glass with his elbow, making a clear circle of light. His lips moved, reading. 'Where did you get this?'

'So you do understand it!'

'Yes, it's Hebrew. *Hebraica veritas*, the original truth uncorrupted by later translation or copying, however faithful in intent. The style of the script is unfamiliar, formal, but the meaning is not difficult. This is very old, Brother William.'

William pointed. He was so excited he felt he might burst. 'Read it to me. What is this word?'

'I am not permitted to tell you. It is the name of God, which may be written but never uttered aloud.'

William hugged himself. It was all he could do not to jump for joy. 'The name of God would never be written lightly. It must be true. Can you tell what it's from?'

Joshua shrugged. 'One of the scriptures. You would call it the Old Testament.'

'Ah, one of yours.'

'Different meanings drawn from the same material. I think it's part of a psalm, perhaps.'

William said eagerly, 'Yes, one of the psalms written by King David personally.'

Joshua caressed the skin with his fingertips. 'If that is so, William, then this is two thousand years old.' His brown eyes looked directly into William's blue gaze. 'Is that possible, Brother William?'

William said, 'Yes.'

'And you are saying there is more?'

'Yes, there is more. There is so much, much more!'

Joshua touched him warningly. 'Be cautious. Be very quiet about this, Brother William. Do not say a word to anyone, neither a Jew nor a Christian.'

William thought about Eleanor. 'You're quite right.'

Joshua returned to the window. He frowned at the lines on the fragment of skin.

William said, 'What is it?'

Joshua went over the sense of it again. 'This cannot be right. It refers to the Messiah. 'And He shall be called a Nazarene . . .' This was written a thousand years before your Christ, yet it predicts your Jesus will be born in Nazareth.'

They stared at one another in silence, the Christian monk and the Jew, listening to the Hebrew shouts of the children playing outside.

It was dark and cold that night in the cathedral.

William shivered on his knees on the hard stone as Matins were sung. Long ago, in the days of St Erconwald whose golden shrine glimmered in the sanctuary shadows, when St Paul's Cathedral was a monastery in all but name, the canons lived lives as dry and dedicated as those of monks. Some monastic solemnities survived from those ancient days of the foundation – for the first time William realised that the normal Christian way of life must seem as threateningly ritual to a Jew as Jewish rituals seemed to him – and among them was the custom of Matins after midnight.

William had prayed on his knees for almost an hour in excruciating discomfort, sleepless, waiting in his place on the left of the sanctuary as he had promised. A circator made the rounds with his lamp, waking snorers. Like penances, prayers and readings, the canonical hours were often performed by substitutes. The Italian pauper priest reading the psalm lost his way, scratched himself, then continued in a different place, from memory. His mind jumbled the words of God and his tongue slurred them and William wanted to scream at him.

The voices and chants were so small that the cathedral was almost silent, a vast darkness starred by a few candles.

Footsteps scraped, echoing. William looked back. A hooded figure in a striped cloak came up the steps of the pulpitum. Head down, the hooded figure finally picked William out amid all the display and ornamention that must seem so mystifying to a not-Christian, crossed the choir and knelt beside him. Every line of Joshua's body betrayed unease, a Jew in a cathedral.

'Don't worry,' William whispered. 'This is sanctuary. No one can touch you here.'

Joshua's hood and sleeves were dusty. He had escaped from his father's house through a window. 'Saving your life may be the death of me,' he whispered in a shaking voice, and William realised how brave he was.

William stood, crossed himself, took a candle and walked behind the tomb of King Sebba. Joshua followed him up the steps set in the wall. When they came to the gallery William took the iron key from his sleeve, opened the library door, and they went inside.

He shut the door behind them, locked it. 'Be silent in here, Joshua.'

Joshua said in a hushed voice, 'I never saw so many books.' He touched a Greek copy of the New Testament bound in black leather and gold, rubies set at each corner. He murmured, 'None of us Jews accept Christ's fantastic story, and we ought to know. But it is beautiful to look at.'

William handed him a second candle. He opened the aumbry and swung aside the lower shelves, went down.

'A mystery within a mystery,' Joshua said.

'Must you always talk?' William preceded him along the catacomb.

'How did you find this place, Brother William?'

'I was shown.'

'Who by?'

William hesitated. 'A vision.' He swung down the creaking ladders.

Both men stood on the pile of chalk boulders. Joshua held up his candle and jumped down, looked round him. He put back his hood and examined the figures daubed on the walls, his face almost touching them. 'There's something—' Then William noticed the drawings for the first time.

'Children's scrawls, without learning or skill,' he scoffed. 'Youngsters must have found their way down here once. Come on. This is the way.'

He scrambled into the tunnel leading downwards. Joshua followed him. William stood by the pile of skins in the second cavern and held up his candleflame high, knowing the impressive effect his revelation of the books would have.

But Joshua cried, '*Ho!*' and jumped forward. He calmed himself, then reached out nervously. He fingered the shape of an enormous tusk drawn in a protective curve along the wall, almost meeting the one that curved from the other side. Both men imagined themselves trapped between those formidable points. The red eyes of the beast staring down at them gleamed and shifted menacingly in the flickering candlelight.

'It's only an elephant!' William said. 'Knights and children returning from the crusade saw them. A tail at each end and horns on their noses.' But still, his voice shook. How did I not see it? he thought. I was too busy looking at the books and I did not see it. I was too busy with the scrolls and with—'I was too busy with Eleanor.' He bit his tongue.

Joshua said, 'Who is Eleanor?'

'No one.'

Joshua asked him again.

'No one,' William said. He dragged Joshua to the scrolls. 'Look. These are what is important.'

Joshua looked. He set his candle in a niche in the wall. There was an opening near the floor, perhaps another tunnel. 'Where does that go?'

William shrugged, he had never thought about it. He watched Joshua kneel by the skins just as he had himself last night, and begin to leaf through them. Some were brittle and Joshua set them aside. Latin translations, too, he set aside at once, together with bound or bifoliate books.

Joshua turned his attention to the scrolls.

He held out his hand for the piece William had torn off and fitted it in its place. Briefly he examined the first column of the document, then let it roll up and replaced it where he had found it.

He opened other scrolls carefully, one by one, then closed them again.

William whispered, 'Are they all Hebrew?'

Joshua lifted out scrolls of copper, silver, gold. He peered carefully at the opening lines of several examples, then put the rest aside. The scrolls sealed with wax or ribbon he also left alone. Other scrolls had rods of cedar or copper pushed through them, so that they could be unrolled and read without touching the precious skin. He reached out, then drew his hand back.

William whispered, 'Tell me.'

Joshua turned suddenly, his face almost desperate. 'It will take months to go through all this. Years.' He settled back to his delicate work. His fingers shook. He blew on them, pressed them together.

With a grating sound he pulled out strangely shaped cylindrical jars made of pottery. Stamped on the sides were three quadrangles inside one another. William whispered, 'What do those mean?'

'They are the highest oath.' Joshua touched them with his fingertips. 'It is the plan of the Temple of the End of Days. An oath sworn on the Temple which will be built at the end of time. Whatever this is, William, it is the truth.'

He pulled the glazed stopper from the end of the jar he held. A scroll wrapped in oatmeal-coloured linen slid into his hand.

On the linen was woven, in blue thread, three quadrangles.

Beneath it was woven a flowering Holy Cross.

'It is the sign of St Matthew,' William whispered, kneeling. 'The

Gospel of St Matthew.' He reached out and laid it reverently across both his hands.

'The seal is unbroken.' Joshua stared with wide eyes, then swallowed. '*Hebraica veritas*, Brother William. *Hebraica veritas*.'

William raised the scroll to his lips and kissed the flowering cross. He prayed, rendering thanks to God that He had chosen William the humble monk, whose walk made men laugh, to be His servant. The scroll was very heavy in his outstretched hands, but William rejoiced in his trembling muscles, for it was well known that the truth was a heavy burden.

Joshua walked round the cavern, from one side of the pile of skins to the other, like the sun round the earth. His cloak fluttered and he wrapped his arms round himself, though it was not cold. 'What drove you to show me these, William?'

'I need you to understand them,' William said. 'I mean I need you to translate so that *I* can understand them, and write them in our blessed Latin as they were meant to be.'

'But suppose these witnesses deny the Christian version of events?'

William said, 'How can that be so? Christianity is the true religion.'

Joshua crouched by the scrolls. 'Suppose they deny the divinity of Jesus the prophet?'

'That's impossible because our Jesus Christ is the Son of God.'

'But, William, just suppose. I know these scrolls will bear out the destiny of the Jews, my people, the Chosen People, I have no doubt of that. But suppose they deny your fundamental faiths of Christianity, the virgin birth and the resurrection?'

'The truth cannot deny what happened.'

'I know, but—'

'Everyone knows the Virgin Mary conceived the baby Jesus through her ear, from the Word of God. The great ideas of the Bible protect themselves, Joshua. The heavenly truths, by their own imperishableness, defeat the mortality of languages with which for a moment they are associated.'

Joshua murmured, 'I wonder if we can understand the truth even if we did hear it. I wonder if God is not so marvellous and so much greater than we can imagine that all the religions of the world, true and false, reveal not so much as His little toenail.' He returned to the David scroll and examined it by the light of his candle in the niche. '"And He shall be called a Nazarene." I have heard of scrolls such as these, you see. The story is well known among my people. In the year 790 an Arab hunter lost his dog near *Khirbet Qumran*, a ruined monastery overlooking the Dead Sea, burnt by the Romans in our failed revolt of 68. These monks, Essenes, were known locally as the Sect of the Caves – and the hunter indeed found his dog fallen into a cave, unhurt. The dog's fall had been broken by hundreds, perhaps thousands, of books. A crowd of Jews came from Jerusalem, including Jews under instruction as Christians, and carried them away. Many of those newly discovered Old Testament scriptures contained prophecies fulfilled in your New Testament, but that are found neither in known Jewish scriptures nor Christian copies. Including, "And He shall be called a Nazarene."'

'What happened to those books?'

'Who knows? They were burnt. If not by the Jews then by Christians.'

'But the truth is irresistible, Joshua. The truth illuminates with a shining light—'

'That's why one side or the other burnt them. These are just pieces of skin, but they are very dangerous, William.'

William laughed. 'You're afraid because you're used to living in fear.' He picked up a skin without looking at it, held it out. 'Read this to me. The truth cannot hurt, Joshua. God surely guided my hand to this scroll just as He guided me here. Read the words He has chosen and learn to live in joy, not in fear.'

Joshua did not move. Then he sighed, held out his hand for the text. Frowning at difficult words, searching for his English, and not revealing the name of God, he translated what he read.

'"And all those willingly offering themselves to His truth shall bring all their knowledge, all their talents, and all their wealth into the Community of God, that they may purify their knowledge in the truth of God's laws, and may use their talents according to His perfect ways and their wealth according to His righteous counsel. And they shall turn neither to the right nor the left. And they shall walk perfectly before Him in faithfulness to His truths that shall be revealed at the dates appointed for their revelation."' He looked up. 'Perhaps you're right, William. It is beautiful.'

'And my skill shall make it more beautiful and more holy. This is not for the glory of Westminster Abbey or St Paul's Cathedral, Joshua. It is simply to the glory of God.' William took his writing pouch and paper from his sleeve. 'Begin.'

To make a book was not easy. It was hard.

There were not enough hours in William's day. Each evening, tired by his day's labours, dozing by the time the hooded, devout figure of Joshua shuffled along the choir, William led the way upstairs. Each time he unlocked the library door, then locked it behind them. With the click of the lock a routine had sprung up between the two young men, the monk and the zealot, a kind of ritual before the night's work. Joshua threw back his hood with a sigh of relief and shared whatever he carried beneath his cloak, sometimes legs of chicken or a couple of apples, and soon William ate even the strange Jewish bread and admitted he found nothing wrong with it. William supplied a half-gallon jug of beer – by universal consent St Paul's beer was the finest in London – or sometimes wine if it was a wine day, and the two sat on the benches eating the meal they missed. 'Does your father never wonder where you are?' William asked.

'He thinks he knows where I am.' Joshua made a foreign gesture. 'He thinks he knows who she is.'

William was amazed. 'And you have persuaded a girl to lie for you?'

'She wished to be with another man. We call it a coincidence of our very different interests to our mutual advantage.'

But Joshua's covering story could not be sustained for more than two hours, three at most, and long before midnight he prepared to hurry out through the deserted cathedral and return to Jewry. For him, too, the work was intensely hard. Often Hebrew words changed their meaning in English and sometimes he held his head. '"Are they then to unsheathe the net?" That can't be right. *Unsheathe* and *empty* are the same word in Hebrew. Are they then to empty the net? That's better. But there's only one letter different between *net* and *sword*, and the interrogative changes the . . . it could mean "Therefore they unsheathe the sword."'

William said, 'Which? Net or sword?'

'Both,' Joshua said decisively. 'Hebrew is often meanings within meaning, statement on first reading, consequence on second. If the swords are unsheathed, *therefore* the nets will be empty. In other words men cannot both fight and fish.'

'So it's a parable about fishing,' William noted.

'It's about the cost of an armed uprising,' said Joshua. 'These men were nationalists.'

After Joshua left, William carried his translated notes into the library and began laboriously to transcribe them. It was hard work.

Hard, precise, difficult, delicate work that took all his skill. William knew he would be blind by the time he was fifty. He worked until his eyes dripped tears and his vision doubled. Exhausted, he concealed his finished papers in the slot below his desk, attended Matins, then staggered with an aching head to his cold carrel and dropped face down in his cot, too tired even to pull his blanket over him, and slept like a dead man.

The bell for Prime clanged, and William's day began again. He hurried through the bustling cathedral, past workmen by a pillar lifting the stone statue of Algar on to a plinth, most munificent of the long line of wealthy St Paul's prebendaries who had swelled the cathedral's holdings of land. William had forged his curly *A* and tailed-off *r* often on spurious documents, and each morning the prebendary's proud marble gaze fixed accusingly on the top of his head, seeming to follow him as he walked beneath, and William ran upstairs.

Here in the library was his home. Here among these books was everything worth having.

William obtained his vellum from the tanners of Cheapside, using only the finest calfskin from stillborn calves. In tubs amid the stinking dusty smoke of Lime Street, where from time immemorial the lime-burners had dismantled and burnt the massive headless pillars and piers of the Roman forum for lime, the hides were immersed in lime baths and scoured to remove the hair. Back in Cheapside craftsmen stretched the precious skins on frames and scraped them with *lunae*, knives curved like the crescent moon. The leaves of smooth vellum were cut to size and chalked for softness.

Each skin made two large pages, four sides of text.

William's stylus pricked the margins, and he ruled the lines between them using his knife with the swiftness and sureness of long experience.

This was his life.

Like most craftsmen he worked fast, completing each broad, intricate line of minuscule and majuscule writing in about a minute. His pen was the long white tail-feather of a swan, his inkhorn the horn of a cow pushed into the hole in the desk. He painted with a brush of marten fur. For the holiest blues he used lapis lazuli from India, fiercely costly, and the minor religious figures and animals made do with indigo or woad. For rubrics he used red lead or insect red, kermes, crushed from rare pregnant insects. For yellow he mixed orpiment, yellow arsenic. William knew he was doing the work of angels.

He was sure of it. God was guiding him.

Late one night, or early one morning, William stared at a page that his toil and skill had completed. Here was the face of a man, there an eagle. He picked out a calf, and here was a lion. They were at one with the ornamentation and illumination, the gold and lapis lazuli, as naturally as though produced without skill. They seemed like daubs rather than careful compositions. But William blinked and leant close, seeing into the secrets of the artistry, the details so delicate and subtle that he had magnified his sight with a crystal to draw them, and he truly could not believe he had achieved such work himself.

But he had. And he would do it again tomorrow night.

The time passed as though it flew, the days of his life flying away like leaves blown by the wind.

Eleanor watched him.

He was a strange one. That was what she liked about him. He wasn't strong, simple and stupid like Peter of Cheap. No, William was worthy of her love. She couldn't put it more clearly than that. He was worthwhile. She moved round the library taking out books when they were requested, putting them away, but her eyes and all her concentration were fixed on the figure of William working so earnestly at his desk.

He ignored her. Eleanor knew that trick. He ignored her to make her think about him.

As she returned someone else's book she leant close. 'I know what you're doing, William.'

He started, then looked at her innocently. 'What's that?'

'You're not looking at me so that I have to look at you. You're learning the ropes, William.'

'The ropes?' The afternoon was darkening with cloud, rain melting the snow.

'Turning into a skilful lover. Making me want you more. I can't stop thinking about you.'

William bowed his head over his work.

When it was dark and everyone had left he commenced his real labour by the light of the lantern. He reached into the paper-slot and pulled out his notes from the night before. Carefully he slid out the illuminated page ready for another wash of colour on certain words, for a three-dimensional effect. From the fireplace came a creaking sound, and a shadow moved. William returned the papers quickly to the slot. The shelves of the aumbry slid back into place with a soft thud.

It was Eleanor. She sat quietly beside him on the bench, but the other way round, leaning back, her elbows on his desk, looking into his face. Then she smiled.

'You have another way in from the outside, don't you,' he said.

'You always want to know everything about everything,' she said happily. 'Even everything about me.' She took his hand and slipped it in her gown. 'That tells you all you need to know, doesn't it?'

Yes, it did. Her nipple felt stiff and juicy and her breast quivered with life as she breathed. William swallowed. Her feminine shape filled his mind, obscuring his thoughts about his work like drifting fog. The sight of her excited him irresistibly and everything jumped up without his being able to control it much. It was simply disgusting and utterly desirable. Eleanor became strangely passive, enfolding him and holding him motionless.

'I do love you, William. Stay with me. Stay with me.'

He shouted her name and closed his eyes.

She cuddled him, murmuring. 'This is the only time you're with me. The only time you don't have books in your eyes.' She yawned and scratched herself, open to him, trusting him as she always did after they had made love. 'My grandmother doesn't approve of you.'

'Do you obey her?'

'No. Her not liking you makes this even better.'

'It is wrong to be a rebel.'

'Is it true a monk does not own even his own body?'

'A monk's body belongs to his abbey. My body is part of the body of the Church.'

'Oh, I'm having the whole Church then.' She chuckled but he did not. He scolded her for irreverence but she tried to get him to talk to her properly, to reveal himself.

'Don't you ever stop talking?' he murmured sleepily.

'My grandmother wants me to marry Peter of Cheap.'

He opened one eye.

'Do you think I should marry a fishmonger, William?'

'Do you love him?'

'No.'

'Is his father wealthy?'

'Yes. I love you, William. I love your nose and your funny ways.
I love the way you smile with the corner of your mouth.'

'What funny ways?'

'Say you love me.'

'Why?'

'I love you to talk about love.'

'You seducing me is not the same as me loving you.'

'You're so clever with cold words. Shall I stroke you and see
the truth?'

'No. *No.*'

'There you are,' she said. 'Why don't you ask me for books
any more?'

'I'm busy with other work.'

She seized him and kissed him hard. 'Don't ignore me again,' she
said, and closed her gown. In a little while she patted his head and
left, and William tried to settle to his work. But instead of the lion
and the eagle he was working on, all he saw was Eleanor.

'I'm in love with her!' he whispered, then fell to his knees, shaking
his head, praying. No, no, I'm in love with God.

After a while he went down to the choir. He led Joshua upstairs,
locked the library door behind them, and they ate chicken legs
with wine.

Joshua stared at the lion and the eagle in the open book on the
desk, the washes of lapis lazuli and gold. He reached out as if to
touch it, then withdrew his hand. 'William, that's the most beautiful
work I've ever seen.'

'Do you see God in it?'

Joshua said, 'Yes, I do. I see love.'

Joshua sat on a rock in the cavern. He had placed it near the niche for
the candle, between the points of the elephant's tusks, where the light
was best. The curved chalk walls glowed around him. He unrolled
the scroll from his right hand, reading the text, rolling it up in his
left hand.

William watched him, the piece of charcoal in his fingers hovering
over the blank paper on his knee. Finally he said, 'Well?'

'This is very strange,' Joshua murmured. 'The Qumran Jews who
wrote this, Essenes, were excluded from the Jerusalem Temple. To
them the whole plan of the Temple, its rituals, sacrifices, moneychangers, even its priesthood, was wrong.' He scratched his head,

then caught the scroll quickly as it rolled up. 'You see, William, these people at Qumran were the founders of Christianity.'

'But they were Jews.'

'The more I see, the less I understand,' Joshua confessed. 'I thought it would be simple. It probably is, if I could just see a little more. Here—' He pointed at the scroll. 'Here is someone called the Teacher of Righteousness.'

William scribbled busily. 'Undoubtedly Jesus Christ.'

'He is opposed by the Man of a Lie, the scoffer—'

William frowned. 'Someone who did not believe? Doubting Thomas? Someone who wanted facts, proof?'

'And here is the Wicked Priest.'

'Obviously Caiaphas! The High Priest Caiaphas, the head of the Jewish religious establishment who sentenced Jesus to death, and had the sentence confirmed by the Roman governor, Pilate.'

Joshua murmured, 'I think this scroll is older than that. "The Wicked Priest plotted against the Teacher of Righteousness and sought to kill him." Does this foresee that Judas Iscariot, Jesus's betrayer, was a priest?'

'Judas was one of the twelve apostles, a preacher, a priest.'

'"But as for him, God will pay him his reward by delivering him into the hand of the ruthless one of the nations." Perhaps these were titles held by different people, passed on.'

'You're right, it's a prediction,' William said. 'Like the other one. How soldiers cannot also be fishermen.'

'That may have been a reference to Peter the Fisherman. The first Pope. The Shoes of the Fisherman . . .'

'This is impossible!' William cried. 'Everything contradicts itself!'

Joshua lifted the scroll. 'This is a prediction of things that were not true, *but that would become true*. Suppose Jesus was at Qumran? He was of the royal line of David through both his mother Mary and his earthly stepfather Joseph, as had been predicted.'

'Royal? But Joseph was only a humble carpenter.'

'No. The Essenes performed menial crafts in the villages, purified by humble tasks, which is not the same thing. Jesus spoke Aramaic and *craftsman* is the same word as *scholar*.'

William whispered, 'How can the future be known to anyone except God?'

'Do you believe in miracles, William?'

'Everyone believes in miracles. Without them there is no Star of Bethlehem, no Virgin Birth, no Walking on the Water, no Resurrection, no Christianity.'

Joshua murmured, 'Then this prediction is also a miracle, because it came true.'

William breathed quickly. He raised his charcoal-stained hand almost in blessing. 'Then one day I shall baptise you, Joshua. You'll see. You'll see.'

'I'm afraid,' Joshua said. He closed the scroll. 'I'm afraid of what I'm finding.' He stood, returned the skin to its place. 'I don't want to do any more tonight.' He gripped William's shoulder. 'Good night, William.'

They went back to the library. William stood on the gallery watching Joshua come out far below and hurry away along the choir. Back at his desk he sat without moving, staring at his completed book. The cover was hard red leather, blind tooled, decorated with as much gold leaf as he could afford. He had already slipped other, smaller volumes into various quiet niches amid the mass of books on the shelves, and added their titles anonymously to the catalogue he was elaborating. *The Prayer of Thanksgiving. The Genesis Apocryphon. The Manual of Discipline.* Some were very short, only a few pages. Others were longer. There would be more.

He placed his catalogue on the book with the red cover. He ran his finger down the list and in meticulously formed script added the title, *The Gospel Witness According to St Simon the Zealot.*

He placed the book beneath a pile of dusty papers, dull records of transactions, in one of the aumbries where it would probably not be found for years. After all, what copyist would think to request a gospel that was not known to exist?

William smiled as he closed the door. He walked slowly downstairs, prayed, and returned to his carrel and his bed where he slept the sleep of the just.

It was the quietest hour of the night. The library was motionless, black except for the row of round windows sweeping fingers of moonlight across the long room. A piece of paper stirred on one of the desks. Its corner lifted in the draught, and it fluttered to the floor.

The doors of the aumbry clicked, opened from the inside. The shelves swung out, thudded softly back into place, then silence fell again.

A cowled figure grew out of the darkness beside the fireplace, stepped forward. It slid its feet round the floorboards that creaked, it knew them all. A moonlit finger rippled over its body bent forward, gleamed beneath the hood.

She pulled it back. The moon shone in her long white hair.

Elfrida looked round her carefully.

She came forward down the library, the moonlight flowing over her from each window, sending her shadow flying over the jumbled bookshelves, then her silhouette moved through the darkness between the desks.

The monk's desk was at the end.

He was a mild meek man of no consequence. A born inheritor of the earth, and her lip curled in contempt. What made him dangerous was Eleanor's love for him. The girl was mad for him, talked of him in her sleep, clasped him in her dreams.

Elfrida knew about girls. They got their way.

She had.

Elfrida knew about men too. Even a monk was a man. No man would resist Eleanor.

Girls were crazy in love. If she really loved him she'd give him everything she had, her heart, her dreams, her self, just to be with him.

Suppose she told him about the cavern?

Elfrida imagined Brother William of Westminster Abbey loose in the cavern. It was the worst nightmare she could imagine.

Idly she picked up one of the charters from his desk.

Innocently and faithfully, Brother William had built his life on deceit. Everything he ever did was a forgery, a lie, a cheat. He had trusted his superiors and followed orders. He had built his house on sand.

She thought, suppose he finds out the truth?

Elfrida knew a believer when she saw one. She wondered, will Brother William believe in knowledge for the sake of knowing, fact for the sake of fact? Will he believe everything has answers?

Will he believe, not in what he is told, but in what he can find out?

She realised sadly, no wonder Eleanor loves him. Such men, fired by the love of God and a good woman, are the very best. Elfrida hardened her heart. But dangerous, dangerous. Let such a man believe that truth is real, there will be no stopping him. He is a bottomless pit who will end God knows where.

She dropped the charter back on his desk but it fell to the floor. She bent to pick it up, saw the sheaf in the paper-slot.

Elfrida helped herself to a handful of papers.

Her expression froze.

She backed into the moonlight, held up the notes so that she could see. In rough charcoal the monk had scrawled a title, *Florilegium*.

Elfrida cursed the moon for not being brighter, squinted her old shortsighted eyes with all her concentration. Her sight made out a scribbled line.

But as for the Wicked Priest – then there were crossings-out – *who will plot to kill the Teacher of Righteousness, God will pay him his reward by delivering him into the hand of the Ruthless One of the nations.*

Elfrida's hands trembled holding the monk's writings. He had found the *Florilegium*.

She knew where he had been.

She knew what Eleanor and William had done.

Elfrida crumpled the paper and shoved it in her sleeve, then she swayed dizzily, her heart murmuring. She clutched the desk for support and jerked down, swept out everything from the slot across the floor, books, papers, notes. The inkhorn dropped, splashed ink.

There was a catalogue.

Her eye fixed on the last entry, the ink so fresh it was still black and glossy.

The Gospel Witness According to St Simon the Zealot.

Elfrida sat without moving on the bench. The moonlight faded and the day grew.

She went down by her usual way and stood in the grey light of dawn. It looked like rain again. She crossed the atrium and walked towards Carter Street and the Creed where the deanery stood. She had known this place all her life and entered easily, taking a back way through the kitchen, then skirted the guards and hangers-on and went silently upstairs. She heard voices and a door opened. A man came out, dressed in black furs, with glittering rings on his fingers.

William stood in the darkness, waving.

Eleanor struggled up from her dream. Something struck her again, though she was still numb from sleep. She was being beaten round her head. She struggled against the hands slapping at her.

'You did it!' her grandmother screamed at her. Eleanor rolled on to the floor, crawled to escape the old woman's flying fists. Elfrida caught her, boxed her ears, clawed Eleanor's hair. 'You did it! *You thought only of yourself!*'

Eleanor screamed back at her, a formless animal scream.

Elfrida paused in mid-slap, then staggered back. The strength went out of her legs and she sat weakly. She said, 'I know everything.'

Eleanor wiped her lip. She looked at her blood smeared on the back of her hand, then stared fiercely at her grandmother. 'I love him. I did it because I love him.'

'That doesn't matter, Eleanor.'

'I'll do it again.'

'Yes.' Elfrida looked up wearily. 'I knew that you would say that.'

'You took Algar down there!' Eleanor said defiantly. 'That's how it was all incorporated into the plans, wasn't it? You showed him.'

Elfrida sighed. 'Algar was a user of men and women, a religious man, a politician. He understood what is possible and what is not, Eleanor. He was a man of the world, not an ignorant monk.'

'William is not an ignorant monk. He's brilliant. You should see—'

'I know what I've seen,' Elfrida said. 'I didn't want to do this. He's been making copies of everything.'

Eleanor's face changed. She stared, wide-eyed, then stumbled to her feet. 'Who did you tell?'

'Stay here.' Elfrida reached out calmly. 'Stay here with me. Don't let them see you. Don't get involved, I beg you.'

Eleanor shouted, 'You betrayed him!'

She ducked under the grasping hand, ran into the street. She was so upset that she ran the wrong way, stopped. She clapped her hands to her cheeks, her mind in a confusion, trying to think clearly, then ran back the other way. It was early and William might still be in his bed.

Elfrida's hand grabbed her from the doorway. 'There's nothing you can do.'

Eleanor shook free. She ran uphill towards the cathedral. It started raining and a builder pushed a barrow along a plank laid in the mud. Her clothes were heavy with wet and mud. She thumped along the planks between piles of melting snow, ditches, foundations being dug, pushed past workmen who grinned at her and called out. The mossy thatch of the chapter house dripped rainwater into her soaked hair. She ran round the back, pushed into William's cold little room.

Too late. Gone.

She laid her hand in his cot. No, perhaps not quite cold.

She ran to the cathedral kitchen house. The stink billowed round her. A slut with a mole on her nose, Mary, peered through the steam and grinned amiably. 'My sweet William? Been and gone, him.'

Eleanor lifted her garb to her knees, ran up the cathedral steps. The nave was a mess of barrows, sand, mortar, masons working on statues, reliefs, gargoyles with snarling faces, horns, talons. She glimpsed Syrus the collator hurrying out, hid behind a pillar, glimpsed his terrified wobbling face like a frightened child running from an angry father. She ran between the ladders of the lantern tower, up the steps of the pulpitum into the choir. Half a dozen monks knelt in prayer. She jerked each one round by his shoulders, stared into his face.

All were different, all strangers.

She ran upstairs, heard William's footsteps climbing above her. She recognised the fast scuff of his sandals, glimpsed the rough-sewn hem of his monk's habit. She hissed upwards, 'William!'

From the top a man's voice called loudly, 'Brother William. You have been busy, I see.'

William made no attempt to run down.

Dean de Langdon waited on the gallery. She heard William reply respectfully. Eleanor hissed but could not stop him going forward from the staircase. The dean went into the library, beckoned William to follow. Eleanor scampered on her toes, reached out to pull him back, but William followed the dean obediently through the library doorway.

She heard Dean de Langdon's voice. 'These papers are your work, monk.'

Eleanor clasped her hands together. Say no!

William murmured, 'Yes, lord.'

He almost sounded relieved. Almost proud.

'Fine work.'

'Yes, lord!'

'Proud of yourself, no doubt.'

Two men with heavy swords pushed Eleanor out, guarded the library door. They ignored her, talking broad peasant French. She could not see past them into the library, only heads and shadows. She went to the staircase but helmets bobbed below her, armed men coming up. The leader caught his sword on a step, showered sparks. Eleanor returned to the library, her cowl pulled over her face, her arms folded inside her garb to make herself bulky. She shuffled forward with an imperious nod at the guards. 'I am the collator. My services are required.'

The guard on her right stopped talking then jerked his head, bored. Probably they only spoke enough English to curse for bread, wine, girls. Eleanor pushed past them.

The library was full of men. Balchus the librarian scurried between them, his face white as a fish's belly with fear. Books and papers were being shifted everywhere, roughly piled on the desks, more being heaved from the shelves. Eleanor knew this mess would take weeks to clear up.

Dean de Langdon glanced up from the slim volume he examined in his gloved hands, then ignored her as a person of no consequence.

Eleanor turned to William's desk. Someone knocked into her, cursed her for an inferior. William sat with his elbows resting on the sloped desktop, turning his swan quill over and over in his hands. He looked concerned but not afraid. Mostly he looked tired. A small book covered with his own minuscule handwriting lay between his elbows, opened like an accusation, as if the exposed text confirmed his guilt. Eleanor slipped towards him, twisted and turned between the sweating stinking priests who pushed past her. She could smell their fear, they were all afraid of the devil in here, but also she sensed their elation at finding the devil's works, their relief at uncovering a plot of the Evil One.

William did not notice her. Eleanor had only a moment. She leant forward across his desk as though reaching for a book, whispered to his ear. 'Oh, William, you fool. What have you done?'

William looked into Eleanor's eyes. For a moment they were so close she could have counted his eyelashes. He looked at her as though marvelling at her. He said, 'I fell in love.'

Someone knocked her aside, spat at William, one of the copyists afraid of being tainted by association with him. They had shared the same room for months and all would be under suspicion. 'We all hated him.'

'Always knew there was something wrong with him,' someone chorused, and the others nodded in agreement.

'Get those idiots out of here,' de Langdon said.

A priest called out, 'More devil's lies, my lord.' He held up something between red covers, held his nose as though the object were made of dung. De Langdon grunted, took the book, turned to William and let it thud unopened on to the desktop.

'More of your blasphemy, Brother William.'

Eleanor knew William must deny any knowledge of it, instantly. She pressed her hands together in prayer. Deny it!

William looked up at de Langdon. He whispered serenely, 'How can it be blasphemy if it is true?'

She knew he was repeating her own words. Eleanor had changed him. He did not realise, or care, that casting such a provocation in the face of the Dean of St Paul's, resplendent in a wealth of furs and glittering rings of favour and rank, a gold chain of office gleaming at his neck, was defiant and disrespectful and another matter entirely. She tried to catch his eye but William thought only of the truth.

De Langdon touched the book. 'You claim these tattle-tales are true?'

William replied calmly, 'I am satisfied that the writer saw with his own eyes what he wrote down. He wrote of the events of each day before retiring for the night. The last entry is for the day of the Crucifixion. Then it simply stops, as though the future ended.'

De Langdon said heavily, 'No, monk. You yourself wrote this tale purporting to be the Gospel of St Simon.'

'I transcribed it.'

'Where from?'

Eleanor felt the blood drain from her face. She stared.

But William remained silent.

De Langdon struck him across the mouth. William stared at him in amazement. He touched his hands to his lips. De Langdon assured him, 'I did not strike you, Brother William, but at the devil within you.'

More slim volumes, some of only a page or two, were pulled by priests from the shelves and thrown down. De Langdon flicked through the pages. 'What's this? Jesus changed the water into wine and *was himself wed* at Cana? Do you say that our Jesus Christ took an earthly wife?'

William murmured, 'That's what it says, lord.'

'That our Jesus Christ, our Lord, married a *Jew*? Satan is in you!'

'God is in me,' William whispered. 'I did it for the glory of God.'

De Langdon grunted, tossed the book down, shrugged. 'Fortunately for me you are not of St Paul's. Any reflection on you will fall badly on the monks of Westminster Abbey, not here.' He smiled, the matter resolved to his satisfaction, then gave a clap to summon his men-at-arms. 'Take him and chain the devil within him until it speaks.'

That evening the Jew Joshua, muffled by a cloak, wore long boots to walk along the foul mire of Cheapside. He pushed through the crowds at the Little Gate into the cathedral precinct. A priest preached hellfire and brimstone under the roofed pulpit of Paul's Cross, but everyone else was getting wet. Serfs and scum at the back of the crowd gossiped excitedly and Joshua pushed behind them, sliding his shoulders quietly along the wall of the charnel house rather than draw attention to himself. Their heat and voices rose around him. A monk had been arrested for treason. No, it was blasphemy. He paused, listening. Someone said it was the crime of false accounting. A fat woman shouted that the monk had been seen with the Devil sitting on his shoulder, whispering what should be written in the Bible of the antiChrist. A girl with a cleft palate cried out in fear, thinking she saw Satan. Joshua walked on quietly. These people were mad. Someone would point at him, the Jew slinking in the shadows of the charnel, and imagine him into Satan. These people even treated themselves in disgusting ways, punishment was their justice. Joshua had seen wives ducked in cesspits for unfaithfulness or ugliness, with his own eyes he had seen Englishmen hanged and cut and burnt alive by Englishmen.

What they did to Jews was worse.

With the crowd in this mood, Joshua knew, it was better to be part of them, to rant and roar as loudly as they. And yet he could not do it. They were shouting rubbish. The Devil and the monk had defiled the Holy Bible with blasphemies and incantations for dark rites. The monk had shown children the Devil's ways. The Devil had taken his body and raped virgins on the altar.

The stories he heard were so ridiculous that Joshua nearly laughed aloud, but it might have been the death of him. Their Christian Devil was always on the prowl, feeding off those he would devour. These people were used to believing what they were told. Only a few shouted, but most people listened and took their whispers home.

Joshua pulled free of the crowd and came round the corner on to the atrium. Rain sheeted down the two huge Norman towers flanking St Paul's entrance. He hooded his face well and climbed the steps. A service had ended and priests chattered about Brother William in the huge draughty porch.

Joshua stopped. Someone else talked of the Westminster monk. Joshua did the bravest thing he had ever done. He asked them gruffly, 'Brother William? Where's that one?'

A pink-faced priest said, 'Do you know him?'

'No, not me!'

The priest pointed at the tower above them. 'He's in that place. They're getting the Devil out of him.'

The priest went with his friends to supper. Joshua stood with the rain pattering on his cloak, dripping from his hood. Then he turned and ran away.

★

'They won't let me see him. They won't say he's there. They won't talk to me.'

Elfrida said, 'I spoke again to Peter of Cheap and I've talked to his father.'

'I don't want to think about marriage!' Eleanor rubbed her eyes, adjusting from the brilliant day in the lane outside to the dimness inside the hovel. Her grandmother lay in her cot looking very old, her bony hands trembling at her neck, licking her lips nervously.

'Eleanor, forget about the monk,' she urged. 'Think of yourself. Don't ask the cathedral authorities about him again.'

Eleanor demanded, 'Why?'

'Don't get involved.' The old woman tried to moisten her lips with her dry tongue.

'*Why?*'

'Yes,' the old woman whined. 'It was me. I told them.'

There was a knife on the table. Eleanor picked it up.

Elfrida lay blinking up at her, her old eyes running with tears. 'Go on. I deserve it.'

Eleanor stood with the knife in her hand. Her hand moved. Elfrida blinked. Eleanor's hand tightened. Then she sighed, dropped the knife at the foot of the cot. 'No, it's worse than that.'

Elfrida gasped, 'I thought you were really going to!'

'You don't know what you've done.' Eleanor opened her clothes. She knelt beside the cot. 'Feel me.'

The two women sat in the dark, only a lamp burning. The cunning light had come back into Elfrida's eyes.

'There's only one thing to do.'

Eleanor whispered, 'I know what to do.'

'You'll have to persuade Peter it's his.'

Eleanor whispered, 'I have never slept with Peter.'

'You'll have to now. It's all for the best.'

'I know what I have to do,' Eleanor whispered.

It was a hot summer day. Doves fluttered round the towers and pinnacles of the cathedral from the huge white dovecotes of the bishop's palace and the deanery garden. Eleanor walked up the cathedral steps carrying a rush basket over her arm, covered with a cloth to keep away flies and thieving fingers. She ignored the busy nave full of builders and turned to her right. She climbed into the chamber beneath the south-west tower and the cold stone closed around her like winter.

The jailer palmed her money, examined her basket and helped himself to a chicken breast, tore a mouthful and walked round her, genially helping himself to squeezes in front and behind. When Eleanor did not resist he lost interest and she followed his broad buttocks heaving ahead of her up the stone steps, dangerous slopes of matted straw. From time to time as they climbed she saw doors cut deep in the wall no higher than her chest, or slit windows through which blew clean warm air from outside, revealing the stench and coldness of the place. The jailer came to a stone platform. He kicked a door to show how strong it was.

She said, 'How long is he here?'

'Monks and priests commit the worst crimes. It's not like murder or rape, see. They've played with men's souls.'

The breath puffing from his flabby stubbled face made Eleanor's stomach churn. She forced herself to smile. 'When will he be released?' she smiled.

The jailer leaned close. 'Christmas Day in Hell, I'd say.' He winked, then took an iron key and twisted it in the lock.

She blurted, 'What would it take to buy that key?'

He pushed the door open with his foot, whispered in her ear as she went inside. 'More than you could pay.'

The room was tiny, not long enough to lie down in, with hardly room to stand. Eleanor squeezed herself into the corner, making room for the door to swing closed. Then she dropped to her knees. William lay curled on straw, his head pressing the outer wall, his feet pushed against the inner wall. He did not move.

'William.'

He jerked, covered his head.

She stroked his shoulder. 'It's me. I've brought you wine. Food.'

He saw her and grinned. His mouth was full of scabs where his teeth had been pulled, but he grinned with his gums. 'Look at you,' he said.

Eleanor wept. She hugged him. 'Chicken – and warm clothes—' She touched his monk's garb and the wool ripped softly under her fingers. She stared. 'Oh, William.'

'It's the Devil. They can't find him.'

She covered William's body with the blanket she had brought. She kissed his face and cried. He grinned, patting her shoulder. 'Don't cry. Don't cry, Eleanor.' He touched her tears with his smooth fingertips. 'Don't cry, you're hurting me.'

She touched his cheeks, spoke earnestly. 'William, listen to me. I tried all the time to get in here. I may not have another chance. You must confess that you are mad so they can get the Devil out of you.'

'The Devil is not in me.'

She whispered, 'Give them what they want. Repent.'

He grinned. 'And make everything a lie.'

'To save your life.'

'This wonderful life.' He brushed the wall with his fingertip, pulled a bloody mark down the stone. 'You don't understand. One day they'll see the truth. I found the truth and I wrote it. You showed me, Eleanor. I repent nothing.'

Eleanor trembled. She took a deep breath. 'William, will you tell them about . . .' She could not say the word. 'About what lies beneath our feet?'

'No. Would they believe it?' He held his finger to his lips. '*Sacerdos in aeternum*. You're right, I have been mad. I won't betray you again.'

'You haven't betrayed me.'

'I don't read Hebrew, Eleanor.'

She stared at him. 'God help us, William, what more have you done?' She clapped her hands to her mouth. 'You let a *Jew* look—'

'A Jew I trust.'

The jailer kicked the door. He made disgusting noises to simulate lovemaking.

William touched her hair tenderly. 'I don't think they'll keep me in here much longer.'

She opened her gown, took his hand and pressed it against her. He touched the swollen curve of her belly wonderingly.

'That's me!'

'I'll always dream I am your wife,' she whispered.

Every day Eleanor, cowled, her girdle untied and garb hanging loose to hide her advanced pregnancy from the new collator, climbed from the choir to the library. The steep steps were by now very arduous and she arrived at the top breathless, which she also had to hide. When she could no longer manage the work at the cathedral, the cathedral would not feed her. Her clothes, supplied by the cathedral, would be taken back. She would not be allowed inside the cathedral or any of the cathedral buildings, her condition making her unclean among men.

None of them cared about someone like her. With luck, no one would ever notice the change in her.

The new collator – Syrus was interrogated, broken, dismissed – was a red-faced jobsman, Alchemidus, who promised much but knew little of the library's workings and cared less. After breakfast beer, the flagon brought up with him hidden between his feet at the lectern, he slept standing up like a horse, and after more beer early in the afternoon he pissed in the empty flagon and slept lying down. This arrangement suited them both very well and gradually, with his help or usually without it, Eleanor returned the books to some sort of order and even began filling out the catalogue William had started. She opened a new page for the charters, then suddenly turned away, put down the quill and did not continue. In truth she had lost heart. The library was a dull and dreary place. It was late afternoon, she had been long hours standing and the baby kicked, bruising her inside. She leant wearily against a shelf and a slim book, dislodged by her elbow, slipped to the floor. She recognised it at once by the style of gold leaf worked on the cover.

She spread her legs and bent at the knee, grunted, snatched it up.

In gold she read, *The Gospel Witness of St Matthew*.

Eleanor's eyes filled with tears. She leafed through the pages. William's minuscule, painstaking work. They had not found it all. Flowering crosses in kermes red. Who knew how many more of his volumes remained hidden on the shelves?

A young man's voice whispered, 'Eleanor.'

Startled, she nevertheless remembered to fold the book into her sleeve as she turned. She stared into a pair of anxious brown eyes staring into her own. More than anxious. They flicked watchfully from side to side, terrified, but determined. That was all she could see of him under the hood.

'How did you know my name?'

'Eleanor. The vision.'

She softened. 'Is that how he spoke of me?'

The stranger glanced round the library. Alchemidus sat by a window, snoring dully. They turned their backs to him, spoke softly. 'I don't know what to do, Eleanor. Did William tell you—'

'Not your name.'

'I am Joshua, son of Abraham.'

'Why did you come back, Joshua?'

'Because I'm ashamed of myself.'

She searched his eyes. 'How did you get up here?'

'I walked through the cathedral. William and I discovered that a Jew is not struck by lightning in a cathedral after all.' He added impatiently, with a flash of humour, 'How else would I get up here?'

William had trusted him. Should she? 'You're brave,' she said.

'Foolish,' he said. 'Has William told anyone but you about me?'

Of course, Joshua had been living in constant terror of arrest. She shook her head. 'No.' Her voice rose. 'He should have confessed he was led into it by you Jews, tricked, exploited. A Jewish plot. I repent, I recant. Anything to live.' She added quietly, 'He's a fool dying for an illusion.'

'I don't know that what you showed him is an illusion.'

She showed the book in her sleeve. 'This. These marks on paper.' She peered under his hood. 'That you don't believe in.'

'I have found things which are very difficult to reconcile with my faith.'

'Suppose your faith and the truth are different.'

'That is what I do not believe.'

She reached up, pushed back his hood a little to see his face. 'If only there was something real, if only it was not just religion. Is there something down there – some *fact* – which will change William's mind?'

'*Hebraica veritas*. Facts don't lie. Truth doesn't take sides.' He sighed, ran his hands back through his curly brown hair. 'Perhaps. Perhaps I could find something—'

She glanced round. Alchemidus muttered, rested his fat red face on his other hand, began his snores again.

Joshua said, 'You see, I'm sure it's simple – if I could just see a little more – I might understand—'

'Then you do believe.'

He hissed, 'I don't know!'

Eleanor took Joshua's hand and led him behind the fireplace. She crouched with a grunt of discomfort, pulled open the doors of the aumbry.

She whispered earnestly, 'I shall be here when you return. God go with you, Joshua.'

It was not so easy.

The first thing, the very first thing Joshua saw in Eleanor's eyes was that she was a woman in love. That was all she was. She wanted to save the man she loved, she didn't want to hear anything else, not common sense, not caution, and Joshua had seen she wouldn't take no for an answer. She might even give him away if he didn't do what she needed.

Joshua had run away once. He wouldn't run away again.

Alone he descended the ladder into the catacomb, covered his mouth and nose against the foul stench, and made his way forward by smoky tallow candlelight, down ladder after ladder leading into the darkness below him, until he came to the bottom.

He held up the candle and looked round him. How had William really not noticed these paintings, so startling, so obvious?

Joshua half crawled, half slid down the tunnel into the cave of the scrolls. As he stood up he realised for the first time that the way in came literally through the mouth of the elephant, and chuckled.

He put the candle in its niche, settled himself comfortably between the tusks of the beast, and worked.

He yawned, examining skin after skin. *If I could just see a little more* . . . the trouble was, the more he saw the less he understood. As he learned more deeply, the things he was sure of began to slip between his fingers. Most things that were certain became uncertain. Even the Christian Gospels disagreed and had to be interpreted. But the Talmud taught that whenever a scriptural passage was repeated, it was only because of some new point contained therein.

Joshua shivered as he read. Above was a warm autumnal day, the winds of October whirling golden leaves along the streets of London, but down here the draught was cool, and he pulled his cloak round him for warmth.

What did all these skins mean? To a Christian, Adam and Eve's story was about how knowledge creates sin. To a Jew it was a story about choice. Which belief was right?

Churches and monasteries were full of books, they copied books, preserved books, lived by books. But when people began thinking for themselves they risked coming under the ban of heresy, as William had. When the Church feared heresy, sooner or later Jews, the ultimate heretics, paid the price. In some other countries Hebrew books were a dangerous possession, and rabbinical writings were burnt by the cartload.

Joshua blinked tiredly at the skins in his lap. What was the truth?

His head snapped back and he yawned, realising he had dozed. The candle was suddenly lower, less than half the length of his finger. He thought, suppose Jesus Christ is not the Teacher of Righteousness?

William instinctively assumed He was. But William was a Christian. That was not the only point of view.

His disciples were the only Jews who believed Jesus was the Messiah. But how deeply had even the Twelve Apostles believed? Peter denied Him three times. None of the others appeared in His defence before the Sanhedrin court. Only John stood near Him at His crucifixion.

Joshua rubbed his face. He was tired.

The candle flickered. He pushed the manuscripts away and stood up, took the candle from the niche. The flame stood upright as he moved. He stopped, and the flame was pulled sideways.

He knelt, put his face into the draught blowing from the opening near the floor he had noticed once before. He put his head inside, holding the candle in front of him.

It led somewhere.

He crawled after the candleflame. The tunnel widened and he stood up in a third chamber. The walls were a chaos of stick figures.

Thousands of stick humans. They looked so simple at first glance. Then he glimpsed patterns that his eye could not quite pull out from all the rocks and people, and whole areas of slightly different detail. The people were different races, tribes perhaps, or generations of the same tribe. They walked in different landscapes, some with yellow feet from sand, others green with grass, some blue. Was that woad? Did the blue mean a river, or the sea? What river? What sea? Most did not carry spears but some did, especially in particular areas of the wall. Why?

He peered closer, then groaned in frustration. He was looking at something but he did not know how to see it.

Some of the figures were slightly smaller. The way they held their arms meant something. They were trying to tell him something. Him, a Jew. He could not imagine what.

These weren't childish daubs. They were precise.

Joshua looked round him in awe. The candle flickered in front of another opening.

He ducked inside, pushed forward into the dark. He coughed in the tallow-smoke and the candle dripped warm fat on his hand, burning down. Still the tunnel went on, its ribbed sides receding in front of him. The candle softened, melting itself, and his hand turned hot and greasy. The tunnel widened.

He crawled forward. Here was another cavern, much larger.

At its centre stood a broad stone slab and on the slab stood a miniature house of gold, encrusted with jewels.

A reliquary.

Joshua stood up. He banged his head on the tunnel roof. Burning tallow splashed over his hand. The candle was a mere stump.

No time. He ducked back into the tunnel, hurrying now, curling his forefinger inside his bent thumb to keep the flame alive in the pool of tallow. He ran through the caverns shielding the flame with his other hand. Halfway up the ladders the last flicker of flame went out, but he knew the way and was not afraid of the dark.

He climbed to the catacomb and from there to the library.

His fingers touched the inside of the aumbry door. He wondered what awaited him on the other side. Then he saw a tiny eyehole. The library was empty, closed. He could see Eleanor's foot.

He opened the door and slipped out quietly. She was sitting on a bench, leaning back, her legs apart.

She said, 'I think I'm starting to have my baby. You've been for ever.'

'Can you walk?'

She grunted, 'If it makes my back hurt less I can.' She put out her arm and he helped her up. 'Did you find anything?' she asked, but he could see her mind was on more pressing business. He helped her forward.

'No.'

She locked the library door behind them. Candles burning on the chantry altars filled the cathedral with an eerie glow, making the marble floor gleam like ice. Eleanor walked more easily now. They moved without discovery among the crowds of worshippers gathering for this or that sermon or canonical hour, women selling candles, scampering children crying out bread and ale, and a man making the cathedral transept a short cut for his mule between Paternoster Row and Carter Street. Then her lips pressed tight and she hung on to Joshua's arm, for the first time revealing his fine showy clothes beneath his cape.

On the steps she pushed him away and left him. She did not want him to discover the hovel in which she lived.

Joshua returned to the cathedral the next day. He waited by the steps on the atrium but she did not appear. He was not surprised, supposing she'd had the child in the night. But he was afraid to go in the library alone, and afraid of being locked in.

He returned to the atrium the following day, and the day after that, then left his vigil for more than a week, working for his father. The Saturday was the Jewish Sabbath, and the day after that the Christian Sabbath, so it was Monday before Joshua could return to the atrium. It was late and he looked anxiously over the heads of the people hurrying home and applesellers shouting red apples, red apples.

Today was the first day of November, All Saints' Day in the Christian calendar, now All Souls' Eve as the light dulled. Bonfires were lit to the dying sun, and church bells would chime until dawn all over London. Only St Paul's was mute, workmen swarming over the lattice of timbers rising from the lantern tower, but such a high spire might never support the weight of bells. Joshua stared up at the massive structure, vast, alien, Christian. Tonight in Christian homes, he knew, apple peel formed initials on the floor to reveal the future. At bedtime girls ate apples sitting at their mirrors, and the ghostly faces of their husbands-to-be peered over their shoulders. Gangs of children and louts banged from door to door, 'souling' for cakes or money. Candles were left burning in every room as guides, for at the clang of midnight the dead would return, able only to squeak like bats until they were offered blood to drink. On every Christian table stood a cup of red wine tonight, and it would be gone by morning.

Joshua waited as long as he could, until it was almost full dark and the only light came from bonfires and braziers. The bells of St Paul's clochier, a tower built near the precinct wall, began to toll, and then the two west towers joined in, their jangling rhythm seeming almost intolerably loud. The last faint line of sunset faded behind Westminster. Eleanor saw him first.

She hurried behind him towards the cathedral without being seen, but then Joshua turned to go home and saw her. He hurried after her. 'Eleanor!'

She hurried faster, then looked away when he caught her up. He stood in front of her but she would not meet his eye.

'Eleanor. Please. I only want to help.'

'Have you not heard?'

'Heard?'

'There is to be a burning tomorrow.'

'No.' His elbows moved and she knew he was running his hands through his hair. 'No. They won't. Not now. Not after all this time.'

'The Papal Bull of Excommunication arrived.' He wouldn't get out of her way, so she walked round him.

'Eleanor. Wait.'

He ran after her, snatched her sleeve, but she pulled away and walked on. 'There's nothing you can do, Jew.' She lifted her skirt and ran up the steps into the cathedral, knowing he would not follow.

Joshua stared after her, then turned away angrily.

Eleanor turned right. Alone she climbed the stairs into the chamber beneath the south-west tower. The jailer came out of his little room set in the twelve-foot thickness of the wall. He grunted. He remembered her.

She said, 'I can afford to pay.'

Eleanor took the iron key and twisted it in the lock. She pushed the door open with her foot.

William lay on the matted straw. Only his eyes moved. He trembled, trying to sit up. She helped him. He whispered, 'Eleanor, as God is my witness, what has happened to you? Have you been attacked?'

She hugged him tight. William was skin and bone, his skin so pale he looked like a man made out of wax. Only his eyes were the same, peering from his gaunt bearded face. She brushed his hair out of them to see him better. She murmured, 'You look so strong.'

'They tell me the Devil is the ape of God. Still can't get him out.' He chuckled, coughed. He touched her skirt. 'You're bleeding.'

'Nothing, it's nothing.'

'Was it the child?'

She held him against her, kissed the top of his head. 'Yes,' she lied.

He nodded his head. 'Was it a difficult birth?'

She wept.

'No, William, not difficult.'

He pulled the rags round his neck. 'Don't want him to see me like this, Eleanor. Don't bring him here.'

'Not him,' she whispered. 'She's a her.'

'Well. What name have you given her?'

'You're her father.'

'Agnes.'

'She looks like you.'

'Better than me, I hope.'

'Yes. Pretty. She'll break some man's heart.'

He whispered, 'Like you.' He raised his fingers to her cheeks. 'Dry your tears.'

'William, listen to me.' She showed him the key. 'Tonight a mule will be waiting on the left side of the atrium. I will meet you at Ludgate. By morning we'll be—'

'How did you get the key?'

She said, 'I did it for you.'

He put his fists to his head. 'No, no, Eleanor.'

After a while she said, 'We'll run. Run away anywhere.'

'Run?' William smiled. 'From myself?'

'*Please*, William.'

'I would be running from myself. That I stand by my own individual identity is the heresy. I have written the truth.'

340

'William, don't. They will murder you and murder your eternal soul by excommunication. No one but me will remember you. No one will ever know your truth.'

'But I am saved,' he said simply. 'More than a thousand years ago Jesus Christ saved me, died for me on the Cross. Don't cry.'

'All that matters is you. Nothing else. I just want to be with you.'

He stroked her hair reassuringly. 'They can't do it, you'll see. I shall spend my life in prison.'

She burst out, 'You've already spent your life in prison!'

He kissed her lips.

'I love you, Eleanor.'

She stood. Then she bent down and laid the key on his straw bed. 'Free yourself.'

Joshua plodded from Jewry into Cheapside, the sun rising behind him hidden in the clouds. The feast of All Souls' Day was one of the many Christian public holidays that made business so difficult through the winter months. He hardly slept and he had forgotten his long boots. He picked his way among the mass of wheel-ruts and slimy pools, the Cheap's markets all shut up, but a few people drifted towards the cathedral. He pulled his scarf across his face lest he was recognised as a Jew. Pigs grunted, disgusting filthy animals roaming forward out of the sidestreets, and he cursed as puddles of their mess slopped over his shoes. Rubbish blew past him, but the many flags and banners that lined the street fluttered cheerfully against the grey sky.

He came into the cathedral precinct and the folkmoot where a clerk read announcements from Paul's Cross, part of the thousand daily minutiae of ordinance and regulation, public and religious, that ruled and guided the lives of ordinary people. Someone had built the front of their house too close to the road. Joshua moved forward with most people, and came to the atrium. He paused, expecting them to go into the cathedral, but instead they walked ahead down Bower Row towards Ludgate, their children scampering beside them. He stood on the hill, looking over the heads of the crowd, following them downhill with his eyes to Ludgate, then across the fields beyond the City wall, joining the crowds from Newgate. Together the black thread of people wandered north along the track towards Smithfield and the fresh white outline of St Bartholomew's Priory.

Eleanor was right. There would be a burning today.

Joshua turned back to the cathedral. Perhaps there was still time. Probably William had not even been taken from his cell yet. From the corner of his eye, as he ran up the steps, Joshua could see the tall green elms west of Bartholomew's, the gallows by the horse-pool where common thieves were hanged and hooked. Only when that show was finished would attention turn to more serious matters.

Joshua crossed from the nave into the choir. The place was sonorous with chanting voices, no doubt every canon of St Paul's was present today, all devoutly religious. Joshua went up to the library, pushed his way inside, found it much busier than he had hoped. He requested a book from the inferior and sat at the desk nearest the aumbry. Several times he got to his feet but each time someone noticed him. The inferior brought his book and slipped it in front of him, kept her hand on it. He glanced up impatiently. A woman with long white hair. She stared into his face, then turned away.

Joshua waited his moment. He glanced at the aumbry doors, but then more people came in and he had to sit back, pretending to read the book.

At the far end of the library the woman with white hair knocked over a horn of ink. She cried out, covering herself with shame for her clumsiness. Alchemidus ran at her, and Joshua opened the aumbry, slipped inside, pulled the door closed behind him.

He waited a moment. Then he felt for the flint and the candle, lit it, and went down into the dark.

Eleanor woke. Her night had been spent sleeplessly waiting at Ludgate, baby Agnes crying, then mouthing the breast, then crying again, and Eleanor had jogged her until her arms ached. The mule chewed hay then hung its head, sleeping.

William did not come.

Eleanor returned home to Sporyer Lane at first light, exhausted by worry. Elfrida was not there. At last the baby slept and Eleanor sat down for a moment. She put her elbows on the table and rested her head in her hands.

She jerked, waking, and it was full daylight, the wind rattling the roof, flapping the blanket in the doorway. She snatched baby Agnes off the table, clutched her tight and ran to the cathedral. Amazingly the baby, little more than a week old, slept peacefully through this rough treatment, a small smile on her lips, her snub nose red with the cold morning.

The jailer grinned at her. Eleanor ran upstairs.

William's cell was empty.

The iron key lay on the straw where he had left it when he was taken away. She picked it up and held it tight, the last thing he had touched.

Joshua held up the candle.

He reached out towards the pile of skins, then did not touch them. He knew he was missing something. He could search through the scrolls, as he had been doing, until he was an old man. It was time to be brilliant. It was time to let God guide his hand, as William had let himself be guided.

On the day of his death William's words seemed very wise. *God*

*surely guided my hand to this scroll just as He guided me here, Joshua.
You're afraid because you're used to living in fear. The truth cannot hurt.
Read the words He has chosen and learn to live in joy, not in fear . . . not
in fear . . .*

Joshua spoke the name of God because there was no one who
could hear him, except God.

'Yahweh, guide my hand as surely as You guided me here.'

He closed his eyes, stretched out his fingers, reached forward. In
his mind's eye he saw the golden house standing on the rock. He
whispered, 'There?'

There was no answer, only the draught from the tunnel.

Joshua stepped back from the skins. He let his arm fall to his side.
God had guided him.

He turned away from the skins and crawled into the tunnel. He
barely noticed the cavern of stick people, scrambled through, went
deeper. The chalky roof of the tunnel scuffed his shoulders, then
rose high as he entered the largest cavern.

The gold reliquary, shaped like a house, gleamed on the slab of
rock in front of him.

More than a house. A temple.

He crossed to it, stared at his face glowing in the ornate patterns of gold and rubies. Then he tilted the candle to drip tallow
on the flat rock, and set the candle in it so that it should not
fall over.

He lifted the golden temple carefully. It was surprisingly heavy.
As he examined it something thumped inside. He peered in the
tiny windows. There was something dark inside it, a relic no doubt.
Probably he was going to all this trouble for the finger-bone of
some forgotten Christian saint, wasting his time. He stuck his finger
through one of the windows, and felt something hairy.

The front was a door. Joshua could not work out how to open
it. On the left he identified hinges, cleverly worked. The right was
secured by a gold rod, but it would not move.

He jerked at it with all his strength, but still it would not move.

He touched it lightly with his fingertips. It turned easily, lifted up,
and the entire front of the building hinged forward. A hairy black
scroll fell into his lap.

Joshua replaced the open reliquary carefully on the rock. He sat
beside it and turned the heavy scroll curiously in his hands. This
was gazelle skin, or possibly goat, obviously flayed from the black
part of the animal. It was wrapped in a broad blue linen ribbon,
much faded. The ribbon was sealed with wax. The wax had been
stamped with the pattern of three quadrangles.

Joshua looked round him. He saw only darkness beyond the circle
of candlelight. He broke the seal.

Beneath it was scrawled, in jagged hurried Aramaic so that Joshua
could still sense the haste in which it had been finished, the quill

scratching so hard that the ink had spattered the words, *Herein Lies the Gospel Witness of Judas Iscariot, His Testament*.

Joshua unrolled the first few columns, draping them over his knees.

Inside the black skin, the scroll was still ivory white.

Joshua bent forward, and began to read.

The archbishop's emissary, Gilbert, the scroll containing the Papal Bull of Excommunication tucked under the archdiaconal robes that hid his chain-mail armour, was attended in front of St Bartholomew's by three hundred Italian priests dressed in rags. The Pope wished them to be found livings at the expense of the English. As always during times of weak rule England was at the mercy of continental politics and senior clergy were more likely to be Spanish or French than English. The peasant-priests, who knew nothing but Latin and country Italian, chattered like birds and the common mob watching the hangings spat at them as they passed. The Cardinal Legate in purple and gold had taken refuge in Bartholomew's, enjoying the hospitality for which Prior Rahere the Dutchman was famous, and showed no sign of coming out. Posts had been planted in front of the priory steps. Rahere, once a canon of St Paul's, was said to be a wicked man though he helped orphans and the sick. There had been several conspiracies to kill him and his priory had a reputation for strangeness, but powerful friends saved him. Half a dozen people were to be burnt today but one had died. She was roped to her pole anyway and burnt dead, she must not cheat justice. The emissary drank a cup of wine. Behind him the crowd roared and something kicked on the gallows. Gilbert's priest confirmed, 'The last one, lord.'

'Tell these Italian scum to sing the *Te Deum*.'

The priest said, 'Pardon, lord?' Gilbert himself was French and difficult to understand.

'Never mind.' Gilbert decided not to wait for the Cardinal Legate. He took the scroll from his armpit, opened it, and began to read.

'Hear me, English, for these are the eternal truths.

'The Pope can be judged by no one.

'The Roman Church has never erred and never will err till the end of time.

'The Roman Church was founded by Christ alone.

'It is written in the Roman law of the great Theodoric that no one can be compelled to believe against his or her will.

'But Christians cannot disbelieve, because they are baptised.'

He glared at the monk tied to the third post. 'Heresy is a sin which merits not only excommunication but also death, for it is worse to corrupt the faith which is the life of the soul than to issue counterfeit coins which minister to the secular life. Since counterfeiters are justly killed by princes as enemies to the common good, so heretics also deserve the same punishment.'

The crowd came forward from the elm trees, pushing round the cart on which he stood. The wind was cold and they wanted to warm themselves at the flames around the dead girl. The smell of human flesh being burnt was strangely mouthwatering, like frying bacon. Gilbert raised his voice, coughing at the smoke, and read out the Bull of Excommunication.

'Do you have anything to say?'

Joshua read the words of Judas Iscariot, his eyes following his finger quickly along the close-set columns of text. *This is the birth-roll of Jesus, son of David—*

His finger skipped to the top of the next column.

Here I send my messenger before your face to prepare the Way for you, the voice of one who cries in the desert, 'Make the Way ready for the Lord—'

Similar so far to other Christian gospels. Joshua unrolled more of the hairy scroll and his finger skipped forward.

So I, Judas the Assassin, tax-collector, scribe of the holy scriptorium and lector, Teacher of Righteousness and leader of my people in the Essene Way, am His humble servant preparing us through purity and holiness for the End of Days and the building of the Temple that we are. And the building of a House of Aaron for the union of supreme holiness with God. And of a House of Community for Israel, for those of us who walk in perfection—

Joshua swallowed. Judas too had been at Qumran. He was important there. *Us,* a priest, perhaps even the head priest as he claimed, the Teacher of Righteousness called the Pope.

Perhaps more important, at first, than Jesus.

Building a House of Community for Israel. A nation.

Joshua swallowed. His heart thudded, he had too little time, he hardly dared to understand what he was reading.

There followed a detailed description of the Temple of the End of Days, after the Sons of Light had vanquished the Sons of Darkness, and of the duties of the priests.

His finger skipped forward.

And I said to him, 'Are you the One?'

Joshua stared. Judas Iscariot, the twelfth apostle, had asked Jesus outright if he was the Messiah.

So he had doubted it.

The part of the scroll that Joshua had read hung down from his left knee to the floor, where it curled loosely.

Jesus answered to me, You know the things which you hear and see. The blind receive their sight, and the lame walk, the lepers are cleansed, the deaf hear, and the poor have good news preached to them. And blessed is he who shall find no stumbling in me. Aram menaht menou.

What did that mean? The text was more difficult to read now, hurried. Joshua pulled out several feet of skin in his impatience, let the dense columns uncoil across the floor.

Here it was. Jesus's peaceful answer had not satisfied Judas the nationalist, with his forge for making swords and his workshops for arrows and spears, hot for an armed uprising against the Romans. He no longer believed Jesus was the One. They were on opposite sides.

Of the High Priest I demanded fifty-two oaths of silver, being the number of the Fathers of the Congregation, the visible talents of the people. And he offered twelve talents stamped with his promise of a time to come, saying he loved Caesar no more than I, but the time was not yet ready—

Judas and the High Priest had haggled over how much Judas would be paid. The coins were much more than money. They were promises.

And so we settled on the number, wrought in the shape of his promise. Caesar wrought on the one side for the present, and the Nation of Israel promised on the other side for the future. And the number of the talents was thirty pieces of silver.

The candleflame fluttered in a sudden draught. Joshua did not take his eyes off the text.

In the Garden of Gethsemane Judas betrayed Jesus with a kiss. '*You are not the One.*'

Jesus was arrested by the *huperetai*, the Sanhedrin police, his ideas discredited, his disciples scattered. Judas returned, victorious, to the monastery.

The writing changed, the point of the quill almost tearing the skin, flicking ink.

Judas did not understand what he found at Qumran.

Something has happened but he does not know what. The busy buildings and courtyards and baptismal pools, all are empty. He stands alone in the storm, then climbs to the scriptorium. Some people run across the potter's field, their clothes flapping in the wind, the dust flying from their feet. Jesus is risen.

The people cry Jesus the prophet is risen from the dead, he is He, He is the true Christ, He is the Messiah, He is the One. He walks the road from Jerusalem to Qumran. He has been seen.

I believe it is not true, but what if it is true?

If it is true, what have I done?

Abide with me, for it is toward evening and the day is far spent, and my heart burns within me.

More was scribbled, much more. The scroll fluttered in Joshua's hands.

Waiting for Him.

He looked up. Shadows moved around him from the flickering candle, and he realised it was his own breath disturbing the flame. He panted for air like a running man. His forehead was icy cold with sweat. Had Judas looked like this, waiting alone in the darkened scriptorium at Qumran for the Christ to come?

The wind blows where it will, and I hear its sound but I cannot tell whence it comes, or whither it goes.

He imagined Judas waiting, the thirty pieces of silver cold in his hand, and the door opens, and His voice speaks.

'*I say to you, it would have been good for you if you had not been born.*'

Joshua struggled to read the writing.

'*I am with you always, to the close of the age.*'

Beneath the last line was written a notice in Latin, in large Roman letters, by a different hand.

THUS ENDS THE BLACK BOOK OF JUDAS ISCARIOT
MURDERER OF GOD

A breeze blew through the cavern. The unravelled skin flapped like a wing above the floor and Joshua tried to roll it up.

'The truth will be revealed in the flames,' William said.

'If you say so,' said the incendiary. He was a kindly talkative man with eleven children, four of them boys. 'Best faggots at the bottom for a hot heart, a layer of bavins above that, and brushwood and dry bramble on top for a quick flame.' He dragged back some brambles that the wind had blown down, pulled a thorn from his thick leather gloves. The smoke from the dead woman blew over them but he was used to it and did not cough. The others had been dragged screaming to the posts but the monk was quiet. 'If you don't mind my advice, sir,' the incendiary muttered appreciatively, 'if I was you, which begging your pardon thank God I'm not, when the heat gets up I'd take a good deep breath of flame, sear my lungs, and drown. Don't suffer, it's not worth it. Fact, that is.'

'I drowned once before,' William murmured. 'I die to live.'

The incendiary put his hands on his hips, stared at the crowd streaming away. 'What's got into them now?'

Eleanor pushed through the crowd running past her. Someone shouted, 'Gold! Gold!' They bumped into her and she held baby Agnes high, trying to protect her. The child woke and gave an infant's piercing, urgent cry.

Somebody shouted, 'Where is it? Where are we going?'

'A gardener told us! A treasure of gold found in a church!'

A woman screamed, 'I dreamt it the other night! It's mine!'

'The crypt of St Martin-in-the-Fields—'

'No,' shouted a heavy man running with a spade, 'it's in the garden, an old tree opened a grave when it fell, I heard it from my nephew. Jewels! Gold! Silver!'

347

Eleanor came through them. She held her baby to the breast but still Agnes cried and cried. The fires burned on the mud in front of Bartholomew's steps, the wind pulling the flames well out to the side, so that the flames jumped by themselves from pyre to pyre. A few people who had not heard the rumour or did not believe it were held back by men on horseback.

Eleanor felt the heat of the fires on her face, scalding her tears. She walked through the ring of ragged priests and horsemen without hearing them. They fell back on each side of her.

Eleanor approached the fire. She held up William's baby.

The child put out its hands as if to be picked up.

Eleanor and William spoke. Their lips moved silently in the roar of the flames.

'I love you.'

William took a breath of flame to the sound of the baby's cry.

The wind filled the cavern, pulled Joshua's cloak, pushed at him, whirled him round. He scrambled for the candle, its flame burning straight and true, grabbed it. He hung on, leaning backward like a man against a storm, was pushed forward one step, then another. His hair fluttered in his eyes, his cloak whipped round him. The wind blew from everywhere, pressed him forward towards the tunnel leading away from here. He ran into the tunnel and the wind stopped.

Joshua stopped, and the wind rose, blew around him like a storm.

He stared back into the cavern. The wind whirled the scroll from side to side. He thought of going back in there. He should leave the scroll neatly.

It was a fake, wasn't it? A clever fake.

The wind blew into his eyes from the cavern. Joshua blinked. He closed his eyes and his mind's eye saw the scroll rolling itself up, blown by the wind, tossed into the golden temple, the door slamming and the gold rod dropping to lock it in place, a miracle.

He crawled away, afraid to look. It was a windy day up above, and that explained the wind. Doubtless there were more caves and caverns than he had found, which explained the circulation of the air. The wind blew him forward through the cave of the stick people and the cavern of the scrolls, whirling round the skins, fluttering his cloak over his head as he crawled into the domed cave.

Joshua climbed the ladders gasping for breath. *Here I send my messenger before your face to prepare the Way for you, the voice of one who cries in the desert, 'Make the Way ready for the Lord, and the building of the Temple that we are, and of a House of Community for Israel.'*

Joshua stopped. The wind roared around him. 'Stop!' he shouted, but the wind thundered like an angry god and he feared being dragged from his hold, whirled through the earth into the sky.

He climbed again, almost running up the ladders.

A House of Community for Israel. Yahweh is with us always.

'It's all true,' he panted. 'The Gospels, all true.'

He ran along the catacomb. He was afraid to go up to the library full of people, but the wind blew him forward past the ladder, past huge old tree roots hanging from the roof, along a short tunnel into a cellar. The stench was appalling. Joshua stared at piles of manure.

He was in the cesspit below the cathedral's latrines.

He crawled forward beneath squares of daylight and a row of white Christian bottoms. He heard the priests murmuring to one another and someone hummed Latin. The opening at the end was brightest, unoccupied. Joshua stuck his head out, then climbed up into a small room with wooden walls, the priests of St Paul's being as shy as the monks of Westminster or Qumran of their privacy. Each latrine was separated from its neighbour by a wooden panel and a door. Joshua pressed his ear to the door.

He lifted the latch, peered out. No one was about. He closed the door behind him and slipped quietly along the row of bowls and pitchers waiting in the lavatory, ran past a startled priest coming in to wash his hands. The priest shouted.

The wind blew, and Joshua ran into a fine sunny day, the river green below Lud's Hill and the sky purest windswept blue above. Whichever way he turned the wind blew him towards London Bridge and the boats for France, and Spain, and Italy, and Cyprus, stepping stones to the Holy Land.

Our land. My land. Israel.

He shouted joyously as he ran. 'It's all true!'

'I think William found the truth in the end,' Eleanor whispered, cuddling Agnes to her as she walked. The baby whimpered. 'I saw it in his eyes.'

'What was it?'

'I don't know. But *he* saw it.' She limped from the darkness of the Creed, laid the baby on the table.

'I'm sorry,' Elfrida said. 'I'm sorry. I'm so sorry I did what I did. I was wrong, but I thought it was for the best.'

'You were jealous.'

'But you did love him, didn't you?'

'Yes. I do.'

'I tried to make amends. That Jewish boy was no good. He's probably down there still for all I know. He never came up.' She lit a taper, raised her gnarled hand, brushed Eleanor's hair from her eyes. 'It's still just us, then.'

'Just the two of us.' Eleanor soothed the crying baby. 'And her. Especially her.'

Elfrida said possessively, 'Never did like that Peter of Cheap anyway. Well, that's settled. All over and done with. She'll be our very own.' She reached for the pot of beer, glanced at Eleanor, frowned, held up the taper. 'Does your face hurt?'

'No, why?'

'Got too close to the fire, I'd say.' Elfrida peered close. 'And your neck. Almighty God, look at you!'

Eleanor looked. She unlaced her clothes. 'Fire got you down the front,' Elfrida whispered, shocked. 'You must be in agony.'

Eleanor pulled her clothes off. The line of raw red skin ran from her forehead to her crotch, and another from her hands up the inside of her arms, across her breasts. 'God help me, look at me. Have I been feeding this to Agnes?' She calmed herself. 'No, it wasn't the fire.'

Elfrida leant forward. She touched the marks reverently. 'I've seen the friars on London Bridge do this. The flagellants. They believe in God so deeply that sometimes, just sometimes, the holy marks appear on them. Mostly they thrash themselves until it happens. But sometimes, all by itself, a friar's forehead bleeds as if from the Crown of Thorns. Or blood flows from their hands and ankles, sometimes their side, as the Bible tells us. The marks of Jesus's suffering on the Cross, real and true.'

Eleanor trembled. 'You're frightening me. What does it mean?'

'I seen it before,' her grandmother said. 'I saw them on my own body, Eleanor, the night your father was born. Only lasted a few heartbeats, but my mother Astrid saw them too, as clear as I did or better. And we didn't say a word about it, I can tell you. I never told a soul.' She caressed the fading marks with her fingertips. 'Yet here they are on you.'

Eleanor quickly unwrapped her baby, pulled open the linen rags that lay next to her skin. 'She's got it too. What should I do? No wonder she was crying!' She cuddled her tight. 'Poor baby.'

Elfrida kissed the baby's head. 'She's all right. It's fading.'

Eleanor sat weakly. 'What have I handed down to her? She looks like me and she looks like William too—'

Elfrida grinned, cooing at the baby the way old people always did. 'Can't help being the child of her parents, can she?' She stood, suddenly businesslike. 'Get your coat on. We'll see what we see.'

Eleanor draped herself in her cape, baby Agnes wrapped warm beneath, and followed her grandmother into the night. The sky was quiet and black after the storm. The temporary planks of the cathedral roof were damaged, covered with canvas until repairs in the morning. The brewer who had sold Elfrida her evening beer, a sober and pious man, had assured her that the thatch roof of the latrines was completely blown off the walls, and one of the joists was lifted so high on the storm that it was found driven twenty-three feet deep into the churchyard. Elfrida had scoffed at him, but he had believed it.

The great iron gates to the cathedral were closed. The two women entered through the small Si Quis door in the north wall. They hurried beneath the statue of Algar and went up to the library, Agnes by now sleeping peacefully, and Elfrida unlocked the door then locked it securely behind them.

They went down.

Nothing had changed. There was no sign of the Jew Joshua. The skins lay piled as they always had been, with nothing to show they had ever been disturbed.

'I wonder how many more marvels William copied and left in the library,' Eleanor whispered.

Elfrida led her further down. The reliquary shaped like a gold house stood on the rock slab, the Black Book rolled up inside, carefully secured by the gold bar.

The old woman knelt. 'All I know is that there is more than I know.'

Eleanor knelt beside her.

The old woman said, 'We are imperfect but this is the truth. There really is God. Every word of the Old Testament is true and every word of the New Testament is true and all the inconsistencies are mistakes by us. God is, and Jesus Christ really literally is His Son. This is what the Black Book says.'

Part Five
Elizabeth

London, 10 September 1666 AD

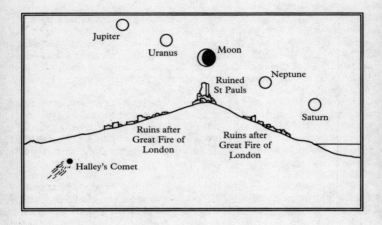

'Crying the Neck,' Harvest Festival
Saturday, 1 September 1666

Elizabeth Ludgate, for the past five childless years Mrs John Barwick, beautiful young wife of the grey-haired Reverend Dr Barwick, DD, Fellow of St John's College and Dean of St Paul's Cathedral, jumped from the window of the cathedral's riverside vicarage in Chiswick, leapt across the flowerbed, hoisted her azure moiré dress above her knees, and ran down the garden on her long white legs.

'Stop thief!'

The driver and postillion waiting beyond the garden gate stared at the dean's wife, mouths gaping, then bent to see past the vagabond running in front of her, their eyes firmly fixed on the amazing sight of those sprinting white legs usually so correctly concealed. Elizabeth's black hair, long enough for her to sit on, slipped from its band and flew behind her in the afternoon sunlight.

'Stop him, you idiots!'

The vagabond, who had slipped into the vicarage through the open window from which Elizabeth pursued him, dodged round the garden clasping to his chest the thick leather satchel snatched from the dean's table. His cap dropped over his eyes and he tripped on an apple root, sprawled on the dry grass. Elizabeth knelt on his back, her eyes shining, her elfin face and high cheekbones glowing as red as the apples on the tree. She flipped him over.

'Got you!'

They stared into one another's faces, both winded, puffing.

She said, 'But you're only a child.'

The child's eyes filled with tears. The driver and postillion seized him officiously, wrestled him to his bare dirty feet. Elizabeth stepped back. She smoothed her dress decorously in place but she had lost her shoes and the grass felt pleasantly warm and soft under her soles. The Presbyterian whose house neighboured the vicarage found her shoes in the flowerbed and picked them up.

'You owe that boy a good birching to improve his ways, Mrs Barwick. The more you make him sorrowful, the more you may be sure that the loving God is giving him his portion. Your husband will know his duty, no doubt.'

Elizabeth looked the man in the eye. She could not remember his last name but only his first, Nehemiah. For her to address him so familiarly – even his wife probably called him *Mr*, or simply husband – would be a great impropriety. She took her shoes. 'No doubt my husband the dean knows his duty better than either of us, sir.' Nehemiah looked so dour that Elizabeth couldn't help smiling, in her mind's eye seeing the thin-lipped Puritan embraced over his wife on their hard bed, whispering conjugal endearments to each other as *Mr* or *Mrs*, each held in place by rank not love, except love for God.

'Mr – ah—' Elizabeth said. Her grin broadened, imagining them.

No man wearing tall heels, especially one of the drab interfering Presbyterians who appreciated simple force of character, liked to be looked directly in the eye and silenced by the smile of a barefoot beautiful woman. The neckline of Elizabeth's dress was cut fashionably low and trimmed with fine Honiton lace, which by its gauzy concealment drew attention to the ripeness of her young breasts. She reached up and plucked an apple from the bough, and all three men followed her supple left-handed movement with their eyes. But instead of eating the fruit, she held it out to the child.

'Do not cry. My husband's papers are worthless but they are of great value him and to St Paul's Cathedral, and thus to me.' She tossed the apple up, caught it in her right hand. 'This for them, child. Fair exchange. You look more in need of food than paper.'

The boy dropped the satchel and caught the apple, skipped back when her left hand ruffled his hair and something flashed in her fingers. He blew a rude noise from the gate, then looked amazed, and pulled a silver coin from his hair. He bowed to her as deeply as a gentleman, and scampered from sight down the dusty lane between fields of ripe Chiswick barley, munching the apple.

'Roman justice,' the Presbyterian insulted her. 'Paying with a silver coin for what you already own.'

She snapped, 'Puritan justice stabled eight hundred horse in the nave of St Paul's, and made a cavalry barracks of the choir.'

'You've made a bad boy into a rogue, madam. With your encouragement, one day he'll hang.' Nehemiah touched his black hat. 'Good day!'

Elizabeth sighed. 'I'd like to kick you on the backside,' she whispered. Her husband watched her from the porch, holding his china coffee bowl in both quivering hands. 'Did you save them entire?' he called fretfully, and she held up the satchel victoriously. 'I mustn't be late, wife . . .'

'There's plenty of time.' In a loud voice Elizabeth instructed the sulking postillion to carry out her portmanteau and the dean's cloak-bag, then pulled on her shoes and went to the old man. He slurped his coffee and she handed the bowl disapprovingly to the maid who had carried his stick, put her arm round her husband and helped him down the steps.

'I know I embarrassed you, John.'

He murmured, 'You look gorgeous like the sun.'

'I know sometimes I'm not ladylike. And I apologise. But I did the right thing.'

He said mildly, 'You always do the right thing, wife. You *do* care for me, don't you?' John Barwick's papery hand patted her arm and he grinned, and from the sentimental shine in his eyes she realised he was proud of her. He tapped his stick on the path. 'I had not left the room for more than ten seconds. The cheek of the boy . . .'

She said, 'That was what I liked about him!'

'My good generous wife,' the dean sighed fondly. 'You are too good, and too generous to others for your own good.' He tried to take the satchel but she insisted. The postillion held open the gate, the driver the carriage door, then slammed it. The carriage rocked as he jumped up on his seat, then rocked again as the postillion took his place standing on the platform behind. The whip cracked.

John asked again, worried, 'Are we late?' He had forgotten he had asked before.

'No, not too late,' Elizabeth repeated.

'We must get to St Paul's with the utmost rapidity! I am never late for a meeting in my life.'

'John, rest. Close your eyes. Remember what your brother Peter ordered. Complete rest.'

'My headache is better. You organise me so completely, wife, that sometimes I feel like your child, not your husband.'

He had not meant to hurt her, and she told herself that to be rebuked for caring was a compliment. 'You have not been well, John.'

'I mean to rest, wife,' he murmured irritably. 'I know. It's so hot.' He stared at the mudbanks passing on their right, the gleaming channels of mud and slime and sewage spreading towards them under the sun, the rising tide that was the reason for their return by carriage not oars against the flood. Seagulls flapped lazily into the hot hazy air, dull white crosses whirling against the smoke of London ahead of them.

Despite the heat his skin felt cold and she laid the rug over his knees. A dean's life was constant toil and worry, more constant and more worrying the nearer to his cathedral he came. John's living at Therfield rectory in Hertfordshire was too far for a man in his sixties who had suffered an apoplectic stroke, but Chiswick was close enough for country air and rest. But somehow he had smuggled this heavy satchel of papers. Elizabeth said decisively, 'Your physician orders you not to work, so my organisation is merely in submission to your brother's orders, because I love you.'

'Yes, wife.'

'And you should not drink coffee. It is your vice.'

'It is my only pleasure.'

'I should be your only pleasure.'

'And the cathedral—'

'The cathedral is your duty, not a pleasure, John. You are worn out, exhausted by your work for the public good . . .'

Elizabeth listened to herself. Low-born and uneducated I am, she thought, but do I not talk on the same level with my husband who loves me? And I hold my own among the exalted men who are his equals, those close friends of high rank and brilliant company who prize his gifts as much as I prize his love. Dr Thomas Turner the Dean of Canterbury sat at supper two nights ago, Dr Layfield too, Dr Pory the archbishop's chaplain and, though late by a first course of skink soup, Archbishop Juxon himself. And John's younger brother Peter, King Charles II's personal physician, all tucking into my own dishes of roasted Lambeth snipes and Tewkesbury mustard with cream and cloves and my own raisin pudding, and me at their table standing my ground in conversation, hearing myself. 'I don't care what you say, gentlemen. Coffee is a vice. Never did gentlemen wear greater breeches or carry less in them of any worth, because of that abominable liquor called coffee – ask any lady—'

'Ho!' Peter the physician had laughed. 'Tell that to the king.'

'Never were ladies prettier,' her husband had smiled at Elizabeth. 'Ladies nowadays are too beautiful. They are our undoing.'

'The last five years have been the happiest of your life, John.' Edward Layfield, John's oldest friend, had pointed his dripping soup spoon. 'Since you wed your wife.'

'Since he returned from exile in The Hague with the king,' Peter said, sipping his Haut Brion claret. 'Exhausted by secret missions and danger. Why are you not a bishop, John? Dean of Durham, now Dean of St Paul's. You should be in the bishop's throne. Damned unfair.'

John murmured, 'Nolo episcopari. The Anglican Church hierarchy was in ruins after the disastrous Puritan interregnum. The king in exile made me his chaplain, and bade me persuade surviving bishops to consecrate new prelates for his restoration and the resurrection of the Church of England. Now, I would be accused of self-interest had I thereby raised my own self to a bishopric, would I not?' He spread his pale hands. 'Thus, nolo episcopari.'

'He was offered the bishopric of Sodor and Man.' Elizabeth found her husband's diffidence infuriating. 'He refused Carlisle outright.'

Peter had said gently, 'Your devotion to your husband does you great credit.'

She said, 'Anyway, we were talking of coffee.'

'We were talking,' John winked at her, 'of my dear wife's anger at the exclusion of women from coffee-houses. That is the vice of coffee which you find most objectionable, wife . . .'

The carriage jolted. John's eyes fluttered and he woke. 'Ah. Where are we?'

'Kensington, I think.'

'Looks less like a country village and more like a part of London every time,' he grumbled. Grand mansions stood among the hayfields rising on their left, beyond the little church. Downhill spread a patchwork of a thousand market gardens and nurseries, the river winding among them like a muddy worm. The colours changed suddenly from summer to autumn, though the trees were still green, as the long golden fields were reaped, burnt black, ploughed brown.

'Wife?'

'Yes, John?'

'Whom are we meeting?'

She said gaily, as though he had not forgotten, 'Your young professor of astronomy—'

He remembered. 'Ah. Chris Wren. And Mr Evelyn of the Royal Commission. And Sir Roger Pratt?'

'Yes, and Mr May, Mr Chicheley, Mr Slingsby—' Elizabeth recited their names effortlessly from memory. 'The Bishop of London, of course. And several expert workmen.'

John nodded wisely. Then he said, 'And the purpose of it, wife?'

She kissed his cheek. 'Your tour of inspection of the cathedral.'

'It is even older than I,' he said sadly. 'And even more decrepit.'

He pointed across the fields to the morass of London, the shambles of Smithfield and the rows of wooden shanties piled up like sticks against the ancient stony rampart of the City, and above that St Paul's stuck out like a rotting, blackened stump of old tooth.

'Even without its spire it is by far the tallest building in London,' he sighed. 'Look, the spires on the little churches all round are pinpricks by comparison with that great tower.' That was true, but the tower was encased in a haze of scaffolding, for it was leaning. But John was carried away by his enthusiasm, as though he had not told her all this many times before. 'Once the great spire of St Paul's was topped by a huge gold ball on which stood a gold cross fifteen feet high, surmounted by a gold eagle. Idolatry! In the pommel of the gold cross was a piece of the True Cross, a stone from the Holy Sepulchre of His Resurrection, and bones taken from eleven thousand virgins.' The dean could no longer remember what he'd had for breakfast, but his learning remained perfect. 'The spire touched the clouds. Lightning struck it every hundred years, burnt it down, burnt it down. The last time was a hundred years ago.'

She said, 'It was not lightning. A plumber left a pan of coals burning while he went down to dinner.'

'Really? I've never heard that. I'm sure it was lightning.'

'Everyone thought so at the time. His name was Solomon.'

'Who told you that? I'm sure it's wrong.'

'My mother—' Elizabeth stopped her tongue. She said, 'Yes, I'm sure you must be right. It was lightning.'

'It was truly a pan of coals?'

359

'Yes.'

'Wife,' he confessed adoringly, 'you are a person of marvels, you constantly surprise me. With so little education, how do you know so much?' He turned awkwardly, keeping his numb left hand to his side, and touched her face tenderly. 'There is so much more to you than I know. You are life itself to me. I love you so much, wife.'

She burst out, 'John, at least when we are alone call me by my name!'

He blinked, then said, 'My own dear Liza.'

She squeezed his hands. 'I'm sorry I was brusque. In your endearments please treat me as a person. Myself. Not as a – position.'

'I'm sorry I am not young, Liza.' He looked out of the window. 'An old man and an old cathedral.'

They jolted in silence for a while, except for the leathery creak of the springs. Elizabeth watched from the window. Noticing her inattention, he squeezed his pince-nez on to his nose and quietly pulled a lapful of yellowed papers and old manuscripts from the satchel.

She turned. 'John, you cannot work now!'

'Can I break the habit of a lifetime? My mind is sufficiently raised to write to the Lord Mayor of London. A most difficult and delicate matter has come up.' He leant back, reading. 'These are the ancient Rights of St Paul's, the *laudabiles consuetudines* which I have sworn to maintain, *Ecclesiae Sancti Pauli Londinium Decanus et Prebendarius Prebendae de Oxgate in Ecclesia predicta* . . .'

Elizabeth dropped the window and thrust her head from his murmuring voice into the easterly breeze, dried mud blowing past her from the road, the wheels rumbling. Farmworkers with backs scalded red by the sun laboured with scythes at fields of golden-black barley, women wearing broad straw hats threshed and winnowed, girls and the youngest children pulled out bolters and weeds, corncockle, goosefoot, and old men and boys tied and piled straw stooks for the stables of London. As the reapers closed towards the last stand of barley she saw hares, rabbits, rats, mice, scattering ahead of the steadily sweeping blades.

A cry went up, 'The Neck! The Neck!'

She called the driver to stop, heard the grunts of the harvesters now, the hiss of their scythes. The watchers hung back, afraid of the last haunted stand of the crop. Many believed the god of the crop fled in the body of a hare. An old man stepped forward. The last ears of barley fell to his scythe and a hare dashed out, chased by dogs. The hare coursed wildly from side to side, leapt the ditch, escaped.

Meanwhile the old man picked up the stalks of the hare's last hiding place in his hands, twisted them into a strange device. Elizabeth gave a low cry. The old man held up a straw baby. He bound it at the neck and waist with blood-coloured ribbon. She whispered, 'What's happening?' John shrugged, reading Latin.

'It's a thanksgiving.'

The reapers formed a circle round the straw baby, swept off their hats and the tips of their fingers touched the stubbled ground. A low, musical, rising cry came up as the old harvester lifted the straw baby slowly above his head. The women and children's voices joined in. They were crying the Neck. The sound of the word rose up like the cries of wolves. Stopped.

John said, 'They're killing the Corn Spirit.'

'Who's the Corn Spirit?' Elizabeth turned back, hearing a burst of laughter. The older men had thrown up their caps and were dancing with the women delightedly.

John said, 'Osiris.'

The old reaper tossed the straw baby into the air. There was a scuffle among the young men to catch it, somebody tripped, another was pushed. Two lads fought for the prize, one was punched and fell. The victor, clutching the straw baby, ran towards the farmer's daughter in the doorway of the farmhouse. At the last moment she lifted a bucket and soused him with water. He snatched a kiss anyway.

John muttered, 'Herodotus wrote of the custom more than two thousand years ago. In Egypt.' He knocked the roof with his stick and the carriage jerked onward. Elizabeth leant from the window until the farmworkers were gone. When she settled back John observed her flushed face over his pince-nez. 'You women, whose chief companions are the forms and faces of outdoor Nature, retain in your souls far more of the pagan fantasy of your remote forebears, in my opinion, than of the systematic religion taught by the race of men at this later date.'

'Yes, I am a woman.'

'You are a lady, my dear, and my wife. Wife of the Dean of St Paul's.'

She said, 'You never snatch a kiss from me.'

He touched the papers. 'At my age more important matters compel my attention. It is particularly ticklish.' He sounded wearied by the journey. 'There is so much to do. My cathedral is ruined by the Puritan revolution, the windows broke, the cloisters and chapter house made a wine cellar and builders' stores, shops built along the walls, the nave used as a bowling alley for ninepins, Paul's Cross torn down.'

She closed the window. 'But the rebuilding—'

'Tinkering is all we can afford. The Bishop of London gives me a hundred pounds a year, the king one thousand but in quarterly payments, in arrears. In the last three years we have spent three thousand five hundred pounds on running repairs, and that only on the portico. A thousand pounds a year! Now even more work is required.'

'So you are seeing Dr Wren in an hour.'

St Martin-in-the-Fields chimed. 'In half an hour.' But he enjoyed her interest. 'I will tell you something amazing. You will not believe me but it is true. A few years ago the Jews offered half a million pounds to buy St Paul's. An incredible sum!' He stared at her. 'You are not surprised.'

'The Jews have always had a close feeling for St Paul's.'

'I cannot imagine why. Naturally, the Church demanded eight hundred thousand pounds, which even the Jews cannot raise.'

'This is the ticklish matter?'

'No, that is much more serious. Sir Thomas Bludworth, the Lord Mayor, and his Court of Aldermen have sent workmen into the cathedral to provide seating for themselves, dignified and formal, that they may be received in worship with the respect due to their rank and station. It is beautiful work, I admit.'

'You are always saying that holiness should be beautiful.'

'But they have mounted the City Arms over a throne made for the Lord Mayor. It is an unprecedented attack on the independence of the Church.'

'Why?'

'Because they are paying for the work! When money is given to the cathedral, it is for *us* to use. By doing their own work they impose their will upon the Church, and I am under the strictest oath to preserve the rights of our Church inviolable. So, I must write to Sir Thomas Bludworth, a proud and bad-tempered man, and insist that the Church pays him for his gift.'

'The City has actually paid its workmen?'

'Last quarter-day.'

She scoffed, 'This is much ado about nothing. Half a century ago Sir Paul Pindar gave thousands of pounds for marble pillars, repairs—'

'This is different. Do you not remember the Puritans abolishing bishops, deans, and chapters, melting crucifixes and the bishop's mitre and crozier to make artillery shells? No, you are too young. I remember St Paul's closed by parliamentary order as a lair of idolatry. I remember my cathedral handed over to the Lord Mayor to be knocked down, and all its lands and revenues stolen and looted by the Lord Mayor and his aldermen.'

'I see. A difficult letter indeed.' Elizabeth seized a pen and ink-bottle from the satchel. 'What do you wish to say?'

'To say, wife? For Bludworth to set up his throne in my cathedral is an intolerable affront!'

She said gently, 'Bludworth is a powerful man. You must not offend him but you must get your way. What tone do you wish to strike?'

'Polite, reasonable, but firm.' The dean leant back sleepily. 'The danger of precedent. The danger that the City might again claim rights in the cathedral, which under God and the king is altogether free. Perhaps some Biblical quotation?'

'To the Right Honourable Sir Thomas Bludworth, Knight—' Elizabeth wrote rapidly. 'My lord, if it did consist with my health I should rather have waited upon you myself, being desirous of testifying my due respects to your place and person, than trouble you with the importunity of this letter . . .'

She glanced at him several times as she wrote. He was asleep. She paid the toll at Piccadilly and he did not wake. Without him, I am nothing, she thought, and pulled the rug to his chin although it was such a hot day. A fly settled on his nose and she brushed it away. A fly settled on his nose, she remembered, when he first came to my father's tavern in the Lydiard – Lud's Yard – by Ludgate, and I served him that cup of Spanish wine, and flicked the fly away with my serviette. I was fifteen when I married him, he late in his fifties, dry as paper, and. funny, and serious, and wise, and I made him young. What makes two people fall in love? We could not have had more happiness than we have.

The carriage rocked between the people along the narrow dusty Strand. At Temple Bar, in the usual confusion at the narrow gate, a jovial City woman riding a mare from Westminster was knocked from its back by a stallion, and the wheels of a cart at once ran over her head. Another quarter of an hour's delay was caused by the accident, and a Puritan moved among the stalled vehicles and dropped sedan chairs thanking God for punishing sin, for she was a wicked woman riding a mare in heat. 'There are no accidents, only signs of God's will.' Children ran among the wagons and carriages selling farthing tankards of water for a penny-farthing each, the summer drought was so dry this year. The carriage jerked beneath the Bar, and John woke.

Elizabeth handed him the long completed letter. 'I managed a quote from Thessalonians. The Lord's command to abstain from even the appearance of evil.'

'One Thessalonians Five Twenty-two.'

She laughed and kissed him.

He whispered, 'I do not know what I would do without you, Liza.'

She thought, what would I be without you?

In front of them the River Fleet disappeared between houses and streets built on mountains of rubbish. All that remained of the steep valley was a gentle slope down, then the gentle slope up to Ludgate and more traffic crammed in the gateway. 'Every gentleman wants a carriage these days,' John grumbled. 'Here we are, the City of Sodom and Gomorrah. Seventy thousand people dead of the plague last year, yet the roads now as busy as ever again, and the buildings as crowded. Repent or be consumed, as Mr Gostelo prints it.'

Elizabeth murmured, 'A consuming fire shall be kindled in the bowels of the earth. A great effusion of blood, fire and smoke shall rise up in the dark habitations of cruelty.'

'I've read Mr Baker's sayings.'

'Mr Baker?'

'Did you not quote him?' He muttered to himself, forgetting her words. 'Did you know that the Pope has sent agents to London, but they have been captured? Their instructions were to set fires to burn the city the day after tomorrow, Monday morning. The Pope fears the restoration of our religion, you see.'

'What has happened to them?'

'Hanged, drawn, quartered.' He looked up longingly. 'I do wish we could clean the cathedral. But it would be black again in a year. This soot!'

The horses struggled to drag the carriage up Ludgate Hill, and the cathedral rose above them black and immense and ancient, as though made of dark soil, old even when it was built.

The carriage slowed at Paul's Gate, crossed the broad dusty space of the atrium, and pulled up at the steps where a group of men waited at the top. Near the convocation house Elizabeth could hear the shouts of children in the school, made from the bishop's ancient ruined palace on the south side and various derelict buildings, but did not see them. The medieval palace built to replace it, standing against the north wall of the cathedral next to the Si Quis door, had long ago crumbled away. The charnel house had been torn down and the five hundred tons of human bones it contained dumped on Bone Hill in Finsbury. But still St Paul's Cathedral stood glimmering darkly above the carriage in the afternoon sun, looking as large as London.

The postillion helped John, who fussed he wanted no help, from the carriage and Elizabeth took her husband's elbow. 'Dr Barwick!' A young man in his early thirties detached himself nimbly from the group in the portico and supported the dean's other elbow. He wore a plume in his hat and his movements climbing the steps were as quick and precise as a bird's, but he seemed kind and steady by nature. 'Dean Barwick, I would not let them start without you, sir. I am a strong pillar of deans, being the son of one.'

'My dear Dr Wren! My wife, as you see, is my other strong pillar.'

'Mrs Barwick.' Wren bowed. He had broad cheekbones, large flashing eyes, a large well-formed nose, a wide expressive mouth. He smiled.

She said, 'And here is poor St Paul's, Dr Wren, which looks in need of even stronger pillars.'

Wren laughed, swept off his hat, bowed. 'Indeed!'

'I see my wife's reputation precedes me,' the dean said dryly. 'It is rare that both strength and wit are found in a woman.'

'They are the most underrated half of the population, sir. Now, my old friend Mr Evelyn you already know.' Wren's introductions cooled slightly. 'Francis Chicheley, Sir Roger Pratt . . .'

364

Elizabeth bent as John whispered to her. 'Dr Wren wishes my support against the ideas of those two. That is why he waited. Our miracle of youth wants to make his reputation. He is a determined fellow and will have his way by one means or another.'

She murmured, 'That makes two of you.'

He chuckled, squeezed her hand, bowed to the bishop, and they walked between the huge iron gates into the cathedral.

'Look at this!' Wren talked excitedly. 'What a mixture of styles! Inigo Jones papering over the Norman portico with Classic stonework. Corinthian columns – Renaissance doorways, stone balls on the pilasters. Ghastly, ghastly frightful work. But here is some Gothic.'

'Crumbling,' Evelyn said.

'Once St Paul's was brilliant with chantry altars,' Wren said. 'Gone. All this stone is black with filth.'

'It even smells rotten,' Elizabeth said.

'Indeed, Mrs Barwick.' He stared up. 'Observe how the walls recede outwards at the top. Six inches at least.'

'Built that way *ab origine*,' Chicheley said.

'For an effect of perspective,' said Pratt.

'I am of quite another judgement!' exclaimed Wren. 'Let us plumb them to establish the straightness of the matter.'

'I agree,' Evelyn said, writing the decision down.

They stood in the crossing peering up at the tower.

'The pillars are shifted,' Pratt said.

'The whole foundation is shifted!' Wren said. 'A new foundation is required. And instead of a spire, I suggest a cupola.'

The bishop said, 'What?'

'A dome.'

'Is that not rather Roman, Dr Wren?'

'I see it as a domed rotunda in the Renaissance style. Covered with copper, crowned with a lantern.'

'I do not recall anything else like it in this country.'

By now Elizabeth recognised Wren's smile. 'Exactly, my lord,' he smiled.

'How exciting!' she said.

Wren left the dean talking with the bishop, seized her elbow. 'You see these columns? Eleven feet in diameter, but they are worthless, filled with crushed stone and rubbish too fine to take the weight. That's why they have settled, and I will alter . . .' They went up the steps past the black marble pillars into the choir. 'Now look at this. Gothic. Original work, thirteenth century, laid on plain solid Norman workmanship. Beautiful. These columns haven't settled at all.'

Elizabeth said, 'They are hollow.'

He turned sharply. 'What?'

She murmured, 'It is only a legend.'

He stared at her. 'I need do no work in here, anyway.' He looked up at the statue of John Donne. 'Here is your husband's predecessor as dean, one of our greatest poets. *Twice or thrice had I loved thee before I knew your face or name—*'

She murmured, '*So in a voice, so in a shapeless flame—*'

'*Angels affect us oft, and worshipped be.*' Chris Wren cleared his throat, looked away from her.

She complimented him, 'For a scientist you are a romantic, Dr Wren. I had thought you gentlemen of reason believed geometry and arithmetic to be the only truths.'

'Truth can only be discovered with certainty by mathematical demonstration, yes.'

'If it does not add up, it cannot be true?'

'I am merely educated in music, Latin, geometry, mathematics, astronomy, and architecture. You have me at a disadvantage, Mrs Barwick.'

She laughed. Then he laughed too, following her.

She walked beneath the statue of Algar and touched its foot, blackened and smoothed by generations of tailors taking their standard measurements from its heel to toe, the English foot. Wren pointed. 'There are the tombs of King Sebba and King Ethelred. What is that door in the wall?'

'There was once a library up there, above the side aisle. It leads nowhere now.'

'You know St Paul's well.'

'Perhaps. It has been my neighbour all my life.'

He looked at her seriously.

'I begin to see I have much to learn, Mrs Barwick.'

She turned, hearing a call. 'Excuse me, Dr Wren. My husband is waiting.'

The heat of the night woke the dean. His wife stood at the open window of the deanery bedroom, the wind blowing her white linen nightclothes round her, fluttering the unbound black wing of her hair. Elizabeth was so beautiful, youth itself, that he longed to touch her, become part of her, make himself young again for her. His spirit burned with an old man's ardour, but his flesh hung limp as vanilla pudding.

He called in a low voice, 'Can you not sleep, wife?'

'I did not mean to wake you, John. I think it is your papist plot.' She threw the leaded window wide and the east wind pushed into the room, sent his papers whirling from the desk by his bed. 'A fire by the Tower of London.'

'Fire? The papists are killed, it cannot be fire. Are there Dutch ships on the river? Nobody warms their house-fire on such a hot night. What hour is it? It cannot be a breakfast-fire—'

'No, it's three in the morning, by St Paul's.' Between the dark bulk of the cathedral standing above her, and the dark abyss of the river winding below her, he glimpsed flames gleaming in the distance. A comet hung like a feather in the eastern sky above the shimmering line.

'It's nothing, wife. I mean Liza. It's the Lord's Day. Come back to bed.'

She murmured, remembering her previous life, before her marriage to the great man. 'Poor people are only just in their beds, in their deepest sleep. I know how they live, John. I am one of them. Saturday is the end of our week's labour, the day of receipts, payments. The markets stay open long after dark for us, and on Sunday morning men lie late with their wives and their children are conceived—'

He drew back. The sudden aching desire he heard in her voice shrivelled him instantly. To physically desire a woman was part of a man's nature, however tiresome it was, but to be physically desired by her was a form of tyranny. His wife's need oppressed him. He snatched his papers, turned over away from her. 'Close the window!' he muttered. 'Go to sleep.'

She knelt beside him on his bed. She was watching him, he could feel the heat of her gaze. She was young and she wanted children. Her sister at the Lydiard had four children, one baby, and another on the way.

Elizabeth lay behind him, kissed the back of his head, wrapped him gently in her arms, and eventually slept.

The dean lay awake. Moisture trickled from his left eye, which always wept since his apoplexy. He stopped his prayers and tried to imagine himself young again, the youth he had given away for service of the Church. Many men worshipped the sexual act like an idol, but he had missed all that and now it was too late, he had not acquired the habit. But he had drunk a jar of water before bed and now the urge to urinate stiffened his desire. He turned awkwardly against his wife's warm enfolding body. She took him effortlessly and undemandingly in her sleep and he uttered low cries, thinking he would die, as his body shuddered with such love for her that he felt his soul rush out of him into her.

He lay exhausted and victorious beside her passive body. She murmured, pulling him to her breast, and he shrank away ashamed of himself.

Very faintly, orange glows flickered on the ceiling.

At breakfast the dean's servant Tom assured them the fire was under control, and Dutchmen, Frenchmen, and anyone heard with a foreign accent near the fire was arrested. The dean took his seat in his private stall in the choir of St Paul's as usual, but when Elizabeth left the cathedral later she saw the fire burning down Cornhill to London Bridge, spreading perhaps halfway towards her along the waterfront. The river wall of London was long gone, replaced by wooden wharves and warehouses, and a thick haze of smoke gusted across the steeply pitched rooftops below her. A cart rumbled beneath the storeys and attics overhanging the road and someone cried out that three hundred houses were burnt. A sick woman was carried by in her bed. A man saw Elizabeth and snorted the smoke with his hairy nostrils. 'Do you smell it, madam? That is the smell of a Popish plot, hatched in the same place where the Gunpowder Plot to blow up Parliament was contrived!' Men ran by with ladders, and he lumbered after them.

The dean came outside. She exclaimed, 'Will our cathedral be safe?'

He looked amazed by her emotional outburst. 'Of course. St Paul's is made of stone. Stone does not burn.'

Dr Wren came limping from Carter Street. 'It is an easterly wind, Mrs Barwick, and an easterly is rare. More like than not it will veer westerly, push the fire back on itself and save us.'

She heard a child crying and said furiously, 'Is that your mathematical conclusion, Dr Wren?'

'I conceive it is the statistical probability.'

'Can you assure then these poor people that their homes are safe?'

'No, Mrs Barwick. No. You show me that I know nothing. I believe it is a serious fire. But it is not a papist plot.'

'Some say,' the dean said sharply, 'that you would say that. Your High Church, not to say Roman sympathies—'

Elizabeth said, 'John!'

'I believe the fire started by accident, Mrs Barwick, at a baker's near London Bridge.' Wren was always watchful. He smiled with very white-seeming teeth, seeing her observe his blackened sooty face and clothes holed by sparks, saw her realise how tired he was. 'I advised that the conflagration be halted by clearing the streets running north from the Dowgate,' he confided wearily to her, 'and then contained south of Watling Street. But the roads are crammed full of people and carts and household goods, and the fire jumps across them all. First the streets must be cleared by the City militia. But the people will not go.'

'London is always on fire,' the dean said firmly, holding on to his hat as the wind gusted. 'This is no different.'

Elizabeth turned her ear to the wind. 'What is that terrible sound? It is not birds and animals burning?'

Wren said, 'It is the screaming of people dragged away from their houses and all they possess for their own safety, dreadful to hear even at this distance. They run back despite armed men, run into their burning homes and carry away what little they can . . .'

The dean said confidently, 'Dr Wren will stop the fire.'

'That is up to the Lord Mayor,' Wren said. 'He will not allow the use of gunpowder to clear fire-breaks, fears the powder falling into the hands of papists. He is an exhausted man. He fights the burning

City with buckets of water and would pull houses down with hooks – but he cannot, for there is a law among the citizens that whoever pulls down a house must rebuild it. So an order must come from the king and council . . .'

'I shall pray,' John said. 'God shall save us.'

'Stone shall save you,' Wren said. 'The cathedral walls are five feet thick, surrounded by the broad gravel of the precinct. I must go back to the fire.'

The dean returned to worship. Elizabeth called, 'Dr Wren?' She ran after him. 'This happens so quickly I can hardly understand it. Where will the fire stop? Where is safe for the homeless people? Inside the cathedral?'

He rubbed his face, making a complete sooty mess of his countenance, out of which his eyes stood brightly. He gazed back past St Paul's, the smoke blowing past him over the City wall towards the Strand, the vast ramshackle pile of Whitehall Palace, and Westminster, to the market gardens of Eia.

'Chiswick,' he said. 'You are safe in Chiswick, Mrs Barwick.'

'You mock me. Do I look the sort to run away?'

He looked at her steadily. 'I am afraid,' he said. 'Perhaps you should run, Mrs Barwick. Everything is chaos. Did you see the comet rise this morning, and the Sun rise beneath it? And late this afternoon the Moon rises as if in counterbalance to the Sun.'

She murmured, 'You understand the Moon and the Sun?'

Someone ran to Wren shouting. Voices babbled to him for help everywhere, and Elizabeth was left standing alone. She returned to the cathedral, and suffered through her husband's plain, orderly, sonorous Anglican celebration of the Lord's Day.

That evening she stood at her window. Night fell like day, white and yellow with fire. The east of the City was fire and smoke. Flames a mile away at London Bridge leapt along the warehouses by the red river, sending stores of tar and brandy rising like fireworks into the smoke. 'The river looks like blood,' she murmured. The mudbanks moved, so many people huddled across them to reach ships and barges, and one lighter burned at its moorings like a candle. 'John, the fire has reached Queenhithe,' she said. 'No one is asleep tonight.' She covered her ears.

She must have slept a little. John shook her and Elizabeth sat up in an armchair. She saw it was day. 'I have unlocked the crypt,' he said. He looked terrified. 'I have given permission for the booksellers of Paternoster Row to hide their books in safety from looters and the fire, if it gets this far. The doors are strengthened, the windows sealed. This cannot be happening.' He went off, and she hurried after him.

Outside, everything had changed. The streets leading to the cathedral were packed solid with refugees, herds of people pushing forward in shock and misery, carts piled high stuck or slipping backward. A wheelbarrow overturned and disappeared under the mass pressing forward, pushed from behind. Everyone was losing someone or something, everyone cried out names and news. Elizabeth seized a child and carried it to its mother. An old man and an old woman embraced as though they had not seen one another for years. The cathedral doors were thrown open and all day carts were pushed along the nave, bundles piled up, furniture, everything that could be carried or dragged, children, dogs, bolts of silk, beds, rope, boxes of money, silver candlesticks, carpets, chests and trunks, a broken door, a pile of dresses, a turner's lathe, a basket of puppies yapping excitedly, a box of shoes, a black and white cow, Elizabeth saw them all brought into the safety of St Paul's Cathedral. A boy stood by the door picking his nose and his mother slapped him then burst into tears, hugged him tight.

Someone called out, 'Cornhill is burnt. The churches are burning. The fire rages all along the waterfront from the Tower of London to Baynard's Castle. God save us all.'

'Baynard's Castle,' a woman shouted, 'that's almost here.' No one could see the castle, the day was so black with smoke pouring over the cathedral from Cheapside. A soldier came by as darkness fell. 'Fire's everywhere from St Paul's south to the river, spreading up. To the east ten thousand houses are burning in Cheapside, spreading down. Fire's coming both ways.'

Elizabeth brushed a spark from her dress. 'The wind will change. It will blow the fire back on its ashes.'

'Fire don't listen to prayers!' The man laughed. 'Fire makes it own weather. Pulls air in from every side to feed itself, backs against the Tower of London in the east, jumps London Wall in the west.'

A gentleman with burnt hair ran into the cathedral. 'They pay a shilling to any man who stays to fight the fire tonight.'

A few tired men stood, kissed their wives goodbye, and followed him. 'Is it night?' someone asked. Elizabeth went into the churchyard, a mass of exhausted refugees lying down around her, heads, shoulders coloured like skinned flesh, the fire coming up from Cheapside laying its glare over them. They tried to move into the shadow of the cathedral, but the shadow swung round as the fire spread along Paternoster Row. Some brave householders and their wives stood up to watch their houses burn. Many more would not leave their homes until the roofs were burning over their heads, then fled into the churchyard and threw themselves down like the dead.

A voice called out, 'Anyone want a cart to save their stuff, I'll sell them an empty cart for thirty pounds in silver, coin only.' Someone cried, 'Done!' As the fire raged closer people began staggering down to Ludgate but it was burning, flames leaping the Fleet river. They beat a path through the embers of Baynard's and Montfichet Castle. Elizabeth returned to the deanery, found Tom the servant busy packing up anything of use, burying it in the knot garden. 'Beg my pardon, Mrs,' he said, filling in the hole, 'but my own wife and children . . .'

'Off you go, Tom. There's a barrow in the shed.'

'Thank'ee, Mrs, I already got it.' All he owned of value was his wife's bed, and he put it across the barrow, laid his young children on top. Elizabeth went indoors, dropped her elbows on the kitchen table, and fell forward into an exhausted sleep.

The dean woke her. The day was dark with smoke. John had conquered his fear and confusion, and he was growing angry. 'What are you doing here, Liza?' he shouted over the roar of the fire. 'In Christ's name, I thought you safe at least!'

The crisis was bringing out the best in him, banishing the lines from his face. 'I don't want to be safe,' she said fiercely. 'I want to be with you.' He clasped her and she said, 'You smell of smoke.'

'London is smoke – the Guildhall is burning – the great statues of Gog and Magog are burnt—' He looked round as the deanery shook to thudding explosions. 'They are using gunpowder at last. I pray for the poor people, everything is consumed by fire. The streets and lanes and alleys are gone. How will anyone know where they once lived when this is finished?'

Elizabeth murmured, 'Fire and blood, the torrents of Satan. And the fiery flames shall eat up the foundations of the earth.'

'Wife? I beg your pardon?'

Elizabeth looked over his shoulder. She stared in horror through the window. St Paul's was not burning, but the stone tower was wreathed in flame from the wooden scaffolding surrounding it.

'John!' She ran outside after her husband, stood beside him in the garden. She took his hand, held him back. 'There's nothing you can do, John.'

There was no water, the fire could not be fought. Teams of firefighters could not even get to the cathedral, the roads blocked by falling houses and flames. John dropped to his knees in prayer to God, his raised hands shadowing his face. As Elizabeth watched the fire take hold she gripped his shoulder so tight he squirmed. Watching the death of the cathedral, she was afraid her husband would die.

All through the afternoon she watched the fire spread downward and along the roofs of the cathedral. The lead melted, poured fire down the walls. The windows burst. Night darkened the distance but the shell of St Paul's burned too bright to look near. The oak roof-beams shimmered above it like a burning cage, then the beams and timbers and vaults fell inwards like thunder.

'My God. All the people. Look at all the people.'

It was one morning after the fire. Elizabeth watched survivors wandering in the ruins. 'Where is everything?' she asked. Only one corner of the deanery remained. Tom was busy digging the dean's silver out of the garden. The sound of his spade was very small.

She recognised the boy who had picked his nose. His mother was alive, he said, though she had lost everything she had. 'Except me,' he added cheerfully, still picking his nose.

'London is gone,' the dean called hoarsely. 'St Paul's is gone.'

Elizabeth helped him climb a heap of rubble, part of the fallen tower-vaulting of the cathedral, five thousand tons of stone split and exploded by intense heat. The roofless pillars stood like rows of huge white legs, holding up nothing. The shell of the great tower was like a gutted torso crouched on widespread feet, held up by its ancient buttresses. Six days, perhaps a week had passed since the height of the fire, but she felt the warmth still glowing uncomfortably through her thick shoes. She held her husband's elbow and they looked round them in silence.

London within the Roman walls was smooth ash and rubble. A jumble of old timber houses and narrow streets huddled in the north-east, saved by the wind. The Tower of London stood alone, steel-grey, the houses round it blown to pieces by gunpowder. The City's north wall had held the fire from Moorfields, but the flames had jumped the western wall and Fleet Street was a black tongue of destruction. A living, rippling serpent of human misery ringed the City, tents, huts, carts, upturned barrows, scraps of sail where two hundred thousand people or more scrabbled for shelter. A few brave souls ventured in to forage for what they had lost, but the streets and landmarks of the City had disappeared. Destitute families scrambled among piles of ash and embers and smoke billowing from cellars still burning, trying to find where they had lived. Someone shouted that a hundred churches were burnt, but someone else cried out it was only eighty-nine. The spires of the City were flattened and a wasteland remained. Elizabeth could not imagine how London would ever be rebuilt. The king must make Oxford or Winchester his capital city, and perhaps in a hundred years grass would begin to grow where the City had been, and peasants would Cry the Neck for Osiris where St Paul's once stood.

The dean pointed. 'I believe we can save the west end of the nave and the portico of my cathedral, wife. Look, something remains of the roof . . .' His enthusiasm grew, even the left side of his mouth lifted in a smile, as though bringing part of himself back to life together with his hope for St Paul's. 'We could use the end of the nave as a choir, with an altar and pulpit—'

She saw Dr Wren and waved. 'We're glad to see you safe, sir,' she called. Something about him always made her want to set him straight. 'And I see you have washed your face.' He grinned, left the man he was speaking with and climbed up to them. But then he did not look at her, only her husband.

'Dean Barwick,' he bowed seriously.

'Look, Wren,' the dean said. He swept out his stick to show the desolation around them. 'A terrible tragedy.'

'A tragedy but also an opportunity,' Wren said.

'Opportunity!' The dean pointed his stick at the portico. 'Perhaps you're right. In fact I was just saying to my wife, perhaps we might recover the west end, eh?'

Wren dug the toe of his shiny shoe into the mound of plaster and dust, strangely delicate in his action, then flicked the toecap clean with a flourish of his kerchief.

'Old St Paul's is finished,' he said flatly. 'It's gone.'

'No, no.'

Wren folded the kerchief into his pocket, jumped nimbly down. The dean gripped Elizabeth's wrist tight and she helped him over the stones. Wren turned by the row of massive headless pillars, each eighty feet high and white as snow, that remained of the nave. He touched one and the surface crumbled. 'We call this calcination. The heat has turned the Caen stone to chalk. Ornaments, friezes, capitals, pinnacles, all are but chalkdust set in the image of their former selves.' He touched a flaking shell of wall. 'The same here. Exploded by the heat. Mind your head – the stone tracery may fall from the window—'

The small party stepped cautiously forward among the beads of stained glass like jewels. Wren led them up the steps of the pulpitum, where a vast tangle of vaulted roof lay crashed into the choir. 'The choir pavement is gone,' he said at once, 'broken down into the crypt. They say a hundred and fifty thousand pounds' worth of books are burnt, and a hundred booksellers ruined. Priceless knowledge lost. It makes my heart ache. They have found charred papers blown as far as Windsor.' Elizabeth felt the heat radiate on her hands and face as he led them round the side. The coffin of a bishop buried in the floor had burst open and spilled him out, red-haired and so dry that the body stood stiff as a plank.

'That's de Braybroke,' the dean said. 'Three hundred years old, by good God.'

They stared into the exposed crypt. Wren said, 'Because of the raised choir, the crypt and St Faith's Church beneath the cathedral are only four feet below ground level.' A fire still burnt down there and he snatched a piece of paper fluttering up, examined it. 'Palladio's *I Quattro Libri dell' Architettura*! I have a copy of the Venetian edition.'

The dean said, 'Four books from St Paul's library survived the fire. Uncounted thousands gone. And the catalogue burnt, so no one even knows how much we have lost.' The two men moved on, talking. Another page of paper flew from the fire and Elizabeth caught it. She read, *The Gospel Witness According to St Simon the Zealot*. She crumpled it in her hand.

'What is it, Mrs Barwick?' Wren called.

'Nothing.' Both men stared at her, so she smiled. 'I was thinking, at least the fire has solved one problem, John. You need worry about Mayor Bludworth's throne no longer.'

John spoke to Wren in a low voice. 'They are creatures of strange emotion. I never know what she will come out with.'

A workman arrived and shovelled matted papers, so tightly packed that they were preserved from the fire, into a barrow. Elizabeth followed the dean and the astronomer to the north side of the choir. Only two statues in their niches had survived the fall of the roof, Donne the poet-dean in his marble shroud, and Algar the prebendary with one of his sandalled feet broken off. Wren examined her face curiously. 'Mrs Barwick? You remain utterly pale. Are you sure you did not hurt your hand?'

'I am sad for all the books that are lost. Who knows what had made its way into the inventories of booksellers?'

'There is to be a commission for the rebuilding of London,' the dean was saying, and Wren had to turn away from her, paying attention to his prospective employer. 'A choir is essential as soon as possible, and I shall ask them, Dr Wren, to order a temporary choir containing pulpit and altar at the west end.' Wren glanced at Elizabeth, then at her clenched hand. The dean continued, 'We shall decide what to do with – all this'– he stared round the vast ruin in despair – 'later.' He tapped his stick, invigorated by his decision. As always it was doubt that had taken the greatest toll on John Barwick's energy, and he looked like a man made ten years younger. 'London must have a place for worship.'

Wren said, 'Sir, I had hoped for more—'

'The income of the entire City of London is twelve thousand pounds a year, Dr Wren. A new St Paul's would alone cost ten times that amount. It is impossible. The Commission for London is dwarfed by its responsibilities and regulations—'

Wren raised his voice. 'Sir, I have already entered the competition for the planning of the new City, and I assure you—'

'It will take two hundred years for London to recover. Trade must first come back – if it ever does—'

'Sir, whatever the final plan, broad new streets are to be driven through the rubble, water conduits laid, cesspits dug, brickpits quarried – London is built on brickearth – brick kilns set up, bricklayers trained, at least thirteen thousand houses built in the first instance. The churches will be rebuilt better, more beautiful than before. They will, sir. The king is determined and will raise taxes to do it.'

'I shall not see a new St Paul's raised in my lifetime,' the dean said. 'You will repair the present nave.'

'Sir, even that small work will cost three thousand pounds or more.'

Elizabeth knew her husband would be stubborn now he had set on his plan. He wanted a place he would live to see. 'Dr Wren, God has left us a holy place to assemble in that we may acknowledge His miraculous mercy.'

Wren did something amazing. He turned to Elizabeth. 'What do *you* think, Mrs Barwick?'

There was only one answer she could give. 'I think what my husband thinks, Dr Wren. I am his flesh and his shadow.'

He bowed. 'Of course you are quite right, Mrs Barwick.'

John laughed. 'She always is, my dear Wren! She always is!' He put his arm round Wren's shoulder. 'Then the matter is settled. A new choir to be made of the portico and west end of the nave, so that in spite of Puritans on the one side and papists on the other, we may re-establish the services and moderation of our Church of England in these difficult times as soon and as visibly as humanly possible.'

It was midnight and Elizabeth stood at her bedroom window. Down Lud's Hill the broad ribbon of the Thames gleamed below her, silvery with the three-quarter moon setting towards the south-west.

'Wife? Liza?'

'I thought I heard something,' she murmured. 'I could not sleep.'

John sat up. 'I remember last time. You frighten me when you are awake. Not another papist plot?'

The moon was in Capricorn, she saw. Inclined among the twinkling stars the planets Jupiter and Uranus shone steadily at an angle above the moon, Neptune and Saturn below. Together the five celestial objects, two planets on each side balanced by the moon in the centre, drew a perfectly straight line across the heavens, a conjunction.

'No, John,' she said. 'Not another papist plot.'

'Are you looking at the sky?'

She span on her heel in exactly the opposite direction, looking past the ruin of St Paul's, its walls blue, shimmering with frozen streams of roof-lead in the moonlight. The comet had yet to rise in the north-east.

She remembered, *Did you see the comet rise this morning, Mrs Barwick? And the Sun rise beneath it? And the Moon rises as if in counterbalance to the Sun* . . .

'What do you see, wife?'

She said emptily, 'I don't know what I see.'

'Why are you so unhappy? Is it because of me?'

She went to him quickly, stroked his dry hands on the bedspread. 'No. It is not you, John. I owe everything to you. You have made me what I am. You are the perfect husband.'

He touched her fingers to his lips. 'You are very kind.'

She looked round as the sound came again. In the moonlight blue dust showered from the top of one of the columns of St Paul's. Stones fell. The column, third from the left in the arcade closest to her, began to lean almost imperceptibly, like a trick of her eye. Then the column gently toppled, breaking in the middle, blowing dust upward, and a massive roaring sound echoed to them as it dropped into a billowing cloud of debris.

They watched the dust settle, blow slowly away on the wind.

'Well, John,' Elizabeth said, 'there goes your choir.'

He whispered numbly, 'It all but by the grace of God fell on the others, knocked them forward like a row of dominoes. They could fall at any moment, I see that now. Dr Wren was right.'

She took pen and paper into the moonlight slanting from the window. 'What shall I write?'

'Write?'

'Dr Wren returned to Oxford . . .' she paused as a clock chimed the quarter-hour past midnight, 'yesterday afternoon.'

John stared out. 'We can proceed no further at the west end, that is certain.'

'To Dr Christopher Wren, Savilian Professor of Astronomy, Oxford—' Elizabeth wrote busily. 'Sir, it is the opinion of all men that we can proceed no further at the west end. What we are to do next is our present deliberation. We can do nothing, resolve on nothing, without you. You will think fit, I trust, to bring with you those excellent drafts and designs you formerly favoured us with. I am, sir, your affectionate John Barwick, Dean of St Paul's.'

The dean sat quietly.

'Yes, dear,' he said. 'That's exactly what I wanted to say. The same as it was before.'

It was winter and Elizabeth blew on her cold hands. She pushed past the bricklayers repairing the deanery with new red bricks and yellow stone, lifted her dress, and jumped the low walls and frosty shrubbery of the knot garden, going her own way rather than follow the muddy path used by the workmen. She strode uphill through New London's teeming confusion.

A whole new City was being invented around her. Old Bower Row, blocked for months by the timber and plaster of fallen houses, had finally been cleared, repaved broader than before, and renamed Ludgate Hill. Most of the minor streets were still blocked, passable only on foot, but along the main thoroughfare empty carts rattled past her towards the summit of Lud's Hill. Heaped full of rubble from the ruined cathedral to pave the new boulevards of London, they returned downhill swaying over bent axles, cruelly overloaded. She dodged aside as mud spurted. Accidents and runaways were commonplace, but anyone with an old cart and a nag made enough money to rebuild their own house, and in the evening the taverns were packed with bricklayers splashing their money, all of them granted the same liberties as freemen of the City.

The precinct wall twice as high as a man, that all Elizabeth's life had kept St Paul's private from the streets around it, was demolished. Without it the hilltop looked strangely bare, the cathedral ruin vast and sad. A royal warrant had been issued for the demolition of the east end, the old choir and the central tower. She saw Dr Wren walking on the steps beneath the great remnant of the portico. Workmen broke the fallen statuary around him with sledgehammers and shovelled the fragments into wheelbarrows. Wren looked small and lonely, a living, vulnerable figure. She watched his colourful clothes threading among the huge toppled heads and hands of the monarchs of England from the days of King Athelbert and King Sabert.

She waved and he waved back, then folded his arms and politely ignored her ankles as she lifted the hem of her dress over the stones.

'Mrs Barwick,' he greeted her so seriously that she laughed.

'Good day, Dr Wren!'

He looked startled, as though already the meeting had not gone as he planned. 'Madam, whatever do I say that is so amusing?'

'It is the way you say my name. As though you are sad to see me.'

'On the contrary—' he started politely, obscuring himself with good manners.

'Surely you have dealt with one of my gender before, Dr Wren? My husband tells me you were elected to your chair of astronomy at the age of twenty-five, and you know everything of architecture, and you assure me that music and philosophy have no secrets from you, and yet you blush—'

'I do not blush.' He pressed his hands to his cheeks.

'Now I have offended you.' She smiled. 'You do—'

'I am not!'

'You are not one of these boring stones after all.'

He said earnestly, 'I have never said I was.'

She shrugged. 'Then do not ignore me. You do not have to play so serious simply because I am alive and thus beneath your notice.'

'I am not sad to see you, I do not ignore you, I do not play serious, and I do not blush, Mrs Barwick.'

'Elizabeth Barwick. Where I come from it is not improper to acknowledge first names.'

He chuckled because she got her way. 'You are an indomitable woman. Let us start again, Elizabeth Barwick—'

She said quickly, 'Only my husband calls me Liza.'

'I did not call you Liza.' He coloured.

She murmured, 'You *are* happier with buildings than people, aren't you? You are too honest, Christopher Wren. I believe during the fire I saw you forget your shyness. You were happy. These huge schemes make you happy. A whole new City to build, broad new streets laid to your plan. They say you will receive commissions to build more churches than anyone else, even Sir Roger Pratt.' She curtseyed. 'I shall go away now, and leave you alone to your happiness. I came merely to bring this letter from my husband.' She took it from her sleeve and held it out.

He took it, then called her back. 'Mrs Barwick, you are right about me, of course. A little.'

'Only a little?'

He broke the seal of the letter, but then did not unfold the page. For the first time he looked directly in her eye. 'I am sure you can save me the trouble of reading its contents.'

'My dear doctor,' she recited breezily from memory, 'I beg you shall visit me that we may prepare some detailed plan of new St Paul's to be proposed to his majesty, starting with the design of the choir on or near the old foundations. This will be the first part of a greater and more magnificent work to follow in stages. I am resolved to frame upon a handsome and noble building suitable to the reputation of the City and the nation, and to take it for granted that money is found to accomplish it. Your affectionate, etcetera, John Barwick, Dean of St Paul's.'

He watched her admiringly. 'Your husband is a man of great will and character. *Take it for granted that money is found*. That has an indomitable sound.'

'Neither my husband nor I can imagine London without St Paul's.'

He sighed. 'So I am to work split in two between the clergy's instructions and the government's money.'

'They say London Bridge was built on wool.'

He stared at her. 'A bridge cannot be built on wool. It is not structurally—'

'The wool tax. New St Paul's will be built on coal. A tax of a shilling a ton, I hear.' She stood beside him on the step. An amazing smoky shanty city was growing out of the ashes of the City below them. Tents gave way to huts, huts to rows of ramshackle tenements, and fine buildings already stood out bright and clean in various stages of completion along wide new roads. Thatch roofs had been banned in the City for three hundred years, and now wooden dwellings were also prohibited, replaced by planning regulations, brick and stone. 'We are building a City of Reason, Liza.' Wren did not notice his mistake in her name. He pointed across the Walbrook valley towards Cornhill, he could not hide his enthusiasm. 'Under the Rebuilding Act, no houses are taller than four floors, all by main roads to have gutters and drainpipes and uniform tile roofs, more streets to be opened, lanes to be not less than fourteen feet wide—'

She did not take her eyes off his face, listening to him. 'Unfortunately your City of Reason will have people in it.' Something thudded heavily among the ruins. She asked, 'What's that noise?'

'It is a battering ram.' He ran up the steps to see how work progressed, remembered her, ran back to her and doffed his hat. Elizabeth put her hand on his forearm and he escorted her up the steps. Men hurried round them under the gigantic ruins of the nave, tiny figures clambered with sledgehammers on top of the crumbling masonry. Orders were shouted. Thirty sweating labourers, their breath hanging over them like fog, thudded a tree trunk into a wall. The stones shook but did not fall. 'Where lead and glass have melted and run down the walls,' Wren muttered, 'they are made almost impenetrable.'

'Look,' she whispered, kneeling. For five hundred years boys and agile young men had paid a penny to climb the tower of Old St Paul's, and carved their names on the leads despite the objections of the Dean and Chapter. Generations of initials, Christian names, hearts and arrows, thousands of tiny desecrations, had been carried down locked in the surface of the molten lead, a river of human lives all forgotten but for this.

Wren leant close to her. 'I know none of these names. Silly scribblings should not be allowed on a sacred building. Matthew Parris. Tom Golden. Solomon. A hundred Toms and Johns and Williams. Agnes inscribed over Eleanor. So many of them.'

'Do they not make you feel sad, and small, and humble?'

He stepped back. 'We shall have to use the gunpowder to knock it down.'

They walked forward between the columns, the sun flickering between them. The shouts of the men faded. She said, 'So you will knock down Old St Paul's—'

'I have carted out ten thousand loads of old stone already. I shall take ninety thousand cartloads more.'

She patted his hand. 'But what St Paul's will you build in its place?'

'Ah.' He glanced at her. 'Everyone has a different opinion. I am having a model made.'

'Mr Cleere's wooden model?'

'I should have known we have no secrets from you. Yes, Mr Cleere is my carver.'

'The dean has already paid him two hundred pounds for his work.'

'You know everything.'

'Is the model the building you would really like to see? It is not very grand.'

He said, 'A model is a model, but a building is a building.'

'I understand you perfectly.'

'I am pushed and pulled in every direction. I have the king's wishes to consider. And your husband. And his grace the bishop. And the great architect Sir Roger Pratt, who because he has travelled in Italy thinks he knows more than I do, and swears the model's nave is too narrow, too gloomy, the number of windows wrong, and he dislikes the dome at the west end—'

'But there's one person you have not mentioned.'

He bowed in deference to her.

'No,' she laughed, 'I do not matter. You have not mentioned yourself. What do *you* believe, Dr Wren?'

He looked cautious. Finally he said, 'I? Believe?'

She tucked her arm in his, pulled him from the flickering sunlight into the vast shadow of the tower. They stared up inside its gutted shell, the square of empty blue sky at the top where the roof had been. She said, 'A building reflects its architect, does it not? If an architect believes nothing, his building is nothing. God made Man in His image, after all.'

'Then I must be narrow, gloomy, unable to count, and lacking even the sense to place a dome in its proper setting!'

She let his anger settle. 'Whisper it to me.'

'What?'

'Your secret plan.'

He whispered. 'Imagine a building of good proportions. Beautiful. With porticoes, and two towers. And a dome on the hilltop conspicuous above the houses.'

'I can see it in my mind's eye.'

He took a piece of charred timber, scored quickly on the wall. Elizabeth stared as a cruciform building and porticoes surmounted with a huge dome took shape under the swift, sure strokes of Wren's small hand.

'That is what I believe.'

It was her husband's invariable rule that he sit in the dean's comfortable horsehair armchair to the right of the fireplace, and that his wife sit facing him from her slightly smaller, more upright patterned chair to the left side of the fireplace. This social arrangement had been traditional, John informed Elizabeth as she helped him into his chair, at least since the creation of the Church of England.

Dean John Barwick in the shadow of his seventieth year was a stickler for tradition.

Did he not realise how many hours he spent sitting in that chair, expecting his young wife to sit faithfully opposite him like an old woman?

He was a stickler for organisation and routine, too. That there was no cathedral left the cathedral's way of life entirely unaffected. The ancient rights and privileges of the Greater Chapter and all the interlocking lesser bodies of St Paul's sailed forward like a great ship, entirely disregarding the loss of the reason for their existence.

Elizabeth gave herself something to do. She was her husband's eyes, his ears, his hands. She supported him like his stick, but she was invisible. One evening she looked up and saw his gaze fixed on her in the firelight.

He said gruffly, 'You're a good wife. A good choice.'

He was so proud of her.

The airy rooms of the convocation house had escaped the fire with only minor damage, and in summer services overflowed into the garden. Elizabeth sat behind the open window, keeping out of the sun, listening to the drone of voices outside. She wrote out John's order to Dr Wren to build new cottages at Amen Corner, housing the cathedral's three residentiary canons. The cathedral's hierarchy was almost infinitely complex. Twelve minor canons, including a warden and two cardinals of the choir, all with their duties and pride, fought like tigers to preach as little as possible yet keep their privileges, benefices and free dinners. Twenty-six absentee prebendaries drew thousands of pounds a year from the cathedral and preached hardly at all. The Dean of St Paul's was also responsible for the sub-dean, the succentor, the sacrist, the receiver, the almoner with eight choirboys from St Paul's School, a crowd of virgers and the three great dignities of treasurer, precentor and chancellor, all under the chapter and the final authority of the bishop as Visitor. And below these important people lay uncounted others.

The rules, tradition, titles and immunities of St Paul's, even in its desolation, were a deliberately impenetrable tangle.

A strong dean was a powerful man.

As always matins and evensong were sung by St Paul's six vicars choral, no longer in holy orders as in ancient times, now constantly irritating John with their modish laziness and bad manners. After Sunday matins, holy communion was celebrated in the convocation house garden, and the seats in shelter – on such a hot day, those in shadow – were jealously allocated, for a fee, by the dean's virger.

John sat watchfully in his stall on the balcony. From time to time he whispered behind his prayer book to Elizabeth. 'Write this. Item, procession very disorderly.' She wrote carefully in the notebook on her knee, knowing that the matter would be raised later with the hapless individuals concerned. 'First comes one vicar choral, then minor canons with four vicars choral in the middle of them, now here another trails after the procession. Who is he?'

Elizabeth saw. 'That's little Mr Manning.' She hid her smile. 'He looks like a sheepdog snapping at their heels.'

'It's not amusing. Item, one minor canon, Mr Snorrey, knelt during absolution.'

Elizabeth wrote, 'Knelt during absolution.'

'The viol was played so execrably that it produced a harsh discord and gave my ear exquisite pain.'

She wrote, 'Exquisite pain.'

'And Mr Ditchley went round the other way.'

'Went the other way.'

He stared at her. 'Whatever have you done to your hair?'

She touched the white locks twisted artfully among her black curls. 'It's fashionable.'

'Not in the dean's wife it isn't,' he said. At the end of the service she helped him up, and together they returned to the deanery. He would be entertained to supper at Amen Corner, but first he must have his nap. She helped him into his armchair, put the rug she had embroidered across his knees, placed his wig on the wooden bust behind him, pulled the white locks out of her hair and threw them in the corner, and sat opposite him clicking her needles loudly.

'I do not care for your friend Dr Wren's desire for a dome,' he said suddenly. 'It is merely a Romish affectation on an English church. A spire was good enough for Old St Paul's. I want a spire.'

She said nothing. Then she said, 'Dr Wren is not my friend. No more than anyone else.'

'I hear your Wren is to be married.'

'I did not know.'

'No one of importance. He has known her since childhood. Her name is Faith, I believe.'

Next morning Elizabeth heard the surveyor-general was returning from Oxford. Tom watched for his coach on the hill. When he brought word Elizabeth finished her tasks and sought Wren out at the convocation house. The hot, hazy weather had increased and a freakish wind promised thunder. In the assembly room the leathery Bishop de Braybroke stood grinning in his coffin, on view to the public for a small fee to the virger. The dean's clerk of works, Tillison, laboured at accounts. When she asked him he shook his head and pointed upstairs. 'Up there, Mrs Barwick. Don't ask *me* what our resident genius is doing. *I* don't know the full part of it. The king likes it, whatever it is.'

She thought, I know what it is.

She went upstairs and knocked on the door. There came sounds of unlocking and Woodroffe, Wren's assistant, an older and very experienced surveyor, stuck his head out. 'Mrs Barwick, I'm sorry, you can't—' She breezed in. It was a long, airy attic with windows facing both south and north. The long calico curtains hanging over the windows blew in the wind, flashing sunlight across the shadowed room, showing the river on her right hand and the cathedral to her left, where workmen swarmed like ants. Though a few great pillars and the tower still stood, the shape of the ruin was definitely lower, smoother, as though it was not beaten down by hammers but sank slowly into the earth of its own will.

Wren called, 'It's quite all right, Mr Woodroffe.' He laid down his brass compasses. 'You've been at work since six this morning, haven't you? Now it's afternoon.'

Woodroffe nodded. 'Ten minutes till we light the fuse, sir.' He jerked his cap on his white head and went out.

'Ten minutes. Very well, Mr Woodroffe.'

Woodroffe called back through the doorway, 'Nine and a half now.'

They listened to his footsteps limp downstairs.

Wren stood among the trestle tables that had been set up along the room. They were covered with large intricate sheets of drawings unrolled on thick paper, held down with smooth beach pebbles. A large oak model of the cathedral that was to have been lay discarded in two parts in the far corner.

Wren obviously worked without his coat, in his shirtsleeves and cuffs. He followed her eyes and put on his coat self-consciously.

'I hear you are to be married, Dr Wren.'

'Yes.'

She smiled and came forward. 'My heartiest congratulations and felicitations! You must be very pleased.'

'Yes.' He drew back.

She did not take her next step, so he drew back no further. She turned instead to the drawings. 'You drew these yourself?'

He glanced, nodded.

'You have a hand and eye for this work. It is delicate penmanship, Dr Wren. And over there is Mr Woodroffe's work, he has a coarser pen.' She teased him, 'You see? I recognise your work already.' She bent forward over the papers and the wind carried the smell of the river to them, blowing her hair over her shoulders, and the curtains flapped in the breeze. 'These are your designs for a Corinthian portico? And instead of towers, statues to stand on the parapet. I presume they are to break the skyline?'

'She looks rather like you,' he said. 'She is hardly younger than you.'

She examined the drawing. 'The dome echoes Bramante's design for St Peter's in Rome, does it not?'

'Mrs Barwick. Elizabeth.'

'Imitation is the sincerest form of flattery. I am sure you will be very happy.'

'Happy!' he said. 'Are you happy?'

'I am.'

He picked up a pencil and actually drew an ornamental line with it, anywhere. 'Yes. Forgive me. We must all make the best we can of the nature God gives us. Everything plain and simple, as once I saw myself. But you fill me with confusion.'

'That I can do nothing about. I was married at the age of fifteen and today I am twenty-four.'

'To an old man with a weepy eye.'

'You are nearly forty and only now to be married.'

He said calmly, 'I wish I was married to you.'

'I take that as a compliment and wish you every happiness.'

He burst out, 'I shall never be happy. I cannot stand still. You have strength and intelligence. You are excitement itself. Everything about you is difficult. Provocative.'

'I love my husband and I owe him everything I have. Before I married him you would not have noticed me. Do you see the girl who serves you a plate of beef and a cup of cheap Spanish wine?'

'The story is well known. Your husband did.'

She studied the plans.

'You ignore me,' he said. 'You feel nothing for me.'

'Because I cannot.'

'I would notice her if she was you.'

'Fortune has treated us another way, Dr Wren.'

'There is no such thing as fortune, only statistics.' He went to a window and stood with his arms crossed, the curtains flapping by his shoulders, surveying the ruins above him. He sighed, 'Today we are blowing up the tower, Mrs Barwick.'

'I thought that was considered too dangerous.'

'Last time we did not use enough gunpowder. Only eighteen pounds. Now I am using thirty-six pounds to pulverise the stone to dust, so that it does not fly.' The clock by the fireplace chimed softly and he seized his hat, recollecting. 'It is nearly time.' The words rushed out of him impulsively. 'I apologise for my intemperate speech, Mrs Barwick. Hearing me rant so stupidly must have embarrassed you even more than I have embarrassed myself. I am covered with shame. Forgive me.'

'You have not been stupid and you must not be ashamed. There is nothing to forgive. You work too hard.'

'And you are too kind.'

She went to the door with him. 'Since we now understand one another perfectly, I shall accompany you.'

'But we must not speak like strangers.'

'We must, in front of strangers.'

He followed her downstairs into the brightness of the sun in the west, and the afternoon heat hit them like a wave. They walked up the path winding between the piles of rubble. He muttered, 'Three minutes, by my reckoning. We have plenty of time.'

'My husband has set his mind on a spire,' Elizabeth said.

Wren stopped dead. He ignored the workmen scurrying round them. 'And you, Mrs Barwick?' He remembered. 'You are your husband's reflection.'

'You understand my loyalty.'

A man ran by pushing a barrow, and now men were leaping down off the walls, sheltering behind heaps of rubble.

Wren said, 'Two minutes—'

He shouted in alarm. Smoke puffed round the wreck of the tower. One great flying buttress, shaped like a leg bent at the knee, straightened and rose up into the air. Stones rained down around them. Wren wrapped her in his arms to protect her. From somewhere on the hillside below came a crash of tiles as a stone block went through someone's roof. The tower shuddered, canting over, then braced itself in a state of balance like a great cow leaning on three legs.

384

Elizabeth said, 'Was that your calculation, Dr Wren?'

He took off his hat and wig. She was surprised to see his own hair was sandy in colour.

'I must peck the whole thing down with pickaxes and hammers! It will take for ever.' He looked so disappointed that she laughed.

The acrid dust blew over them in the wind. The tower leant above them, appearing to rise higher as they came beneath. They heard shouts and then Woodroffe beckoned from the crossing, almost entirely flattened around the buttress fallen into it. He picked his way through the rubble, calling, 'Dr Wren. Come over here, sir. Look at this.'

They scrambled after him into the gap where one of the great windows had been. 'Be careful, Mrs Barwick. Do not stand too close to the edge there.'

Where the knuckle of the buttress had landed, the floor had collapsed into a pit.

'It's another one of them,' Woodroffe grunted. He spat the dust from his mouth. 'Pardon my spit, madam.'

Wren stared down into the mess of fallen flagstones and timbers. A few shards of marble flashed white.

'It's nothing,' Elizabeth said. 'Suppose the tower falls?'

But he saw something, slid down, picked out a marble figurine. He cleaned it with his kerchief. 'An altar statue,' he called up. 'So the legend is true.'

'Legend, Dr Wren?'

'The *Domum qui fuit Diane*. That St Paul's was built over a temple to the goddess Diana. I believed it no more than the story that Westminster Abbey is built over a temple to Apollo. But now—'

Elizabeth put out her hand for Woodroffe's support and swung herself down. Wren wrapped the figurine in both hands.

'The goddess wears no clothes, Mrs Barwick.'

She said, 'I have seen a naked woman before, Dr Wren.' He blushed scarlet. He had not.

It was darker down here. Gradually evening sunlight stretched fingers under the tower, made a lid of glowing light over the pit. Wren foraged in the shadows. The workmen drifted away. Woodroffe called down, 'The other places had ox-heads in, sir, turned to stone by age. Deer skulls, hare, I don't know what.' Wren called him to come down, but Woodroffe remained adamant. 'Too old for that sort of thing, sir. I'm back to the drawings while I've got daylight.'

'Very well.' Woodroffe hobbled from sight. Wren scooped a handful of bone, excited as a schoolboy. 'What's this?' he muttered. 'Shell? Oysters?'

They were alone. Elizabeth leaned back against the side of the pit, watching him. She said, 'It's bone.'

'Ah yes. Pagan sacrifice.'

'Or merely the remains of a meal.'

Without his wig, she thought, he does not look like other men. I am seeing him as he is. As only his wife will see him, or his servant. The private man.

She said, 'And you will truly erect the new cathedral exactly over these foundations?'

He examined a new find. 'Yes. The crossing will be precisely where we are standing now. The cathedral's east–west axis will be backed six and one half degrees to the north, to make the angle more imposing from Ludgate Hill.' He glanced at her in the failing light. 'You were right, by the way. Some of the old pillars were hollow.'

She thought, do I trust him? I like him, but that's not the same as trusting him. Do I love him? I love my husband. A woman cannot love two men at once. I cannot feel like this.

I cannot seduce a man on the eve of his marriage, he will never forget me. When he makes love to his wife, it will be me he loves.

God help me, I can. I am a wicked woman. I am not me, I am my need. I ache for my own child as deeply as he desires his cathedral. Our ambitions coincide.

But do I trust him?

She said, 'You'll promise a spire to the dean, a dome to the king. Plan your cathedral as a Greek cross for Sir Roger Pratt, a Latin cross for the bishop.'

'You know what I want, Elizabeth. I drew it for you. You alone know the truth.'

'Do I? Do I know you at all?'

He stepped back on the floor of crushed bone. It creaked, moving slightly beneath his heels.

She said, 'How deep must you dig your foundations?'

'What is wrong? I have yet to take careful soundings of the subsoil. If I find sand and gravel over clay, as I expect in London, the immense weight of the cathedral will require foundations forty feet deep.'

'Dr Wren,' she cried out, 'you should leave here.'

He looked up at the tower. The sun had left it completely, its black bulk leant ponderously above them against the dark sky. The first stars glimmered in the open, airy space where the great buttress once stood.

'If the tower was going to fall it would have fallen already. But I admit, the feeling is exciting.' He stopped as though he had heard himself say something extraordinary. 'I must be mad talking like this.' He stepped towards her, tripped, tore the knee of his breeches. He felt like a fool, looked back for what had caught him, pulled something out from the rubble.

It was a skull as big as his body, with curved horns.

Elizabeth dug. She grasped the figurine in both hands like a pickaxe, and the slope of rubble in front of her began to give way at the top.

She plunged her hands into the hole, hauling back, and Wren cleared away. Dust and bricks, brickearth and hardcore, mortar and broken flagstone, pieces of distinctive green and black marble floor from the old cathedral, cascaded back around her. What had once been the roof of the pit was now piled over its floor. She coughed, waving her hand against the dust, leant forward into the gap showing above the rubble, and pulled out a candle and flint.

She lit the candle.

She and Wren stood in the candlelit hollow with the stars above them, darkness around them on the hilltop. Distantly they heard singing from a tavern.

She pulled down more debris, crawled forward.

'It's a family crypt,' Wren said.

'It's a catacomb.'

He peered round. 'We shall destroy this. The new building is through here.'

She scrambled back into the pit, returned to the corner where Wren had stood. She handed him the candle and scooped with her hands, scraping back armfuls of dust and bone. The outline of a wooden hatch, much battered, was revealed.

She opened it, showering dust.

She took the candle, lifted her dress to her knee so that she did not trip, and climbed down into the ground.

Wren stood beside her on the platform in the dark. He touched the railing and it crumbled to dust. He brushed the wood-dust from his hands. The platform creaked. She held up the candle and he stared round, his eyes enlarged by the darkness.

'I've heard of such places, Mrs Barwick. A house under ground. It's said many churches have a labyrinth beneath them. Secrets that are not revealed to the general laity of ordinary people.'

She whispered, 'You are talking of the Freemasons.'

'I would not have believed this until now.'

She leant where the railing had been, held the candle out into the dark, tilted it. Wren leant out, he had no fear of heights. From the flame a burning ribbon of wax dropped down to the centre of the earth.

He shuddered with vitality, terror, excitement. They stared up at the tiny stars framed above them, the sparks fading far below, making darkness visible.

'My God,' he whispered. 'My God Liza. Here is my cathedral.'

She pulled him a footstep to one side, held up the candle to the slanting stone broken from the roof of the pit by the fall of Old St Paul's.

Wren reached upward with both hands. 'Aram menaht menou.' His fingertips caressed the groups of intricate wavy lines, moved forward to the patterns of tiny holes pecked in the hard stone.

He whispered, 'These are stars. Constellations familiar *and* strange.

387

Changed. Here is the Sun. Here is the Moon.' He looked around him in wonder. 'There is more?'

'I have much more to show you.' She lifted the candle high. He craned his head back, stared straight up. Eight letters were worried deep into the stone, so deep they were shadowed by the light, and moved as she moved the light. His lips moved reverently.

RESURGAM.

'Latin, Dr Wren. I shall rise again.'

Elizabeth's first priority was to sleep with her husband. She cried out passionately and writhed sufficiently to provoke his spasm. She was almost sure he was impotent, though she was certain the idea had not occurred to him. He thought of her entirely as his dutiful wife and assistant, not as the mother of children, and thought of himself as a father of the Church not the father of a bundle of actual warm human flesh. They had been married for nine years and not been blessed, yet each year her body had cried out to be filled with child.

She stroked John's sleeping face gently. She would not have hurt him for the world.

She thought, he will never know our child is not his.

Even I will never know quite for sure.

Again she counted the days since her last course of the moon, and counted the days to the next.

Fourteen days to wait and see.

In the morning she watched John wash his face and hands as usual. He grinned at her, slapped her rump goatishly, and went into his other room to be dressed by Tom.

Fourteen days later nothing happened.

Nothing happened on the fifteenth day, or the sixteenth.

Weeks passed, and nothing happened.

Elizabeth waited for the second month to make certain. She thought of what was growing inside her night and day, she was obsessional about any tiny change in her feelings, woke up hot in the night and knew it was because of her baby, felt an itch in her leg and knew it was her baby. Her baby was invading her body, and she gloried in every moment, knowing this was why she had been born.

'My Lord!' John sat up in his armchair. 'You are quite certain of your condition, wife?'

She nodded demurely. 'Two months gone already.'

'This is marvellous news, my dear! And I am seventy years old. People will be so impressed!' His face fell. 'Shall I live to see my child?'

She kissed his forehead. 'Of course. I shall pray for it. It takes a mere seven months from now, not a lifetime.'

'When my son is ten years old, I shall be eighty. When he is twenty, I will be an old man.' He brightened, hugged her tight. 'You are a marvel, Liza. You have made me feel young again.'

But Elizabeth's child was not a son. She was a daughter.

'My daughter, Abigail.' The dean held her proudly in front of the worshippers in the assembly room. 'And I in my seventy-second year!' He had taken as his text St Matthew 18:3, *Except ye become as little children, ye shall not enter into the Kingdom of Heaven*. Rain pattered down the window panes, audible only because it was the Lord's Day and the hee-hawing fretsaws in the attic, where Cleere and twelve joiners worked in secret on the cathedral's Great Model, were silent. The dean shuffled, turned to Elizabeth, handed her child into her lap, then kissed her face in public with trembling lips.

At night he would not let her lie alone, but pestered her with attentions.

Elizabeth rocked on the hard chair by the bedroom window, her baby wrapped round with soft wool shawls in her lap, protected from the night wind. She bent forward, lifted aside the shawl from the sleeping face with her little finger, breathed the child's breath.

'Abby, my Abby. Without you I am nothing. You are who I am. You are my life.'

When Abby was toddling Elizabeth visited her sister in the Lydiard. The cramped medieval yard she remembered was gone, of course, replaced by brick houses with whitewashed window sills. Bella's youngest son was seven years old and took Abby's hand dutifully. Bella's husband was an upholsterer and the two women walked to Smithfield to fetch horsehair from the Shambles. The whole area was a vast factory for turning animals into useful products. Elizabeth and Bella followed their children between the steaming stockyards lined with butcher's shops, tanneries, boneyards, soap-boilers, lard-makers and a hundred others, coming to Skinners Row. From Mr Flenser they purchased a half-hundredweight of hair of standard length, bound in loops of its own hair for ease of carrying, and distributed it among the children. They swung the rest over their shoulders and retraced their footsteps talking busily, exchanging news and exclamations – Bella had always been the excitable sister – about their children. 'Jethro will be just like his father,' she prattled, 'and as for Zachariah, lazy feckless boy, I don't know what I'll do with him, his father beats him but he doesn't learn, he—'

Elizabeth looked up, hearing a rope creak.

'—should send him to sea to fight the Dutch, but he—'

Elizabeth stared. The blackened face and protruding tongue of a man gaped down on her from Holborn Gallows. His body slowly rotated in the wind. His hands and heels were tied. She recognised something about his eyes, which the birds had not yet taken.

Elizabeth was sure this was the boy to whom she'd given an apple and a silver shilling in the Chiswick vicarage garden long ago, grown into a man.

She grabbed Abby to her, buried the child's face in her dress. 'Don't look.'

Bella said, 'Whatever is the matter?' She turned away, prattling, 'They say the king has converted his religion to the Roman Catholics in secret—'

A stern self-satisfied voice returned to haunt Elizabeth. *You've made a bad boy into a rogue, madam. With your encouragement, one day he'll hang.*

Elizabeth left her sister to talk to herself. She hurried Abby home and they did not go out again that day, or all week.

For John's favourite dinner his cook, Miss Blencowe, boiled a ragoût of boeuf à la mode, highly seasoned and seethed for four hours to soften it. He had acquired his taste for foreign food in exile, and his mind often now returned to those days. Suddenly he stopped whatever he had been saying about the past and his silence made Elizabeth look up. He called Tom to move the candelabrum to one side so that he could see her, spoke to her down the length of the table. 'Why aren't you eating?' he called. 'You seem disturbed.'

'I saw a hanged man. I thought I recognised him. I didn't want Abby to see him.'

John listened with his hand cupped to his right ear, grown slightly deaf. 'We're all sinners.' He nodded for Tom to serve another scoop of beef.

She said impatiently, 'Yes I know, but we aren't all criminals.'

'Roman Catholics are criminals. The wolf in the confessional wears priest's robes.'

'They say the king—'

'If that rumour is true, his action is a crime. I do not believe it. We are an Anglican nation under an Anglican king.'

His voice had risen. She murmured, 'Yes, husband.'

'Anyway, your friend Christopher Wren has received his knighthood.'

'I'm pleased.'

'His honour will reflect well on the cathedral. They say he is a Freemason.'

'I'm sure your cathedral will be worthy of him.'

'My spire is certain. I have seen Sir Chris's plans for it. For all his marriage to that wife of his—'

'Faith.'

'Your memory is excellent. She has given him no child, you know.' He wiped his face on his napkin. 'Now I am hungry for bed.' He reached out for her hand and pulled her upstairs, where after they had undressed he pawed her as best he could.

Afterwards Elizabeth wrapped herself in a gown and knelt beside her daughter's truckle-bed. Abby was three years old, nearly four. Her hair spread black over her bolster and would be as long as her mother's. Her eyes, flickering in a dream, were her mother's blue. But her hands were tiny, with long delicate fingers, whereas Elizabeth's hands were straightforward, strong and direct. Abby smiled in her sleep, her mouth expressive in her elfin face.

So Sir Chris's wife had not given him a child.

'I must not see him again,' Elizabeth said aloud. She rubbed her knuckles against her forehead and prayed.

Old St Paul's was almost gone. The great pillars and buttresses were hammered down chip by chip, the last lines of wall levelled to rubble and pounded flat, so the top of the hill looked smooth enough for bowls. This late in the evening, nearly at midsummer, no one moved on the summit except Elizabeth. The seemingly endless procession of carts taking away stone had ceased, and many of them lay broken about the site, abandoned between the workmen's huts waiting for workmen and builders' stores waiting to be filled. It was the calm before the storm. The foundation stone would be laid in the next few days, and no one who saw the new cathedral started thought to live to see its completion. Old St Paul's took more than two hundred years to build, and no doubt the building of New St Paul's would be a constant activity all the rest of their lives and beyond.

'Liza.'

She turned. 'Sir Chris?'

Wren's thin lips broke into that particular wide, expressive smile. 'Why do you pretend to be surprised? You knew I would be here. You must have seen me many times here, in the distance.'

She heard her voice confess more easily than she could have believed to the truth. 'The more I am determined not to see you, the more I hope I will. When I come round a corner I think I may see you standing in front of me.'

'But you have succeeded in avoiding me.'

'I have tried to get you out of my mind for both our sakes.'

'Now here I am.'

'I must go—'

He interrupted her. 'You haven't changed, Liza. Not one whit. You always wear your hair differently, just as you always did. Each time I glimpse you, across a crowded room perhaps, your hair is up, or down, or curled, or in the French fashion, and yet you are the same. You are—' He laughed at himself. 'You. You are simply you.'

'You have more lines in your face. You look tired.'

'I have no time for anything but work. Oh, to do nothing for five minutes!' He put out his arm. 'Walk with me. For five minutes.'

He matched the length of his stride to hers. They talked of the weather.

She said, 'I have a daughter.'

'I've seen. Your husband is so proud.'

'You know the truth.'

'I have spoken to Abby sometimes. A word or two from a stranger. She's pretty.'

'Is that all?'

'Liza, she is the most perfectly pretty little thing who ever lived. She makes me laugh. She has my humour.' He stopped himself.

She said quietly, 'Are you angry?'

He whispered, 'Yes, because you know what you do to me. Because I love you, sometimes I almost hate you. I adore you. God help me, it is always *your* face I see. Whatever I feel about you – I am a busy man during the days – always, always it is a strong feeling. I cannot help it. I am not a man of strong emotions but you make me one.'

'You should be.'

'Yes, I have my work. All this.' He kicked the dust. He could not put into words what he felt for her, yet she knew much of New London rising below them had come from his mind. The distant stone needle of his Monument to the Great Fire was nearly finished, his Customs House rebuilt, his bright new churches of St Dunstan and St Vedast complete, St Edmund and St Bride and St Lawrence in Jewry all under way, his tall steeple for St Mary-le-Bow already pointing high above the surrounding buildings, St Stephen's dome standing amid a mass of scaffolding in the Walbrook valley.

She whispered, 'Forgive me. I used you.'

'I'll never forgive you. I worship you, Liza. I meant what happened to happen. I dream of you, I hold you.'

She admitted fiercely, 'I wanted what happened. I did not mean to hurt you so badly.'

'I,' he said, looking round him on the field of bleached and rollered stone, 'have learnt always to want the impossible. You have taught me this. When I met you I believed that everything in the universe, under God, was preordained and rational. The stars in their courses, the orbits of the planets. That everything could one day be perfectly known and subjected to mathematical analysis and conclusion, even people. You have shown me how immoral that would be. Because even immoral acts could be predicted. But they would still happen and we would still want them to. I would still lie with you, be naked with you. Science is not truth, it is merely uniformity. Liza, you showed me how little I know, can ever know.'

'You talk like a mathematician in love.'

'Yes. I do.'

They walked together carefully, his hand guiding her arm, not letting their bodies touch. She said, 'That is enough of us. Talk of St Paul's.'

'How can I talk of my work without talking of you?'

A raven swept over their heads, one of the new black variety brought to London by the king. It landed, pecked for worms in the stone. Wren watched attentively.

'There are certain matters I have decided,' he said as they walked on. 'I will not drive foundations into the clay after all. But the fine sand and gravel above it is too unstable to take St Paul's weight. However, covering that I have found a cap of firm brickearth, six feet thick, barely beneath the surface soil.' He stamped his foot as they walked downhill. 'I will build the cathedral on this.'

'I understand what you are saying. Anything beneath the brickearth will remain undisturbed. Undiscovered.'

'I have removed less than fifty thousand cartloads of rubble, half what I originally proposed. The rest is built up to make this raft of stone. So even the crypt need not intrude below the layer of brickearth.'

They walked downhill through the cool evening air, the river below them a mass of dirty sails and oars pulling the boats like insects. London Bridge stood astride the slack water like a centipede. The smaller boats crept beneath its legs. The setting sun made glinting eyes of the windows in the bridge houses.

He said, 'I do now have a son, in Oxford. Also named Chris. Not yet seven months old.'

'I'm pleased for you.'

'Yes.'

He opened the double door to the convocation house and went upstairs ahead of her. 'Here's something you must see, Liza.' He took a bundle of keys from his pocket, selected one. But it was the wrong one and would not fit the lock. He tried another, unlocked the door and bowed her ahead of him. She went first into the attic.

Elizabeth gasped. 'This is the Great Model? I heard it cost almost a thousand pounds, and entranced the king.'

Standing nearly twenty feet long, on a table specially constructed to support its weight, the model of New St Paul's looked perfect to the tiniest detail. 'Oak,' Wren said, watching her eyes. 'Cleere's work. The gilding is by the king's sergeant-painter, the ornaments and cherubims are plaster. Evelyn's little Dutchman, Grinling Gibbons, carved the statues.'

She glanced at him under her lashes. 'This is not what you showed me.'

He grinned. 'Ah. You alone I have no secrets from.'

'You have no intention of building this. It has two domes, not the spire you promise my husband. But there are no towers. And where is the choir for daily services?'

He shrugged, opened a drawer, pulled out a sheaf of plans. 'Look. Everyone sees what they want to see. The king has approved this design, similar to the model.' He held up plans with the royal warrant of approval pinned to them. 'But his majesty has kindly allowed me to make variations from time to time, as I see proper. Since *this* design has two domes, one on top of the other, surmounted by a steeple, you may be sure it is one of the variations that I intend not to proceed.' He flourished another set of papers, this time showing no domes and a tall tiered steeple. 'Your husband's choice, which I have shown to him. The important thing is to get the work started, Liza. This morning I issued contracts to the two senior masons to begin work on the choir. We lay the foundation stone next week, on Midsummer's Day.' He replaced the papers. He beckoned her to another drawer, unlocked it. He turned to her seriously. 'But these are my private drawings, Liza.'

He laid them on a table. These drawings were painstaking, she saw, formed in hair-fine lines of brown ink. The dome was painted blue like the sky. Every detail and ornament was precise, even to the two western towers, supposedly unplanned.

'This . . . then what you really intend is much larger than anything you have said,' she whispered. 'It's very grand. And it is lovely.'

'Best that the people who will pay for it do not know how much it will cost,' he sighed. 'New St Paul's will take thirty years to rise to the level of the dome. By then everyone who matters now will not, it will be for our children to decide. The outer walls are two feet thicker than in the public plans, the aisles narrower. The upper walls are false to support the dome. And all will be built together, not pecked at piecemeal.' He replaced the papers in the drawer, locked it, then took her hand. 'And this. This secret is what you will want to see.'

He crouched, tugging her forward with a smile, and ducked under the table supporting the Great Model. It was hollow and they stood up in the interior, their heads inside the dome, their faces almost touching.

'We're like giants standing with our feet deep in the earth,' she murmured, looking round her at the piers, arches, the ring of columns and the great circular gallery that almost touched her eye, but he only looked at her.

'I love you and I always will,' he whispered.

'These beautiful colours, and one dome carried inside another. So complex yet so simple. It's almost confusing. Yet delightful.'

'Like you.'

'You mustn't talk like this.'

'There is not another building like it in this country. Unique. I have changed it since . . . what happened. I have done it for you. Planned it like this for you.'

'But won't narrower side aisles make the circle of eight piers and arches supporting the dome's weight uneven in their spacing?'

'They are hollow, Liza.'

'The irregularity will look very odd. Everyone will notice.'

He took her face in his hands and kissed her. She neither resisted nor responded.

He murmured, 'I wish we could have been young for ever.'

Sir Christopher Wren, holding a silver trowel of symbolic mortar, assisted by Dean John Barwick with his white shoulder-length hair blowing in the wind, and the Bishop of London with his *pallium* blown over one side of his head, laid the foundation stone of St Paul's to mark the south-east corner of the new cathedral. Elizabeth stood on the hilltop hand in hand with Abby, watching, both in their best bottle-green dresses. They were the only females present. Their hair blew in the wind, restrained at first by green ribbons, but the wind unknotted and unravelled them. Abby laughed, five years old, catching at one ribbon that flew free, then ran after it between the assembled dignitaries. Plump aldermen and hobnobbing clerics snatched at the ribbon, but the wind fluttered it past them. Sir Christopher Wren caught it.

He held it out to her with a deep bow, but instead Abby turned with folded arms and waited for him to tie it in her hair. He laughed and did so, not very skilfully. Someone applauded, then everyone at the back joined in, believing the foundation stone to have been laid, eager to get out of the wind and pitch into the food. Abby curtseyed, very self-possessed, and ran back to her mother. The dignitaries accompanied the bishop to the convocation house for glasses of claret, oysters, and ten or twelve types of marinaded meat.

A hundred workmen scurried on to the site. Windbreaks were erected around a second foundation stone to be laid on the north-east side in the masonic tradition. Abby crouched, played a pebble game. She could hear her mother dealing briskly with someone who wanted to bother Papa with a matter of no importance. Fed up with her game, Abby crept forward and peeped between the windbreaks.

Various strange implements were arranged around the foundation stone. She saw a tall beaker of gold. A gold spade. A silver scythe. Abby smiled, seeing a golden Sun and a silver Moon placed on stands with three legs. A builder's square and a compass. She crawled forward curiously, then drew back as gentlemen appeared. Most of these gentlemen she had seen before, friends who would pat her head or smile to her, or wink, as they talked business with her father the Dean of St Paul's, or Sir Christopher Wren, or her mother. Once Mr Pierce had given her an orange and kissed her forehead.

But now they were dressed in strange ceremonial clothes, with signs pinned to them, carrying secret symbols she did not understand.

Abby watched quiet as a mouse. The voice of the wind thundered in the windbreaks.

Two more gentlemen came forward. They bowed on bended knee to the Sun and Moon. One held up his right hand, the other his left, and together they made a sign as if crossing themselves. As they turned away she recognised Joshua Marshall, the Master Mason to the Crown who would build the cathedral's choir. The younger man – though he looked very old to Abby – was Thomas Strong, another master mason, who would build the apse and the east wall. The two men would be jointly responsible, under Wren, for building the eight massive piers supporting the dome and for the foundations beneath them. Mr Woodroffe was not there. Mr Evelyn wore a strange hat. He bowed to the golden Sun and his hat fell off. Abby covered her mouth and giggled. She slipped back with a child's quickness when someone turned, frowning. A man's hand appeared, pulled a flapping canvas windbreak across the gap. She was not seen.

The canvas made such a noise in the wind that she could not hear what they were saying, only their chanting voices.

Abby found a gap on the other side and peeped through. Someone had lifted the gold pitcher and poured a thick fluid of liquid cement like a libation across the foundation stone. He looked up and she recognised Sir Christopher Wren.

A hand gripped Abby's shoulder. She almost screamed. But it was only her mother. Elizabeth pulled her away, put her finger to her lips. 'Sssh, Abby.'

Abby asked, 'What are they doing?'

'They are Freemasons, Abby. They are blessing the building in their own way.'

Abby played at running up and down. The windblown dust stung her legs. Labourers arrived carrying stakes over their shoulders for boundary markers, great reels of string, shovels and all sorts of tools she had never seen before.

After a while the gentlemen came into the open, looking very ordinary, their cravats fluttering in the wind. Workmen removed the windbreaks and most of the gentlemen walked off to eat. Sir Christopher remained. He smiled at Abby. He seemed to have a special affection for her, and Abby was pleased. She liked to be liked.

'Now, Abby,' he told her, 'I must mark the crossing, the exact centre of the dome. Between that and the foundation stone –' he meant the masonic foundation stone – 'all other measurements and geometry of the cathedral shall be derived.' She slipped her right hand in his and walked with him across the dusty plateau. Mother held her other hand. Abby swung comfortably between the two adults, enjoying their attention.

'Don't scuff your best shoes!' Mother said, but she smiled, and Abby realised she was very happy. Normally Mother was too busy to be happy, or at least to show happiness.

Sir Christopher lifted Abby over the tapes and markers into a wide featureless area. Abby could not imagine that a place so big could ever be enclosed inside a building. The three of them walked forward to the middle.

Mother and Sir Christopher stopped.

'Here,' Sir Christopher said. He called out to a workman for a marker, but the wind blew his words away. 'Here is the exact centre.'

Abby bent down. There was a stone with dust blown over it. She scuffed it with her shoe.

'I said—' Mother said.

Abby knelt. Her childish hands swept at the dust, and it blew away.

She read the strange word with difficulty, running her finger in each letter to understand it.

RESURGAM.

Abby asked the two grown-ups, 'What does it mean?'

'It means, I—' Sir Christopher looked round, irritated, as his name was called.

Mr Woodroffe limped across the stones towards them. He looked very ill. He did not say anything.

Wren went very pale. 'Whatever is it, Edward?'

'News has just come from Oxford, sir. There's smallpox there. Your son lives.' Woodroffe held his hands to his face against the wind. 'Sir, your wife is dead.'

That her father should be a very old man with flowing white hair to his shoulders, a long stick, and the manner of a more or less affectionate tyrant, seemed entirely natural to Abby. As she grew up she could imagine no other life but service to her father. The striding figure of Dean John Barwick, his shepherd's crook clenched in one gnarled fist and the other discreetly clasping his daughter's shoulder for support, was a familiar presence all round the interminable building site that was St Paul's. In winter she and her mother endured mud to the knee to support the old man on his tours of inspection, in summer choking clouds of dust.

The Portland stone foundations of St Paul's, six feet deep in the brickearth, rose out of the mud and dust all of a piece, a maze of wall-lines like a puzzle gradually revealing itself, a jigsaw pattern leading from the portico steps in the west to the curve of the apse in the east. Pillars began to grow from the brickearth.

'Where's my choir?' grumbled the dean. 'Where are my walls? I want to hold a service in my new choir before I die.'

'Papa, they aren't *your* walls,' Abby said crossly. 'They're everybody's.'

'I expect Sir Christopher knows that if he completes one part before another,' Mother added diplomatically, 'the flow of subscriptions will dry up.' Abby hid her smile. No one handled Papa as wisely as Mother.

As usual on a Saturday, the dean spied a thin, nimble figure. 'Sir Christopher! Where's my choir?'

'We mustn't bother him, John,' Mother said. 'He knows what he's doing. You said so yourself.'

'Did I?' The dean railed against old age with every ounce of his vitality. 'Forty thousand pounds, he spent last last year! What do I see for it? Endless work on the foundations – yet the nave only to the height of my knee – the crossing no higher – and where is my choir? And I suspect he plans to put the altar at the central point, as the Catholics do. Ours is a reformed religion. The pulpit is most important, not the altar.'

Sir Christopher came over. He bowed at the dean and Elizabeth, smiled at Abby. His hands were inky, his knees and elbows covered with dust. He had married for a second time very soon, almost hastily, after the death of his first wife. His pretty daughter Jane was sometimes looked after by Abby. Now Wren was a widower for the second time. The stains on his lapels were cookshop gravy and his coat was wrinkled, one button missing. The dean muttered unrepentantly and Elizabeth said, 'You are worrying my husband, Sir Christopher. You are overworked.'

'I am my work.'

The dean said, 'Why is he not hurrying forward my choir? Ask him that.'

Wren looked weary. King Charles had died a Roman Catholic and his brother, King James, was a loyal subject to the interests of that religion. The Bishop of London had been suspended by the king's Catholic Ecclesiastical Commission for preaching Protestant views. Four Catholic bishops had been consecrated over the English by the Pope. Now King James insisted St Paul's be rebuilt with side chapels instead of aisles, the altar placed at the crossing beneath the dome, and the choir made as large as the nave so as many people as possible should hear the murmur of the mass and see the Elevation of the Host. The sermons of Anglican preachers would be rendered almost inaudible by such an arrangement.

'Sir, I beg you to be patient,' Wren said. 'I am torn in two.'

'What?' the dean queried Elizabeth. 'He can hardly expect patience from a man my age, with the troubles I have.'

Elizabeth touched Sir Christopher's thin arm. 'When you have finished work, come to supper. You need feeding.'

Abby said, 'And I shall sew your buttons.'

Wren watched the two females escort the dean away. 'I think that old man will live for ever,' he told the foreman.

'Yes, sir,' the foreman said respectfully, 'but what about them stones? Will you put a Lady Chapel on the east end, like the king's man says? I got a hundred labourers waiting with shovels, sir.'

'What I will do,' Wren said, 'is order you to erect scaffolding as high as it will go, and drape it all over with tarred canvas.'

The foreman scratched his crotch. 'But Londoners won't see their new cathedral coming up, though, sir, will they?'

Wren glanced at him. 'Exactly. No one will, and I shall do what I shall do.'

Rain or shine, the dean sat at his window staring uphill at the vast pile of scaffolds and tarred canvas that hid all work on the hilltop from view, imagining the great Anglican cathedral rising up inside, seeing the work progress in his mind's eye. Supposedly because of the builders' problems with theft, a high wall of wooden planks had been erected round the site. Whenever one gate or another was opened the dean craned forward, trying to glimpse what lay beyond. His gaze was attracted to Abby strolling with a young fop in the garden below. 'Wife!'

Elizabeth came over. 'What's the matter, John?' He pointed, and she laughed. 'Did you not know? He is her young man from Ave Maria Lane, Daniel, a clerk at the Navy Office. He has pursued her for months.' Her eyes softened. 'Look how he looks at her.'

'That's what I mean! And she just laughs! Shamelessly flirting!'

'You shamelessly flirted once.'

'I did not.'

'Oh, you've always been too old for that sort of thing, I suppose?'

'She,' the dean muttered, 'is certainly too young.'

'She is eighteen years old. Much older than I when I married you.'

'That was different,' he muttered. 'I was old enough to be your father.'

Elizabeth watched them walk the lawns among the rosebushes and apple trees. The young lovers slipped their hands together, as happy as could be, and she knew precisely what thoughts were going through their minds. 'No,' she said. 'Nothing changes. There's no difference at all.'

It took John a little while to realise he had lost the argument. 'You women always club together,' he accused her, and turned his deaf left ear to Elizabeth's laughter.

King William, a Protestant, was invited to the throne by popular acclaim. King James fled for his life to Catholic Ireland and the covers were finally taken off St Paul's. The dean, almost blind, peered at the blaze of white stone.

''Tis a Roman Catholic building! Stained glass next!'

Abby and her mother, almost carrying his frail weight, walked the old man to Sir Christopher, who bowed.

'Welcome, sir. You will not be disappointed.'

The group walked forward, Daniel walking shyly six feet behind, though Abby hissed at him to keep up.

Along almost its whole length, the cathedral had risen above the level of the first-storey windows and niches for statues. Wren had ignored certain of the old king's instructions and confabulated others. The nave was shorter, with two side chapels at the west end, but he agreed that one should be used as the consistory court, the other for morning prayers, and not to proceed with the other side chapels. Workmen swarmed on the massive west portico. 'And here, dean, we've built a special entrance for you.'

The dean barked, 'What is it?'

'The Dean's Door, sir. The cherubs, wreaths and scrolls are carved by Mr Kempster. Such fine work I have paid him an extra twenty pounds from the accounts.' Wren pushed the double doors open and they went inside. The nave was a building lot and the crossing was wide to the sky.

The dean leant on his stick. His eyes followed the clouds dimly. 'Here my steeple will stand.' Abby saw her mother and Wren exchange glances. There was some sort of close bond between the two of them. She had always sensed it.

Wren led them forward. 'The masonry of the choir is almost finished, sir. A temporary roof is in place.'

'Then it's ready for services.' The dean turned to his wife. 'It's more than twenty years since I last heard a service in the choir of St Paul's.' He looked round him with streaming eyes. Workmen were winching the marble effigy of Dean John Donne into a niche on the south side of the choir. Algar's statue, of blackened Caen stone seeming strangely ancient among the smooth white Portland blocks, had already been set in place in the north wall. Dreamily the dean's eyes followed the curve of the apse. He blinked away his tears.

Wren asked, 'Is my work unsatisfactory, sir?'

'Satisfactory!' the dean said. 'Satisfactory, Sir Christopher.'

Five weeks later Dean John Barwick stood in the choir with a temporary altar set up behind him, Abby and Daniel standing together in front of him. The acoustics of the new cathedral were perfectly suited to the old man's high, silvery voice. 'It is with great gladness that we are gathered here today,' he smiled, 'for no one could be happier to join these two young people in this place than I . . .'

A month and a day later, nine months before Abby's first daughter was born, he died peacefully in his sleep. He was ninety-two.

Abby stood on the star at the exact centre of the crossing, remembering.

Her mother had asked to meet her here, and commands from Mother were always obeyed. It was a hot summer day, but always cool in the cathedral.

Abby had walked to St Paul's from Whitehall. As an afterthought – or had he planned it from the beginning, as Mother said? – Wren had added two towers at the western end. The great dome was cased not in copper but in lead, which gave it a burnished bluish glow under the heat-hazy sky.

Daniel was at work, as always, and Abby's boys, young men hoping for Oxford or Cambridge, were at the Cathedral School. Her elder daughters had made reasonably hopeful marriages, one to the first officer of the Navy ship *Atropos*. After a lean time on half-pay he was at sea the last two years, and hoped for his own vessel if the war with France kept hot.

Abby opened the gate in the cast-iron railing that surrounded the cathedral. Wren had wanted wrought iron, Mother said, but he was an old man now and unable to exert his will on the fashions of modern taste. Abby climbed the steps into the cathedral.

It was quiet in the nave. Voices whispered around her, so perfectly did the cavernous arches and curves and saucer-domes carry sound, but she recognised no one. A few paupers and beggars sat, heads nodding, on distant seats behind the pillars, and she heard the murmur of someone doing business.

Abby stood on the star that marked the centre of the crossing.

Resurgam.

She remembered standing here as a child on a windy bare field of stone, wondering how a building could ever enclose such an enormous space.

She craned back her head, looking up.

The eight massive piers around her, each one fifty-three feet six inches distant from her, supported seventy thousand tons of dome hundreds of feet above her head. It looked as light as air. At the top the lantern admitted daylight in some mysterious manner, the dome being much larger outside than inside the building. Painters were still busy up there, tiny foreshortened figures on the scaffolding. Someone called and they went away for their dinner. It must be the middle of the day.

She waited.

A black-skirted virger came from the south transept. Sunlight made a halo in his hair from the window behind him and his feet shuffled breezily on the tessellated marble, the only sound. He nodded to her, crossed in front of the great screen shutting off the choir, the huge pump-organ above it, then shuffled from sight in the direction of the Lord Mayor's vestry. After a while a door slammed, filling the cathedral with echoes.

Behind her Mother's voice said, 'Well, Abby? What do you see?'

Abby jumped. 'You made me jump!'

Mother smiled with her eyes. She wore a beauty-spot on her powdered face, her silver hair was piled up in the latest court fashion. Even on such a hot day she wore fur. She took Abby's elbow, turned her round and round on the star like a child. 'Tell me what you see.'

'I see the cathedral. The dome turns above me.' Abby stopped. 'Are you well, Mother? Have you spoken to the doctor again?' Abby waited, then said, 'Tell me what *you* see.'

Mother looked around her. 'Love.'

'Yes, God's love.'

'I see love.'

Abby shivered. 'Mother, you're not dying, are you? You won't die.'

Mother shook her head. 'I won't die.'

She laid her hand on her daughter's elbow, drew her forward from the centre of the dome towards the choir screen. The two women passed beneath the carved wooden arch into the choir. Mother murmured, '*Twice or thrice had I loved thee before I knew your face or name—*'

Abby knew the poem. '*So in a voice, so in a shapeless flame—*'

'*Angels affect us oft, and worshipped be.*'

The statue of Algar stood in its niche in the great north-east pier of the dome. Mother stopped. She touched its foot.

'Abby,' she whispered urgently, 'do you remember that day on the hilltop, when the wind blew?'

'I was just thinking of it. I found the stone.'

'Always know more than others think you do,' Mother whispered. 'And always keep it to yourself. Your real father built this building. Abby, I'm sorry, I'm sorry. This is the truth. There is more to it than you know.'

She touched the foot of the statue.

With a grating sound the statue of Algar began to move, and swung slowly aside to reveal darkness.

Part Six

Angela

London, Christmas Day 1999 AD

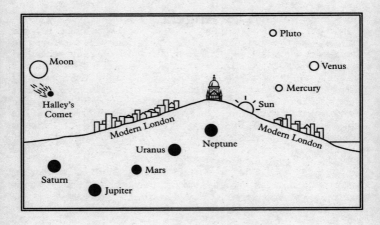

Christmas Day, 1940

His son was born on Christmas Day.

Bernard Lydiard came out of St Paul's at dawn, blinking at the sunlight streaming past him after the gloom inside. He stood waiting thoughtfully, looking across the atrium and wondering what had changed. He had been alert all night but he did not look tired, a tall man, very broad across the shoulder, so that the ARP messenger girl gave him a second glance from beneath her steel helmet. His eyes were blue, cool and deep. His black hair was long enough to make a sergeant-major shout, and he had long powerful hands too. The white band round his upper arm was circled by ST PAUL'S WATCH in black letters. 'Where's your gas mask, chum?' she called.

Bernard looked at her without a word. He reached out and touched the lamp post with his fingertips.

Gus, still sprightly despite a white moustache and steel-grey hair, came down the steps. Beside Bernard's height he looked very short, so he stood several steps up. 'Don't worry about this one, love,' he said. 'Not on the same level as you and me, he's not.'

'I don't like being looked at like that when I'm being helpful,' the girl pouted.

'You've got to talk to him with *very long words*,' Gus said. 'Educated, see. Studied Logic. Greek. Hebrew. Philology—'

Bernard muttered, 'Stamp collecting.'

'Shut up, Bernard. Semitic Studies. That's Jews to you and me, love. Honours degree.' Gus grinned at the pretty girl.

She said obstinately, 'Looking right through me, he is. Not a nutter, is he?'

Bernard said, 'Something's changed.'

Gus chuckled, 'He's married, sorry, love, and probably got a family by now, if the way his wife Rose looked last evening's anything to go by. Me now, I'm single, no attachments—' The girl walked off. 'Ta, love,' Gus called after her. ''Bye then. Same place tomorrow morning, look forward to it.'

'Her name's Doreen,' Bernard said.

'Looks up in awe!' Gus clapped his hands to his cheeks. He was nearly sixty but with Bernard, who was twenty-five, he played the younger man. 'How did you get that, Sherlock?'

'Stitched on the shoulder strap of her gas mask.'

'Talking of which, you're a brave fool going out without yours.

What about Rose? Don't you think of her? I know you do. But suppose—'

'Hitler won't gas London.'

'I saw gas in the last little lot,' Gus said, fingering his strap. 'Thank you.'

Bernard lit a Passing Cloud. It was a woman's cigarette, one of Rose's, she must have slipped it in his overcoat pocket. One more token of her love. He wondered what he had done for her and could not think of anything. It was a mystery why she loved him, bathed him in her love like warm milk, so that without his thinking of her she was always there. If it had not been wartime he could have bought flowers from one of the little Ludgate shops, handed her the bunch and watched her smile.

All were shut on Christmas morning. He wished he had thought of it yesterday.

'Maybe you're a father by now,' Gus said. He eyed the cigarette.

The lorry by the statue of Queen Anne started up and drove off in a cloud of exhaust smoke, its light ack-ack anti-aircraft gun bouncing over the kerb behind it. They watched the vehicle freewheel down Ludgate Hill, under the London, Chatham and Dover Railway viaduct, then labour smokily uphill into sight again along Fleet Street.

Bernard walked to the lamp post on the other end of the balustrade and touched it with his left hand.

As always – cows produced milk despite Christmas Day – a milkman's dray swayed past the vast warehouses lining the south side of St Paul's Churchyard, but this morning he saw no vans bearing copies of *The Times* racing from Printing House Square. A couple of chatty nurses wearing steel helmets walking to work at the Bridewell Hospital waved to him. The local bobby cycled past and nodded acknowledgment at Bernard, Virger Lydiard's son. Bernard remembered the cigarette and handed it to Gus.

'I'll just put this pin through the stub, then it won't burn my lips,' Gus said. 'Are we standing here all day, Bernard? Shall I put out a collection box?'

Bernard looked round him, and quite suddenly realised what the change was. He said, 'They're gone.' The fluttering, swirling clouds of pigeons he remembered all his childhood at St Paul's, waiting for his father to come out, were finally gone. 'Eaten, probably,' he said.

He stood aside to let the volunteers by, the St Paul's Watch standing down. Old men and young invalids like himself dressed in civvies, doing their bit, pushed past the sandbagged walls. Even the orange Belisha beacons by the crossing across the road were dark, part of the blackout. Bernard touched them. Someone said, ''Morning, Bernard. Merry Christmas. See you tonight.' The yawning men plodded wearily past him, blinking as he had at the

406

sun, shoes and knees and elbows and faces grey with cathedral filth.

Bernard turned. Gus was watching him.

Christmas morning, and nothing at all had happened last night. Having nothing to do made the long hours of darkness drag out almost for ever. Most men found a corner to lay their heads, then woke up because of the quiet. The Royal Observer Corps watching from the dome boiled tea and fingered their binoculars, staring towards the east, waiting. Nothing. The air raid sirens hadn't gone off once. Not a bomb, not a fire, not a scare, not a sound. That was the worst.

'Come on,' Gus said, 'time to go home, see if you're a proud father yet.'

Bernard looked up. The sky was a perfect arch of winter blue, clean of aeroplanes and vapour trails, patchworked with herds of enormous soft barrage balloons like silver elephants. They tugged gently at their ropes over the silent City. 'Ladies' underwear,' Gus said. 'That's what they're made of. Makes you think. A hundred thousand silk knickers in each one.' He had turned to this sort of talk since his wife Margie was killed by a landmine, one of the first. They had been married for thirty-seven years. Gus said quietly, 'Are you all right, Bernard?'

'It was overwork. That's all.'

He crossed the atrium, Gus hurrying after him, and walked along the empty cabstand at the north side of the cathedral, touched the lamp post. Cutting across into Paul's Alley by the chapter house, they took the covered way beneath someone's bedroom into Paternoster Row. The famous old street was quiet and empty, lined with the shut-up premises of booksellers, Bible warehouses, map publishers and music publishers, theology publishers and bookbinders, tiny antiquarian bookshops like Gus's with grimy bow windows hinting at the shadows of books within. The windows of the houses above were blacked out. Bernard touched the lamp post on the corner.

'Will you stop that!' Gus exploded.

Bernard looked genuinely confused. 'Stop?'

'What are you doing, counting them? Found any missing? You're as bad as a dog, you are. You'll start peeing on them next.'

Bernard explained. 'They're lucky.'

Gus scoffed, 'If you miss one a bomb will fall on your head?'

'Some people believe that,' Bernard said sensibly. 'I don't say I do. It just seems silly to risk it.'

'They're cutting them down, you know. They're going the same way as the cathedral railings, being made into destroyers and engines.'

Ivy Lane, directly opposite them, was hardly wider than an alley. Gus said he wished the pub on the corner was open. Bernard reached out to the lamp post. Gus said, 'Don't!'

Bernard's hand trembled. He closed his fingers into a fist, pushed it into his pocket.

'That's better,' Gus said. The houses along Ivy Lane were tall and very narrow, little more than a door and a window surrounded by black brick, hundreds of years old. The two men's footsteps sounded so loud that they looked behind them.

'You get used to it,' Bernard muttered. 'This was my father's house. I've lived here all my life. I wasn't born until he was nearly fifty—'

'Fifty's young. I wouldn't mind being fifty again.'

'My mother was his second wife, much younger. He was fifty-three when my sister came along.'

'I thought you were an only child. She can't have been welcome to him at his age.'

'Mum was determined to have a girl.' Bernard looked back. '*You* haven't got used to it. Christ, it sounds as though we're being followed.'

'You ought to hear the noise when kids are playing.' Bernard stopped at his door, reached for the handle, and the door opened. Rose had been waiting.

She grinned, pushed her knuckles into the small of her back. She liked Gus. 'Merry Christmas, Gus,' she smiled. Bernard pecked her cheek. He didn't notice she'd had her chestnut hair shingled.

Gus looked at her tummy. 'My God, Rose, you look like you're any minute now.'

'She's never been on time for anything,' Bernard snorted. Rose straightened his collar affectionately, interrupting him.

'Come in, Gus, cup of tea?'

'Thank you warmly, and no. Beddy-byes.'

'Don't go home and mope.'

'Me!' Gus said brightly. 'I sleep. Merry Christmas.' He had been a bookseller all his life, starting from a barrow. Now he kept a little house above his premises in White Hart Street, beyond Paternoster Square. He was a friendly man who didn't quite fit in wherever he went. He pointed at her. 'It's a boy.'

Rose was fascinated, excited, gullible. 'How can you tell?'

Bernard said, 'He can't tell, he hasn't got any children.'

'I always wanted a son,' Gus said. 'Always regretted—' His eyes filled and he turned away. 'I like your new hair. Close the door, keep the warmth in. See you tonight, Bernard.'

Rose called, 'Fried bread—' but Gus was already waving, gone.

'You'll have the fried bread, and I've got a nice egg for you, a real one,' Rose told Bernard. She could not get round him in the tiny hall, so he went first into the kitchen. 'How are you, dear?' She kissed his nose.

'I mustn't touch lamp posts, Gus says.'

'Good. That's good.' She heaved herself between the table and the range. 'Anything happen?'

'Quiet night.'

'Get out the frying pan for me, there's a dear. Did you sleep?'

'No.'

'I don't sleep without you,' she said. She fried the precious egg carefully, then put her hands to her face. 'I don't sleep without you!' She turned to him impulsively, covering him with warmth and the odd knobbly pregnant shape of her, kissing his face. 'Now I've burnt your egg.' She waited for him to wipe her eye but he did not take out his handkerchief.

He tried to reassure her. 'It doesn't matter. You always burn my egg.'

She blew her nose on her apron. 'I wish I could give you an egg every day. You don't eat enough!'

'Now, Rose, don't start. Turkey for lunch.' One Christmas turkey was not rationed, though Rose had complained to Mr Bonser the butcher in Newgate Street that it was a pigeon. He'd given her the *London Look*. Londoners reserved it for strangers. Dr Winter had given her the *London Look* when she said she was afraid and she wanted to have her baby in hospital. London hospitals were for people who needed them, war-wounded and people who deserved it, and unbearable images of amputees and blinded airmen filled Rose's imagination. She felt awful just for asking the doctor for reassurance. She had never been outside the Cambridge village of Grantchester until she met Bernard, then an undergraduate. After his parents' crash they had moved here to his mother and father's house, full of childhood memories for him she could never share. The wallpaper, the carpets, every flutter of the curtains was Bernard's life, Bernard himself. Bernard's child would be born in the same house as Bernard and his sister Angela, in the same front bedroom, perhaps the same bed. With all her heart Rose had wished for a new bed but they had no money. Her job as a cleaner bought his textbooks, not a bed of her own. She was four years older than he and she had been afraid of having her first baby after thirty. Before his breakdown Bernard always expected more of her – she was sure – than she could provide, more passion, more wit, more beauty, more style. But now he needed mothering. She had never been able to understand his work, Bernard was so clever, brilliant, everyone said so, but now plain old she had him all to herself. Rose stroked his hair as he ate, then laid her other hand comfortingly across the top of her tummy. After all, he couldn't do what she was about to do. He would never know what it was like to feel a baby inside himself.

'I don't think it'll happen until the New Year,' she murmured happily. 'It'll be a nineteen forty-one baby.' Bernard finished his egg and she sat on his lap in front of the little cooker, stroking his hair, her lips against his forehead, until he slept.

She got up and went to the loo in the garden, then came back and watched him. Needing to go to the loo again washed over her in slow waves. Mrs Carter had slipped her a small brown paper bag of allotment sprouts and she peeled the last of the potatoes, giving herself something to do. She loved to work round Bernard, thinking about him, having him home. She hoped she wouldn't need the toilet during lunch. She found a cushion for his head. There was a knock on the door and she answered it, vegetable knife in her hand. A woman was standing on the step.

Rose was so startled that she said, 'Oh!'

'It's me,' Angela said, picking up her suitcase in her left hand. She kissed Rose's cheek as she came past her into the house. 'Heavens, Rosie, you're low! You're almost hanging between your knees. Any minute now. Call the hospital.'

Rose remembered to close the door and followed her along the hall. 'I thought you were in Portsmouth, Angela?'

Angela was a tall dark-haired woman of twenty-one, almost twenty-two. She wore a dark red woollen overcoat which she took off and hung on the hook without needing to look where the hook was. Underneath she was wearing a dark red angora dress, silk stockings, and dark red shoes. She glanced at Rose and smiled.

'Obviously not, Rosie dear.' She dropped her suitcase on the second step of the stairs, again without looking. 'Can I doss in the old back room? It's only me.'

'But – your husband—' Rose struggled to remember his name. She had met him once, something in the Navy, very dashing, with two rows of gilt buttons. 'Quentin—'

'Quentin is no longer with us.'

Rose gasped. She clapped her hand to her mouth, afraid of waking Bernard. 'Those terrible raids!' she whispered frantically. She wanted to hug Angela to show her sympathy, but Angela put a cigarette in a green jade holder that did not match her dress, and lit a match. The flame showed briefly in her eyes.

'He was killed by the husband of the woman he was found in bed with. It happens, and one can't blame all these guns this time. A shovel, they think.' She went into the kitchen. 'Wake up, Bernard.'

Bernard rubbed his face. 'Angela?'

Angela held out her arms.

'I'm sorry, I'm terribly sorry.' Rose pushed by. 'I have to go to the loo—'

'Is it lunchtime yet?' Bernard yawned. 'What are you doing here, Angela?'

Angela told him. 'Rosie put me in the back room.'

'Yes, of course. She was going to put the baby in there but it can sleep with us. Not that I sleep at nights.'

'Or during the day by the look of you. Doesn't she feed you?' Angela sat by the table and pushed her hands through her hair, destroying the set, and with her hair hanging she looked suddenly terribly vulnerable. 'How are you, Bernard?'

'Coping.' Bernard tried to smile. 'At least it keeps me out of the army.'

'You don't lie to me.'

'Sometimes I'm depressed. A little depressed.'

'A little. Like being sat on by a big black elephant.'

'It's good to see you, Angela.'

'Yes. Us. The good old days. God, I was happy here.' Her voice shook. 'I've had some rather bad news, I'm afraid.'

'I heard. Quentin—'

'No, not that loathsome bastard, my ex-husband. It's me.' She stubbed out her cigarette. Her red lips quivered, stretched. She put her fists in her eyes. 'It's me. I wanted . . . it turns out I was pregnant. A few months. Something went wrong, very wrong. I won't go into the plumbing.' She rubbed her face with the palms of her hands. 'I can't have a baby.'

'Oh, Angela.'

She searched her handbag for mirror, lipstick. 'Don't tell that little wife of yours.'

'No, of course not.'

'Don't want to upset her. Difficult time.' Angela gummed her lips, ran a comb through her hair, returned the mirror to her handbag. 'There, I didn't cry.'

'Stay here as long as you want. My doctor says time is the great healer.'

'Talking of time, what's happened to you-know-who? I hope she hasn't fallen down it.'

Bernard went down the garden. He cleared his throat, then knocked on the privy door. Through the gap Rose said in a terrified voice, 'I think it's happening! Bernard!' She was ashamed to be seen crouching over the hole. 'I don't know what to do. I'm frightened.'

Bernard helped her to the house. Angela pushed aside the kitchen chairs, seeing at once what was happening, and led the way upstairs knowing which way to go. 'Oh,' Rose groaned. She didn't want Angela to overhear that she only wanted her husband beside her, not a woman she didn't know. 'Oh,' Rose said. Her waters broke on the stairs. 'Oh, Bernard.'

Angela opened the bedroom door and took over. 'Don't worry, I've done this at the hospital. No place for husbands here.' She closed the door firmly in Bernard's face, then opened it an inch. 'Hot water. Towels. Aspirin. Enjoy your lunch, isn't that what men do?'

Bernard went down and brought back the things Angela had asked for. He knocked on the door.

'Leave them outside,' came Angela's voice.

Bernard sat around. He poured himself a Guinness and put the turkey in the oven. He looked for vegetables but there weren't any,

411

then he saw them peeled where Rose had left them, waiting in a saucepan on the draining board. He thought about her. Angela didn't call down. Occasionally the floorboards creaked upstairs. He went up and waited at the door, then came back down. He boiled the potatoes and the sprouts, then cut a slice or two of turkey. He wasn't hungry. He ate. Angela knew what she was doing. She always did.

Angela ran downstairs. Her hair had fallen in a tangle over her shoulders. 'Bernard? I should call Dr Winter.'

Bernard telephoned from the kiosk in Paternoster Row. It was getting dark. He really ought to be setting off for St Paul's. He went upstairs to tell Angela he must be getting to work. Rose gave an awful scream.

Angela's voice came, rising raggedly. 'Call on Jesus. Trust in Jesus!'

That awful, arching cry came again, then Rose's panting breaths.

Bernard put his hands over his ears. He was intensely distressed. He went and phoned for the doctor again, then waited downstairs.

Old Winter arrived at about five o'clock, a chubby red-faced little man smelling of Christmas pudding. He went upstairs.

Angela came down. She looked terrible. She lit a cigarette and put it out. Bernard said, 'You've got her blood on your hands.'

'It's all right. Everything's all right. Don't worry, Bernard.' She moved round the kitchen putting things in a bowl, threw more towels on top, and carried them upstairs.

Bernard remembered to pull the blackouts. He put a candle on the kitchen table and sat by it. The glow was more comforting than electric light. He heard Rose screaming. Her screams filled the house.

'Jesus! Jesus! Oh, Jesus!'

There was silence.

Bernard stood at the foot of the stairs.

Old Dr Winter came out. He stood on the top landing in his shirtsleeves. One side of his braces had slipped down to his elbow. He carried a white bundle in his arms.

He came downstairs, spoke to Bernard gently. 'Rose is fine.'

'I understand,' Bernard said.

'Bernard, your son is dead. He was born dead.' Winter held out the bundle tenderly. 'But your daughter is alive.'

My son is dead. Bernard reached out and touched a lamp post.

Gus tried to be kind. 'Better they don't live sometimes. I'm sorry.'

Bernard realised something else. 'I never saw him.'

'Doctor knows best, chum. You'll get over it quicker.'

Bernard said, 'It's so horrible I don't want to get over it. If only I'd seen my boy. Held him in my arms. What colour were his eyes?'

Gus stepped back as a darkened car rattled along Paternoster Row, its slitted headlights barely gleaming. He tried to cheer Bernard up. 'Twins run in the family, do they?'

Bernard said distractedly, 'In Rose's family.'

'Still, you've got the girl.'

'Emma.'

They crossed the road. 'Rose can't be that tired, then, if she's choosing names?'

'Angela liked it.'

'You mean *Angela* chose your daughter's name?'

'I suppose they both liked it. Rose is asleep now and Angela's holding the baby.' Bernard smiled in the dark. 'Emma keeps trying to suckle on her and Angela keeps saying, there's nothing for you in there, little one, my tit's dry as a bone. The baby makes her laugh. Angela's not had an easy time of it lately,' he explained.

They came down Paul's Alley and the cathedral hovered above the crooked rooftops, black as a hole cut among the stars. Bernard touched the lamp post. 'My son was born on Christmas Day,' he murmured, 'and on Christmas Day he died.'

'You never saw him, chum, so you'll get over it. Best to have nothing to remember.' Gus was thinking about his wife and their thirty-seven years together. 'I've got over it, didn't I? Life's a bitch and then you're dead. That's all there is to it. Don't think about it, that's my advice.'

A tiny light winked high above the dome. Someone was lighting a cigarette.

Bernard said, 'You're an atheist.'

'So's the Archbishop of Canterbury and the Pope. Power, that's all they want. That's not how they start off, Bernard, but it's how they end up. It's power.'

'Don't talk like this, Gus. Not tonight.'

'Margie died so *fast*. I waved from the end of the street and she was gone. Dust, that's all. A huge cloud of dust.'

'Then how can you be an atheist?'

'I don't know,' Gus said. 'I don't know what else to do. I prayed to God until my knees were raw, and I can tell you straight from the horse's mouth, Bernard, there's nothing there. Now here I am guarding a blooming cathedral. Makes you laugh, don't it.'

Bernard touched a lamp post.

'No,' he said. As they walked down the churchyard St Paul's made a huge dark mass on his left, nothing visible except its blackness, an absence rather than a presence. Yet, as always, Bernard felt comforted to be back here. He sensed its weight. He murmured, 'My mother used to say, you always carry the place you're born inside you.'

Gus was thinking about cigarettes. 'Oh? Where were you born?'

They reached the steps and Bernard touched the lamp post on the balustrade. 'Here.'

Gus said, 'You're joking. What, not actually in the cathedral?'

Bernard nodded. They stepped through the small door set in the huge door and he closed it behind them, echoing. 'Just here in fact.' He took a few paces into All Souls' Chapel on their left, turned by the large marble Lord Kitchener apparently sleeping, awaiting the resurrection or his country's call. 'My father called the national monuments in St Paul's disgusting heaps of trash. Kitchener wasn't put in until after the Great War. Father was the dean's virger. During evensong my mother watched him in the procession, and she made the mistake of kneeling for prayers in her condition. She couldn't quite make it outside. I was born on half a dozen chairs pushed together, just here.'

Gus grinned. 'Jigger me, I'll never look at this place the same way.'

'It's supposed to be haunted, you know. A cowled figure crosses the chapel and melts into the solid stonework.' He pointed at the niche in the north-eastern corner. 'Two accounts say a secret stairway led directly to the dome. My father told visitors that's ridiculous, since the dome is hundreds of feet away along the nave.'

'But people have seen the ghost?'

'You can't see its feet. It emits a high, tuneless whistle. So they say.'

'You've seen it?'

'No, no.'

There was only a single, dim electric light bulb.

'Do you believe in ghosts, Bernard?'

'I suppose I believe some people have seen them.'

'Margie would've found some way to get in touch if there was ghosts,' Gus said. 'There's nothing. I don't deceive myself.' He turned away abruptly. 'Come on, I'm late.'

They walked along the nave. The crossing rose in front of them, the huge dark vacant space of the dome curving above it, the great circle of windows boarded or removed. Even during the day the cathedral was almost impenetrably gloomy, its stones layered with generations of sooty filth. The black walls absorbed the glow of the tiny light bulbs strung here and there along the emptiness of the interior. Bernard's breath streamed over his shoulders like a dim white scarf in the bitter cold. The stoves in the crypt were not lit, saving fuel, and no heat rose through the bronze gratings set in the floor. In the distance an officer with a torch crossed the choir. The wooden screen that once obscured the choir stalls had been taken down in the last century and his torchlight flashed briefly across the elephantine pink marble reredos erected behind the altar by the Victorians, Christ on Calvary towering as high as the clerestory. The officer turned, startled, hearing their footsteps, but did not see them.

Bernard crossed the nave, stepping over the fire hoses laid along the side aisles. As a child he had often accompanied his father's tours of St Paul's – sixpence for the virger's boy from doting ladies in feathered hats – and he probably knew as much of the cathedral as his father had. He knew that grey-black stone was Portland and brown-black was Ketton. He knew that the mains water pressure feeding the hilltop always dropped during a raid, and he knew the hoses would be useless once the old three-thousand-gallon cistern in the south choir-aisle roof, designed to provide hydraulic pressure for the choir organ, was exhausted. Bombs had fallen all round St Paul's but by a miracle the cathedral survived unharmed, so far. A landmine in the churchyard and a bomb striking the atrium had each failed to explode. The St Paul's Watch kept a round-the-clock vigil, prowling the cathedral's miles of passageways, rooftops and balconies with stirrup pumps, buckets of sand, fireproof blankets, and quiet camaraderie hundreds of feet above the ground. If the cathedral burnt, so would they.

Bernard led the way up the broad, curving staircase set in the south-west transept pillar. Visitors and worshippers had carved thousands of names in the limewashed walls. From the Whispering Gallery the two men looked down into the crossing. Gus puffed, cursing cigarettes. The floor seemed very far below.

They ducked through a narrow door and climbed a circular staircase set like a stone screw in the wall. 'Stainless steel chains were wrapped round the dome ten years ago to stop it spreading,' Bernard said. 'Traffic vibration. The ground beneath the cathedral is a Sacred Area by Act of Parliament. No sewers, no Underground tunnels – that was to be the Piccadilly & City Tube. The proposed course of the Central Line was diverted under Newgate Street. No tramcar subways. No telephone lines. Nothing.'

They came to an iron platform, the inner dome curving away beneath them, the skin of the outer dome arching above them in a maze of support timbers. Their feet clanged on the iron ladders crisscrossed over the cone of whitewashed bricks rising from the peak of the inner dome below, taking the weight of the stone lantern high above. The ladders zigzagged between the domes, their angle increasing, leaning towards the centre of the cathedral.

Bernard said, 'Wren's wooden stairs were replaced with cast iron at the same time as Victorian firefighting equipment was installed.'

'You aren't making me look down,' Gus puffed.

They came to the Golden Gallery, stepped into the night air. Beyond the balustrade London spread below them vast and black in every direction, a solid invisible mass of houses and factories stretching to the distant ring of hills. Hardly a light showed all the way from Vaudey in the east to Hammersmith in the west, Hampstead Hill in the north to the Downs in the south. Bernard knew he was looking at millions of people but he could not see them, they might as well not have been there. A few stars gleamed in the Thames. The moon would not rise until five in the morning.

'Bingo, it's not Christmas Day any more,' someone said, and Bernard's grief washed over him.

The Royal Observer Corps brewed tea behind their sandbags, pointed at a light shining in the east. They could not make out if it was an aircraft or a balloon. 'That's Neptune,' Bernard said. 'It's a planet.'

The old men blew on their hands. 'I don't like this quiet,' someone muttered. 'Cuppa, chum?'

Here I am drinking tea, Bernard thought, and my son is dead. 'Thanks,' he said. He could hardly bear to be alive.

Later Gus lit a gasper behind his hands, passed it across. 'Cheer up, mate.' The men were silent now. Gus must have told them what happened and they didn't know how to say anything.

Gus said, 'Christmas is over. Two Woodbines says Jerry'll come across tonight. What do you think, Bernard?'

Bernard said, 'They won't be over tonight.'

'Personal friend of Herr Goering, is he, just got off the Fat Man's blower?' The corporal shook his head, spat over the great curve of dome falling away below them.

'They'll come on Sunday night. No moon. At low tide. And they'll bomb the water mains first.'

Gus said, 'Take it easy, Bernard.'

'That's what *I'd* do,' Bernard said savagely. 'Wouldn't you?'

He leant back against the cold stone and closed his eyes. He couldn't bear to be near the men, their eyes and ears, their murmuring, embarrassed voices, their dullness. They were all decent sorts. Bernard went down to the small balcony encircling the top of the inner dome, sat alone. He pushed his legs through the railings, and rested his head against his forearms. He stared down into the crossing, tiny between his swinging feet.

'There is no God,' he whispered.

The bombers did not come.

A little before dawn he returned to Gus in the lantern room at the peak of the cathedral. Across the southern sky he saw Mercury, Venus, the crescent moon, Mars and Neptune stretched in conjunction above the sunrise like a pointing finger.

The bombers did not come the next night. Or the next.

On Sunday the air raid warning sirens wailed over London at teatime, shortly before sunset. Cigarettes were put out and the St Paul's Watch stood to the fire-posts in the cathedral. Bernard climbed to the Golden Gallery beneath the lantern, ball and cross as usual. Below him five million people hurried towards the air raid shelters or the Underground, children with their mothers into Morrison shelters in the front rooms or Anderson shelters in the garden, carrying their tea on trays if they could, budgerigars in their cages, dogs on leads, rabbits in hutches, and small girls determinedly clutched their cats. Most people were getting more fed up with the winter weather than with bombs.

Again the bombers did not come, and the all-clear sounded in the dark.

'False alarm,' came the corporal's voice. 'Time for a fag, lads.'

Bernard leant on the railing on the gallery's other side, facing not to the east but the south-west. In the sun's fading afterglow, still visible from the top of St Paul's, a faint drifting stain showed among the colours, yellow, orange, purple-red, of sunset over the home counties.

'Look, Gus.'

''Strewth,' Gus said.

Now the bombers made a curling line turning towards their target, black dots swelling but not moving, heading straight for London and the observers. 'Corporal,' Bernard shouted. A few seconds later sirens went off all over the City. The bombers weaved along the line of the river dropping white shadows, parachute bombs. The odd rhythmic beat of Nazi engines roared suddenly loud, close overhead, so that everyone high on the dome instinctively crouched. 'It's all right, they're not interested in us,' Bernard said. 'They're bombing the pumping stations.' Explosions lifted mud and water and buildings along the river's edge. Searchlights lanced upward, ack-ack guns thumped and popped, tracer arched into the night sky, but the bombers were gone.

'And the tide's going out,' Gus whispered, remembering. 'I wish you weren't always right, Bernard.'

Bernard thought of Rose clutching their new-born baby in the Morrison shelter in the parlour, no doubt trying to keep Emma asleep despite the bells of the fire engines and ambulances tearing along Newgate Street and Ludgate, and all the whistles and sirens. Rose hated noises and shocks. Not for the first time Bernard thanked goodness she had Angela with her for company.

What had his son died of? His nameless son. Born dead, going nameless into eternity.

'We're really going to catch it now, aren't we,' Gus said. 'You were right. Christ, Bernard, I wish I didn't know. Knowing only makes it worse.'

Bernard felt in his pocket. His hand trembled. He touched a Passing Cloud, and a warm sensation of love washed over him, knowing whose fingers had put it there. Rose had delicate fingers, sensitive and quite naughty when she felt like it, and he saw her as real and desirable as though she stood here. But he had loved his son too. Neither he nor Rose had spoken of their son, his memory was an invisible wall between them. It was better. They would each slowly forget in their own way, slightly separated.

He blinked. The streets below had disappeared. Everything was total darkness.

And then the flames began.

There was no more time. Suddenly incendiary bombs rattled on the cathedral roof. One old soldier dumped a bucket of sand on the shoddy metal stick sputtering between his feet, calmly winked at Bernard and stepped over it to deal with the next. Bernard kicked another stick over the edge, heard it clatter down the dome's curve, fall harmlessly into the churchyard. A fire had started in one of the skylight balconies. He swung himself over the parapet and slid down the roof, dropped into the balcony. He glimpsed the glare of burning phosphorus in the smoke, then abruptly it went out. Gus, his head and shoulders sticking out of a tiny door, was just finishing off the job. 'Busy night, chum,' he said, wiping his moustache tiredly. They had been on the go for hours and his teeth and eyes looked very white in his smokestained face. Men with a fire hose leant out from the Stone Gallery, spraying the long roof of the nave below. The flow of water slowed to a trickle, stopped. Someone was overcome by smoke, not from inside the cathedral but the air outside. He was carried away and Bernard turned off the hose. The corridors, gilded balconies and great galleries of the cathedral flickered with reflected flame and smoke blowing over the dome. St Paul's must be standing among the smokeclouds like a beacon.

Bernard muttered, 'High explosive south of the river, firebombs north.'

'They can't get water out of the river because the tide's out,' someone called, 'they're sucking mud.'

Bernard put his hand in his pocket but he had smoked the cigarette or given it away. Instead his fingers touched the milky-possety handkerchief he'd wiped on Emma's face, burping her after her feed. He crumpled it to his nose, inhaling the scent of his daughter. He was more than a husband now, he was a father. He stared through the smoke, thinking he saw a couple of shops burning in Paternoster Row. He was mad to keep his family in London, but most people did.

He tripped across Gus, who was lying down against one of the walls. 'I'm just tired,' Gus said. Bernard sat beside him and leant back, closed his eyes. Someone was shaking his shoulder. He woke and followed the man to a fire, but it was only a piece of blackout curtain burning in a gallery doorway. They pulled it down and trod on it. The other man saw a canister bouncing down the steps. It trailed sparks and smoke. He grabbed a bucket of water from the rack. Bernard shouted, 'No!'

The sulphur bomb burst into a fierce blue light at the water's touch, too bright to look near, and splashed sizzling drops of fire. Lumps of burning sulphur splashed with the water in all directions, clinging to wet clothes, and the man who had woken Bernard screamed, pulling at his coat, then his hair, then his face.

Bernard wrapped him in a blanket. Stretcher-bearers manhandled him downstairs. Bernard never saw him again.

Bernard sat on one of the tiny circular stairs closed to the public. The wedge-shaped steps were almost too steep to hold him so he leant back on his elbows. He was looking down into the crossing. From this height the ranks of choir stalls lining the choir looked like beautifully carved toys. The statues of Algar and Donne were no larger than marionettes, the two survivors of Old St Paul's, one from its beginning, the other from very nearly its end. A figure appeared down there in the dim, smoky light, and there was something so familiar about its purposeful walk that for a moment Bernard ached with longing, remembering the brisk strides of his father, Gregory Lydiard, as though he was still alive. The dean's virger always carried his silver wand of office in the crook of his arm, his boyish smiling face scrubbed pink as a choirboy's above his black gown. Father had worked with Simpson in the cathedral library, above the Chapel of St Michael and St George. 'No man knows more of St Paul's,' Father said, 'than I do, except William Sparrow Simpson.' And Mother always smiled her quiet, loyal smile and said, 'Yes, dear.' Father had helped Simpson, then an old man, begin to locate, collect and edit the ancient statutes of St Paul's, at first known only from a single manuscript catalogue, from copies long ago scattered in various libraries. Gradually they had been found and brought together. But Father's greatest discovery was when twenty-one steps of the Geometrical Staircase leading to the library pulled away from the wall – almost sending him to his death – and revealed to his peering eye, as he clung by his fingers to the bolt-holes in the stone, a forgotten garret in the tower. The room was a mass of ancient charters, wills, leases and registers not seen since the Great Fire, many of them half burnt or badly decayed, still with ash clinging to them, still smelling of smoke. Cataloguing them was Father's life's work, for a fee of twenty pounds a year, and it was still not complete when he died.

The figure wore a hood over its head, perhaps brown, or perhaps that was the all-pervading gloom and dirt. The foreshortened shape bobbed at the altar and paused, in prayer perhaps, or contemplation. Dust drifted from the roofs and arches, and Bernard realised that the Nazis were now dropping high-explosive bombs north of the river, spreading the flames that had taken hold.

Bernard stared. The hooded stranger was gone.

He looked each way. The crossing and transepts were deserted, the nave empty but for several firemen at the far end, by the doors.

He dropped down a step or two, trying to see into the ambulatory. Nothing.

Bernard heard a rising whistle and clapped his hands over his head. Everyone knew that sound.

The bomb burst inside the cathedral.

He opened his eyes, coughing. He was deaf, everything was silent. A wave of stained windows blew along the choir below him like glass knives, slid into the crossing, piled up as though the empty pews were breakwaters. Bits of stone and marble and rubble bounced from wherever they had been thrown by the force of the explosion.

Bernard limped down. He had hurt his knee, he did not remember how. On the floor of the cathedral the dust was chokingly thick. He began to hear his feet crunching on glass and looked down to see the hands of saints, and heads in golden haloes, breaking beneath his boots. The flying glass must have cut the stranger to ribbons. Bernard pushed forward. 'Where are you?' he coughed. 'Are you all right? Call out if you can, so I can find you.'

There was no sign or sound of the man. Bernard twisted his head, locating the steps where he'd been sitting, found the line of sight. Exactly here. Bernard stepped forward between the statues of Algar and Donne into the choir, twisting his ankles on lumps of marble. The bomb had burst near the huge pink marble reredos, shattering it. The altar was gone, carried down with the floor into the crypt below. Bernard picked up broken boards, lumps of marble or plaster, searching for a body underneath.

He looked round. 'Where the hell are you,' he said.

From the corner of his eye, he thought he saw the statue of Algar move. Bernard turned slowly. The hooded figure slipped away from the niche and he called after it, 'Hey, you!' The folds covering its head and shoulders were white with dust. Bernard shouted, 'You there. Stop!' The stranger ignored him. Bernard gritted his teeth at the pain in his knee, ran a few steps. The stranger heard his footsteps and ran. A piece of paper fluttered from beneath the hem of the garment. Bernard glimpsed a red shoe. He stopped. 'Angela?'

He stared after the running figure. Men hurrying along the nave towards the scene of the explosion held out their arms. The figure swerved, then disappeared in the direction of the Lord Mayor's vestry, which had its own steps to the outside.

The men shrugged, pushed past Bernard. 'All right, mate? Not too shook about?'

He grinned to show he was fine. He watched them dig in the rubble for survivors, in case anyone had been in the crypt. He drew back step by step.

Bernard picked up the piece of dropped paper. He knew at once it was different. It was skin.

The writing was in square Hebrew text, following the ancient scribal custom with books considered to be Holy Scripture. Bernard's lips moved. '"Are they then to unsheathe the net . . ."' He looked up.

'You know, don't you,' Gus said. He stood without moving a muscle. 'You look like you've seen a ghost.'

Bernard crumpled the fragment in his pocket. 'Know?'

'You mean you don't know?' Gus gripped Bernard's hands. 'Sit down over here, Bernard. The warden just told me. Your house has been hit.' He gripped tight. 'There's nothing you can do. Don't go there, Bernard.'

Bernard ran through the streets. He shouted. The streets were gone, taped off because of unexploded bombs. Paternoster Row was smouldering ruins. A policeman bent with his hands on his knees, talking kindly to a little flat-capped boy in the thin dawn light. The boy had lost his dog. Ivy Lane was gone.

Bernard's house was gone. Men crawled carefully in the ruins, one of them with a stethoscope. He was listening for survivors. Someone held Bernard back. He found himself sitting on a piece of wall.

Rose confessed, 'I only popped out for a moment to make a cup of tea. You don't know what it's like, feeding a baby.'

Bernard shouted, '*Where's Emma?*'

'You don't have to shout!' Rose burst into tears. 'I left her in the Morrison shelter. She was sleeping at last. The men say there's a chance. They say it's amazing sometimes.'

Bernard shouted at her. 'You stupid cow, why didn't you take my daughter into the kitchen with you?' He put his hands over his mouth. 'I'm sorry, I'm sorry.'

'If only you'd been here,' she said. She burst into tears again. 'Angela was asleep upstairs. She called our Morrison poky.' Rose sounded mortally offended. 'She said she'd rather die in a bed, preferably with a bottle of good brandy and a man. I said I had to think of Emma. I called her a self-centred bitch.' She hicked tearfully. 'Now I'm sorry.'

Angela's voice came from behind them, 'And I'm sorry I called you a milky little house-mouse.'

'Angela!' Rose hugged her. Angela looked straight at Bernard across the top of Rose's head.

'I suppose this is the time for us all to say we're sorry. I couldn't sleep, I went for a walk.' She nodded at the men working. 'The little one?'

Bernard shook his head.

'Oh my God,' Angela said.

Half the men took their shovels and went on to the next house. A warden put up tapes.

A bustling woman took them over to a lorry and insisted on handing out mugs of tea. She said something about a church hall. 'No sugar,' Angela said. Even holding a fireclay mug and a slab of bread and marge between her painted nails, her red shoes peeping beneath the hem of her plaid cape, she was the centre of the street. Every man was aware of her, except Bernard.

'My son is dead,' Bernard muttered. 'My daughter is dead. I might as well be dead.'

Angela said, 'Don't speak like that in front of Rose.'

They watched Mrs Horsell dug out from the pub, her hands laid over her chest as peacefully as though she was asleep, her eyes full of wall-plaster and glass.

Bernard turned and looked where the rooftops had been. The cathedral's dome stood dark against the dawn, seeming very high, showing no sign of damage. His distress came out of him as anger. 'What were you doing there, Angela?'

Rose said in a high voice, 'Why shouldn't she walk into your precious cathedral, Bernard? To pray, obviously. I ought to be praying. But you're too clever to believe in anything, aren't you. Hold my hand. Why weren't you with me? What about me? God, I'm going to be sick.'

Bernard sat her on an angle of garden wall. 'Put your head between your knees. That's better.' He spoke without looking round. 'Angela, I know you were there.' He kept his head down, he knew he would believe anything Angela said once he let her catch his eye. It had been that way even when they were children. Little girls liked to be mysterious, and Angela was all girl.

'I don't give a damn what you think, Bernard,' Angela said.

Bernard stared at her, baffled. 'Why are you denying it?'

'You don't know as much as you think you do. You're an arrogant man. You think you know it all.'

Bernard reached into his pocket. 'Well, you forgot this.'

Angela hesitated. She took the scrap of vellum gently between her fingers. 'I don't even know what it is,' she murmured.

'It's Hebrew.'

Angela said, 'But it's not really old, is it, Bernie?'

Bernard shrugged. He sat beside Rose, held her limp hand.

Angela murmured, 'Then Mother was right.'

'Mum?' Bernard said, surprised. 'She couldn't even speak French, let alone Hebrew. All Mum cared about was the price of bread, clean children and a clean house, and keeping Father happy. That was her whole life. That was all she knew.' He realised Angela wasn't listening to him.

'Bernie, tell me what it says!'

He shrugged. 'Something about nets.'

'Is that all?'

Bernard took it back, put it in his pocket. 'You were there in the cathedral, Angela. You were underneath the bomb. It's a wonder you weren't killed.'

Someone shouted. The man with a stethoscope knelt on a wall that had fallen forward in one piece. He reached beneath him into a window. He called for men with shovels to clear a space, then reached down for a second time.

The kneeling man pulled up a baby by the heels. It swung from his fist as silent as a doll. Someone pulled the shawls off, revealing the naked body of a little girl. Rose shrieked, '*Emma!*'

Emma moved. Her baby-face screwed up bright red, she clenched her chubby fists, and then she emitted a piercing cry as though she had just been born for the second time.

'It's a miracle,' Angela said.

'Come up to bed, Bernard,' Rose said.

Bernard sounded surprised. 'I can't, I'm on duty at St Paul's tonight.' Emma had finally gone to sleep in his lap after her baby-bath in the regulation two inches of water. Even asleep she looked determined to make trouble. She had long black eyelashes. Bernard sat like a statue in case he woke her.

'Yes, I know that you are on duty, Bernard.' Rose flushed red to the tips of her ears. Angela sat on the sofa leafing through *Life* magazine, one knee crossed over the other, perfect silk stockings as usual. Where did she get them? Grubby little men in backstreets, probably, Angela always got what she wanted. Rose said, 'Come up and say goodnight, Bernard, that's all.' She tried to pass a secret husband-and-wife signal. 'I'll get ready for bed, all right?'

'I'll be up,' Bernard said, and the door closed. Angela leafed, crossed her legs the other way. Remarkably Gus's little bookshop had survived the raid unharmed, though the terraces all round were flattened from the Oxford Arms passage to the Four Nuns, and now he called it his house-all-alone. The bath and piping of its bombed neighbour still clung improbably, complete with wallpaper, to one wall. Gus had insisted they stay as long as they wanted. 'You're the only friends I got left, anyway.' The parlour was over the shop, a couple of bedrooms above it, and Bernard and Rose had the attic. Gus liked talking to Angela. Remembering Margery comforted him, his memories rushed out of him as though he were living his life again. Angela could be a good listener when she wanted. She glanced up, listening to Rose's footsteps go upstairs.

'You're popular tonight, Bernard,' she said. She put down the magazine, touched the baby. 'You're holding her wrong.'

'For God's sake don't wake her!'

'I won't wake the little darling.' Angela pulled the baby's head up in the crook of Bernard's arm. 'There, that's better. Told you she wouldn't wake.'

Bernard looked down at his daughter's sleeping face. 'Sometimes I realise how much I almost lost. Sometimes it just washes over me.'

Angela smiled and Bernard smelt her perfume. 'You haven't got over it, Bernie.'

'What?'

'She's alive.'

Bernard touched his daughter's black hair with his fingertip. 'No. I'll never get over it. I'll never forget how lucky I am.'

'Give her to me.' Angela held out her arms authoritatively. 'You dash on upstairs to the little wife, go on. She's dying for you.'

Bernard sat without moving. 'And I'll never forget my son. Angela, I can't touch *him*—' He stirred his fingertip in the strands of girlish baby hair. 'But I'll never forget him.'

'You're so unhappy, Bernard. You're as atheist as poor Gus is.'

'Yes. I am unhappy. And I'm happy. I don't know what I am, sis.'

'Your son's name was Bernard, wasn't he?'

'He didn't have a name. He didn't have time.'

'He's a part of you for ever, though. He has his father's name. Bernard.'

'Bernard,' Bernard whispered. He looked straight into Angela's clear blue eyes, as cool and deep as his own, like looking into his own eyes in a mirror in a darkened room. 'Angela, may I ask you a question?'

She gave their childhood answer. 'Only if it's personal.'

'How far along was your baby when it went wrong?'

'Ah.' Angela sighed. 'Her name was Angela.'

'I'm sorry, sis.'

Angela took Emma into her arms. 'I'll look after her while you're gone.'

Bernard stood. 'I'll put her in the cot when I go,' he whispered. 'I won't be a minute.'

'I know how long you'll be,' Angela said.

Bernard went upstairs. The attic floor creaked as Rose came swiftly to him. She put her hands behind his head and kissed him. As she raised her arms her nightdress opened and her breasts lifted towards him, her nipples and aureoles almost black in the single candlelight. Her pubic hair was black. She pulled his hand down so he could feel what he was getting, and suddenly Bernard wanted her, wanted her very badly. They stumbled past the cot and he fell on top of her on the bed.

He pushed down into her as she arched against him. Bernard gasped.

'There,' Rose murmured. She held his head between her breasts, lay back among her curls of chestnut hair, sucked him deeper into her with her hips. 'Here's one thing Angela can't do for you.'

Bernard came out of St Paul's at dawn. Gus blinked at the sunlight streaming past them after the gloom inside, yawned, stretched. 'I'm off home.'

'I've got the Army Medical Review Board at eleven,' Bernard said.

'They'll make you wait. Get some shut-eye. Don't turn up before two.'

'I won't be long,' said Bernard. 'I'll stay here a while.'

'Maybe Angela will fry me an egg,' Gus said cheerfully. He waved as he crossed the road. 'Good luck!'

Bernard turned back into the cathedral. He walked through the main door among the early worshippers. St Paul's termed all visitors worshippers. A temporary altar had been set up in the crossing and he stopped, listening to their footsteps echo away from him up the nave. Then he settled back by one of the pillars where he could watch the door.

A few worshippers left, looking at their watches, hurrying to start the day. Girls primped by with lines drawn up the backs of their legs as though they wore nylons. A smart peremptory woman in a good hat went into the Chapel of St Dunstan for private prayer and holy communion. A sailor with one leg hobbled past, looking at no one as though not to be seen. A man in a wheelchair was carried up the steps by his pals. A couple of strolling RAF airmen smoked pipes, hands in pockets. Now several people came in speaking a foreign language, Polish perhaps. Bernard found a chair, sat with his elbows on his knees. Soon he recognised most of those who had gone in coming out. The sailor came by, ignored him. The cathedral fell silent.

A group of workmen came inside, calling, 'Anyone home?' There was no one around to tell them what to do. They didn't see Bernard. They heard pickaxes clinking in the bomb-damaged choir and made out the men working there, went to join them.

A man with an umbrella came in, shook off the drops. 'Change of weather!' he snorted to no one in particular. It must be raining outside. The light between the doors was grey and smooth.

A small boy came in with his mother. 'But, Mum,' he begged her. She was willowy, very pale, her eyes tearful. The boy kept saying he wanted to play in the snow. The snowflakes on his cap didn't melt, it was so cold in the cathedral. She dragged him up the aisle. 'But, Mum,' he whined. Gradually his complaints faded. Later they came out, and the boy ran forward into the snow. Bernard's eyes flickered. He yawned. He put his right elbow on his knee, rested his face on his hand. His body knew he was supposed to be asleep.

The man with the umbrella left. Bernard glanced at his watch and gave up. He got to his feet, then shrank back behind the pillar as footsteps walked briskly past. He circled the stone behind her, recognising her clothes, recognising her brisk walk. His sister's plaid hood and shoulders were covered with snow. She thought he was snoring in bed in the attic.

It was her after all, though she had denied coming here. *I couldn't sleep, I went for a walk.* Why had Angela lied at first about being in St Paul's that night? Then finally she had admitted, *Mother was right.* Whatever it was Angela had found in the cathedral, that scrap of vellum had surprised her as much as Bernard. *I don't even know what it is.*

And his own voice saying, *It's a wonder you weren't killed.*

How was she still alive?

She walked up the nave and Bernard kept alongside her in the side aisle, the columns sweeping between them. Angela threw back her hood, sending snow sliding from her shoulders. She looked mature and beautiful, her lips fashionably crimson. Mature, beautiful, sterile. Once they'd sworn the oath children always swore, with a pin and blood, and hope to die, they'd never have secrets from each other when they grew up. But being grown up was more complicated than boys and girls believed. Adults always had secrets, and however much they revealed there were always more. Last night Bernard had even wondered, briefly, if Rose was somehow a little jealous of Angela. It was a ridiculous idea. It was impossible for a man to see into the strange secrets of a woman's mind.

As she walked Angela worked her fingers one by one out of her brown leather gloves, revealing smooth white hands. Rose did the washing up, not Angela, except a token rinse of the teacups. Rose always wanted to do it, she was fierce about it, insisted. Bernard hid behind one of the eight great piers supporting the dome. Angela became small, walked into the crossing.

She paused, watching the workmen clear rubble from the choir. A whistle blew and they sat at a table set up by the statue of Algar. They gulped from mugs, ate sandwiches. Bernard heard a burst of male laughter.

Angela turned away abruptly. She returned along the nave and he supposed she was leaving the cathedral. Instead, she changed course by Wellington's monument and walked into the north aisle. For a moment Bernard thought she was going to pray in St Dunstan's chapel, but she walked past the door into All Souls'.

Bernard slipped quietly along the wall of St Dunstan's. He moved forward until he saw into All Souls', the chapel where he had been born. He saw the soles of Angela's feet in her dark red shoes. She was kneeling.

The monumental effigy of Lord Kitchener lay in full marble regalia on its plinth. Between its riding boots and the altar Angela knelt on the little brown prayer cushion. The two enormous silver candlesticks that usually stood there had been removed for safekeeping but the small candlesticks on each side of the crucifix remained. The high window, set back several feet in the thickness of the wall, had been boarded against the danger of flying glass and the chapel was murky as an old photograph.

Angela stood. Bernard pulled back as her hand appeared on the far wall, below the window. She reached into the brass grate commemorating the dead. Her wrist turned as though feeling for something, slid inside almost to the elbow.

The flagstones tingled beneath Bernard's feet. Something had moved.

Her hand withdrew. Bernard glimpsed her. She had pulled the hood over her head.

The niche in the north-east corner had opened. It was a door.

Angela ducked inside. The stones swung, closing. Bernard ran forward. He grabbed one of the small candlesticks, thrust it into the narrow gap. The door stopped.

He used his foot as a wedge, shoved his shoulder into the opening, pushed. The door would neither open nor close. He squeezed his hand inside, grabbed something warm and soft, pulled out a handful of plaid. Angela's face struggled in the gap. 'Let me go!'

Bernard said, 'You're the ghost.'

She tugged. 'For God's sake, Bernard, let me go, let me go—'

'I've got you.'

They heard footsteps approaching from the nave. Their raised voices had been heard.

She hissed, 'For God's sake, Bernard, you don't know what you're doing!' She banged his knuckles with an electric torch, but it rattled loudly. 'For God's sake!' she whispered, then fell back. Bernard stumbled inside, slipped to his knees. The door rumbled, sliding closed.

It was dark inside.

'Turn on the bloody torch,' Bernard said.

She said, 'I can't. I've lost the bloody batteries.'

'You can't have lost the bloody batteries,' Bernard said furiously. His voice sounded so angry that he didn't recognise himself. He chuckled. They both laughed.

They heard muffled voices in the chapel, someone thought they had heard something. Then there was nothing. Bernard heard Angela breathing.

'Wait a minute,' he said. He clicked his lighter, picked up the candlestick, lit the candle. They looked for the batteries that had fallen from the torch.

Angela snapped the torch on. Its light lit her face from below, her eyes intensely blue, her nose sending a black spike of shadow up her forehead.

'You bastard, pushing your way in,' she said.

They stood in a short corridor, the stones pressing close on both sides. He looked round him. 'What's this?'

She shrugged. 'What do you think?'

'What I don't understand,' he said, pushing forward, 'is why Father never told *me* about this place.'

Angela let him push past, shone the torch beam on the back of his head. She drawled, 'Why should Father know of it?'

'Of course he did.' Bernard turned, squinted against the torchlight. 'No one knew St Paul's like Father. He was dean's virger for twenty-four years. But why did he tell *you?*'

He sounded so hurt that Angela said impulsively, 'It wasn't him. It was Mother.'

'Mother?' Bernard came to a circular stone staircase. Steps led both up and down. 'She didn't know anything except raising children, and obedience to Father.'

Angela came to a decision. 'That's what I used to think. Mum never had his education. Never had a job, except being his wife. Never interrupted him, always deferred to him. He was a bit of a tyrant, wasn't he?'

Bernard frowned. He said, 'Father?'

He had never thought of it that way. My father was a tyrant.

'You're blind, Bernard.' Angela sighed. 'There was much more to Mum than we knew. Mum's own mum couldn't write, I don't think. Grandmama never had money, not with the size of her family. Eight boys. But there was something between those two. The two females. Something about them knew a lot more than educated people, I think.'

Bernard held the silver candlestick above his head. He peered round the stairs winding upward. 'The secret staircase,' he said. 'So it is true. There is a secret way along the roof of the nave to the dome.'

'I don't care. I think there's probably more than we can imagine.' Angela pointed the torch beam on the steps going down. 'That's all I know. That's all Mum said.'

'What did she say exactly?'

'She said she knew the truth.'

Bernard went down. He thought to come out in the crypt, but the steps went down farther than he expected, to a second corridor. Angela flashed the torch both ways, then turned right.

'We're beneath the crypt,' Bernard called. He sounded as excited as a little boy. Angela shook her head, remembering him. She grinned, flashing the torch to annoy him.

She led him forward. The snowflakes melted on her shoulders, trickling. It was warmer down here than in the cathedral. The corridor turned from time to time, following the line of the foundations. Other, narrower passageways joined it. Angela shone the torch, they glimpsed ways stretching into darkness, floors of beaten brickearth. Great blocks of stone curved down into the labyrinth, the foundations of the great columns supporting the crypt and the weight of the cathedral above.

Angela glanced round. She whispered, 'This wasn't added afterwards, was it?'

'No,' Bernard murmured. 'I think this is why the cathedral was built as it was. My God.'

Angela walked forward. 'Maybe we're beneath the Treasury now.' She bent, the roof was lower. A dusty passage came from their left. 'I know where I am. Algar's that way.'

'So that's how you got down the other night.'

'The English foot.' She grinned provocatively. 'I'm not telling you everything.' She pointed the torch into the darkness ahead of them.

The stone walls gave way to dark clay. They stepped down on to a floor which crunched. Bernard knelt.

'Mosaic. Roman,' he muttered. 'Can't be.'

He held up the candlestick, then followed Angela's torch into the dark. Cobwebs were lifted into his face by the draught. The flickering candleflame revealed niches about seven feet long, eighteen inches high, carved into the wall. He touched a name and it crumbled to dust. Exsuperius. He came to another. Restitutus. Another, Theon. 'It's a catacomb, sis.'

Angela said, 'You mean these really are dead people?'

'Restitutus was a British bishop in Roman times. Exsuperius I've never heard of. Theon's name is known only from an account by Geoffrey of Monmouth, writing a thousand years later. He's thought to be no more of a real historical figure than King Arthur.' He touched a dry bone. 'He *was* thought. My God, sis, there's my university thesis here.'

Angela shone the torch in his eyes. 'Swear the oath.' She pulled his hands down. 'Look at me. Mum made me swear when she was dying, after the crash. I was called from school. I swore on her deathbed. You protect what I will show you with your life.'

He looked at the walls. He struggled to understand. 'What – dead bodies?'

She shone the light in her own eyes. 'Swear.' She held out her finger.

Bernard touched her fingertip. 'Hope to die.'

Angela looked at him tenderly. 'When you see,' she said, 'you'll believe.'

She took his hand in hers, led him forward. The catacomb ended in a plain wooden door. The style reminded Bernard of doors in the cathedral above them. Angela turned the key. She twisted the handle, and the door opened.

Bernard went first. He came down some steps into a small room lined with stone.

Angela looked up. 'We're directly beneath the crossing. The exact centre of the dome.' She closed the door behind them.

The centre of the room was taken up by a curved cast-iron banister protecting a circle of stone steps going down into the floor. He touched the cool iron. 'Jean Tijou's work. Just like in the cathedral.'

'This is the cathedral,' Angela said.

Bernard gripped the candlestick and went down to the landing below. The roof was low, made of the floor of the little room above. In it a stone slab had been set in mortar. 'It's a petroglyph,' he said.

Along the surface were strange wavy patterns that defied Bernard's intellect. They were disorderly and he could not make them out. Dots had been pecked in the stone at random, or perhaps they were natural flaws in the stone. But beside them, a word had been carved in Roman letters.

RESURGAM.

'You realise how many phoenixes are carved in the cathedral?' Angela murmured. 'Rising from the ashes. Look at this one, carrying *aram menaht menou* in its talons above the flames. Every St Paul's Cathedral there has ever been has been burnt.'

Bernard looked around him. 'Every St Paul's that we know of.'

Angela shone the torch over the edge. Wooden steps led downwards, beautifully finished, round and round through the pale torch beam into the darkness. She led him down.

Bernard marvelled. 'This is William Kempster's work. Kempster was a Freemason. In his lifetime the Geometrical Staircase in the south-west tower was called the Dean's Stair, but this must be the true Geometrical Staircase. Wren paid Kempster extra money from the accounts simply for "good work". It was this work.'

Angela flashed the torchlight. 'Mind your step.' She paused. 'Bernard?'

Bernard's small figure crouched high above her, examining the wall. 'This is impossible,' he called down. 'This shaft was dug from below. The marks are all on the undersides of the rocks. It's impossible.'

Angela continued down. Bernard caught her up. 'It's an engineering feat,' he said. She saved her breath. Water cascaded past her, rushed beneath the steps, flowed into the wall.

The stairs came down into a dome of chalk.

Steps had been cut in the chalk boulders that long ago must have fallen from the roof.

Bernard looked around him, but Angela looked at Bernard.

'Whatever was Wren playing at?' he muttered. 'Was it something to do with Freemasonry? Masonic ritual?' He pushed past her, glanced round the walls. 'Nothing. No sign of that. Perhaps it was a burial shaft, or a well.'

She murmured, 'Sixty years ago, cave paintings were found in Spain. When people knew what to look for, they found them in France too.'

He glanced at the marks on the walls. 'Graffiti. Wren's workmen, probably, or their kids.'

Angela was surprised to hear him sound so stupid. 'Look at them properly.'

He shrugged. 'Not my field.'

She hid her exasperated smile. Sometimes it seemed to her that those who knew most knew least. She took Bernard's hand and guided him past the wall. 'Look,' she said, 'here's another way out.'

He held her back in case it was dangerous, then climbed awkwardly down the slope into the second cavern. She crawled after him.

Bernard stared at the pile of scrolls.

'This is impossible,' he repeated. 'It's impossible. I'm not believing this. I can't.'

He walked round the brown, leathery pile in the middle of the cavern, then reached out.

Angela watched the piece of skin uncurl in his hand.

The scepticism in Bernard's eyes was replaced by a different emotion. Angela had never seen it before in a man's eyes, not for real. But she had dreamt of it, and knew it was true when she saw it.

The expression was love. Bernard's eyes filled with love, reading. 'My good God,' he said.

Angela wondered if Rose had ever seen that look in his eyes, and was sure she had not.

She leant against him tenderly, brother and sister, her head resting against his shoulder. The words he read so easily made little sense to her, but she saw he understood them.

'That,' she said. 'That's what you protect with your life. That's all I know.'

'My God,' he murmured, reading. He looked at his wristwatch. 'Two o'clock! I'm late for the Army Medical Review Board.'

Lieutenant Bernard Lydiard was posted to Hut 3 of the Foreign Office's GC&CS codebreaking headquarters at Bletchley Park, forty miles from London. His head of department was Alfred Dilwyn Knox, brother of the famous Admiralty cryptanalyst Monsignor Ronald Knox, the Catholic theologian and domestic prelate to the Pope. Alfred Knox was brilliant, as tall as Bernard with the same distracted manner, but his black hair was turning white, he wore thick glasses, and he was dying of cancer. After the demanding cryptological and deciphering tasks of the day, Knox set about the work he loved, translating seven hundred verses of Herodas from the original third-century papyrus unearthed at Fayum at the turn of the century. It had taken him eight years and his strength was almost exhausted. A close friendship sprang up between Bernard and the old man. When Knox was ill at home in Hughenden, Bernard often cycled over with drafts of the latest work which Knox would unbundle eagerly in bed. 'Is it my Herodas?'

Bernard said, 'Sorry, sir, it's the *Bismarck* again.' Rose loved to hear that laconic story. Knox and Bernard had deciphered the Luftwaffe codes for the *Bismarck*'s air escort, and so the Nazi battle cruiser had been located and sunk. Her husband, in his quiet way, was a hero. His work saved lives.

Rose said, 'You're doing really important work, aren't you, Bernard.' She brushed his uniform.

'It's not as important as fighting.'

Rose hated him to run himself down. 'You're going to be a really important man when the war's over.' She sounded like any of the young hopeful wives, the 'Bletchley widows'. She added brightly, 'You're doing what you're good at. This could be the best thing that ever happened to us. Mr Knox will help your career afterwards. That's the way it's done, it's who you know that matters, not what. He's a Fellow of King's College, isn't he?'

'And a Companion of the Order of St Michael and St George.'

'There you are,' Rose said.

'I don't think he'll live that long,' Bernard said. 'I think I'll have to finish the Herodas for him.'

Emma watched them from beneath her long lashes. She listened. She didn't understand many of their words, but she heard their emotions loud and clear. Mummy got in a state before Daddy came home on leave, wiping her hands on her apron, doing her face. Emma's earliest memories were of waiting with Mummy at the window for Daddy to come home. As soon as he came in sight near the house-all-alone they ran downstairs to Amen Corner and Mummy kissed Daddy as though she was fighting him, then she lifted Emma into his arms with motherly pride and Daddy had to carry her upstairs, sometimes finding a piece of chocolate for her in his sleeve, or a doll made out of old socks, like a magic trick, and those were the happiest moments of Emma's life.

Often Angela was waiting at the top of the stairs, and Mummy fell silent. Mummy was called Mummy but Aunt Angela was always Angela. She and Emma had an *understanding*. 'Don't call me Aunt, it sounds stuffy,' she'd told Emma in her definite way, then smiled, and so Emma smiled too. She liked Angela. Mummy called her 'your aunt'.

Once Angela looked flustered. Gus had asked her to marry him. Emma was old enough to be excited. 'Are you going to?'

'Yes,' Angela said. She touched Emma's cheek with her thumb. 'Then I shall be near you.'

'Will you wear white?'

'Absolutely not,' Angela said firmly. 'It's wartime, and besides, he's old.' Emma knew that this admission was part of the *understanding*. Angela always told her the truth. She was marrying Gus not because she loved him, but because she wanted to keep close to Emma.

Emma liked that. Angela was lively, and she was fun.

Emma sensed that Mummy hated Angela's marriage. For a while Mummy took Emma to a lodging in Bletchley village to be near Daddy, but the landlady was horrid and Daddy was never home until after bedtime anyway. Emma cried because she'd lost her schoolfriends and Angela too. And Mummy cried because she couldn't make Daddy understand that she didn't want to come back to London and the house-all-alone, and Emma's aunt.

'Aunt Angela is just your daddy's sister,' Mummy said tearfully. 'She's not *close* to you, like I am.'

'Being close to Angela doesn't make me less close to you,' Emma pointed out.

'You're even starting to sound like your aunt,' Rose said miserably.

'You're wrong,' Angela said, overhearing. 'She sounds like her father.'

'How can she?' Rose sulked. 'She hardly sees him. Each time he comes home she's two inches taller, and he's a different rank.'

Angela smiled at Emma, and winked.

She often took Emma for walks in London. Sometimes they sat in the gardens of St Paul's churchyard. Emma wriggled closer on the bench. 'Now I really am close to you, aren't I,' she said.

'I love you, Emma.'

'Mummy loves me too.'

Angela whispered, 'I think we understand one another.'

Emma nodded. She understood whispered secrets.

Angela shielded her eyes from the April sun glinting between the barrage balloons, though the war in Europe was almost over. She turned to the child. 'It will be different for you, Emma. I never had an education.'

'But you know lots.'

'Yes, but it's instinct. Girls my age mostly don't have *education*. I mean going on from school, universities, degrees.'

'Like Daddy.'

'Girls your age will,' Angela said. 'Look at all women have won in this war. It will seem perfectly natural to you. You'll expect it. You'll demand it.'

Emma wasn't interested. 'Why don't you and Gus have children?'

Angela told her the truth.

'Good,' Emma said. 'I'm all you've got.'

Angela gave an amazed laugh. It was a relationship between equals. 'Come on,' she said, getting to her feet, 'let's see if I can find you one of those American ices.'

On St Paul's Day, 25 January 1948, Bernard knelt in prayer in the cathedral with his hands clasped in front of him. His face was lean and eager, almost bony, his black hair beginning to recede from his high pale forehead. His deep cool eyes had not changed but he looked slightly shabby in his utility demob suit, its lapels cut narrow to save cloth and its pockets lined with rough hessian. His shoes showed patches worn through the outer soles but the toecaps were army-bright. It was late in the evening and the perpetual grimy filth of the cathedral added to the gloom, so that the black-gowned virger who collected hymn sheets among the murky choir stalls was visible only by his hacking cough. The cough moved between the ornate, time-blackened stalls until it reached the end, then Bernard heard the soft scuff of shoes towards the vestry. Silence fell.

Bernard stood and walked to the statue of Algar. The prebendary's right foot, exactly 30.48 centimetres from heel to the tip of its toe, had been the basis of English measurement for eight hundred years.

Bernard looked round him carefully. He took the smooth dark stone in his hand, twisted hard, pushed hard. The foot moved slightly in its stone sandal, then the statue turned aside, and Bernard stepped into the darkness.

The statue swung closed behind him.

Bernard felt in his pocket, took out a torch, followed its beam round the narrow steps set in the pillar. He came out below the crypt and turned left, came to Wren's door. The key was already in the lock.

Bernard went down.

He climbed awkwardly down the slope into the second cavern. He tried to keep the chalk off his suit, then brushed himself down.

'Heard you were in London,' Angela said. 'Staying in the Old Paulines' Club in Pall Mall, I suppose, so you didn't have to see me.'

Bernard jumped, seeing for the first time the huge tusks of the mammoth encircling him, its tiny red eyes looking down on him. He had scrambled out of its mouth. 'You gave me a turn!' he said.

Angela, in an incongruous touch, had brought a deckchair down into the cavern. She watched him across the pile of scrolls with her legs crossed, wearing a navy blue lambswool dress with a red silk scarf, her navy blue overcoat open in the cool dry air. 'Me, Bernard dear, or the elephant?'

Bernard calmed himself. 'It's not an elephant, sis, it's a mammoth.'

'You knew I was here, of course.'

'The key was in the door.'

'No fooling our Bernard. Your daughter's as clever as you, you know.'

'You haven't seen Emma for almost a year.'

'Yes, Rose has been successful in keeping her away from me.' Angela pulled up a second deckchair with her foot in invitation.

'I wish you and Rose would be friends.' Bernard circled the scrolls. He would not sit. 'I don't know what's going on between you two.' She had learnt that there were many ways into the cathedral and this time she had not bothered to disguise the deckchair frame as a camera tripod.

Bernard was taking his doctorate in oriental studies at King's College. The move to Cambridge meant a small shabby digs in Grantchester, and though the village Rose had known as a child looked the same, all the people had changed, and she did not like

Emma's school. Rose would not admit anything of this to Bernard. She was simply unhappy. Nevertheless, Rose thought anything was better than living in London and coming home to see Angela waiting on the stairs, and the pleasure on Emma's face at the sight of her aunt.

'I've been waiting,' Angela said shrewdly. 'Knew you'd come. I know more about men than you do, Bernard. Coming down here is like going with a whore. Hard the first time but then you come back again and again and again.' She unstoppered a chromium-plated hip flask, sipped, held it out. 'Brandy.'

'No, thanks.'

'Seven years.' She flicked her fingers at the cavern. 'You still haven't forgiven Mother for knowing more than Father. Our great father.' She nodded at the scrolls. 'You still don't believe.'

Bernard cleared his throat. 'I do believe.'

'Ah, I thought I saw you bobbing at the altar. But you don't hold on to lamp posts any more. Religion's the same thing, you know. Insurance. Hope. Faith. Submission.'

'I am . . . I think I am . . . no longer an atheist.'

Angela shrugged. 'Gus will be disappointed. What's happened? A blazing light on the road to Damascus?'

Bernard touched the scrolls. 'I don't know, Angela. Something has changed. I don't know what I am. But I do know there's something real. There must be.'

'You atheists always end up sucking on the Pope's ring harder than anyone else.' Angela sipped brandy. Bernard took the cap and screwed it on the hip flask. He crouched to explain something to her, then couldn't stay still. He walked up and down in front of the scrolls.

'Listen to me, Angela. I've met a friend from my GC&CS days in the war, Miles Copeland. I bumped into him and his wife by chance last night in Piccadilly. If you believe in chance. We had a few martinis at the Troc, then a few more. He's American, OSS when I knew him, now CIA. He showed me some pictures.' He reached into his inside pocket, pulled out a sheaf of glossy photographs. 'Thirty of them. You haven't seen these, neither have I.'

'How you little boys do love to play your games.'

'Miles snapped them on the roof of the American Legation in Damascus. They'd been brought to him for sale by an Egyptian merchant.'

Angela glanced at the first half-dozen. 'It's gibberish.'

'It's scrolls like these.'

Angela stood angrily, touched the pile of skins. 'But these are a hundred years old at least. And probably older than Wren's cathedral. They aren't some grubby Egyptian forgery. Whatever they are, these are real. Mother believed that with all her heart. They're the truth, Bernard.'

'How can we know? You believe it because she did. That's not enough.' Bernard took the photos. 'These aren't forgeries. This is part of the Book of Daniel, a text the Zealots revered.' His finger moved. '"Thy people shall be delivered, every one that shall be found written in the Book. And many of them that sleep in the dust of the earth shall awake, some to everlasting life, and some to shame and everlasting contempt. And they that be wise shall shine as the brightness of the firmament, and they that turn many to righteousness shall be as the stars for ever and ever. But thou, O Daniel, shut up the words, and seal the Book, even to the End of Days."' He turned to another photograph. 'This is the Genesis Apocryphon.' He flicked through them. 'The others are unknown. Startling. Perhaps revolutionary. Documents from the birthplace of Christianity.'

'But that's impossible.'

'That's what I said when you showed me here.' Bernard slapped the photographs down on top of the skins.

'I wish I hadn't!' Angela cried despairingly. 'Mother was right. Give a man an inch and he takes a mile. I should know. Give men anything and they screw it up. My daughter would have been almost old enough to understand. You don't have to do anything, Bernard. Don't screw it up. Leave it alone. It's not yours.'

'Something has happened and it can't be ignored.' He flapped the photographs.'Corroboration. Answers.'

'Just because something *can* be done doesn't mean it *must* be done.'

'Yes, it does.'

'You don't know where it's leading you.'

'You're right,' he said slowly, 'I don't. Miles thinks this Damascus business started about a year ago. The location's being kept secret – they're pretending the scrolls were found in a library – but the truth is that a Bedouin boy, Mahomet, lost his goat in the desert near a patch of ancient ruins, a *khirbet*, believed to be the place once called Qumran. A Biblical monastery on a cliff overlooking the Dead Sea. Searching for his goat, Mahomet found a cave. A cave full of pots.' He held up one of the manuscript jars inscribed with three quadrangles. 'Like this. Inscribed with three quadrangles.'

'How many?'

'At least forty. Most of them have been emptied and the contents burnt, or sold into the bazaars, and the tribes use the jars for carrying water.'

'Oh my God.'

'I believe these skins came from the same place. This is knowledge, Angela. The Dead Sea Scrolls will confirm, or more likely give the lie to, the scrolls here. The priests of the École Biblique have already found a second cave at Qumran, the cliffs are riddled with caverns. The Dead Sea Scrolls may well show that the Gospels are true, that every word of Christianity is true in *fact* as well as faith. Professor Albright says they're older than the Nash Papyrus. There's not the slightest doubt they're genuine.'

'You're completely out of your head.' Angela stared at him. 'How many people are involved in this Dead Sea find?'

'The Americans, the British, the Jews, the Arabs, the French, the Jesuits, the Vatican. You can imagine the interest of the holy fathers is intense. They have everything to gain or everything to lose by the interpretation of perhaps a single word in any one of the Scrolls. Everyone wants control. Jerusalem is divided into British, Arab, and Jewish sectors. An independent State of Israel may be declared, in which case the Arabs will declare war. The Palestine Archaeological Museum is in Arab Jerusalem. The Bedouin pitch tents where they please, and they're turning up stuff all the time and selling it wherever they can to whoever they can for whatever they can get.'

Angela took her hip flask back. 'It's all so simple for you, isn't it, Bernard.' A vein pulsed in her throat as she drank. 'Secrets to be revealed, not kept. Trouble to be found, not hidden. Pride is a sin, Bernard, even intellectual pride. You don't know what you're doing.'

'Angela, in Israel today they're finding – not the face of God, but perhaps the face of Jesus Christ. We can begin to see the outlines of what really happened. I'll believe in that. The proof of Christ. And it's happening in our lifetime.'

'God save us,' Angela said. 'What are you going to do?'

Bernard said, 'I want to get out there if I can.'

But first, there were his studies to finish.

Dr Bernard Lydiard was appointed to the Department of Oriental Studies at Queen Mary College, his Ph.D. thesis *A Linguistic Study of Uncial Script in the Magdalen Fragments*, and settled at once to his work. For Rose it was more difficult. The East End of London round the college was a wasteland of bomb sites, shattered buildings and grim terraced streets. Rose put her foot down. 'I have no intention of living here or letting Emma go to school here.' Bernard pulled strings at the cathedral – the chapter, all old men with long memories, had not forgotten his father's work on the ancient charters of St Paul's – and a place was found for Emma at the Colet, the St Paul's Preparatory School for Girls in Hammersmith. Rose rented a house close by the tennis courts, and Bernard rode to work every day on the Tube, examining texts in the racketing, roaring gloom by the light of an illuminated magnifying glass. One of the administrators lived nearby and often rode with him, calling out 'Mile End!' when the brakes squealed.

'Thank you,' Bernard said absent-mindedly.

But this morning the man stuck with him. 'I hear you're applying for the international team.'

'What international team?'

'The Dead Sea Scrolls. Father de Vaux is assembling an international team to store and examine them in east Jerusalem. You're not Jewish, are you?'

'No.' The train doors slammed open and they crossed the platform.

'De Vaux won't have any Jews. The École Biblique are Catholic priests and they've nominated most of the team members, various fathers and monsignors and professors from theological seminaries in America, France, Germany, here. Magdalen College got one nominee, Allegro – he's even younger than you, still in his twenties – and we get the other. You. The priests need an agnostic or two to leaven the bread.' The administrator gave a crafty administrative smile, stopped a horse-float on the Mile End Road and bought a bottle of milk to go with his lunch. 'A year in the sun. Lucky chap.'

When Bernard got home that evening, late as usual, Rose opened the door. She said, 'She's here.'

'Who?'

She hissed, 'Your sister.'

'Have you given her a drink?'

Rose closed the door behind him. 'I wouldn't give her the time of day. She's all over Emma already.'

Angela sat at the table by the window helping Emma with her homework. 'That's wrong,' Emma giggled. 'You've got it wrong. You need help. Don't you know what a square root is?'

Angela laughed.

Emma rubbed out, shaking her head. 'It's the number which multiplied by itself gives the product.'

Angela saw Bernard and stood. 'My God,' Bernard said, 'whatever's the matter?'

Angela burst into tears. 'Gus is dead.' Emma hugged her. 'I didn't want to upset you,' Angela croaked. 'I'm sorry.'

Rose looked angry. 'I'll take Emma for a walk.' Bernard found some cooking brandy and gave Angela his handkerchief, sat beside her on the sofa. Rose put on her hat, caught his eye, and Bernard followed her into the hall. 'She's just making a fuss,' Rose whispered. 'She just wants to get back in. She never loved him.'

'Don't be silly, Rose. She was married to the man for ten years.'

Angela overheard. 'I miss him now he's gone.'

Bernard slammed the door and went back to her.

Angela said, 'You see, it was so sudden.'

'I knew he'd had a stroke.'

'Yes, but this time he hit his head on the side of the basin when he fell. It was awful. I knew at once. I've always hated that basin sticking out, I should have made him get rid of it. I've broken it with a hammer. That little house meant so much to all of us. They're going to knock it down, you know. They're going to make

438

it into a huge paved square ringed with skyscrapers. I do miss him so much.'

'You stay here as long as you like.'

Angela licked her lips distastefully. 'This is the most disgusting brandy. I'll buy Rose some proper stuff.'

That night Rose got Bernard alone in bed. She was furious. 'I won't have her here. If she stays I'm going.'

Bernard said reasonably, 'But Emma likes her.'

Tears trickled down Rose's cheeks. 'That's what I mean.'

'Give me a few days,' Bernard said. 'Something may come up.' He looked down at his pyjamas. 'In fact, I think it just has.'

Rose turned away, bored. She put out the light.

Her voice came. 'You heard what I said.'

Bernard sighed.

Ten days he later pushed between the workmen rebuilding the college, wiped the clay off his shoes, and faced three priests behind the long table in an echoing lecture room. Father de Vaux, bearded and gaunt, gestured at a stool. Bernard rested his briefcase against a leg of the stool and sat. De Vaux introduced the other two priests.

'So, a cryptanalyst,' de Vaux smiled. 'Perfect.'

'I've already published six articles in important journals, the *Revue Biblique*, the *Biblical Archaeological Review*, *Philology Today*—'

'Yes, yes, I know all that. A cryptanalyst with a knowledge of Hebrew, Aramaic and the various scripts will be most useful. There are many fragments. We have just discovered a further eight hundred scrolls in Cave Four at Qumran.'

'A year's work at least,' Bernard said. 'It's a jigsaw, that's all.'

The priest on the left interrupted. 'A year? Years. Decades.'

Bernard asked eagerly, 'What date does palaeographic evidence give for the scrolls?'

'I am not prepared to divulge that information.'

'Are they from the lifetime of Christ?'

The priest on the left said, 'We shall not divulge our information until we are certain of our conclusions. They are, of course, much older. Documents from the lifetime of Christ would be exceedingly dangerous for Christianity. Who knows what use might be made of them? The Jews – the Muslims – muckraking journalists—'

The priest on the right said, 'Any stick now seems big enough to use against Christianity and dislodge belief in the uniqueness of Jesus, which is sacrosanct.'

'Yes,' Bernard said. 'I understand.'

'They are much too sensitive to be entrusted to the public or the academic community before exhaustive and definitive scholarship has been completed.' De Vaux asked, 'Do you believe in God, Dr Lydiard?'

Bernard had expected this question. 'I believe God is more than everything. I believe God is all. I believe God is gods, all gods. God is all thoughts that were ever thought. God is the world and the future and the past. God is every particle, every wave, every atom. God is the Sun and the Moon and the fleck of sleep in the corner of your eye. God is every man, every woman, every child, every colour, every creed, every love. God is.'

De Vaux rubbed his eye. 'That doesn't sound like a religion. It's a prayer.'

'Thank you, Father.'

The priest on the right said, 'We are certain that the various stages in the religious history of mankind form a deliberate narrative. History is directly and supernaturally guided by God to lead to the ultimate and definitive age.'

'The messianic age inaugurated by Jesus Christ,' said the priest on the left.

'Yes,' Bernard said.

'Today it is incumbent on biblical scholars to show the steps by which God steadily led stone age man, Palaeolithic man, and ancient pagan man to the capability of measuring up to the social and moral facts of our Christian Church.'

'Yes.'

'The Pope has been infallible since 1870,' de Vaux said. 'These social and moral facts cannot be questioned. They are indisputably the truth.'

'Yes,' Bernard said.

'Good.' De Vaux stood and held out his hand. 'Welcome to the team, Dr Lydiard. Jerusalem is beautiful in the spring.'

Angela bought a house near the St Paul's School for Girls. 'I like the area, that's all,' she told Rose. 'The shops. The river.'

'The school,' Rose said.

'We'll be in Jerusalem nine months of the year,' Bernard told Rose. 'It's not fair to dislocate Emma's education. She can join us in the school holidays. Two months in summer, a month at Easter and Christmas. And we'll be home three months of the year. That's only five months away from her.'

'I don't know,' Rose said.

'It's for Emma's sake,' Angela said. 'The time will be over before you know it. You've got to put Emma first.'

Rose was outraged. 'Of course I do!'

'Yes, of course you will,' Angela soothed.

Rose said miserably, 'I don't want to go to Jerusalem.'

Angela chuckled. 'You wouldn't put yourself in the way of your husband's career, would you? You aren't that sort of wife.'

Rose looked wounded. 'No, I suppose not.'

'That's settled then. You go off and enjoy yourself among the olive groves.'

Rose whispered, 'All I've ever wanted is a home.'

440

Angela looked at Emma with an expression of intense love, Bernard's girl now twelve years old, shy, growing up, her lustrous black hair flowing like a black wing when unbound – though in school it was always tied back – already almost beautiful, and the same age to the month Angela's own daughter would have been.

'I know you better than anyone,' Angela whispered. She looked down at the sleeping girl, then stroked Emma's hair across the pillow with her knuckles. 'I love you more than your mother does, I love you more than she knows how to. She went to Jerusalem without you. I'd die for you, I'll never leave you. Without you I'm nothing.' She knelt, inhaled the breath from the girl's nostrils. 'I love you, darling. You're the only person I've ever loved. Not the men I married. Not the ones I flirt with to keep myself young. I love you even more than I love Bernard. You are my life, my hope, my light. You are the future. Without you I never lived.'

Angela packed Emma off to school each morning, Angela waited for her at the school gates, Angela cheered her during hockey. It was Angela who told Emma the things she needed to know about growing up. It was Angela who tended broken bones and broken hearts. Angela drove Emma calmly to Fulham Hospital for the appendicitis operation – Rose flew back in a panic from Jerusalem three days too late, when Emma was already home, and Emma gave an adolescent cringe and said, 'Oh, Mummy,' embarrassed by Rose's tears.

Rose told Angela, 'You've changed her.'

'Don't you see she's almost an adult? School's changed her, not me. She has a sweetheart. She goes shopping. She listens to forty-fives not your old seventy-eights. She knew who James Dean was even before he died.'

'She's still my little girl,' Rose said.

Angela said, 'And she wants to go to university.'

'My God,' Bernard said when he landed at the airport, 'she'll meet people like us.'

'You're the one who's changed, professor.' Angela drove him back to her house. Bernard's work kept him almost entirely in Jerusalem and he no longer bothered to keep a London flat.

He said, 'You know, Rose insists Emma comes back with us to Jerusalem. Emma can go to the American School.'

Angela said definitely, 'Not if she wants to go to Somerville.' She raised her eyebrows. 'Biblical Studies. Like father, like daughter.'

'Rose will crucify me.'

'No, she blames me, I think.' Angela turned into the narrow residential street by the river, parked beneath a plane tree. 'How's it going out there, Bernard?'

'Good.'

'Really? I hear your colleague Dr Allegro is writing a book called

The Sacred Mushroom and the Cross and is searching for a publisher. The origins of Christianity are an edible fungus, he says.'

'My colleague has been isolated and discredited.'

'I'm not surprised.'

'Over another matter, in fact. He accused the team leaders of not wanting to publish their results, of not even allowing the texts of the Dead Sea Scrolls be seen.'

'That's ridiculous. Surely they have to?'

'Not even for the most serious academic research. They can spin it out for ten years if they want to. A Copper Scroll has been discovered. Precious materials mean an important text. The Copper Scroll is corroded and was sliced open at the Manchester College of Technology. It's an inventory of treasure and its hiding places in the ruins of Qumran. So many gold bars "in the cistern under the Salt", and "thirty talents of silver under the western *pinna* of the temple", and so on. The Essene monastery was very rich. Perhaps twenty or thirty tons of gold altogether. Twice that weight of silver.'

'My God. No wonder they're keeping it quiet.'

'We're not sure of the layout of the ruins yet. No trace of treasure has been found so far. Only a few jars of holy resin for anointing the faithful, from a particular tree, now extinct.'

'Then you are finding some marvels.'

'I think there's so much more we don't know. Some researchers believe Jesus was an Essene. That some or perhaps all of the twelve apostles were. But then why should Judas betray Jesus for a mere thirty pieces of silver? It doesn't make sense.'

'Don't sound so disillusioned and depressed. You remember how you used to cling on to the lamp posts?'

'I'm going to start that up again, I think,' he sighed. 'No, I think there may not be any real answers. Not in this life.' He got out of the car, then got back in again.

'What is it, Bernard?'

He said quietly, 'Have you been back to St Paul's?'

Angela shook her head.

He whispered, 'Could there have been any treasure there, once?'

'The skins are the treasure.'

'I know. But.'

'You think they came from Qumran? They can't be that old.'

'I think that Mother's skins come actually from inside the holy scriptorium, the library of Qumran. Perhaps they were being worked over on one particular day, not in store. The scrolls I'm examining in Jerusalem are different, the library's stock, not work in progress. I think they were buried en masse at a different time.'

'I found one or two gold coins down there. A tiny Greek statue, quite pretty. Nothing that meant much to me. Perhaps in one of the other caverns—'

'Others?'

442

'Didn't you see?'

He clenched his fists. 'I spend fourteen hours a day poring over the Dead Sea Scrolls. I'm one of the few allowed to look at them. I know almost everything there is to know. I'm so close to seeing what it's about that sometimes I almost feel I can touch it. Touch Christ. And then I realise I don't know anything. Zero. Ask me about the Manichaean heresy, or Herodian or Isaiah A or Late Hasmonean semi-formal script, or the War of the Sons of Light and Darkness, or the seating arrangement at the Last Supper, I'll go on for hours. But I'm missing something and it's staring me in the face.'

Angela patted his shoulder. 'Poor chap.'

He pointed at his large head, spoke ruefully in his Neddy Seagoon voice. 'What a magnificent brain, but he was walking backwards to Christmas.'

They looked through the windscreen as Emma, tall with long legs showing beneath her floral print skirt, ran along the pavement. 'You two always have your heads together,' she laughed. She pulled her father from the car and hugged him, kissed him on the lips. 'What secrets are you muttering? You'll drive Mummy wild with jealousy.'

The three of them looked up guiltily and waved at the window where Rose watched them.

Rose wore furs even at the dinner table. She found London very cold. 'I do wish you well at Somerville, Emma,' she said in the voice of a mother who knows she has lost her daughter. She kissed her cheek. 'Now, wouldn't it be nice if you came out for a short holiday with us in Jerusalem before—'

'I've got my exams,' Emma said. She looked up, met her mother's eye. 'I've got my exams, Mummy.'

The night before Angela drove her niece to the university, she drove her into the City, up Ludgate Hill, and parked by the tourist bureau. Angela always forgot to lock the car. It had never been stolen but Emma went back with the key, then both women crossed the road. 'This open space in front of St Paul's is called the atrium,' Angela said.

'Why should they call it that?'

'I don't know. Your grandfather was a virger here. Dean's virger.'

'I suppose Daddy must have mentioned him. I wish he'd cleaned the place. It's so dirty.'

They went inside. Angela stood at the centre of the crossing. 'When we're young we know it all, Emma, and when we're old we realise we don't know anything.' She looked round her, then reached out towards the statue of Algar.

'But the more you look, Emma, the more you see.'

Twenty years after the Dead Sea Scrolls were discovered, the Six Day War burst across the Holy Land like a tidal wave. Dr Emma

Lydiard, living in a kibbutz in T-shirt and jeans, was digging at an ossuary discovered during roadworks east of Tel-Aviv when the news came. Her first thought was of her father working at the scrollery in east Jerusalem. Rumours flew about that Arab soldiers had shot the priests of the international team and ransacked the scrolls, then word came that Jewish soldiers taking control of the quarter had lined the priests up in the courtyard to deter snipers. Emma knew where to go to get reliable information. She telephoned Angela in London.

'You know your father,' Angela reassured her authoritatively. 'I expect this hostage scare was started by de Vaux, he hates the Jews. I expect your father will be hanging on to the lamp posts, but he always lands on his feet.' She added attentively, 'It's your mother I'm more worried about.'

'Oh, she's all right if she's got Daddy to hang on to,' Emma said briskly. She held the phone tighter. 'By the way, I'm getting married.'

'Am I the first to know?'

'Of course you are. His name's Isaac. He's here on the kibbutz, an exchange student with Hebrew University.' Emma's voice giggled suddenly.

'An Israeli boy?'

'Well, Golders Green, actually, or he'd be in the army getting shot at. His father's a meat wholesaler on the Finchley Road, near the traffic lights.'

'Is Isaac a serious boy?'

'Very serious.'

'I've never heard you giggle like that before.'

'That, Angela,' Emma explained, 'is because it's so serious.'

'So he's converting his religion to agnostic, is he?'

'Oh no,' Emma said brightly. 'I'm going to be a Jew. I know all about it. He's teaching me.'

Angela knew better than to try to change her mind.

'I should tell your father first,' she said. 'Let him break the news to your mother.'

The line crackled. 'You know I always do what you tell me,' came Emma's voice, then the connection broke.

Angela sat back in her armchair. A Boeing thundered overhead towards Heathrow, following the line of the river. 'My God,' she whispered, putting the phone down. 'How You do like to move in mysterious ways.'

In fact Emma was not married for three years, because his parents were horrified their little Isaac was marrying a Gentile. That she was a mature woman thirty years old, a doctor of Biblical Studies at London University, and her father was the Professor Bernard Lydiard who worked on the Dead Sea Scrolls, mollified them not at all. They were afraid that the Scrolls undermined Judaism. 'I don't think so,' Bernard assured them. The house to which he and Rose had been invited was quiet and substantial in one of the side roads behind Hendon Hall, candles on the table, and various breads laid out. Bernard had been prepared to talk with his hosts about meat prices, but he was treated with formal politeness, both invited and excluded. Emma, wearing her long pale dress, winked at him.

Isaac's father said, 'If the Scrolls do not undermine Judaism, then surely they must undermine Christianity.'

Bernard said, 'I do not believe that is necessarily a consequence. Religions do not win or lose. It's not a competition.'

'You do not live in the real world, Professor.'

A woman's voice spoke. 'If there is nothing to fear, then why have these public treasures been hidden, concealed, obstructed from the public view for almost a quarter of a century?'

Bernard was aware of Isaac's mother looking at him intently. She had been in Dachau.

'It would not surprise me,' he confessed, 'if the Scrolls were kept from view for another quarter of a century. It is not necessarily a conspiracy. Scholars refuse to let others see their material until it is safely published under their own names. Others blame the Israeli government, who now control the Scrolls.'

'Always blame the Jews!' Isaac's mother exclaimed. 'Always an easy target.'

'It is a conspiracy,' Isaac's father said, nodding.

Bernard shook his head. 'I believe that knowledge, the truth, if it can be proved, is the most powerful force in the world. Stronger than armies, hotter than the atom bomb. If the Dead Sea Scrolls did contain some great truth that overturned everything, perhaps it is better they should remain hidden. But I do not believe they do. I have given their study nearly twenty years of my life, and I should know.'

'But still,' Isaac's father said, 'you speak only of belief, not the sure knowledge that comes with faith.'

'These are delicious,' Rose told Isaac's mother. 'Will you let me have the recipe?'

Angela sat in the dark.

She had been down here long enough to feel the darkness stretching out all around her, like a meditation. She sat on a rug laid on the chalk floor, her legs crossed in the lotus position, her fingertips resting lightly on her knees. The faint draught that was always in the cavern blew around her, on the back of her right shoulder and the front of her left shoulder, round and round, as if she were the centre of everything.

Her eyelids fluttered, her mouth opened slightly. She heard the voice of the wind. The wind called her. She knew it was an illusion. Her hair rippled over her eyes, caressing her. She heard voices calling, footsteps. The wind picked her up, turned her round, set her gently down again as she had been. She heard a baby crying.

The wind stopped.

Silence.

Angela remembered to breathe again. She drew air into her lungs, felt the effort of it. Her legs were stiff. She pushed back her hair, realising it hung over her face. She blinked her eyes at the dark, then yawned. She must have been down here for more than an hour.

She heard distant footsteps. She listened, the footsteps echoing slightly, the descending clack of shoes on wooden stairs. A faint gleam of torchlight outlined the mouth of the mammoth, showing the ribbing beyond, then the light flashed in her eyes, suddenly brilliant.

A human form, long legs and long hair, slid down. Angela held up her hand against the light.

Emma said, 'You were waiting for me.'

Angela grunted. She opened an old shopping bag marked 'Souvenirs of St Paul's Cathedral Shop' beneath the Cathedral's logo, the crossed swords of St Paul with the words *Ecclesia Cathedralis Sancti Pauli Londinensis*. She rummaged under St Paul's tourist guides and St Paul's fridge magnets, came up with a small Camping-Gaz lantern. She struck a match and touched it to the mantle, set the lantern beside her and adjusted its glare to a kindly glow.

'I didn't know if it was you or your father.'

Emma was startled. 'He knows? Then why isn't he here? With what he knows – with his skills—'

Angela put out her hand to be helped up, dusted her slacks, stretched.

'Why is your father studying boring old Dead Sea Scrolls in a specially lit, air-conditioned, fireproof vault in an Israeli museum?' She shrugged. 'Because he's afraid to be here.'

Emma touched the skins. 'But they're exciting, not frightening.'

'Exactly. He knows the Dead Sea Scrolls are safe. The new Catholic leader of the international team says that Judaism is a Christian heresy, that the solution is a mass conversion to Christianity. But he would say that, wouldn't he? There are other views, opposite views, no doubt. But that is all human chatter, not truth. Your father feels safe working on the Scrolls, they are his life's work, an intellectual exercise. A puzzle two thousand years out of date, irrelevant, exciting, worthwhile, not quite real. He is content. Undisturbed. Safe.'

'But you thought I might be him.'

'He is at the height of his powers. I live in hope that the worm will turn.' Angela sat in the deckchair, gestured Emma to sit beside her. 'Two thousand years is long enough. No one is more qualified than he to make sense of these.'

Emma sat. She turned out the torch. The lantern hissed companionably.

She said, 'I have a secret from my husband. A secret I cannot share with him, though I love him.'

'Nothing changes. I had secrets from both of mine.'

'I'm pregnant. I'm going to have a baby.'

Angela looked at her sharply. 'I thought I heard a baby cry.'

'Not yet!' Emma laughed. 'Not for another seven months.'

'So it goes on,' Angela smiled. 'And on, and on.' She kissed Emma's forehead. 'I'm so pleased for you.'

'I've agreed the child will be brought up as a Jew.'

'Fair enough.'

'I can feel it inside me. Me, alone. I can't share that with Isaac however hard I try. He's my husband but he thinks in a completely different way. He's a Jew, sure and certain, chosen by God. I'm afraid to die. I never realised life was so close to death.'

Angela said, 'Every day of our lives.' She touched her fingers to Emma's tummy. 'Boy or girl?'

'If he's a boy Isaac names him, if she's a girl I do.'

Angela leant back with a groan for her own unborn child. 'I remember the day you were born, Emma. It seems like yesterday. You had a brother. A twin.'

Emma sat without moving. 'Yes,' she said. 'I've always felt there was something missing from my life.'

'There isn't now.' Angela felt the warmth beneath her fingertips.

'Alexandra,' Emma said, sounding more cheerful. 'You're up early, by the way.'

'Early? It's late.'

'It's early. It's morning.'

Angela was confused. 'I must have lost track of time. I've been down here all night. I can't have been.'

'You've been asleep.'

'I came down here to pray.'

Emma hugged herself. 'So did I. Isn't that amazing? I thought it was my secret.' She turned up the lantern as though to banish all shadows, smiling at Angela, then her face froze. 'Oh my God.'

She reached out, touched Angela's forehead, her nose, her chin. The raised red mark went into the open neck of Angela's Marks & Spencer blouse.

'What is it?' Angela said frantically. She undid the buttons with shaking fingers.

The red mark burnt a line down her tummy, disappeared under her slacks. Another was scorched from each hand to her brassiere. Angela unclipped it and her breasts pulled forward.

The two women stared at the lines joined between her bare breasts.

Angela whispered, 'It's a cross.'

They watched. Slowly, the shape faded.

It was gone.

The two women hugged each other, shaking.

Alexandra played in the back garden of the terraced house in Hampstead, a chubby black-haired infant with her mother's blue eyes and a saucy smile. Bernard closed his eyes in the warm afternoon sunshine. Isaac and Emma called one another doctor. 'Another cup of tea, doctor?'

'I'll get it, doctor.' Isaac stood up from the swing-sofa by the little fishpond.

'Doctor,' Alexandra said. She frowned intently, trying to catch a goldfish with a twig.

Isaac said, 'More tea for you, professor?'

'Professor,' Alexandra said.

'Thank you.' Bernard handed up his teacup. Isaac went into the house.

Emma said, 'So, Grandpa.'

'I know, I know,' Bernard said. His hair was silver, to his shoulders, and he looked exactly like a learned professor. 'Don't frown at me like that. You look just like your daughter.'

'So, how much longer are you insiders going to sit on them?'

'I don't know what you mean,' Bernard said glumly. He knew.

'Your precious Scrolls. Angela says you're such a brave man. She tells me little things all the time, you know. I didn't know you slid down the dome of St Paul's to put out a fire.'

'As it turned out it had already been put out. It was a very little fire anyway.'

'So, when are you going to bravely publish them?'

'We hope to have the Scrolls in print with the Oxford University Press by the twenty-first century.'

Emma gaped. 'I can't believe you.'

'Well, some time in the twenty-first century, anyway,' Bernard said. 'Probably by the end of it.'

'Don't mock yourself,' Emma said. 'Stop it. Stop smiling.'

He made a face, shrugged.

She said, 'I've been down there. I know all about it, Dad. Angela showed me. Something happened.' She explained briefly.

'It's her time of life,' Bernard said.

'She was fifty-five, for God's sake, she had the change years ago. There's something important down there, Dad, and you're trying to ignore it. Sit on it like you're sitting on those Scrolls.'

'What do you want me to do? Resign?'

'There's more, I'm sure of it. I've looked, I know a little. I wonder what Jesus really said on the Cross. All of it. What He really looked like, what He really said. All of what He said when He preached, not just the little bits that have come down to us. He would have preached all day, and it's all gone.' She begged him, 'There was so much more. It's down there. We need you.'

'The fact of life, Emma, is that academics in their sixties without a sound record of publications and papers don't resign.'

'Just look at them. Dad. Please.'

'I haven't got time.' Bernard looked at his watch. 'I'm meeting your mother for dinner. We're seeing the new Ayckbourn at the National.'

'Coward.'

'No, Ayckbourn.'

'Ha ha.'

Bernard jumped to his feet, white-lipped. 'That's enough, Emma.' He pushed angrily past Isaac, who was returning. The teacups rattled.

''Bye-bye,' Alexandra waved.

Bernard sighed. He came back, picked her up, tweaked her nose and apologised to Emma. 'I'll think about it,' he said.

Isaac looked interested. 'What's this?'

'Resigning,' Emma said. 'Don't worry about it, doctor. It's just a family row.'

Isaac sat beside her, ran his hands back through his curly hair. 'We don't have family rows.'

'That's because you do what you're told,' Emma said.

On St Paul's Day, 25 January 1990, Professor Bernard Lydiard finally resigned from the international team of scholars studying the Dead Sea Scrolls. It was his seventy-fifth birthday. His associates regretted that the distinguished professor had thrown his life's work away by his ultimatum of impossible demands. 'One. The Department of Antiquities in Israel must be provided with photographic plates of all unpublished Scrolls. Two, a fascimile edition must be issued forthwith to all scholars who ask for it, irrespective of race or religion. Three, the Editors and Associates must cease to be an obstacle to publication and become a source of information.' Behind closed doors the international team muttered that Professor Lydiard was old and tired, perhaps senile. The word Alzheimer's was mentioned. They issued a statement deploring his tirade, saying his retirement for medical reasons was very sad. They spoke well of him in speeches, fought for his places on committees, scrambled for privileged access to his texts and his corner office, and forgot him.

Emma parked on a double yellow line by the Green outside St Paul's School for Girls, waiting for Alexandra to come out. A finger tapped her shoulder. 'I'm sorry, I've only stopped here for a minute—' Emma turned. 'Dad!' She hugged him.

'You thought I was the traffic warden, didn't you. You're guilty.'

She straightened his tie. 'Look at you, wearing a white jacket in this weather.'

'I've just come from the airport.' He nodded at his taxi. 'You heard?'

'Yes!' Emma paid off the taxi, threw Bernard's suitcase in the back of her old Cortina. 'Yes, of course I heard. I was lecturing at the University of Michigan. Great excitement. The Lydiard Ultimatum.'

'I lost.'

'Of course you did. But you went down with all guns blazing. I'm so proud of you, Dad.'

Alexandra ran across the road. 'My goodness, it can't be,' Bernard said.

'Our little Alex,' Emma agreed.

'She's as tall as me.'

'Grandad!' Alex cried. Bernard grunted as she hugged him. 'We all read about you in the papers. There was a little photograph in the *Evening Standard*, in the middle. Monica said you were amazingly handsome.' She waved. 'There she is! I'll just dash and make her *sooo* envious.'

Bernard got into the car, sat beside his suitcase. Emma turned round in the driver's seat. After a moment of quietness she said, 'Well?'

'She's beautiful. They live so fast nowadays.'

'You know that's not what I meant.'

'I'm sorry. It's a habit. I've been running away all my life.'

'But now you've come back, haven't you.'

'Your poor mother thinks I've retired.'

'But you haven't.'

'Emma, when I was interviewed for the international team, one of the priests made a remark I've never forgotten. He told me the history of mankind is a deliberate narrative. A *récit* directly and supernaturally guided by God to lead to an ultimate and definitive age. History is a series of steps by which God leads us upward, he said, and educates us to measure up to the heightened morality of the Christian Church.'

Emma adjusted the rearview mirror, did her face. 'I'm familiar with the view. History is preordained by God, new information is not revealed until Man is ready to respond to each new stage.'

Alex got into the front seat. 'That's sexist, Mummy. What about Woman?' She twisted over the back of the seat. 'Monica's busting to meet you.'

Bernard glanced at Emma's face in the mirror. 'Does Alex know?'

'No. Not yet. She's too young.'

'Know what about?' Alex sulked. 'You old people are always talking about sex, it's gross.' She grinned. 'I bet Mummy was one of those sex-crazed hippy druggies in the sixties.'

Emma coloured. 'I was not.'

'We weren't talking about sex,' Bernard said. 'We talked about knowledge.'

Alex did up her safety belt. 'Same thing,' she said cheerfully. 'We

450

do have Religious Education. I have read the Bible. All that knowing and begetting. The greatest story ever told.' She pointed at the tennis courts. 'I'm playing Amanda at tennis. Drop me off, would you? Her mum'll bring me home.'

Emma stopped the car. Her eyes met Bernard's in the mirror.

'You'll stay with us, of course.'

'You know where we'll go first,' Bernard said.

Angela found a party of American tourists filling All Souls' Chapel. She turned away and walked as far as the crossing, but saw the evening prayer service had ended and at least thirty boy choristers from the cathedral choir school were filing past the statue of Algar. She turned back past the seated worshippers and slow herds of drifting tourists, came to the pillar behind the Light of the World. She paused, out of sight, seeing but unseen.

St Paul's Cathedral, for all its sudden vistas of open spaces and airy vaults, was at heart a place of nooks and crannies, niches and small stairways and secret ways half hidden behind pillars and inside walls. The more she looked, the more she saw. Like an iceberg, from the Lantern Room downwards St Paul's hid most of itself inside itself, the complex void between the domes, the huge library with its fireplace, the private rooms and garrets, the chimneys and recesses and inconsequential-seeming doorways to soaring galleries, even the hollows and byways of the massive crypt, all were hidden from public view. The Grand Master of Freemasonry revealed everything, concealed everything. A visitor could wander in Wren's cathedral all day and see almost nothing of it. An Austrian tourist looked round, thinking she saw someone, but Angela was gone.

Far below, Angela arrived down the steps. 'Bernard?' The cavern beneath the chalk dome was empty but she heard sounds of movement. She rubbed her aching legs – the climb downstairs seemed longer every time – then ducked through to the next cave. Bernard was lost in his work, pen in hand.

'Angela.' He kissed her. He had rolled up his shirtsleeves and looked slightly embarrassed at being found. 'Well, I knew it wouldn't be long before Emma told you I was here.'

'I knew the moment I read of your resignation in the evening paper.' She opened her innocuous London Dungeon tourist bag. 'I brought you a Thermos of coffee. Strong and sugary. The way you like it.' She poured a cup for each of them, uncharacteristically shy, watching him work. 'Well, Bernard? Are these just hoaxes after all?'

'You know they aren't, Angela.'

'I've never known. I *feel*.' They stood by the pile of skins and Bernard's spiral-bound notes, sipping coffee.

'It's exactly as I thought,' Bernard said. 'These skins are from the scriptorium at Qumran. They were still being worked on when they were taken, they're unfinished. Sometimes in the middle of a sentence.'

'How did they get here?'

He chuckled. 'God knows.'

'God's Will.' Angela's lips moved. 'Call on Jesus. Trust in Jesus.'

For a moment Bernard looked appalled. He remembered his son being born. 'My son, my dead son,' he said. 'I remember you saying those words to Rose.'

'Bernard, I'm sorry. I'd forgotten.'

He turned back to his work. 'Roman churches often had a Deep Room beneath them for pagan worship. Tradition has it the Romans built a church here to St Paul in the second century. But Wren specifically wrote that having changed all the foundations of Old St Paul's, he found no trace of any Roman temple.'

'He would, wouldn't he.'

'Anyway, these have been here at least since medieval times.' Bernard held up a damaged scroll. 'My professional life has come full circle, back to my doctoral thesis. There's an apocryphal medieval work at Magdalen College, one of many, beautifully illuminated but of no significance, from outside the canon. *The Gospel Witness of St Simon the Zealot*. It was believed to be the work of some crazy medieval sect. This is its original. The Gospel Witness of the Apostle Simon, the Zealot.'

'Neither crazy nor medieval.'

He touched it reverently. 'From the lifetime of Christ. Impossible to say accurately without accelerator mass spectroscopy dating, but the script is uncial, a form which died out in the middle of the first century. In the medieval copy, fragments of scroll were found between the pages.' He showed a jagged edge where the skin he held was torn. 'I bet my pension these pieces were torn from here. The script is in the same style as some other Magdalen fragments given to the college in the 1890s, bought by a chaplain in an Egyptian market. That's another confirmation.'

Angela touched the skin. She whispered, 'Lifetime of Christ.'

'Lifetime of Christ.'

'Formidable erudition, professor. Congratulations.'

Bernard bowed. 'Thanks, sis.'

She said tenderly, 'You haven't called me that for years.'

They stood in silence for a while. Bernard said quietly, 'I don't know what I'm going to find here. I don't think I'm a believer. I'm a don't-know, sis. No, I'm more than that, I'm a don't-care. I don't care if God is a lobster if He's the truth. I just want to have something to believe in. Something that isn't a lie.'

'Angela said you were working down here. She's at evensong, she says she hardly sees you nowadays.' Emma spoke from the passageway leading down to the scroll cavern. She had watched her father work for ten minutes or more without his becoming aware of her.

Bernard glanced up at her over his reading glasses, then continued with his transcription. The two Camping-Gaz lanterns that were always lit down here hissed, casting their glow on each side of him.

'Come in, Emma.' At last he put the cap on his gold pen. 'Rose thinks I'm working at the British Museum.'

'Poor Mother.' She crossed the room, touched the scrolls with her fingertips. 'Happy birthday.'

He looked genuinely surprised. 'Is it my birthday?'

'Of course it is.' She crouched by his knee and peered up at his face, then kissed him lightly on the lips. 'You don't look any older.'

'Virtuous living.'

'I mean it. You don't look a day older than when you came back from Jerusalem.'

'One forgets which birthday it is.'

'It's eighty.'

He touched the work in front of him. 'I never thought I'd be enjoying myself so much at my age. I thought it was all stiff bones and the horizon closing in. But it isn't. I feel . . . free.'

She settled beside him, glanced over his notes. 'That's because you're doing what you're good at. What's this?'

'At first I still thought the Teacher of Righteousness must be Jesus. But that view imposes historical hindsight. The Teacher of Righteousness may have been the founder or head of Qumran. To him Jesus, the historical Jesus, the man, may have been the Man of a Lie. An opponent to be discredited if there was a struggle for power.'

Emma frowned. 'I thought St Paul was the Man of a Lie. I thought James, the leader of the early Church, was against St Paul. The opponent may have been St Paul.'

'No, that was thirty years later. These are eyewitness accounts, diaries, of the life and ministry of Christ. They simply stop, unfinished, in the first week of April in AD 30, when the twelve apostles went with Jesus to Jerusalem, to the Last Supper. There's nothing about Judas's betrayal, nothing after the Crucifixion. Not one word. The apostles were scattered. For them Christianity was over. It took St Paul to re-invent it years later.'

Emma said, 'Do you hear footsteps?'

'It's Angela.' Bernard went forward as his sister came into the cavern, embraced her. 'Happy birthday,' Angela said, very smart in navy blue with a silver brooch. 'I thought Emma was never coming back.'

'I watched him work for a few minutes,' Emma said.

Angela said, 'A few hours, my dear.' They all looked at their watches. Bernard's watch started beeping and he couldn't stop it. 'They'll be closing the cathedral in a hour. One day someone's going to find out about us, you know.'

'We were talking,' Bernard said. 'I think I'm getting somewhere.'

Angela glanced at his notes. 'Have you tried the other caverns?'

'I'm too old to go crawling through tunnels at my age,' Bernard said.

But Emma looked round the walls. 'There's more?'

Angela turned the page. 'There's always more.'

Emma crouched between the wall and the floor. She looked back at Bernard, called. 'There's something here.' She pulled his hand. 'Come on, let's have a look, it can't do any harm.' She took one of the lanterns and moved forward. 'It really is a tunnel.' Outfaced by his daughter, Bernard watched her light fade between the ribbed, chalky walls of the tunnel. He swore, ducked down and crawled after her. Emma stood up in a third cavern.

She held up the lantern, showing the chalk walls scrawled with thousands of stick figures and daubs of rough colour. Bernard glanced round him, grunted. 'Looks like Wren's workmen got through here. With their children.'

'Look at them,' she whispered.

He found another tunnel, beckoned her. Emma bent and followed him, the lantern swinging from her hand.

Bernard stood up in another cavern. The light grew as the lantern illuminated the cavern's murky walls curving into the distance, its roof rising to a jagged peak hidden by shadows.

A gold house, bright and untarnished, stood on a rock in the centre of the cavern.

'Wait for me,' Angela called.

Without thinking, Bernard lifted the gold rod. The front of the house swung open.

Something black flopped forward, uncoiled over his hands and wrists. Bernard staggered, then took the weight. 'It's *heavy*.'

Emma stepped back. 'What's that disgusting smell?'

Angela covered her mouth. 'It's made of fish skin.'

'It's not fish.' Bernard calmed them, laid the skin over the rock. 'It's gazelle skin, just like the others. It's a scroll, that's all. I've been dealing with scrolls all my life.'

The ends fluttered where they hung down near the floor.

Bernard grabbed one end, cursed the draught. He held the skin down with the palm of his hand, his reading glasses forgotten in his pocket, squinted close to the ink-spattered text.

THUS ENDS THE BLACK BOOK OF JUDAS ISCARIOT
MURDERER OF GOD

He looked up at the two women.

'It's the only Gospel Witness that's finished.' He touched the words with shaking fingers. 'And it was finished after the Crucifixion.'

Bernard said, 'Each time I think I know it all, I find I know nothing.'

He looked round. He was talking to himself. Weeks and months he had spent on this Gospel Witness, complex, vulnerable, flawed, this peculiarly human story of one man's faith and doubt and decision that was telling him so much. He had thought Emma was sitting here with him, as she often was, but the cavern was empty. He was alone.

But he did not feel alone.

He took off his reading glasses and rubbed his eyes. Emma came down. She sounded amazed. 'Are you still here?'

Bernard bent to his work. He was back at the beginning again.

Herein Lies the Gospel Witness of Judas Iscariot, His Testament.

All was plain to Bernard now. Judas, claiming to be the Teacher of Righteousness, a powerful and important man, had become a follower of Jesus, his disciple. *His humble servant preparing us through purity and holiness for the End of Days and the building of the Temple that we are.* Judas believed Jesus was his Messiah, his Christ, the Son of God. Judas even wrote the name of Jesus as KS, meaning *Kyrios*, Lord. But Jesus was not a warrior, he was a teacher, a healer, a lamb. *Are you the One?* All Jesus would answer in response to Judas's growing doubt was, *You know the things which you hear and see. The blind receive their sight, and the lame walk, the lepers are cleansed, the deaf hear, and the poor have good news preached to them. And blessed is he who shall find no stumbling in me. Aram menaht menou.*

And so Judas betrayed peaceful Jesus for the good of Israel, the nation that would rise up against Rome. The Chosen People at last forging their own destiny, under God. Yes, yes, Bernard thought, I've almost got it. Judas would be the Messiah, leading his people to war.

Aram menaht menou. Bernard came back to these three last words, the most difficult to read and so probably the least important. But he could not get the sense of them in Hebrew or Aramaic. He wrote them backwards, searching for a code, or pesher, the p-sense. Neither did the phrase work, quite, in Syriac or Greek. He could not deduce the meaning from the context. Perhaps a miswritten form of *Maranatha*, Our Lord, come. Perhaps a blessing.

He thought, I've heard them before, somewhere. Somewhere quite different. But he could not think where.

Emma said, 'You're working too hard.' She put her hands on his shoulders, her face beside his. 'Mother must think she's a widow. Come up into the sun.'

Bernard nodded. He got to his feet, staggered. 'You're quite right, my dear.' She found his coat for him, screwed the cap on his pen for him. He put his arm through hers and they went to the steps. His feet dragged. 'I feel so exhausted,' he said.

'You don't look it. You look like a young man of seventy-five.'

He found the stairs a fearful climb. 'Add ten years.'

'You should take a holiday,' she said.

They came slowly towards the platform near the top. Bernard looked down. 'I still don't understand how this was dug. I know it's impossible yet here it is.'

'It's the middle of the afternoon, Dad. The cathedral will still be busy with tourists. We'll use one of the quiet ways out.'

Bernard looked up.

He reached up towards the stone set in the roof. '*Resurgam*,' he muttered.

Blinking, his eyes followed the pattern of dots and holes, the wavy lines. 'You know, Emma, research by the Central Intelligence Agency into drug-induced behaviour shows that stone age man was . . . well, stoned.'

She laughed.

'Literally, my girl. Stoned out of his skull. Magic mushrooms. Maybe Allegro was right. These wavy lines match the patterns scrawled by people under the influence of hallucinogenic drugs.' He frowned. 'Or religious ecstasy. Religious trance.'

Emma said, 'Prayer.'

Bernard's fingertips touched the stone, moved along the lines, his fingers too big to fit inside them, came to markings at the edge.

'This is an ogam stone,' he said.

She grinned and tugged him forward, but he pulled her back. 'Cup-and-ring marks,' he whispered. 'They represent the Sun. My God, how have I missed it? Magical Sun-symbols carved in hope of bringing back the sun in times of deteriorating climate. Common.' His eyes moved rapidly. 'Here are spirals, perhaps an astronomical function. Like the ones at Fajada Butte, New Mexico. Others in Ireland. Everywhere in Britain. Once this stone stood in sunlight.' He let go of Emma, stood on tiptoe.

Bernard's tongue licked between his lips, flecks of dust fell from his fingers on to his glasses. 'Yes. This part here is later. The stone was worked on at all different times, different people, perhaps different cultures. No, *developing* cultures. Yes, yes, history *is* a narrative, a series of steps by which God leads us upward towards the morality of the Christian Church.' His breath came rapidly. 'Yes. This is ogam script, very ancient, but not nearly as old as the stone. Vowels are one, two, three, four or five lines across the edge. Here is A. Other letters are made by a varying number of lines slanted to the left or right of the edge. Here's R—'

Emma laughed at him. 'Slow down. You're overexcited.' But he shrugged her off. 'Sit down for a minute,' she said, concerned.

Bernard staggered back.

'It's been here all the time,' he said. '*Aram menaht menou.*' He cried out, 'The Black Book says, *Here I send my messenger before your face to prepare the Way for you, the voice of one who cries in the desert, "Make the Way ready for the Lord—"'* He turned to her. 'For the building of the Temple that we are.'

'Dad, please. Calm down.' Emma stopped, staring. The stone phoenix carved by Wren's mason clasped the same message in its claws as it flew up, reborn, from its fiery death.

Bernard spoke rapidly. 'The Messianic age will be inaugurated by Jesus Christ. Blessed by Him. *Aram menaht menou.* Three words. What do they mean? Could it be a reference to the Temple at the End of Days?'

Emma stared at her father. 'Three quadrangles . . .'

'Yes, but it's more than that. I've almost got it—' Bernard clapped his hands to his head. 'The Book of Daniel. The Zealot text says, *Thy people shall be delivered, every one that shall be found written in the Book. And many of them that sleep in the dust of the earth shall awake, some to everlasting life, and some to shame and everlasting contempt. And they that be wise shall shine as the brightness of the firmament, and they that turn many to righteousness shall be as the stars for ever and ever. But thou, O Daniel, shut up the words, and seal the Book, even to the End of Days!'*

Emma said eagerly, 'In the Black Book Judas hears Jesus say, "Blessed is he who shall find no stumbling in me. *Aram menaht menou.*" Yes, it's a blessing. A blessing and a promise.' She shrugged helplessly. 'But what does it mean?'

Bernard's hands dropped to his sides. He stood in silence, then suddenly turned from Emma and hobbled down the stairs so fast she was terrified he would fall, his thin white hair flying over his shoulders. She called down, 'Dad!'

Emma followed him as fast as she could. She found her father gazing at the walls of the cavern beneath the chalk dome. She watched quietly, afraid to interrupt. He turned slowly in a circle, amazed by how much he had missed, then reached out to her.

'A religion isn't about God. It's about people. People believing in God, people having faith. Look at them all, Emma. I never noticed them. Look at all the people. So many of them.'

Bernard blinked in the spring sunlight. Emma guided him to a bench in St Paul's churchyard, sat beside him. She took her Vodafone from her handbag, talked into it. Big red buses rumbled past, streams of taxis, a coach braked in the coach rank and added German tourists to the French and Japanese. Bernard watched them moving past. He spoke in a loud voice. 'Who am I?'

Emma put her hand on his, her chin over the mouthpiece to block her voice from her call. 'Don't speak so loudly. They'll hear you.'

Bernard stood on the seat. 'Who are we? Where are we going? These are questions we all ask whatever our language. We are a family. A family rushing forward through time. We're all part of it, though our own lives are as brief as the flash of salmon in a waterfall. Where do we come from, where do we go? We're a family, the answer's in our blood. We the people. Inside us all the time, we have only to look to see. *Aram menaht menou.*'

Emma closed the phone and put it back in her bag. 'Dad, it's all right. They understand. Sit down.'

Bernard sat. He called out to a startled Japanese, 'I believe in Jesus. Jesus is in me. Jesus will come again.' The man beamed, bowed politely. A party of brown-faced children scuttled past, the teacher keeping between his flock and Bernard.

'He's just an old man,' Emma said, 'he's harmless,' then hated herself for saying it. Well over a thousand spy cameras overlooked every movement in the City, many of them capable of counting the hairs in Bernard's nose, and doubtless they were observed at this very moment, either by humans or by computers running face-recognition programs. The ancient walls of the City were gone but an electronic ring of steel was erected in their place. There was little physical crime in the City, but in their glass towers people lived in terror of it, in terror of fear itself. For their sake microphones listened, and sniffer probes for explosives detected the contents of pockets. The security agency responsible for the cathedral would intervene if he made a disturbance.

Bernard whispered, 'I'm cold.' Emma took off her coat, draped it round his shoulders. He asked, 'What year is it?'

'It's the spring. March. The twenty-fourth of March.'

'Yes, but what year?'

'It's nineteen ninety-nine, Dad. I love you.'

'It's gone, Emma. My life is gone. I had it once but it's gone. The years have gone so fast I've forgotten them. I've had my birthday, haven't I?'

She hugged him. 'Your birthday's in January.'

He nodded. 'I suppose I was working.' He blew his nose.

'I've telephoned Mother and we'll get a taxi to take you home.'

He looked at the cathedral. 'I am home.'

Bernard pushed the coat off his shoulders and walked across the grass, scattering pigeons in front of him. 'I am home. This is my home!'

He turned and stared up at the cathedral, vast and clean and pale grey above him, the dome as blue as the sky. The sun glinted off the gold ball and cross at the summit.

'It's a religious place,' he said. 'That's it. This is a religious place.'

A taxi pulled up and Rose got out. 'What's the old fool done now?'

'He's all right,' Emma said. 'He ought to rest.'

Rose glanced at the cathedral. The cool wind blew so that strands of her fur stole tickled her chin, and she pushed it down irritably.

She pursed her lips. 'Silly old fool,' she said, then took his arm affectionately. 'He's always coming back here. Religious mania, he's got.'

'Nine months till Christmas,' Bernard said. Then he said, 'My God.' He pressed the palms of his hands to his temples. 'Oh my God. *And they that turn many to righteousness shall be as the stars for ever and ever.*'

'I can't stop here all blooming day you know,' the taxi driver said.

Bernard opened the door, pushed Emma inside. 'Take us to the Royal Astronomical Society, Burlington House, Piccadilly,' he told the driver. 'Come on, Rose!' He beckoned furiously.

Rose hesitated, peering through the door. Then she shook her head, drew back. 'No. No, Bernard. I won't go.'

'The twenty-fifth of March, nineteen ninety-nine,' Bernard muttered. He held a large sheaf of transparencies rolled under his arm, adjusted the lantern to maximum brightness as he came to Wren's door. 'The Angel Gabriel didn't tell Mary she was pregnant until August, when her condition was obvious. The Holy Ghost had come to her and the power of the Highest overshadowed her nine months before Christmas. St Luke says for God nothing shall be impossible.'

Emma said, 'Actually pregnancy lasts two hundred and sixty-six days, not nine months. Though Alexandra took a month longer,' she admitted.

'You're missing the point.' Bernard went into the stone room, waited for Emma at the head of the steps, then they descended together to the platform below. Bernard peered up at the roof. 'Just a moment.' He touched the holes pecked into the surface, then unrolled one of the transparencies and pressed it over the stone. He was disappointed at once. The black dots on the transparency, stars, did not match the pattern of holes in the stone.

'It was just a thought,' he said. 'The RAS has a huge library of star maps.'

Emma stared up at the marks on the stone. 'You thought those marks were *stars*?'

'I hoped, that's all,' he murmured. 'I hoped it was an answer.'

'Too neat, professor,' Emma said.

'Einstein said God does not play dice.'

'Stephen Hawking says God plays dice all the time.' Emma took the transparency and held it another way. 'The stars move, don't they?'

'Over thousands of years, yes. The planets appear to move much more quickly. And then there are special phenomena, comets, novas, supernovas . . .'

She stared at her father between her raised arms. 'You're not looking for the Star of Bethlehem, are you?' She shook the transparency to make her point. 'But this is the modern sky. If the stars move—'

Bernard crouched, flicked through the transparencies, pulled out another. 'Here we are. Bethlehem, Christmas, 1 BC.'

The black marks speckled across the transparency hid the holes in the stone.

Bernard swallowed.

His voice trembled. 'Halley's Comet rose at sunset. It was high in the sky all night. It set due west of Bethlehem at dawn.' He pointed with his fingertip. 'Exactly there.'

Emma gazed up. 'This stone was a prediction. A prediction of something that *was* in the future, but is now in the past. Something that really happened. The birth of Christ, the Star of Bethlehem. I don't believe it.'

'Of course you do.' Bernard took the transparency and rolled it with the others. 'Or it's an amazing coincidence.'

He touched Emma's hand and they went down to the caverns below.

He stood waiting for her under the chalk dome, looked round him at the walls covered with drawings of women and children.

'There's a lifetime of study just in here.'

Emma said quietly, 'I wonder if we are looking at the past, or what's to come.'

'These places are discovered all the time,' Bernard said. 'Two or three years ago the first Neanderthal shrine was located.'

'Neanderthals worshipped gods? Incredible.'

'And look at the vast system of cave paintings just discovered at Vallon-Pont d'Arc. More than thirty thousand years old.'

Bernard slid awkwardly, as always, into next cavern. The skins were exactly as he always left them, neatly ordered, but he had never felt so aware of someone standing behind him. He turned, but saw only the mammoth, and Emma coming forward from its mouth.

Bernard ducked down. He crawled into the next cavern on aching knees, stood up among the stick figures drawn in charcoal amid daubs of green, yellow, blue, and lines of dark blue. 'It's obvious,' he said. 'It's a map. How did I never realise it before? It's so obvious.'

'You're not going to say these people are stars, are you?'

'I think they're real people.' He gestured at the colours. 'Green woodlands and grassland. Yellow desert. Blue seas. The darker lines are rivers. How did we never see it?'

Emma looked at him. She said, 'They have dots for eyes.'

Bernard gave an exclamation. He rummaged through the transparencies.

'No, not that one again,' Emma said. 'This.' She pulled out a different star map, held out her arms at full stretch, pressed it to the wall.

Bernard adjusted it slightly, and the eyes disappeared.

He whispered, 'Their eyes are stars.'

She nodded downward, unable to move her hands, then pressed her knee to the wall. 'But it doesn't match down there. That line of dots.'

He fumbled through the sheaf, unrolled one of the sheets, put a sticky tab on each corner, pressed it over the transparency below. 'The planets, all in a row. Here is the sun. Here is the moon.'

She jerked her head, pointing. 'There should be something more.'

He found the final transparency, which contained only one large hairy star. He placed it over the maps beneath, and the final mark on the wall disappeared. 'It isn't a star,' he said. 'It's Halley's Comet.'

Emma breathed quickly. 'But *when* is it?'

Bernard stepped back. He gazed at the overlaid maps with an expression of awe.

'It's next Christmas Day.'

'I won't go,' Rose said. 'It's wrong. I won't do it. And it's ridiculous. Caves beneath St Paul's.'

'No, no,' Bernard said gently, 'it's much more than that.'

'Today's March the twenty-fifth. You might at least have waited for April Fools' Day.'

'Please come, Rose. Please.'

'I'm too old for any of your silliness,' Rose said. 'I'm tired and I've had enough.'

'Emma will be there. She'll bring Isaac. And Alexandra will be there too. Our whole family. They all know.'

'And Angela?'

'Yes.'

'Then I won't go,' Rose said spitefully. 'She stole my baby. Don't expect me to forgive that woman.' Her hairy lips trembled. 'Go away, Bernard. I'm fed up with you. I'm fed up with your dreams. You've spent your life in a dream, you've never done anything worthwhile, you never stood up for me.' She clenched her fists and her knuckles stood out. 'Go away from me!'

He went out and closed the door.

'Bernard,' she whispered.

It was a hazy, sunny afternoon. Bernard, Angela, Emma and Isaac got out of the taxi in front of St Paul's, and Isaac paid. 'Have you ever been in a synagogue, Bernard?'

'Yes, once. When you married Emma.'

'That's once more than I've been in a cathedral,' Isaac said. He looked fit, and ran his hands back through his short grey hair.

Bernard said, 'Where you're going is a lot holier than a cathedral.' He led them to the north-west corner of St Paul's, to a blocked doorway hardly distinguishable among the filled-in windows and

461

empty niches along the rest of the wall. Bernard said, 'In Wren's plans it's called the Si Quis door. I don't know why.' He did something with his hand and shoulder, the angle of the doorstone changed slightly, and he slipped inside. The others crowded after him. The door shut and Bernard shone a torch.

He led the way down.

Rose got out of her taxi. By the time she had counted out the money to pay the driver, Bernard and the others had disappeared as though they had never been. She looked inside the cathedral but there was no sign of them. She waited on the steps. The sun was pleasant.

'Now you know,' Bernard said. 'I trust in Jesus. I believe in Jesus. I believe Jesus will be born again. *Aram menaht menou.*'

Alex turned by the skins. She said, 'Do you mean the modern equivalents of Mary and Joseph are . . . you know . . . doing it, right now?'

Bernard shook his head. 'Mary didn't sleep with Joseph until after Jesus was born.'

Isaac said, 'You mean God is . . .'

'I think the word is *overshadowing*,' Angela said.

'That's right,' Bernard said. 'The power of the Holy Ghost is somewhere near. Somewhere in this world. I think we should pray.'

'I feel a bit of a fool,' Isaac said.

'Perhaps,' Bernard said. 'But suppose you're wrong?'

Emma took her husband's elbow. 'This is a very special place, Isaac. Not a cathedral, not a synagogue, not a mosque. I think it's beyond religion.'

Bernard got down on his knees. 'Let us pray quietly,' he said.

They knelt. It was intensely quiet in the cavern.

Alex unclasped her hands. She put back her long black hair. 'Perhaps it's me.'

'Alex!' Angela said.

'You aren't a virgin,' Emma said.

'Yes, I am, actually.'

Emma raised her eyebrows.

'It's not like it was in your day.' Alex shrugged. 'We don't all have wicked pasts and sleep around for the sake of it. We've got better things to do.'

'It's a virgin birth,' Bernard said. 'Conception without the intervention of a man. After her marriage Mary herself simply asked the angel how her pregnancy could be, *seeing I know not a man.* Present tense.'

'You're missing the point again,' Angela said. Her eyes were closed. 'Trust in Jesus.'

'Give me faith,' Bernard whispered. 'Let me see.'

'We've been down here for hours,' Alex said. Her hair kept

blowing in her eyes and she put it back irritably. 'Where's that wind coming from?'

Rose crossed to the edge of the steps, stared towards the river. The river was sunny, grey-green, white around the bows of the pleasure boats. Thunder growled and she wished she had brought her umbrella. Pigeons swirled round her, hoping for bread, and she waved them away with her stick.

For the first time she noticed the cloud above St Paul's.

The cloud slowly rotated, like a huge grey whirlpool. She imagined the force of the wind.

She stood looking up with her mouth open.

A man bumped into her, apologised, went on his way.

Lightning flickered in the cloud but no rain fell. People coming out of the cathedral squinted in the bright sunlight. A kid chased a McDonald's bag against the wind.

'It's a storm,' Rose muttered.

'Do you feel anything?' Isaac asked.

'There's nothing,' Alex yawned.

'Wait,' Angela said.

'No, there's nothing after all,' Emma said.

'What did you expect?' Bernard asked. 'Peals of bells and angels singing the Magnificat?'

Alex said, 'Yes.'

Rose looked up at the cloud. Lightning flickered from the expanding mass, lightning-strikes lit the streets of London like striding footprints, silhouetting the church spires and office blocks in sharp relief. Queenhithe. London Bridge, suddenly black and sharp as the Thames glowed for a moment brilliant yellowish-green beneath its arches, as if illuminated from far below. Southwark. Greenwich. The hills of Vaudey. A sudden, last, breathtaking flash.

Nothing. It was a sunny day. Rose sat down.

'*Big* disappointment,' Alex said. 'Unless,' she added sweetly, 'I'm pregnant. But then, how would anyone know He was the Son of God?'

'Don't you dare speak like that,' Angela said.

'You'd know,' Bernard said.

Bernard lay on his bed. He heard the front door close, footsteps in the hall.

He covered his eyes with his hands. Rose stood in the doorway. She called softly, 'Are you all right, dear?'

'Nothing happened.'

Rose hesitated. Then she turned away. 'It's all for the best,' she said. She went into the kitchen of their Bankside flat, made a cup of tea, and sat looking at it.

Nine months later Bernard sat up in bed, slowly, so as not to awaken Rose. Her breathing did not change. He swung his legs out of bed, fetched his clothes, shuffled into the bathroom in his slippers and pyjamas, and dressed himself quietly. In his living room, beyond the glass sliding door and his snowy balcony, the Thames glinted under chains of streetlights. Beyond them the dome of St Paul's, floodlit, moon-coloured, rose up among the darkened office blocks.

Seven o'clock on Christmas morning.

He shrugged on his overcoat, wound a muffler round his neck, put on the flat cap he always wore in winter. He kissed Rose on the top of her sleeping head, closed the door, and took the stairs down not the lift.

Old snow speckled the road along Bankside. He walked towards the footbridge.

Nothing moved, only the figure of an old man dwindling from sight.

Rose turned from the window. She put her trembling hands, clawed with age and arthritis, to her withered face.

She thought, what do I believe?

The same as everyone else, I suppose. I *want* to see. I *want* to have courage. I *want* to believe.

If only it was easy.

She looked again from the window. She could hardly see Bernard now. His tiny form turned towards the footbridge.

Rose dressed as quickly as she possibly could. She forgot her bra and put her knickers on back to front. Her fingers did not have the strength to do up the zip on her dress. She let it hang, pulled her fur coat over it, then forgot her shoes and had to come back for them, hobbled out wearing one black, one brown.

She went down into the street. It was empty.

She raised her eyes across the river, where the floodlit dome of St Paul's hung like a huge setting moon above its image in the river.

Rose hobbled towards the footbridge. Suddenly a huge letter flashed on to the dome.

The letter was *W*.

Rose knew she was seeing the Word of God. She stood rooted to the spot.

The next letter flashed into view. *I*.

The letters were made of light, brilliantly bright and clear. *S*. Rose clasped her hands in prayer.

PA.

Rose stared. *WISPA*. She was not seeing the Word of God revealed after all. It was an advertisement for a chocolate bar.

Bernard climbed Lud's Hill. He came up the broad pedestrian precinct from the river. There was a Christmas tree in the gardens, pretty with coloured lights. He waited at the road, a single car's headlights approaching.

The cathedral towered above Bernard. It looked ancient, vast and pale. Dawn drew a bright blue line across the south-eastern sky.

The car stopped. 'Emma?'

Emma got out. 'It just felt right to come,' she said. 'That's all.'

Isaac turned off the headlights, got out of the driver's side. He said, 'She's right.'

'She's always right,' Angela said, getting out of the back. 'Happy Christmas, Bernard.'

'It was our idea,' Emma said. She put her arm through Angela's.

Angela patted her hand. 'It's always us.'

'Get over the road,' Bernard said. 'They'll be opening the cathedral in a moment.'

As they crossed the atrium an engine clattered, brakes squealed. A cab drew up at the kerb. The door flew open and Alexandra got out, streamers in her hair, holding a champagne bottle by the neck. Laughter came from the back of the cab, someone wearing a paper crown, dinner jackets, girls in sparkly dresses, all drunk. Alex handed back the champagne to the clutching hands, the door slammed, and the cab pulled away trailing black fumes.

Alex turned. She grinned with one corner of her mouth, and suddenly Bernard saw himself in her. She pulled the streamers from her hair.

'Knew you'd be here,' she said.

Bernard looked at them. 'My sister, my daughter, my grand-daughter,' he said. 'Three generations of you.'

They waited on the steps. Due west, down Ludgate Hill front of them, the full moon set towards the horizon over Westminster, Halley's Comet pointing beneath it like a diamond pendant from a pearl.

Bernard turned. In the south-east sky the sun rose like a locomotive pulling a chain of planets, Saturn in the north, Jupiter, Mars, Uranus, Neptune. Pushing Mercury, brilliant Venus, and invisible Pluto in front of its brilliant glare.

Bernard touched Emma's shoulder and they looked together. 'That's it exactly,' he said.

A virger opened the doors of St Paul's. It was cool and empty in the cathedral.

The group walked slowly towards the crossing.

Rose watched them. She peered round one of the great piers that supported the dome. They moved near the statue of Algar.

Bernard reached out to its foot, then he turned and looked straight into Rose's eyes.

He murmured something to the others, came to her. He touched her but she shook her head.

'Rose, come with us,' he said.

She turned away from him.

He said, 'I won't go without you.'

Rose wept. 'You will,' she said. 'You know you will.'

She hobbled away. When she looked back, they were gone.

'Jesus is born again today,' Angela said, 'somewhere in the world.'

'I suppose to every mother her baby is special,' Alex said.

'Shut up,' Emma said angrily. 'You can't possibly imagine just how special each baby is. You've never had one. You haven't even had a man.'

'If that's how you feel, darling Mother—' Alex wandered into the next cavern, stood up among the stick people. She couldn't understand how Bernard believed he saw a map in it.

The wind blew in her face. Isaac came through behind her. 'I don't like this place,' he said. He wore a black jacket, white shirt, conservative tie. He kissed her forehead solicitously. 'Are you warm enough? We can go home soon.'

Alex ducked down into the warm wind. 'There's another tunnel,' she pointed out.

She crawled through. Whatever the lighting system was, it was superb, showing no shadows.

Alex stood up in front of a gold house.

Light shone around her as though it poured from the walls, as though the darkness of the earth had turned to light.

A long scroll of black skin, perfectly black, lay rolled loosely on the rock on which the gold house rested.

She touched the skin, and it stuck to her own skin. She could not peel it from her fingers.

The scroll began to uncoil, flapping round her as though a wind blew from the floor.

Isaac crawled into the cavern. He stood up in front of the gold house, saw no sign of his daughter. He called out.

'Alex?'

There was no reply. He reached out towards the gold house, recognising the plan of the Temple.

His fingers lifted the gold rod, and the Temple blossomed open, gleaming with gold, towards him.

'*It's true,*' he whispered. '*It's all true.*'

Bernard stood next to the scrolls with his eyes closed. He felt dizzy, as though he was being picked up and turned round, as though he was supported on air. He was very afraid that he was dying, had suffered a heart attack perhaps, and this was the feeling of dying.

He kept his eyes tight shut.

He whispered, '*Are you the One?*'

Angela wondered where Bernard had gone. The tunnel into the next cavern seemed taller than she remembered, and she walked through.

'Hundreds of you,' she said. 'Thousands. Stars for eyes.'

The stars moved.

Emma was lost. She had taken a wrong turn somewhere. Each tunnel she took led to a different cavern, and when she turned back after a few footsteps she found herself in a new place she did not know.

The tunnels grew larger, wider, taller, until she no longer touched their sides with her outstretched hands. She came into a cavern as large as a cathedral. In the centre of it a gold house stood on a rock.

Emma shivered, feeling pain and darkness. She was utterly alone.

She realised that the rock walls of the cathedral were covered with animals, more than she knew how to recognise. Reindeer, and creatures with huge horns like cattle, bears, tiny rugged horses, all worked cunningly into the shapes of the chalk boulders that made up the walls.

Someone called her name.

Her name was called again. 'Yes?' Emma looked round her wildly. 'Who's there? Is anybody there?'

The wall moved, the leg of a deer became a woman's leg, a snarling bear's head became her smiling face.

'Emma, what ever is the matter?' Angela smiled. 'Didn't you see me? I was standing beside you all the time.'

She led Emma forward. The walls narrowed and the mouth of the tunnel was blocked by chalk boulders. In the gaps between them something gleamed, a hidden mirror. They pulled away the rocks. Emma reached forward. The mirror rippled slightly as her hand slipped inside.

A little water sprayed around her wrist. She pulled her hand out, licked the drops, pushed her hand inside again.

'It's water,' she said. 'It's water standing up.'

She pushed her face inside, slid forward as though she were being born. Bubbles burst around her. She stood beneath cliffs so high that the sky above them looked no wider than a strip of blue ribbon, and beside her the Thames foamed in a torrent of icy green.

Rose came down the steps of St Paul's into the sunlight and traffic. She had been inside most of the day, until a kindly virger spoke to her.

'I'm waiting,' Rose had tried to fob him off. 'I'm waiting for someone.'

'And who is that, my dear?'

'I don't know,' Rose was forced to admit. 'I'm afraid I don't know.'

As she came down the steps, she felt the ground tremble.

The cavern shook. Whatever is happening, Bernard thought, it's real. It's really happening.

The wind roared like a storm in the earth, burning hot. 'It's the prophecy in the Prayer of Thanksgiving,' he whispered. *Fire and blood, the torrents of Satan. And the fiery flames shall eat up the foundations of the earth, and the rocks shall burn like rivers of pitch.*

The wind stopped. Bernard whispered, '*Are you the One?*'

He listened to his breaths panting in his mouth, the wheeze of his heart.

The Book of Daniel had prophesied, *And many of them that sleep in the dust of the earth shall awake—*

Bernard pulled himself slowly to his feet beside the tunnel to the next cavern. Behind him, he heard the rocks creak. The rough dirty smell of an animal filled the cave.

Bernard turned. He crouched, terrified.

The mammoth charged forward. Chalkdust spurted from its feet. Meat hung from its mouth. Its tusks enclosed Bernard, its enormous body crashed into the wall above his head.

Bernard ran into the tunnel as fast as he could. Behind him came a gathering roar like the sound of a stampede. He squeezed himself into a niche in the rocks, bent his shoulders, hurt his head.

A deer with huge antlers dashed along the tunnel, chalkdust flying from its slotted hooves. Its gentle brown eyes stared in panic. Bernard saw elk, bison with broad black shoulders, wild animals surging from side to side like the waves of a living sea to fit in the tunnel, wolves, tall low-browed men, apes, birds, more than his mind knew shapes or names for.

Silence fell. The dust settled.

A baby mammoth trotted by, no larger than a small pony, its trunk raised and the whites of its eyes showing. It looked warily at Bernard, then trumpeted for its mother, tail twitching, and trotted smartly from sight.

Bernard began to understand. He whispered, '*It's all true.*'

Angela and Emma stood by the river winding below the cliffs. They saw Alex in the cavern, beckoned her, and Alex stepped forward in a cloud of bubbles. She gasped, then put back her head and gazed in wonder at the snowy cliffs of London.

'Everything's alive,' Angela said. 'She's Gaia. Everything that lives

468

remembers, and is remembered. Our planet is alive. Everything that ever happened is still happening.'

'We were surrounded by marvels,' Emma said. 'All our lives are a part of something marvellous, and we never realised.'

The three women stood hand in hand. There was a noise like a stampede. Animals poured from the cliffs, heads tossing, hooves pounding. Spreading out, they stretched to the horizon like a carpet of life.

Alex looked back into the cave. Its white walls shone. The gold house gleamed on its rock in the centre.

'There's more,' she said. 'There's much more. Quick!'

She tugged the others after her towards her father.

Isaac stared at the Temple. Its glorious gold rose on each side of him, shimmering brighter than the sun with the purity of the promised three gold quadrangles, the House of the Laver, the House of Altar Utensils, the rows of gold spikes along each golden roof. He knew he was seeing Heaven, the Heaven God had promised His people. The holy light burnt into his eyes, flinging the shadows of his human imperfection away from him so that everything was darkness and gold and glory. He stood at the centre, blinded by perfection, filled with an emotion of utter joy and righteousness. Everything he had believed, the faith of the Chosen People for more than three thousand years, was proved true. The Temple contained nothing unclean, no human frailty, only pure worship. So deep was his joy that he hardly felt the wind blowing through the floor, or noticed the Black Book unrolling around him.

Rose stood on the kerb. She wished a taxi would come so that she could get home. As the ground rumbled she looked down at her feet, realising for the first time she wore mismatched shoes. Dust and pebbles blew up through the joins between the paving stones, stinging her legs. Her handbag was lifted away from her side. The statue of Queen Anne fell with a crash, then the pieces flew up into the air from the ground.

Rose heard a terrible sound behind her.

She was afraid to look round.

She looked.

Rose looked up and saw the dome of St Paul's splitting in half. The gold Christian cross tottered and fell inside as the dome opened like a mouth. She saw the roof-beams exposed as the dome fell away, the great columns and colonnades and piers collapsed one by one. Rose clapped her hands over her ears. She screamed, but she could not hear herself. The thunder of the falling cathedral bruised her feet. The nave collapsed, blowing a cloud of fine white plaster-dust and chips of mosaic into the blue sky. A huge block of stone tumbled slowly towards her, shattered a bench, bounded ponderously over her head, left deep gouges in the roadway as it crashed downhill between the buses bringing worshippers to pray.

Rose stood on the bare hilltop among the piles of stones.

She heard an approaching roar like a whirlwind. Deep below the earth, something was beginning.

Far below, the three women struggled to return the skin to the Temple. The Black Book bannered like a wing above the floor, the wind roared.

Alex caught one end of the scroll. Emma reached out, grabbed Angela's hand, then Alex's wrist. They grasped hands. Bernard limped forward, caught one end of the scroll, and together they struggled to drag it down.

Rose stared quietly at the whirlwind rising from the rubble of the cathedral. Something moved.

Satan stood up from the earth. Rose recognised him at once though he was made of red wind, his horns and cloven hooves, his fierce distorted mouth. But his eyes were as she had never imagined, not mocking but knowing, and sad, and conniving.

The wind lifted him up and other faces and giant shapes rose up beneath him, each standing on the shoulders of the others like a vast totem, eastern gods and Asian gods, Greek gods and northern gods, gods of ice and gods of palm fronds, desert gods and forest gods, water gods and gods of fire, more than Rose could tell or say, gentle gods and fierce gods, gods of earth and wind, stern Mithras, silver Diana the huntress, huge blunt women with bulging breasts and bellies, primitive gods of fog and mist, half-formed, haunted, incoherent shadows from the dawn of Neanderthal time.

Beneath them were even more, inchoate, loved.

A huge tree grew out of the ground. Its spreading branches covered the sky. Rose knew she saw the beginning of the world.

The leaves of the Tree of Knowledge bore fruit, then were gone.

Rose heard a child's prayer. She heard their innocent voices clearly, a girl and boy.

'And now I lay my head to sleep, I pray the Lord my soul to keep.'

Bernard pushed the Black Book into the doorway of the gold Temple. Together they forced the scroll inside. The foul stinking skin felt as soft and warm as living flesh.

'What have we done?' Isaac said in a desolate voice.

The door slammed, the wind stopped, the gold rod dropped in place.

Bernard looked around him. Nothing moved. He spoke calmly.

'It's all true, Isaac, don't you see? We are all the Chosen People.

Each of us is the Temple. All land is the Holy Land. It's everywhere. It's all of us. It's the whole world.'

They waited in a circle, Angela, Emma, Alex, Isaac, Bernard, then joined hands.

Beneath the blue sky, a man walked towards Rose along the pavement. His shadow rippled over the piles of rubble in the dawn light. Grit scuffed His sandals and flecked His toenails, which were neatly trimmed. He wore a white gown, woven without a seam, and His brown hair fell to His shoulders in curls, as though recently unbraided. His eyes, also brown, were large and gentle, yet determined too, and she was utterly certain who He was.

Rose burst into tears.

She dropped to her knees at His feet. Her joints cracked with arthritis.

Rose took His hand in both her hands. She kissed His wrist. She laid her head on the comfort of His forearm.

He said to her, 'It is all true.'

She said, 'Yes, Lord.'

He said to her, 'I am the beginning and the end. I am with you always, till the close of the age.'

Rose heard a long, gentle sigh behind her, the low grinding of stones rising into place.

She knew what He had done. Rose was afraid to look and see.

He lifted her, and she stood up easily beside Him, as though she were young.

He said to her, '*Aram menaht menou*. This is my will, that my people may live.'

Rose looked. Nothing had changed. Everything was new. The cathedral stood in the morning sunlight, its gold cross glinting on the peak of the lantern above the dome.

Far below, Bernard looked up from the circle. He stood. He looked at the others, then began to laugh.

'I understand everything now,' he said. 'I am alive. I do not die.'

Epilogue

London, Midsummer's Day

Fifteen thousand years later nothing moved, only the wind sweeping across the two hills, and the wind was hard.

Far below, by the river, a human figure appeared. A man was witless or lost to come out on such a night. Clad in flapping skins, the figure clambered upward from the darkness of the river-gorge to the darkness over the plain.

Pale with snow, the greater of the two hills rose in front of her. She bowed to the wind, and climbed.

She patted her face to find her left hand, pulled off her glove. Her bare fingers traced the comforting pattern of grooves worn across the stone that stood out of the hilltop. The pattern felt slightly warm, and was free of snow.

Her fingers moved with the prayer offered since the beginning of time until now, its end. The hills and the wind and the sky would live for ever, but love had only a day.

Her fingers wore at the stone. Flesh and blood were harder than stone.

Worn almost as deep as her fingertips could reach, the grooves formed a pattern across the stone. Even the meaning of *word* was long lost, but nothing had changed.

The tiny figure prayed on the hilltop, watching, waiting. And all the while her fingers worked busily, keeping hope and love alive, following the word.

RESURGAM

London, Midsummer's Day 17,000 years AD

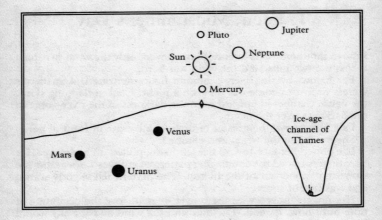